PRAISE FOR THE EXTRAORDINARY NOVELS OF
JOHN CROWLEY

ÆGYPT

"A dizzying experience, achieved with unerring security of technique . . . The narrative startles the reader again and again with the eloquent rightness of the web of coincidences that structure it."

—*The New York Times Book Review*

"Extraordinary."

—*Los Angeles Times*

"*Ægypt* is a must; it is a land of questions, more questions and mysteries, because crafting mysteries is what John Crowley, an original moralist of the same giddy heights occupied by the likes of Thomas Mann and Robertson Davies, does best."

—*San Francisco Chronicle*

And the three novels collected in
JOHN CROWLEY: THREE NOVELS

THE DEEP

"Extraordinary . . . It has genuine beauty."

—Ursula K. Le Guin

"An honest and sensitively written fantasy."

—*Chicago Daily News*

"Crowley writes with style and wit, creates characters that live and breathe."

—*New York Newsday*

ENGINE SUMMER

"A strikingly original and involving book . . . with uncommon sensitivity and grace."
—*The Washington Post Book World*

"*Engine Summer* has strong, believable characters, an ingenious, well-made plot and a resolution that is intellectually and dramatically satisfying."
—*The New York Times Book Review*

"Reminiscent of Tolkien's and Bradbury's gentle mysticism . . . This is the sort of book people take to their hearts, reread and recommend."
—*Publishers Weekly*

BEASTS

"This haunting, thought-provoking novel . . . is extraordinarily touching, mingling a sense of hope with a pervasive mood of despair."
—*Booklist*

"Crowley has enough genuine imagination for ten ordinary science fiction writers."
—Kirkus *Reviews*

"Unforgettable."
—Gerald Jonas, *Penthouse*

LITTLE, BIG

BANTAM BOOKS BY JOHN CROWLEY

THREE NOVELS BY JOHN CROWLEY
Beasts
The Deep
Engine Summer

ÆGYPT
LOVE & SLEEP

John Crowley
LITTLE, BIG

BANTAM BOOKS
NEW YORK · TORONTO · LONDON · SYDNEY · AUCKLAND

*This edition contains the complete text
of the original hardcover edition.*
NOT ONE WORD HAS BEEN OMITTED.

LITTLE, BIG
A Bantam Book

PUBLISHING HISTORY
Bantam hardcover edition published 1981
Bantam trade paperback edition / September 1994

ACKNOWLEDGMENTS
Lines from Lark Rise to Candleford *by Flora Thompson;
published 1954. By permission of Oxford University Press.*

Lines from "For the Marriage of Faustus and Helen" from The
Complete Poems and Selected Letters and Prose of Hart Crane *by
Hart Crane, edited by Brom Weber; copyright 1933, © 1958, 1966
by Liveright Publishing Corporation, also published by Oxford
University Press. By permission of W.W. Norton, Inc. and Laurence
Pollinger, Ltd.*

*(Note: Every effort has been made to locate the copyright owners of
material reproduced in this book. Omissions brought to our
attention will be corrected in subsequent editions.)*

ISBN 0-553-37397-8

Published simultaneously in the United States and Canada

*Bantam Books are published by Bantam Books, a division of Bantam
Doubleday Dell Publishing Group, Inc. Its trademark, consisting of
the words "Bantam Books" and the portrayal of a rooster, is Regis-
tered in U.S. Patent and Trademark Office and in other countries.
Marca Registrada. Bantam Books, 1540 Broadway, New York, New
York 10036.*

PRINTED IN THE UNITED STATES OF AMERICA

FFG   0 9 8 7 6 5 4 3 2

For Lynda
*who first knew it
with the author's love.*

Contents

LITTLE, BIG
or,
The Fairies' Parliament

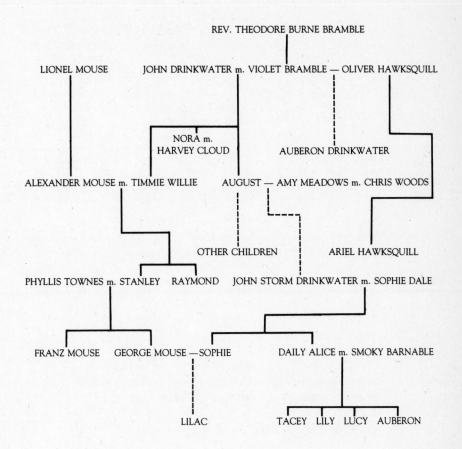

REV. THEODORE BURNE BRAMBLE

LIONEL MOUSE   JOHN DRINKWATER m. VIOLET BRAMBLE — OLIVER HAWKSQUILL

NORA m.
HARVEY CLOUD   AUBERON DRINKWATER

ALEXANDER MOUSE m. TIMMIE WILLIE   AUGUST — AMY MEADOWS m. CHRIS WOODS

OTHER CHILDREN   ARIEL HAWKSQUILL

PHYLLIS TOWNES m. STANLEY   RAYMOND   JOHN STORM DRINKWATER m. SOPHIE DALE

FRANZ MOUSE   GEORGE MOUSE —SOPHIE   DAILY ALICE m. SMOKY BARNABLE

LILAC   TACEY   LILY   LUCY   AUBERON

A little later, remembering man's earthly origin, 'dust thou art and to dust thou shalt return,' they liked to fancy themselves bubbles of earth. When alone in the fields, with no one to see them, they would hop, skip and jump, touching the ground as lightly as possible and crying 'We are bubbles of earth! Bubbles of earth! Bubbles of earth!'

—Flora Thompson,
Lark Rise

Book One

EDGEWOOD

I

Men are men, but Man is a woman.
—Chesterton

On a certain day in June, 19—, a young man was making his way on foot northward from the great City to a town or place called Edgewood, that he had been told of but had never visited. His name was Smoky Barnable, and he was going to Edgewood to get married; the fact that he walked and didn't ride was one of the conditions placed on his coming there at all.

Though he had left his City room early in the morning it was nearly noon before he had crossed the huge bridge on a little-used walkway and come out into the named but boundaryless towns on the north side of the river. Through the afternoon he negotiated those Indian-named places, usually unable to take the straight route commanded by the imperious and constant flow of traffic; he went neighborhood by neighborhood, looking down alleys and into stores. He saw few walkers, even indigenous, though there were kids on bikes; he wondered about their lives in these places, which to him seemed gloomily peripheral, though the kids were cheerful enough.

Somewhere to Elsewhere

The regular blocks of commercial avenues and residential streets began gradually to become disordered, thinning like the extremes of a great forest; began to be broken by weedy lots as though by glades; now and then a dusty undergrown woods or a scruffy meadow announced that it was available to be turned into an industrial park. Smoky turned that phrase over in his mind, since that seemed truly the place in the world where he was, the industrial park, between the desert and the sown.

He stopped at a bench where people could catch buses from Somewhere to Elsewhere. He sat, shrugged his small pack from

3

his back, took from it a sandwich he had made himself—another condition—and a confetti-colored gas-station road map. He wasn't sure if the map were forbidden by the conditions, but the directions he'd been given to get to Edgewood weren't explicit, and he opened it.

Now. This blue line was apparently the cracked macadam lined with untenanted brick factories he had been walking along. He turned the map so that this line ran parallel to his bench, as the road did (he wasn't much of a map reader) and found, far off to his left, the place he walked toward. The name Edgewood didn't appear, actually, but it was *here* somewhere, in this group of five towns marked with the legend's most insignificant bullets. So. There was a mighty double red line that went near there, proud with exits and entrances; he couldn't walk along that. A thick blue line (on the model of the vascular system, Smoky imagined all the traffic flowing south to the city on the blue lines, away on the red) ran somewhat nearer, extending corpuscular access to towns and townlets along the way. The much thinner sclerotic blue line he sat besidé was tributary to this; probably commerce had moved there, Tool Town, Food City, Furniture World, Carpet Village. Well . . . But there was also, almost indistinguishable, a narrow black line he could take soon instead. He thought at first that it led nowhere, but no, it went on, faltering, seeming at first almost forgotten by the mapmaker in the ganglia, but then growing clearer in the northward emptiness, and coming very near a town Smoky knew to be near Edgewood.

That one, then. It seemed a walker's road.

After measuring with his thumb and finger the distance on the map he had come, and how far he had to go (much farther), he slung on his pack, tilted his hat against the sun, and went on.

A Long Drink of Water

She was not much in his mind as he walked, though for sure she hadn't been far from it often in the last nearly two years he had loved her; the room he had met her in was one he looked into with the mind's eye often, sometimes with the trepidation he had felt then, but often nowadays with a grateful happiness; looked in to see George Mouse showing him from afar a glass, a pipe, and his two tall cousins: she, and her shy sister behind her.

It was in the Mouse townhouse, last tenanted house on the block, in the library on the third floor, the one whose mullioned windows were patched with cardboard and whose dark rug was worn white in pathways between door, bar and windows. It was that very room.

4

She was tall.

She was nearly six feet tall, which was several inches taller than Smoky; her sister, just turned fourteen, was as tall as he. Their party dresses were short, and glittered, hers red, her sister's white; their long, long stockings glistened. What was odd was that tall as they were they were shy, especially the younger, who smiled but wouldn't take Smoky's hand, only turned away further behind her sister.

Delicate giantesses. The older glanced toward George as he made debonair introductions. Her smile was tentative. Her hair was red-gold and curly-fine. Her name, George said, was Daily Alice.

He took her hand, looking up. "A long drink of water," he said, and she began to laugh. Her sister laughed too, and George Mouse bent down and slapped his knee. Smoky, not knowing why the old chestnut should be so funny, looked from one to another with a seraphic idiot's grin, his hand unrelinquished.

It was the happiest moment of his life.

It had not been, until he met Daily Alice Drinkwater in the library of the Mouse townhouse, a life particularly charged with happiness; but it happened to be a life suited just right for the courtship he then set out on. He was the only child of his father's second marriage, and was born when his father was nearly sixty. When his mother realized that the solid Barnable fortune had largely evanesced under his father's management, and that there had been therefore little reason to marry him and less to bear him a child, she left him in an access of bitterness. That was too bad for Smoky, because of all his relations she was the least anonymous; in fact she was the only one of any related to him by blood whose face he could instantly bring to memory in his old age, though he had been a boy when she left. Smoky himself mostly inherited the Barnable anonymity, and only a streak of his mother's concreteness: an actual streak it seemed to those who knew him, a streak of presence surrounded by a dim glow of absence.

They were a large family. His father had five sons and daughters by his first wife; they all lived in anonymous suburbs of cities in those states whose names begin with an I and which Smoky's City friends couldn't distinguish from one another. Smoky confused the catalogue himself at times. Since his father was supposed by them to have a lot of money and it was never clear what he intended to do with it, Dad was always welcome in their houses, and after his wife's departure he chose to sell the house Smoky was born in and travel

Anonymity

from one to another with his young son, a succession of anonymous dogs, and seven custom-made chests containing his library. Barnable was an educated man, though his learning was of such a remote and rigid kind that it gave him no conversation and didn't reduce his natural anonymity at all. His older sons and daughters regarded the chests of books as an inconvenience, like having his socks confused in the wash with theirs.

(Later on, it was Smoky's habit to try to sort out his half-siblings and their houses and assign them to their proper cities and states while he sat on the toilet. Maybe that was because it was in their toilets that he had felt most anonymous, anonymous to the point of invisibility; anyway, he would pass the time there shuffling his brothers and sisters and their children like a pack of cards, trying to match faces to porches to lawns, until late in life he could deal out the whole of it. It gave him the same bleak satisfaction he got from solving crossword puzzles, and the same doubt—what if he had guessed words that crossed correctly, but weren't the words the maker had in mind? The next-week's paper with the solution printed would never arrive.)

His wife's desertion didn't make Barnable less cheerful, only more anonymous; it seemed to his older children, as he coalesced in and then evaporated from their lives, that he existed less and less. It was only to Smoky that he gave the gift of his private solidity: his learning. Because the two of them moved so often, Smoky never did go to a regular school; and by the time one of the states that began with an I found out what had been done to Smoky by his father all those years, he was too old to be compelled to go to school any more. So, at sixteen, Smoky knew Latin, classical and medieval; Greek; some old-fashioned mathematics; and he could play the violin a little. He had smelled few books other than his father's leather-bound classics; he could recite two hundred lines of Virgil more or less accurately; and he wrote in a perfect Chancery hand.

His father died in that year, shriveled it seemed by the imparting of all that was thick in him to his son. Smoky continued their wanderings for a few more years. He had a hard time getting work because he had no Diploma; at last he learned to type in a shabby business school, in South Bend he later thought it must have been, and became a Clerk. He lived a lot in three different suburbs with the same name in three different cities, and in each his relatives called him by a different name—his own, his father's, and Smoky—which last so suited his evanescence that he kept it. When he was twenty-one, an unknown thrift of his father's threw down some belated money on him, and he took a bus to the City, forgetting as soon as he was past the last one all the cities his relatives had lived in, and all his relatives too, so that long afterwards he had to reconstruct them face by lawn; and once arrived in the City, he dispersed utterly and gratefully in it like a raindrop fallen into the sea.

      He had a room in a building that had once been the rectory of the very old church that stood revered and vandalized behind it. From his window he could see the churchyard where men with Dutch names turned comfortably in their old beds. In the morning he got up by the clock of sudden traffic—which he could never learn to sleep through as he had the long thunder of Midwestern trains—and went to work.

Name & Number

      He worked in a wide, white room where the little sounds he and the others made would rise to the ceiling and descend again strangely altered; when someone coughed, it was as though the ceiling itself coughed, apologetically, with covered mouth. All day long there Smoky slid a magnifying bar down column after column after column of tiny print, scrutinizing each name and its attendant address and phone number, and marking red symbols next to those that were not the same as the name and address and phone number typed on each card of stack after stack of cards that were piled daily next to him.

      At first the names he read were meaningless to him, as deeply anonymous as their phone numbers. The only distinction a name had was its accidental yet ineluctable place in the alphabetical order, and then whatever idiot errors the computer could dress it in, which Smoky was paid to discover. (That the computer could make as few errors as it did impressed Smoky less than its bizarre witlessness; it couldn't distinguish, for instance, when the abbreviation "St." meant "street" and when it meant "saint," and directed to expand these abbreviations, would without a smile produce the Seventh Saint Bar and Grill and the Church of All Streets.) As the weeks fell away, though, and Smoky filled up his aimless evenings walking block after block of the City (not knowing that most people stayed inside after dark) and began to learn the neighborhoods and their boundaries and classes and bars and stoops, the names that looked up at him through the glass bar began to grow faces, ages, attitudes; the people he saw in buses and trains and candy stores, the people who shouted to each other across tenement shaftways and stood gaping at traffic accidents and argued with waiters and shopgirls, and the waiters and shopgirls too, began to mill through his flimsy pages; the Book began to seem like a great epic of the City's life, with all its comings and goings, tragedies and farces, changeful and full of drama. He found widowed ladies with ancient Dutch names who lived he knew in high-windowed buildings on great avenues, whose husbands, Estates of, they managed, and whose sons had names like Steele and Eric and were intr dcrtrs and lived in Bohemian neighborhoods; he read of a huge family with wild Greek-sounding names who lived in several buildings on a noisome block he had walked once, a family that grew and discarded members every time he passed them in the alphabet—Gypsies, he decided at last; he knew of men whose wives and teenage daughters had private phones (on which they cooed with their lovers) while their men made calls on the many phones of the financial firms that bore their names; he grew suspicious of men who used their first initials and middle names because he found them all to be bill collectors, or lawyers whose bsns had the same address as their rsdnce, or city marshals who also sold used furniture; he learned that almost everyone named Singleton and everyone named Singletary lived in the northern black city where the men had for first names the names of past presidents and the women had gemlike names, pearl and ruby and opal and jewel, with a proud Mrs. before it—he imagined them large and dark and glowing in small apartments, alone with many clean children. From the proud locksmith who used so many A's in his tiny shop's name that he came first to Archimedes Zzzyandottie who came last (an old scholar who lived alone, reading Greek newspapers in a shabby apartment) he knew them all. Beneath his sliding bar a tiny name and number would rise up like flotsam borne up a beach by waves and tell its story; Smoky listened, looked at his card, found them the same, and was turning down the card even as the distorting glass threw up the next tale. The reader next to him sighed tragically. The ceiling coughed. The ceiling laughed, loudly. Everyone looked up.

A young man who had just been hired had laughed.

"I've just found," he said, "a listing here for the Noisy Bridge Rod and Gun Club." He could barely finish it for laughing, and Smoky was amazed that the silence of every other proofreader there didn't hush him. "Don't you get it?" The young man appealed to Smoky. "It sure would be a noisy bridge." Smoky suddenly laughed too, and their laughter rose to the ceiling and shook hands there.

His name was George Mouse; he wore wide suspenders to his wide pants, and when the day was done, he threw around himself a great woolen cloak whose collar trapped his long black hair, so that he must reach back and flip it out, like a girl. He had a hat like

Svengali's, and eyes like him too—dark-shadowed, compelling, and humorous. It wasn't a week later that he was fired, to the relief of every pair of bifocals in the white room, but by then he and Smoky had become, as only Smoky in the whole world it seemed could any longer say with all seriousness, fast friends.

With George as his friend, Smoky began a course of mild debauchery, a little drink, a little drugs; George changed his clothes, and his patterns of speech, to a City tattersall, and introduced him to Girls. In not too long a while, Smoky's anonymity became clothed, like the Invisible Man in his bandages; people stopped bumping into him on the street or sitting on his lap in buses without apology—which he had attributed to his being very vaguely present to most people.

A City Mouse

To the Mouse family—who lived in the last tenanted building of a block of buildings the first City Mouse had built and which they still mostly owned—he was at least present; and more than for his new hat and his new lingo he thanked George for that family of highly distinguishable and loudly loving folk. In the midst of their arguments, jokes, parties, walkings-out-in-bedroom-slippers, attempts at suicide and noisy reconciliations, he sat unnoticed for hours; but then Uncle Ray or Franz or Mom would look up startled and say, "Smoky's here!" and he would smile.

"Do you have country cousins?" Smoky asked George once as they waited out a snowstorm over café-royale in George's favorite old hotel bar. And indeed he did.

"They're very religious," George told him with a wink as he led him away from the giggly girls to introduce him to their parents, Dr. and Mrs. Drinkwater.

"Not a practicing doctor," said the Doctor, a wrinkled man with woolly hair and the unsmiling cheerfulness of a small animal. He was not as tall as his wife, whose generously-fringed and silken shawl trembled as she shook Smoky's hand and asked him to call her Sophie; she in turn wasn't as tall as her daughters. "All the Dales were tall," she said, looking up and inward as though she could see them all somewhere above her. She had given her surname therefore to her two great daughters, Alice Dale and Sophie Dale Drinkwater; but Mother was the only one who ever used the names, except that as a child Alice Dale had been called by some other child Daily Alice and the name

At First Sight

had stuck, so now it was Daily Alice and plain Sophie, and there was nothing for it, except that anyone looking at them could certainly see that they were Dale; and they all turned to look at them.

Whatever religion it was that they practiced didn't prevent them from sharing a pipe with Franz Mouse, who sat at their feet since they two took up all of a small divan; or from taking the rum-punch Mom offered them; or from laughing behind their hands, more at what they whispered to each other than at anything silly Franz said; or showing, when they crossed their legs, long thighs beneath their spangled dresses.

Smoky went on looking. Even though George Mouse had taught him to be a City man and not afraid of women, a lifetime's habit wasn't so easily overcome, and he went on looking; and only after a decent interval of being paralyzed with uncertainty did he force himself to walk the rug to where they sat. Eager not to be a wet blanket—"Don't be a wet blanket, for God's sake," George was always telling him—he sat down on the floor by them, a fixed smile on his face and a bearing that made him look (and he was, he was stunned to feel as Daily Alice turned to look at him, visible to her) oddly breakable. He had a habit of twiddling his glass between thumb and forefinger so that the ice trembled rapidly and chilled the drink. He did it now, and the ice rattled in the glass like a bell rung for attention. A silence fell.

"Do you come here often?" he said.

"No," she said evenly. "Not to the City. Only once in a while, when Daddy has business, or . . . other things."

"He's a doctor."

"Not really. Not any more. He's a writer." She was smiling, and Sophie beside her was giggling again, and Daily Alice went on with the conversation as though the object were to see how long she could keep a straight face. "He writes animal stories, for children."

"Oh."

"He writes one a day."

He looked up into her laughing eyes clear and brown as bottle glass. He had begun to feel very odd. "They must not be very long," he said, swallowing.

What was happening? He was in love, of course, at first sight, but he had been in love before and it had always been at first sight and he had never felt like this—as though something were growing, inexorably, within him.

"He writes under the name of Saunders," Daily Alice said.

He pretended to search his memory for this name, but in fact he was searching within for what it was that made him feel so

10

funny. It had extended now outward to his hands; he examined them where they lay in his houndstooth lap, looking very weighty. He interlaced the ponderous fingers.

"Remarkable," he said, and the two girls laughed, and Smoky laughed too. The feeling made him want to laugh. It couldn't be the smoke; that always made him feel weightless and transparent. This was the opposite. The more he looked at her the stronger it grew, the more she looked at him the more he felt . . . what? In a moment of silence they simply looked at each other, and understanding hummed, thundered within Smoky as he realized what had happened: not only had he fallen in love with her, and at first sight, but she at first sight had fallen in love with him, and the two circumstances had this effect: his anonymity was being cured. Not disguised, as George Mouse had tried to do, but cured, from the inside out. That was the feeling. It was as though she stirred him with cornstarch. He had begun to thicken.

He had gone down the narrow back stairs to the only john in the house that still worked, and stood looking into the wide, black-flecked mirror of that stone place.

The Young Santa Claus

Well. Who would have thought it. From the mirror a face looked out at him, not unfamiliar really, but still as though seen for the first time. A round and open face, a face that looked like the young Santa Claus, as we might see him in early photographs: a little grave, dark-moustached, with a round nose and lines by the eyes already where little laughing birds had walked though he wasn't yet twenty-three. All in all, a face of sunny disposition, with something in the eyes still blank and unresolved, pale and missing, that would, he supposed, never fill in. It was enough. In fact it was miraculous. He nodded, smiling, at his new acquaintance, and glanced at him again over his shoulder as he left.

As he was going up the back stairs, he met Daily Alice coming down, suddenly, at a turning. Now there was no idiot grin on his face; now she wasn't giggling. They slowed as they approached each other; when she had squeezed past him she didn't go on but turned to look back at him; Smoky was a step higher than she, so that their heads were in the relation dictated by movie kisses. His heart pounding with fear and elation, and his head humming with the fierce certainty of a sure thing, he kissed her. She responded as though for her too a certainty had proved out, and in the midst of her hair and lips and long arms encircling him, Smoky added a treasure of great price to the small store of his wisdom.

11

There was a noise then on the stair above them and they started. It was Sophie, and she stood above them eyes wide, biting her lip. "I have to pee-pee," she said, and danced by them lightly.

"You'll be leaving soon," Smoky said.

"Tonight."

"When will you come back?"

"I don't know."

He held her again; the second embrace was calm and sure. "I was frightened," she said. "I know," he said, exulting. God she was big. How was he to handle her when there was no stair to stand on?

A Sea Island

As a man well might who had grown up anonymous, Smoky had always thought that women choose or do not choose men by criteria he knew nothing of, by caprice, like monarchs, by taste, like critics; he had always assumed that a woman's choice of him or of another was foregone, ineluctable and instant. So he waited on them, like a courtier, waited to be noticed. Turns out, he thought, standing late that night on the Mouse stoop, turns out not so; they—she anyway—is flushed with the same heats and doubts, is like me shy and overcome by desire, and her heart raced like mine when the embrace was at hand, I know it did.

He stood for a long time on the stoop, turning over this jewel of knowledge, and sniffing the wind which had turned, as it infrequently does in the City, and blew in from the ocean. He could smell tide, and shore and sea detritus, sour and salt and bittersweet. And realized that the great City was after all a sea island, and a small one at that.

A sea island. And you could forget so basic a fact for years at a time if you lived here. But there it was, amazing but true. He stepped off the stoop and down the street, solid as a statue from breast to back, his footsteps ringing on the pavement.

Correspondence

Her address was "Edgewood, that's all," George Mouse said, and they had no phone; and so because he had no choice, Smoky sat down to make love through the mails with a thoroughness just about vanished from the world. His thick letters were consigned to this Edgewood place, and he waited for reply until he couldn't wait anymore and wrote another, and so their letters crossed in the mail as all true lovers' letters do; and she saved them and tied them with a lavender ribbon, and years later her grandchildren found them and read of those old people's improbable passion.

"I found a park," he wrote, in his black, spiky goblin's hand; "there's a plaque on the pillar where you enter it that says Mouse Drinkwater Stone 1900. Is that you all? It has a little pavilion of the Seasons, and statues, and all the walks curve so that you can't walk straight into the middle. You walk and walk and find yourself coming back out. Summer's very old there (you don't notice, in the city, except in parks), it's whiskery and dusty, and the park is little, too; but it all reminded me of you," as if everything did not. "I found an old pile of newspapers," said her letter which crossed his (the two truckdrivers waving to each other from their tall blue cabs on the misty morning turnpike). "There were these comic strips about a boy who dreams. The comic strip is all his dream, his Dreamland. Dreamland is beautiful; palaces and processions are always folding up and shrinking away, or growing huge and out of hand, or when you look closely turn out to be something else—you know—just like real dreams, only always pretty. Great-aunt Cloud says she saved them because the man who drew them, his name was Stone, once was an architect in the City, with George's great-grandfather and mine! They were 'Beaux-Arts' architects. Dreamland is very 'Beaux-Arts'. Stone was a drunkard—that's the word Cloud uses. The boy in the dreams always looks sleepy and surprised at the same time. He reminds me of you."

After beginning thus timidly, their letters eventually became so face-to-face that when at last they met again, in the bar of the old hotel (outside whose leaded windows snow fell) they both wondered if there had been some mistake, if somehow they had sent all those letters to the wrong person, this person, this unfocused and nervous stranger. That passed in an instant, but for a while they had to take turns speaking at some length, because it was the only way they knew; the snow turned to blizzard, the cafe-royale turned cold; a phrase of hers fell in with one of his and one of his with one of hers and, as elated as if they were the first to discover the trick of it, they conversed.

"You don't get—well—bored up there, all alone all the time?" Smoky asked, when they had practiced a while.

"Bored?" She was surprised. It seemed like an idea that hadn't before occurred to her. "No. And we're not alone."

"Well, I didn't mean . . . What sort of people are they?"

"What people?"

"The people . . . you're not alone with."

13

"Oh. Well. There used to be a lot of farmers. It was Scotch immigrants at first there. MacDonald, MacGregor, Brown. There aren't so many farms now. But some. A lot of people up there now are our relatives, too, sort of. You know how it is."

He didn't, exactly. A silence fell, and rose as they both started to speak at once, and fell again. Smoky said: "It's a big house?"

She smiled. "Enormous." Her brown eyes were deliquescent in the lamplight. "You'll like it. Everybody does. Even George, but he says he doesn't."

"Why?"

"He's always getting lost there."

Smoky smiled to think of George, the pathfinder, the waymaker through sinister night streets, baffled in an ordinary house. He tried to remember if in a letter he'd used the joke about city mice and country mice. She said: "Can I tell you something?"

"Sure." His heart beat fast, with no reason to.

"I knew you, when we met."

"What do you mean?"

"I mean I recognized you." She lowered her furry red-gold lashes, then stole a quick look at him, then looked around the somnolent bar as though someone might overhear her. "I'd been told about you."

"By George."

"No, no. A long time ago. When I was a kid."

"About me?"

"Well not about you exactly. Or about you exactly but I didn't know that till I met you." On the plaid tablecloth, she cupped her elbows in her hands, and leaned forward. "I was nine; or ten. It had been raining for a long time. Then there was a morning when I was walking Spark in the Park—"

"What?"

"Spark was a dog we had. The Park is, you know, the grounds around. There was a breeze blowing, and it felt like the rain was going to end. We were all wet. Then I looked west: there was a rainbow. I remembered what my mother said: morning rainbow in the west, then the weather will be best."

He imagined her very vividly, in a yellow slicker and high widemouthed boots, and her hair finer even and curlier than now; and wondered how she knew which way west was, a problem he still sometimes stumbled over.

"It was a rainbow, but bright, and it looked like it came down just—there, you know, not far; I could see the grass, all spar-

14

kling and stained every color there. The sky had got big, you know, the way it does when it clears at last after a long rainy time, and everything looked near; the place the rainbow came down was near; and I wanted more than anything to go stand in it—and look up—and be covered with colors."

Smoky laughed. "That's hard," he said.

She laughed too, dipping her head and raising the back of her hand to her mouth in a way that already seemed heartstirringly familiar to him. "It sure is," she said. "It seemed to take *forever*."

"You mean you—"

"Every time you thought you were coming close, it would be just as far off, in a different place; and if you came to that place, it would be in the place you came from; and my throat was sore with running, and not getting any closer. But you know what you do then—"

"Walk away from it," he said, surprised at his own voice but Somehow sure this was the answer.

"Sure. That isn't as easy as it sounds, but—"

"No, I don't suppose." He had stopped laughing.

"—but if you do it right—"

"No, wait," he said.

"—just right, then . . ."

"They don't really come down, now," Smoky said. "They don't, not really."

"They don't *here*," she said. "Now listen. I followed Spark; I let him choose, because he didn't care, and I did. It took just one step, and turn around, and guess what."

"I can't guess. You were covered in colors."

"No. It's not like that. Outside, you see colors inside it; so, inside it—"

"You see colors outside it."

"Yes. The whole world colored, as though it were made of candy—no, like it was made of a rainbow. A whole colored world as soft as light all around as far as you can see. You want to run and explore it. But you don't dare take a step, because it might be the wrong step—so you only look, and look. And you think: Here I am at last." She had fallen into thought. "At last," she said again softly.

"How," he said, and swallowed, and began again. "How did I come into it? You said someone told you . . ."

"Spark," she said. "Or someone like him."

She looked closely at him, and he tried to compose his features into a semblance of pleasant attention. "Spark is the dog," he said.

"Yes." She had become reluctant, it seemed, to go on. She picked up her spoon and studied herself, tiny and upside down, in its concavity, and put it down. "Or someone like him. Well. It's not important."

"Wait," he said.

"It only lasted a minute. While we stood there, I *thought*—" guardedly, and not looking at him "—I thought Spark said . . ." She looked up at him. "Is this hard to believe?"

"Well, yes. It is. Hard to believe."

"I didn't think it would be. Not for you."

"Why not for me?"

"Because," she said, and cradled her cheek in her hand, her face sad, disappointed even, which silenced him utterly, "because you were the one Spark talked about."

Make-Believe

It was probably only because he had nothing at all left to say, that in that moment—or rather in the moment after that moment—a difficult question or delicate proposition which Smoky had been mulling over all day tumbled out of his mouth in a far from finished form.

"Yes," she said, not raising her cheek from her hand but with a new smile lighting her face like a morning rainbow in the west. And so when the false dawn of the City's lights showed them the snow piled deep and crisp and even on their window-ledge, they lay with the deep crisp bedclothes up around their necks (the hotel's heat had failed in the sudden cold) and talked. They hadn't yet slept.

"What," he said, "are you talking about?"

She laughed and curled her toes against him. He felt strange, giddy, in a certain way he hadn't felt since before puberty, which was odd, but there it was: that feeling of being filled up so full that the tips of his fingers and the top of his head tingled: shone, maybe, if he were to look at them. Anything was possible. "It's make-believe, isn't it," he said, and she turned over smiling and fitted their bodies together like a double *s*.

Make-believe. When he was a kid, when he and others found some buried thing—neck of a brown bottle, tarnished spoon, a stone even that bore half an ancient spike-hole—they could convince themselves it was of great age. It had been there when George Washington was alive. Earlier. It was venerable, and immensely valuable. They convinced themselves of this by a collective act of will, which at the same time they concealed from each other: like make-believe, but different.

16

"But see?" she said. "It was all meant to be. And I knew it."

"But why?" he said, delighted, in torment; "why are you so sure?"

"Because it's a Tale. And Tales work out."

"But I don't know it's a tale."

"People in tales *don't* know, always. But there they are."

One winter night when he was a boy, boarding then with a half-brother who was half-heartedly religious, he first saw a ring around the moon. He stared up at it, immense, icy, half as wide as the night sky, and grew certain that it could only mean the End of the World. He waited thrilled in that suburban yard for the still night to break apart in apocalypse, all the while knowing in his heart that it would not: that there is nothing in this world not proper to it and that it contains no such surprises. That night he dreamt of Heaven: Heaven was a dark amusement park, small and joyless, just an iron Ferris wheel turning in eternity and a glum arcade to amuse the faithful. He awoke relieved, and never after believed his prayers, though he had said them for his brother without rancor. He would say hers, if she asked him to, and gladly; but she said none, that he knew of; she asked instead assent to something, something so odd, so unencompassable by the common world he had always lived in, so—he laughed, amazed. "A fairy tale," he said.

"I guess," she said sleepily. She reached behind her for his hand, and drew it around her. "I guess, if you want."

He knew he would have to believe in order to go where she had been; knew that, if he believed, he could go there even if it didn't exist, if it was make-believe. He moved the hand she had drawn around her down her long flesh, and with a little sound she pressed herself against him. He searched himself for that old will, long in disuse. If she went there, ever, he didn't want to be left behind; wanted never to be farther from her than this.

In May at Edgewood Daily Alice in the dark of the woods sat on a shining rock that jutted out over a deep pool, a pool made by the fall of water down a cleft in high rock walls. The stream that hurtled ceaselessly through the cleft to plunge into the pool made a speech as it did so, a speech repetitive yet always full of interest; Daily Alice listened, though she had heard it all before. She looked a lot like the girl on the soda bottle, though not so delicate and lacking wings.

Life is Short, or Long

"Grandfather Trout," she said to the pool, and again:

"Grandfather Trout." She waited then, and when nothing came of this, took up two small stones and plunged them into the water (cold and silky as only falling water held in stone pools seems to be) and knocked them together, which within the water made a sound like distant guns and hung longer than sounds hang in air. Then there swam out from somewhere in the weed-bearded hidey-holes along the bank a great white trout, an albino without speckle or belt, his pink eye solemn and large. The repeated ripples caused by the water-fall made him seem to shudder, his great eye to wink or maybe tremble with tears (can fish cry? she wondered, not for the first time).

When she thought she had his attention, she began to tell him how she had gone to the City in the fall and met this man in George Mouse's house, and how she had known instantly (or at least decided very quickly) that he would be the one that it had been promised she would "find or make up," as Spark had long ago put it to her. "While you slept through the winter," she said shyly, tracing the quartz muscle of the rock she sat on, smiling but not looking at him (because she spoke of whom she loved), "we, well we met again, and made promises—you know—" She saw him flick his ghostly tail; she knew this to be a painful subject. She stretched out her great length on the cool rock and, chin in hands and eyes alight, told him about Smoky in terms glowing and vague, which didn't seem to move the fish to enthusiasm. She took no notice. It *must* be Smoky that had been meant, it could be no other. "Don't you think so? Don't you agree?" More cautiously then: "Will they be satisfied?"

"No telling," Grandfather Trout said gloomily. "Who's to say what's in their minds?"

"But you said . . ."

"I bring their messages, daughter. Don't expect any more from *me*."

"Well," she said, put out, "I won't wait forever. I love him. Life is short."

"Life," said Grandfather Trout as though his throat were thick with tears, "is long. Too long." He turned his fins carefully and with a motion of his tail slid backwards into his hiding place.

"Tell them I came, anyway," she shouted after him, her voice small against the waterfall's. "Tell them I did my part."

But he was gone.

She wrote to Smoky: "I'm going to get married," and his heart turned cold where he stood by the letter-box, until he realized she meant to him. "Great-aunt Cloud has read the cards very care-fully, once for each part, it's to be Midsummer Day and this is what

you have to do. Please *please* follow all these instructions *very carefully* or I don't know what might happen."

Which is how Smoky came to be walking not riding to
Edgewood, with a wedding-suit in his pack old not new, and food
made not bought; and why he had begun to look around himself for a
place to spend the night, that he must beg or find but not pay for.

He had not known how suddenly the industrial park
would quit and the country begin. It was late afternoon and he had turned westerly, and the road had
become edgeworn, and patched like an old shoe in
many shades of tar. On either side the fields and farms
came down to meet the road; he walked beneath

*Trumps Turned
at Edgewood*

guardian trees neither farm nor road that cast multifold shadows now
and then over him. The gregarious weeds that frequent roadsides,
dusty, thick and blowsy, friends to man and traffic, nodded from
fence and ditch by the way. Less and less often he would hear the
hum of a car; the hum would grow intermittently, as the car went up
and down hills, and then suddenly it would be on him very loud and
roar past surprised, potent, fast, leaving the weeds blown and chuckling furiously for a moment; then the roar would just as quickly
subside to a far hum again, and then gone, and the only sounds the
insect orchestra and his own feet striking.

For a long time he had been walking somewhat uphill, but
now the incline crested, and he looked out over a broad sweep of
midsummer country. The road he stood on went on down through it,
past meadows and through pastures and around wooded hills; it disappeared in a valley near a little town whose steeple just showed
above the bursting green, and then appeared again, a tiny gray band
curling into blue mountains in whose cleft the sun was setting amid
roly-poly clouds.

And just then a woman on a porch at Edgewood far away
turned a trump called the Journey. There was the Traveler, pack on
his back and stout stick in his hand, and the long and winding road
before him to traverse; and the Sun too, though whether setting or
rising she had never decided. Beside the cards' unfolding pattern, a
brown cigarette smoldered in a saucer. She moved the saucer and
put the Journey in its place in the pattern, and then turned another
card. It was the Host.

When Smoky reached the bottom of the first of the rolling
hills the road stitched up, he was in a trough of shadow, and the sun
had set.

On the whole he preferred finding a place to sleep to asking for one; he had brought two blankets. He had even thought of finding a hay-barn to sleep in, as travelers do in books (his books), but the real hay-barns he passed seemed not only Private Property but also highly functional and crowded with large animals. He began to feel, in fact, somewhat lonely as the twilight deepened and the fields grew vague, and when he came on a bungalow at the bottom of the hill he went up to its picket fence and wondered how he might phrase what he thought must be an odd request.

Junipers

It was a white bungalow snuggled within bushy evergreens. Roses just blown grew up trellises beside the green dutch door. White-painted stones marked the path from the door; on the darkling lawn a young deer looked up at him immobile in surprise, and dwarves sat cross-legged on toadstools or snuck away holding treasure. On the gate was a rustic board with a legend burned on it: The Junipers. Smoky unlatched the gate and opened it, and a small bell tinkled in the silence. The top of the dutch door opened, and yellow lamplight streamed out. A woman's voice said "Friend or foe?" and laughed.

"Friend," he said, and walked toward the door. The air smelled unmistakably of gin. The woman leaning on the door's bottom half was one of those with a long middle age; Smoky couldn't tell where along it she stood. Her thin hair might have been gray or brown, she wore cat's-eye glasses and smiled a false-toothed smile; her arms folded on the door were comfortable and freckled. "Well, I don't know *you*," she said.

"I was wondering," Smoky said, "am I on the right road for a town called Edgewood?"

"I couldn't tell you," she said. "Jeff? Can you tell this young man the way to Edgewood?" She awaited an answer from within he couldn't hear, and then opened the door. "Come in," she said. "We'll see."

The house was tiny and tidy and stuffed with stuff. An old, old dog of the dust-mop kind sniffed at his feet, laughing breathlessly; be bumped into a bamboo telephone table, shouldered a knickknack shelf, stepped on a sliding scatter rug and fell through a narrow archway into a parlor that smelled of roses, bay rum and last winter's fires. Jeff put down his newspaper and lifted his slippered feet from their hassock. "Edgewood?" he asked around his pipe.

"Edgewood. I was given directions, sort of."

20

"You hitching?" Jeff's lean mouth opened like a fish's to puff as he perused Smoky doubtfully.

"No, walking actually." Above the fireplace was a sampler. It said:

> I will Live in a House
> By the side of the Road
> & Be a Friend to Man.
> Margaret Juniper 1 9 2 7

"I'm going there to get married." Ahhh, they seemed to say.

"Well." Jeff stood. "Marge, get the map."

It was a county map or something, much more detailed than Smoky's; he found the constellation of towns he knew of, neatly outlined, but nothing for Edgewood. "It should be somewhere around these." Jeff found the stub of a pencil, and with a "hmmm" and a "let's see," connected the centers of the five towns with a five-pointed star. The pentagon enclosed by the lines of the star he tapped with the pencil, and raised his sandy eyebrows at Smoky. An old map-reader's trick, Smoky surmised. He discerned the shadow of a road crossing the pentagon, joining the road he walked, which stopped for good here at Meadowbrook. "Hmmm," he said.

"That's about all I can tell you," Jeff said, re-rolling the map.

"You going to walk all night?" Marge asked.

"Well, I've got a bedroll."

Marge pursed her lips at the comfortless blankets strapped to the top of his pack. "And I suppose you haven't eaten all day."

"Oh, I've got, you know, sandwiches, and an apple . . . "

The kitchen was papered with baskets of impossibly luscious fruit, blue grapes and russet apples and cleft peaches that protruded like bottoms from the harvest. Marge moved dish after steaming dish from stove to oilcloth, and when it was all consumed, Jeff poured out banana liqueur into tiny ruby glasses. That did it; all his polite remonstrance with their hospitality vanished, and Marge "did up the davenport" and Smoky was put to bed wrapped in an earth-brown Indian blanket.

For a moment after the Junipers had left him, he lay awake looking around the room. It was lit only by a night-light that plugged right into the outlet, a night-light in the shape of a tiny, rose-covered cottage. By its light he saw Jeff's maple chair, the kind whose orange paddle arms had always looked tasty to him, like glossy hard

21

candy. He saw the ruffled curtains move in the rose-odorous breeze. He listened to the dust-mop dog sigh in his dreams. He found another sampler. This one said, he thought but could not be sure:

The Things that Make us Happy
Make us Wise.

He slept.

You may observe that I do not put
a hyphen between the two words.
I write "country house," not
"country-house." This is deliberate.

—V. Sackville-West

Daily Alice awoke, as she always did, when the sun broke in at her eastward windows with a noise like music. She kicked off the figured coverlet and lay naked in the long bars of sun for a time, touching herself awake, finding eyes, knees, breasts, red-gold hair all in place and where she had left them. Then she stood, stretched, brushed the last of sleep from her face, and knelt by the bed amid the squares of sun and said, as she had every morning since she could speak, her prayers:

> O great wide beautiful wonderful World
> With the wonderful waters around you curled
> And the beautiful grass upon your breast
> O World you are beautifully dressed.

Devotions done, she tilted the tall standing mirror that had been her great-grandmother's so that she could see her whole length in it, asked the usual question of it and got the right reply this morning; sometimes it was equivocal. She belted around herself a long brown gown, did a turn on her toes so that its frayed edges flew out, and went out wary into the still cold hall. She passed her father's study and listened briefly to his old Remington click-clacking about the adventures of mice and rabbits. She opened the door to her sister Sophie's room; Sophie was tangled in her bedclothes, a long golden hair in her parted lips, and her sleeping hands closed like a

A Gothic Bathroom

23

LITTLE, BIG

baby's. The morning sun was just then looking in at this room, and
Sophie stirred, resentful. Most people look odd asleep; foreign, not
themselves. Sophie asleep looked most like Sophie, and Sophie liked
sleep and could sleep anywhere, even standing up. Daily Alice stayed
awhile to watch her, wondering what her adventures were. Well, she
would hear later, in detail.

At the end of a whorl of hall was the Gothic bathroom,
the only one in the house with a tub long enough for her. Stuck as it
was at a turning of the house, the sun hadn't yet reached it; its
stained windows were dim and its cold tile floor made her stand
tiptoe. The gargoyle faucet coughed phthisically, and deep within
the house the plumbing held conference before allowing her some
hot water. The sudden rush had its effect, and she gathered up her
brown skirts around her waist and sat on the somewhat episcopal
hollow throne, chin in hand, watching the steam rise from the
sepulchral tub and feeling suddenly sleepy again.

She pulled the chain, and when the loud clash of contrary
waters was done she unbelted and stepped from her gown, shuddered,
and climbed carefully into the tub. The Gothic bathroom had filled
with steam. Its sort of Gothic was really more woodland than church;
the vaulting of it arched above Daily Alice's head and interlaced like
meeting branches, and everywhere carven ivy, leaves, tendrils and
vines were in restless biomorphic motion. On the surface of the
narrow stained-glass windows, dew formed in drops on cartoon-
bright trees, and on the distant hunters and vague fields which the
trees framed; and when the sun on its lazy way had lit up all twelve of
these, bejewelling the fog that rose from her bath, Daily Alice lay in
a pool in a medieval forest. Her great-grandfather had designed the
room, but another had made the glass. His middle name was Comfort, and that's what Daily Alice felt. She even sang.

While she scrubbed and sang, her bridegroom came on,
footsore and surprised at the fierceness of his muscles'
retaliation for yesterday's walk. While she breakfasted
in the long and angular kitchen and made plans with
her busy mother, Smoky climbed up a buzzing, sunshot mountain and down into a valley. When Daily
Alice and Sophie were calling to each other through intersecting
halls and the Doctor was looking out his window for inspiration,
Smoky stood at a crossroads where four elder elms stood like grave
old men conversing. A signboard there said EDGEWOOD and
pointed its finger along a dirt road that looped down a shadowy
tunnel of trees; and as he walked it, looking from side to side and

From Side
to Side

24

wondering what next, Daily Alice and Sophie were in Daily Alice's room preparing what Daily Alice next day would wear, while Sophie told her dream.

"I dreamt that I had learned a way of saving time I didn't want to spend, and having it to spend when I needed it. Like the time you spend waiting in a doctor's office, or coming back from someplace you didn't enjoy going to, or waiting for a bus—all the little useless spaces. Well, it was a matter of taking them and folding them up, like broken boxes, so that they took up less room. It was really an easy trick, once you knew you could do it. Nobody seemed surprised at all when I told them I'd learned how; Mother just nodded and smiled, you know, as though of course everybody learns at a certain age how to do these things. Just break it along the seams; be careful not to lose any; fold it flat. Daddy gave me this enormous envelope of sort of marbled paper to put it all in, and when he gave it to me I remembered seeing envelopes like that around, and wondering what they were for. Funny how you can make up memories in dreams to explain the story." While she talked, Sophie's quick fingers were dealing with a hem, and Daily Alice couldn't always hear her because she talked with pins in her mouth. The dream was hard to follow anyway; Daily Alice forgot each incident as soon as Sophie told it, just as though she were dreaming them herself. She picked up and put down a pair of satin shoes, and wandered out onto the tiny balcony of her oriel window. "I got frightened then," Sophie was saying. "I had this big dreary envelope stuffed with unhappy time, and I didn't know how to get any out and use it when I wanted it without letting all the dreary waiting and stuff out. It seemed maybe I'd made a mistake starting this. Anyhow . . ." Daily Alice looked down the front way, a brown drive with a tender spine of weed, all trembling in leaf shadow. Down at the end of the drive, gateposts grew up with a sudden curve from a wall, each topped with a pitted ball like a gray stone orange. As she looked, a Traveler turned hesitantly in at the gate.

Her heart turned over. She had been so happily calm all day that she had decided he wasn't coming, that Somehow her heart knew he wouldn't come today and that therefore there was no reason for it to sink and hammer in expectation. And now her heart was taken by surprise.

"Then it all got mixed up. It seemed there wasn't any time that wasn't being broken flat and put away, that I wasn't doing it any more, that it was happening by itself; and that all that was left was

25

awful time, walking down halls time, waking up in the night time, nothing doing time. . . ."

Daily Alice let her heart hammer, there being nothing she could say to it anyway. Below, Smoky came closer, slowly, as though in awe, she could not tell of what; but when she knew that he saw her, she undid the brown robe's belt and shrugged the robe from her shoulders. It slid open down her arms to her wrists and she could feel, like cool hands and warm, the shadows of leaves and the sun on her skin.

There was a hot flush in his legs that began with the soles of his feet and traveled midway up his shins, as though the long friction of his journey had heated them. His bitten head hummed with the noonday, and there was a sharp, threadlike pain in the inside of his right thigh. But he stood in Edgewood; there was no doubt. Even as he came down the path toward the immense and many-angled house, he knew he wouldn't ask the old woman on the porch for directions, because he needed none; he had arrived. And when he came close to the house, Daily Alice showed herself to him. He stood staring, his sweat-stained pack dangling in his hand. He didn't dare respond—there was the old woman on the porch—but he couldn't look away.

"Lovely, isn't it?" the old woman said at last. He blushed. She sat upright smiling at him from her peacock chair; there was a little glass-topped table by her, and she was playing solitaire. "I say—lovely," she repeated, a little louder.

"Yes!"

"Yes . . . so graceful. I'm glad it's the first thing you see, coming up the drive. The casements are new, but the balcony and all the stonework are original. Won't you come up on the porch? It's difficult to talk this way."

He glanced up again, but Alice was gone now; there was only a fanciful housetop painted with sunlight. He ascended to the pillared porch. "I'm Smoky Barnable."

"Yes. I'm Nora Cloud. Won't you sit?" She picked up her cards with a practiced hand and put them into a velvet bag; the velvet bag she then put into a tooled box.

"Was it you then," he said sitting in a whispering wicker chair, "who put these conditions on me about the suit and the walking and all?"

"Oh, no," she said. "I only discovered them."

"A sort of test."

The side note in the margin reads: Led Astray

"Perhaps. I don't know." She seemed surprised by the suggestion. She took from her breast pocket, where a neat and useless handkerchief was pinned, a brown cigarette, and lit it with a kitchen match she struck on her sole. She wore a light dress of the sort of print proper to old ladies, though Smoky thought he had never seen one quite so intensely blue-green, or one with leaves, tiny flowers, vines, so intricately intertwined: as though cut from the whole day. "I think prophylactic, though, on the whole."

"Hm?"

"For your own safety."

"Ah, I see." They sat in silence awhile, Great-aunt Cloud's a calm and smiling silence, his expectant; he wondered why he wasn't taken within, introduced; he was conscious of the heat rising from his shirt's open neck; he realized it was Sunday. He cleared his throat. "Dr. and Mrs. Drinkwater at church?"

"Why, in a sense, yes." It was odd the way she responded to everything he said as though it were a notion that had never occurred to her before. "Are you religious?"

He had been afraid of this. "Well," he began.

"The women tend to be more so, don't you think?"

"I guess. No one I grew up with cared much about it."

"My mother and I felt it far more strongly than my father, or my brothers. Though they suffered from it, perhaps, more than we."

He had no answer for this, and couldn't tell if her close inspection of him just then awaited one, or didn't, or was merely short sight.

"My nephew also—Dr. Drinkwater—well of course there are the animals, which he does pay close attention to. He pays very close attention there. The rest seems to pass him by."

"A pantheist, sort of?"

"Oh no. He's not that foolish. It just seems to"—she moved her cigarette in the air—"pass him by. Ah, who's here?"

A woman in a large picture hat had turned in at the gate on a bicycle. She wore a blouse, printed like Cloud's but more patent, and a pair of large jeans. She dismounted inexpertly and took a wooden bucket from the bike's basket; when she tilted her picture hat back, Smoky recognized Mrs. Drinkwater. She came up and sat heavily on the steps. "Cloud," she said, "that is forever the last time I will ever ask you for advice about berrying again."

"Mr. Barnable and I," said Cloud merrily, "were discussing religion."

"Cloud," said Mrs. Drinkwater darkly, scratching her

ankle above a slip-on sneaker frayed about the big toe, "Cloud, I was led astray."

"Your bucket is full."

"I was led astray. The bucket, hell, I filled that the first ten minutes I got there."

"Well. There you are."

"You didn't say I would be led astray."

"I didn't ask."

There was a pause then. Cloud smoked. Mrs. Drinkwater dreamily scratched her ankle. Smoky (who didn't mind not being greeted by Mrs. Drinkwater; in fact hadn't noticed it; that comes from growing up anonymous) had time to wonder why Cloud hadn't said *you didn't ask*. "As for religion," Mrs. Drinkwater said, "ask Auberon."

"Ah. There you see. Not a religious man." To Smoky: "My older brother."

"It's all he thinks about," Mrs. Drinkwater said.

"Yes," Cloud said thoughtfully, "yes. Well, there it is, you see."

"Are you religious?" Mrs. Drinkwater asked Smoky.

"He's not," Cloud said. "Of course there was August."

"I didn't have a religious childhood," Smoky said. He grinned. "I guess I was sort of a polytheist."

"What?" said Mrs. Drinkwater.

"The Pantheon. I had a classical education."

"You have to start somewhere," she replied, picking leaves and small bugs from her bucket of berries. "This should be *nearly* the last of the foul things. Tomorrow's Midsummer Day, thank it all."

"My brother August," Cloud said, "Alice's grandfather, he was perhaps religious. He left. For parts unknown."

"A missionary?" Smoky asked.

"Why yes," Cloud said, again seeming newly struck with the idea. "Yes, maybe so."

"They must be dressed by now," Mrs. Drinkwater said. "Suppose we go in."

An Imaginary Bedroom

The screen door was old and large, its wood pierced and turned a bit to summery effect, and the screen potbellied below from years of children's thoughtless egress; when Smoky pulled its porcelain handle, the rusty spring groaned. He stepped across the sill. He was inside.

The vestibule, tall and polished, smelled of cool trapped night air and last winter's fires, lavender sachets in brass-handled linen closets, what else? Wax, sunlight, collated seasons, the June day outside brought in as the screen groaned and clacked shut behind him. The stairs rose before him and above him, turning a half-circle by stages to the floor above. On the first landing, in the light of a lancet window there, dressed now in jeans made all of patches, her feet bare, his bride stood. A little behind her was Sophie, a year older now but still not her sister's height, in a thin white dress and many rings.

"Hi," said Daily Alice.

"Hi," Smoky said.

"Take Smoky upstairs," Mrs. Drinkwater said. "He's in the imaginary bedroom. And I'm sure he wants to wash up." She patted his shoulder and he put his foot on the first stair. In later years he would wonder, sometimes idly, sometimes in anguish, whether having once entered here he had ever again truly left; but at the time he just mounted to where she stood, deliriously happy that after a long and extremely odd journey he had at last arrived and that she was greeting him with brown eyes full of promise (and perhaps then this was the journey's only purpose, his present happiness, and if so a good one and all right with him) and taking his pack and his hand and leading him into the cool upper regions of the house.

"I could use a wash," he said, a little breathless. She dipped her big head near his ear and said, "I'll lick you clean, like a cat." Sophie giggled behind them.

"Hall," Alice said, running her hand along the dark wainscoting. She patted the glass doorknobs she passed: "Mom and Dad's room. Dad's study—shhh. My room—see?" He peeked in, and mostly saw himself in the tall mirror. "Imaginary study. Old orrery, up those stairs. Turn left, then turn left." The hallway seemed concentric, and Smoky wondered how all these rooms managed to sprout off it. "Here," she said.

The room was of indiscernible shape; the ceiling sank toward one corner sharply, which made one end of the room lower than the other; the windows there were smaller too; the room seemed larger than it was, or was smaller than it looked, he couldn't decide which. Alice threw his pack on the bed, narrow and spread for summer in dotted swiss. "The bathroom's down the hall," she said. "Sophie, go run some water."

"Is there a shower?" he asked, imagining the hard plunge of cool water.

"Nope," Sophie said. "We were going to modernize the plumbing, but we can't find it anymore. . . ."

"Sophie."

Sophie shut the door on them.

First she wanted to taste the sweat that shone on his throat and fragile clavicle; then he chose to undo the tails of her shirt, that she had tied up beneath her breasts; then, but then impatient they forgot about taking turns and quarreled silently, eagerly over each other, like pirates dividing treasure long sought, long imagined, long withheld.

Alone together at noon they ate peanut-butter and apple sandwiches in the walled garden at the back front of the house.

"The back front?"

In the Walled Garden

Opulent trees looked over the gray garden wall, like calm spectators leaning on their elbows. The stone table they sat at, in a corner beneath a spreading beech, was marked with the coiled stains left by caterpillars crushed in other summers; their cheerful paper plates lay on its thickness flimsy and ephemeral. Smoky struggled to clear his palate; he didn't usually eat peanut-butter.

"This used to be the front," Daily Alice said. "Then they built the garden and the wall; so the back became the front. It was a front anyway. And now this is the back front." She straddled the bench, and picked up a twig, at the same time drawing out with her pinkie a glittering hair that had blown between her lips. She scratched a quick five-pointed star in the dirt. Smoky looked at it, and at the tautness of her jeans. "That's not really it," she said, looking birdwise at her star, "but sort of. See, it's a house all fronts. It was built to be a sample. My great-grandfather? Who I wrote you about? He built this house to be a sample, so people could come and look at it, from any side, and choose which kind of house they wanted; that's why the inside is so crazy. It's so many houses, sort of put inside each other or across each other, with their fronts sticking out."

"What?" He had been watching her talk, not listening; she saw it in his face and laughed. "Look. See?" she said. He looked where she pointed, along the back front. It was a severe, classical facade softened by ivy, its gray stone stained as though by dark tears; tall, arched windows; symmetrical detail he recognized as the classical Orders; rustications, columns, plinths. Someone was looking out one tall window with an air of melancholy. "Now come on." She took a big bite (big teeth) and led him by the hand along that front, and as they passed, it seemed to fold like scenery; what had looked flat became out-thrust; what stuck out folded in; pillars turned pilasters and disappeared. Like one of those ripply pictures children play with, where a face turns from grim to grin as you move it, the back front altered, and when they reached the opposite wall and turned to look back, the house had become cheerful and mock-Tudor, with deep curling eaves and clustered chimneys like comic hats. One of the broad casement windows (a stained piece or two glittered among the leaded panes) opened on the second floor, and Sophie looked out, waving. "Smoky," she called, "when you've finished your lunch, you're to go talk to Daddy in the library." She stayed in the window, arms folded and resting on the sill, looking down at him smiling, as though pleased to have brought this news.

"Oh, aha," Smoky called up nonchalantly. He walked back to the stone table, the house translating itself back into Latin beside him. Daily Alice was eating his sandwich. "What am I going to say to him?" She shrugged, mouth full. "What if he asks me what are your prospects, young man?" She laughed, covering her mouth, the way she had in George Mouse's library. "Well, I can't just tell him I read the telephone book." The immensity of what he was about to embark on, and Doctor Drinkwater's obvious responsibility to impress it on him, settled on his shoulders like birds. He wavered suddenly, doubted doubts. He looked at his big beloved. What anyway *were* his prospects? Could he explain to the Doctor that his daughter had cured Smoky's anonymity as if in one blow—one glancing blow—and that that was enough? That the marriage service once completed (and whatever religious commitments they would like him to make made) he intended to just live happily ever after, like other folks?

She had taken out a little jackknife and was peeling a green apple in one segmented curling ribbon. She had such talents. What good was he to her?

"Do you like children?" she asked, without taking her eyes from her apple.

It was dim in the library, according to the old philosophy of keeping a house shut up on hot summer days to keep it cool. It was cool. Dr. Drinkwater wasn't there. Through the draped, arched windows he could just glimpse Daily Alice and Sophie talking at the stone table in the garden, and he felt like a boy kept indoors, bad or sickly. He yawned nervously, and looked over nearby titles; it didn't appear that anyone had taken a book from these laden shelves in a long time. There were sets of sermons, volumes of George MacDonald, Andrew Jackson Davis, Swedenborg. There were a

Houses & Histories

couple of yards of the Doctor's children's stories, pretty, shoddily bound, with repetitious titles. Some nicely bound classics propped against an anonymous laureled bust. He took down Suetonius, and brought down with it a pamphlet that had been wedged between the volumes. It was old, both dog-eared and foxed, illustrated with pearly photogravure, and titled *Upstate Houses and Their Histories.* He turned its pages carefully so as not to break the old glue of the binding, looking at dim gardens of black flowers, a roofless castle built on a river island by a thread magnate, a house made of beer vats.

He looked up, turning the page. Daily Alice and Sophie were gone; a paper plate leapt from the table and spun balletically to the ground.

And here was a photograph of two people sitting at a stone table, having tea. There was a man who looked like the poet Yeats, in a pale summer suit and spotted tie, his hair full and white, his eyes obscured by the sunlight glinting from his spectacles; and a younger woman in a wide white hat, her dark features shaded by the hat and blurred perhaps by a sudden movement. Behind them was part of this house Smoky sat in, and beside them, reaching up a tiny hand to the woman, who perhaps saw it and moved to take it and then again perhaps not (it was hard to tell), was a figure, personage, a little creature about a foot high in a conical hat and pointed shoes. His broad inhuman features seemed blurred too by sudden movement, and he appeared to bear a pair of gauzy insect wings. The caption read "John Drinkwater and Mrs. Drinkwater (Violet Bramble;) elf. Edgewood, 1912." Below the picture, the author had this to say:

"Oddest of the turn-of-the-century folly houses may be John Drinkwater's *Edgewood*, although not strictly conceived as a folly at all. Its history must begin with the first publication of Drinkwater's *Architecture of Country Houses* in 1880. This charming and influential compendium of Victorian domestic architecture made the young Drinkwater's name, and he later became a partner in the famed landscape-architecture team of Mouse, Stone. In 1894 Drinkwater designed Edgewood as a kind of compound illustration of the plates of his famous book, thus making it several different houses of different sizes and styles collapsed together and quite literally impossible to describe. That it presents an aspect (or aspects) of logic and order is a credit to Drinkwater's (already waning) powers. In 1897 Drinkwater married Violet Bramble, a young Englishwoman, daughter of the mystic preacher Theodore Burne Bramble, and in the course of his marriage, came completely under the influence of his wife, a magnetic spiritualist. Her thought informs later editions of *Architecture of Country Houses*, into which he interpolated larger and larger amounts of theosophist or idealist philosophy without however removing any of the original material. The sixth and last edition (1910) had to be printed privately, since commercial publishers were no longer willing to undertake it, and it still contains all the plates of the 1880 edition.

"The Drinkwaters assembled around them in those years a group of like-thinking people including artists, aesthetes, and world-weary sensitives. From the beginning the cult had an Anglophile twist, and interested correspondents included the poet Yeats, J. M. Barrie, several well-known illustrators, and the sort of 'poetic' personality that was allowed to flourish in that happy twilight before the Great War, and that has disappeared in the harsh light of the present day.

"An interesting sidelight is that these people were able to profit from the general depopulation of the farms in that area at that time. The pentagon of five towns around Edgewood saw the heels of improverished yeoman farmers driven to the City and the West, and the bland faces of poets escaping economic realities who came to take their houses. That all who still remained of this tiny band were 'conscientious objectors' at the time of their country's greatest need is perhaps not surprising; nor is the fact that no trace of their bizarre and fruitless mysteries has survived to this day.

"The house is still lived in by Drinkwater's heirs. There is reputed to be a genuine folly summer house on the (very extensive) grounds, but the house and grounds are not open to the public at any time."

Elf?

"So we're supposed to have a chat," Dr. Drinkwater said. "Where would you like to sit?" Smoky took a club chair of buttoned leather. Dr. Drinkwater, on the chesterfield, ran his hand over his woolly head, sucked his teeth for a moment, then coughed in an introductory kind of way. Smoky awaited his first question.

Doctor Drinkwater's Advice

"Do you like animals?" he said.

"Well," Smoky said, "I haven't known very many. My father liked dogs." Doctor Drinkwater nodded with a disappointed air. "I always lived in cities, or suburbs. I liked listening to the birds in the morning." He paused. "I've read your stories. I think they're

. . . very true to life, I imagine." He smiled what he instantly realized to be a horridly ingratiating smile, but the Doctor didn't seem to notice. He only sighed deeply.

"I suppose," he said, "you're aware of what you're getting into."

Now Smoky cleared his throat in introduction. "Well, sir, of course I know I can't give Alice, well, the splendor she's used to, at least not for a while. I'm—in research. I've had a good education, not really formal, but I'm finding out how to use my, what I know. I might teach."

"Teach?"

"Classics."

The doctor had been gazing upward at the high shelves burdened with dark volumes. "Um. This room gives me the willies. Go talk to the boy in the library, Mother says. I never come in here if I can help it. What is it you teach, did you say?"

"Well, I don't yet. I'm—breaking into it."

"Can you write? I mean write handwriting? That's very important for a teacher."

"Oh, yes. I have a good hand." Silence. "I've got a little money, an inheritance. . . ."

"Oh, money. There's no worry there. We're rich." He grinned at Smoky. "Rich as Croesus." He leaned back, clutching one flannel knee in his oddly small hands. "My grandfather's, mostly. He was an architect. And then my own, from the stories. And we've had good advice." He looked at Smoky in a strange, almost pitying way. "That you can always count on having—good advice." Then, as if he had delivered a piece of it himself, he unfolded his legs, slapped his knees, and got up. "Well. Time I was going. I'll see you at dinner? Good. Don't wear yourself out. You've got a long day tomorrow." He spoke this last out the door, so eager was he to go.

The Architecture of Country Houses

He had noticed them, behind glass doors up behind where Doctor Drinkwater had sat on the chesterfield; he got up now on his knees on the sofa, turned the convolute key in its lock, and slid open the door. There they were, six together, just as the guidebook had said, neatly graduated in thickness. Around them, leaning together or stacked up horizontally, were others, other printings perhaps. He took out the slimmest one, an inch or so thick. *Architecture of Country Houses.* Intaglie cover, with that "rustic" Victorian lettering (running biaswise) that sprouts twigs and leaves. The olive color of dead foliage. He riffled the heavy leaves. The Perpendicular,

Full or Modified. The Italianate Villa, suitable for a residence on an open field or campagna. The Tudor and the Modified Neo-classical, here chastely on separate pages. The Cottage. The Manor. Each in its etched circumstances of poplars or pines, fountain or mountain, with little black visitors come to call, or were they the proud owners come to take possession? He thought that if all the plates were on glass, he could hold them all up at once to the mote-inhabited bar of sunlight from the window and Edgewood would appear whole. He read a bit of the text, which gave careful dimensions, optional fancies, full and funny accounting of costs (ten-dollar-a-week stonemasons long dead and their skills and secrets buried too) and, oddly, what sort of house suited what sort of personality and calling. He returned it.

The next one he drew out was nearly twice as thick. Fourth edition, it said, Little, Brown, Boston 1898. It had a frontispiece, a sad, soft pencil portrait of Drinkwater. Smoky vaguely recognized the artist's hyphenated double name. Its chock-full title page had an epigraph: I arise, and unbuild it again. Shelley. The plates were the same, though there were a set of Combinations that were all floorplans and labeled in a way Smoky couldn't comprehend.

The sixth and last edition, great and heavy, was beautifully bound in art-nouveau mauve; the letters of the title stretched out shuddered limbs and curling descenders as though to grow; the whole seemed as though reflected in a rippled lily-pond surface all in bloom at evening. The frontispiece was not Drinkwater now but his wife, a photograph like a drawing, smudged like charcoal. Her indistinct features. Perhaps it wasn't the art. Perhaps she was as he had been, not always fully present; but she was lovely. There were dedicatory poems and epistles and a great armor of Prefaces, Forewords and Prolegomena, red type and black; and then the little houses again just as before, looking now old-fashioned and awkward, like an ordinary small town swept up in a modern mania. As though Violet's amanuensis were struggling for some last grasp of reason over the pages and pages studded with capitalized abstractions (the type had grown smaller as books had grown thicker), there were marginal glosses every page or so, and epigraphs, chapter headings, and all paraphernalia that makes a text into an object, logical, articulated, unreadable. Tipped in at the end against the watered endpapers was a chart or map, folded over several times, a thick packet in fact. It was of thin paper, and Smoky at first couldn't see how to go about unfolding it; he began one way, winced at the little cry it made as an old fold tore slightly, began again. As he glimpsed parts of it, he could see it was an immense plan, but of what? At last he had the whole unfolded; it lay crackling across his lap face down, he had only to turn it face up. He stopped then, not sure he wanted to see what it was. *I suppose,* the Doctor had said, *you're aware of what you're getting into.* He lifted its edge, it rose up lightly like a moth's wing so old and fine it was, a shaft of sunlight pierced it and he glimpsed complex shapes studded with notions; he laid it down to look at it.

Just Then

"Will she go, then, Cloud?" Mother asked, and Cloud answered, "Well it appears not so;" but she wouldn't add any more, only sat at the far end of the kitchen table, the smoke of her cigarette an obscurity in the sunlight. Mother was powdered to the elbows in the process of pie-making, not a mindless task though she liked to call it that, in fact she found that at it her thoughts were often clearest, notions sharpest; she could do things when her body was busy that she could at no other time, things like assemble her worries into ranks, each rank commanded by a hope. She remembered verse sometimes cooking that she had forgotten she knew, or spoke in tongues, her husband's or her children's or her dead father's or her unborn, clearly-seen grandchildren's, three graduated girls and a lean unhappy boy. She knew the weather in her elbows, and mentioned as she slipped the old glass pie-plates into the oven which breathed its heated breath on her that it would storm soon. Cloud made no answer, only sighed and smoked, and dabbed at the dew at her wrinkled throat with a little hankie which she then tucked neatly back into her sleeve. She said: "It will be lots clearer later," and went slowly from the kitchen and through the halls to her room to see if she might be able to close her eyes for a while before dinner had to be prepared; and before she lay down on the wide featherbed that for a few short years had been hers and Henry Cloud's she looked out toward the hills and yes, white cumulus had begun to assemble itself that way, climbing like imminent victory, and no doubt Sophie was right. She lay and thought: At least he came all right, and contradicted none of it. Beyond that she couldn't tell.

Just then where the Old Stone Fence divides the Green Meadow from the Old Pasture which goes down rocky and leaping with insects to the margin of the Lily Pond, Doctor Drinkwater in a wide-awake hat stopped, panting from his climb; slowly the roar of his own blood diminished in his ears and he could begin to listen to the scene in progress of his only drama, the interminable conversations of birds, cicada's semitune, the rustle and thump of a thousand creatures' entrances and exits. The land was touched by the hand of man, though that hand was in these days mostly withdrawn; way down beyond the Lily Pond he could see the dreaming roof of Brown's barn, and knew this to be an abandoned pasture of his enterprise, and this wall his ancient marker. The scene was variegated by man's enterprise, and room made for many houses large and small, this capacious wall, that sunny pasture, that pond. It all seemed to the Doctor just what was truly meant by the word "ecology," which he saw now and then misused in the dense columns that bordered his chronicles of this place in the City paper; and as he sat on a warm lichened stone utterly attentive, a Little Breeze brought him news that by evening a mountain of cloud would break in pieces here.

Just then in Sophie's room on the wide featherbed where for many years John Drinkwater lay with Violet Bramble, their two great-grandchildren lay. The long pale dress that next day Daily Alice would put on, and then presumably not again ever completely put off, was hung carefully from the top of the closet door, and made in the closet door mirror another like it, which it pressed back to back; and below it and around it were all things proper to it. Sophie and her sister lay naked in the afternoon heat; Sophie brushed her hand across her sister's sweat-damp flank, and Daily Alice said "Ah, it's too hot," and felt hotter still her sister's tears on her shoulder. She said: "Someday soon it'll be you, you'll choose or maybe be chosen, and you'll be another June bride," and Sophie said, "I'll never, never," and more that Alice couldn't hear because Sophie buried her face against her sister's neck and murmured like the afternoon; what Sophie said was, "He'll never understand or see, they'll never give him what they gave us, he'll step in the wrong places and look when he should look away, never see doors or know turnings; wait and see, you just wait and see"; which just then Great-aunt Cloud was pondering, what they would see if they waited, and what their mother also felt though not with the same plain curiosity but a sort of maneuvering within of the armies of Possibility; and what Smoky too, left alone for what he imagined was the general Sunday siesta, day of rest, in the black and dusty library with the whole plan before him, just then trembled with, sleepless and erect as a flame.

III

There was an old woman
Who lived under the hill
And if she's not gone
She lives there still.

I t was during a glad summer toward the end of the last
century that John Drinkwater, while on a walking tour
of England ostensibly to look at houses, came one
twilight to the gates of a red-brick vicarage in Cheshire. He had lost
his way, and his guidebook, which he had foolishly knocked into the
millrace by which he had eaten his lunch hours before; he was
hungry, and however safe and sweet the English countryside he
couldn't help feeling uneasy.

In the vicarage garden, an unkempt and riotous garden,
moths glimmered amid a dense cascade of rosebushes,
and birds flitted and rustled in a gnarled and
domineering apple tree. In the tree's crook someone
sat and, as he looked, lit a candle. A candle? It was a
young girl in white, and she cupped the candle with
her hands; it glowed and faded and then glowed again. She spoke,
not to him: "What's the matter?" The candleglow was extinguished,
and he said, "I beg your pardon." She began to climb quickly and
expertly down from the tree, and he stood away from the gate so as
not to look importunate and prying when she came to speak to him.
But she didn't come. From somewhere or everywhere a nightingale
began, ceased, began again.

He had come not long before to a crossroads (not a literal
crossroads, though many of those too in his month's walk where he
had to choose to go down by the water or over the hill, and found it
not much use as practice for the crossroads in his life). He had spent

Strange
Insides

a hateful year designing an enormous Skyscraper that was to look, as exactly as its hugeness and use allowed, like a thirteenth-century cathedral. When he had first submitted sketches to his client it had been in the nature of a joke, a fancy, a red herring even, meant to be dismissed, but the client hadn't understood that; he wanted his Skyscraper to be just this, just what it eventually would become, a Cathedral of Commerce, and nothing John Drinkwater could think of, brass letterbox like a baptismal font, grotesque bas-reliefs in Cluniac style of dwarves using telephones or reading stone ticker tape, gargoyles projecting from the building at such a height that no one could ever see them and wearing (though even *that* the man had refused to recognize) his client's own headlamp eyes and porous nose—nothing was too much for him and now it would all have to be executed just as he had conceived it.

While this project dragged on, a change attempted to come over him. Attempted, because he resisted it; it seemed a thing apart from him, a thing he could almost but not quite name. He first noticed it as an insinuation into his crowded yet orderly day of peculiar daydreams: abstract words merely, that would suddenly be spoken within him as though by a voice. *Multiplicity* was one. Another on another day (as he sat looking out the tall windows of the University Club at the sooty rain) was *combinatory*. Once uttered, the notion had a way of taking over his whole mind, extending into the work-place there and into the countinghouse, until he was left paralyzed and unable to take the next long-prepared and well-thought-out step in the career everyone described as "meteoric."

He felt he was lapsing into a long dream, or perhaps awaking from one. Either way, he didn't want it to happen. As a specific against it (he thought) he began to take an interest in theology. He read Swedenborg and Augustine; he was soothed most by Aquinas, could sense the Angelic Doctor building stone by stone the great cathedral of his *Summa*. He learned then that at the end of his life Aquinas regarded all that he had written as "a heap of straw."

A heap of straw. Drinkwater sat at his broad board in the long skylit offices of Mouse, Drinkwater, Stone and stared at the sepia photographs of the towers and parks and villas he had built, and thought: a heap of straw. Like the first and most ephemeral house the Three Pigs in the story built. There must be a stronger place, a place where he could hide from whatever this wolf was that pursued him. He was thirty-nine years old.

His partner Mouse found that after he had been some months at his drawing board he had gotten no further with firm plans for the Cathedral of Commerce, had been sitting instead hour after hour doodling tiny houses with strange insides; and he was sent abroad for a while, to rest.

Strange insides . . . By the path that led up from the gate to the fanlighted door of the vicarage he could see a machine or garden ornament, a white globe on a pedestal surrounded by rusted iron hoops. Some of the hoops had sprung and lay fallen on the path, obscured in weeds. He pushed the gate and it opened, making a brief song on its hinges. Within the house a light was moving, and as he came up the weedy path he was hailed from the door.

For It Was He

"You are not welcome," said Dr. Bramble (for it was he). "You are none of you, any more. Is that you, Fred? I shall have a lock to that gate, if people can't have better manners."

"I'm not Fred."

His accent made Dr. Bramble stop to think. He raised his lamp. "Who are you then?"

"Just a traveler. I'm afraid I've lost my way. You don't have a telephone."

"Of course not."

"I didn't mean to barge in."

"Mind the old orrery there. It's all fallen, and a dreadful trap. American?"

"Yes."

"Well, well, come in."

The girl was gone.

Strange and Shaded Lanes

Two years later, John Drinkwater was sitting sleepily in the overheated and spiritually-lit rooms of the City Theosophical Society (he never guessed that any of the ways his crossroads pointed out would lead him there, but there he was). A subscription was being raised for a course of lectures by variously enlightened persons, and among the mediums and gymnosophists who were awaiting the Society's decision, Drinkwater found the name of Dr. Theodore Burne Bramble, to speak on the Smaller Worlds within the Large. As soon as he read the name he saw, at once and unsummoned, the girl within the apple tree, the light within her cupped hands going dim. *What's the matter?* He saw her again come into the dusky dining room, unintroduced by the vicar who couldn't bring himself to break his paragraph long enough to speak her name, only nodded and pushed aside a pile of mildewed books and sheaves of papers tied with blue tape so that there was room for her to put down (without raising her eyes to him) the tarnished tea service and cracked plate of kippers. She might have been daughter or ward or servant or prisoner—or keeper even, for Dr. Bramble's ideas were odd and obsessive enough, though mildly expressed.

"Paracelsus is of the opinion, you see," he said, and paused to light his pipe; Drinkwater managed to say, "The young lady is your daughter?"

Bramble shot a look behind him as though Drinkwater had seen some member of the Bramble family he didn't know about; then he agreed, nodding, and went on: "Paracelsus, you see . . ."

She brought white port and ruby, unsummoned, and when that was gone Dr. Bramble was inflamed enough to speak of some of his personal sorrows, how his pulpit had been taken from him because he would speak the truth as he learned it, and how they came around now to taunt him and tie tins to his dog's tail, poor dumb creature! She brought whiskey and brandy and at last he didn't care and asked her her name. "Violet," she said, not looking at him. When Dr. Bramble finally showed him to a bed, it was only because if he had not Drinkwater would have got out of earshot; as it was he had ceased to understand anything Dr. Bramble was saying. "Houses made of houses within houses made of time," he found himself saying aloud when just before dawn he awoke from a dream of Dr. Bramble's kindly face and with a fierce burning in his throat. When he tipped up the ewer at his bedside a discomfited spider crawled out, and he stood at the window unrelieved, pressing the cool porcelain to his cheek. He looked out at the wind-ordered islands of mist that lay between the lacy cutout trees, and watched the last fireflies extinguishing themselves. He saw her returning from the barn, shoeless and in her pale dress, with a bucket of milk in each hand that threw out drops on the ground at her every step however carefully she walked; and he understood, in a moment of knifelike clarity, how he would go about making a sort of house, a house that a year and some months later became the house Edgewood.

And here now in New York was her name before him, whom he had thought never to see again. He signed the subscription.

He knew that she would accompany her father, knew this the moment he read the name. He knew, somehow, that she would be even more lovely and that her never-cut hair would be two years longer. He didn't know that she would arrive three months pregnant by Fred Reynard or Oliver Hawksquill or some other not welcome at the parsonage (he never asked the name); it didn't occur to him that she, like him, would be two years older, and have come upon hard

41

crossroads of her own, and gone a ways down strange and shaded lanes.

"Paracelsus is of the opinion," Dr. Bramble told the theosophists, "that the universe is crowded with pow- ers, spirits, who are not quite immaterial—whatever that means or meant, perhaps made of some finer, less tangible stuff than the ordinary world. They fill up the air and the water and so on; they surround us on every side, so that at our every movement" —he moved his long-fingered hand gently in the air, causing turmoil amid his pipesmoke—"we displace thousands."

Call Them Doors

She sat by the door, just out of the light of a red-shaded lamp, bored or nervous or both; her cheek was in her palm and the lamp lit the dark down of her arms and turned it blond. Her eyes were deep and feral, and she had a single eyebrow—that is, it extended without a break across her nose, unplucked and thick. She didn't look at him, or when she did didn't see him.

"Nereids, dryads, sylphs, and salamanders is how Paracel- sus divides them," Dr. Bramble said. "That is to say (as we would express it) mermaids, elves, fairies, and goblins or imps. One class of spirit for each of the four elements—mermaids for the water, elves for the earth, fairies for the air, goblins for the fire. It is thus that we derive the common name for all such beings—'elementals.' Very regular and neat. Paracelsus had an orderly mind. It is not, however, true, based as it is on the common error—the old, the great error that underlies the whole history of our science—that there are these four elements, earth, air, fire, water, out of which the world is made. We know now of course that there are some ninety elements, and that the old four are not among them."

There was a stirring at this among the more radical or Rosicrucian wing of the assembly, who still set great store by the Four, and Dr. Bramble, who desperately needed this appearance to be a success, gulped water from a goblet beside him, cleared his throat, and tried to march on to the more sensational or revelatory parts of his lecture. "The question is really," he said "why, if the 'elementals' are not several kinds of being but only one, which I believe, why they manifest themselves in such various forms. *That they do manifest themselves, ladies and gentlemen, is no longer open to doubt.*" He looked meaningfully at his daughter, and many there did also; it was her experiences, after all, that lent Dr. Bramble's notions what weight they had. She smiled, faintly, and seemed to contract beneath their gaze. "Now," he said. "Collating the various experi-

42

ences, both those told of in myth and fable and those more recent ones verifiable by investigation, we find that these elementals, while separable into two basic *characters,* can be any of several different sizes and (as we might put it) densities.

"The two distinct characters—the ethereal, beautiful, and elevated character on the one hand, and the impish, earthy, gnomelike character on the other, is in fact a sexual distinction. The sexes among these beings are much more distinct than among men.

"The differences observed in size is another matter. What are the differences? In their sylphlike or pixie manifestation they appear no bigger than a large insect, or a hummingbird; they are said to inhabit the woods, they are associated with flowers. Droll tales are spun of their spears of locust-thorns and their chariots made of nut-shells drawn by dragonflies, and so on. In other instances, they appear to be a foot to three feet in height, wingless, fully-formed little men and women of more human habits. And there are fairy maidens who capture the hearts of, and can apparently lie with, humans, and who are the size of human maidens. And there are fairy warriors on great steeds, banshees and pookahs and ogres who are huge, larger by far than men.

"What is the explanation for this?

"The explanation is that the world inhabited by these beings is not the world we inhabit. It is another world entirely, and it is enclosed within this one; it is in a sense a universal retreating mirror image of this one, with a peculiar geography I can only describe as *infundibular.*" He paused for effect. "I mean by this that the other world is composed of a series of concentric rings, which as one penetrates deeper into the other world, grow larger. The further in you go, the bigger it gets. Each perimeter of this series of concentricities encloses a larger world within, until, at the center point, it is infinite. Or at least very very large." He drank water again. As always when he began to explain it all, it began to leak away from him; the perfect clarity of it, the just-seizable perfect paradox of it, which sometimes rang like a bell within him, was so difficult— maybe, oh Lord, impossible—to express. The unmoved faces before him waited. "We men, you see, inhabit what is in fact the vastest outermost circle of the converse infundibulum which is the other world. Paracelsus is right: our every movement is accompanied by these beings, but we fail to perceive them not because they are intangible but because, out here, they are too small to be seen!

"Around the inner perimeter of this circle which is our daily world are many, many ways—call them doors—by which we can enter the next smaller, that is larger, circle of their world. Here the inhabitants appear the size of ghost-birds or errant candle-flames. This is our most common experience of them, because it is only through this first perimeter that most people ever pass, if at all. The next-innermost perimeter is smaller, and thus has fewer doors; it is therefore less likely anyone would step through by chance. There, the inhabitants will appear fairy-children or Little People, a manifestation correspondingly less often observed. And so on further within: the vast, inner circles where they grow to full size are so tiny that we step completely *over* them, constantly, in our daily lives, without knowing we do so, and never enter there at all—though it may be that in the old heroic age, access there was easier, and so we have the many tales of deeds done there. And lastly, the vastest circle, the infinity, the center point—Faëry, ladies and gentlemen, where the heroes ride across endless landscapes and sail sea beyond sea and there is no end to possibility—why that circle is so tiny it has no door at all."

He sat, spent. "Now." He put his dead pipe between his teeth. "Before I proceed to certain evidences, certain demonstrations, mathematical and topographical" —he patted a messy pile of papers and place-marked books beside him—"you should know that there are individuals to whom it is given to be able to penetrate at will, or nearly, the small worlds I have discussed. If you require *firsthand* evidence of the general propositions I have laid down, my daughter Miss Violet Bramble . . ."

The company, murmuring (it was this they had come for), turned toward where Violet sat in the light of the red-shaded lamp.

The girl was gone.

No End to Possibility

It was Drinkwater who found her, huddled on the landing of the stairs that led up from the Society's rooms to a lawyer's office on the next floor. She didn't stir as he climbed toward her, only her eyes moved, searching him. When he moved to light the gas above her, she touched his shin: "Don't."

"Are you ill?"

"No."

"Afraid?"

She didn't answer. He sat down beside her and took her hand. "Now, my child," he said paternally, but felt a thrill as though some current ran through her hand to his. "They don't want to hurt you, you know, they won't badger you. . . ."

"I am not," she said slowly, "a circus show."

"No." How old could she be, to have to live so—fifteen,

sixteen? Closer to her now, he could see that she was weeping softly; big tears formed in the dark pools of her eyes, trembled at the thick lashes, and tumbled one by one down her cheek.

"I feel so sorry for him. He hates to do this to me and yet he does it. It's because we're desperate." She said it quite simply, as though she had said "It's because we're English." She hadn't released his hand; perhaps she hadn't noticed it.

"Let me help." That had sprung to his lips, but he felt any choice about her was anyway beyond him; the two years of vain struggle that lay between the twilight he saw her in the apple tree and now seemed to shrivel into a mote and blow away. He must protect her; he would take her away, somewhere safe, somewhere. . . . She would say nothing further, and he could not; he knew that his well-built life, masoned and furnished over forty careful years, had not weathered the wind of his dissatisfaction: he felt it crumble, the foundations slipped, vast cracks appeared, the whole edifice of it caved in with a long noise he could almost hear. He was kissing the warm salt tears from her cheek.

"Perhaps," John Drinkwater said to Violet when all their boxes and trunks had been piled in the doorway for the servant to put away, and Dr. Bramble had been installed in a comfortable chair on the wide marmoreal porch, "you'd like to take a turn around the house."

A Turn Around the House

Wisteria had been trained up the tapering columns of the porch, and their crystalline green leaves, though the summer was young, already curtained the scenes he offered them with his hand, the broad lawn and young plantings, the view to a pavilion, the distant sheet of water arched by a neat classical bridge.

Dr. Bramble declined, already drawing an octavo volume from his pocket. Violet murmured her assent (how demure she must now be, in this great place; she had expected log cabins and red Indians; she really knew very little). She took the arm he offered her—a builder's strong arm she thought—and they went out across the new lawn, walking a gravel path between stone sphinxes set at intervals to guard the way. (The sphinxes were cut by his Italian stonemason friends, the same who were just then cutting garlands of grapes and queer faces all across the facades of his partner Mouse's City blocks; they were cut quickly in soft stone that the years would not be kind to, but that was all to come.)

"You must stay on now as long as you like," Drinkwater said. He had said it in Sherry's restaurant where he had taken them after the lecture ended inconclusively, when he had first shyly but insistently invited them. He had said it again in the mean and odorous hotel lobby when he came to collect them, and in Grand Central Station beneath the great twinkling zodiac which (Dr. Bramble couldn't help but notice) ran the wrong way across the night-blue ceiling. And again in the train as she nodded in a doze beneath the silk rosebud which nodded too in its railroad bud-vase.

But how long did she like?

"It's very kind of you," she said.

You will live in many houses, Mrs. Underhill had told her. *You will wander, and live in many houses.* She had wept hearing that, or rather later when she thought of it on trains and boats and in waiting rooms, not knowing how many houses were many or how long it took to live in one. For sure it would take an immensity of time, for since they had left the vicarage in Cheshire six months ago they had lived only in hotels and lodgings, and seemed likely to go on doing so; how long?

As in a drill, they marched up one neat stone path, turned right, marched along another. Drinkwater made an introductory noise to announce he was about to break the silence they had fallen into.

"I'm so interested in these, well, experiences of yours," he said. He raised an honest palm. "I don't mean to pry, or upset you if it upsets you to talk of them. I'm just very interested."

She said nothing. She could only tell him that they were all over in any case. Her heart for a moment grew great and hollow, and he seemed to sense it, because he pressed the arm he held, very slightly. "Other worlds," he said dreamily. "Worlds within worlds." He drew her to one of the many small benches set against a curving, clipped wall of box-hedge. The complex housefront beyond, buff-colored and patent in the late afternoon sun, seemed to her severe yet smiling, like Erasmus' face in a frontispiece she had seen over Father's shoulder.

"Well," she said. "Those ideas, about worlds within worlds and all that, those are Father's ideas. I don't know."

"But you've been there."

"Father says I have." She crossed her legs and covered an old ineradicable brown stain on her muslin dress with interlaced fingers. "I never expected this, you know. I only told him about . . . all that, what had happened to me—because I hoped to lift his spirits. To tell him it would be all right, that all the troubles were part of the Tale."

"Tale?"

She grew circumspect. "I mean I never expected this. To leave home. To leave . . ." Them, she almost said, but since the night at the Theosophical Society—the last straw!—she had resolved not to speak any more about them. It was bad enough to have lost them.

"Miss Bramble," he said. "Please. I certainly wouldn't pursue you, pursue your . . . your tale." That wasn't true. He was rapt before it. He must know it: know her heart. "You won't be bothered here. You can rest." He gestured toward the cedars of Lebanon he had planted in that careful lawn. The wind in them spoke in a childish gabble, faint presage of the great grave voice they would speak in when they were grown. "It's safe here. I built it for that."

And she did feel, despite the deep constraints of formality that seemed laid on her here, a kind of serenity. If it had all been a terrible error telling Father about them, if it had inflamed not settled his mind and sent the two of them out on the road like a pair of itinerant preachers, or a gypsy and his dancing bear more nearly, to make their living entertaining the mad and the obsessed in glum lecture-halls and meeting rooms (and counting afterwards their take, good Lord!) then rest and forgetfulness were the best issue it could have. Better than they could have expected. Only . . .

She rose, restless, unreconciled, and followed a radiating path toward a kind of stage-set wing of arches that protruded from a corner of the house. "I built it," she heard him say, "for you really. In a way."

She had passed through the arches and come around the corner of the house, and suddenly out of the plain pillared envelope of the wing a flowered valentine was unfolded and offered her, whitewashed and American, bright with flowerbeds and lacy with jigsaw work. It was a wholly different place; it was as though the severe face of Erasmus had tittered behind his hand. She laughed, the first time she had laughed since she had shut the wicket on her English garden forever.

He came almost at a run, grinning at her surprise. He tilted his straw hat on the back of his head and began to talk with animation about the house, about himself; the quick moods came and went in his big face. "*Not* usual, no," he laughed, "not a thing about it's usual. Like here: this was to be the kitchen-garden, you see, where anybody'd put a kitchen-garden, but I've filled it with flowers. The cook won't garden, and the gardener's a great one with flowers, but says he can't keep a tomato alive. . . ." He pointed with his bamboo walking-stick at a pretty, cut-out pumphouse—"Just like," he said, "one my parents had in their garden, and useful too"—and then the pierced, ogee arches of the porch, which broad grape-leaves had begun to climb. "Hollyhocks," he said, taking her to admire some that the bumblebees were engaged on. "Some people think hollyhocks are a weed. Not me."

" 'Ware heads, there!" called out a broad, Irish voice above them. A maid upstairs had flung open a window, and shook a dust mop in the sun.

"She's a great girl," Drinkwater said, indicating her with his thumb. "A great girl . . ." He looked down at Violet, dreamy again, and she up at him, as the dust-motes descended in the sun like Danae's gold. "I suppose," he said gravely, the bamboo stick swinging pendulum-fashion behind his back, "I suppose you think of me as old."

"You mean you think that's so."

"I'm not, you know. Not *old*."

"But you suppose, you expect . . ."

"I mean I think . . ."

"You're supposed to say 'I guess,' " she said, stamping her small foot and raising a butterfly from the sweet William. "Americans always say 'I guess,' don't they?" She put on a bumpkin basso: "I guess it's time to bring the cows in from the pasture. I guess there'll be no taxation without representation.—Oh, *you* know." She bent to smell flowers, and he bent with her. The sun beat down on her bare arms, and as though tormenting them made the garden insects hum and buzz.

"Well," he said, and she could hear the sudden daring in his voice. "I guess, then. I guess I love you, Violet. I guess I want you to stay here always. I guess . . ."

She fled from him along the flagged garden path, knowing that next he would take her in his arms. She fled around the next corner of the house. He let her go. *Don't let me go,* she thought.

What had happened? She slowed her steps, finding herself in a dark valley. She had come behind the shadow of the house. A sloping lawn fell away down to a noiseless stream, and just across the stream a sudden hill arose straight up, piney and sharp like a quiver of arrows. She stopped amid the yew trees planted there; she didn't know which way to turn. The house beside her was as gray as the yews, and as dreary. Plump stone pillars, oppressive in their strength, supported flinty stringcourses that seemed purposeless, covert. What should she do?

She glimpsed Drinkwater then, his white suit a paleness loitering within the stone cloister; she heard his boots on the tiles of it. In a change, the wind pointed the yews' branches toward him, but she wouldn't look that way, and he, abashed, said nothing; but he came closer.

"You mustn't say those things," she said to the dark Hill, not turning to him. "You don't know me, don't know . . ."

"Nothing I don't know matters," he said.

"Oh," she said, "oh . . ." She shivered, and it was his warmth that caused it; he had come up behind her, and covered her now with his arms, and she leaned against him and his strength. They walked on together thus, down to where the full-charged stream ran foaming into a cave's mouth in the hillside and was lost. They could feel the cave's damp and stony breath; he held her closer, protecting her from what seemed the cold infection of it that made her shiver. And from within the circle of his arms she told him, without tears, all her secrets.

"Do you love him, then?" Drinkwater said when she had done. "The one who did this to you?" It was his eyes that were bright with tears.

"No. I didn't, ever." It had never till this moment mattered. Now she wondered what would hurt him more, that she loved the one who had done this to her or did not (she wasn't even absolutely certain which one it was, but he would never, never know that). Sin pressed on her. He held her like forgiveness.

"Poor child," he said. "Lost. But no more. Listen to me now. If . . ." He held her at arm's length, to look into her face; the single eyebrow and the thick lashes seemed to shutter it. "If you could accept me . . . You see, no stain on you can make me think less of you; I'd still be unworthy. But if you could, I swear the child will be raised here, one of mine." His face, stern with resolve, softened. He almost smiled. "One of ours, Violet. One of many."

Now at last the tears came to her eyes, wondering tears at his goodness. She hadn't before thought of herself as in terrible trouble; now he had offered to save her from it. What goodness! Father had hardly noticed.

Lost, though, yes; that she knew herself to be. And could she find herself here? She left his touch again, and went around the next corner of the house, beneath beetling arcades grotesquely carved and thick castellations. The white ribbons of her hat, which she held now in her hand, trailed across the damp emerald grass. She could sense him following at a respectful distance.

"Curious," she said out loud when she had rounded the corner. "How very curious."

The stonework of the house had changed from grim gray

to cheerful brickwork in eye-intriguing shades of red and brown, with pretty enamel plaques set here and there, and white woodwork. All the Gothic heaviness had been stretched, pulled, pointed, and exploded into deep-curving, high-sweeping eaves, and comical chimney pots, and fat useless towers, and exaggerated curves of stacked and angled brick. It was as though—and here the sun shone again too, picking out the brickwork, and winking at her—it was as though the dark porch and soundless stream and dreaming yews had all been a joke.

"What it is," Violet said when John, hands behind his back, came up to her, "is many houses, isn't it?"

"Many houses," he said, smiling. "Every one for you."

Through a silly piece of cloistery archwork she could see a bit of Father's back. He was still ensconced in his wicker chair, still looking out through the curtain of wisteria, presumably still seeing the avenue of sphinxes and the cedars of Lebanon. But from here, his bald head could be a dreaming monk's in a monastery garden. She began to laugh. *You will wander, and live in many houses.* "Many houses!" She took John Drinkwater's hand; she almost kissed it; she looked up laughing at his face, that seemed just then to be full of pleasant surprises.

"It's a great joke!" she said. "Many jokes! Are there as many houses inside?"

"In a sense," he said.

"Oh, show me!" She pulled him toward the white arched door that was hinged with neat brass Gothic e's. In the sudden darkness of the brief, painted vestibule within, she lifted his big hand to her lips in an access of gratitude.

Beyond the vestibule, there was a vision of doorways, long lists of arches and lintels through which underscorings of light were painted by unseen windows.

"However do you find your way about?" Violet asked, on the threshold of all this.

"Sometimes I don't, in fact," he said. "I proved that every room needed more than two doors, but couldn't ever prove that any could get along with only three." He waited, unwilling to hurry her.

"Perhaps," she said, "one day, you'll be thinking of such a thing, and not be able to get out at all."

Hands on the walls and going slowly, as though she were blind (but in fact only marveling), Violet Bramble stepped into the pumpkin-shell John Drinkwater had made to keep her in, which he had first transformed into a golden coach for her delight.

50

After moonrise Violet awoke in a large and unfamiliar bedroom, feeling the pressure of cold light and the sound of her name called. She lay deathly still for a long moment on the tall bed, holding her breath, waiting for the tiny call to come again; but it didn't come. She threw off the coverlet and climbed down from the tall bed and across the floor. When she opened the casement she thought she heard her name again.

Tell Me the Tale

Violet?

Summer odors invaded the room, and a host of small noises from which she couldn't sort out the voice, if it was one, that had called her, if it had. She pulled her big cloak from the steamer trunk which had been put in her room, and quickly, quietly left the room on the balls of her feet. Her white calico nightgown billowed in the stale air which came searching up the stairways for the window she had left open.

"Violet?"

But that was only her father, perhaps asleep, as she passed his room, and she didn't answer.

It took some time of cautious creeping (feet growing cold on the uncarpeted stairs and halls) to find which way went down and out. And when at last she found a door flanked by windows which showed the night, she realized she had no idea which way she was faced. Did it matter?

It was that grand, still garden. The sphinxes watched her pass, their identical faces mobile in the aqueous moonlight. A frog spoke from the fishpond's edge, but not her name. She went on, across the spectral bridge and through a screen of poplars like frightened heads of hair on end. Beyond was a field, crossed by a kind of hedge, not a proper hedge, a line of bushes and small sighing trees, and the piled stones of a crude wall. She followed this, not knowing where she was going, feeling (as Smoky Barnable would years hence) that she may not have left Edgewood at all, only turned down some new illusory outdoor corridor of it.

She went what seemed a long way. The hedge beings, rabbits and stoats and hedgehogs (did they have such creatures here?) didn't speak, but they have no voices, or don't use them, she didn't know which. Her naked feet were cold at first in the dew, then numb; she drew the cloak over her nose, though it was a mild night, for the moonlight seemed to chill her.

Then, without knowing which foot had taken the step or when, she began to feel she was in familiar places. She looked up at

51

the moon, and could tell by its smile that she was somewhere she had never been but knew, somewhere elsewhere. Ahead the sedgy, flower-starred meadow rose up to a knoll, and there grew an oak tree and a thorn together, in deep embrace, inseparable. She knew, her feet quickening and her heart too, that there would be a path around the knoll, and it would lead to a small house built underside.

"Violet?"

Lamplight shone from its round window, and a brass face on the round door held a knocker in its teeth. But the door opened as she came to it: no need to knock.

"Mrs. Underhill," she said, trembling between joy and hurt, "why didn't you tell me this is how it was to be?"

"Come in, child, and ask me not; if I'd known more than I said I'd have said it."

"I thought," Violet said, and for a moment couldn't speak, couldn't say that she had thought never to see her, never to see any of them again, not a single glowing person in the gloom of the garden, not one small secret face sipping at the honeysuckle. The roots of oak and thorn that made Mrs. Underhill's house were lit by her little lamp, and when Violet raised her eyes to them and sighed a long shuddering sigh to keep from weeping, she inhaled the black odor of their growing. "But how . . ." she said.

Tiny, bent Mrs. Underhill, who was mostly shawl-bound head and great slippered feet, raised an admonitory finger as long almost as the needles she knitted with. "Don't ask me how," she said. "But there it is."

Violet sat at her feet, all questions answered or at least not mattering any more. Only—"You might have told me," she said, her eyes starred with happy tears," that all the houses I'm to live in are one house."

"Are they," Mrs. Underhill said. She knitted and rocked. The scarf of many colors between her needles grew quickly longer. "Time past, time to come," she said comfortably. "Somehow the Tale gets told."

"Tell me the Tale," Violet said.

"Ah, if I could I would."

"Is it too long?"

"Longer than any. Why, child, they'll have put you long beneath the earth, and your children, and your children's children, before that Tale's all told." She shook her head. "That's common knowledge."

"Does it have," Violet asked, "a happy ending?" She'd asked all this before; these weren't questions, but exchanges, as though she and Mrs. Underhill passed back and forth, with compliments, the same gift: each time expressing surprise and gratitude.

"Well, who's to say," Mrs. Underhill said. The scarf grew longer, row by row. "It's a Tale, is all. There are only short ones and long ones. Yours is the longest I know." Something, not a cat, began to unravel Mrs. Underhill's fat ball of yarn. "Stop that, bold thing!" she said, and beat at it with a knitting needle she drew from behind her ear. She shook her head at Violet. "Not a moment's peace in centuries."

Violet got up and cupped her hand to Mrs. Underhill's ear. Mrs. Underhill leaned close, grinning, ready for secrets.

"Are they listening?" Violet whispered.

Mrs. Underhill put her fingers to her lips. "I think not," she said.

"Then tell me truly," Violet said. "How do you come to be here?"

Mrs. Underhill started in surprise. "I?" she said. "Whatever do you mean, child? I've been here all the time. It's you who've been in motion." She took up her whispering needles. "Use your sense." She leaned back in her rocker; something caught beneath the tread shrieked, and Mrs. Underhill grinned maliciously.

"Not a moment's peace," she said, "in centuries."

After his marriage, John Drinkwater began to retire, or retreat, more and more from an active life in architecture. The buildings he would have been called on to build came to seem to him at once heavy, obtuse, and lifeless, and at the same time ephemeral. He remained with the firm; he was constantly consulted, and his ideas and exquisite initial sketches (when reduced to ordinariness by his partners and their teams of engineers) continued to alter the cities of the east, but they were no longer his life's work.

All Questions Answered

There were other schemes to occupy him. He designed a folding bed of astonishing ingenuity, in effect an entire bedroom disguised as or contained within a sort of wardrobe or armoire, which in a moment—a quick motion of brass catches and levers, a shift of heavy counterweighting—became the bed which made the bedroom a bedroom. He enjoyed that idea, a bedroom within the bedroom, and even patented his scheme, but the only buyer he ever found was his partner Mouse, who (chiefly as a favor) installed a few in his City apartments. And then there was the Cosmo-Opticon: he spent a happy year working on this with his friend the inventor Henry Cloud, the only man John Drinkwater had ever known who could actually *sense* the spin of the earth on its axis and its motion around the sun. The Cosmo-Opticon was an enormous, hideously expensive stained-glass-and-wrought-iron representation of the Zodiacal heavens and their movement, and the movement of the planets within them. And it did move: its owner could sit within it on a green plush seat, and as great weights fell and clockwork ticked over, the dome of many-colored glass would move just as the heavens did in their apparent motion. It was a measure of Drinkwater's abstraction that he thought there would be a ready market for this strange toy among the wealthy.

And yet—strange—no matter how he removed himself from the world, no matter how he poured the rich gains of his working life into such schemes, he flourished; his investments turned over at a great rate, his fortune only increased.

Protected, Violet said. Taking tea at the stone table he had placed to overlook the Park, John Drinkwater looked up at the sky. He had tried to feel protected. He had tried to repose himself within the protection she was so certain of, and to laugh at the world's weather from within it. But in his heart he felt unsheltered, bare-headed, abroad.

In fact, as he grew older, he became more and more concerned with the weather. He collected almanacs scientific and not so, and he studied the daily weather surmise in his paper though it was the divination of priests he didn't entirely trust—he only hoped, without having reason to, that they were right when they read the omens Fair and wrong when they read them Foul. He watched the summer sky especially, could feel as a burden on his own back any far-off cloud that might obscure the sun, or that might bring others after it. When fluffy harmless cumulus trod the sky like sheep, he was at ease but watchful. They could combine suddenly into thunderheads, they could drive him indoors to listen to the dull fall of rain on his roofs.

(As they seemed just now to be doing, over in the west, and he powerless to stop them. They drew his eye, and each time he looked they were piled that much higher. The air was dense and palpable. There was then little hope that rain and storm would not begin soon. He was not reconciled.)

In the winter, he wept often; in the spring he was desperately impatient, rageful when he found heaps of winter still piled in the corners of April. When Violet spoke of spring she meant a time of flowers and baby animals—a notion. A single clear day in April was like what she had in mind, he supposed. Or May, rather, because it had become clear to him that her idea of the qualities of months differed from his: hers were English months, Februaries when the snow melted and Aprils when flowers burst, not the months of this harsher exile place. May, there, was like June here. And no experience of these American months could change her mind: or even reach it, he sometimes thought.

Perhaps that conspiracy of cloud on the horizon was stationary, a kind of decoration merely, like the high-piled clouds behind country scenes in his children's picture books. But the air around him belied that: laden and sparkling with change.

Violet thought (or did she?—he spent hours grappling with her cryptic remarks, with Dr. Bramble's elaborate explications for a guide, and yet he wasn't sure) that it was always spring There. But spring is a change only. All seasons, collated into a string of fast-following days like changes of mood. Was that what she meant? Or did she mean the notional spring of young grass and new-unfurled leaves, changeless single equinoctial day? There is no spring. Perhaps it was a joke. There would be precedent for that. He felt sometimes that all she said to his urgent inquiries was a joke. Spring is all seasons and no season. It's always spring There. There is no There. A humid wave of despair washed over him: a thunder mood, he knew, and yet . . .

It wasn't that he loved her less as they grew older (or rather as he grew older and she grew up); only that he lost that first wild certainty that she would *lead him somewhere,* a certainty that he had because for sure she had been there herself. He couldn't, as it happened, follow. After a bitter year he knew that. Better years followed. He would be Purchas to her pilgrims: he would tell her journeys to the world, her traveler's tall tales of marvels he would never see. She had intimated to him (he thought) that without the house he had built the whole Tale could not be told, that it was the beginning and perhaps the end, in some way, like the house that Jack built, cause of a chain. He didn't understand, but he was satisfied.

And there was no time when (even after years, after three children, after who knows how much water under what crumbling bridges) his heart would not swell when she came up to him and put her small hands on him suddenly and whispered in his ear *Go to bed, old Goat*—Goat she called him for his shameless ceaselessness—and he would mount the stairs and await her.

And look what he possessed now, all framed against the vertiginous height of cloud forming.

Here were his daughters Timothea Wilhelmina and Nora Angelica come home from a swim. And his son (her son, his) Aube-ron stalking across the lawn with his camera as though seeking some-

55

thing to strike with it. And his baby August in a sailor suit, who had never smelled the sea. He had named him for that month when the year stands still and blue day follows blue day, when for a while he stopped looking at the sky. He looked at the sky now. The white clouds were being edged with somber gray, sagging like old men's sad eyes. Yet still before him his shadow lay amid the shadows of leaves. He shook his newspaper and changed the way his legs were crossed. Enjoy, enjoy.

Among many other and odder beliefs, his father-in-law was sure that a man can't think or feel clearly if he can see his own shadow. (He thought also that looking at oneself in the mirror immediately before retiring caused bad, or at least troubling, dreams.) He always sat in the shade or faced into the sun, as he now sat in the wrought-iron love seat by "The Syrinx" with a stick between his knees to rest his hairy hands on, and a gold chain glowing on his stomach as the sun played with it. August sat at his feet listening or perhaps only politely seeming to listen to the old man, whose voice reached Drinkwater as a murmur, one murmur among many, the cicadas, the lawn mower Ottolo pushed in widening circles, the piano in the music room where Nora was practicing now, her chords running together like tears down a cheek.

She liked mostly the feel of the keys beneath her fingers, liked the thought of them being solid ivory and ebony. "What are they made of?" "Solid ivory." She

Gone, She Said

stroked them in harmonic sets of six and eight at a time, no longer really practicing, only testing the plangency as her fingertips tested the smoothness. Her mother wouldn't notice it was no longer Delius she was playing or trying to play, her mother had no ear, she said so herself, though Nora could see the shapely whorl of her mother's ear where she sat cheek in hand at the drum table, playing her cards or looking at them anyway. For a moment her long earrings were still, till she looked up to take another card from the pile and everything moved, earrings shook, necklaces swung. Nora slid from her polished stool and came to stare at her mother's work.

"You should go outside," Violet said to her without looking up. "You and Timmie Willie should go down to the lake. It's so hot."

Nora didn't say that she had just returned from there, because she had told her mother that already, and if she hadn't understood then, there seemed no reason to insist on it. She only looked down at what her mother had laid out.

"Can you make a house of cards?" she asked.

"Yes," Violet said, and went on looking. This way Violet had of seizing first not the most obvious sense of what people said to her but some other, interior echo or reverse side of it was a thing that baffled and frustrated her husband, who sought in her sybilline responses to ordinary questions some truth he was sure Violet knew but couldn't quite enunciate. With his father-in-law's help, he had filled volumes with his searchings. Her children, though, hardly noticed it. Nora shifted from foot to foot for a moment waiting for the promised structure, and when it didn't appear forgot it. The clock on the mantelpiece chimed.

"Oh." Violet looked up. "They must have had their tea already." She rubbed her cheeks as though suddenly waking. "Why didn't you say something? Let's go see what's left."

She took Nora's hand and they went to the French doors that led out to the garden. Violet picked up a wide hat that lay on the table there, but stopped when she had it on, and stood looking out into the haze. "What is it in the air?" she said.

"Electricity," Nora said, already crossing the patio. "That's what Auberon says." She squinted her eyes. "I can see it, all red and blue squiggles, when I do this. It means a storm."

Violet nodded, and started across the lawn slowly, as though making progress through an unfamiliar element, to where her husband waved to her from the stone table. Auberon had just done taking a picture of Grandy and the baby, and now he brought his instrument toward the table, making a motion to gather his mother into his field of focus. He went about his picture-taking solemnly, as though it were duty not pleasure. She felt a sudden pity for him. This air!

She sat, and John poured her tea. Auberon put his camera before them. The vast cloud defeated the sun, and John looked up at it, resentful.

"Oh! Look!" Nora said.

"Look!" Violet said.

Auberon opened the camera's eye, and closed it again.

"Gone," Nora said.

"Gone," Violet said.

The advancing edge of the occluded front swept invisibly across the lawn, stirring hair and turning lapels and leaves to show their pale undersides. It cut through the broken front of the house, lifting a card on the card-table and riffling the pages of five-finger exercises on the piano. It swung the tassels of scarves hung on sofas, it snapped the edges of drapes. Its cold oncoming wedge rose up through the second floor and the third and then thousands of feet into the air, where the rainmaker minted his first fat drops to throw on them.

"Gone," August said.

IV

Insnar'd in flowers, I fall on grass.
—Marvell

All on a summer morning Smoky dressed himself to wed, in a white suit of yellowed linen or alpaca that his father had always said once belonged to Harry Truman, and there were the initials on the inside pocket, HST; it was only when he came to consider it for a wedding suit (old not new) that he realized the initials could after all stand for somebody else, and that his father had kept up the joke through his life and then perpetuated it beyond without cracking a smile. The sensation wasn't unknown to Smoky. He had wondered if his education weren't the same kind of posthumous fun (revenge on his betraying mother?) and though Smoky could take a joke, he did as he shot his cuffs at himself in the bathroom mirror feel a little at a loss and wish his father had given him some man-to-man advice on weddings and marriage. Barnable had hated weddings and funerals and christenings, and whenever one seemed imminent would pack socks, books, dog, and son and move on; Smoky had been to Franz Mouse's wedding reception and danced with the starry-eyed bride, who made him a surprising suggestion; but that was a Mouse wedding after all and the couple were separated already. He knew there must be a Ring, and he patted his pocket where he had it; he thought there should be a Best Man, though when he wrote so to Daily Alice she wrote that they didn't believe in that; and as for Rehearsals, she said when he mentioned them, "Don't you want it to be a surprise?" The only other thing he was sure of was that he shouldn't see his bride till she was led up the aisle (what aisle?) by her father. And so he wouldn't, and didn't peek in the direction he thought her room lay (he was wrong) when he went to the john. His walking shoes stuck out thick and unfestive from beneath his white cuffs.

The wedding was to be "on the grounds," he had been told, and Great-aunt Cloud, as oldest there, would conduct him to the place—a chapel, Smoky surmised, and Cloud with that surprised air said yes, she supposed that's exactly what it was. It was she Smoky found waiting for him at the top of the stairs when at last he shyly emerged from the bathroom. What a comforting presence he found her, large and calm in a June dress with a bunch of late violets at her bosom and a walking-stick in her hand. Like him she wore hard shoes with a glum expression. "Very, very good," she said, as though a hope had proved out for her; she held him at arm's length and inspected him through blue-tinted glasses for a moment, and then offered him her arm to take.

A Suit of Truman's

"I think often of the patience of landscape gardeners," Cloud said as they went through the knee-deep sedge of what she called the Park. "These great trees, some of them, my father planted as infants, only imagining the effect they would have, and knowing he would never live to see the whole. That beech—I could almost join hands around it when I was a girl. You know there are fashions in landscape gardening—immensely long fashions, since the landscapes take so long to grow. Rhododendrons—I called them rum-de-dum-dums when I was a child, helping the Italian men to plant these. The fashion passed. So difficult to keep them cut back. No Italian men to do it for us, so they grow jungly and—ouch!— watch your eyes here.

The Summer House

"The plan goes, you see. From where the walled garden is now you once looked out this way and there were Vistas—the trees were various, chosen for, oh, picturesqueness, they looked like foreign dignitaries conversing together at an embassy affair—and between them the lawns, kept down you know, and the flower-beds and fountains. It seemed that you would any moment see a hunting party appear, lords and ladies, hawks on their wrists. Look now! Forty years since it's been properly cared for. You can still see the pattern, what it all was meant to look like, but it's like reading a letter, a letter from oh a long time ago, that's been left out in the rain and all the words have run together. I wonder if he grieves at it. He was an orderly man. See? The statue is 'The Syrinx.' How long till the vines pull it down, or the moles undermine it? Well. He would understand. There are reasons. One doesn't want to disturb what likes it this way."

"Moles and things."

"The statue is only marble."

"You could—ouch—pull up these thorn-trees, maybe."

She looked at him as though, unexpectedly, he had struck her. She cleared her throat, patting her clavicle. "This is Auberon's lane," she said. "It leads to the Summer House. It's not the directest way, but Auberon ought to see you."

"Oh yes?"

The Summer House was two round red brick towers squat as great toes, with a machicolated foot between them. Was it intended to look ruined, or was it really ruined? The windows were out of scale, large and arched and cheerfully curtained. "Once," Cloud said, "you could see this place from the house. It was thought, on moony nights, to be very romantic. . . . Auberon is my mother's son, though not my father's—my half-brother, then. Some years older than I. He's been our schoolmaster for many years, though he's not well now, hasn't been out of the Summer House much for, oh, a year? It's a pity. . . . Auberon!"

Closer now he could see the place had stretched out habitation's hands around it, a privy, a neat vegetable garden, a shed from which a lawn mower peeked out ready to roll. There was a screen door, rhombic with age, for the central toothed entrance, and board steps at a slant, and a striped canvas sling-chair in the sun there by the birdbath, and a small old man in the chair who, when he heard his name called, jumped up or at least rose up in agitation—his suspenders seemed to draw him down into a crouch—and made for his house, but he was slow, and Cloud had come near enough to stop him. "Here's Smoky Barnable, who's going to marry Daily Alice today. At least come and say hello." She shook her head for Smoky to see her patience was tried, and led him by the elbow into the yard.

Auberon, trapped, turned at the door with a welcoming smile, hand extended. "Well, welcome, welcome, hm." He had the distracted chuckle of troubled old people who look within, keeping watch on failing organs. He took Smoky's hand and almost before they touched sank again gratefully in his sling-chair, motioning Smoky to a bench. Why was it that within this enclosure Smoky felt a troubling of the sunlight? Cloud sat in a chair by her brother, and Auberon put his white-haired hand over hers. "Well, what's happened?" she said indulgently.

"No need to say," he said undertone, "not before . . ."

"Member of the family," Cloud said. "As of today."

Auberon, his throat still making soundless chuckles, looked at Smoky. Unprotected! That's what Smoky felt. They had stepped into this yard and lost something they had had in the woods; they had stepped out of something. "Easy enough to test," Auberon said, striking his bony knee and rising. He retreated into the house rubbing his fingers together.

"It's *not* easy," Cloud said to no one, looking up at the blank sky. She had lost a portion of her ease. She cleared her throat again, contemplated the gray birdbath, which was supported by a number of carved figures, gnomes or elves, with patient bearded faces, who seemed in the act of bearing it away. Cloud sighed. She glanced at a tiny gold watch that was pinned to her bosom. It had little curling wings on either side. Time flies. She looked at Smoky and smiled apologetically.

"Now, aha, aha," Auberon said, coming out with a large, long-legged camera veiled with a black cloth. "Oh, Auberon" Cloud said, not impatiently but as though this weren't necessary and anyway an enthusiasm she didn't share; but he was already thrusting its spiked toes into the ground by Smoky, adjusting its tibiae to make it stand straight, and bending its mahogany face upon Smoky.

For years that last photograph of Auberon's lay on a table in the Summer House, Auberon's magnifying glass beside it; it showed Smoky, in his suit of Truman's that glowed in the sunlight, his hair fiery, and half his face sun-struck and blind. There were Cloud's dimpled elbow and ringed ear. The birdbath. The birdbath: could it be that one of those long soapstone faces had not before been there, that there was an arm too many supporting the garlanded bowl? Auberon didn't complete the study, come to a decision; and when years later a son of Smoky's blew the dust from the old image and took up Auberon's work again it was still inconclusive, proving nothing, a silvered paper blackened by a long-past midsummer sun.

Woods and Lakes

Beyond the Summer House they descended a concave lane, quickly swallowed up in a wood tangled and somnolent, moist from the rain. It seemed the kind of wood grown to hide a sleeping princess till her hundred years were up. They hadn't been long within it when there was a rustle or a whisper beside them, and with a suddenness that startled Smoky, a man stood on the path ahead of them. "Good morning, Rudy," Cloud said. "Here's the groom. Smoky, Rudy Flood." Rudy's hat looked as though it had been fought with, punched and pummelled; its upturned brim gave his broad bearded face an open look. Out of his open green coat a great belly came, tautening his white shirt. "Where's Rory?" Cloud asked.

"Down the path." He grinned at Smoky as though they shared a joke. Rory Flood his tiny wife appeared in a moment as he had, and a big girl in floppy jeans, big baby in her arms punching the air. "Betsy Bird," Cloud said, "and Robin. And see here are Phil Fox and two cousins of mine, Stones, Irv and Walter. Clouds on their mother's side." More came on the path from right and left; the path was narrow, and the wedding guests walked it two by two, dropping back or moving up to handle Smoky and bless him. "Charles Wayne," Cloud said. "Hannah Noon. Where are the Lakes? And the Woods?"

The path came out into a wide, sloping glade, the marge of a dark lake that still and moatlike surrounded an island where aged trees grew. Leaves floated flat on its surface, and frogs fled from their feet as they came down among its pools. "It's certainly," Smoky said remembering the guidebook, "an extensive estate."

"The further in you go, the bigger it gets," said Hannah Noon. "Have you met my boy Sonny?"

Across the lake a boat was coming, laying out lacquered ripples. Its carved prow was intended for a swan, but it was gray and eyeless now, like the dark swan on the dark lake of northern legend. It struck the bank with a hollow rattle of oarlocks, and Smoky was pushed forward to board with Cloud, who was still explaining who was who of the laughing wedding-guests. "Hannah's distantly related," she said. "Her grandfather was a Bush, and her grandfather's sister married one of Mrs. Drinkwater's uncles, a Dale. . . ." She saw that he wasn't listening, though his head was nodding mechanically. She smiled and put her hand on his. The lake island, shadowed by its trees, seemed made of changeful green glass; myrtle grew on its gentle slopes. At its center was a round gazebo, its pillars slim as arms, softly domed and greenly garlanded. There, a tall girl in white stood among others, holding a ribboned bouquet.

They were greeted and handed out of the leaking swan by many hands. Around the island people were sitting together, opening picnic baskets, placating shouting children; few of them seemed to notice Smoky's arrival. "Look who we've got here, Cloud," said a slim chinless man who made Smoky think of the poets the guidebook had disliked so much. "We've got Dr. Word. Where is he now? Doctor! Got some more champagne?" Doctor Word in a tight black suit had a look of unreasoning terror on his badly shaven face; his golden glassful trembled and bubbles rose. "Nice to see you, Doctor," Cloud said. "I think we can promise no wonders. Oh, settle down, man!" Dr. Word had tried to speak, choked, spluttered. "Pound his back, someone. He's not our minister," Cloud said confidentially to

Smoky. "They come from the outside, and tend to get very nervous. A wonder any of us is married or buried at all. Here's Sarah Pink, and the little Pinks. How do you do. Ready?" She took Smoky's arm, and as they went up the flagged path toward the gazebo a harmonium began to play, like a tiny weeping voice, music he didn't know but that seemed to score him with sudden longing. At its sound the wedding-guests gathered, talking in low voices; when Smoky reached the low worn steps of the gazebo, Doctor Word had arrived there too, glancing around, fishing a book from his pocket; Smoky saw Mother, and Doctor Drinkwater, and Sophie with her flowers behind Daily Alice with hers; Daily Alice watched him unsmiling and calm, as though he were someone she didn't know. They stood him beside her; he began to put his hands in his pockets, stopped, clasped them behind his back, then in front of him. Doctor Word fluttered the pages of his book and began to speak quickly, his words shot through with champagne and tremblings and the harmonium's unceasing melody; it sounded like "Do you Barble take this Daily Alice to be your awful wedded life for bed or for worse insidious in stealth for which or for poor or to have unto whole until death you do part?" And he looked up inquiringly.

"I do," Smoky said.

"I do too," Daily Alice said.

"Wring," Doctor Word said. "And now you pounce you, man on wife."

Aaaah, said all the wedding guests, who then began to drift away, talking in low voices.

There was a game she had played with Sophie in the long hallways of Edgewood, where she and Sophie would stand as far apart as was possible to get and still see each other. Then they would walk slowly together, slowly and deliberately, looking always each at the other's face. They kept on, at the same pace, not laughing or trying not to, till their noses touched. It was like that with Smoky, though he had started far off, too far to be seen, coming from the City—no farther, out there where she had never been, far away, walking towards her. When the swan boat picked him up, she could easily cover him with her thumbnail if she chose to; then the boat drew closer, Phil Flowers hauling on the oars, and she could see his face, see that it was indeed he. At the water's edge he was lost for a moment; then there was a murmur of expectation and appreciation around her and he reappeared, led by Cloud, much larger now, the new wrinkles visible at his knees, his strong veined hands she loved.

Touching Noses

Larger. There were violets in his buttonhole. She saw his throat move, and at that moment came Music. When he had come to the stairs of the pavilion she could no longer take in his feet if she looked resolutely at his face, and she did—for a moment everything around his face darkened and swam, his face orbited towards her like a pale smiling moon. He mounted the steps. He stood beside her. No touching noses. That would come. It might she thought take years; maybe they never would—their marriage was after all a Convenience, though she had never, would never, need not now ever explain that to him because, just as the cards had promised, she knew now she would choose him over anybody else, whether the cards chose him or not, or whether they who had promised someone like him to her thought he was unnecessary now or even wrong. She would defy them to have him. And it was they who had first seen fit to send her out to find him! She wanted with all her being to continue to find him now, to put her arms around him and search; but the stupid minister began to mutter—she felt anger at her parents who had thought *him* necessary, for Smoky's sake they said, but she already knew Smoky better than that. She tried to listen to the man, thinking how much better it would be to marry touching noses: to proceed from great distances together till it was as in the old halls when the walls and pictures glided by changefully on the edge of vision but Sophie's face kept constant, growing, the eyes widening, freckles expanding, a planet, then a moon, then a sun, then nothing at all visible except the onrushing map of it, the great eyes starting to cross at the last moment before their two noses rushed vastly headlong together to collide soundlessly.

"A little unreal," he said. There were grass stains on Truman's suit, and Mother noted them with worry as she repacked a picnic basket. "They won't come out," she said. He drank champagne, which seemed to make the unreality acceptable, normal, even necessary; he sat in a haze like the lengthening afternoon's, pacific and happy. Mother tied up the basket, and then saw a plate staring up at her from the grass; when the job had been all redone, Smoky with a sense of *déjà vu* pointed out a fork she hadn't seen. Daily Alice linked her arm with his. They had been all over the island several times, seeing friends and relatives, being made much of. "Thank you," several of them said when she presented Smoky, and when they gave her gifts. Smoky, after his third glass of champagne, wondered if this saying of things backwards (Cloud was always doing it) needn't be looked at case by case, so to speak, but was in the way of a

Happy Isles

general, well, a general . . . She leaned her head on his padded shoulder, and the two of them supported each other, hello'd out. "Nice," he said to no one. "What do they say when something's outdoors?"

"Al fresco?"

"Is that it?"

"I think so."

"Are you happy?"

"I think so."

"I am."

When Franz Mouse had been married, he and his bride (what was her name?) had gone together to a storefront photo studio. There, as well as the formal nuptial exposure, the photographer had thrown in a few goof pictures taken with props of his own: a papier-mâché ball-and-chain for Franz's leg, a rolling pin he encouraged the bride to brandish over him. Smoky reflected that he knew just about that much of married life, and laughed aloud.

"What," Alice inquired.

"Do you have a rolling pin?"

"You mean to roll out dough? I guess Mother does."

"That's all right, then." He had the giggles now, the stream of laughter arising from a point in his diaphragm as the bubbles rose from an invisible point in his glass. She caught it from him. Mother, standing above them arms akimbo, shook her head at them. The harmonium or whatever it was began again, stilling them as though it had been a cool hand laid on them or a voice suddenly beginning to speak of some long-past sadness; he had never heard music like it, and it seemed to catch him, or rather he it, as though he were a rough thing drawn across the silk of it. It was a Recessional, he thought, not remembering how he knew the word; but it was a Recessional meant seemingly not for him and his bride, but for the others. Mother sighed a great sigh, having fallen momentarily silent as the whole island had; she picked up her picnic basket, motioned Smoky to sit still who had half-risen with deep reluctance to help her. She kissed them both and turned away smiling. Around the island others were going down to the water; there was laughter, and a far-off shout. At the water's edge he saw pretty Sarah Pink helped into the swan boat, and others waiting to embark, depart, some holding glasses and one with a guitar over his shoulder; Ruby Flood flourished a green bottle. The music and the late afternoon charged their glad departure with melancholy, as though they left the Happy Isles for somewhere less happy, unable till they left to realize their loss.

Smoky stood his near-empty glass at a drunken angle in
the grass, and feeling made of music head to foot, turned to lay his
head in Daily Alice's lap. In doing so, he happened to catch sight of
Great-aunt Cloud at the lake's margin speaking with two people he
seemed to know but for a moment couldn't identify, though he felt
great surprise to see them there. Then the man made a fish's mouth
to puff on his pipe, and helped his wife into a rowboat.

Marge and Jeff Juniper.

He looked up into Daily Alice's placid and certain face,
wondering why every deepening of these daily mysteries left him less
inclined to probe them. "The things that make us happy," he said,
"make us wise."

And she smiled, and nodded, as who should say: yes,
those old truths are really true.

Sophie parted from her parents as they went arm in arm
through the hushing wood, talking quietly to each
other of what has been, as parents do whose eldest
child has just been married. She took a path of her
own, which went away uncertainly, eventually leading back the way they had come. Evening began to
fall as she walked, though what it seemed to do was not fall but well
up from the ground, beginning with the dense ferns' velvet undersides turning black. Sophie could see day go from her hands; they
became indistinct by degrees, and life then light went from the
bunch of flowers she still for some reason carried. But she felt her
head to be still above the rising dark, until the path before her grew
obscure and she breathed an evening coolness, and was submerged.
Evening next reached the birds where they sat, stilling bird by bird
their furious battle-of-the-hands and leaving whispering silence in
the middle air. Still the sky was as blue as noon, or nearly, though
the path was so dark she stumbled, and the first firefly reported for
work. She took off her shoes (bending her knee in mid-step and
reaching behind her to pull off one by the heel, hopping a step, and
taking off the other) and left them on a stone, hoping without giving
it much thought that the dew would not spoil their satin.

She wanted not to hurry, though her heart against her will
hurried anyway. Brambles implored her lacy dress to stay, and she
thought of taking it off too, but did not. The wood, looked through
lengthwise the way she went, was a tunnel of soft darkness, a perspective of fireflies; but when she looked out its less dense sides she
could see a lapidary blue-gone-green horizon flawed by a pale brush of
cloud. She could also see, unexpectedly (it was always unexpected)

A Sheltered
Life

the top or tops of the house, far off and moving farther off—so it seemed as the air between grew hazier. She went on more slowly into the tunnel into evening, feeling a kind of laughter constrict her throat.

When she came close to the island, she began to feel Somehow accompanied, which was not wholly unexpected, but still it made her flush with sensitivity, as though she had fur and it had been brushed to crackling.

The island wasn't really an island, or not quite one; it was teardrop-shaped, and the long tail of it reached up into the stream which fed the lake. Coming to it here, where the stream at its narrowest swept around the teardrop's tail to swell and ripple the lake, she easily found a way to step from rock to rock that the water rushed over making silken water-pillows where it seemed she could lay her heated cheek.

She came onto the island, beneath the gazebo which stood abstracted, looking the other way.

Yes, they were around her in numbers now, their purpose, she couldn't help but think, like hers: just to know or see or be sure. But their reasons surely must be different. She had no reasons that she could name, and perhaps their reasons had no names that could be spoken either, though she seemed to hear—doubtless only the stream and the blood sounding in her ears—a lot of voices speaking nothing. She went with care and great silence around the gazebo, hearing a voice, a human voice, Alice's, but not what it said; and a laugh, and she thought she knew what it must be saying. Why had she come? Already she began to feel a horrid blind dark pressure at her heart, a wall of great weight building, but she went on and came to a higher place shielded by glossy bushes and a cold stone bench; there she knelt without a sound.

The last green light of evening went out. The gazebo, as though it had been waiting and watching for it, saw the gibbous moon pull itself above the trees and spill its light over the wrinkled water and through the pillars and onto the couple there.

Daily Alice had hung her white gown on the hands of a bush, and now and again its sleeve or hem would move in the breeze which began when the sun set; seeing it with a corner of his vision Smoky would think there was someone else near the gazebo where they lay. There were these lights then: darkening sky, fireflies, phosphorescent blossoms that seemed to shine not by reflection but by some mild inward light of their own. By them he could sense more than see her long geography beside him on the cushions.

"I'm really very innocent," he said. "In lots of ways."

"Innocent!" she said with false surprise (false because of course it was for that innocence that he was here now, and she with him). "You don't *act* innocent." She laughed, and so did he; it was the laugh Sophie heard. "Shameless."

"Yes, that too. The same thing, I think. Nobody ever told me what to be ashamed of. Afraid of—they don't have to teach that. But I got over that." With you, he might have said. "I've had a sheltered life."

"Me too."

Smoky thought that his life had been not sheltered at all, not when Daily Alice could say the same thing about hers. If hers were sheltered, his was naked—and that's how it felt to him. "I never had a childhood . . . not like you had. In a way I never was a child. I mean I was a kid, but not a child. . . ."

"Well," she said, "you can have mine then. If you want it."

"Thank you," he said; and he did want it, all of it, no second left ungarnered. "Thank you."

The moon rose, and by its sudden light he saw her rise too, stretch herself as though after labor, and go to lean against a pillar, stroking herself absently and looking across to the massed darkness of the trees across the lake. Her long thews were silvered and insubstantial (though they were not insubstantial; no; he was still trembling slightly from their pressure). Her arm up along the pillar drew up her breast and the blade of her shoulder. She rested her weight on one long leg, locked back tensely; the other bent. The twin fullnesses of her nates were thus set and balanced like a theorem. All this Smoky noted with an intense precision, not as though his senses took it in, but as though they rushed toward it endlessly.

"My earliest memory," she said, as though in down payment on the gift she had offered him, or maybe thinking of something else entirely (though he took it anyway), "my earliest memory is of a face in my bedroom window. It was night, in summer. The window was open. A yellow face, round and glowing. It had a wide smile and sort of *penetrating* eyes. It was looking at me with *great interest.* I laughed, I remember, because it was sinister but it was smiling, and made me want to laugh. Then there were hands on the sill, and it seemed the face, I mean the owner of it, was coming in the window. I still wasn't scared, I heard laughter and I laughed too. Just then my father came in the room, and I turned away, and when I looked again the face wasn't there. Later on when I reminded Daddy about it, he said that the face was the moon in the window; and the hands on the sill were the curtains moving in the breeze; and that when I looked back a cloud had covered the moon."

"Probably."

"It's what *he* saw."

"I mean probably . . ."

"Whose childhood," she said turning to him, her hair afire with moonlight and her face matte and blue and for a moment frighteningly not hers, "is it that you want to have?"

"I want to have yours. Now."

"Now?"

"Come here."

She laughed, and came to kneel with him on the cushions, her flesh cooled now by moonlight but no less wholly her flesh for that.

As Quietly As She Had Come

Sophie saw them coupling. She felt with intense certainty what moods Smoky made come and go in her sister, though they were not the moods she had known Daily Alice to feel before. She saw clearly what it was to make her sister's brown eyes grow dense and inward, or leap to light: saw it all. It was as though Daily Alice were made of some dark glass which had always been partly opaque, but now, held up before the bright lamp of Smoky's love, became wholly transparent, so that no detail of Alice could be hidden from her as she watched them. She heard them speak—a few words only, directions, triumphs—and each word rang like a crystal bell. She breathed her sister's breath, and at each quickening of it Alice was fired further with distinctness. Strange way to possess her, and Sophie couldn't tell if the breath-robbing heat she felt at it were pain, or daring, or shame, or what. She knew that no force could make her look away; and that if she did she would still see, and just as clearly.

And yet all this time Sophie was asleep.

It was the sort of sleep (she knew every kind, but had no name for any one) in which it seems your eyelids have grown transparent, and you look through them at the scene you saw before they closed. The same scene, but not the same. She had, before her eyes closed, known or felt anyway that there were others around come also to spy on this marriage. Now in her dream they were quite concrete; they looked over her shoulders and her head, they crept with cunning to be near the gazebo, they lifted atomies of children above the myrtle leaves to see the wonder of it. They hung in the air on panting wings, wings panting in the same exaltation as that which

70

they witnessed. Their murmuring didn't disturb Sophie, for their interest, as intense as hers, was in nothing else like it; while she felt herself braving deeps, not certain she would not drown in contrary tides of wonder, passion, shame, suffocating love, she knew that those around her were urging those two—no, cheering them on— to one thing only, and that thing was Generation.

A clumsy beetle rattled past her ear, and Sophie woke.

The living things around her were dim analogs of those in her dream: murmuring gnats and glinting glowworms, a distant nightjar, hunting bats on rubber wings.

Far off, the gazebo was white and secret in the moonlight. She thought she could see, at moments, what might be the movements of their limbs. But no sound; no actions that could be named, or even guessed at. A stillness utterly private.

Why did it cut her more deeply than what she dreamed she had witnessed?

Exclusion. But she felt immolated between them as surely now when she could not see them as when she dreamed she could; was as uncertain she would survive it.

Jealousy: a waking jealousy. No, not that either. She had never been conscious of owning so much as a pin, and you can be jealous only when what is yours is taken. Nor betrayal either: she had known all from the start (and knew more now than they would ever know she knew); and you can only be betrayed by the false, by liars.

Envy. But of Alice, or Smoky, or both?

She couldn't tell. She only felt that she glowed with pain and love at once, as though she had eaten live coals for sustenance.

As quietly as she had come she went, and numbers of others presumably after her even more quietly.

The stream that fed the lake fell down a long stony distance like a flight of stairs from a broad pool carved by a tall waterfall high up within the woods.

Spears of moonlight struck the silken surface of that pool, and were bent and shattered in the depths. Stars lay on it, rising and falling with the

Suppose One Were a Fish

continual arc of ripples which proceeded from the foamy falls. So it would appear to anyone at the pool's edge. To a fish, a great white trout almost asleep within, it seemed very different.

Asleep? Yes, fish sleep, though they don't cry; their fiercest emotion is panic, the saddest a kind of bitter regret. They sleep wide-eyed, their cold dreams projected on the black and green interior of the water. To Grandfather Trout it seemed that the living water and its familiar geography were being shuttered and revealed to him as sleep came and went; when the pool was shuttered, he saw inward interiors. Fish-dreams are usually about the same water they see when they're awake, but Grandfather Trout's were not. So utterly other than trout-stream were his dreams, yet so constant were the reminders of his watery home before his lidless eyes, that his whole existence became a matter of supposition. Sleepy suppositions supplanted one another with every pant of his gills.

Suppose one were a fish. No finer place to live than this. Falls continually drowning air within the pool so that it was a pleasure simply to breathe. Like (supposing one were not a water-breather) the high, fresh, wind-renewed air of an alpine meadow. Wonderful, and thoughtful of them so to provide for him, supposing that they thought of his or anyone's happiness or comfort. And here were no predators, and few competitors, because (though a fish couldn't be supposed to know it) the stream above was shallow and stony and so was the stream below, so that nothing approaching him in size came into the pool to contest with him for the constant fall of bugs from the dense and various woods which overhung. Really, they had thought of everything, supposing they thought of anything.

Yet (supposing that it was not his choice at all to be a swimmer here) how condign and terrible a punishment, bitter an exile. Mounted in liquid glass, unable to breathe, was he to make back-and-forth forever, biting at mosquitoes? He supposed that to a fish that taste was the toothsome matter of his happiest dreams. But if one were not a fish, what a memory, the endless multiplication of those tiny drops of bitter blood.

Suppose on the other hand (supposing one had hands) that it was all a Tale. That however truly a satisfied fish he might appear to be, or however reluctantly accustomed to it he had become, that once-on-a-time a fair form would appear looking down into the rainbow depths, and speak words she had wrested from malign secret-keepers at great cost to herself, and with a strangulating rush of waters he would leap—legs flailing and royal robes drenched—to stand before her panting, restored, the curse lifted, the wicked fairy weeping with frustration. At the thought a sudden picture, a colored engraving, was projected before him on the water: a bewigged fish in a high-collared coat, a huge letter under his arm, his mouth gaping open. In air. At this nightmare image (from where?) his gills gasped and he awoke momentarily; the shutters shot back. All a dream. For a while he gratefully supposed nothing but sane and moonshot water.

Of course (the shutters began to drift closed again) it was

possible to imagine he was one of them, himself a secret-keeper, curse-maker, malign manipulator; an eternal wizard intelligence housed for its own subtle purposes in a common fish. Eternal: suppose it to be so: cetainly he has lived forever or nearly, has survived into this present time (supposing (drifting deeper) this to be the present time); he has not expired at a fish's age, or even at a prince's. It seems to him that he extends backwards (or is it forwards?) without beginning (or is it end?) and he can't just now remember whether the great tales and plots which he supposes he knows and forever broods on lie in the to-come or lie dead in the has-been. But then suppose that's how secrets are kept, and age-long tales remembered, and unbreakable curses made too. . . .

No. They know. They don't suppose. He thinks of their certainty, the calm, inexpressive beauty of their truth-telling faces and task-assigning hands, as unrefuseable as a hook deep in the throat. He is as ignorant as a fingerling; knows nothing; he wouldn't care to know—wouldn't care to ask them, even supposing (another inward window slides open silently) they would answer, whether on a certain night in August a certain young man. Standing on these rocks which lift their dry brows into the perishing air. A young man struck by metamorphosis as this pool was once struck by lightning. For presumably some affront, you have your reasons, don't get me wrong, it's nothing to do with me. Only suppose this man imagines remembering, imagines his only and final memory to be (the rest, all the rest, is supposition) the awful strangulated gasping in deadly waterlessness, the sudden fusing of arms and legs, the twisting in air (air!) and then the horrible relief of the plunge into cold, sweet water where he ought to be—must now be forever.

And suppose he cannot now remember *why* it happened: only supposes, dreaming, that it did.

What was it he did to hurt you so?

Was it only that the Tale required some go-between, some *maquereau,* and he came close enough to be seized?

Why can't I remember my sin?

But Grandfather Trout is deep asleep now, for he could not suppose any of this if he were not. All shutters are shut before his open eyes, the water is all around and far away. Grandfather Trout dreams that he's gone fishing.

V

what thou lovest well is
thy true heritage
what thou lovest well shall
not be reft from thee.

—*Ezra Pound*

T he next morning, Smoky and Daily Alice assembled packs more complete than Smoky's City pack had been, and chose knobbed sticks from an urn full of walking-sticks, umbrellas, and so on that stood in the hall. Doctor Drinkwater gave them guides to the birds and the flowers, which in the end they didn't open; and they took along also George Mouse's wedding present, which had arrived that morning in the mail in a package marked Open Elsewhere and would turn out to be (as Smoky hoped and expected) a big handful of crushed brown weed odorous as a spice.

Everyone gathered on the porch to see them off, making suggestions as to where they should go and whom of those that hadn't been able to get to the wedding they

Lucky
Children

ought to visit. Sophie said nothing, but as they were turning to go, she kissed them both firmly and solemnly, Smoky especially as if to say So there, and then took herself quickly away.

While they were gone, Cloud intended to follow them by means of her cards, and report, insofar as she could, on their adventures, which she supposed would be small and numerous and just the kind of thing these cards of hers had always been best for discovering. So after breakfast she drew the glass table near the peacock chair on that porch, and lit a first cigarette of the day, and composed her thoughts.

She knew that first they would climb the Hill, but that was because they said they would. She saw with the mind's eye the way they went up over the well-trodden paths to the top, to stand there then and look out over morning's domain and theirs: how it stretched green, forested and farmed across the county's heart. Then they would go down the wilder far side to walk the marches of the land they had looked at.

She laid down cups and wands, squires of coins and kings of swords. She guessed that Smoky would be falling behind Alice's long strides as they crossed the sun-whitened pastures of Plainfield; there Rudy Flood's brindled cows would look up at them with lashy eyes, and tiny insects would leap from their footfalls.

Where would they rest? Perhaps by the quick stream that bites into that pasture, undermining the upholstered tussocks and raising infant willow groves by its sides. She laid the trump called the Bundle within the pattern and thought: Time for lunch.

In the pale tigery shade of the willow-grove they lay full-length looking into the stream and its complex handiwork in the bank. "See already," she said, chin in hands. "Can't you see apartments, river-houses, esplanades or whatever? Whole ruined palaces? Balls, banquets, visiting?" He stared with her into the fretwork of weed, root, and mud which striped sunlight reached into without illuminating. "Not now," she said, "but by moonlight. I mean isn't that when they come out to play? Look." Eye level with the bank, it was just possible to imagine. He stared hard, knitting his brows. Make-believe. He'd make an effort.

She laughed, getting up. She donned her pack again that made her breasts stand. "We'll follow the brook up," she said. "I know a good place."

So through the afternoon they went up and slowly out of the valley, which the gurgling stream in malapert pride had taken over from some long-dead great river. They drew closer to forest, and Smoky wondered if this were the wood Edgewood is on the edge of. "Gee, I don't know," Alice said. "I never thought about it."

"Here," she said at last, wet and breathless from the long climb up. "This is a place we used to come to."

It was like a cave cut in the wall of the sudden forest. The crest they stood on fell away down into it, and he thought he had never looked into anywhere so deeply and secretly The Wood as this. For some reason its floor was carpeted with moss, not thick with the irregulars of the forest's edge, shrub and briar and small aspen. It led inward, it drew them inward into whispering darkness where the big trees groaned intermittently.

Within, she sat gratefully. The shade was deep, and deepened as the afternoon perceptibly passed. It was as still and as stilling as a church, with the same inexplicable yet reverent noises from nave, apse, and choir.

"Did you ever think," Alice said, "that maybe trees are alive like we are, only just more slowly? That what a day is to us, maybe a whole summer is to them—between sleep and sleep, you know. That they have long, long thoughts and conversations that are just too slow for us to hear." She laid aside her stick and slid one by one the pack-straps from her shoulders; her shirt was stained where she had worn them. She drew up her big knees glossy with sweat and rested her arms on them. Her brown wrists were wet too, and damp dust was caught in their golden hair. "What do you think?" She began to pluck at the heavy thongs of her high-top shoes. He said nothing, only took all this in, too pleased to speak. It was like watching a Valkyrie disarm after battle.

When she knelt up to force down her creased, constricting shorts he came to help.

By the time Mother snapped on the yellow bulb above Cloud's head, changing her card-dream from evening blue to something harsh and not quite intelligible, she had discerned what most of her cousins' journey might be like in the days to come, and she said: "Lucky children."

"You'll go blind out here," Mother said. "Dad's poured you a sherry."

"They'll be all right," Cloud said, shutting up the cards and getting up with some difficulty from the peacock chair.

"They did say, didn't they, that they'd stop in at the Woods'."

"Oh, they will," Cloud said. "They will."

"Listen to the cicadas still going," Mother said. "No relief."

She took Cloud's arm and they went in. They spent that evening playing cribbage with a polished folding board, one missing ivory peg replaced with a matchstick; they listened to the knock and rasp of great stupid June bugs against the screens.

Some Final Order

In the middle of the night Auberon awoke in the summer house and decided he would get up and begin to put his photographs in order: some final order.

He didn't sleep much anyway, and was beyond the age when getting up in the night to do some task seemed inappropiate or vaguely immoral. He had lain a long time listening to his heart, and grown bored with that, and so he found his spectacles and sat up. It was hardly night anyway; Grady's watch said three o'clock, yet the six squares of the window were not black but faintly blue. The insects seemed asleep; in not too long the birds would begin. For the moment though it was quite still.

He pumped up the pressure lamp, his chest wheezing each time he drove in the plunger. It was a good lamp, looked just like a lamp, with a pleated paper shade and blue Delft ice skaters around its base. Needed a new mantle, though. Wouldn't get one. He lit it, turned it down. Its long hiss was comforting. Almost as soon as it was lit it began to sound as though it were running down, but in fact it would continue running down for a long time. He knew the feeling.

It wasn't that the photographs were in no order. In fact he spent much of his time with their ordering. But he always felt that *their own* order, which wasn't chronological, or by size, or by some description of subjects, had always escaped him. They seemed to him sometimes individual frames taken from a motion picture, or several motion pictures, with lacunae long or short between the frames he had; and that if they were filled in, they would make scenes: long, story-telling pans, various and poignant. But how was he to tell if he had constituted even the frames he had aright, since so many others were missing? He always hesitated to disturb the after all quite rational cross-referenced order he did have in order to discover some other that might not be there at all.

He took out a portfolio labeled Contacts, 1911-1915. They were, though the label didn't specify it, his earliest pictures. There had been others, of course, early failures that he had destroyed. In those days, as he never tired of saying, photography was like a religion. A perfect image was like a gift of grace, but sin would always be swiftly punished. A sort of Calvinist dogma, where you never knew when you were right, but must be constantly vigilant against error.

Here now was Nora on the whitewashed porch of the kitchen, in creased white skirt and shirt. Her scuffed high-top shoes seemed too large for her. White cotton, white porch-pillars, darkness of her summer skin, fairness of her summer hair, her eyes startlingly pale from the shadowless brightness that fills whitewashed porches on sunny days. She was (he looked at the date on the picture's back) twelve. No, eleven.

Nora, then. Was there a way to begin with Nora (where his pictures began although of course the plot might not) and follow her, going away from her as a motion picture might when some other entered the frame, and follow that one?

Timmie Willie, for instance, and here she was by the X-gate that led out of the Park in that same summer, perhaps on that same day. Not quite sharp, for she would never be still. She was probably talking, telling where she was going, while he said Keep still. There was a towel in her hand: swimming. Hang your clothes on the hickory limb. It was a fine clear image, except that wherever the sun struck something, it flared: the weeds flamed whitely, one shoe of hers shone, the rings burned that she loved to wear even at that age. Hussy.

Which had he loved more?

Hung from Timmie Willie's wrist by a black strap was the small, leather-bound Kodak he let them borrow. Be careful with it, he told them. Don't break it. Don't open it up to look inside. Don't get it wet.

He traced with a forefinger Timmie Willie's single eyebrow, denser in this picture even than it had been in life, and suddenly missed her desperately. As though riffled by some inward dealer a deck of later pictures passed through his mind. Timmie Willie posed in winter at the frosty window of the music room. Timmie and Nora and tall Harvey Cloud and Alex Mouse in the dawn on a butterfly expedition, Alex wearing plus-fours and a hangover. Nora with dog Spark. Nora a bridesmaid at Timmie and Alex's wedding. Alex's roadster and glad Timmie standing in it waving, holding its canted windshield and wearing the most hopeful of ribboned hats. And in time Nora and Harvey Cloud married with Timmie present looking already pale and wasted, he blamed the City; and then gone, not seen again; the moving camera must pass and follow others.

Montage, then: but how was he to explain Timmie Willie's sudden absence from these groups of faces and festivals? His first pictures seemed to lead him right through his entire collection, branching and proliferating; and yet there was no way for any single picture to tell its whole story without a thousand words of explanation.

He thought wildly of printing them all on lantern-slides, and packing them together, packing more and more until their stained darknesses overlapped and nothing at all could be seen, no light came through: yet it would all be there.

No. Not all.

For there was another divergence it could take, symmetrical dark root to these patent everyday branches. He turned again to the picture of Timmie Willie at the X-gate, the camera on her wrist:

the moment of divergence, the place or was it time where the parting came.

He had always thought of himself as rational, common-sensical, an employer of evidences and a balancer of claims; a changeling, it seemed, in a family of mad believers and sybils and gnomic fancifiers. At the teacher's college where he had learned about the sci-entific method and logic, he had also been given a new Bible, that is Darwin's *Descent of Man;* in fact it was between its pages of careful Victorian science that he flattened Nora and Timmie Willie's camera-work when the finished prints had dried into scrolls.

Can You
Find the Faces

When Nora at evening with a new pink flush on her brown cheekbones had brought him the camera, breathless with some excitement, he had indulgently taken it to his red-lit cell in the basement, extracted the film, washed it in amnionic fluid, dried it and printed it. "You mustn't *look* at them, though," Nora said to him, "because, well," dancing from foot to foot, "in some of them we were—Stark Naked!" And he had promised, thinking of the Muslim letter-readers who must cover their ears when they read letters for their clients, so as not to overhear the contents.

They *were* naked by the lake in one or two, which inter-ested and disturbed him profoundly (your own sisters!). Otherwise for a long time he didn't look carefully at them again. Nora and Timmie Willie lost interest; Nora had found a new toy in Violet's old cards, and Timmie met Alex Mouse that summer. And so they lay between the pages of Darwin, facing the closely-reasoned arguments and the engravings of skulls. It was only after he had developed an impossible, an inexplicable picture of his parents on a thundery day that he searched them out again: looked closely at them: examined them with loupe and reading-glass: studied them more intently than he ever had the "Can You Find the Faces" pictures in *St. Nicholas* magazine.

And he found the faces.

He was rarely thereafter to see a picture anything like as clear and unambiguous as that picture of John and Violet and that other at the stone table. It was as though that one were a goad, a promise, to keep him searching through images far more subtle and puzzling. He was an investigator, without prejudice, and wouldn't say that he was "allowed" that one glimpse, that it was "intended" to make his life a search for further evidences, for some unambiguous answer to all the impossible puzzlement. Yet it had that effect. As it happened, he had nothing else pressing for his life to be about.

For there had to be, he was a certain of it, an explanation. An *explanation,* not airy talk like Grandy's of worlds-within-worlds or cryptic utterances out of Violet's subconscious.

He thought at first (even hoped, glass in hand) that he was wrong: tricked, deluded. Discounting the one singular image at the stone table—scientifically speaking an anomaly and therefore without interest—might not all these others be, oh, an ivy vine twisted into the shape of a claw-hand, light falling on a celandine so as to make a face? He knew light had its gifts and its surprises; could not these be among them? No, they could not. Nora and Timmie Willie had caught, by accident or design, creatures that seemed on the point of metamorphosis from natural to outlandish. A bird's face here and yet that claw which gripped the branch was a hand, a hand in a sleeve. There wasn't any doubt about it when you studied it long enough. This cobweb was no cobweb but the trailing skirt of a lady whose pale face was collared in these dark leaves. Why hadn't he given them a camera of higher resolution? There appeared to be crowds of them in some pictures, receding into the unfocused background. What size were they? All sizes, or else the perspective was Somehow distorted. As long as his little finger? As big as a toad? He printed them on lantern slides and threw them on a sheet, and sat before them for hours.

"Nora, did you when you went to the woods that day"—careful, mustn't prejudice her answer—"see anything, well, *special* to take pictures of?"

"No. Nothing *special.* Just . . . well, not special."

"Maybe we could go out again, with a good camera, see what we could see."

"Oh, Auberon."

He consulted Darwin, and the glimmer of a hypothesis began to be seen as though far off but coming closer.

In the primeval forests, by some unimaginable eon-long struggle, the race of Man separated itself from its near cousins the hairy apes. It appeared that there had been more than one attempt so to differentiate a Man, and that all of them had failed, leaving no trace behind except for the odd anomolous bone. Dead ends. Man alone had learned speech—fire—tool-making, and so was the only sapient one to survive.

Or was he?

Suppose a branch of our old family tree—a branch that seemed doomed to wither—had in fact not died out but survived, survived by learning arts just as new to the world but utterly different from the tool-making and fire-building of its grosser cousins, us. Suppose that instead they had learned concealment, smallification, disappearance, and some way to blind the eyes of beholders.

Suppose they had learned to leave no trace; no barrow, flint, glyph; no bone, no tooth.

Except that now Man's arts had caught up with them, had discovered an eye dull enough to see them and record the fact, a retina of celluloid and silver-salts less forgetful, less confusable; an eye that couldn't deny what it had seen.

He thought of the thousands of years—hundreds of thousands—it had taken men to learn what they knew, the arts they had invented out of absolute dark animal ignorance; how they had come to cast pots, amazing thing, whose clumsy shards we find now amid fires cold a millennium and the gnawed bones of prey and neighbors. This other race, supposing it existed, supposing data *proving* its existence could be found, must have spent those same millennia perfecting its own arts. There was the story Grandy told, that in Britain the Little People were those original inhabitants driven to littleness and secret wiles by invaders who carried iron weapons— thus their ancient fear and avoidance of iron. Maybe so! As (he turned Darwin's dense and cautious pages) turtles grow shells, zebras paint themselves in stripes; as men, like babies, grasped and gabbled, these others retreated into learned crafts of undiscoverability and track-covering until the race that planted, made, built, hunted with weapons no longer noticed their presence in our very midst—except for the discountable tales of goodwives who left dishes of milk on the sill for them, or the drunkard or the madman from whom they could not or chose not to hide.

They could not or chose not to hide from Timmie Willie and Nora Drinkwater, who had taken their likeness with a Kodak.

From that time on his photography became for him not an entertainment but a tool, a surgical instrument that would slice out the heart of the secret and bring it before his scrutiny. Unfortunately, he discovered that he himself was barred from witnessing any further evidences of their presence. His photographs of woods, no matter of what spooky and promising corners, were only woods. He needed mediums, which endlessly complicated his task. He continued to believe—how could he not?—that the lens and the salted film behind it were impassive, that a camera could no more invent or falsify images than a frosted glass could make up fingerprints. And yet if someone were present with him when he made what seemed to him

These Few
Windows

random images—a child, a *sensitive*—then sometimes the images grew faces and revealed personages, subtly perhaps, but study revealed them.

Yet what child?

Evidences. Data. There were the eyebrows, for one thing. He was convinced that the single eyebrow which some, but not all of them, had inherited from Violet had something to do with it. August had had it, thick and dark over his nose, where it would sometimes grow a spray of long hairs like those over a cat's nose. Nora had had a trace of it, and Timmie Willie had had it, though when she became a young woman she shaved and plucked it constantly. Most of the Mouse children, who looked most like Grandy, hadn't had it, nor John Storm nor Grandy himself.

And Auberon lacked it too.

Violet always said that in her part of England a single eyebrow marked you as a violent, criminal person, possibly a maniac. She laughed at it, and at Auberon's idea of it, and in all the encyclopaedic explanations and conflations of the last *Architecture* there was nothing about eyebrows.

All right then. Maybe all that about eyebrows was just a way for him to discover why it was that he had been excluded, couldn't see them though his camera could, as Violet could, as Nora had for a time been able to. Grandy would talk for hours about the little worlds, and who might be admitted there, but had no reasons, no *reasons*; he'd pore over Auberon's pictures and talk about magnification, enlargement, special lenses. He didn't know quite what he was talking about, but Auberon did make some experiments that way, looking for a door. Then Grandy and John insisted on publishing some of the pictures he had collected in a little book—"a religious book, for children," John said, and Grandy wrote his own commentary, including his views on photography, and made such a hash of it that no one paid the slightest attention to it, not even—especially—children. Auberon never forgave them. It was hard enough to think of it all impartially, scientifically, not to suppose you were mad or deeply fooled, without the whole world saying you were. Or at least the few who cared to comment.

He came to the conclusion that they had reduced his struggle in this way—a children's book!—just in order to further exclude him. He had allowed them to do it because of his own deep sense of exclusion. He was *outside*, in every way; not John's son, not truly the younger children's brother, not of Violet's placid mind but not brave and lost like August; without the eyebrow, without belief.

He was as well a lifelong bachelor, without wife or progeny; he was in fact almost a virgin. Almost. Excluded even from that company, yet he had never possessed anyone he had ever loved.

He felt now little anguish over all that. He had lived his whole life longing for unattainables, and such a life eventually achieves a balance, mad or sane. He couldn't complain. They were all exiles here anyway, he shared that at least with them, and he envied no one's happiness. He certainly didn't envy Timmie Willie, who had fled from here to the City; he didn't dare envy lost August. And he had always had these few windows, gray and black, still and changeless, casements opening on the perilous lands.

He closed the portfolio (it released a perfumy smell of old, broken black leather) and with it the new attempt at classification of these and the long sequence of his other pictures, ordinary and otherwise, up to the present day. He would leave it all as it was, in discrete chapters, neatly but oh inadequately crossreferenced. The decision didn't dismay him. He had often in his late life attempted this reclassification, and each time come to this same conclusion.

He patiently did up the knots of 1911-1915 and got up to take from its secret place a large display-book with a buckram cover. Unlabeled. It needed none. It contained many late images, beginning only ten, twelve years ago; yet it was companion to the old portfolio which contained his first. It represented another kind of photography he did, the left hand of his life-work, though the right hand of Science had for a long time not known what this left hand was doing. In the end it was the left hand's work which mattered; the right had shriveled. He became, perhaps had always been, left-handed.

It was easier to discover when he had become a scientist than to discover when he had ceased to be one; the moment, if there was one, when his flawed nature had betrayed him and, without divulging it, abandoned the great search in favor of—well, what? Art? Were the precious images in this buckram book art, and if they weren't did he care?

Love. Did he dare call it love?

He placed the book on the black portfolio, from which it grew, as a rose from a black thorn. He saw that he had his whole life piled up before him, beneath the hissing lamp. A pale night moth destroyed itself against the lamp's white mantle.

Daily Alice said to Smoky in the mossy cave in the woods: "He'd say, Let's go out in the woods and see what we can see. And he'd pack up his camera, sometimes he'd take a little one, and sometimes the big one, the wood and brass one with legs. And we'd pack a lunch. Lots of times we'd come here.

"We only came out on days that were hot and sunny so we could take off all our clothes—Sophie and me would —and run around and say Look and Look and sometimes Oh it's gone when you weren't really sure you'd seen anything anyway. . . ."

To See What He Could See

"Take off your clothes? How old were you?"

"I don't remember. Eight. Till I was maybe twelve."

"Was that necessary? To do the looking?"

She laughed, a low sound for she was lying down, full length, letting whatever breeze that came by have its way with her—naked now too. "It wasn't *necessary*," she said. "Just fun. Didn't you like to take your clothes off when you were a kid?"

He remembered the feeling, a kind of mad elation, a freedom, some restraint discarded with the garments: not a feeling quite like grown-up sexual feelings, but as intense. "Never around grown-ups though."

"Oh, Auberon didn't count. He wasn't . . . well, one of *them*, I guess. In fact I suppose we were doing it all for him. He got just as crazy."

"I bet," Smoky said darkly.

Daily Alice was quiet for a time. Then she said: "He never hurt us. Never, never made us do anything. *We* suggested things! He wouldn't. We were all sworn to secrecy—and *we* swore *him* to secrecy. He was—like a spirit, like Pan or something. His excitement made us excited. We'd run around and shriek and roll on the ground. Or just stand stock still with a big buzz just filling you up till you thought you'd burst with it. It was magic."

"And you never told."

"No! Not that it mattered. Everybody knew anyway, except oh Mom and Dad and Cloud, anyway they never said anything; but I've talked to lots of people, later on, and they say Oh you too? Auberon took you to the woods to see what he could see?" She laughed again. "I guess he'd been at it for years. I don't know anybody who resented it, though. He picked them well, I guess."

"Psychological scars."

"Oh, don't be stupid."

He stroked his own nakedness, pearly in the moonlight, drying in the licking breeze. "Did he ever see anything? I mean, besides . . ."

"No. Never."

"Did you?"

"We thought we did." She was of course sure they had: on brave luminous mornings walking expectant and watchful, waiting to be led and feeling (at once, at the same moment) the turning they must take that would lead to a place they had never been but which was intensely familiar, a place that *took your hand* and said *We're here.* And you must look away, and so would see them.

And they would hear Auberon behind them somewhere and be unable to answer him or show him, though it was he who had brought them here, he who had spun them like tops, tops that then walked away from him, walked their own way.

Sophie? he would call. Alice?

The Summer House was all blue within except where the lamp glowed, with less authority now. Auberon, dusting his fingers rapidly against his thumbs, went around the little place peering into boxes and corners. He found what he wanted then, a large envelope of marbled paper, last one of many he had had once, in which French platinum printing-papers had long ago been mailed to him.

But There
It Is

A fierce pain no worse than longing stitched up his torso, but went away again, more quickly than longing used to when he felt longing. He took the album of buckram and slipped it into the marbled envelope. He undid his ancient Waterman's (he'd never allowed his students to write with ball points or any of that) and wrote in his schoolmarm hand—shuddery now as though seen under water—*For Daily Alice and Sophie.* A great pressure seemed to enlarge his heart. He added: *And for no one else.* He thought of adding an exclamation, but didn't; only sealed it tightly. The black portfolio he put no name on. It was—all the rest of it was—for no living person anyway.

He went out into his yard. Still the birds for some reason had not begun. He tried to urinate at the lawn's edge but could not, gave up, went to sit on the canvas chair damp with dew.

He had always imagined, without of course ever believing it, that he would know this moment. He imagined that it would come at their time, unphotographable twilight; and that years after he had surrendered it all, grown hopeless, bitter even, in that twilight one would come to him, stepping through the gloaming without sound and without causing the sleeping flowers to nod. A child, it would seem to be, discarnate flesh glowing as in an antique platinum print, whose silver hair would be as though on fire, lit by

85

the sun which had just set or perhaps hadn't yet risen. He wouldn't speak to it, unable to, stone dead already it may be; but it would speak to him. It would say: "Yes, you knew us. Yes, you alone came close to the whole secret. Without you, none of the others could have come near us. Without your blindness, they couldn't have seen us; without your loneliness, they couldn't have loved each other, or engendered their young. Without your disbelief, they couldn't have believed. I know it's hard for you to think the world could work in this strange way, but there it is."

By noon next day, clouds had gathered, fitting themselves together resolutely and without haste, seeming when they had put out all the sky to be almost low enough to touch.

In the Woods

The road they walked between Meadowbrook and Highland wound up and down amid an aged forest. The well-grown trees stood close together, their roots it must be all interlaced below; above the road, their branches met and grappled together, so it seemed the oaks grew maple leaves and the hickories oak leaves. They suffered great choking garments of ivy, especially the riddled and fibrous trunks of the dead, propped against their old neighbors, unable to fall.

"Dense," Smoky said.

"Protected," Daily Alice said.

"How do you mean?"

She held out a hand, to see whether the rain had begun, and her palm was struck once, then again. "Well, it's never been logged. Not anyway in a hundred years."

The rain came on steadily, without haste, as the clouds had; this wasn't to be some fickle shower, but a well-prepared day's rain. "Damn," she said. She pulled a crumpled yellow hat from her pack and put it on, but it was apparent they were in for a wetting.

"How far is it?"

"To the Woods' house? Not *too* far. Wait a minute though." She stopped, and looked back the way they had come, then the way they were going. Smoky's bare head began to itch from the drops. "There's a shortcut," Alice said. "A path you can take, instead of going all the way around by the road. It *ought* to be right around here, if I can find it."

They walked back and forth along the apparently impassable margin. "Maybe they've stopped keeping it up," she said as they searched. "They're kind of strange. Solitary. Just live out here all by themselves and almost never see anybody." She stopped before an ambiguous hole in the undergrowth and said: "Here it is," without confidence, Smoky thought. They started in. The rain ticked in the leaves steadily, the sound growing less discontinuous and more a single voice, surprisingly loud, drowning out the sounds their own progress made. It was dark as night beneath the trees beneath the clouds, and not lightened by the silver shimmer of the rain.

"Alice?"

He stood still. All he could hear was the rain. So intent on making his way along this supposed path that now he'd lost her. And surely he had lost the path too, if there had ever been one. He called out again, a confident, no-nonsense call, no reason to get excited. He got no reply, but just then saw between two trees a true path, quite patent, an easy winding way. She must have found it and just got quickly on ahead while he floundered in the creepers. He took the path and went along, pretty well wet now. Alice should any moment appear before him, but she didn't. The path led him deeper and deeper beneath the crackling forest; it seemed to unroll before his feet, he couldn't see where it led, but it was always there to follow. It brought him eventually (long or short time he couldn't tell, what with the rain and all) to the edge of a wide, grassy glade all ringed with forest giants slick and black with wet.

Down in the glade, seeming insubstantial in the dripping mist, was the oddest house he had ever seen. It was a miniature of one of Drinkwater's crazy cottages, but all colored, with a bright red tile roof and white walls encumbered with decoration. Not an inch of it hadn't been curled or carved or colored or blazoned in some way. It looked, odder still, brand new.

Well, this must be it, he thought, but where was Alice? It must have been she, not he, who had got lost. He started down the hill toward the house, through a crowd of red and white mushrooms that had come out in the wetness. The little round door, knockered and peepholed and brass-hinged, was flung open as he came close, and a sharp small face appeared around its edge. The eyes were glittering and suspicious, but the smile was broad.

"Excuse me," Smoky said, "is this the Woods'?"

"Indeed it is," the man said. He opened the door wider. "And are you Smoky Barnable?"

"Well I am!" How did he know that?

"Won't you come right on in."

If there are more than the two of us in there, Smoky thought, it'll be crowded. He passed by Mr. Woods, who seemed to be wearing a striped nightcap, and was presenting the interior to Smoky with the longest, flattest, knobbiest hand Smoky had ever seen. "Nice of you to take me in," he said, and the little man's grin grew wider, which Smoky wouldn't have thought possible. His nut-brown face would split right in two at the ears if it went on growing.

Inside it seemed much larger than it was, or was smaller than it looked, he couldn't tell which. He felt laughter for some reason rise up in him. There was room in here for a grandfather clock with a cunning expression, a bureau on which pewter candlesticks and mugs stood, a high fluffy bed with a patchwork quilt more varied and comical than any he had ever seen. There was a round, much polished table with a splinted leg, and a domineering wardrobe. There were moreover three more people, all quite comfortably disposed: a pretty woman busy at a squat stove, a baby in a wooden cradle who cooed like a mechanical toy whenever the woman gave the cradle a push, and an old, old lady, all nose and chin and spectacles, who rocked in a corner and knitted quickly on a long striped scarf. All three of these noticed his arrival, but seemed to *take* no notice.

"Sittee down," said Mr. Woods. "And tell us your history."

Somewhere in the blue joyful surprise that filled Smoky to the chin a small voice was trying to say *What on earth*, but it exploded at that moment like a stepped-on puff-ball and went out. "Well," he said, "I seem to have lost my way—that is Daily Alice and I had—but now I've found you, and I don't know what's become of her."

"Right," said Mr. Woods. He had put Smoky in a high-backed chair at the table, and now he took from a cupboard a stack of blue-flowered plates which he dealt out around the table like cards. "Take some refreshment," he said.

As though on cue, the woman drew out from the oven a tin sheet on which a single hot-cross bun steamed. This Mr. Woods put on Smoky's plate, watching him expectantly. The cross on the bun was not a cross, but a five-pointed star drawn in white icing-sugar. He waited a moment for others to be served, but the smell of the bun was so rich and curranty that he picked it up and ate it without pause. It was as good as it smelled.

"I'm just married," he said then, and Mr. Woods nodded. "You know Daily Alice Drinkwater."

"We do."

"We think we'll be happy together."

"Yes and no."

"What?"

"Well what would you say, Mrs. Underhill? Happy to-gether?"

"Yes and no," said Mrs. Underhill.

"But how . . ." Smoky began. An immense sadness flew over him.

"All part of the Tale," Mrs. Underhill said. "Don't ask me how."

"Be specific," Smoky said challengingly.

"Oh, well," said Mr. Woods. "It's not like that, you know." His face had grown long and contemplative, and he rested his chin in the great cup of one hand while the long fingers of the other strummed the table. "What gift did she give you, though? Tell us that."

That was very unfair. She had given him everything. Her-self. Why should she have to give him any other gift? And yet even as he said it, he remembered that she had on their wedding night offered him a true gift. "She gave me," he said proudly, "her child-hood. Because I didn't have one of my own. She said I could use it any time I liked."

Mr. Woods cocked an eye at him. "But," he said slyly, "did she give you a bag to put it in?" His wife (if that's who she was) nodded at this stroke. Mrs. Underhill rocked smugly. Even the baby seemed to coo as though it had scored a point.

"It's not a matter of that," Smoky said. Since he had eaten the hot-star bun, emotions seemed to sweep him alternately like swift changes of season. Autumnal tears rose to his eyes. "It doesn't matter anyway. I couldn't take the gift. You see"—this was difficult to explain—"when she was young she believed in fairies. The whole family did. I never did. I think they still do. Now that's crazy. How could I believe in that? I *wanted* to—that is, I wanted to *have* be-lieved in them, and seen them, but if I never did—if the thought never occurred to me—how can I take her gift?"

Mr. Woods was shaking his head rapidly. "No, no," he said. "It's a perfectly fine gift." He shrugged. "But you have no bag to put it in is all. See here! *We'll* give you gifts. Real ones. No holding back on essential parts." He flung open a humpbacked chest bound with black iron. It seemed to glow within. "See!" he said, drawing out a long snake of a necklace. "Gold!" The others there looked at Smoky, smiling in approval of this gift, and waiting for Smoky's amazed gratitude.

"It's . . . very kind," Smoky said. Mr. Woods draped the glowing coils around Smoky's neck, once, again, as though he meant to strangle him. The gold was not cold as metal should be but warm as flesh. It seemed to weight his neck, so heavy it was, to bend his back.

"What more?" Mr. Woods said, looking around him, finger to his lips. Mrs. Underhill with one of her needles pointed to a round leather box on top of the cupboard. "Right!" Mr. Woods said. "How about this?" He fingered the box from its high place till it fell into his arms. He popped open the lid. "A hat!"

It was a red hat, high-crowned and soft, belted with a plaited belt in which a white owl's feather nodded. Mr. Woods and Mrs. Underhill said Aaaaah, and watched closely as Mr. Woods fitted it to Smoky's head. It was as heavy as a crown. "I wonder," Smoky said, "what became of Daily Alice."

"Which reminds me," Mr. Woods said with a smile, "last but not least but best . . ." From under the bed he drew out a faded and mouse-chewed Gladstone carpetbag. He brought it to the table and placed it tenderly before Smoky. A sadness seemed to have entered him too. His great hands stroked the bag as though it were beloved. "Smoky Barnable," he said. "This is in my gift. She couldn't give it, no matter that she wanted to. It's old but all the more capacious for that. I bet there's room in it for . . ." A doubt came over him, and he snapped open the crossbones catch of the bag and looked inside. He grinned. "Ah, plenty of room. Not only for her gift, but pockets too for your unbelief, and whatever else. It'll come in handy."

The empty bag was heaviest of all.

"That's all," said Mrs. Underhill, and the grandfather clock struck sweetly.

"Time you were going," said Mrs. Woods, and the baby choked impatiently.

"What's become of Alice?" Mr. Woods said thoughtfully. He turned twice around the room, looking out the small deep windows and peering into corners. He opened a door; beyond it Smoky glimpsed utter darkness and heard a long, sleepy whisper before Mr. Woods closed it quickly. He lifted his finger and his eyebrows went up with a sudden idea. He went to the tall wardrobe that stood on claw feet in the corner; he threw open its doors, and Smoky saw the wet woods he had come through with Alice—and, far off, loitering in the afternoon, Alice herself. He was shown into the wardrobe.

"It was very nice of you," he said, stooping to enter. "Giving me all this stuff."

"*Forget it,*" said Mr. Woods, his voice sounding distant

and vague. The wardrobe doors shut on him with a long noise like a far great low-voiced bell. He walked through the wet underbrush, slapped at by branches, his nose starting to run.

"What on earth," Daily Alice said when she saw him.

"I've been in the Woods'," he said.

"I guess you have. Look at you."

A thick tangle of creeper had Somehow got twined around his neck; its tenacious prickles tore his flesh and plucked at his shirt. "Damn," he said. She laughed, and began to pull leaves from his hair.

"Did you fall? How did you get dead leaves all in your hair? What's that you've got?"

"A bag," he said. "It's all right now." He raised to show her the long-dead hornet's nest he carried; its fine paper-work was broken in places and showed the tunneled interior. A ladybug crawled from it like a spot of blood and flew away.

"Fly away home," Daily Alice said. "It's all right now. The path was there all the time. Come on."

The great weight he felt was his pack, sodden with rain. He wanted desperately to put it down. He followed her along a rutted trail, and soon they came to a great littered clearing below a crumbling bank of clay. In the midst of the clearing was a brown shack with a tarpaper roof, tied to the woods by a dripping clothesline. A pickup truck sat wheelless on concrete blocks in the yard, and a black-and-white cat prowled, looking damp and furious. A woman in apron and galoshes was waving to them from the wire-bound chicken house.

"The Woods," Daily Alice said.

"Yes."

And yet, even when they had coffee in front of them, and Amy and Chris Woods were talking of this and that, and his discarded pack lay puddling the linoleum, still Smoky felt press on him a weight given him, which he could not shake off, and which gradually came to seem as if it had always been there. He thought he could carry it.

Of the rest of that day, and the rest of their adventures on that journey, Smoky later on would remember very little. Daily Alice would remind him later of this or that, in the middle of a silence, as though she rehearsed that journey often when her mind had nothing else to do, and he'd say, "Oh yes," and perhaps really remember what she spoke of and perhaps not.

On that same day Cloud on the porch by the glass table, thinking only to complete her pursuit of those same adventures,

91

turned up a trump called the Secret, and when she prepared to put it in its place gasped, began to tremble; her eyes filled with sudden tears, and when Mother came to call her for lunch, Cloud, red-eyed and still surprised that she had not known or suspected, told her without hesitation or doubt what she had learned. And so when Smoky and Daily Alice returned, brown, scratched and happy, they found the blinds drawn in the front windows (Smoky didn't know this old custom) and Doctor Drinkwater solemn on the porch. "Auberon is dead," he said.

Rooks (Smoky supposed) fled home across a cloud-streaked chilly sky toward naked trees which gestured beyond the newly-turned furrows of a March field (he was quite sure it was March). A split-rail fence, nicely cracked and knotholed, separated the field from the road, where a Traveler walked, looking a bit like Dante in Doré, with a peaked hood. At his feet were a row of white, red-capped mushrooms, and the Traveler's face had a look of alarm—well, surprise—because the last small mushroom in the row had tilted up its red hat and was looking at him with a sly smile from beneath the brim.

By the Way

"It's an original," Doctor Drinkwater said, indicating the picture with his sherry glass. "Given to my grandmother Violet by the artist. He was an admirer of hers."

Because his childhood books had been Caesar and Ovid, Smoky had never seen the man's work before, his pollarded, faced trees and evening exactness; he was struck by it in ways he couldn't analyze. It was called *By the Way*, like a whisper in his ear. He sipped his sherry. The doorbell (it was the kind where you turn a key to make the noise, but what a noise) rang, and he saw Mother hurry by the parlor door, wiping her hands on her apron.

He had made himself useful, less affected as he was than the rest of them. He and Rudy Flood dug the grave, in a place on the grounds where these Drinkwaters lay together. There was John. Violet. Harvey Cloud. It was a fiercely hot day; above the maples burdened with awesome weight of leaves there hung a vapour, as though the trees panted it out with their soft breathing in the fainting breeze. Rudy expertly shaped the place, his shirt plastered with sweat to his great stomach; worms fled from their spades, or from the light, and the cool, dark earth they turned out turned pale quickly.

And the next day people arrived, all the guests from his wedding or most of them, appearing in their sudden way, some wearing the same clothes they had worn for the wedding since they

hadn't expected another Drinkwater occasion so soon; and Auberon
was buried without minister or prayer, only the long requiem of the
harmonium, which sounded now calm and somehow full of gladness.

"Why is it," Mother said returning from the door with a
sky-blue Pyrex dish covered with foil, "that everyone thinks you're
starving after a funeral? Well, it's very kind."

Great-aunt Cloud tucked her damp hankie away in a black
sleeve. "I think of the children," she said. "All there
today, year after year of them—Frank Bush and
Claude Berry were in his very first class after the Decision."

Good Advice

Doctor Drinkwater bit on a briar pipe he
really seldom used, took it out and stared hard at it, as though
surprised to find it was inedible.

"Decision?" Smoky said.

"Berry et al. vs. Board of Ed," Doc said solemnly.

"I guess we can eat this now," Mother came in to say.
"Sort of pot luck. Bring your glasses. Bring the bottle, Smoky—*I'm*
having another." And at the dining table Sophie sat in tears because
she had set without thinking a place for Auberon, who always came
to eat on this day, Saturday. "How *could* I just *forget*," she said
through the napkin covering her face. "He loved us so much. . . ."
Still with the napkin over her face, she went quickly out. Smoky
seemed hardly to have seen her face since he arrived, only her retreating back.

"She and you were his favorites," Cloud said, touching
Daily Alice's hand.

"I suppose I'll go up and see Sophie," Mother said, irreso-
lute by the door.

"Sit down, Mother," Doc said softly. "It's not one of those
times." He helped Smoky to one of the three bowls of potato salad
there were among the funeral offerings. "Well. Berry et al. It was
thirty some years ago. . . ."

"*You* lose track of time," Mother said. "It's more like
forty-five."

"Anyway. We're very out-of-the-way up here. Rather
than trouble the State about our kids and all, we'd set up a little
private school. Nothing fancy at all. But it began to appear that our
school had to meet Standards. State Standards. Now the kids could
read and write as well as any, and learned their math; but the Standards said they had to learn as well History, and Civics whatever that
is or was, and a lot of other stuff we just didn't think was necessary. If

you know how to read, the World of Books is open to you, after all; and if you like to read, you'll read. If you don't, you'll forget whatever anybody *makes* you read, anyway. People around here aren't ignoramuses; just have an idea—or rather a lot of different ideas—about what's important to know, and very little of it's taught in school.

"Well, it turns out that our little school was closed down, and all the kids went outside to school for a couple of years. . . ."

"They said our Standards didn't fit our students for the real world," Mother said.

"What's so real about it?" Cloud said testily. "What I've seen lately doesn't seem so real to me."

"This was forty years ago, Nora."

"Hasn't gotten any realer since then."

"I went to the public school for a while," Mother said. "It didn't seem so bad. Only you always had to be there at exactly the same time every day, spring or winter, rain or shine; and they didn't let you out till exactly the same hour every day, as well." She marveled, looking back on it.

"How was the Civics and all that," Daily Alice asked, squeezing Smoky's hand under the table because the answer was a venerable clincher.

"You know what?" Mother said to Smoky. "I don't remember a single thing about them. *Not a single thing.*"

And that was just how the School System had appeared to Smoky. Most of the kids he had known forgot everything they learned in school as soon as they left those (to him) mysterious halls. "Boy," he'd say, "you ought to go to school with my father. He never lets you forget a thing." On the other hand, when they questioned him about schoolroom fixtures like the Pledge of Allegiance or Arbor Day or Prince Henry the Navigator, he was made of ignorance. They thought he was strange, when they noticed him at all.

"So Claude Berry's dad got in trouble for keeping him out of the public school, and it became a case," Cloud was saying. "All the way to the State Supreme Court."

"Bent our bank accounts out of shape," Doc said.

"And eventually was decided in our favor," Mom said.

"Because," Cloud said, "It was a religious thing, we claimed. Like the Amish, do you know about them?" She smiled slyly. "Religious."

"A landmark decision," Mom said.

"Nobody's heard of it, though," Doc said, wiping his lips. "I think the court surprised itself by the way it decided, and it was kept quiet; don't want to start people thinking, get their wind up, so to speak. But *we*'ve had no trouble since then."

"We had good advice," Cloud said, lowering her eyes; and they all consented silently to that.

Smoky, taking another glass of sherry and arguing from ignorance, began talking about a loophole in the Standards he knew of—that is, himself—and the superior education he'd anyway received, and how he wouldn't have it any other way, when Doctor Drinkwater suddenly struck the table with his palm, gavel-style, and beamed on Smoky, the light of a bright idea in his eyes.

"What about that?" Daily Alice said to him much later when they lay in bed.

"What?"

"What Dad suggested."

What About It

They had just the sheet over them in the heat, which only since midnight had begun to break apart into breezes. The long white hills and dales made by her body shifted cataclysmically and settled into a different country. "I don't know," he said, feeling muzzy and thoughtless, helpless against sleep. He tried to think of some more pointed answer, but instead fell off into sleep. She shifted nervously again and he was snatched back.

"What."

"I think of Auberon," she said quietly, wiping her face on her pillow. He took her up then, and she hid her face in the hollow of his shoulder and sniffed. He stroked her hair, running his fingers soothingly through it, which she loved as much as a cat does, until she slept. And when she was asleep, he found himself staring into the sparkling phantasmal ceiling, surprised by sleeplessness, not having heard of the rule whereby one spouse can trade a restlessness for the other's sleep—a rule spelled out in no marriage contract.

Well, what about it then?

He had been taken in here, adopted, it seemed not an issue that he would ever leave. Since nothing had before been said about their future together, he hadn't thought about it himself: he was unaccustomed to having a future is what it was, since his present had always been so ill-defined.

But now, anonymous no more, he must make a decision. He put his hands behind his head, carefully so as not to disturb her still-fresh sleep. What sort of a person was he, if he was now a sort of person? Anonymous, he had been as well everything as nothing; now he would grow qualities, a character, likes and dislikes. And did he

95

like or dislike the idea of living in this house, teaching at their school, being—well, religious he supposed was how they would put it? Did it suit his character?

He looked at the dim range of snowy mountains which Daily Alice made beside him. If he was a character, she had made him one. And if he was a character, he was probably a minor one: a minor character in someone else's story, this tall story he had got himself into. He would have his entrances and exits, contribute a line of dialogue now and then. Whether the character would be crabby schoolmaster or something else didn't seem to matter much, and would be decided along the way. Well then.

He examined himself carefully for feelings of resentment at this. He did feel a certain nostalgia for his vanished anonymity, for the infinity of possibilities it contained; but he also felt her breathing next to him, and the house's breathing around him, and in rhythm with them he fell asleep, nothing decided.

While the moon smoothly shifted the shadows from one side of Edgewood to the other, Daily Alice dreamed that she stood in a flower-starred field where on a hill there grew an oak tree and a thorn in deep embrace, their branches intertwined like fingers. Far down the hall, Sophie dreamed that there was a tiny door in her elbow, open a crack, through which the wind blew, blowing on her heart. Doctor Drinkwater dreamed he sat before his typewriter and wrote this: "There is an aged, aged insect who lives in a hole in the ground. One June he puts on his summer straw, and takes his pipe and his staff and his lamp in half his hands, and follows the worm and the root to the stair that leads up to the door into blue summer." This seemed immensely significant to him, but when he awoke he wouldn't be able to remember a word of it, try as he might. Mother beside him dreamed her husband wasn't in his study at all, but with her in the kitchen, where she drew tin cookie-sheets endlessly out of the oven; the baked things on them were brown and round, and when he asked her what they were, she said "Years."

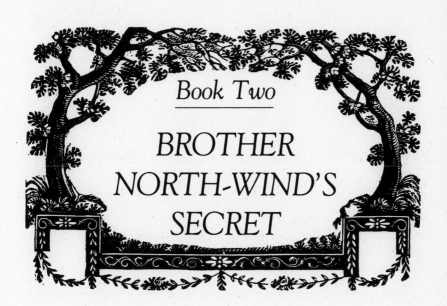

Book Two

BROTHER NORTH-WIND'S SECRET

I

The shepherd in Virgil grew at
last acquainted with Love, and found
him to be a native of the rocks.

—Johnson

After John Drinkwater's death in 1920, Violet, unable to
bear or even believe in the thirty years and more of life
without him promised her by her cards, retreated for a
long time to an upstairs room. Her thick dark hair, turned prema-
turely white, and her elfin thinness, grown more pronounced because
of a sudden distaste she took in that year to most food, gave her the
appearance of great and fragile age, though she didn't seem aged; her
skin remained unlined for many more years, and her dark, liquid eyes
never lost the infant, feral innocence which John Drinkwater had
first seen in them in the last century.

It was a nice room, facing in several directions at once. In
one corner, half the interior of a dome (all the interior
it had, though its exterior was whole) made a win-
dowed retreat, and she had a big buttoned chaise
there. Elsewhere, her bed, hung with the gauzy curtains and covered with the eiderdowns and ivory-
colored laces with which the mother she had never known had
clothed her own sad marriage bed; a broad oxblood-colored
mahogany table, piled up with John Drinkwater's papers, which she
had at first thought to put in some order, and maybe publish, he had
loved to publish, but which in the end she only left piled there under
the gooseneck brass lamp; the humpbacked cracked leather trunk
from which they had come and into which, years later, they would go
again; a couple of splayed velvet armchairs, napless and cozy, by the
fire; and those small things—her silver and tortoiseshell combs and

Retreats and
Operations

99

brushes, a painted music-box, her strange cards—which her children and grandchildren and visitors would later remember as being the chief furnishings of the room.

Her children, except August, didn't resent this abdication of Violet's. She had not often been wholly present anyway, and this seemed only the natural continuation of her daily abstraction. They all, except August, loved her deeply and uncritically, and would contest with each other over who would bring up her frugal and as often as not uneaten meals, make up her fire, read her her mail, or be the first to bring her news.

"August found a new use for his Ford," Auberon told her as they looked together through some pictures he had taken. "He took a wheel off, and hitched it with a belt to Ezra Meadows' saw. Then the engine will turn the saw, and cut wood."

"I hope they don't go far," Violet said.

"What? Oh, no," he said, laughing at the image she must have, of a tooth-wheeled Model T tearing through the woods, felling trees as it went. "No. The car is put up on logs, so the wheels just go around but don't go anywhere. It's just to saw with, not to drive around."

"Oh." Her slim hands touched the teapot, to see if it were still warm. "He's very clever," she said, as though she meant something else.

It was a clever idea, though not August's; he had read of it in an illustrated mechanics magazine, and persuaded Ezra Meadows to try it out. It proved to be a little more laborious than the magazine described it, what with leaping in and out of the driver's seat to alter the blade's speed, cranking each time the engine stalled out on a knot in the wood, and shouting What? What? back and forth with Ezra over the racket it made; and August had little interest in the production of sawn wood anyway. But he loved his Ford, and anything it could be made to do, from bouncing obliviously down railroad tracks to skimming and whirling like a four-wheeled Nijinsky over a frozen lake, he made it do. Ezra, suspicious at first, at least didn't have the airy contempt for Henry Ford's masterpiece which his family or people like the Flowers had; and making such a to-do in Ezra's yard brought out from her chores more than once his daughter Amy. Once with a dishclout in her hand, abstractedly wiping a white-speckled black tin frying pan as she stared; again with her hands and apron floured. The belt of the saw broke, and went flapping wildly. August cut the engine.

"There now, Ezra, look at that. Look at that stack." The fresh yellow wood, rough-cut and burned in brown arcs here and there by the blade's insistence, gave out its sweet odor, resin and pastry. "That would have taken you a week by hand. What do you think of that?"

"It's all right."

"What do you think, Amy? Pretty nice?" She smiled, and looked shy, as though it were she he was praising.

"It's all all right," said Ezra. "Gwan, git." This to Amy, whose expression changed to a hurt hauteur as sweet to August as her smile; she tossed her head and went, slowly, so as not to appear dismissed.

Ezra helped him bolt back the wheel of the Ford in silence; an ungrateful silence, August thought, though maybe the farmer was afraid that if he opened his mouth the subject of payment might come up. He was in no danger; for August, unlike the youngest son in all the old tales, knew he couldn't demand, in return for the accomplishment of an impossible task (the sawing of a couple hundred board feet in a single afternoon), the hand of his beautiful daughter.

Rolling home along the familiar roads, raising the familiar dust, August felt sharply the congruence (which everyone else saw as a contradiction) of his car and this deep summer. He made a small, unnecessary adjustment to the throttle, and tossed his straw hat on the seat next to him; he thought that if the evening were fine he might drive to some spots he knew of, and do some fishing. He was conscious of a bliss that stole over him not infrequently now, had first stolen over him when he had first acquired his car, first bent up its bat-wing hood and seen the engine and drive-train, humble and useful like his own internal organs. It was a sense that at last what he knew of the world was sufficient to his being alive in it: that the world and what he knew of it were one. He called this feeling "growing up," and it did feel like growing, though in moments of mad elation he would wonder if what he was growing into weren't a Ford, or perhaps Ford: there was no other instrument, and no other man, so serenely purposeful and complete, August thought, so sufficient to the world and so self-sufficient: it would have been a destiny he could welcome.

Everyone else seemed bent on thwarting it. When he told Pop (he called his father Pop to himself and to Amy, though he had never said it to John's face) that what was needed in this area was a garage, which could dispense gas and make repairs, and sell Fords, and had laid out the literature he'd got from the Ford company about what it would cost to set up such an agency (he hadn't proposed himself as agent, he knew he was too young at sixteen for that, but he would be happy just pumping the gas and making repairs, very happy), his father had smiled and not considered it even for five minutes, had sat nodding while August explained it to him only because he loved his son, and loved to indulge him. And then he said: "Would you like a car of your own?"

Well, yes; but August knew he had been treated like a boy, though he had made his proposal as carefully as any man; and his father, whose concerns were so weirdly childish, had smiled at it as though it were a child's mad desire, and bought him the car only to allay it.

But it was not allayed. Pop didn't understand. Before the war, things were different. Nobody *knew* anything. You could go walking in the woods and make up stories and see things if you wanted. But there was no excuse now. Now knowledge was there to be had, real knowledge, knowledge of how the world operates and what must be done to operate it. Operate. "The operator of a Ford Model T will find setting the spark simple and convenient. The operation is performed in this way. . . ." And August drew these knowledges on, reasonable and close-fitting, over the mad muddle of his childhood, as one draws on a duster over a suit of clothes, and buttoned them up to the neck.

A Swell Idea

"What you need," he told his mother that afternoon, "is some fresh air. Let me take you out for a drive. Come on." He came to take her hands, to lift her from the chaise, and though she gave him her hands they both knew, for they had enacted all this several times the same way, that she wouldn't rise and certainly wouldn't ride. But she kept his hands in hers. "You can bundle up, and anyway with the roads around here you can't go more than fifteen miles an hour. . . ."

"Oh, August."

"Don't 'oh, August' me," he said, allowing himself to be drawn down to sit by her, but turning his face away from her lips. "There's nothing wrong with you, you know, I mean nothing really *wrong*. You're just brooding." That it should be he, the baby, who was compelled to speak sternly to his mother as to a mopey child, when there were older children who ought to be doing it, annoyed him, though it didn't her.

"Tell me about sawing wood," she said. "Was little Amy there?"

"She's not so little."

102

"No, no. She's not. So pretty."

He supposed he blushed, and he supposed she saw it. He found it embarrassing, almost indecent, that his mother should see that he regarded any girl with other than amused indifference. In fact toward few girls did he feel amused indifference, if the truth were known, and it was known: even his sisters plucked lint from his lapels and brushed back his hair, thick and unruly as his mother's, with knowing smiles when he mentioned ever so casually that during the course of an evening he might drop in at the Meadows' or the Flowers'. "Listen, Ma," he said, faintly peremptory, "now really listen. Before, you know, Papa died, we talked about the garage, and the agency and all that. He didn't like it so well, but that was four years ago, I was very young. Can we talk about it again? Auberon thinks it's a swell idea."

"He does?"

He hadn't put up any objections; but then he had been behind the darkroom door, in his dim red-lit hermit's cell, when August had discussed it with him. "Sure. You know, everybody's going to have an automobile soon. Everybody."

"Oh, dear."

"You can't hide from the future."

"No, no, that's true." She gazed out the windows at the sleeping afternoon. "That's true." She had taken a meaning, but not his: he drew out his watch and consulted it, to draw her back.

"So, well," he said.

"I don't know," she said, looking into his face not as though to read it, or to communicate with it, but as though it were a mirror: that frankly, that dreamily. "I don't know, dear. I think if John didn't think it was a good idea . . ."

"That was *four years* ago, Ma."

"Was it, was it four. . . ." She made an effort, and took his hand again. "You were his favorite, August, did you know that? I mean he loved all of you, but . . . Well, don't you think he knew best? He must have thought it all out, he thought everything all out. Oh, no, dear, if he was sure, I don't think I could do better, really."

He stood up suddenly and thrust his hands into his pockets. "All right, all right. But don't blame him, that's all. You don't like the idea, you're afraid of a simple thing like a car, and you never wanted me to have anything at all anyway."

"Oh, August," she began to say, but clapped her hand over her mouth.

"All right," he said. "I guess I'll tell you, then. I think I'll

103

go away." A lump rose to his throat, unexpectedly; he had expected to feel only defiance and triumph. "Maybe to the City. I don't know."

"What do you mean?" In a tiny voice, like a child just beginning to understand a huge and terrible thing. "What do you mean?"

"Well really," he said, rounding on her, "I'm a grown man. What do you think? That I'll just hang around this house for the rest of my life? Well, I won't."

The look in her face, of shocked helpless anguish, when all he'd said was what any twenty-year-old might say, when all he felt was the dissatisfaction any ordinary person might feel, made confusion and frustrated common sense boil up in him like a lava. He rushed to her chair and knelt before her. "Ma, Ma," he said, "what is it? What on earth is it?" He kissed her hand, a kiss like a furious bite.

"I'm afraid, that's all. . . ."

"No, no, just tell me what's so terrible. What's so terrible about wanting to advance yourself, and be, and be *normal*. What was so wrong"—it was spilling out now, that lava, he neither desired to stop it now nor could if he chose—"about Timmie Willie going to the City? It's where her husband lives, and she loves him. Is this such a swell house that nobody should ever think of living anyplace else? Even married?"

"There was so much room. And the City's so far. . . ."

"Well, and what was so wrong when Aub wanted to join the Army? There was a war. Everybody went. Do you want us all to be your babies forever?"

Violet said nothing, though her big pearly tears, like a child's, trembled at her lashes. She suddenly missed John very much. Into him she could pour all the inarticulate perceptions, all the knowings and unknowings she felt, which, though he couldn't understand them really, he would receive reverently; and out of him would come then the advice, warnings, notions, the clever decisions she could never have made. She ran her hand through August's matted, elf-locked hair, no comb could conquer it, and said, "But you know, dear, you know. You remember, don't you? You do, don't you?"

He laid his cheek in her lap with a groan, and she continued to stroke his hair. "And autos, August—what would they think? The noise, and the smell. The—the boldness. What must they think? What if you drove them away?"

"No, Ma, don't."

"They're brave, August, you remember the time, when you were a little boy, the time with the wasp, you remember how brave the little one was. *You* saw. What if—what if it angered them, wouldn't they plan something, oh something so horrid. . . . They could, you know they could."

"I was just a little kid."

"Do you all forget?" she said, not as though to him, but as though questioning herself, questioning a strange perception she had just then had. "Do you all really forget? Is that it? Did Timmie? Do you all?" She raised his face in her hands to study it. "August? Do you forget, or . . . You mustn't, you mustn't forget; if you do . . ."

"What if they didn't mind?" August said, defeated. "What if they didn't care at all? How can you be so sure they'd mind? They've got a whole world to themselves, don't they?"

"I don't know."

"Grandy said . . ."

"Oh, dear, August, I don't know."

"Well," he said, extracting himself from her, "then I'll go ask. I'll go ask their permission." He rose. "If I ask their permission, and they say it's all right, then . . ."

"I don't see how they could."

"Well, if they do?"

"How could you be sure? Oh, don't, August, they might lie. No, promise me you won't. Where are you going?"

"I'm going fishing."

"August?"

When he was gone the tears rose again to her eyes. She brushed away impatiently the hot drops that rolled down her cheeks, rolled down because she couldn't explain: nothing she knew could be said, there were not the words, when she tried the very saying of it made what she said into lies or stupidities. They're brave, she had said to August. They might lie, she had said. None of that was true. They weren't brave, and they couldn't lie. Such things were true only when said to children, as it's true when you say "Grandy's gone away" to a child, when Grandy is dead, when there is no more Grandy to come or go. And the child says: Where did he go? And you think of an answer a little less true than the first, and so on. And yet you have spoken truly to it, and it has understood, at least as much as you have.

But her children weren't children any more.

105

So many years she had tried to form what she knew into language with John, grown-up language, nets to catch the wind, the Meaning of it all, the Intention, the Resolution. Oh great good man! And he had come as close to understanding it as intelligence, unwearying application, orderliness of mind and attention to detail could get.

But there wasn't any Meaning, or any Intention, or any Resolution. To think that way about them was like trying to do some task while you looked only in a mirror: force them as you might, your hands do the opposite of what they are told to do, away from not toward, left not right, forward not back. She sometimes thought that thinking of them at all was just that: was looking at yourself in a mirror. But what could that mean?

She *didn't* want her children to be babies forever, this country seemed full of people furious to grow up and though she hadn't ever sensed herself growing up she didn't care to prevent it in others, only she was afraid: if her children forgot what they had known as children, they were in danger. She was sure of that. What danger? And how on earth was she to warn them?

There were no answers, none. All that was within the power of mind and speech was to become more precise in how the questions were put. John had asked her: Do fairies really exist? And there wasn't any answer to that. So he tried harder, and the question got more circumstantial and tentative, and at the same time more precise and exact; and still there were no answers, only the fuller and fuller form of the question, evolving as Auberon had described to her all life evolving, reaching out limbs and inventing organs, reticulating joints, doing and being in more and more complex yet more and more compact and individuated ways, until the question, perfectly asked, understood its own answerlessness. And then there was an end to that. The last edition, and John died still waiting for his answer.

And yet there *were* things she knew. On the oxblood-colored mahogany table stood John's tall black typewriter, bony and carapaced like an old crustacean. For August's sake, for all of their sakes, she ought to say what she knew. She went to it, sat before it, rested her hands on its keys as a pianist might, thoughtfully, before beginning some soft, sad, almost inaudible nocturne; then realized there was no paper in it. This took a while to find; and her notepaper, when she had rolled a piece within the typewriter's jaws, looked small and shrinking and unready to receive the blows of the keys. But she began, using two fingers, and spelled out this:

violets notes about them

—and beneath this, the word Grandy had used to write on the desultory journals he kept:

tacenda

Now what? She advanced the paper, and wrote:

they mean no good to us

She thought about this for a moment, and then directly under it, she added:

they mean us no harm either.

She meant that they didn't care, that their concerns weren't ours, that if they brought gifts—and they had; if they arranged a marriage or an accident—and they had; if they watched and waited—and they did, none of that was with any reason to aid or hurt mortals. Their reasons were their own—if they had reasons at all, she sometimes thought they didn't, any more than stones or seasons have.

they are made not born

She considered this, cheek in hand, and said "No," and carefully x'd out "made" and wrote "born" above it, then x'd out "born" and wrote "made" above it, and then saw that neither was truer than the other. Useless! Was there any thought about them she could have whose opposite wasn't true? She skipped a space, sighing, and wrote:

no two doors to them are the same

Is that what she meant? She meant that what was a door for one person wouldn't be a door for another. She meant also that any door, once passed through, ceased to be a door ever after, could not even be returned by. She meant that no two doors ever led to the same place. She meant that there were no doors to them at all. And yet: she found, on the topmost rank of keys, an asterisk (she hadn't known the machine carried one) and added it to her last sentence, so it read:

no two doors to them are the same*

And beneath that she wrote:

*but the house is a door

This filled up her little notepaper, and she drew it out and read over what she had written. She saw that what she had was a sort

107

of precis of several chapters of the last edition of the *Architecture*, deprived of the billowing draperies of explanation and abstraction, nude and frail but no more help than ever. She crushed it slowly in her hands, thinking she knew nothing at all and yet knew this: that the fate that awaited her and all of them awaited them here (why was she dumb to say why she knew it?), and so they must cling to this place, and not stray far from it, she supposed that she herself wouldn't ever leave it again. It was the door, the greatest of doors, it stood Somehow, by chance or design, on the very edge or border of Elsewhere, and it would in the end be the last door that led that way. For a long time it would stand open; then for a time after that it would at least be able to be opened, or unlocked, if you had the key; but there would come a time when it would be closed for good, not be a door at all any more; and she wanted none of those whom she loved to be standing outside then.

The south wind blows the fly in the fish's mouth, says the Angler, but it didn't seem to blow August's well-tied and tempting examples into any. Ezra Meadows was **What You Most Want** sure that fish bite before rain; old MacDonald had always been sure they never do, and August saw that they do and don't: they bite at the gnats and mosquitoes settling like dust-motes over the water, driven down by altering pressure (Change, said John's ambivalent barometer) but not at the Jack Scotts and Alexandras August played over them.

Perhaps he wasn't thinking hard enough about angling. He was trying, without exactly trying to try, to see or notice something, without exactly noticing or seeing it, that would be a clue or a message; trying to remember, at the same time as he tried to forget he had ever forgotten, how such clues or messages had used to appear, and how he had used to interpret them. He must also try not to think This is madness; nor to think that he did this only for his mother's sake. Either thought would spoil whatever might happen. Over the water a kingfisher shot, laughing, iridescent in the sun, just above the evening which had already obscured the stream. I'm not mad, August thought.

A similarity between fishing and this other enterprise was that no matter where along the stream you stood, there seemed to be, just down there, where the stream spilled through a narrow race around stones, or just beyond the tresses of the willows, the perfect spot, the spot you had all along intended to go to. The feeling wouldn't diminish even when, after some thought, you realized that the perfect spot was one where, a few minutes ago, you had been standing, standing and looking longingly at the spot you now stood in and wanting to be amid the long maculations of its leaf shadows, as you now were, and yet; and just as August did realize this, as his desires were so to speak in transit between There and Here, something seized his line and nearly snatched the pole from his abstracted hand.

As startled as the fish itself must be, August played him clumsily, but had him after a struggle; netted him; the leaf-shadows were absorbed into evening vagueness; the fish looked up at him with the dull astonishment of all caught fish; August removed the hook, inserted his thumb in the bony mouth, and neatly broke the fish's neck. His thumb, when he withdrew it, was coated with slime and cold fish-blood. Without thinking, he thrust the thumb into his own mouth and sucked it. The kingfisher, making another laughing sortie just then, eyed him as he arrowed over the water and then up into a dead tree.

August, fish in his creel, went to the bank and sat, waiting. The kingfisher had laughed at *him*, not at the world in general, he was sure of that, a sarcastic, vindictive laugh. Well, perhaps he was laughable. The fish was not seven inches long, hardly breakfast. So? Well? "If I had to live on fish," he said, "I'd grow a beak."

"You shouldn't speak," said the kingfisher, "until you're spoken to. There are manners, you know."

"Sorry."

"First *I* speak," said the kingfisher, "and you wonder who it is that's spoken to you. Then you realize it's me; then you look at your thumb and your fish, and see that it was the fish's blood you tasted, that allowed you to understand the voices of creatures; *then* we converse."

"I didn't mean . . ."

"We'll assume it was done that way." The kingfisher spoke in the choleric, impatient tone August would have expected from his upshot head-feathers, his thick neck, his fierce, annoyed eyes and beak: a kingfisher's voice. Halcyon bird indeed!

"Now you address me," the kingfisher said. " 'O Bird!' you say, and make your request."

"O Bird!" August said, opening his hands imploringly, "Tell me this: Is it okay if we have a gas station in Meadowbrook, and sell Ford cars?"

"Certainly."

"What?"

"Certainly!"

It was so inconvenient speaking in this way to a bird, a

kingfisher seated on a branch in a dead tree at no more conversational a distance than any kingfisher ever was, that August imagined the bird as seated beside him on the bank, a sort of kingfisher-like person, of a more conversable size, with his legs crossed, as August's were. This worked well. He doubted that this kingfisher was a kingfisher at all anyway.

"Now," said the kingfisher, still bird enough to be unable to look at August with more than one eye at a time, and that one bright and smart and pitiless, "was that all?"

"I . . . think so. I—"

"Yes?"

"Well, I thought there might be some objection. The noise. The smell."

"None."

"Oh."

"On the other hand," said the kingfisher—a laugh, a raucous laugh, seemed always just beneath his words—"since you're here, and I'm here, you might ask for something else altogether."

"What?"

"Oh, anything. What you most want."

He had thought—right up until he had voiced his absurd request—that he was doing just that: but, with a terrible rush of heat that took his breath away, he knew that he hadn't, and that he could. He blushed fiercely. "Well," he said, stammering, "over in Meadowbrook, there's, there's a farmer, a certain farmer, and he has a daughter . . ."

"Yes yes yes," said the kingfisher impatiently, as though he knew well enough what August wanted, and didn't want to be bothered with having it spelled out circumstantially. "But let's discuss payment first, reward after."

"Payment?"

The kingfisher cocked his head in short, furious changes of attitude, sometimes eyeing August, sometimes the stream or the sky, as though he were trying to think of some really cutting remark in which to couch his annoyance. "Payment," he said. "Payment, payment. It's nothing to do with you. Let's call it a favor, if you prefer. The return of certain property that—don't get me wrong—I'm sure fell into your hands inadvertently. I mean—" for the briefest moment, and for the first time, the kingfisher showed something like hesitation, or trepidation "—I mean a deck of cards, playing cards. Old ones. Which you possess."

"Violet's?" said August.

"Those ones."

"I'll ask her."

"No, no. She thinks, you see, the cards are *hers*. So. She mustn't know."

"You mean steal them?"

The kingfisher was silent. For a moment he disappeared altogether, although that may only have been August's attention wandering from the effort of imagining him, to the enormity that he had been commanded to perform.

When he appeared again, the kingfisher seemed somewhat subdued. "Have you given any further thought to your reward?" he said, almost soothingly.

In fact he had. Even as he had grasped the fact that he could in some sense ask Amy of them (without even trying to imagine how they could make good on such a promise) he had ceased to desire her quite so intensely—small presage of what would happen when he did possess her, or anyone. But what one could he choose then? Was it possible he could ask for—"All of them," he said in a small voice.

"All?"

"Any one I want." If sudden horrid strength of desire hadn't whelmed him, shame would never have allowed him to say it. "Power over them."

"You have it." The kingfisher cleared his throat, looking away, and combed his beard with a black claw, as though glad this unclean bargaining was done. "There is a certain pool up in the woods above the lake. A certain rock which juts out into the pool. Put the cards there, in their bag in their box, and take the gift you find there. Do it soon. Goodbye."

Evening was dense yet clear, presage of a storm; the confusions of sunset were over. The pools of the stream were black, with steady glassy ribs raised by the continuous current. A black flutter of feathers in a dead tree was a kingfisher preparing for sleep. August waited on the bank till he had been returned, by an evening path, to the place he had started out from; then he gathered up his gear and went home, eyes wide and blind to the beauties of a stormgathering evening, feeling faintly sick with strangeness and expectation.

The velvet bag in which Violet's cards were kept was of a dusty rose color that had once been vivid. The box had once held a set of silver coffee-spoons from the Crystal Palace, but those had long since been sold, when she and her father wandered. To bring those strange huge oblongs drawn or printed centuries be-

Something
Horrific

111

fore out of this cozy box, with a picture of the old Queen and the Palace itself done on the cover in different woods, was always an odd moment, like the drawing aside of an arras in an old play to reveal something horrific.

Horrific: well, not quite, or not usually, though there were times when, as she laid out a Rose or a Banner or some other shape, she felt afraid: felt that some secret might be revealed which she didn't want to know, her own death or something even more dreadful. But—despite the weird, minatory images of the trumps, engraved with dense black detail like Dürer's, baroque and Germanic—the secrets revealed were oftenest not terrible, oftenest not even secret: cloudy abstractions merely, oppositions, contentions, resolutions, common as proverbs and as unspecific. At least so she had been told the fall of them should be interpreted, by John and those of his acquaintance who knew card reading.

But the cards they knew weren't these cards, exactly; and though she knew no other way of laying them out or interpreting them than as the Tarot of the Egyptians was laid out (before she was instructed in those methods she used just to turn them down anyhow and stare at them, often for hours) she often wondered if there weren't some more revelatory, simpler, Somehow more useful manipulation of them she could make.

"And here is," she said, turning one up carefully top to bottom, "a Five of Wands."

"New possibilities," Nora said. "New acquaintances. Surprising developments."

"All right." The Five of Wands went in its place in the Horseshoe Violet was making. She chose from another pile—the cards had been sorted, by arcane distribution, into six piles before her—and turned a trump: it was the Sportsman.

This was the difficulty. Like the usual deck, Violet's contained a set of twenty-one major trumps; but hers—persons, places, things, notions—were not the Greater Trumps at all. And so when the Bundle, or the Traveler, or Convenience, or Multiplicity, or the Sportsman fell, a leap had to be made, meanings guessed at which made sense of the spread. Over the years, with growing certainty, she had assigned meanings to her trumps, made inferences from the way in which they fell among the cups and swords and wands, and discerned—or seemed to discern—their influences, malign or beneficent. But she could never be sure. Death, the Moon, Judgement— those greater trumps had large and obvious significance; what did one make though of the Sportsman?

He was, like all people pictured in her cards, musclebound

in a not quite human way and striking an absurd, orgulous pose, toes turned out and knuckles on hip. He seemed certainly overdressed for what he was about, with ribbons at his knees, slashes in his jacket, and a wreath of dying flowers around his broad hat; but that was for sure a fishing pole over his shoulder. He carried something like a creel, and other impedimenta she didn't understand; and a dog, who looked a lot like Spark, lay asleep at his feet. It was Grandy who called this figure the Sportsman; underneath him was written in Roman capitals P I S C A T O R.

"So," Violet said, "new experiences, and good times, or adventures outdoors, for someone. That's nice."

"For who?" Nora asked.

"For *whom*."

"Well, for whom?"

"For whomever we're reading this spread for. Did we decide? Or is this only practice?"

"Since it's coming out so well," Nora said, "let's say it's for someone."

"August." Poor August, something good ought to be in store for him.

"All right." But before Violet could turn another card, Nora said "Wait. We shouldn't joke with it. I mean if it didn't *start* being August—what if we turn up something awful? Wouldn't we worry it might come true?" She looked out over the tangled spread, feeling apprehensive for the first time before their power. "Do they always come true?"

"I don't know." She stopped dealing them out. "No," she said. "Not for *us*. I think they might predict things that *could* happen to us. But—well, we're protected, aren't we?"

Nora said nothing to this. She believed Violet, and believed Violet knew the Tale in ways she couldn't imagine; but she had never felt herself to be protected.

"There are catastrophes," Violet said, "of an ordinary kind, that if the cards predicted them I wouldn't believe them."

"And you correct *my* grammar!" Nora said, laughing. Violet, laughing too, turned the next card: the Four of Cups, reversed.

"Weariness. Disgust. Aversion," Nora said. "Bitter experience."

Below, the ratchety doorbell rang. Nora leapt up.

"Now, who could that be?" Violet said, sweeping up the cards.

"Oh," Nora said, "I don't know." She had gone to the mirror hastily, and pushed her heavy golden hair quickly into place, and smoothed her blouse. "It *might* be Harvey Cloud, who said he might stop by to return a book I loaned him." She stopped her hurry, and sighed, as though annoyed at the interruption. "I guess I'd better go see."

"Yes," Violet said. "You go see. We'll do this again another day."

But when, a week later, Nora asked for another lesson, and Violet went to the drawer where her cards were kept, they weren't there. Nora insisted she hadn't taken them. They weren't in any other place that Violet might absentmindedly have put them. With half her drawers turned out and papers and boxes littering the floor from her search, she sat on the edge of the bed, puzzled and a little alarmed.

"Gone," she said.

"I'll do what you want, August," Amy said. "Whatever you want."

Anthology of Love

He bent his head down onto his upraised knees and said "Oh, Jesus, Amy. Oh, God, I'm so sorry."

"Oh, don't swear so, August, it's terrible." Her face was as misty and tearful as the shorn October cornfield in their view, where blackbirds hunted corn, rising at unseen signals and settling again elsewhere. She put her harvest-chapped hands on his. They both shivered, from the cold and from chill circumstance. "I've read in books and such that for a while people love people and then they don't any more. I never knew why."

"I don't know why either, Amy."

"I'll always love you."

He raised his head, so flooded with melancholy and tender regret that he seemed to have turned to mist and autumn himself. He'd loved her intensely before, but never so purely as now when he told her he wouldn't be seeing her any more.

"I just wonder why," she said.

He couldn't tell her it was mostly a matter of scheduling, nothing to do with her really, only the most pressing engagements he had elsewhere—oh Lord, pressing, pressing . . . He had met her here, beneath the brown bracken, at dawn when she wouldn't be missed at home, to break off with her, and the only acceptable and honorable reason he could think of for that was that he didn't love her any more, and so that was the reason which, after long hesitations and many cold kisses, he had given her. But when he did so, she was so brave, so acquiescent, the tears that rolled down her cheeks so salty, that it seemed to him that he'd said it only to see how good, how loyal, how meek she was; to animate with sadness and imminent loss his own flagging feelings.

"Oh, don't Amy, Amy, I never meant . . ." He held her, and she yielded, shy to trespass where he had only a moment ago said she was forbidden, not wanted; and her shyness, her big eyes searching him, afraid and wildly hopeful, undid him.

"You shouldn't, August, if you don't love me."

"Don't say it, Amy, don't."

Near to weeping himself, just as though he truly wouldn't ever see her again (though he knew now he must and would), on the rustling leaves he entered with her into new sad sweet lands of love, where the awful hurts he had inflicted on her were healed.

There was no end to Love's geography, apparently.

"Next Sunday? August?" Timid, but sure now.

"No. Not next Sunday. But . . . Tomorrow. Or tonight. Can you . . ."

"Yes. I'll think of a way. Oh, August. Sweetness."

She ran, wiping her face, pinning her hair, late, in danger, happy, across the field. This, he thought, in some last resisting stronghold of his soul, is what I've come to: even the end of love is only another spur to love. He went the other way to where his car, reproachful, awaited him. The mist-sodden squirrel tail that now adorned it hung limply on its staff. Trying not to think, he cranked the car into life.

What the hell was he to do anyway?

He had thought that the ardent sword of feeling that had gone through him when he first saw Amy Meadows after acquiring his gift was only the certainty that desire was at last to be fulfilled. But he proceeded to make a fool of himself over her, certainty or no certainty; he braved her father, he told desperate lies and was nearly caught out in them, he waited hours on the cold ground beyond her house for her to free herself—they had promised him power over women, he realized bitterly, but not over their circumstances—and though Amy acceded to all his plans, his nighttime meetings, his schemes, and matched his importunities one for one, not even her shamelessness lessened his sense of not being at all in charge here, but at the beck and call of desire more demanding, less a part of himself and more a demon that rode him, than he had been before.

The sense grew, over the months, as he wheeled the Ford around the five towns, to a certainty: he drove the Ford, but was himself driven, steered, and shifted without let.

Violet didn't inquire why he had dropped the notion of

building a garage in Meadowbrook. Now and then he complained to her that he used almost as much gas getting to and from the nearest garage as he put in his tank when he got there, but this didn't seem to be a hint or an argument, in fact he seemed less argumentative altogether than he had been. It might be, she thought, that his almost haggard air of being concerned quite elsewhere meant that he was hatching some even more unlikely scheme, but Somehow she thought not; she hoped that what appeared to be guilty exhaustion in his face and voice when he lounged silent at home didn't mean he was practicing some secret vice; certainly something had happened. The cards might have told her what, but the cards were gone. It was probably, she thought, only that he was in love.

That was true. If Violet hadn't chosen to seclude herself in an upstairs room, she would have had a notion of the swath her younger son was cutting through the young girls, the standing harvest of the pentacle of five towns around Edgewood. Their parents knew, a little; the girls themselves, among themselves, told of it; among them a glimpse of August's T, with the bright jaunty squirrel tail flying from a whippy rod at the windscreen, meant a day's consternation, a night's hot tossing, a wet pillow in the morning; they didn't know—how could they guess? All their hearts were his—that August's days and nights were spent much as theirs were.

He hadn't expected this. He had heard of Casanova, but hadn't read him. He had imagined harems, the peremptory clap of a sultan's hands which brings the acquiescent object of desire as quickly and impersonally as a dime brought a chocolate soda at the drugstore. He was astounded when, without his mad desire for Amy lessening in the slightest, he fell deeply in love with the Flowers' eldest daughter. Ravened by love and lewdness, he thought of her continually, when he wasn't with Amy; or when he wasn't thinking about—how could it be—little Margaret Juniper, who wasn't even fourteen. He learned, though slowly, what all great harrowed lovers learn: that love is what most surely compels love—is perhaps, except for brute force, the only thing that does, though only (and this was the terrible gift he had been given) when the lover truly believes, as August could, that when his love is strong enough it must surely be returned—and August's was.

When, with shame in his heart and trembling hands he had laid down by the rock pool what he had tried to deny to himself was his mother's most precious possession, the cards, and picked up what lay there for him, only a squirrel's tail and probably no gift at all but only the remnants of an owl's or a fox's breakfast, this is madness, it was only the dense weight of virgin hope that had allowed him to

tie it to his Ford, expecting nothing. But they had kept their promise, oh they had, he was on the way to becoming an entire anthology
of love, with footnotes (there were a pair of step-ins under his seat,
he could not remember who had stepped out of them); only, as he
drove from drugstore to church, from farmhouse to farmhouse, with
the hairy thing flying from his windscreen, he came to know that it
did not and had not ever contained his power over women: his power
over women lay in their power over him.

The Flowers came on Wednesdays, usually, bringing
armloads of blossoms for Violet's room, and though
Violet always felt somewhat ashamed and guilty in the
presence of so many decapitated and slowly expiring
blooms, she tried to express admiration and wonder at
Mrs. Flowers' green thumb. But this visit was Tues-
day, and there were no flowers.

Darker Before
It Lightened

"Come in, come in," Violet said. They were standing,
unwontedly shy, at her bedroom door. "Will you take some tea?"
"Oh, no," said Mrs. Flowers. "Just a few words."
But when they were seated, exchanging glances with one
another (though unable apparently to look at Violet) they said nothing for an uncomfortably long time.
The Flowers had come up just after the War to take Mr.
MacGregor's old place, "fleeing," as Mrs. Flowers put it, the City;
Mr. Flowers had had position and money there, but just what position wasn't clear, and how it had made him money was even less
clear, not because they chose to hide it but because they seemed to
find commonplaces of daily life hard to converse about intelligibly.
They had been members with John of the Theosophical Society; they
were both in love with Violet. Like John's, their lives were full of
quiet drama, full of vague yet thrilling signs that life was not as the
common run supposed it to be; they were among those (it surprised
Violet how many there were, and how many gravitated toward
Edgewood) who watch life as though it were a great drab curtain
which they are sure is always about to rise on some terrific and
exquisite spectacle, and though it never did quite rise, they were
patient, and noted excitedly every small movement of it as the actors
took their places, strained to hear the unimaginable setting being
shifted.
Like John, they supposed Violet to be one of those actors,
or at least to have been behind the curtain. That she couldn't see it
that way at all made her only the more cryptic and entrancing to
them. Their Wednesday visits made matter for a whole evening's

quiet talk, inspiration for a whole week's reverent and watchful life.

But this wasn't Wednesday.

"It's about happiness," Mrs. Flowers said, and Violet had to stare puzzled at her for a moment until she reheard this as "It's about Happiness," the name of their eldest daughter. The younger ones were named Joy and Spirit. The same confusion happened when their names came up: our Joy is gone for the day; our Spirit came home covered with mud. Folding her hands and raising eyes that Violet now saw were red from weeping, Mrs. Flowers said, "Happiness is pregnant."

"Oh my."

Mr. Flowers, who with his thin boyish beard and great sensitive brow reminded Violet of Shakespeare, began speaking so softly and indirectly that Violet had to lean forward to hear. She got the gist: Happiness was pregnant, so Happiness had said, by her son August.

"She cried all night," Mrs. Flowers said, her own eyes filling. Mr. Flowers explained, or tried to. It wasn't that they believed in worldly shame or honor, their own marriage bond had been sealed before any words or formulas had been spoken; the flowering of vital energies is always to be welcomed. No: it was that August, well, didn't seem to understand it the way they did, or perhaps he understood it better, but anyway to speak frankly they thought he'd broken the girl's heart, though she said he said he loved her; they wondered if Violet knew what August felt, or—or if she knew (the phrase, so loaded with common and wrong meaning, fell out anyway, with a clang, like a horseshoe he had had in his pocket) what the boy intended to do about this.

Violet moved her mouth, as though in answer, but no answer came out. She composed herself. "If he loves her," she said, "then . . ."

"He may," Mr. Flowers said. "But he says—she says he says—that there's someone else, someone with, well, a prior claim, someone . . ."

"He's promised to another," Mrs. Flowers said. "Who's also, well."

"Amy Meadows?" Violet said.

"No, no. That wasn't the name. Was that the name?"

Mr. Flowers coughed. "Happiness wasn't sure, exactly. There might be . . . more than one."

Violet could only say "Oh dear, oh dear," feeling deeply their consternation, their brave effort not to censure, and having no idea how to answer them. They looked at her with hope, hope that

118

she would say something that would fit all this too into the drama they perceived. But in the end she could only say, in a tiny voice, with a desperate smile, "Well, I suppose it's not the first time it ever happened in the world."

"Not the first time?"

"I mean not the *first* time."

Their hearts leapt up. She *did* know: she knew precedents for this. What could they be? Krishna fluting, seed-scattering, spirit-incarnating—avatars—what? Something they had no inkling of? Yes, brighter and stranger than they could know. "Not the first time," said Mr. Flowers, his unlined brow raised. "Yes."

"Is it," said Mrs. Flowers, almost whispering, "part of the Tale?"

"Is what? Oh, yes," Violet said, lost in thought. What had become of Amy? What on earth was August up to? Where had he found the daring to break girls' hearts? A dread came over her. "Only I didn't know this, I never suspected. . . . Oh, August," she said, and bowed her head. Was this their doing? How could she know? Could she ask him? Would his answer tell her?

Seeing her so lost, Mr. Flowers leaned forward. "We never, never meant to burden you," he said. "It wasn't—it wasn't that we didn't think, that we weren't sure it wasn't, or wouldn't be, all right. Happiness doesn't *blame* him, I mean it's not that."

"No," said Mrs. Flowers, and put her hand gently on Violet's arm. "We didn't *want* anything. It wasn't that. A new spirit is always a joy. She'll be ours."

"Maybe," Violet said, "it'll be clearer later."

"I'm sure," Mrs. Flowers said. "It is, it *is* part of the Tale."

But Violet had seen that it would not be clearer later. The Tale: yes, this was part of the Tale, but she had suddenly seen, as a person alone in a room reading or working at the end of day sees, as she raises her eyes from work that has for some reason grown obscure and difficult, that evening has come, and that's the reason; and that it would long grow darker before it lightened.

"Please," she said, "have tea. We'll light the lights. Stay awhile."

Outside she could hear—they could all hear—a car, chugging steadily toward the house. It slowed as it approached the drive—its voice was distinct and regular, like the crickets'—and changed gears like changing its mind, and chugged onward.

How long is the Tale? she had asked, and Mrs. Underhill had said: you and your children and your children's children will all be buried before that Tale's all told.

She took hold of the lamp cord, but for a moment didn't pull it. What had she done? Was this her fault, because she hadn't believed the Tale could be so long? It was. She would change. She would correct what she could, if there were time. There must be time. She pulled the cord, which made the windows night, and the room a room.

The Last Day of August

The enormous moon which August had taken Margaret Juniper out to see rise had risen, though they hadn't noticed its ascent. The harvest moon, August had insisted this was, and had sung a song about it to Marge as they sped along; but it wasn't the harvest moon, amber and huge and plenteous as it was, that would be next month's; this was only the last day of August.

Its light was on them. They could look at it now, August was too dazed and replete to do anything else, even to comfort Marge who wept quietly—perhaps, who could tell, even happily—beside him. He couldn't speak. He wondered if he would ever speak again, except to invite, except to propose. Maybe if he kept his mouth shut . . . But he knew he wouldn't.

Marge raised a moonlit hand, and stroked the moustache he had begun to grow, laughing through her tears. "It's so handsome," she said. He twitched his nose like a rabbit under her fingers. Why do they always rub it wrong, turn it uncomfortably underside-over, should he shave it so they can't? Her mouth was red and the flesh around it flushed from kissing and from weeping. Her skin against his was as soft as he had imagined it would be, but flecked with pinkish freckles he hadn't expected, not her slim white thighs though, bare on the sweat-slick leather of the seat. Within her opened blouse her breasts were small and new-looking, capped with large changeable nipples, seeming to have just been extruded from a boyish chest. The little hair was blond and stiff and small, like a dot. Oh God the privacies he had seen. He felt the strangeness of unbound flesh strongly. They ought to be kept hidden, these vulnerabilities, these oddities and organs soft as a snail's body or its tender horns, the exposure of them was monstrous, he wanted to recase hers in the pretty white underthings that hung around the car like festoons, and yet even as he thought this be began to rise again.

"Oh," she said. She hadn't, probably, got much of a gander at his engorgement in the rush of her deflowering, too much else to think about. "Do you do it right away again?"

He made no answer, it had nothing to do with him. As well ask the trout struggling on the hook if he liked to go on with that activity or cease it. A bargain is a bargain. He did wonder why, though one knows a woman better and she has picked up anyway the rudiments, the second time often seems more difficult, more ill-fitting, more a matter of inconvenient knees and elbows, than the first. None of this prevented his falling, as they coupled, more deeply in love with her, but he hadn't expected it to. So various they are, bodies, breasts, odors, he hadn't known about that, that they would be as individual, as charged with character, as faces and voices. He was surfeited with so much character. He knew too much. He groaned aloud with love and knowledge, and clung to her.

It was late, the moon had shrunk and grown chill and white as it climbed the sky. With how sad steps. Her tears fell again, though she didn't seem to be exactly weeping, they seemed a natural secretion, drawn forth by the moon perhaps; she was busy putting away her nakedness, though she couldn't take it back from him any more. She said to him calmly: "I'm glad, August. That we had this one time."

"What do you mean?" A hoarse beast's voice, not his own. "This one time?"

She brushed the tears from her face with the flat of her hand, she couldn't see to fasten her garters. "Because I can always remember this now."

"No."

"At least remember this." She threw her dress into the air, very agilely causing it to settle over her head; she wiggled, and it descended over her like a curtain, the last act. "August, no." She shrank against the door, clasping her hands together, drawing up her shoulders. "Because you don't love me, and that's all right. No. I know about Sara Stone. Everybody knows. It's all right."

"Who?"

"Don't you dare." She looked at him warningly. He wasn't to spoil this with lies, with coarse denials. "You love her. That's true and you know it." He said nothing. It was true. A collision was taking place inside him of such magnitude he could only witness it. The noise of it made it hard to hear her. "I'll never ever do it with anyone else, ever." Her bravery exhausted, her lip began to tremble. "I'm going to go off and live with Jeff, and I'll never love anyone else, and just remember this always." Jeff was her kindly brother, a rose gardener. She turned her face away. "You can take me home now."

He took her home, without another word.

Being filled with clamor is like being void. Void, he watched her climb down from the car, watched her shatter the moonshadows of leaves and be shattered by them as she went away,

121

not looking back, he would not have seen her if she had looked. Void, he drove away from the shaded, shuddering crossroads. Void, he drove toward home. It didn't feel like a decision, it felt like void, when he turned off the gray pebble-glittering road, bounced through the ditch, climbed a bank, and steered the Ford (dauntless, unfazed) out into the silvered pond of an uncut pasture, and then further on, the void slowly filling with resolution that felt also like void.

The car sputtered out of gas. He choked it, prodded it, urged it a little further, but it died. If there was a God damn garage within ten miles of here it would be convenient as hell. He sat for a while in the cooling car, imagining his destination without exactly thinking about it. He did wonder (last lamplit window of common thought, flickering out) if Marge would think he'd done it for her. Well he would have, in a way, in a way, he would have to put stones in his pockets, heavy ones, and just relax. Wash it all away. The thunder of void resolution was like the cold thunder of the falls, he seemed already to hear it, and wondered if he would hear nothing else through eternity; he hoped not.

He got out of the car, detached the squirrel tail, it ought to be returned, maybe they would Somehow return the payment he had made for it; and, slipping and stumbling in his patent-leather seducer's shoes, he made for the woods.

"Mother?" Nora said, astonished, stopping in the hall with an empty cup and saucer in her hands. "What are you doing up?"

Strange Way to Live

Violet stood on the stairs, having made no sound coming down that Nora heard; she was dressed, in clothes which Nora hadn't seen for years, but she had the air of someone asleep, somnambulating.

"No word," she said, as though sure there would not be, "about August?"

"No. No, no word."

Two weeks had passed since a neighbor had told them of seeing August's Ford abandoned in a field, open to the elements. Auberon, after long hesitation, had suggested to Violet that they call the police; but this notion was so far from anything Violet could imagine about what had happened that he doubted she even heard: no fate August was reserved to could possibly be altered, or even discovered, by police.

"It's my fault, you know," she said in a small voice. "Whatever it is that's happened. Oh, Nora."

Nora rushed up the stairs to where Violet had sat down suddenly as though fallen. She took Violet's arm to help her rise, but Violet only grasped the hand she offered and squeezed it, as though it were Nora who needed comforting. Nora sat beside her on the stair. "I've been so wrong," Violet said, "so stupid and wrong. And now see what's come of it."

"No," Nora said. "What do you mean?"

"I didn't see," Violet said. "I thought . . . Listen now, Nora. I want to go to the City. I want to see Timmie and Alex, and have a long visit, and see the baby. Will you come?"

"Of course," Nora said. "But . . ."

"All right. And Nora. Your young man."

"What young man?" She looked away.

"Henry. Harvey. You mightn't think I know, but I do. I think—I think you and he should—should do what you like. If ever anything I said made you think I didn't want you to, well, it's not so. You must do exactly as you like. Marry him, and move away . . ."

"But I don't want to move away."

"Poor Auberon, I suppose it's too late—he's missed his war now, and . . ."

"Mother," Nora said, "what are you talking about?"

She was silent a time. Then: "It's my own fault," she said. "I didn't think. It's very hard though, you know, to know a little, or to guess a little, and not want to—to help, or to see that things come out right; it's hard not to be afraid, not to think some small thing— oh, the smallest—that you might do would spoil it. But that's not so, is it?"

"I don't know."

"It isn't. You see"—she clasped her pale, thin hands together, and closed her eyes—"it *is* a Tale. Only it's longer and stranger than we imagine. Longer and stranger than we *can* imagine. So what you must do—" she opened her eyes "—what you must do, and what I must do, is forget."

"Forget what?"

"Forget a Tale is being told. Otherwise—oh, don't you see, if we didn't know the little that we do, we'd never interfere, never get things wrong; but we *do* know, only not enough; and so we guess wrong, and get entangled, and have to be put right in ways—in ways so odd, so—oh, dear, poor August, the smelliest, noisiest garage would have been better, I know it would have been . . . ."

"But what about a special fate, and all that," Nora said, alarmed at her mother's distress, "and being Protected, and all?"

123

"Yes," Violet said. "Perhaps. But it doesn't matter, because we can't understand that, or what it means. So we have to forget."

"How can we?"

"We can't." She stared straight in front of her. "But we can be silent. And we can be clever against our knowledge. And we can—oh, it's so strange, such a strange way to live—we can keep secrets. Can't we? Can you?"

"I think. I don't know."

"Well, you must learn. So must I. So must we all. Never to tell what you know, or think, because it's never enough, and it won't be true anyway for anyone but you, not in the same way; and never hope, or be afraid; and never, never take their side against us, and still, Somehow, I don't know how, trust them. We must do that from now on."

"How long?"

Before Violet could answer this, if she could, or would, the door of the library, which they could see through the fat banisters, opened a crack, and a wan face looked out, and withdrew.

"Who's that?" Violet asked.

"Amy Meadows," Nora said, and blushed.

"What's she doing in the library?"

"She came looking for August. She *says*—" Nora now clasped her hands and shut her eyes "—she says she's going to have August's baby. And she wondered where he was."

The Seed. She thought of Mrs. Flowers: *Is it the Tale?* Hopeful, astonished, glad. She nearly laughed, giddily. "Well, so do I," she said. "So do I." She leaned out between the banisters and said, "Come out, dear. Don't be afraid."

The door opened, just enough to let Amy pass, and though she shut it behind her softly, it boomed resoundingly as it latched. "Oh," she said, not having at first recognized the woman on the stair, "Mrs. Drinkwater."

"Come up," Violet said. She patted her lap, as she might to attract a kitten. Amy mounted the stairs to where they sat halfway to the landing. Her dress was homemade, and her stockings were thick, and she was even prettier than Violet remembered. "Now. What is it?"

Amy sat on the stair below them, a miserable huddle, with a big loose bag in her lap, like a runaway's. "August's not here," she said.

"No. We . . . don't know where he is, exactly. Amy, now everything's going to be all right. You're not to worry."

"It's not," Amy said softly. "It's not going to ever be all right again." She looked up at Violet. "Did he run off?"

"I think he did." She put her arm around Amy. "But he'll come back, possibly, probably . . ." She brushed Amy's hair aside which had fallen lankly and sadly over her cheek. "You must go home now for a while, you see, and not worry, and everything will turn out for the best, you'll see."

At that Amy's shoulders began to heave, softly and slowly. "Can't," she said, in a small high weeping voice. "Daddy's put me out. He's sent me away." Slowly, as though unable not to, she turned and put her sobbing head in Violet's lap. "I didn't come to bother him. I didn't. I don't care, he was wonderful and good, he was, I'd do it all again and I wouldn't bother him, only I got no place to go at all. No place to go."

"Well, well," Violet said, "well, well." She exchanged a glance with Nora, whose eyes had filled too. "Of course you have a place. Of course you do. You'll stay here, that's all. I'm sure your father will change his mind, the silly old fool, you can stay here as long as you need to. Now don't cry any more, Amy, don't. Here." She took a lace-edged hanky from her sleeve, and made the girl look up and use it, looking levelly into her eyes to stiffen her. "Now. That's better. As long as you like. Will that be all right?"

"Yes." Still a squeak was all she could manage, but her shoulders had stopped heaving. She smiled a little, ashamed. Nora and Violet smiled for her. "Oh," she said, sniffing, "I almost forgot." She tried with trembling fingers to undo her bundle, dabbed her face again and gave Violet back her sodden hanky, not much help for storms like Amy's, and managed to work open the bundle. "A man gave me something to give you. On my way here." She rooted among her belongings. "He seemed real mad. He said to say, 'If you people can't keep your bargains, there's no use dealing with you at all.'" She drew out and placed in Violet's hands a box that bore on its cover a picture of Queen Victoria and the Crystal Palace, done in different woods.

"Maybe he was joking," Amy said. "A funny, birdy man. He winked at me. Is it yours?"

Violet held the box, whose weight told her that the cards, or something like them, were within.

"I don't know," she said. "I really don't know."

There were footsteps climbing the stairs of the porch just then, and the three of them fell silent. The footsteps crossed the porch, with a squishy squeak as though sodden. Violet took Amy's hand, and Nora Violet's. The screen-door spring sang, and there was a figure against the cloudy oval glass of the door.

Auberon opened the door. He wore waders, and an old hat of John's stuck full of flies. He was whistling as he came into the hall, about packing up your troubles in an old kit bag, but stopped when he saw the three women huddled on the stair, inexplicably, halfway to the landing.

"Well!" he said. "What's up? Any word from August?" They didn't answer, and he held up to show them four fat speckled trout neatly strung. "Supper!" he said, and for a moment they were all motionless, a tableau, he with the fish, they with their thoughts, the rest only watching and waiting.

The cards had altered in their time elsewhere, Violet found, though just how she couldn't at first define. What meaning they had once had seemed to have clouded over, to have become powdered or dusty with obscurity; the patent, even funny quadrilles of meaning the figures had once joined hands in whenever she laid them out, the Oppositions and Influences and so on—they would have none of it any more. It was only after she and Nora had investigated them for a long time that she discovered that they had not lost power but gained it: they could no longer do what they had done, but they could, if interpreted correctly, predict with great accuracy the small events of Drinkwater daily life: gifts, and colds, and sprains; the itineraries of absent loved ones; whether it would rain on a picnic—that sort of thing. Only now and again did the deck throw up anything more startling. But it was a great help. They *would* grant us that, Violet thought; that gift in exchange . . . In fact she supposed (much later on) that to bestow this diurnal exactness of her deck was why they had taken it from her in the first place, unless they just couldn't help bestowing it. There was no catching up with them, no, not ever.

No Catching Up

August's offspring would in the course of time be settled around the five towns, some with their mothers and grandmothers, some with others, changing names and families as they moved, as in a game of musical chairs: when the music stopped, in fact, two of the children (by a process so charged with emotion, and so complex in its jointure of shame, regret, love, indifference and kindliness that the participants would never be able to agree later on how it had happened) had changed places in two different dishonored households.

When Smoky Barnable came to Edgewood, August's descendants, disguised under several names, had come to the dozens.

There were Flowers, and Stones, and Weeds; Charles Wayne was a grandson. One though, left out in the game, had found no seat: that was Amy's. She stayed at Edgewood, while in what she called her tummy there grew a boy, recapitulating in his ontogeny the many beasts, tadpole, fish, salamander, mouse, whose lives he would later describe in endless detail. They called him John Storm: John after his grandfather, but Storm after his father and his mother.

II

*Hours and days and months and years
go by; the past returns no more,
and what is to be we cannot know; but
whatever the time gives us in which
to live, we should therefore be content.*

—Cicero

Jolly, round, red Mr. Sun lifted his cloudy head over the purple mountains and cast long, long rays down into the Green Meadow." Robin Bird read it out in a proud, piping voice; he knew this book almost by heart. "Not far from the Stone Fence that separates the Green Meadow from the Old Pasture, a family of Meadow Mice awoke in their tiny house in the grass, Mother, Father, and six pink, blind babies.

Robin Bird's Lesson

"The head of the household rolled over, opened his eyes, twitched his whiskers, and went out to the doorstep to wash his face in the dew caught in a fallen leaf. As he stood there looking out at the Green Meadow and the morning, Old Mother West-wind hurried by, tickling his nose and bringing him news of the Wild Wood, the Laughing Brook, the Old Pasture and the Great World all around him, confused and clamorous news, better than any *Times* at breakfast.

"The news was the same as it had been for many days now: the world is changing! Soon things will be very different than you smell them today! Prepare yourself, Meadow Mouse!

"The Meadow Mouse, when he had learned as much as he could from the coy Little Breezes that travel in Mother West-wind's company, scampered along one of his many paths through the long

128

grass to the Stone Fence, where he knew of a place he could sit and see but not be seen. When he had come to this secret place, he settled back, thrust a grass-spear between his teeth, and chewed thoughtfully.

"What was the great change in the world that Mother West-wind and all her Little Breezes talked of these days? What did it mean, and how was he to prepare himself?

"To the Meadow Mouse, the Green Meadow could not have been a better place to live than it was just then. All the grasses of the meadow were pouring forth their seed for him to eat. Many plants that he had thought were nasty had suddenly unfolded dry pods of sweet nuts for him to gnaw on with his strong teeth. The Meadow Mouse was happy and well-fed.

"And now was all that to change? He wondered and puzzled and thought, but he could make no sense of it.

"You see, children, the Meadow Mouse had been born in the Springtime. He had grown up in the Summer when Mr. Sun smiles his broadest and takes his time to cross the blue, blue sky. All in the space of that single Summer, he had grown to his full size (which wasn't very great), and had married, and had babies born to him; soon they too would be grown.

"Now can *you* guess what the great change was, that the Meadow Mouse couldn't possibly know about?"

All the younger children called out and waved their hands, because unlike the older children they thought they were actually supposed to guess.

"Okay," Smoky said, "everybody knows. Thank you, Robin. Now let's see. Can you read for a while, Billy?" Billy Bush stood up, less confident than Robin, and took the battered book from him.

"Well," he read, "the Meadow Mouse decided he had better ask someone older and wiser than himself. The wisest creature he knew was the Black Crow, who came to the Green Meadow sometimes in search of grain or grubs, and always had a remark to make to anyone who would listen. The Meadow Mouse always listened to what the Black Crow had to say, though he stayed well away from the Black Crow's glittering eye and long, sharp beak. The Crow family was not known for eating mice, but on the other hand they were known to eat almost anything that came to hand, or to beak you might say.

"The Meadow Mouse had not been sitting and thinking

The End of
the World

129

for very long when out of the blue sky came a heavy flapping of wings and a raucous call, and the Black Crow himself landed in the Green Meadow not far from where the Meadow Mouse sat!

" 'Good Morning, Mr. Crow,' the Meadow Mouse called out, feeling quite safe in his snuggery in the wall.

" 'Is it a good morning?' said the Black Crow. 'Not many more days you'll be saying that.'

" 'Now that's just what I wanted to ask you about,' the Meadow Mouse said. 'It seems that a great change is coming over the world. Do you feel it? Do you know what it is?'

" 'Ah, foolish Youth!' said the Black Crow. 'There is indeed a change coming. It is called Winter, and you'd better prepare for it.'

" 'What will it be like? How shall I prepare for it?'

"With a glint in his eye, as though he enjoyed the Meadow Mouse's discomfort, the Black Crow told him about Winter: how cruel Brother North-wind would come sweeping over the Green Meadow and the Old Pasture, turning the leaves gold and brown and blowing them from the trees; how the grasses would die and the animals that lived on them grow thin with hunger. He told how the cold rains would fall and flood the houses of small creatures like the Meadow Mouse. He described the snow, which sounded rather wonderful to the Meadow Mouse; but then he learned of the terrible cold that would bite him to the bone, and how the small birds would grow weak with cold and tumble frozen from their perches, and the fish would stop swimming and the Laughing Brook laugh no more because its mouth was stopped with ice.

" 'But it's the End of the World,' cried the Meadow Mouse in despair.

" 'So it would seem,' said the Black Crow gaily. "For some folks. Not for *me*. I'll get by. But you had better prepare yourself, Meadow Mouse, if you expect to stay among the living!'

"And with that the Black Crow flapped his heavy wings and took to the air, leaving the Meadow Mouse more puzzled and much more afraid than he had been before.

"But as he sat there chewing his grass-blade in the warmth of the kindly Sun, he saw how he might learn to survive the awful cold that Brother North-wind was bringing to the world."

"Okay, Billy. You know," Smoky said, "you don't have to say 'thee' every time you say 'the,' t-h-e. Just say 'the,' like you do when you're talking."

Billy Bush looked at him as though for the first time understanding that the word on paper and the word he said all day were the same. "The," he said.

"Right. Now who's next?"

"What he thought he would do," Terry Ocean read (too old really for this, Smoky thought), "was to go around the Great World as far as he could go and ask every creature how he intended to prepare himself for the coming Winter. He was so pleased with this plan that he filled himself full of the seeds and nuts that were so sadly plentiful all around, said goodbye to his wife and children, and set off that very noon.

Brother North-wind's Secret

"The first creature he came to was a fuzzy caterpillar on a twig. Though caterpillars are not known for being clever, the Meadow Mouse put the question to him anyway: What would he do to prepare himself for the Winter that's coming?

" 'I don't know about Winter, whatever that may be,' the caterpillar said in his tiny voice. 'A change is certainly coming over *me*, though. I intend to wrap myself up in this lovely white silken thread I seem to have just learned how to spin, don't ask me how; and when I'm all wrapped up and stuck well on to this comfortable twig, I'll spend a long time there. Maybe forever. *I* don't know.'

"Well, that didn't seem like much of a solution to the Meadow Mouse, and with pity in his heart for the foolish caterpillar, he went on with his journey.

"Down at the Lily Pond, he met creatures he had never seen there before: great gray-brown birds with long graceful necks and black beaks. There were many of them, and they sailed across the Lily Pond dipping their long heads beneath the water and eating what they found there. 'Birds!' said the Meadow Mouse. 'Winter's coming! How do you intend to prepare yourselves?'

" 'Winter's coming indeed,' said an old bird in a solemn voice. 'Brother North-wind has chased us from our homes. There the cold is already sharp. He's at out backs now, hurrying us on. We'll outfly him, though, fast as he is! We'll fly to the South, farther South than he's allowed to go; and there we'll be safe from Winter.'

" 'How far?' the Meadow Mouse asked, hoping perhaps he could outrun Brother North-wind too.

" 'Days and days and days, flying as fast as we can,' said the old one. 'We're late already.' And with a great beating of his wings he arose from the pond, tucking his black feet neatly against his white stomach. The others rose up after him, and together they flew off honking toward the warm South.

"The Meadow Mouse went on sadly, knowing he couldn't outrun the winter on broad strong wings like theirs. So absorbed was he in these thoughts that he nearly stumbled over a brown Mud Turtle at the Lily Pond's edge. The Meadow Mouse asked him what he would do when the Winter came.

" 'Sleep,' said the Mud Turtle sleepily, wrinkled like an old brown man. 'I'll wrap myself in the warm mud deeper than Winter can reach, and sleep. In fact I'm getting sleepy now.'

"Sleep! That didn't sound like much of an answer to the Meadow Mouse. But as he continued on his way, he was to hear the same answer from many different creatures.

" 'Sleep!' said the Grass Snake, the Meadow Mouse's enemy. 'You'll have nothing to fear from _me_, Meadow Mouse.'

" 'Sleep!' said the Brown Bear. 'In a cave or a strong house of branches. Sleep for good.'

" 'Sleep,' squeaked his cousin the Bat when evening came. 'Sleep upside down, hanging by my toes.'

"Well! Half the world was simply going to go to sleep when Winter came. This was the oddest answer the Meadow Mouse heard, but there were many others too.

" 'I'll store nuts and seeds in secret places,' said the Red Squirrel. 'That's how I'll get by.'

" 'I'll trust the People to feed me when there's nothing left.' said the Chickadee.

" 'I'll build,' said the Beaver. 'I'll build a house to live in with my wife and children, down beneath the frozen stream. Now may I get on with it? I'm very busy.'

" 'I'll steal,' the Raccoon with his burglar mask said. 'Eggs from the People's barns, garbage from their cans.'

" 'I'll eat _you_,' said the Red Fox. 'See if I don't!' And he chased the poor Meadow Mouse and nearly caught him before the Meadow Mouse reached his private hole in the old Stone Fence.

"As he lay there panting, he could see that during his travels the great change called Winter had grown more evident in the Green Meadow. It was not so green now. It had grown brown and yellow and white. Many seeds had ripened and fallen or flown away on little wings. Overhead the Sun's face was hidden by grim gray clouds. And still the Meadow Mouse had no plan to protect himself from cruel Brother North-wind.

" 'What will I do?' he cried aloud. 'Shall I go live with my cousin in Farmer Brown's barn, and take my chances with Tom the cat and Fury the dog and the mousetraps and the poisons? I wouldn't last long. Shall I start off to the South and hope I outrun Brother North-wind? Surely he'll catch me unprotected and freeze me with his cold breath far from home. Shall I lie down with my wife and children and pull the grasses over my head and try to sleep? Before long I'd wake up hungry, and so would they. Whatever will I do?'

"Just then a glittering black eye looked in at him where he sat, so suddenly that he jumped up with a cry. It was the Black Crow.

" 'Meadow Mouse,' he said, as gaily as ever, 'whatever you do to protect yourself, there's one thing you should know which you do not.'

" 'What is it?' asked the Meadow Mouse.

" 'It's Brother North-wind's secret.'

" 'His secret! What is it? Do you know it? Will you tell it to me?'

" 'It is,' the Black Crow answered, 'the one good thing about Winter, which Brother North-wind wants no living creature to know. And yes, I know it; And no, I will not tell it to you.' For the Black Crow guards his secrets as closely as he guards the shiny bits of metal and glass he finds and saves. And so the ungenerous creature went laughing off to join his brothers and sisters in the Old Pasture.

"The one good thing about Winter! What could it be? Not the cold or the snow or the ice or the flooding rains.

"Not the hiding and scavenging and deathlike sleep, and the running away from enemies desperate with hunger.

"Not the short days and long nights and pale, absentminded Sun, all of which the Meadow Mouse didn't even know about yet.

"What could it be?

"That night, while the Meadow Mouse lay huddled for warmth with his wife and children in their house in the grass, Brother North-wind himself came sweeping across the Green Meadow. Oh, what great strides he took! Oh, how the brown, thin house of the Meadow Mouse rattled and shook! Oh, how the grim gray clouds were ripped and torn and flung from the face of the frightened Moon!

" 'Brother North-wind!' the Meadow Mouse cried out. 'I'm cold and frightened! Won't you tell me the one good thing about Winter?'

" 'That's my secret,' Brother North-wind said in a great icy voice. And to show his strength he squeezed a tall maple tree till all its green leaves turned orange and red, and then he blew them all away. Which done, he strode away across the Green Meadow leaving

133

the Meadow Mouse to tuck his cold nose into his paws and wonder what his secret was.

"Do *you* know what Brother North-wind's secret is?

"Of course you do."

"Oh. Oh." Smoky came to himself. "I'm sorry, Terry, I didn't mean to make you go on and on. Thank you very much." He suppressed a yawn, and the children watched him do so with interest. "Um, now could everybody take out pens and paper and ink, please? Come on, no groaning. It's too nice a day."

The Only Game Going

Mornings it was reading and penmanship, the penmanship taking more time since Smoky taught them (could only teach them) his own Italic hand, which if done right is supremely lovely, and if done even a little wrong is illegible. "Ligature," he would say sternly, tapping a paper, and its frowning maker would begin again. "Ligature," he said to Patty Flowers, who through the whole of that year thought he was saying "Look at you," an accusation she couldn't reply to but couldn't avoid; once in a fit of frustration at this she drove her pen-point through the paper, so fiercely it stuck in the desk like a knife.

Reading was a pickup affair with books from the Drinkwater library, *Brother North-wind's Secret* and the rest of Doc's tales for the younger and whatever Smoky thought appropriate and informative for the older. Sometimes, bored to tears with their halting voices, he simply read to them himself. He enjoyed that, and enjoyed explicating the hard parts and imagining aloud why the author had said what he had. Most of the kids thought these glosses were part of the text, and when they were grown, the few who read to themselves the books Smoky had read to them sometimes found them lean, allusive and tightlipped, as though parts were missing.

Afternoons was math, which often enough became an extension of penmanship, since the elegant shapes of Italic numbers interested Smoky as much as their relations. There were two or three of his students who were good at figures, perhaps prodigies Smoky thought because they were in fact quicker at fractions and other hard stuff than he was; he would get them to help teach the others. On the ancient principle that music and mathematics are sisters, he sometimes used the anyway somnolent and useless butt-end of the day to play to them on his violin; and its mild, not always certain songs, and the stove's smell, and the winter foregathering outside, were what Billy Bush later remembered of arithmetic.

He had one great virtue as a teacher; he didn't really

understand children, didn't enjoy their childishness, was baffled and shy before their mad energy. He treated them like grown-ups, because it was the only way he knew of treating anyone; when they didn't respond like grown-ups, he ignored it and tried again. What he cared about was what he taught, the black ribbon of meaning that was writing, the bundles of words and the boxes of grammar it tied up, the notions of writers and the neat regularity of number. And so that was what he talked about. It was the only game going during school hours—even the cleverest kids found it hard to get him to play any other—and so when they had all stopped listening at last (it happened soonest on fine days, as when snow came tumbling hypnotically out of the sky or when sun and mud came together) he just let them go, unable to think of any way to amuse them further.

And went home himself then through the front gate of Edgewood (the schoolhouse was the old gatehouse, a gray Doric temple with for some reason a grand rack of antlers over the door) wondering whether Sophie had got up from her nap yet.

He lingered on this day to clean out the smaller stove; it would need lighting tomorrow, if the cold kept up. When he had locked the door he turned from the tiny temple and stood in the leaf-littered road that ran between it and the front gate of Edgewood. This road hadn't been the one he had taken to reach Edgewood at first, nor this the gate he had gone in at. In fact no one ever used the front gate any more, and the sedge-drowned drive that led for half a mile through the Park was now only kept a path by his diurnal journeys, as though it were the habitual trail of a large and heavy-footed wild beast.

The One Good Thing About Winter

The tall entrance gates before him, green wrought-iron in a '90's lily pattern, stood or leaned eternally open, lashed to earth by weed and undergrowth. Only a rusted chain across the drive now suggested that this was still the entrance to somewhere, and not to be entered upon by the uninvited. To his left and his right the road ran away down an avenue of horse-chestnuts heartbreakingly golden; the wind tore fortunes from them and scattered them spendthrift. The road wasn't used much either, except by the kids walking or biking from here and there to school, and Smoky wasn't sure exactly where it led. But he thought that day, standing ankle-deep in leaves and for some reason unable to pass through the gates, that one branch of it must lead to the cracked macadam from Meadowbrook, which joined the tarred road that went past the Junipers', which eventually joined the traffic-loud fugue of feeder roads and expressways roaring into the City.

135

What if he were now to turn right (left?) and start off back that way, empty-handed and on foot as he had come, going backwards as in a film run the wrong way (leaves leaping to the trees) until he was where he had started from?

Well, for one thing he was not empty-handed.

And he had grown increasingly certain (not because it was sensible or even possible) that once on a summer afternoon having entered through the screen door into Edgewood, he had never again left: that the various doors by which he had afterwards seemed to go out had led only to further parts of the house, cleverly by some architectural enfoldment or trompe-l'oeil (which he didn't doubt John Drinkwater was capable of) made to look and behave like woods, lakes, farms, and distant hills. The road taken might lead only back around to some other porch at Edgewood, one he had never seen before, with wide worn steps and a door for him to go in by.

He uprooted himself from the spot, and from these autumnal notions. The circularity of roads and seasons: he had been here before. October was the cause.

Yet he stopped again as he crossed the stained white bridge that arched the sheet of water (stucco had been broken here, showing the plain brickwork beneath, that should be fixed, winter was the cause). Down in the water, drowned leaves turned and flew in the current, as the same leaves turned and flew in the busy sea of air, only half as fast or slower; sharp orange claws of maple, broad blades of elm and hickory, torn oak inelegant brown. In the air they were too fast to follow, but down in the mirror-box of the stream they did their dance with elegiac slowness for the current's sake.

What on earth was he to do?

When long ago he had seen that he would grow a character in the place of his lost anonymity, he had supposed that it would be like a suit of clothes bought too large for a child, that the child must grow into. He expected a certain discomfort at first, an ill-fittingness, that would go away as his self filled up the spaces, took the shape of his character, until at last it would be creased for good in the places where he bent and worn smooth where it chafed him. He expected, that is, for it to be singular. He didn't expect to have to suffer more than one; or, worse, to find himself done up in the wrong one at the wrong time, or in parts of several all at once, bound and struggling.

He looked toward the inscrutable edge of Edgewood which pointed toward him, windows lit already in the fleeting day; a mask that covered many faces, or a single face that wore many masks, he didn't know which, nor did he know it about himself.

What was the one good thing about Winter? Well, he knew the answer to that; he'd read the book before. If Winter comes, Spring can't be far behind. But oh yes, he thought; yes it can; far behind.

In the polygonal music room on the ground floor Daily Alice, hugely pregnant for the second time, played checkers with Great-Aunt Cloud.

The Old Age of the World

"It's as though," Daily Alice said, "each day is like a step, and every step takes you further away from—well, from when things made more sense. When things were all alive, and made signs to you. And you can no more not take a step farther away than you could not live through a day."

"I think I see," Cloud said. "But I think it only seems so."

"It isn't just that I've outgrown it." She was stacking up her captured red men in even piles. "Don't tell me that."

"It'll always be easier for children. You're an old lady now—children of your own."

"And Violet? What about Violet?"

"Oh, yes. Well. Violet."

"What I wonder is, maybe the world is growing older. Less all alive. Or is it only my growing older?"

"Everybody always wonders that. I don't think, really, anyone could feel the world grow older. Its life is far too long for that." She took a black man of Alice's. "What maybe you learn as you grow older is that the world *is* old—very old. When you're young, the world seems young. That's all."

That made sense, Daily Alice thought, and yet it couldn't explain the sense of loss she felt, a sense that things clear to her were being left behind, connections broken around her, by her, daily. When she was young, she had always the sense that she was being teased: teased to go on, ahead, follow somewhere. That was what she had lost. She felt certain that never again would she spy, with that special flush of sensibility, a clue to their presence, a message meant only for her; wouldn't feel again, when she slept in the sun, the brush of garments against her cheek, the garments of those who observed her, who, when she woke, had fled, and left only the leaves astir around her.

Come hither, come hither, they had sung in her childhood. Now she was stationary.

137

"Your move," Cloud said.

"Well, do you do that consciously?" Daily Alice asked, only partly of Cloud.

"Do what?" Cloud said. "Grow up? No. Well. In a sense. You see it's inevitable, or refuse to. You greet it or don't—take it in trade, maybe, for all you're going to lose anyway. Or you can refuse, and have what you've got to lose snatched from you, and never take payment—never see a trade is possible." She thought of Auberon.

Through the windows of the music room, Daily Alice saw Smoky trudging home, his image refracted jerkily as it passed from one old rippled pane into the next. Yes: if what Cloud said were true, then she had taken Smoky in trade—and what she had traded for him was the living sense that it was they, they themselves, who had led her to him, they who had chosen him for her, they who had plotted the quick glances that had made him hers, the long engagement, the fruitful and snug marriage. So that though she possessed what she had been promised, she had lost in return the sense that it had been promised. Which made what she possessed—Smoky, and ordinary happiness—seem fragile, losable, hers only by chance.

Afraid: she felt afraid: yet how could it be, if the bargain had been truly struck, and she had done her part, and it had cost her so much, and they had gone to such trouble to prepare it all, that she could lose him? Could they be that deceitful? Did she understand so little? And yet she was afraid.

She heard the front door close, solemnly, and a moment later she saw Doc in a red plaid jacket come out toward Smoky, carrying two shotguns and other equipment. Smoky looked surprised, then shot up his eyes and smacked his forehead as though remembering something he'd forgotten. Then, resigned, he took one of the guns from Doc, who was pointing out possible ways they might take; the wind blew orange sparks from his pipe-bowl. Smoky turned away with him outward toward the Park, Doc still pointing and talking. Once, Smoky looked back, toward the upstairs windows of the house.

"Your move," Cloud said again.

Alice looked down at the board, which had grown disjunct and patternless. Sophie came through the music-room then, in a flannel gown and a cardigan of Alice's, and for a moment the two women stopped their game. It wasn't that Sophie distracted them; she seemed oblivious of them; she noticed them, but took no notice. It was that as she passed they both seemed to feel the world intensely around them for a moment: the wind, wild, and the earth, brown, outside; the hour, late afternoon; the day and the house's progress through it. Whether it was this sudden generality of feeling which

Sophie caused, or Sophie herself, Daily Alice didn't know; but something just then became clear to her which had not been clear before.

"Where's he going?" Sophie said to no one, splaying a hand against the curved glass of the bay as though it were a barrier or the bars of a cage she had just found herself to be in.

"Hunting," Daily Alice said. She made a king, and said "Your move."

It was only once or so an autumn that Doctor Drinkwater unlimbered one of a number of shotguns his grandfather had kept in a case in the billiard room, cleaned it, loaded it, and went out to shoot birds. For all his love of the animal world—or perhaps because of it—Doc felt he deserved as much as the Red Fox or the Barn Owl to be a carnivore, if it was in his nature to be so; and the unaffected joy with which he ate flesh, chewing the bones and gristle and licking with delight the grease from his fingers, convinced him it was in his nature. He thought however that he ought, if he was to be a carnivore, to be able to face killing what he ate rather than that the bloody work should always be done elsewhere and he enjoy only the trimmed and unrecognizable products. One shoot or two a year, a few bright-plumaged birds blasted mercilessly from the sky, and brought home bleeding and open-beaked, seemed to satisfy his scruples; his woodcraft and stealth made up for a certain irresolution at the moment the grouse or pheasant thundered from the brush, and he usually managed to supply a good harvest-home, and thus to think of himself as an unflinching predator when he tucked into the beef and lamb the rest of the year.

Often these days he took Smoky along, having convinced him of the logic of this position. Doc was left-handed and Smoky right-handed, which made it less likely that they'd shoot each other in their blood-lust, and Smoky, though inattentive and not very patient, turned out to be a natural shot.

"We're still," Smoky asked as they crossed a stone fence, "on your property?"

"Drinkwater property," Doc said. "Do you know, this lichen here, the flat, silvery kind, can live to be hundreds of years old?"

"Yours, Drinkwater's," Smoky said, "is what I meant."

"Actually, you know," Doc said, cradling his weapon and choosing a direction, "I'm not a Drinkwater. Not by *name*." It reminded Smoky of the first words Doc had ever said to him: "Not a *practicing* doctor," he'd said.

139

"Technically I'm a bastard." He tugged his checked cap further over his forehead and considered his case without rancor. "I was illegitimate, and never legally adopted by anybody. Violet raised me, mostly, and Nora and Harvey Cloud. But never got around to going through the formalities."

"Oh?" said Smoky, with a show of interest, though in fact he knew the story.

"Skeletons," Doc said, "in the old family wardrobe. My father had a what, a liaison, with Amy Meadows, you met her."

He plowed her, and she cropp'd, Smoky quoted, almost, unforgivably, aloud. "Yes," he said. "Amy Woods now."

"Married to Chris Woods now many years."

"Mmm." What memory tried to enter Smoky's consciousness, but at the last moment changed its mind, and withdrew? A dream?

"I was the result." His Adam's apple moved, whether from emotion or not Smoky couldn't tell. "I think if you sort of spread out around that brake there, we're coming to some good spots."

Smoky went where he was told. He held his gun, an old English over-and-under, at the ready, the chased safety off. He didn't, like the rest of the family, much enjoy long aimless walks outdoors, especially in the wet; but if they had a token purpose, like today's, he could go on in discomfort with the best of them. He would like though to pull a trigger at least, even if he hit nothing. And even as he was dwelling absently on this, two brown cannonballs were fired from the tangled thicket ahead of him, pounding the air for altitude. Smoky gave a startled cry, but was raising his gun even as Doc shouted "Yours!", and as though his barrels were tied by strings to their tails, followed one, fired, followed the other and fired again; lowered his gun to watch, astonished, both birds tumble through the air and fall to earth with a crackle of brown weed and a definitive thump. "Damn," he said.

"Good *shot,*" Doc cried out heartily, with only a small pang of guilty horror in his heart.

Coming back in a wide circle toward the house, with a bag of four and the evening growing cold as winter, they passed a thing that had puzzled Smoky before: he was used to seeing the ruins of half-started projects around the place, greenhouses, temples, forlorn yet somehow appropriate, but what was an old car doing rusting away to unrecognizability in the middle of a field? A very old car too: it must have been there fifty years, its half-buried spoked wheels as

Responsibilities

lonesome and antique as the broken wheels of prairie schooners sunken on Midwestern prairies.

"A Model T, yes," Doc said. "My father's once."

With it in view, they stopped at a stone wall to pass back and forth, as hunters will, a warming flask.

"As I grew up," Doc said, wiping his mouth on his sleeve, "I started to ask how I had come about. Well, I did get it out of them about Amy and August, but you see Amy has always wanted to pretend it all never happened, that she's just an old friend of the family, even though everybody was well aware, even Chris Woods, and even though she used to cry whenever I went to visit her. Violet—well. She seemed to have forgotten August altogether, though you never knew with her. Nora only said: he ran off." He passed the flask back. "I eventually got up the courage to ask Amy what the story had been, and she got, well, shy and—*girlish* is the only way to put it. August was her first love. Some people never forget, do they? I'm proud of that, in a way."

"Used to be thought a love-child was special," Smoky threw in. "Very good or very bad. Pearl in *The Scarlet Letter.* Edmund in . . ."

"I was at the age when you want to be sure of all this," Doc went on. "Just who you are, exactly. Your identity. You know." Smoky in fact didn't. "I thought: My father ran off, without leaving, so far as I knew, a trace. Mightn't I do the same? Mightn't it be in my nature too? And perhaps if I found him, after who knows what adventures, I would make him acknowledge me. Grasp his shoulders in my hands—" here Doc made a gesture which the flask in his hand kept from being as poignant as it ought to have been "—and say *I am your son.*" He sat back, and drank moodily.

"And did you run off?"

"I did. Sort of."

"And?"

"Oh, I didn't get far, really. And there was always money from home. I got a doctor's degree, even though I've never practiced much; saw something of the Great World. But I came back." He smiled shyly. "I suppose they knew I would. Sophie Dale knew I would. So she says now."

"Never did find your father," Smoky said.

"Well," Doc said, "yes and no." He contemplated the pile in the field. Soon it would be only a shapeless hillock where no grass grew; then nothing. "I suppose it's true, you know, that you set out on adventures and then find what you've been looking for right in your own backyard."

141

Below and beside them, unmoving in his secret place in the stone wall, a Meadow Mouse observed them. What were they about? He smelled the reek of their slaughter, and their mouths moved as though consuming vast provender, but they weren't eating. He squatted on the coarse pad of lichen he and his ancestors had squatted on for time out of mind and wondered: wondering made his nose twitch furiously and his translucent ears cup themselves toward the sounds they made.

"It doesn't do to inquire into some things too deeply," Doc said. "Into what's given. What can't be changed."

"No," Smoky said, with less conviction.

"We," Doc said, and Smoky thought he knew whom of them that "we" included and whom of them it didn't, "have our responsibilities. It wouldn't do just to run off on some quest and pay no attention to what others might want or need. We have to think of them."

The Meadow Mouse in the midst of his wonderings had fallen asleep, but awoke with a start as the two great creatures stood and collected their inexplicable belongings.

"Sometimes we don't entirely understand," Doc said, as though it were wisdom he had arrived at after some cost. "But we have our parts to play."

Smoky drank, and capped the flask. Could it really be that he intended to abdicate his responsibilities, throw up his part, do something so horrid and unlike himself, and so hopeless too? What you're looking for is right in your own backyard: a grim joke, in his case. Well, he couldn't tell; and knew no one he could ask; but he knew he was tired of struggling.

And anyway, he thought, it wouldn't be the first time it ever happened in the world.

Harvest-Home

The day of the game supper, when the birds had hung, was something of an occasion every year. Through that week, people would arrive, and be closeted with Great-aunt Cloud, and pay their rents or explain why they couldn't (Smoky wasn't amazed, having no sense of real property and its values, at the great extent of the Drinkwater property or the odd way in which it was managed—though this yearly ceremony did seem very feudal to him). Most of those who came brought some tribute too, a gallon of cider, a basket of white-rayed apples, tomatoes in purple paper.

The Floods and Hannah and Sonny Noon, the largest (in every way) of their tenants, stayed to the supper. Rudy brought a duck of his own to fill out the feast, and the lavender-smelling lace tablecloth was laid. Cloud opened her polished box of wedding-silver (she being the only Drinkwater bride anyone had ever thought to give such to, the Clouds had been careful about these things) and the tall candles shone on it and on the facets of cut-crystal glasses, diminished this year by one small heartrending crash.

They set out a lot of sleepy, sea-dark wine that Walter Ocean made every year and decanted the next, his tribute; in it, toasts were made over the glistening bodies of the birds and the bowls of autumn harvest. Rudy rose, his stomach advancing somewhat over the table's edge, and said:

> "Bless the master of this house
> The mistress bless also
> And all the little children
> That round the table go."

Which that year included his own grandson Robin, and Sonny Noon's new twins, and Smoky's daughter Tacey.

Mother said, glass aloft:

> "I wish you shelter from the storm
> A fireplace, to keep you warm
> But most of all, when snowflakes fall
> I wish you love."

Smoky began one in Latin, but Daily Alice and Sophie groaned, so he stopped, and began again:

> "A goose, tobacco and cologne:
> Three-winged and gold-shod prophecies of Heaven
> The lavish heart shall always have, to leaven,
> To spread with bells and voices, and atone
> The abating shadows of our conscript dust."

" 'Abating shadows' is good," said Doc. "And 'conscript dust'."

"Didn't know you were a smoker though," Rudy said.

"And I didn't know, Rudy," Smoky said expansively, inhaling Rudy's Old Spice, "you were a lavish heart." He helped himself to the decanter.

"I'll say one I learned as a kid," said Hannah Noon, "and then let's get down to it:

> "Father Son and Holy Ghost
> You eat the fastest, you get the most."

After dinner, Rudy sorted through some piles of ancient records as heavy as dishes that had lain long disused and circled with arcs of dust in the buffet. He found treasures, greeting old friends with glad cries. They stacked them on the record player and danced.

Seized by the Tale

Daily Alice, unable after the first round to dance any more, rested her hands on the great prie-dieu of stomach she had grown and watched the others. Great Rudy flung his little wife around like a jointed doll, and Alice supposed he'd learned over the years how to live with her and not break her; she imagined his great weight on her—no, probably she would climb up on him, like climbing a mountain.

> Dunkin' donuts, yubba yubba
> Dunkin' donuts, yubba yubba
> Dunkin' donuts—splash! in the coffee!

Smoky, bright-eyed and loose-limbed, made her laugh with his cheerfulness, like a sun; a sunny disposition, is that what was meant by that? And how did he come to know the words to these crazy songs, who seemed never to know anything that everybody else knew? He danced with Sophie, just tall enough to take her properly, footing it gallantly and inexpertly.

> The pale moon was rising above the green mountains
> The sun was declining beneath the blue sea

Like a sun: but a small sun, which she had within her, warming her from the inside out. She was conscious of a feeling she had had before, a sense that she was looking at him, and at all of them, from some way off, or from a great height. There had been a time when she seemed to herself to be snug, and small, within the large house of Smoky, a safe inhabitant, room to run in yet never leave his encompassment. Now she oftener felt otherwise: over time it was he who seemed to have become a mouse within the house of her. Huge: that's what she felt herself to be becoming. Her perimeters expanded, she felt that eventually she would be contiguous almost with the walls of Edgewood itself: as large, as old, as comfortably splayed on its feet and as capacious. And as she grew huge—this suddenly struck her—the ones she loved diminished in size as surely as if they walked away from her, and left her behind.

"Ain't misbehavin'," Smoky sang in a dreamy, effete falsetto, "savin' all my love for you."

Mysteries seemed to accumulate around her. She rose heavily, saying No, no, you stay, to Smoky who had come to her,

144

and went laboriously up the stairs, as though she carried a great, fragile egg before her, which she did, almost hatched. She thought perhaps she had better get advice, before winter came and it was no longer possible.

But when she sat on the edge of her bed, still faintly hearing the high accents of the music below, which seemed to be endlessly repeating *tin-cup, top-hat,* she saw that she knew what advice she would get if she went to get it: it would only be made clear to her again what she already knew, what only grew dim or clouded now and again by daily life, by useless hopes and by despairs equally useless—that if this were indeed a Tale, and she in it, then no gesture she or any of them could make was not a part of it, no rising up to dance or sitting down to eat and drink, no blessing or curse, no joy, no longing, no error; if they fled the Tale or struggled against it, well, that too was part of the Tale. They had chosen Smoky for her and then she had chosen him for herself; or, she had chosen him and then they had chosen him for her; either way it was the Tale. And if in some subtle way he moved on or away and she lost him now, by inches, by small daily motions she only now and then even perceived for certain, then his loss to her, and the degree of that loss, and each one of the myriad motions, looks, lookings-away, absences, angers, placations and desires that made up Loss, sealing him from her as layers of lacquer seal the painted bird on a japanned tray or as layers of rain freeze deeper the fallen leaf within the winter pond, all of it was the Tale. And if there were to come some new turning, some debouchment of this shaded lane they seemed just now to be walking, if it opened up quite suddenly into broad, flower-starred fields, or even if it only brought them to crossroads where fingerboards stated cautiously the possibilities of such fields, then all that too would be the Tale; and those whom Daily Alice thought wise, whom she supposed to be endlessly relating this tale. Somehow at the same pace as Drinkwater and Barnable lives fell away day by day, hour by hour—those tellers couldn't be blamed for anything told of in it, because in fact they neither spun nor told it really, but only knew how it would unfold in some way she never would; and that should satisfy her.

"No," she said aloud. "I don't believe it. They have powers. It's just that sometimes we don't understand how they'll protect us. And if *you* know, you won't say."

"That's right," Grandfather Trout seemed gloomily to reply. "Contradict your elders, think you know better."

She lay back on her bed, supporting her child with interlaced fingers, thinking she did not know better, but that advice would anyway be lost on her. "I'll hope," she said. "I'll be happy. There's something I don't know, some gift they have to give. At the right time it'll be there. At the last moment. That's how Tales are," and she wouldn't listen to the sardonic answer she knew the fish would give to this; and yet when Smoky opened the door and came in whistling, his odor a meld of the wine he had drunk and Sophie's perfume he had absorbed, something which had been growing within her, a wave, crested, and she began to weep.

The tears of those who never cry, the calm, the levelheaded ones, are terrible to see. She seemed to be split or torn by the force of the tears, which she squeezed her eyes shut against, which she forced back with her fist against her lips. Smoky, afraid and awed, came immediately to her as he might to rescue his child from a fire, without thought and without knowing quite what he would do. When he tried to take her hand, speak softly to her, she only trembled more violently, the red cross branded on her face grew uglier; so he enveloped her, smother the flames. Disregarding her resistance, as well as he could he covered her, having a vague idea that he could by tenderness invade her and then rout her grief, whatever it was, by main strength. He wasn't sure he wasn't himself the cause of it, wasn't sure if she would cling to him for comfort or break him in rage, but he had no choice anyway, savior or sacrifice, it didn't matter so long as she could cease suffering.

She yielded, not at first willing to, and took handfuls of his shirt as though she meant to rend his garments, and "Tell me," he said, "tell me," as though that could make it right; but he could no more keep her from suffering this than he would be able to keep her from sweating and crying aloud when the child within her made its way out. And there was no way anyway for her to tell him that what made her weep was a picture in her mind of the black pool in the forest, starred with golden leaves falling continuously, each hovering momentarily above the surface of the water before it alighted, as though choosing carefully its drowning place, and the great damned fish within too cold to speak or think: that fish seized by the Tale, even as she was herself.

III

Come, *let me see thee sink into a dream*
Of quiet thoughts, protracted till thine eye
Be calm as water when the winds are gone
And no one can tell whither.
                    —Wordsworth

I t's George Mouse," Smoky said. Lily clinging to his pants-leg looked out the front way where her father pointed. Above the fist stuck in her face, her long-lashed eyes made no judgment on George coming up through the mist, his boots spraying puddles. He wore his great black cloak, his Svengali's hat limp with rain; he waved a hand at them as he came up. "Hey," he said, squishily mounting the stairs. "Heeeeeey." He embraced Smoky; beneath his hat-brim his teeth shone and his dark-rimmed eyes were coals. "This is what's-her-name, Tacey?"

"Lily," Smoky said. Lily retreated behind the curtain of her father's pants. "Tacey's a big girl now. Six years old."

"Oh my God."

"Yes."

"Time flies."

"Well, come in. What's up? You should have written."

"Didn't decide till this morning."

"Any reason?"

"Wild hair up my ass." He chose not to tell Smoky of the five hundred milligrams of Pellucidar he had taken and which were now coldly ventilating his nervous system like the first day of winter, which this was, seventh winter solstice of Smoky's married life. The great capsule of Pellucidar had put him on the gad; he had got out the Mercedes, one of the last tangibles of the old Mouse

Time Flies

147

affluence, and driven north till all the gas stations he passed were bankrupt ones; he parked it then in the garage of a deserted house, and, breathing deeply of the dense and moldy air, set off on foot.

The front door closed behind them with a solid sound of brass fittings and a rattle of the oval glass. George Mouse decaped grandly, a gesture that made Lily laugh and that halted Tacey in her headlong rush down the hall to see who had come. Behind her came Daily Alice in a long cardigan, her fists making bulges in the pockets. She ran to kiss George, and he pressing her felt a dizzying and inappropriate rush of chemical lust that made him laugh.

They all turned toward the parlor where yellow lamplight already shone, and saw themselves in the tall hall pier-glass. George stopped them by it, holding a shoulder of each, and studied the images: himself, his cousin, Smoky—and Lily who just then appeared between her mother's legs. Changed? Well, Smoky had regrown the beard he had started and then amputated when George first knew him. His face looked gaunter, more what George could only call (since the word was just then rushed to him by importunate messenger) more *spiritual*. SPIRITUAL. Watch out. He got a grip on himself. Alice: a mother twice over, amazing! It occurred to him that seeing a woman's child is like seeing a woman naked, in the way it changes how her face looks to you, how her face becomes less the whole story. And himself? He could see the grizzle in his moustache, the lean stoop of his stringbean torso, but that was nothing; it was the same face that had always looked out from mirrors at him since he had first looked in.

"Time flies," he said.

In the parlor, they were all preparing a long shopping list. "Peanut butter," Mother said, "stamps, iodine, soda-water—lots of it, soap pads, raisins, tooth powder; chutney, chewing gum, candles, George!" She embraced him; Doctor Drinkwater looked up from the list he was making.

A Definite Hazard

"Hello, George," said Cloud from her corner by the fire. "Don't forget cigarettes."

"Paper diapers, the cheap ones," Daily Alice said. "Matches—Tampax—3-in-One Oil."

"Oatmeal," Mother said. "How are your people, George?"

"No oatmeal!" Tacey said.

"Good, good. Mom's, you know, hanging on." Mother shook her head. "I haven't seen Franz for, oh, a year?" He put bills on the drum-table where Doc wrote. "A bottle of gin," he said.

Doc wrote "gin," but pushed aside the bills. "Aspirin," he remembered. "Camphorated oil. Antihistamine."

"Somebody sick?" George asked.

"Sophie's got this strange fever," Daily Alice said. "It comes and goes."

"Last call," Doc said, looking up at his wife. She stroked her chin and clucked in an agony of doubt, and at last decided she would have to go too. In the hall, pursued by all of their last-minute needs, he tugged a cap over his head (his hair had gone almost white, like dirty cotton-wool) and put on a pair of pink-framed glasses his license said he had to wear. He picked up a brown envelope of papers he must deal with, announced himself ready, and they all went out onto the porch to see them off.

"I hope they'll be careful," Cloud said. "It's very wet."

From within the coach-house, they heard a hesitant grinding. Then an expectant silence, followed by a firmer start, and the station wagon backed warily out into the drive, making two soft and delible marks in the wet leaves. George Mouse marveled. Here they all were intently watching nothing more than an old guy very gingerly handling a car. The gears ground and an awed silence fell. George knew of course that it wasn't every day they got the car out, that it was an occasion, that doubtless Doc had spent the morning wiping cobwebs from the old wood sides and chasing chipmunks away who were thinking of nesting under the apparently immobile seats, and that he now put on the old machine like a suit of armor to go out and do battle in the Great World. Had to hand it to his country cousins. Everybody he knew in the City bitched endlessly about the Car and its depredations; his cousins had never handled this twenty-year-old woodie anyhow but infrequently and with the greatest respect. He laughed, waving goodbye with the rest, imagining Doc out on the road, nervous at first, shushing his wife, changing gears with care; then turning onto the great highway, beginning to enjoy the smooth slipping-by of brown landscape and the sureness of his control, until some monster truck roars by and nearly blows him off the road. The guy's a definite hazard.

He certainly didn't want, George said, to stay indoors; he'd come up for fresh air and stuff, even if he hadn't picked the best day for it; so Smoky put on a hat and galoshes, took a stick, and went with him to walk up the Hill.

Up on
the Hill

Drinkwater had tamed the Hill with a footpath, and stone steps where it was steepest, and rustic seats at lookout places, and a stone table at the top where views and lunch could be taken together. "No lunch," George said. The fine rain had stopped—had halted, it seemed, in mid-fall, and hung, stationary, in the air. They went up the path which circled the tops of trees that grew in the ravines below, George admiring the pattern of silver drops on leaf and twig and Smoky pointing out the odd bird (he had learned the names of many, particularly odd ones).

"No but really," George said. "How's it going?"

"Slate junco," Smoky said. "Good. Good." He sighed. "It's just hard when winter comes."

"God, yes."

"No, but harder here. I don't know. I wouldn't have it any different. . . . You just can't bear the melancholy, some evenings." Indeed it seemed to George that Smoky's eyes might brim with tears. George breathed deeply, glorying in the wetness and the wood. "Yes, it's bad," he said happily.

"You're indoors so much," Smoky said. "You draw together. And there's so many people there. You seem to get wound around each other more."

"In that house? You could lose yourself for days in there. For days." He remembered an afternoon like this one when he was a kid, when he had come up here for Christmas with the family. While searching for the stash he knew must be somewhere awaiting the great morning, he got lost on the third floor. He went down a strange staircase narrow as a chute, found himself Elsewhere amid strange rooms; draughts made a dusty tapestry in a sitting room breathe with spooky life, his own feet sounded like other's feet coming toward him. He began to shout after a while, having lost the staircase; found another; lost all restraint when he heard far off Mom Drinkwater calling to him, and ran around shouting and throwing open doors until at last he opened the arched door of what looked like a church, where his two cousins were taking a bath.

They sat on one of Drinkwater's seats of bent and knobby wood. Through the screen of naked trees they could see across the land a great gray distance. They could just make out the gray back of the Interstate lying coiled and smooth in the next county; they could even hear, at moments, carried on the thick air, the far hum of trucks: the monster breathed. Smoky pointed out a finger or Hydra's head of it which reached out tentatively through the hills this way, then stopped abruptly. Those bits of yellow, sole brightness on the scene, were sleeping caterpillars—the man-made kind, earth-movers and -shakers. They wouldn't come any closer; the surveyors and purveyors, contractors and engineers were stalled there, mired, bogged in indecision, and that vestigial limb would never grow bone and muscle to punch through the pentacle of five towns around Edgewood. Smoky knew it. "Don't ask me how," he said.

But George Mouse had been thinking of a scheme whereby all the buildings, mostly empty, on the block his family owned in the City might be combined and sealed up to make an enormous, impenetrable curtain-wall—like the hollow wall of a castle—around the center of the block, where the gardens were. The outbuildings and stuff inside the block could be torn down then and all the garden-space transformed into a single pasture or farm. They could grow things there, and keep cows. No, goats. Goats were smaller and less fussy about their food. They gave milk and there would be the odd kid to eat. George had never killed anything larger than a cockroach, but he had eaten kid in a 'Rican diner and his mouth watered. He hadn't heard what Smoky said, though he had heard Smoky talking. He said, "But what's the story? What's the real story?"

"Well, we're Protected, you know," Smoky said vaguely, digging the black ground with his stick. "But there's always something that's got to be given in return for protection, isn't there?" He hadn't understood any of that in the beginning; he didn't suppose he understood it any better now. Though he knew some payment had to be made, he wasn't sure whether it had been made, or was to be made, or had been deferred; whether the vague sense he had in winter of something being wrung from him, of being dunned and desiccated and having sacrificed much (he couldn't say what exactly) meant that the Creditors had been satisfied, or that the goblins he sensed peeking in the windows and calling down the chimneys, clustering under the eaves and scrabbling through the disused upper rooms were reminding him and all of them of a debt unpaid, tribute unexacted, goblin principal earning some horrid interest he couldn't calculate.

But George had been thinking of a plan to represent the basic notions of Act Theory (that he had read of in a popular magazine and which seemed to him just then to make sense, a lot of sense) by means of a *display of fireworks:* how the various parts of an Act as the theory explained them could be expressed in the initiation, rising whistle, culminating starburst and crackling expiration of a colored bomb; and how in combination fireworks could represent "entrained" Acts, multiple Acts of all kinds, the grand Act that is Life's rhythm and Time's. The notion faded in sparks. He shook Smoky's shoulder and said, "But how goes it? How are you getting on?"

"Jesus, George," Smoky said standing. "I've told you all I

can. I'm freezing. I bet it freezes over tonight. There might be snow for Christmas." He knew in fact there would be; it had been promised. "Let's go get some cocoa."

It was brown and hot, with chocolate bubbles winking at the brim. A marshmallow Cloud had plopped in it turned and bubbled as though dissolving in joy. Daily Alice instructed Tacey and Lily in the arts of blowing gently on it, picking it up by the handle, and laughing at the brown moustaches it made. The way Cloud watched over it it grew no skin, though George didn't mind a skin; his mother's had always had a skin, and so had that they served from urns in the basement of the Church of All Streets, a nondenominational church she had used to take him and Franz to, always, it seemed, on days like this.

Cocoa and a Bun

"Have another bun," Cloud said to Alice. "Eating for two," she said to George.

"You don't mean it," George said.

"I think so," Alice said. She bit the bun. "I'm a good bearer."

"Wow. A boy this time."

"No," she said confidently. "Another girl. So Cloud says."

"Not I," Cloud said. "The cards."

"We'll name her Lucy," Tacey said. "Lucy Ann and Anndy Ann de Bam Bam Barnable. George has *two* moustaches."

"Who'll take this up to Sophie?" Cloud said, setting a cup and a bun on a black japanned tray of great age that showed a silver-haired, star-spangled sprite drinking Coke.

"Let me," George said. "Hey, Aunt Cloud. Can you do the cards for me?"

"Sure, George. I think you're included."

"Now if I can find her room," he said giggling. He took up the tray carefully, noting that his hands had begun to shake.

Sophie was asleep when he came into her room by pushing the door open with his knee. He stood unmoving in the room, feeling the steam rise from the cocoa and hoping she would never wake. So strange to feel again those adolescent peeping-tom emotions—mostly a trembling weakness at the knees and a dry thickness in the throat—caused now by conjunction of the mad capsule and Sophie deshabille on the messy bed. One long leg was uncovered and the toes pointed toward the floor, as though indicating the appropriate one of two Chinese slippers that peeped from beneath a discarded kimono; her breasts soft with sleeping had come out of her ruffled 'jammies and rose and fell slightly with her breathing, flushed (he thought tenderly) with fever. Even as he devoured her though she seemed to feel his gaze, and without waking she pulled her clothes together and rolled over so her cheek lay on her closed fist. It made him want to laugh, or cry, so prettily she did it, but he restrained himself and did neither, only set down the tray on her table cluttered with pill bottles and crushed tissues. He moved onto the bed a big album or scrapbook to do it, and at that she woke.

"George," she said calmly, stretching, not surprised, thinking perhaps she was still asleep. He laid his swarthy hand to her brow gently. "Hi, cutie," he said. She lay back amid the pillows; her eyes closed, and for a moment she wandered back to dreamland. Then she said *Oh* and struggled up to kneel on the bed and come full awake. "George!"

"Feeling better?"

"I don't know. I was dreaming. Cocoa for me?"

"For you. What were you dreaming?"

"Mm. Good. Sleeping makes me hungry. Does it you?" She wiped away her moustache with a pink tissue she plucked from a box of them; another took its place pertly. "Oh, dreams about years ago. I guess because of that album. No you can't." She took his hand from it. "Dirty pictures."

"Dirty."

"Pictures of me, years ago." She smiled, ducking her head Drinkwater-style, and peeked at him over her cocoa cup with eyes still crinkled with sleep. "What are you doing here?"

"Came to see you," George said; once he had seen her, he knew it to be true. She didn't respond to his gallantry; she seemed to have forgotten him, or remembered suddenly something else entirely; the cocoa cup stopped halfway to her lips. She put it down slowly, her eyes looking at something he couldn't see, something within. Then she seemed to wrest herself from it, laughed a quick, frightened laugh and took George's wrist in a sudden grip as though to stay herself. "Some dreams," she said, searching his face. "It's the fever."

She had always lived her best life in dreams. She knew no greater pleasure than that moment of passage into the other place, when her limbs grew warm and heavy and the sparkling darkness behind her lids became ordered and doors opened; when conscious thought grew owl's wings and talons and became other than conscious.

The Orphan Nymphs

153

Starting from the simple pleasure of it, she had become practiced in all its nameless arts. The first thing was to learn to hear the small voice: that fragment of conscious self which like a guardian angel walks with the eidolons of self with which we replace ourselves in Dreamland, the voice that whispers *you are dreaming.* The trick was to hear it, but not attend to it, or else you wake. She learned to hear it; and it told her that she could not be hurt by dream wounds, no matter how terrible; she woke from them always whole and safe—most safe because warm in bed. Since then she had feared no bad dreams; the dream Dante of her leaned on the dreaming Virgil and passed through horrors delightful and instructive.

Next she found she was one of those who can awake, leap the gap of consciousness, and arrive back in the same dream she had awakened from. She could build also many-storied houses of dream; she could dream that she woke, and then dream that she woke from that dream, each time dreaming that she said *Oh! It was all a dream!* until at last and most wonderful she woke to wakefulness, home from her journey, and breakfast cooking downstairs.

But soon she began to linger on her journeys, go farther, return later and more reluctantly. She worried, at first, that if she spent half the day as well as all the night in Dreamland, she would eventually run out of matter to transmute into dreams, that her dreams would grow thin, unconvincing, repetitious. The opposite happened. The deeper she journeyed—the farther the waking world fell behind—the grander and more inventive became the fictive landscapes, the more complete and epical the adventures. How could that be? Where if not from waking life, books and pictures, loves and longings, real roads and rocks and real toes stubbed on them, could she manufacture dreams? And where then did these fabulous isles, gloomy vast sheds, intricate cities, cruel governments, insoluble problems, comical supporting players with convincing manners, come from? She didn't know; gradually she came not to care.

She knew that the real ones, loved ones, in her life worried about her. Their concern followed her into dreams, but became transformed into exquisite persecutions and triumphal reunions, so that was how she chose to deal with them and their concern.

And now she had learned the last art, which squared the power of her secret life and at the same time hushed the real ones' questions. She had Somehow learned to raise at will a fever, and with it the lurid, compelling, white-hot dreams a fever brings. Flushed with the victory of it, she hadn't at first seen the danger of this double dose, as it were; too hastily she tossed away most of her waking life—it had lately grown complex and promiseless anyhow—and retired to her sickbed secretly, guiltily exulting.

Only on waking was she sometimes—as now when George Mouse saw her look within—seized by the terrible understanding of the addict: the understanding that she was doomed, had lost her way in this realm, had, not meaning to, gone too far in to find a way out —that the only way out was to go in, give in, fly further in—that the only way to ameliorate the horror of her addiction was to indulge it.

She grasped George's wrist as though his real flesh could wake her truly. "Some dreams," she said. "It's the fever."

"Sure," George said. "Fever dreams."

"I ache," she said, hugging herself. "Too much sleep. Too long in one position. Something."

"You need a massage." Did his voice betray him?

She bent her long torso side to side. "Would you?"

"You bet."

She turned her back to him, pointing out on the figured bed-jacket where it hurt. "No no no honey," he said as though to a child. "Look. Lie down here. Put the pillow under your chin—right. Now I sit here—just move a little—let me take my shoes off. Comfy?" He began, feeling her fever-heat through the thin jacket. "That album," he said, not having for a moment forgotten it.

"Oh," she said, her voice low and gruff as he pressed the bellows of her lungs. "Auberon's pictures." Her hand reached out and rested on the cover. "When we were kids. Art pictures."

"Art pictures like what?" George said, working the bones where her wings would be if she had wings.

As though she couldn't help it she raised the cover, put it down again. "*He* didn't know," she said. "*He* didn't think they were dirty. Oh, they're not." She opened the book. "Lower. There. Lower more."

"Oho," George said. George had once known these naked, pearl-gray children, abstracted here and more carnal for not being flesh at all. "Let's take this shirtie off," he said. "That's better. . . ."

She turned the album's pages with abstracted slowness, touching certain of the pictures as though she wished to feel the texture of the day, the past, the flesh.

Here were Alice and she on the stippled stones by a waterfall which plunged madly out-of-focus behind them. In the hazy foreground leaves, some law of optics inflated droplets of sunlight into dozens of white disembodied eyes round with wonder. The naked children (Sophie's dark aureoles were puckered like unblown flowers, like tiny closed lips) looked down into a black, silken pool.

What did they see there that kept their lashy eyes lowered, that made them smile? Below the image, in a neat hand, was the picture's title: *August*. Sophie's fingers traced the ray of lines where Alice's thigh creased at the pelvis, lines tender and finely-drawn as though her skin were thinner then than it would become. Her silver calves lay together, and her long-toed feet, as though they were beginning to be changed into a mermaid's tail.

Small pictures clipped to the pages with black corners. Sophie wide-eyed, open-mouthed, feet wide apart and arms high, all open, a Gnostic's X of microcosmic child-woman-kind, her yet-uncut hair wide too and white—thus golden in fact—against an obscure cave of summer-dark trees. Alice undressing, stepping one-footed from her white cotton panties, her plump purse already beginning to be clothed with crisp fair hair. The two girls opening through time like the magic flowers of nature films as George hungrily looked through Auberon's eyes, double-peeping at the past. Stop here a minute. . . .

She held the page open there, while he went on, shifting his position and his hands; her legs opening across the sheets made a certain sound. She showed him the Orphan Nymphs. Flowers twined in their hair, they lay full length entwined on the grassy sward. They had their hands to each other's cheeks, and their eyes were heavy and they were on the point of kissing open-mouthed: acting out lonely consolation, it might be, for an art-picture of innocence at once orphaned and faëry, but not acting; Sophie remembered. Her nerveless hand slipped from the page and her eyes too lost their grasp of it; it didn't matter.

"Do you know what I'm going to do," George asked, unable not to.

"Uh-huh."

"Do you?"

"Yes." An exhalation only. "Yes."

But she didn't, not really; she had leapt across that gap Consciousness again, had saved herself from falling there, had landed safely (able to fly) on the far side, within that pearl-toned afternoon that had no night.

"As in any deck," Cloud said, taking their velvet bag from the tooled case and then the cards themselves from the bag, "there are fifty-two cards for the fifty-two weeks of the year, four suits for the four seasons, twelve court cards for the twelve months and, if you count them right, three hundred and sixty-four pips for the days of the year."

The Least Trumps

"A year's got three-sixty-five," George said.

"This is the old year, before they knew better. Throw another log on the fire, will you, George?"

She began to lay out his future as he fooled with the fire. The secret he had within him—or above him asleep actually—warmed his center and made him grin, but left his extremities deathly cold. He unrolled the cuffs of his sweater and drew his hands within. They felt like a skeleton's.

"Also," said Cloud, "there are twenty-one trumps, numbered from zero to twenty. There are Persons, and Places, and Things, and Notions." The big cards fell, with their pretty emblems of sticks and cups and swords. "There's another set of trumps," Cloud said. "The ones I have here are not as great as those; those have oh the sun and the moon and large notions. Mine are called—my mother called them—the Least Trumps." She smiled at George. "Here is a Person. The Cousin." She placed that in the circle and thought a moment.

"Tell me the worst," George said. "I can take it."

"The worst," said Daily Alice from the deep armchair where she sat reading, "is just what she can't tell you."

"Or the best either," said Cloud. "Just a bit of what might be. But in the next day, or the next year, or the next hour, that I can't tell either. Now hush while I think." The cards had grown into interlocking circles like trains of thought, and Cloud spoke to George of events that would befall him; a small legacy, she said, from someone he never knew, but not money, and left him by accident. "You see, here's the Gift; here the Stranger in this place."

Watching her, chuckling at the process and also helplessly at what had occurred to him that afternoon (and which he intended to repeat, creeping quiet as a mouse when all were asleep), George didn't notice Cloud fall silent before the completing pattern; didn't see her lips purse or her hand hesitate as she placed the last card in the center. It was a Place: the Vista.

"Well?" George said.

"George," she said, "I don't know."

"Don't know what?"

"Exactly." She reached for her box of cigarettes, shook it and found it empty. She had seen so many displays, so many possible falls had grown into her consciousness that sometimes they overlapped; with a sense like *déjà vu*, she felt she was looking not at a single arrangement but at one of a series, as though some old display she had made were to be labeled "Continued," and here, without warning, was the continuation. Yet it was all George's fall too.

"If," she said, "the Cousin card is you." No. That wouldn't do. There was something, some fact she didn't know.

George of course knew what it was, and felt a sudden strangulation, a fear of discovery absurd on the face of it but intense anyway, as though he had walked into a trap. "Well," he said, finding voice. "That's enough anyway. I'm not sure I want to know my every future move." He saw Cloud touch the Cousin card; then the Thing called Seed. Oh Christ, he thought; and just then the station wagon's hoarse horn was heard in the drive.

"They'll need help unloading," Daily Alice said, struggling to rise from the grasp of her armchair. George jumped up. "No no, honey, oh no, not in your condition. You sit tight." He went from the room, cold hands thrust in his sleeves like a monk.

Alice laughed and picked up her book again. "Did you scare him, Cloud? What did you see?"

Cloud only looked down at the pattern she had made.

For some time now she had begun to think she had been wrong about the Least Trumps, that they were not telling her of the small events of lives close to her—or rather that those small events were parts of chains, and the chains were great events; very great indeed.

The Vista card in the center of her pattern showed a meeting of corridors or aisles. Down each corridor was an endless vista of doorways, each one different, an arch then a lintel then pillars and so on till the artist's invention ran out and the fineness of his woodcutting (which was very fine) could no longer make distinctions. You could see, down those aisles, other doors which led off in other directions, perhaps each showing vistas as endless and various as this one.

A juncture, doorways, turnings, a moment only when all the ways could be seen at once. This was George—all this. He was that vista, though he didn't know it and she couldn't think how to tell him. The vista wasn't *his*: he was the vista. It was *she* who looked down it at the possibilities. And could not express them. She only knew—for sure now—that all the patterns she had ever cast were parts of one pattern, and that George had done or would do—or was at that moment doing—something that made an element in that pattern. And in any pattern, the elements do not stand alone; they are repeated, they are linked. What could it be?

Around her in the house the sounds of her family came, calling and hauling and treading the stairs. But it was into this place that she stared, into the prospect of endless branchings, corners, corridors. She felt that perhaps she was *in* that place; that there was a

door just behind her, that she sat here between it and the first of the
doors pictured on the card; that if she turned her head she might see
an endless prospect of arch and lintel behind her too.

All night especially in cold weather the house was accustomed to speak softly to itself, perhaps because of its
hundreds of joints and its half-floors and its stone
parts piled on wooden. It tocked and groaned, grunted
and squeaked; something gave way in an attic and fell,
which caused something to come loose in a cellar and
drop. The squirrels in the airspaces scratched and the mice explored
the walls and halls. One mouse late at night went on tiptoe, a bottle
of gin under his arm and a finger on his lips, trying to remember
where Sophie's room might be. He nearly tripped on an unexpected
step; all steps in this house were unexpected.

Only Fair

Within his head it was still noon. The Pellucidar had not
worn off, but it had turned evil, as it will do, not prodding flesh and
consciousness any the less, but now with a cruel malice and not in
fun. His flesh was contracted and defensive and he doubted that it
would uncoil even for Sophie supposing he could find her. Ah: the
lamp over a painting had been left on, and by it he saw the doorknob
he wanted, he was sure of it. He was about to step quickly to it when
it turned, spookily; he stepped back into the shadows, and the door
opened. Smoky came out, an old dressing gown over his shoulders
(the kind, George noticed, that has a braided edge of dark and light
hues around the collar and pocket) and shut the door carefully and
silently. He stood for a moment then, and seemed to sigh; then he
went off around the corner.

Wrong damn door, George thought; imagine if I'd gone
into their room, or is it the kids' room? He went away, utterly
confused now, searching hopelessly through the coiled nautilus of
the second floor, tempted once to go down a floor; maybe in his
madness he had gotten onto a matching upper floor and forgotten he
had done so. Then Somehow he found himself in front of a door that
Reason told him must be hers, though other senses disputed it. He
opened it in some fear and stepped inside.

Tacey and Lily lay sweetly asleep beneath the sloping
ceiling of a dormer room. By the nightlight he could see spectral
toys, the glittering eye of a bear. The two girls, one still in a jailhouse
crib, didn't stir, and he was about to shut the door on them when he
knew there was someone else in the room, near Tacey's bed. Someone . . . He peered around the edge of the door.

Someone had just drawn from within the fine folds of his

159

night-gray cloak a night-gray bag. George couldn't see his face for the wide Spanish night-gray hat he wore. He stepped to the crib where Lily lay, and with fingers clothed in night-gray gloves took from his bag a pinch of something, which delicately he dispensed from between thumb and finger above her sleeping face. Sand descended in a dull-gold trickle to her eyes. He turned away then and was putting away his bag when he seemed to sense George turned to stone at the doorway. He glanced at him over the tall collar of his cloak, and George looked into his placid, heavy-lidded, night-gray eyes. Those eyes regarded him for a moment with something like pity, and he shook his heavy head, as who should say *Nothing for* you, *son; not tonight.* Which was after all only fair. And then he turned around, the tassel swinging on his hat, and went away with a low snap of his cloak to elsewhere and others more deserving.

So when George at last found his own cheerless bed (in the imaginary bedroom as it happened) he lay sleepless for hours, his withered eyeballs starting from his head. He cradled the gin bottle in his arms, tugging now and again at its cold and acid comfort, the night and day growing confused and raggedy on the still-burning Catherine-wheel of his consciousness. Only he did come to understand that the first room he had tried to enter, the one he saw Smoky come out of, was indeed Sophie's, had to be. The shudder-starting rest of it dissolved as the sparkling synapses one by one mercifully began to burn out.

Toward dawn he watched it begin to snow.

Heaven in ordinarie, man well drest,
The milkie way, the bird of Paradise,
Church-bels beyond the starres heard,
*   the souls blood,*
The land of spices; something understood.

—George Herbert

C hristmas," said Doctor Drinkwater as his red-cheeked face sped smoothly toward Smoky's, "is a kind of day, like no other in the year, that doesn't seem to succeed the days it follows, if you see what I mean." He came close to Smoky in a long, expert circle and slid away. Smoky, jerking forward and backward, hands not neatly clasped behind like Doc's but extended, feeling the air, thought he saw. Daily Alice, whose hands were inside an old tatty muff, went by him smoothly, glancing once at his unprogress and making, just to be mean, a laughing, swooping figure as she went away, which was however outside his ken, since his eyes couldn't seem to leave his own feet.

"I mean," Doctor Drinkwater said, reappearing beside him, "that every Christmas seems to follow imme-diately after the last one; all the months that came between don't figure in. Christmases succeed each other, not the falls they follow."

> Agreement
> with Newton

"That's right," said Mother, making stately progress around. Behind her, like the wooden ducklings attached to wooden ducks, she drew her two granddaughters. "It seems you just get through one and there's another."

"Mmm," said Doc. "Not what I meant exactly." He veered off like a fighter plane, and slipped an arm through Sophie's

161

arm. "How's every little thing," Smoky heard him say, and heard her laugh before they swept off, listing both together.

"Getting better every year," Smoky said, and suddenly turned around involuntarily. He was back in Daily Alice's path, collision course, nothing he could do. He wished he'd strapped a pillow to his ass as they do in comic postcards. Alice grew large, and halted abruptly and expertly.

"Do you think Tacey and Lily should go in?" she said.

"I leave that up to you." Mother drew them past again on their sled; their round, fur-circled faces were bright as berries; then they were gone again, and so was Alice. Let the womenfolk consult, he thought. He had to master the simple forward progress; they were making him dizzy, appearing and disappearing like that. "Woops," he said, and would have lost it, but Sophie appearing suddenly behind him bore him up, propelled him forward. "How have you been?" he said nonchalantly; it seemed the thing, to greet each other as they all went around.

"Unfaithful," she said; the cold word made a small cloud on the air.

Smoky's left ankle buckled, and his right runner just then sped away on its own. He spun around and landed hard on the ice, on the rudimentary tail so vulnerable on one so fleshless behind. Sophie was circling him, her laughter almost making her fall too.

Just sit here a while till my tail freezes up, Smoky thought. Sit gripped in ice like the feet of bushes until some thaw comes. . . .

The previous week's snow had not cleaved to earth, it was a night's fall only, the rain returned heavily the next morning and George Mouse went sloshing off in it hollow-eyed and confused, having caught, they all thought, Sophie's bug. The rain continued like unassuageable grief, flooding the low broad lawn where the sphinxes decayed mumchance. Then the temperature tumbled, and Christmas Eve morning the world was all iron-gray and glaring in ice, all the color of the iron-gray sky where the sun made a white smear only behind the clouds. The lawn was hard enough to skate on; the house looked like a miniature house for a model railroad, set beside a pond made from a compact-mirror.

Still Sophie circled him. He said: "What do you mean? Unfaithful?"

She only smiled secretly and helped him up, then turned and with some occult motion he saw but could never copy whispered away effortlessly.

He'd do better if he could figure out how the others got around that unalterable law which said that if one skate slid forward, the other had to slide backward. It seemed he could zip zip back and forth in one place forever and be the only one here in agreement with Newton. Till he fell down. There is no perpetual motion. Yet just at that moment he began Somehow to get it, and, numb-bummed, made his way across the ice to the steps of the porch, where Cloud sat in state on a fur rug guarding the boots and the thermos.

"So where's this promised snow?" he said, and Cloud displayed her own brand of secret smile. He wrung the neck of the thermos and decapitated it. He poured lemon tea charged with rum into one of the nested cups the cap contained, and one for Cloud. He drank, the steam melting the cold in his nostrils. He felt bleakly, recklessly dissatisfied. Unfaithful! Was that some kind of joke? The jewel of great price which he had had from Daily Alice long ago, in the midst of their first embrace, darkened as pearls can do and turned to nothing when he tried to hang it on Sophie's throat. He never knew what Sophie felt, but couldn't believe, though he'd learned it to be so of Daily Alice, that Sophie didn't know either: that she was torn, bewildered, and withal half-dreaming as much as he. So he only watched her come and go with seeming purpose, and wondered, imagined, supposed.

She came across the lawn with her hands behind her back, then made a foot-across-foot turn and sailed up to the porch. She turned just where the frozen pond ran out, and engraved the ice with a small shower of crystals when she stopped. She sat beside Smoky and took his cup from him, her breath quick with exertion. In her hair Smoky noticed something, a tiny flower, or a jewel made to look like one; he looked closer and saw it was a snowflake, so whole and perfect he could count its arms and tell its parts. As he was saying "A snowflake," another fell beside it, and another.

Different families have different methods, at Christmas, of communicating their wishes to Santa. Many send letters, mailing them early and addressing them to the North Pole. These never arrive, postmasters having their own whimsical ways of dealing with them, none involving delivery.

Letters to Santa

Another method, which the Drinkwaters had always used though no one could remember how they had hit on it, was to burn their missives in the study fireplace, the tiled one whose blue scenes of skaters, windmills, trophies of the hunt seemed most appropriate, and whose chimney was the highest. The smoke then (the children always insisted on running out to see) vanished into the North, or at least into the atmosphere, for Santa to decipher. A complex procedure, but it seemed to work, and was always done on Christmas Eve when wishes were sharpest.

Secrecy was important, at least for the grown-ups' letters; the kids could never resist telling everybody what they wanted and for Lily and Tacey the letters had to be written by others anyway, and they had to be reminded of the many wishes they'd had as Christmas neared but which had grown small in the interim and slipped through the coarse seine of young desire. Don't you want a brother for Teddy (a bear)? Do you still want a shotgun like Grampa's? Ice skates with double blades?

But the grown-ups could presumably decide these things for themselves.

In the expectant, crackling afternoon of that Eve of ice Daily Alice drew her knees up within a huge armchair and used a folded checkerboard resting on her knees for a desk. "Dear Santa," she wrote, "please bring me a new hot-water bottle, any color but that pink that looks like boiled meat, a jade ring like the one my great-aunt Cloud has, for the right middle finger." She thought. She watched the snow fall on the gray world, still just visible as day died. "A quilted robe," she wrote; "one that comes down to my feet. A pair of fuzzy slippers. I would like this baby to be easier than the other two to have. The other stuff is not so important if you could manage that. Ribbon candy is nice, and you can't find it anywhere any more. Thanking you in advance, Alice Barnable (the older sister)." Since childhood she had always added that, to avoid confusion. She hesitated over the tiny blue notepaper nearly filled with these few desires. "P.S.," she wrote. "If you could bring my sister and my husband back from wherever it is they've gone off together I would be more grateful than I could say. ADB."

She folded this absently. Her father's typewriter could be heard in the strange snow-silence. Cloud, cheek in hand, wrote with the stub of a pencil at the drum-table, her eyes moist, perhaps with tears, though her eyes often seemed bedimmed lately; old age only, probably. Alice rested her head back against the chair's soft breast, looking upward.

Above her, Smoky charged with rum-tea sat down in the imaginary study to begin his letter. He spoiled one sheet because the rickety writing-table there rocked beneath his careful pen; he shimmed the leg with a matchbook and began again.

"My dear Santa, First of all it's only right that I explain about last year's wish. I won't excuse myself by saying I was a little drunk, though I was, and I am (it's getting to be a Christmas habit, as

164

everything about Christmas gets to be a habit, but you know all about *that*). Anyway, if I shocked you or strained your powers by such a request I'm sorry; I meant only to be flip and let off a little steam. I know (I mean I assume) it's not in your power to give one person to another, but the fact is my wish was granted. Maybe only because I wanted it then more than anything, and what you want so much you're just likely to get. So I don't know whether to thank you or not. I mean I don't know whether you're responsible; and I don't know whether I'm grateful."

He chewed the end of his pen for a moment, thinking of last Christmas morning when he had gone into Sophie's room to wake her, so early (Tacey wouldn't wait) that blank nighttime still ruled the windows. He wondered if he should relate the story. He'd never told anyone else, and the deep privacy of this about-to-be-cremated letter tempted him to confidences. But no.

It was true what Doc had said, that Christmas succeeds Christmas rather than the days it follows. That had become apparent to Smoky in the last few days. Not because of the repeated ritual, the tree sledded home, the antique ornaments lovingly brought out, the Druid greenery hung on the lintels. It was only since last Christmas that all that had become imbued for him with dense emotion, an emotion having nothing to do with Yuletide, a day which for him as a child had had nothing like the fascination of Hallowe'en, when he went masked and recognizable (pirate, clown) in the burnt and smoky night. Yet he saw that it was an emotion that would cover him now, as with snow, each time this season came. She was the cause, not he to whom he wrote.

"Anyway," he began again, "my desires this year are a little clouded. I would like one of those instruments you use to sharpen the blades of an old-fashioned lawn mower. I would like the missing volume of Gibbon (Vol. II) which somebody's apparently taken out to use as a doorstop or something and lost." He thought of listing publisher and date, but a feeling of futility and silence came over him, drifting deep. "Santa," he wrote, "I would like to be one person only, not a whole crowd of them, half of them always trying to turn their backs and run whenever somebody"—Sophie, he meant, Alice, Cloud, Doc, Mother; Alice most of all—"looks at me. I want to be brave and honest and shoulder my burdens. I don't want to leave myself out while a bunch of slyboots figments do my living for me." He stopped, seeing he was growing unintelligible. He hesitated over the complimentary close; he thought of using "Yours as ever," but thought that might sound ironic or sneering, and at last wrote only "Yours &c.," as his father always had, which then seemed ambiguous and cool; what the hell anyway; and he signed it: Evan S. Barnable.

Down in the study they had gathered with eggnog and their letters. Doc had his folded like true correspondence, its backside pimpled with hard-struck punctuation; Mother's was torn from a brown bag, like a shopping list. The fire took them all, though—rejecting only Lily's at first, who tried with a shriek to throw it in the fire's mouth, you can't really throw a piece of paper, she'd learn that as she grew in grace and wisdom—and Tacey insisted they go out to see. Smoky took her by the hand, and lifted Lily onto his shoulders, and they went out into the snowfall made spectral by the house's lights to watch the smoke go away, melting the falling snowflakes as it rose.

When he received these communications, Santa drew the claws of his spectacles from behind his ears and pressed the sore place on the bridge of his nose with thumb and finger. What was it they expected him to do with these? A shotgun, a bear, snowshoes, some pretty things and some useful: well, all right. But for the rest of it . . . He just didn't know what people were thinking anymore. But it was growing late; if they, or anyone else, were disappointed in him to-morrow, it wouldn't be the first time. He took his furred hat from its peg and drew on his gloves. He went out, already unaccountably weary though the journey had not even begun, into the multicolored arctic waste beneath a decillion stars, whose near brilliance seemed to chime, even as the harness of his reindeer chimed when they raised their shaggy heads at his approach, and as the eternal snow chimed too when he trod it with his booted feet.

Soon after that Christmas, Sophie began to feel as though her body were being unwrapped and repacked in a completely different way, a set of sensations that was vertiginous at first when she didn't suspect its cause, and then interesting, awesome even, when she did, and at last (later on, when the process was completed and the new tenant fully installed and making itself at home) comfortable: deeply so at times, like a new kind of sweet sleep; yet expectant too. Expectant! The right word.

Room for One More

There wasn't much her father could say when eventually Sophie's condition was admitted to him, he being just such a one as she carried himself. Being a father, he had to go through motions of solemnity that never quite amounted to censure, and there was never any question of What was to be Done with It—he shuddered to think what would have happened if anyone had thought that kind of thought when he was growing inside Amy Meadows.

"Well, my God, there's room for one more," Mother said, drying a tear. "It's not like it was the first time it ever happened in the world." Like the rest of them, she wondered who the father was, but Sophie wasn't saying, or rather in her smallest voice and with eyes downcast, was saying she wouldn't say. And so the matter had eventually to be dropped.

Though of course Daily Alice had to be told.

It was to Daily Alice that she took her news first, or next to first; her news, and her secret.

"Smoky," she said.

"Oh, Sophie," Alice said. "No."

"Yes," she said, defiant by the door of Alice's room, unwilling to enter further in.

"I can't believe it, that he would."

"Well, you better," Sophie said. "You'd better get used to it, because it's not going away."

Something in Sophie's face—or maybe only the horrid impossibility of what she said—made Alice wonder. "Sophie," she said softly after they had regarded each other in silence for a time, "are you asleep?"

"No." Indignant. But it was early morning; Sophie was in her nightgown; Smoky had only an hour ago stepped down from the tall bed, scratching his head, to go off to school. Sophie had waked Alice: that was so unusual, so reverse of the usual, that for a moment Alice had hoped . . . She lay back against the pillow, and closed her eyes; but she wasn't asleep either.

"Didn't you ever suspect?" Sophie asked. "Didn't you ever think?"

"Oh, I guess I did." She covered her eyes with her hand. "Of course I did." The way Sophie said it made it seem she would be disappointed if Alice hadn't known. She sat up, suddenly angry. "But this! I mean the two of you! How could you be so *silly?*"

"I guess we just got carried away," Sophie said levelly. "You know." But then she lost her brave look before Alice's, and dropped her eyes.

Alice pushed herself up in the bed and sat against the headboard. "Do you have to stand over there?" she said. "I'm not going to hit you or anything." Sophie still stood, a little unsure, a little truculent, looking just like Lily did when she'd spilled something all over her and was afraid she was being summoned for something worse than having it wiped off. Alice waved her over impatiently.

Sophie's bare feet made small sounds on the floor, and when she climbed up on the bed, a strange shy smile on her face, Alice sensed her nakedness under the flannel nightie. It all made her think of years ago, of old intimacies. So few of us, she thought, so much love and so few to spend it on, no wonder we get tangled up. "Does Smoky know?" she asked coolly.

"Yes," Sophie said. "I told him first."

That hurt, that Smoky hadn't told her: the first sensation that could be called pain since Sophie had entered. She thought of him, burdened with that knowledge, and she innocent of it; the thoughts stabbed her. "And what does he intend to do?" she asked next, as in a catechism.

"He wasn't . . . He didn't . . ."

"Well, you'd better decide, hadn't you? The two of you."

Sophie's lip trembled. The store of bravery she had started out with was running out. "Oh, Alice, don't be this way," she pleaded. "I didn't think you'd be this way." She took Alice's hand, but Alice looked away, the knuckles of her other hand pressing her lips. "I mean, I know it was hateful of us," she said, watching Alice's face, trying to gauge it. "*Hateful.* But, Alice . . ."

"Oh, I don't hate you, Soph." As though not wishing to, but unable not to, Alice's fingers curled themselves closely among Sophie's, though still she looked away. "It's just, well." Sophie watched a struggle taking place within Alice; she didn't dare speak, only held her hand tighter, waiting to see what issue it would have. "See, I thought . . ." She fell silent again, and cleared her throat of an obstruction that had just arisen there. "Well, you know," she said. "You remember: Smoky was chosen for me, that's what I used to think; I used to think that's what our story was."

"Yes," Sophie said, lowering her eyes.

"Only lately, I can't seem to remember that very well. I can't remember them. How it used to be. I can *remember*, but not . . . the feeling, do you know what I mean? How it used to be, with Auberon; those times."

"Oh, Alice," Sophie said. "How could you forget?"

"Cloud said: when you grow up, you trade what you had as a child for what you have as a grown-up. Or if you don't, you lose it anyway, and get nothing in return." Her eyes had grown tears, though her voice was steady; the tears seemed less part of her than part of the story she told. "And I thought: then I traded them for

Smoky. And they arranged that trade. And that was okay. Because even though I couldn't remember them any more, I had Smoky." Now her voice wavered. "I guess I was wrong."

"No!" Sophie said, shocked as if by a blasphemy.

"I guess it's just—ordinary," Alice said, and sighed a tremulous sigh. "I guess you were right, when we were married, that we wouldn't ever have what you and I had once; wait and see, you said. . . ."

"No, Alice, no!" Sophie gripped her sister's arm, as if to hold her back from going further. "That story was true, it *was* true, I always knew it. Don't, don't ever say it wasn't. It was the most beautiful story I ever heard, and it all came true, just as they said it would. Oh, I was so jealous, Alice, it was wonderful for you and I was so jealous. . . ."

Alice turned to face her. Sophie was shocked by her face: not sad, though tears stood in her eyes; not angry; not anything. "Well," Alice said, "I guess you don't have to be jealous any more, anyway." She pulled Sophie's nightgown up over the ball of her shoulder from which it had slipped. "Now. We have to think what to do. . . ."

"It's a lie," Sophie said.

"What?" Alice looked at her, puzzled. "What's a lie, Soph?"

"It's a lie, it's a lie!" Sophie almost shouted, tearing it out from within her. "It isn't Smoky's at all! I lied to you!" Unable any longer to bear her sister's foreign face, Sophie buried her head in Alice's lap, sobbing. "I'm so sorry. . . . I was so jealous, I wanted to be part of your story, that's all; oh, don't you see he never would, he couldn't, he loves you so much; and I wouldn't have, but I—I missed you. I *missed* you. I wanted to have a story too, I wanted . . . Oh, Alice."

Alice, taken by surprise, only stroked her sister's head, automatically comforting her. Then: "Wait a minute, Sophie. Sophie, listen." With both her hands she raised Sophie's face from her lap. "Do you mean you never . . ."

Sophie blushed; even through her tears that could be seen. "Well, we did. Once or twice." She held up a forestalling palm. "But it was all my fault, always. He felt so bad." She brushed back, with a furious gesture, her hair, glued to her face with tears. "He always felt so *bad*."

"Once or twice?"

"Well, three times."

"You mean you . . ."

169

"Three—and a half." She almost giggled, wiping her face on the sheet. She sniffed. "It took him *forever* to get around to it, and then he always got so tied in knots it almost wasn't any fun."

Alice laughed, amazed, couldn't help it. Sophie seeing her, laughed too, a laugh like a sob, through her sniffing. "Well," she said, throwing up her hands and letting them fall in her lap; "well."

"But wait a minute," Alice said. "If it wasn't Smoky, who was it?

"Sophie?"

Sophie told her.

"No."

"Yes."

"Of all people. But—how can you be sure? I mean . . ."

Sophie told her, counting off the reasons on her fingers, why she was sure.

"George Mouse," Alice said. "Of all people. Sophie, that's practically incest."

"Oh, come on," Sophie said dismissively. "It was only one time."

"Well, then he . . ."

"No!" Sophie said, and put her hands on Alice's shoulders. "No. He's not to know. Never. Alice, promise. Cross your heart. Don't ever tell, ever. I'd be so embarrassed."

"Oh, *Sophie!*" What an amazing person, she thought, what a strange person. And realized, with a rush of feeling, that she had for a long time missed Sophie, too; had forgotten what she was like, even; had even forgotten she missed her. "Well what do we tell Smoky then? That would mean he . . ."

"Yes." Sophie was shivering. Tremors ran around her rib-cage. Alice moved aside, and Sophie pulled down the bedclothes and scrambled in, her nightgown riding up, into the pocket of warmth Alice had made. Her feet against Alice's legs were icy, and she wiggled her toes against Alice to warm them.

"It's not true, but it wouldn't be so terrible, would it, to let him think so? I mean it's got to have a father Somehow," Sophie said. "And not George, for heaven's sake." She buried her face against Alice's breasts, and said, after a time, in a tiny voice, "I wish it *was* Smoky's." And after another time: "It ought to be." And after a longer time still: "Just think. A baby."

It seemed to Alice that she could feel Sophie smile. Was that possible, to feel a smile when someone's face was pressed against you? "Well, I guess, maybe so," she said, and drew Sophie close. "I can't think what else." What a strange way to live, she thought, the way they lived; if she grew to be a hundred she'd never understand it. She smiled herself, bewildered, and shook her head in surrender. What a conclusion! But it had been so long since she had seen Sophie happy—if this was happiness she felt, and damn if it didn't seem to be—she could only be happy with her. Night-blooming Sophie had flowered in the day.

"He *does* love you," Sophie's muffled voice said. "He'll love you for ever." She yawned hugely, shuddering. "It *was* all true. It was all true."

Maybe it was. A kind of perception was stealing over her, entwining itself in her as Sophie's long, familiar legs were twining in hers: perhaps she *had* been wrong, about the trade; perhaps they had stopped teasing her to follow them only because she had long since arrived wherever it was they had been teasing her to come. She hadn't lost them, and yet needn't follow any more because here she was.

She squeezed Sophie suddenly, and said "Ah!"

But if she was here, where was she? And where was Smoky?

When it was Smoky's turn, Alice sat on the bed to receive him, as she had Sophie, but propped up on pillows like an Oriental queen, and smoking a brown cigarette of Cloud's as she now and then did when feeling grand. "Well," she said, grandly. "Some fix."

A Gift They Had to Give

Strangled with embarrassment (and deeply confused, he had thought he had been so careful, they say it's always possible, but how?) Smoky walked around the room picking up small objects and studying them, and putting them down again. "I never expected this," he said.

"No. Well, I guess it's always unexpected." She watched Smoky go back and forth to the window to peep through the curtains at the moon on the snow, as though he were a renegade looking out of his hideout. "Do you want to tell me what happened?"

He turned from the window, his shoulders bent with the weight of it. For so long he had dreaded this exposure, the crowd of ill-dressed characters he had been impersonating caught out, made to stand forth in all their inadequacy. "It was all my fault, first of all," he said. "You shouldn't hate Sophie."

"Oh?"

"I . . . I forced myself on her, really. I mean I plotted it, I . . . like a, like a, well."

"Mmm."

All right, ragamuffins, show yourselves, Smoky thought; it's all up with you. With me. He cleared his throat; he plucked his beard; he told all, or nearly all.

Alice listened, fooling with her cigarette. She tried to blow out with the smoke the lump of sweet generosity she tasted in her throat. She knew she mustn't smile while Smoky told his story, but she felt so kindly toward him, wanted so much to take him in her arms and kiss the soul she saw clearly rising to his lips and eyes, so brave and honest he was being, that at last she said, "You don't have to keep stalking around like that. Come sit down."

He sat, using as little of the bed he had betrayed as he could. "It was only once or twice, in the end," he said. "I don't mean . . ."

"Three times," she said. "And a half." He blushed fiercely. She hoped that soon he would be able to look at her, and see that she would smile for him. "Well, you know, it's probably not the first time it ever happened in the world," she said. He still looked down. He thought it probably was. The shameful self sat on his knees like a ventriloquist's dummy. He had it say:

"I promised I'd take care of it, and all. And be responsible. I had to."

"Of course. That's only right."

"And it's over now. I swear it, Alice, it is."

"Don't say that," she said. "You never know."

"No!"

"Well," she said, "there's always room for one more."

"Oh don't."

"I'm sorry."

"I deserve it."

Shyly, not wanting to intrude on his guilt and repentance, she slipped an arm through his and interlaced her fingers with his. After a tormented pause, he did turn to look at her. She smiled. "Dummy," she said. In her eyes brown as bottle-glass he could see himself reflected. One self. What was happening? Under her gaze something wholly unexpected was taking place: a fusing, a knitting-together of parts that had never been able to stand alone but which all together made up him. "You dummy," she said, and another foetal and incompetent self retreated back within him.

"Alice, listen," he said, and she raised a hand to cover his mouth, almost as if to prevent the escape of what she had put back. "No more," she said. It was astonishing. Once again she had done it to him: as she had first in George Mouse's library so long ago, she had invented him: only this time not out of nothing, as then, but out of falsehoods and figments. He felt a cold flash of horror: what if, in his foolishness, he had gone so far as to lose her? What if he had? What on earth would he have done then? In a rush, before her no-shaking head could stop him, he offered her the rod of correction, offered it without reservation; but she had only asked him for it so that she could, as she then did, give it back to him unused with all her heart.

"Smoky," she said. "Smoky, don't. Listen. About this kid."

"Yes."

"Do you hope it's a boy or a girl?"

"Alice . . . !"

She had always hoped, and almost always believed, that there was a gift they had to give, and that in time—their own time—they would give it. She had even thought that when at last it came, she would recognize it: and she had.

Like a centrifuge, with infinite slowness accelerating, spring flung them all outward in advancing circles as it advanced, seeming (though how it was possible they couldn't tell) to untangle the tangled skein of them and lay their lives out properly around Edgewood like the coils of a golden necklace: more golden as it grew warmer. Doc, after a long walk one thawing day, described how he had seen the beavers break out of their winter home, two, four, *six* of them, who had spent months trapped beneath the ice in a room hardly larger than themselves, imagine; and Mother and the rest nodded and groaned as though they knew the feeling well.

Old World Bird

On a day when Daily Alice and Sophie were digging happily in the dirt around the back front, as much for the feel of the cool, reborn earth under their nails and in their fingers as for any improvements they might make in the flower beds, they saw a large white bird descend lazily out of the sky, looking at first like a page of wind-borne newspaper or a runaway white umbrella. The bird, which carried a stick in its long red beak, settled on the roof, on a spoked iron mechanism like a cartwheel which was part of the machinery (rusted and forever stopped) of the old orrery. The bird stepped around this place on long red legs. It laid its stick there, cocked its head at it and changed its place; then it looked around itself and began clacking its long red bill together and opening its wings like a fan.

"What is it?"

"I don't know."

"Is it building a nest there?"

"Starting to."

"You know what it looks like?"

"Yes."

"A stork."

"It couldn't be a stork," Doc said when they told him. "Storks are European, or Old World, birds. Never cross the big water." He hurried out with them, and Sophie pointed with her trowel to where there were now two white birds and two more nest-sticks. The birds were clacking at each other and entwining their necks, like newlyweds unable to stop necking long enough to do housework.

Dr. Drinkwater, after disbelieving his eyes for a long time and making certain with binoculars and reference-works that he wasn't mistaken, that this wasn't a heron of some kind but a true European stork, *Ciconia alba*, went with great excitement to his study and typed out in triplicate a report of this amazing, this unprecedented sighting to send to the various bird-watching societies he more or less belonged to. He was searching for stamps for these, saying "amazing" under his breath, when he stopped and grew thoughtful. He looked at the memos on his desk. He dropped his search for stamps and sat down slowly, looking upward at the ceiling as though he could see the white birds above him.

The stork had indeed come a great distance and from another country, but remembered crossing no big water. The situation here suited her very well, she thought; from the high housetop she could see a great distance, looking with her red-rimmed eyes along the way her beak pointed. She thought she could even see, on clear hot days that brought breezes to ruffle her sun-heated plumage, almost as far as her own long-awaited liberation from this bird-form which for time out of mind she had inhabited. Certainly she once did see as far as to the awakening of the King, who slept and would sleep some time longer within his mountain, his attendants asleep too around him, his red beard grown so long in his long sleep that tendrils of it twisted like ivy around the legs of the feast-table whereon he snored face down. She saw him snuffle, and move, as though tugged at by a dream that might startle him awake: saw this with a leap of her heart, for surely after his awakening, some distance farther on, would come her own liberation.

Unlike some others she could name, though, she would have patience. She would hatch once again from her pebbled eggs a

Lucy, then
Lilac

brood of quilly young. She would step with dignity among the weeds of the Lily Pond and slay for their sakes a generation of frogs. She would love her current husband, a dear he was, patient and solicitous, a great help with the children. She would not *long*: longing was fatal.

And as they all set off on the long and dusty road of that year's summer, Alice was brought to bed. She named her third daughter Lucy, though Smoky thought it was too much like the names of her two others, Tacey and Lily, and he knew that he at least would spend the next twenty or thirty years calling each of them by the others' names. "That's all right," Alice said. "This is the last, anyway." But it wasn't. There was still a boy for her to bear, though even Cloud didn't yet know that.

Anyway, if Generation was the thing they wanted, as Sophie had once perceived as she sat huddled and dreaming by the pavilion on the lake, this was a gratifying year for them: after the equinox came with a frost that left the woods dusty and gray but let summer linger, spectral and so endless that it summoned distrait crocuses from the ground and called the restless souls of Indians from their burial mounds, Sophie had the child which was attributed to Smoky. Compounding confusion, she named *her* daughter Lilac, because she dreamed that her mother was coming into her room bearing a great branch of it heavy with odorous blue blooms, and awoke then to see her mother come into her room bearing the newborn girl. Tacey and Lily came too, Tacey carrying carefully her three-month-old sister Lucy to see the baby.

"See, Lucy? See the baby? Just like you."

Lily raised herself up on the bed to peer closely into Lilac's face where she lay nestled now against cooing Sophie. "She won't stay long," she said, after studying it.

"Lily!" Mom said. "What a terrible thing to say!"

"Well, she won't." She looked to Tacey: "Will she?"

"Nope." Tacey shifted Lucy in her arms. "But it's okay. She'll come back." Seeing her grandmother shocked, she said. "Oh, don't worry, she's not going to *die* or anything. She's just not going to *stay.*"

• "And she'll come back," Lily said. "Later."

"Why do you think all that?" Sophie asked, not sure she was yet quite in the world again, or hearing what she thought she heard.

The two girls shrugged, at the same time; the same shrug, in fact, a quick lift of shoulders and eyebrows and back again, as at a simple fact. They watched as Mom, shaking her head, helped Sophie induce pink-and-white Lilac to nurse (a delightful, easefully painful feeling) and with her sucking Sophie fell asleep again, dopey with exhaustion and wonderment, and presently so did Lilac, feeling perhaps the same; and though the cord had been cut which joined them, perhaps they dreamed the same dream.

Next morning the stork left the roof of Edgewood and her messy nest. Her children had already flown without farewell or apology—she expected none—and her husband had gone too, hoping they would meet again next spring. She herself had waited only for Lilac's arrival so that she could bring news of it—she kept her promises—and now she flew off in quite a different direction from her family, following her beak, her fanlike wings cupping the autumn dawn and her legs trailing behind like bannerets.

Striving like the Meadow Mouse to disbelieve in Winter, Smoky gorged himself on the summer sky, lying late into the night on the ground staring upward, though the month had an R in it and Cloud thought it bad for nerve, bone, and tissue. Odd that the changeful constellations, so mindful of the seasons, should be what he chose of summer to memorize, but the turning of the sky was so slow, and seemed so impossible, that it comforted him. Yet he needed only to look at his watch to see that they fled away south even as the geese did.

Little, Big

On the night Orion rose and Scorpio set, a night as warm almost as August for reasons of the weather's own but in fact by that sign the last night of summer, he and Sophie and Daily Alice lay out in a sheep-shorn meadow on their backs, their heads close together like three eggs in a nest, as pale too as that in the night light. They had their heads together so that when one pointed out a star, the arm he pointed with would be more or less in the other's line of sight; otherwise, they would be all night saying *That* one, *there*, where I'm *pointing*, unable to correct for billions of miles of parallax. Smoky had the star-book open on his lap, and consulted it with a flashlight whose light was masked with red cellophane taken from a Dutch cheese so its bightness wouldn't blind him.

"Camelopardalis," he said, pointing to a dangling necklace in the north, not clear because the horizon's light still diluted it. "That is, the Camelopard."

"And what," Daily Alice asked indulgently, "is a camelopard?"

"A giraffe, in fact," Smoky said. "A camel-leopard. A camel with leopard's spots."

"Why is there a giraffe in heaven?" Sophie asked. "How did it get there?"

"I bet you're not the first to ask that," Smoky said, laughing. "Imagine their surprise when they first looked up over there and said, My God, what's that giraffe doing up there?"

The menagerie of heaven, racing as from a zoo breakout through the lives of the men and women, gods and heroes; the band of the Zodiac (that night all their birth-signs were invisible, bearing the sun around the south); the impossible dust of the Milky Way rainbow-wise overarching them; Orion lifting one racing foot over the horizon, following his dog Sirius. They discovered the moment's rising sign. Jupiter burned unwinking in the west. The whole spangled beach-umbrella, fringed with the Tropics, revolved on its bent staff around the North Star, too slowly to be seen, yet steadily.

Smoky, out of his childhood reading, related the interlocking tales told above them. The pictures were so formless and incomplete, and the tales, some at least, so trivial that it seemed to Smoky that it must all be true: Hercules looked so little like himself that the only way anyone could have found him was if he'd got the news about Hercules being up there, and was told where to look. As one tree traces its family back to Daphne but another has to be mere commoner; as only the odd flower, mountain, fact gets to have divine ancestry, so Cassiopeia of all people is brilliantly asterized, or her chair rather, as though by accident; and somebody else's crown, and another's lyre: the attic of the gods.

What Sophie wondered, who couldn't make the patterned floor of heaven come out in pictures but lay hypnotized by their nearness, was how it could be that some in heaven were there for reward, and others condemned to it; while still others were there it seemed only to play parts in the dramas of others. It seemed unfair; and yet she couldn't decide whether it was unfair because there they were, stuck forever, who hadn't deserved it; or unfair because, without having earned it, they had been saved—enthroned—need not die. She thought of their own tale, they three, permanent as a constellation, strange enough to be remembered forever.

The earth that week was making progress through the discarded tail of a long-passed comet, and each night a rain of fragments entered the air and flamed whitely as they burned up. "No bigger than pebbles or pinheads some of them," Smoky said. "It's the air you see lit up."

But this now Sophie could see clearly: these were falling stars. She thought perhaps she could pick one out and watch and see it fall: a momentary bright exhalation, that made her draw breath, her heart filled with infinitude. Would that be a better fate? In the grass her hand found Smoky's; the other already held her sister's, who pressed it every time brightness fell from the air.

Daily Alice couldn't tell if she felt huge or small. She wondered whether her head were so big as to be able to contain all this starry universe, or whether the universe were so little that it would fit within the compass of her human head. She alternated between these feelings, expanding and diminishing. The stars wandered in and out of the vast portals of her eyes, under the immense empty dome of her brow; and then Smoky took her hand and she vanished to a speck, still holding the stars as in a tiny jewel box within her.

So they lay a long time, not caring to talk any more, each dwelling on that odd, physical sensation of ephemeral eternity—a paradox but undeniably felt; and if the stars had been as near and full of faces as they seemed, they would have looked down and seen those three as a single asterism, a linked wheel against the wheeling dark sky of the meadow.

There was no entrance but a tiny hole at the window corner where the solstice-midnight wind blew in, piling dust on the sill in a little furrow: but that was room enough for them, and they entered there.

Solstice Night

There were three then in Sophie's bedroom standing close together, their brown-capped heads consulting, their pale flat faces like little moons.

"See how she sleeps away."

"Yes, and the babe asleep in her arms."

"My, she holds it tight."

"Not so tight."

As one, they drew closer to the tall bed. Lilac in her mother's arms, in a hooded bunting against the cold, breathed on Sophie's cheek; a drop of wetness was there.

"Well, take it, then."

"Why don't you if you're so anxious."

"Let's all."

Six long white hands went out toward Lilac. "Wait," said one. "Who has the other?"

"You were to bring it."

"Not I."

"Here it is, here." A thing was unfolded from a drawstring bag.

"My. Not very like, is it."

"What's to be done?"

"Breathe on it."

The breathed on it in turns as they held it amidst them. Now and again one looked back at sleeping Lilac. They breathed till the thing amid them was a second Lilac.

"That'll do."

"It's very like."

"Now take the . . ."

"Wait again." One looked closely at Lilac, drawing back ever so slightly the coverlet. "Look here. She has her little hands tight wound up in her mother's hair."

"Holding fast."

"Take the child, we'll wake the mother."

"These, then." One had drawn out great scissors, which gleamed whitely in the night-light and opened with a faint snicker. "As good as done."

One holding the false Lilac (not asleep but with vacant eyes and unmoving; a night in its mother's arms would cure that) and one reaching ready to take away Sophie's Lilac, and the third with the shears, it was all quickly done; neither mother nor child awoke; they nestled what they had brought by Sophie's breast.

"Now to be gone."

"Easily said. Not the way we came."

"Down the stairs and out their way."

"If we must."

Moving as one and without sound (the old house seemed now and again to draw breath or groan at their passing, but then it always did so, for reasons of its own) they gained the front door, and one reached up and opened it, and they were outside and going quickly with a favorable wind. Lilac never waked or made a sound (the wisps and locks of gold hair still held in her fists blew away in the quick wind of their passage) and Sophie slept too, having felt nothing; except the long tale of her dream had altered, at a turning, and become sad and difficult in ways she hadn't known before.

Smoky was wrenched awake by some internal motion; as soon as his eyes were wide open, he forgot whatever it was that had awakened him. But he was awake, as awake as if it were midday, irritating state, he wondered if it was something he ate. The hour was useless four o'clock in the morning. He shut his eyes resolutely for a while, unconvinced that sleep could have deserted him so completely. But it had; he could tell because the more he watched

In All Directions

179

the eggs of color break and run on the screen of his eyelids the less soporific they became, the more pointless and uninteresting.

Very carefully he slipped out from under the high-piled covers, and felt in the darkness for his robe. There was only one cure he knew of for this state, and that was to get up and act awake until it was placated and went away. He stepped carefully over the floor, hoping he wouldn't step into shoes or other impedimenta, there was no reason to inflict this state on Daily Alice, and he gained the door, satisfied he hadn't disturbed her or the night at all. He'd just walk the halls, go downstairs and turn on some lights, that should do it. He closed the door carefully behind him, and at that Daily Alice awoke, not because of any noise he'd made but because the whole peace of her sleep had been subtly broken and invaded by his absence.

There was already a light burning in the kitchen when he opened the back-stairs door. Great-aunt Cloud made a low, shuddering sound of startled horror when she saw the door open, and then "Oh," she said, when only Smoky looked around it. She had a glass of warm milk before her, and her hair was down, long and fine and spreading, white as Hecate's; it had been uncut for years and years.

"You gave me a start," she said.

They discussed sleeplessness in low voices, though there was no one their voices could disturb from here but the mice. Smoky, seeing she too wanted to bustle some to overcome wakefulness, allowed her to warm milk for him; to his he added a stiff measure of brandy.

"Listen to that wind," said Cloud.

Above them, they heard the long gargle and whisper of a flushed toilet. "What's up?" Cloud said. "A sleepless night, and no moon." She shivered. "It feels like the night of a catastrophe, or a night big news comes, everybody awake. Well. Just chance." She said it as another might say God help us—with that same degree of rote unbelief.

Smoky, warmed now, rose and said "Well," in a resigned sort of way. Cloud had begun to leaf through a cookbook there. He hoped she wouldn't have to sit to watch bleak dawn come; he hoped he wouldn't himself.

At the top of the stairs he didn't turn toward his own bed where, he knew, sleep didn't yet await him. He turned toward Sophie's room, with no intention but to look at her a while. Her restfulness calmed him sometimes, as a cat's can, made him restful too. When he opened her door, he saw by the moon-pale night-light that someone sat on the edge of Sophie's bed.

"Hi," he said.

"Hi," said Daily Alice.

There was an odd smell in the air, a smell like leaf mold, or Queen Anne's-lace, or perhaps the earth under an upturned stone. "What's up?" he asked softly. He came to sit on the other side of the bed.

"I don't know," she said. "Nothing. I woke up when you left. I felt like something happened to Sophie, so I came to see."

There was no danger that their quiet talk would waken Sophie; people talking near her in her sleep only seemed to comfort her, to make her deep draughts of breath more regular.

"Everything's all right, though," he said.

"Yes."

Wind pressed on the house, beating it in fitful anger; the window boomed. He looked down at Sophie and Lilac. Lilac looked quite dead, but after three children Smoky knew that this scary appearance, especially in the dark, wasn't reason for alarm.

They sat silent on either side of Sophie. The wind spoke suddenly a single word in the chimney's throat. Smoky looked at Alice, who touched his arm and smiled quickly.

What smile did it remind him of?

"Everything's okay," she said.

He remembered Great-aunt Cloud smiling at him as they sat troubled on the lawn of Auberon's summer house the day he was married: a smile meant to be comforting, but which was not. A smile against distance, that only seemed to increase distance. A signal of friendship sent out of infrangible foreignness; a hand waved far off, from across a border.

"Do you smell a funny smell?" he said.

"Yes. No. I did. It's gone now."

It was. The room was full only of night air. The sea of wind outside raised small currents in it which now and again brushed his face; but it didn't seem to him as though this were Brother North-wind moving around them, but as though the many-angled house itself were under sail, making progress through the night, plowing steadily into the future in all directions.

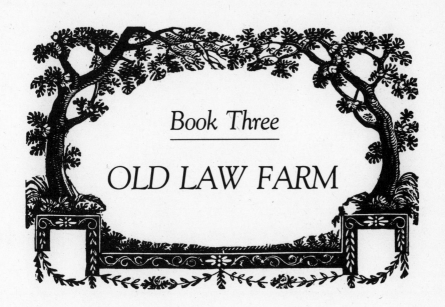

Book Three

OLD LAW FARM

Twenty-five years passed.

On a night late in the autumn, George Mouse stepped out the window of what had been the third-floor library of his townhouse and through a small covered bridge, which connected his window with the window of what had once been a kitchen in a tenement that adjoined his building. The ex-kitchen was dark and cold; George Mouse's breath was manifest in the light of his lantern. As he walked, rats or mice moved away from him and his light, he heard their scratches and rustlings but saw nothing. Without opening a door (there hadn't been a door for years) he went out into the hallway and started carefully down the stairs, carefully because the stairs were rotten and loose where they weren't missing altogether.

On the floor below there were light and laughter; people greeted him as they went in and out of apartments with the makings of a communal dinner; children chased along the halls. But the first floor was dark again, unused now except for storage. George, holding his lantern aloft, peered down along the dark hall to the outer door, and could see its great bar in place, its chains and locks secure. He went around the stairs to the door which led to the basement, taking out as he went an enormous bunch of keys. One,

Keeping People Out

185

specially marked, dark as an old penny, unlocked the ancient Segal lock of the basement.

Every time he opened the basement door, George fretted over whether he shouldn't put a nice new padlock on it; this old lock was a toy by now, an elder's grip, anyone could break it. He always decided that a new lock would only make people wonder, and a shoulder against the door would satisfy curiosity, new padlock or no.

Oh, they had all grown very circumspect in this matter of keeping people out.

Down the stairs, even more carefully, God knew what lived down here amid the rusted pipe and old boilers and fabulous detritus, he had once stepped on something large, soft and dead and nearly broken his neck. At the bottom of the stairs he hung up his lantern, went to a corner, and maneuvered an old trunk so that he could stand on it and reach a high, ratproof shelf.

He had had the gift, predicted long ago by Great-aunt Cloud (left him by a stranger, and not money), for a long time before he learned how he could have come by it. Even before he learned, he was in his Mouse way secretive about it, the result of growing up on the street and youngest in a nosy family. Everyone admired the potent, musky hashish George seemed always to be provided with, and all desired to have some; but he would not (could not) introduce them to his dealer (who was long dead). He kept everyone happy with free bits, and the pipe was always full at his place; but though sometimes, after a few pipes of it, he would look around at his stupefied company and feel guilt for his gloating, and his great, his hilarious, his astonishing secret would burn within him to be spilt, he never told, not a soul.

It was Smoky who, inadvertently, revealed to George the source of his great good fortune. "I read somewhere," Smoky said (his usual entry into conversation), "that oh fifty or sixty years ago, your neighborhood was a Middle Eastern neighborhood. Lots of Lebanese. And the little candy stores and places like that sold hashish, right out in the open. You know, along with the toffee and halvah. For a nickel, you could buy a lot. Big hunks. Like chocolate bars."

And indeed they were very much like chocolate bars. . . . George had felt like a cartoon mouse suddenly struck over the head with the great, well-worn mallet of Revelation.

Ever afterward, when he went down to take from his hoard, he had imagined himself a goat-bearded Levantine, hook-nosed and skull-capped, a secret pederast who gave free baklava to the olive boys of the streets. Fussily he would arrange the old trunk and climb on it (lifting the frayed skirts of an imaginary dressing gown) and lift the lid of the wooden crate stenciled with curling letters.

Not much left. Time to reorder soon.

Beneath a thick covering of silvered paper, layer upon layer of lay. The layers were separated by yellow oiled paper. The bars themselves were wrapped tightly too in a third sort of oily paper. He took out two, considered a moment, and put one reluctantly back. It would not, though he had exclaimed so in awe many years ago when he had discovered what it was, last forever. He replaced the layer of oiled paper and then the layer of silvered paper; he drew back on the stout lid, and pushed in place the ancient shapeless nails; he blew across it to resettle the dust. He got down, and studied the bar in the lantern's light as he had the very first by electric light. He peeled away its paper carefully. It was as black as chocolate, and about the size of a playing card, an eighth of an inch thin. It bore on it a convolute impress: A trademark? Tax stamp? Mystic sign? He had never decided.

He pushed the trunk he had used for a stepladder back into its place in the corner, took up the lantern and started up the stairs. In his cardigan pocket was a piece of hashish something like a hundred years old, and, George Mouse had long ago decided, not reduced in potency by age at all. Improved, perhaps, like vintage port.

He was relocking the cellar door when there came a pounding at the street door, so sudden and unexpected that he cried out. He waited a moment, hoping it was some madman's momentary whim and wouldn't come again. But it did. He went to the door, listened at it without speaking, and heard frustrated cursing outside. Then, with a growl, the someone grabbed at the bars and began to shake them.

News from
Home

"That's no use, that's no use," George called. The shaking stopped.

"Well, open the door."

"What?" It was a habit of George's, when stuck for an answer, to act as though he hadn't heard the question.

"*Open* the *door!*"

"Now, you know I can't just open the door, man. You know what it's like."

"Well, listen. Can you tell me which of these buildings is number two-twenty-two?"

"Who wants to know?"

"Why does everybody in this city answer everything with a question?"

"Huh?"

"Why can't you open the door and talk to me like a god DAMN human being?"

Silence. The horrid depths of frustration in that outcry touched George's heart, and he listened at the door to see if there would be more; he tingled secretly at the safety he felt behind the door's fastness.

"Can you tell me," the someone began, and George could hear his rage strangled down into politeness, "please, where I can find, or if you know, the Mouse house or George Mouse?"

"Yes," George said. "I am him." That was risky, but surely even the most desperate bill-collectors and process-servers weren't abroad this late. "Who are you?"

"My name is Auberon Barnable. My father . . ." But already the clankings and scrapings of locks and shootings of bolts drowned him out. George reached into the darkness and pulled the person standing on the threshold into the hall. With quick skill he reslammed and barred and bolted the door, and then raised his lamp to look at his cousin.

"So you're the baby," he said, noting with perverse pleasure how ill this remark sat on the tall youth. The moving lantern made his expression changeful, but it wasn't really a changeful face; it was narrow and tight; in fact the whole of him, slim and neat as a pen in pipe-rack black clothes that fit him well, was somewhat rigid and aloof. Just pissed off, George thought. He laughed, and patted his arm. "Hey, how's the folks? How's Elsie, Lacy, and Tilly, whatever their names are? What brings you here?"

"Dad wrote," Auberon said, as though unwilling to waste effort answering all this if it had already been done.

"Oh yeah? Well, you know how the mail's been. Look, look. Come on. We don't have to stand in the hall. Colder than a witch's tit here. Coffee and something?"

Smoky's son shrugged shortly. "Be careful on the stairs," George said, and the lamplight threaded them both back through the tenement and over the little bridge till they stood together on the threadbare rug where Auberon's parents had first met.

Somewhere along their route, George had picked up an old three-and-a-half-legged kitchen chair. "Did you run away from home? Have a seat," he said, motioning Auberon to a tattered wing-back.

"My father and mother know I left, if that's what you

mean," Auberon said, a bit haughtily, which was understandable, George thought. Then he shrank back in the chair; George had with a grunt and a wild look raised the broken chair over his head, and, his face twisted with exertion, brought it down on the stone hearth. It fell clattering to pieces. "Did they approve?" George asked, tossing the chair-parts into the fire.

"Of course." Auberon crossed his legs and plucked at his trouser-knee. "He wrote. I told you. He said to look you up."

"Oh, yeah. Did you walk?"

"No." With some contempt.

"And you came to the City to . . ."

"To seek my fortune."

"Aha." George hung a kettle over the fire and took down a precious can of contraband coffee from a bookshelf. "Any glimpse yet what form it might take?"

"No, not exactly. Only . . ." George mmm-hmmm'd encouragingly as he prepared the coffeepot and set out mismatched cups. "I wanted, I want to write, or be a writer." George raised his eyebrows. Auberon was twisted around in the wing-back chair as though these admissions were escaping him against his will, and he were trying to hold them in. "I thought television."

"Wrong coast."

"What?"

"They do all that television out on the Sunny, the Golden, the West Coast." Auberon locked his right foot behind his left calf and declined to answer this. George, searching for something in the bookshelves and drawers and beating his many pockets, wondered how that antique desire could have made its way to Edgewood. Odd how the young take to these dying trades so hopefully. When he was young, when the last poets were prattling incommunicado, glowworms gone out in their dells of dew, boys of twenty-one set out to be poets. . . . At length he found what he was looking for: a gift-shop dagger-shaped letter-opener chased with enamel which he had found years ago in an abandoned apartment and sharpened to a fine edge. "Takes a lot of ambition, that television," he said, "and drive, and the failures are many." He poured water into the coffeepot.

"How would you know?" his cousin said swiftly, as though he had heard that adult wisdom often before.

"Because," George said, "I haven't got those qualities, and I haven't failed in that field cause I don't, to wit, QED. Coffee's running through." The boy didn't crack a smile. George put the coffeepot on a trivet that bore a joke in Pennsylvania Dutch argot, and broke out a tin box of cookies, mostly broken. He also took from his cardigan pocket the brown square of hashish. "Like a taste?" he said, not at all grudgingly, he thought, showing Auberon the square. "Best Lebanese. I think."

"I don't use drugs."

"Oh, aha."

Judging nicely, George cut off a corner with his Florentine instrument, pierced the fragment with its point, and dunked it in his cup. He sat turning the knife in the cup and looking at his cousin, who was blowing on his coffee with single-minded intensity. Ah, it was lovely to be old and gray, and to have learned to ask neither for too much nor too little. "So," he said. He lifted the knife from his coffee to see that the fragment had nearly dissolved. "Tell us your history."

Auberon was mum.

"Come on, let's have it." He slurped the fragrant brew eagerly. "News from home."

It took a deal of questioning, but as the night wore down, Auberon did speak phrases, yield anecdotes. It was enough for George; his laced coffee finished, he heard a whole life in Auberon's sentences, complete with amusing detail and odd conjunctions; pathos, even magic, even. He found himself looking into his cousin's closed heart as into the halved shell of a coiled and chambered nautilus.

What George Mouse Heard

He'd left Edgewood early, awakening just before dawn, as he'd intended to—it was an ability he shared with his mother, that he could wake when he chose. He lit a lamp; it would be another hour or two before Smoky shuffled down to the basement to start up the generator. There was a trembling tightness around his diaphragm, as though something struggled for release or escape there. He knew the phrase "butterflies in your stomach," but is one of those people to whom phrases like that communicate nothing. He has had butterflies in his stomach as he'd had the willies, and the jitters; more than once he has been beside himself; but has always thought these experiences were his alone, and never knew they were so common as to have names. His ignorance allowed him to compose poetry about the weird feelings he felt, a handful of typewritten pages which as soon as he was dressed in the neat black suit he put carefully into the green canvas knapsack along with his other clothes, his toothbrush, what else? An antique Gillette, four bars of soap, a copy of *Brother North-wind's Secret,* and the testamentary stuff for the lawyers.

He walked through the sleeping house for what he solemnly imagined was the last time, on his way to an unknown destiny. The house seemed in fact to be quite restless, tossing and turning in an unquiet half-dream, opening its eyes, startled, as he passed. A watery, wintery light lay along the corridors; the imaginary rooms and halls were real in the gloom.

"You look as though you hadn't shaved," Smoky said uncertainly when Auberon came into the kitchen. "You want some oatmeal?"

"I didn't want to wake up everybody, running the water and everything. I don't think I can eat."

Smoky went on fussing with the old wood stove anyway. It always amazed Auberon as a child to see his father go to bed at night in this house and then appear at his desk in the schoolhouse next morning as though translated, or as though there were two of him. The first time he got up early enough to catch his father with frowzy hair and a plaid robe, on his way between sleep and school, it was as though he had caught out a conjurer; but in fact Smoky always made his own breakfast, and though for years the glossy white electric range has stood cold and useless in the corner, like a proud old housekeeper unwillingly retired, and Smoky was as unhandy with fires as he was about most things, he went on doing it; it only meant he had to get up earlier to begin.

Auberon, growing impatient with his father's patience, bent down before the stove and got it angrily flaming in a moment; Smoky stood behind him, hands in his robe pockets, admiring; and in a while they sat opposite each other with bowls of oatmeal, and coffee too, a gift from George Mouse in the City.

They sat for a moment, hands in laps, looking not into each other's eyes but into the brown Brazilian eyes of the two coffee cups together; and then Smoky, with an apologetic cough, got up and got the brandy bottle from a high shelf. "It's a long walk," he said, and spiked the coffee.

Smoky?

Yes; George could see that there could well have grown in him in the last years a sort of constriction of feeling sometimes that a nip can untangle. No problem really; just a nip, so he can begin to ask Auberon if he's sure he has enough money, if he's got Grandpa's agents' address and George Mouse's address and all the legal instruments and so on about the inheritance and so on. And yes he does.

Even after Doc died, his stories continued to be published in the City's evening paper—George read them even before he read the funnies. Besides these posthumous stories squirreled away like winter nuts, Doc left a mess of affairs as thick and entangling as any briar patch; lawyers and agents pursued his intentions there, and might for years. Auberon had a special interest in these thorny matters because Doc had specified a bequest to him, enough to live for a year or so and write unhampered. Doc had hoped, actually—though he was too shy to say so—that his grandson and the best friend of his last years might take up the little adventures, though Auberon was at a disadvantage there—he would have to make them up, unlike Doc, who for years had been getting them firsthand.

There's a certain embarrassment, George could easily imagine, in learning that you can talk to animals. No one knew how long Doc's conviction was in growing, though some of the grown-ups could remember his first claiming it was so, shyly, tentatively, as a joke they supposed, a lame sort of joke, but then Doc's jokes weren't ever very funny except to millions of children. It took later the form of a metaphor or puzzle: he recounted his conversations with salamanders and chickadees with a cryptic smile, as though inviting his family to guess why he spoke so. In the end, he ceased trying to hide it: what he heard from his correspondents was just too interesting not to recount.

Since all this was happening as Auberon was coming into consciousness, it only seemed to him that his grandfather's powers were growing surer, his ear more keen. When, on one of their long walks together through the woods, Doc at last stopped pretending that what he heard the animals say was made up, and admitted that he was passing on conversations he heard, they both felt a lot better. Auberon never much liked let's-pretend, and Doc had hated lying to the child. The science of it escaped him, he said; maybe it was only a result of his long devotion; anyway, it was only certain animals he could understand, small ones, the ones he knew best. Bears, moose, the scarce and fabulous cats, the solitary, long-winged predators he knew nothing of. They disdained him, or couldn't discourse, or had no use for small talk—he couldn't tell.

"And insects and bugs?" Auberon asked him.

"Some, but not all," Doc answered.

"Ants?"

"Oh, yes, ants," Doc said, "sure."

And taking his grandson's hands where they knelt together beside a new yellow hill, he gratefully translated for him the mindless shoptalk of the ants within.

192

Auberon was asleep now, on the bursting loveseat, curled beneath a blanket, as who would not be who had risen as early and come as far in as many ways as he had today; but George Mouse, subject to tics and exulting on the giddy chutes and ladders of High Thought, kept watch over the boy and continued to overhear his adventures.

George Mouse Goes on Overhearing

When, oatmeal untasted but coffee finished, he went out the great front door, Smoky's hand paternally on his shoulder though it was higher than his own, Auberon saw that he wasn't to make his getaway without goodbyes. His sisters, all three, had come to see him off; Lily and Lucy were walking up the drive arm-in-arm, Lily bearing her twins fore-and-aft in canvas carriers, and Tacey was just turning in at the end of the drive on her bike.

He might have known, but hadn't wished this sendoff, wished it less than anything because of the formal finality his sisters' presence always lent to whatever partings or arrivals or conjunctions they attended. How the hell anyway had they known this was to be the morning? He had only told Smoky late last night, and sworn him to secrecy. A certain familiar rage rose in him whose name he didn't know was rage. "Hi, hi," he said.

"We came to say goodbye," Lily said. Lucy shifted the front twin and added, "And give you some things."

"Yeah? Well." Tacey turned her bike neatly at the porch stairs and dismounted. "Hi, hi," Auberon said again. "Did you bring along the whole county?" But of course they hadn't brought anyone else; no one else's presence was necessary, as theirs was.

Perhaps because their names were so similar, or because so often in the community they appeared and acted together, but people around Edgewood always found it hard to distinguish among Tacey, Lily, and Lucy. In fact they were very different. Tacey and Lily were descendants of their mother and her mother, long, big-boned and coltish, though Lily had inherited from somewhere a head of fine straight blond hair, straw spun into gold as the princess in the story spun it, where Tacey's was curly reddish-gold like Alice's. Lucy, though, was all Smoky's; shorter than her sisters, with Smoky's dark curls and Smoky's cheerful bemused face and even something of Smoky's congenital anonymity in her round eyes. But in another sense it was Lucy and Lily who were a pair: the sort of sisters who can finish one another's sentences, and feel even at a distance one another's pains. For years the two of them kept up a running series of seemingly pointless jokes; one would ask, in a serious tone, a silly question, and the other would just as seriously give an even sillier answer, and then they would (never cracking a smile) give the joke a number. The numbers ran into the hundreds. Tacey, perhaps because she was the oldest, was remote from their games; she was a naturally regal and private person who cultivated intensely a number of passions, for the alto recorder, for raising rabbits, for fast bikes. On the other hand, in all complots, plans, and ceremonies that dealt with grownups and their affairs, it had always been Tacey who was priestess, and the younger two her acolytes.

(In one thing all three were alike: they each had only one eyebrow, running over their noses from outer eye-corner to outer eye-corner without a break. Of Smoky and Alice's children, only Auberon was without it.)

Auberon's memories of his sisters would always be of their playing at the mysteries, birth, marriage, love, and death. He had been their Baby when he was very young, chivvied around from imaginary bath to imaginary hospital endlessly, a living doll. Later he was compelled to be Bridegroom, and finally Departed when he was old enough to be pleased simply to lie there while they ministered to him. And it was not only play; as they grew older, all three seemed to develop an instinctive grasp of the scenes and acts of quotidian life, of the curtains rising and rung down in the lives around them. No one remembered telling them (they were aged four, six, and eight then) that the youngest of the Bird girls was to be married to Jim Jay over in Plainfield, but they appeared at the church in jeans with bunches of wildflowers in their hands and knelt decorously on the church steps while inside the bride and groom took their vows. (The wedding photographer, waiting outside for the couple to appear, took a whimsical picture of the three darlings which later won a prize in a photo contest. It looked posed. In a sense, it was.)

From an early age, they had all three learned needlework, becoming more skilled and taking up in turn more difficult and esoteric branches of it as they got older, tatting, silk embroidery, crewel-work; what Tacey learned first from Great-aunt Cloud and her grandmother she taught to Lily, and Lily to Lucy; and as they sat together expertly doing and undoing with thread (often in the many-sided music room where the sun came in at all seasons) they kept up among themselves a constant calendar of the passings, pledges, partings, parturitions expected (announced or not) among the people they knew. They made knots, they snipped threads, they knew all; it came to pass that no sad or glad occasion was unknown to them, and few went forward without the three of them present. Those that did seemed incomplete, unsanctioned. Their only brother's departure for his appointment with destiny and lawyers was not to be one of those.

"Here," said Tacey, plucking from her bike's basket a small package done up in ice-blue paper, "take this, and open it when you get to the City." She kissed him lightly.

"Take this," Lily said, giving him one wrapped in minty-green, "and open it when you think of it."

"Take this," Lucy said. Hers was wrapped in white. "Open it when you want to come home again."

He gathered these together, nodding, embarrassed, and put them in his duffle. The girls said nothing more about them, only sat for a while with him and Smoky on the porch, across which dead leaves blew unswept, gathering up under the seats of wicker chairs (which ought to go in the basement, Smoky thought; an old chore of Auberon's; he felt a chill of foreboding, or loss, but thought it to be the somber November gloaming only). Auberon, who was young and solitary enough to think that he might have escaped his house without anyone being the wiser, that no one paid much attention to his movements, sat constrainedly with them watching dawn grow; then he slapped his knees, rose, shook his father's hand, kissed his sisters, promised to write, and at last stepped off southward into the sounding sea of leaves, striking for the crossroads where a bus could be hailed; he didn't look back at the four who watched him go.

"Well," Smoky said, remembering his own journey to the City at an age near Auberon's, "he'll have adventures."

"Lots," Tacey said.

"It'll be fun," Smoky said, "probably, possibly. I remember . . ."

"Fun for a while," Lily said.

"Not much fun," Lucy said. "Fun first, though, at least."

"Dad," said Tacey, seeing him trembling, "you shouldn't sit out here in your 'jammies, for God's sake."

He rose, pulling his bathrobe around him. This afternoon he would have to get in the porch furniture, before snow piled absurdly in its summery seats.

Shifting focus, George Mouse watched from a niche in the Old Stone Fence as Auberon came across the Old Pasture, short-cutting his way toward Meadowbrook. The Meadow Mouse in that niche, grass blade between his teeth and gloomy thoughts in his mind, watched the human come toward him, crunching

A Friend of the Doctor's

great twigs and dead leaves by the hundreds beneath his boots. Ah, the great and clumsy feet of them! The shod feet, larger and harder even than the Brown Bear's of ancient memory! Only the fact that they had only two each, and came around rarely and singly near his home, allowed the Meadow Mouse to feel somewhat more kindly toward them than toward the house-wrecking Cow, his personal behemoth. As Auberon came closer, passing indeed very close to the niche where he huddled, the Meadow Mouse had a surprise. This was the boy—grown huge—who had once come with the Doctor who was the Meadow Mouse's great-great-grandfather's friend; the very same boy that the Meadow Mouse as a tiny mousling had once observed, hands on his bare and scabby knees peering intently into the familial home as the Doctor took down Great-great-grandfather's memoirs, which were so famous now not only among generations of Meadow Mice but throughout the Great World as well! His natural timidity overcome by a rush of family feeling, the Meadow Mouse put his nose out of the niche in the wall and attempted a greeting: "My great-great-grandfather knew the Doctor," he called out. But the fellow went right on.

The Doctor could talk with the animals, but the boy, apparently, could not.

A Shepherd in the Bronx

When Auberon was standing by the crossroads ankle-deep in golden leaves, and Smoky was standing abstracted before his tribe who puzzled that he had fallen silent, chalk to board, between noun and predicate, Daily Alice beneath her figured quilt (yes! George Mouse gasped at the breadth and length of his own Mental Sympathies) dreamed that her son Auberon, who lived in the City now, had telephoned to tell her how he was getting on.

"For a while I was a shepherd in the Bronx," the disembodied and still secretive voice was saying, "but when November came, I sold the flock;" and as he told her of it, she could see the Bronx he spoke of: its green, cropped sea-hills, a space of clean, windy air between those hills and the low wet clouds. It was as though she had been there herself when he shepherded, and had followed the delicate prints and black droppings along the rutted ways to pasturage, her ears full of their complainings, nose full of the smell of their wet wool on misty mornings. Vivid! She could see her son when (as he told her) he would stand staff in hand on a promontory there and look off to the sea, and to the west from where the weather came, and to the south across the river, to the dark wood that covered the sea-island there, and wonder . . .

In the fall then he changed his leathers and gaiters for a decent suit of black and his crook for a walking-stick, and though he had never decided on it in so many words, he and the dog Spark (a good sheepdog whom Auberon could have sold with the flock but couldn't part with) set out along the Harlem River till they came to a place where they could cross (near 137th Street). The aged, aged ferryman had a beautiful great-grandaughter brown as a berry and a gray, flat, knocking, groaning boat; Auberon stood up in the bows as the ferry drifted along its line downstream to a mooring on the opposite side. He paid, the dog Spark leapt out before him, and he stepped off into the Wild Wood without looking back. It was late afternoon; the sun (he could glimpse it now and then, a dull yellow glow behind gray clouds) seemed so cold and cheerless he almost wished for night.

Deeper in, he retracted this wish. Somehow he had turned the wrong way between St. Nicholas Park and Cathedral Parkway, and found himself climbing stony uplands written on by lichen. The great trees clinging to the rocky places with their knuckled toes groaned and chuckled at him as he passed, and made bole-faces in the twilight. Panting on a high rock, he saw between the trees the gray sun go out. He knew he was still far uptown, and now night had come; he was cold, and how many warnings had he always had about night in this place? He felt small. In fact he was growing small. Spark noticed it, but made no remark.

The night as it will do brought forth creatures. Auberon began foolishly to hurry, which made him stumble, which caused the creatures to come close, thousand-eyed in the complex darkness all around. Auberon collected himself. Mustn't show them your fear. He took a grip on his stick. Looking neither right nor left, he toiled downtown; he walked, didn't walk as appropriate. Once or twice he caught himself gawking up at the immense trees scraping the night sky (for sure he had grown much smaller) but lowered his eyes quickly; he didn't want to appear a stranger here or someone who didn't know what was what; he couldn't keep, though, from glancing around himself at those who, grinning or knowing or indifferent, glanced at him as he passed.

Where was Spark, he wondered as he pulled himself from a tangled deadfall into which he had sunk hip-deep. Now he could have climbed onto the dog's back and gotten on much faster. But Spark had developed a contempt for his newly-small master and had gone off in the direction of Washington Heights to try his fortune alone.

Alone. Auberon remembered the three gifts his sisters had

given him. He took from his canvas knapsack the one Tacey had given him and tore its ice-blue wrapping with trembling fingers.

It was a combination pen and flashlight, one end to see by and the other to write with. Handy. It even had its little battery: he pressed its button, and it burned. A few snowflakes drifted in the beam; a few faces that had come close withdrew. And by the light he saw that he stood before a tiny door in the woods; his journey was done. He knocked, and knocked again.

Look at the Time George Mouse shuddered vastly. The effort of Mental Sympathy and the wearing off of his dose had him feeling a little ashen. It had been fun, but good Lord, look at the time! In a few hours he would have to be up again for milking. For sure Sylvie (brown as a berry, but not home yet, unless he missed his guess) wouldn't be up for it. Gathering up his hash-dispersed limbs, which ached with pleasant tiredness (long trip), he stitched them back roughly where they belonged on his consciousness and rose. Getting too old for this. He made certain his cousin had blankets enough, raked up the fire, and (already forgetting in the main what he had perceived behind his cousin's dark and shapely lids) took up the lamp and made his way to his own cluttered bedroom, yawning uncontrollably.

The Club Meets Some city blocks away at that hour, before the narrow townhouse of Ariel Hawksquill which faced a small park, large and silent cars of another era one by one drew up and let out each a single passenger, and drove away to where cars like that await their masters. Each of the visitors rang Hawksquill's bell and was admitted; each must take off his gloves finger by finger, so well they fitted; each gave them to the servant inside his hat, and some had white scarves that whistled faintly as they drew them from their necks. They gathered in Hawksquill's parlor floor which was chiefly library; each crossed his legs as he sat. They exchanged a few words in low voices.

When Hawksquill at last entered, they rose for her (though she motioned that they shouldn't) and sat again, each tugging at his trouser-knee as he recrossed his legs.

"I guess we can say," one said, "that this meeting of the Noisy Bridge Rod and Gun Club is now open. For new business."

Ariel Hawksquill awaited their questions. She was in this year nearing the height of her powers, her figure angular, hair iron-gray, manner sharp and deliberate as a cockatoo's. She was imposing, if not quite the intimidating figure she would become; and everything about her, from dun shoes to ringed fingers, suggested powers—powers the Noisy Bridge Rod and Gun Club at least was well aware she possessed.

"The new business, of course," another member said, smiling toward Hawksquill, "being the matter of Russell Eigenblick. The Lecturer."

"What," a third asked Hawksquill, "do you think now? What are your impressions?"

She put her fingertips together, like Holmes. "He is and is not what he seems," she said in a voice as precise and dry as a parchment page. "More clever than he appears on television, though not so large. The enthusiasm he arouses is genuine, but, I can't help thinking, evanescent. He has five planets in Scorpio; so did Martin Luther. His favorite color is billiard-cloth green. He has large, moist, falsely sympathetic brown eyes, like a cow. His voice is amplified by miniature devices concealed in his clothing, which is expensive but doesn't fit well. He wears, beneath his pants, boots to his knees."

They absorbed this.

"His character?" one asked.

"Contemptible."

"His manners?"

"Well . . ."

"His ambitions?"

This she was for a moment unable to answer, yet it was this question which the puissant bankers, board chairmen, bureaucratic plenipotentiaries and retired generals who met under the aegis of the Noisy Bridge Rod and Gun Club most wanted answered. As the secret guardians of a touchy, wilful, aging republic suffering in the more or less permanent grip of social and economic depression, they were minutely sensitive to any attractive man, preacher, soldier, adventurer, thinker, thug. Hawksquill was well aware that her insights had led to the putting away of more than one such. "He has no interest in being President," she said.

One of the members made a noise that indicated: if he does not, he could not have any other ambition that could truly alarm us; and if he does, he is helpless, because for some years the regular succession of shadowy presidents has been solely the concern of the Club, whatever the people or the Presidents may have thought. It was a brief noise, made in the throat.

"It's difficult to describe precisely," Hawksquill said. "On the one hand his self-importance seems ludicrous, and his aims so

huge as to be dismissable entirely, like God's. On the other hand . . .
He claims, for instance, often and with a particular expression that
seems to hint at large secrets, to be 'in the cards.' An old catch
phrase: and yet Somehow (I'm afraid I can't say quite how) I think
his words are exact, and that he *is* in the cards, in some cards, only I
don't know which ones." She looked over her slow-nodding listen-
ers, and felt sorry to puzzle them, but she was puzzled herself. She had
spent weeks with Russell Eigenblick on the road, in hotels, on
planes, transparently disguised as a journalist (the hard-faced paladins who surrounded Eigenblick saw easily through the disguise, but
could see nothing within); but she was less able now to offer a
suggestion as to the disposition of his case than when she had first
heard his name, and laughed.

Fingertips on her temples, she walked carefully through
the perfectly-ordered new wing which she had added over the last
weeks to her memory mansion to contain her investigation of Russell
Eigenblick. She knew at what turnings he himself should appear, at
the head of which staircases, at the nexus of which vistas. He would
not appear. She could picture him with the ordinary or Natural
Memory. She could see him against the rain-streaked window of a
local train, talking indefatigably, his red beard wagging and his curling eyebrows ascending and descending like a ventriloquist's dummy's. She could see him haranguing the vast ecstatic dove-moaning
audiences, real tears in his eyes and real love poured forth from
them to him; she could see him rattling a blue teacup and saucer on
his knee at a women's club meeting after another interminable lecture, with his steely disciples, each holding his own cup and saucer
and cake, around him. The Lecturer: it was they who insisted on his
being called that. They arrived first and made arrangements for the
Lecturer's appearance. The Lecturer will stand here. No one must
use this room but the Lecturer. There must be a car for the Lecturer.
And *their* eyes never filled with tears as they sat behind his lectern,
faces as composed and expressionless as their black-socked ankles.
All this she had quarried from Natural Memory and by artifice constructed into a fine Palladian wing of her memory mansion, where it
ought all to make a new and subtle sense; she expected to be able to
turn a marble corner and find him *there*, framed in a vista, suddenly
revealed and revealing what he was, which she had known all along
but had not known she knew. That was how it was intended to work,
how it had always worked in the past. But now the Club waited,
silent and unstirring, for her disposition; and between the pillars and
on the belvederes there stood the disciples, neatly dressed, holding
each the emblem to identify himself which she had given him—

train-ticket stub, golf club, purple mimeo sheets, dead body. *They* were clear enough. But *he* would not appear. And yet the whole wing was, yes, for sure, him; and it was chill, and pregnant.

"What about these lectures?" a member said, interrupting her survey.

She looked at him coldly. "God," she said. "You have transcripts of them all. Is that what I'm to concern myself with? Can you read?" She paused then, wondering whether her contempt was merely a mask for her own failure to encompass her quarry. "When he speaks," she said more graciously, "they listen. What he says you know. The old amalgam designed to touch every heart. Hope, a limitless hope. Common sense, or what passes for it. Wit that releases. He can draw tears. But many can. I think . . ." It was as close as she could come now to a definition, and was not close: "I think he is less or more than a man. I think we are Somehow dealing not with a man but with a geography."

"I see," said a member, brushing a moustache pearly-gray like his tie.

"You do not," Hawksquill said, "because I do not."

"Snuff him out," another said.

"His message," said another, drawing from his supple case a sheaf of papers, "is not one we object to, though. Stability. Vigilance. Acceptance. Love."

"Love," said another. "All things degenerate. Nothing works any more, everything misfires." There was a desperate quaver in his voice. "There is no force left on earth found stronger than love." He burst into strange sobs.

"Do I see, Hawksquill," someone said calmly, "decanters on your sideboard there?"

"One is cut-glass, and has brandy," Hawksquill said. "The other is not, and has rye."

They calmed their associate with a taste of brandy, and declared the meeting closed, *sine die,* with Hawksquill's commission continued and the new business unresolved; and left her house in greater puzzlement than they had felt since the society whose secret pillars they were had first begun perversely to sicken and waste.

When she had shown them out, Hawksquill's servant stood in the hall, gloomily contemplating what seemed to be a pale stain of dawn showing in the barred glass of the door, and complaining inwardly of her state, her subservience, her brief glows of night-time consciousness worse almost than having none at

Pictured
Heavens

all. All this while the gray light grew, and seemed to stain the unmoving servant, to subtract the living light from her eyes. She raised a hand in an Egyptian gesture of blessing or dismissal; her lips sealed. When Hawksquill passed her on her way upward, day had come, and the Maid of Stone (as Hawksquill named this ancient statue) was all marmoreal again.

Hawksquill climbed up within the tall, narrow house, four long flights (a daily exercise that would keep her strong heart beating till great old age) and arrived at a small door at the very top of the house, where the stairs narrowed sharply and ran out. She could hear the steady noise of the great mechanism beyond the door, the drop of heavy weights inch by inch, the hollow clicks of catchments and escapements, and felt her mind already soothed. She opened the door. Daylight, many-colored and faint, poured out; the music of the spheres, like soft-soughing wind among clicking bare branches, became distinct. She glanced at her old, square-faced wristwatch, and bent to enter.

That this City house was one of only three in the world equipped with a complete Patent Cosmo-Opticon or Theatrum Mundi in more-or-less working order, Hawksquill had known before she bought it. It had amused her to think that her house would be capped by such an enormous and iron-bound talisman of her mind's heavens. She had been prepared, though, neither for its great beauty, nor—when it had been set in motion, and she had adjusted it in certain long-thought-out ways—for its usefulness. She had been unable to learn much about the Cosmo-Opticon's designer, so she couldn't tell what he had conceived its function to be—entertainment only, probably—but what he hadn't known she supplied, and so now when she bent to enter the tiny door she entered not only a stained-glass-and-wrought-iron Cosmos exquisitely detailed and moving with spanking exactness in its clockwork rounds, but one which presented to Hawksquill the actual moment of the World-Age that was passing as she entered.

In fact, though Hawksquill had corrected the Cosmo-Opticon so that it accurately reflected the state of the real heavens outside it, it was still not quite exact. Even if its maker had been aware of it, there was no way to build into a machine of cogs and gears as gross as this one the slow, the vast fall of the Cosmos backward through the Zodiac, the so-called precession of the equinoxes—that unimaginably stately grand tour which would take some twenty thousand years longer, until once again the spring equinox coincided with the first degrees of Aries: where conventional astrology for convenience's sake assumes it always to be, and

202

where Hawksquill had found it fixed in her Cosmo-Opticon when she had first aquired the thing. No: the only true pictures of time were the changeful heavens themselves, and their perfect reflection within the powerful consciousness of Ariel Hawksquill, who knew what time it was: this engine around her was in the end a crude caricature, though pretty enough. Indeed, she thought, taking the green plush seat in the center of the universe, very pretty.

She relaxed in the warm pour of winter sun (by noon it would be hot as hell inside this glass egg, something else its designer hadn't apparently taken into account) and gazed upwards. Blue Venus trine with blood-orange Jupiter, each blown-glass figured sphere borne between the Tropics on its own band; the mirror-surfaced Moon just declining below the horizon, and tiny ringed Saturn, milky-gray, just rising. Saturn in the ascendant house, proper for the sort of meditation she must now make. Click: the Zodiac turned a degree, lady Libra (looking a little like Bernhardt in her finely-leaded art-nouveau draperies, and weighing something in her scales that had always seemed to Hawksquill to be a bunch of lush Malaga grapes) lifted her toes out of the austral waters. The real Sol burned so hotly through her that her features were obscured. As they of course were in the blank blue sky of day, burned out entirely and invisible, but still of course there behind his brightness, of course, of course. . . . Already she felt her thoughts becoming ordered as the undifferentiated light of heaven was ordered by the colors and marked degrees of the Cosmo-Opticon; she felt her own Theatrum Mundi within open its doors, and the stage manager strike the stage three times with his staff to signal the curtain rising. The enormous engine, star-founded, of her Artificial Memory began to lay out for her once again the parts of the problem of Russell Eigenblick. And she felt, sharp-set for the work, that there had not ever been among all the strange tasks her powers had been bent upon a task as strange as this one, or one which was more important to her herself; or one that would require her to go as far, dive as deep, see as widely, or think as hard.

In the cards. Well. She would see.

> . . . *la que, en volto comenzando humano,*
> *acaba en mortal fiera,*
> *esfinge bachillera,*
> *que hace hoy a Narciso*
> *escos solicitar, desdeñar fuentes . . .*

—*De Gongora*, Soledades

Auberon was awakened first by the crying of a cat.
"An abandoned child," he thought, and went back to sleep. Then the bleating of goats, and the raucous, strangled reveille of a cock. "Damn animals," he said aloud, and was again returning to sleep when he remembered where he was. Had he really heard goats and chickens? No. A dream; or some City noise transformed by sleep. But then cockcrow came again. Pulling the blanket around him (it was deathly cold in the library, the fire long since out) he went to the mullioned window and looked down into the yard. George Mouse was just returning from the milking, in high black rubber boots, carrying steaming milk-pail. From a shed roof a scrawny Rhode Island Red lifted his clipped wings and gave the cry again. Auberon was looking down on Old Law Farm.

Of all George Mouse's fantastic schemes, Old Law Farm had had the virtue of necessity. These dark days, if you wanted fresh eggs, milk, butter, at less than ruinous prices, there was nothing for it but to supply them yourself. And the square of long-empty buildings was uninhabitable anyway, so its outside windows were blinded with tin or blackened plywood, its doors stopped with cinder block, and it became the hollow castle wall around a farm. Chickens now roosted in the degraded interiors, goats laughed and bewailed in

Old Law Farm

204

the garden apartments and ate orts from claw-foot bathtubs. The nude brown vegetable garden which Auberon looked out on from the library windows and which took up much of the old backyards within the block was rimy this morning; orange pumpkins showed beneath the remains of corn and cabbage. Someone, small and dark, was going carefully up and down the wrought-iron fire escapes and in and out of frameless windows. Chickens squawked. She wore a sequined evening gown, and shivered as she collected eggs in a gold lamé purse. She looked disgusted, and when she called out something to George Mouse he only pulled his wide hat down further over his face and galoshed away. She came down into the yard, stepping amid the mud and garden detritus on fragile high heels. She shouted a word after George, flinging up an arm, then tugged her fringed shawl angrily around her shoulders. The lamé purse over her arm just then gave way under its load of eggs, and one by one they began to fall out as though laid. At first she didn't notice, then cried out—"Oh! Oh! Yike!"—and turned to prevent more from falling; turned her ankle as a heel gave way; and burst into laughter. She laughed as the eggs fell through her fingers, laughed bent over, slipped in egg-slime and nearly fell, and laughed harder. She covered her mouth, delicately; but he could hear the laugh—deep and raucous. He laughed too.

He thought then—seeing those eggs break—that he would find out where breakfast was happening. He tugged his wrinkled and spiralled suit into something like its right shape; he screwed his knuckles into his eyes, and ran his hand through his proud hair—an Irish comb, Rudy Flood always called that. But then he had to choose the door, or the window he had come in by. He remembered passing somewhere where food was cooking on his way into the library, and so he took up his bag—didn't want it inspected or stolen—and crept out onto the rickety bridge, shaking his head at the ridiculous crouch he must make. The boards groaned under him and drab light came in through the cracks. Like an impossible passageway in a dream. What if it fell under him, dropping him down the airshaft. And the window at the other end might be locked. God this was stupid. What a *stupid* way to get from one place to another. He tore his jacket on a protruding nail and hunkered furiously back the way he had come.

Out with ruffled dignity and smutty hands through the solid old doors of the library and down the winding stairs. In a statue-niche at a turning a pinch-faced silent-butler in a pillbox hat stood, holding out a corroded ashtray. At the bottom of the stairs, a hole had been knocked in the wall, a brick-toothed rent that led into the next building, perhaps the building George had originally admit-

205

ted him to, or was he disoriented now? He went through the hole, into a building of another kind, not faded elegance but aged poverty. The number of coats of paint these stamped-tin ceilings had had, the layers of linoleum one over another on these floors: it was impressive, almost archaeological. A single dim bulb burned in the hall. There was a door whose many locks were all open, and music coming from within, and laughter and odors of cooking; Auberon approached it, but was overcome by shyness. How did you approach the people of this place? He would have to learn; he who had rarely seen around him a face he hadn't known since babyhood was surrounded now by no one but strangers, millions of them.

But he didn't feel like going in that door just now.

Angry at himself but unable to change his mind, he wandered away down the hall. Daylight showed through the opaque glass imbedded with chicken wire of a door at the hall's end, and he shot its bolt and opened it; he found himself looking out over the farmyard in the middle of the block. In the buildings around it were dozens of doors, each different, each obstructed by a different sort of barrier, rusted gates, chains, wire fencing, bars, locks, or all of those, and yet looking fragile and openable. What was behind them? Some stood wide, and through one he glimpsed goats. There came out from it then a small, a very small man, a bandy-legged black man with enormously strong arms, who carried on his back a great burlap sack. He hurried across the yard at a quick pace despite his short legs (he was no bigger than a child) and Auberon called out to him: "Excuse me!"

He didn't stop. Deaf? Auberon set out after him. Was he naked? Or wearing some coverall the same color as himself? "Hey," Auberon called, and this stopped the man. He turned his big dark flat head to Auberon, and grinned widely; his eyes were mere slits above his broad nose. Boy, the people here get positively medieval, Auberon thought; effects of poverty? He was about to frame a question, sure now the man was idiotic and wouldn't understand, when with a long black sharp-nailed finger the man pointed behind Auberon.

He turned to look. George Mouse had just opened a door there, releasing three cats; he shut it again before Auberon could call him. He started for that door, tripping in the ruts of the garden, and turned back to wave thanks to the little black man, but he was gone.

At the end of the hall to which the door led him he paused, smelling cooking, and listened. Inside he could hear what sounded like an argument, the clash and rattle of pots and dishes, a baby crying. He pushed on the door, and it swung open.

The girl he had seen dropping eggs stood at the stove, still in her golden gown. A child of almost visionary beauty, its face streaked with dirty tears, sat near her on the floor. George Mouse presided at a large circular dining table, beneath which his muddy boots took up a lot of room. "Hey," he said. "Grits, my man. Sleep well?" He rapped with his knuckles at the place next to his. The baby, only momentarily intrigued by Auberon, prepared himself for another round of crying by sputtering tiny bubbles from his angelic lips. He tugged at the girl's gown.

The Bee or the Sea

"Ay, *coño,* man," she said mildly, "take it easy," just as she might have to a grown-up; the kid looked up at her as she looked down, and they seemed to come to an understanding. He didn't cry again. She rapidly stirred a pot with a long wooden spoon, an action she did with her whole body, making her gold-clad bottom snap neatly back and forth. Auberon was watching this closely when George spoke again.

"This is Sylvie, my man. Sylvie, say hello to Auberon Barnable, who's come to the City to seek his fortune."

Her smile was instant and unfeigned, sun bursting from clouds. Auberon bowed stiffly, aware of the blear in his eye and the shadow on his cheek. "You want some breakfast?" she said.

"Sure he does. Sittee downee, cousin."

She turned back to the stove, plucking from the little ceramic auto where they rode one of two top-hatted figures labeled Mr. Salty and Mr. Peppy, and shook him vigorously over the pot. Auberon sat down, and folded his hands in front of him. This kitchen looked out through diamond-paned windows at the farm-yard, where now someone, not the strange man Auberon had seen, was driving the goats amid the decaying vegetation—with a yardstick, Auberon noted. "Do you," he asked his cousin, "have a lot of tenants here?"

"Well, they're not exactly tenants," George said.

"He takes them in," Sylvie said, looking fondly at George. "They got no place else to go. People like me. Because he has a good heart." She laughed, stirring. "Little lost squirrels and stuff."

"I sort of met someone," Auberon said, "a black guy sort of, out in the yard . . . ." He saw that Sylvie had stopped her stirring, and had turned to him. "Very short," Auberon said, surprised at the silence he'd made.

"Brownie," Sylvie said. "That was Brownie. You saw Brownie?"

"I guess," Auberon said. "Who . . ."

"Yeah, old Brownie," George said. "He's kind of private. Like a hermit. Does a lot of work around the place." He looked at Auberon curiously. "I hope you didn't . . ."

"I don't think he understood me. He went off."

"Aw," Sylvie said gently. "Brownie."

"Did you, well, take him in too?" Auberon asked George.

"Hm? Who? Brownie?" George said, having fallen into thought. "Nah, old Brownie's always been here, I guess, who the hell knows. So listen," he said, definitely changing the subject, "what are you up to today? *Negocio?*"

From an inside pocket Auberon took out a card. It said PETTY, SMILODON & RUTH, *Attorneys-at-law,* and gave an address and phone number. "My grandfather's lawyers. I've got to see about this inheritance. Can you tell me how to get there?"

George puzzled over this, reading the address aloud slowly as though it were esoteric. Sylvie, hiking her shawl over her shoulder, brought a battered, steaming pot to the table. "Take the bee or the sea," she said. "Here's your nasties." She banged the pot down. George inhaled the steam gratefully. "She don't eat oatmeal," he said to Auberon, with a wink.

She had turned away, her face, her whole body in fact, showing aversion very graphically, and (changing utterly in an instant) picked up with easy grace the child, who was in the process of sword-swallowing a ball-point pen. "*Que jodiendo!* Look at this implement. C'mere, you, look at these fat cheeks, so cute, don't they make you want to *bite* 'em? Mmmp." She sucked his fat brown cheeks avidly as he struggled to escape, eyes screwed tight. She sat him down in a rickety high-chair whose decals of bear and rabbit were all but worn away, and set food before him. She helped him eat, opening her mouth when he did, closing it around an imaginary spoon, cleaning the excess neatly from his face. Watching her, Auberon caught himself opening his own mouth in assistance. He snapped it shut.

"Hey, sport model," George said to Sylvie as she finished with the baby. "You going to eat or what?"

"*Eat?*" As though he had made an indecent suggestion. "I just *got* here. I'm going to *bed,* man, and I'm going to *sleep.*" She stretched, she yawned, she offered herself wholeheartedly to Morpheus; she scratched her stomach lazily with long painted nails. The gold gown showed a small shadowed hollow where her navel was. Auberon felt that her brown body, however perfect, was too small to contain her; she shot out from it all over in flashes and spikes of intelligence and feeling; even her impersonation now of exhaustion and debility exploded from her like a brilliance.

"The bee or the sea?" he said.

Riding racketing uptown on the B train underground, Auberon—with no experience at all of such things to guide him—tried to puzzle out what relation there might be between George and Sylvie. He was old enough to be her father, and Auberon was young enough to find the possibility of that kind of May-December coupling unlikely and repellent. Yet she had been making breakfast for him. What bed did she go to, when she went to bed? He wished, well, he didn't know quite what he wished, and just then an emergency occurred on the train which threw all that out of his mind. The train began shaking violently to and fro; it screamed as though tormented; it was apparently about to burst apart. Auberon leapt up. Loud metallic knockings beat on his ears, and the lights shuddered and went out. Clutching a cold pole, Auberon waited for the imminent collision or derailment. Then he noticed that no one on the train seemed the least concerned; stony-faced, they read foreign-language newspapers or rocked baby carriages or rooted in shopping bags or chewed gum placidly, my God those asleep didn't even stir. The only thing they seemed to find odd was his own leaping up, and this they only glanced at furtively. But here was the disaster! Outside the almost comically filthy windows he saw another train, on a parallel track, sweeping toward them, whistles and iron shrieks, they were about to sideswipe, the yellow windows (all that was visible) of the other train rushed at them like eyes aghast. At the last possible instant the two trains shifted minutely and resumed their furious parallel, inches from one another's flanks, racing madly. In the other train Auberon could see placid overcoated riders reading foreign newspapers and rooting in shopping bags. He sat down.

An aged black man in ancient clothes, who through all of this had been lightly holding a pole in the middle of the car, was saying as the noise diminished, "Now don't get me wrong—don't get me wrong," holding out a long, gray-palmed hand to the passengers in general, whom, studiously ignoring him, he was reassuring. "Don't get me wrong. A well-dressed woman's sumpm to see, now, y'know, y'know, a thing of beauty's, yunnastan, a joy fevvah; what I'm talkin 'bout's a woman who wears a *fuh*. Now don't get me wrong—" a deprecatory shake of the head to forestall criticism "—but y'see a woman who wears a *fuh* takes on the propensities of that animal. Y'see. Takes on the propensities of the animal of whose *fuh* she wears.

A Wingéd Messenger

Thass right." He struck a casual, raconteur's pose and glanced around
at his hearers with benign intimacy. As he pushed aside his unspeak-
able overcoat to place his knuckles on his hip, Auberon saw the
heavy swing of a bottle in the pocket. "Now I was in Saks Fiff
Avenue thutha day," he said, "and there was ladies pricin' a coat
made from the fuh of the *sable.*" He shook his head to think of it.
"Now, now, of all th'animals in God's creation the *sable* animal has
got to be the lowest. The sable animal, my friends, will eat its own
children. Y'hear what I'm sayin'? Thass right. The sable is the dirt-
iest, low-downest, meanest—the sable is a meaner and a lower thing
than a mink, people, than a *mink,* and surely you know where the
mink is at. Well! And here was these nice ladies, wouldn't hurt a fly,
feelin' up this coat made of the sable animal, yas yas, ain't it fine—"
He laughed, delicately, unable to check his amusement any longer.
"Yas, yas, the propensities of the animal, no doubt about it . . ." His
yellow eyes fell on Auberon, the only one there who'd followed him
with any attention, wondering if he were right. "Mmm-mmm-
mmm," he said, absently, his discourse done, a half-smile on his face;
his eyes, wise, humorous, and reptilian at once, seemed to find
something amusing in Auberon. The train just then turned a shrieking corner, propelling the man forward down the car. He gavotted
away neatly, never falling, though without balance, the bottle-
weighted pocket clanking on the poles. As he passed, Auberon heard
him say "Fans and furred robes hide all." He was brought up by the
train's coming to a halt, began to dance backward; the doors slid
open, and a final lurch of the train tossed him out. Just in time,
Auberon recognized his own stop, and leapt out also.

Clamor and acrid smoke, urgent announcements that
were a garble of static and drowned anyway by the metal roar of trains
and the constant echo and re-echo. Auberon, utterly disoriented,
followed herds of riders upward along stairs, ramps, and escalators,
and found himself still apparently underground. At a turning, he
caught a glimpse of the black man's overcoat; at the next—which
seemed intent on leading him downward again—he was beside him.
He seemed now preoccupied, walking aimlessly; the garrulousness he
had shown in the train was gone. An actor offstage, with troubles of
his own.

"Excuse me," Auberon said, fishing in his pocket. The
black man, with no surprise, held out a hand to receive what Auberon would offer, and with no surprise withdrew the hand when
Auberon came up with only the card of Petty, Smilodon & Ruth.
"Can you help me find this address?" He read it. The black man
looked doubtful.

"A tricky one," he said. "Seems to mean one thing, but it don't. Oh, tricky. Take some findin'." He shuffled off, bent and dreaming, but his hand down at his side motioned with a quick motion that Auberon should follow. "Ever'man I will go with thee," he muttered, "and be thy guide, in thy mose need to be by thy side."

"Thanks," Auberon said, though not quite sure this was meant for him. He grew less sure as the man (whose gait was quicker than it looked, and who gave no warning at turnings) led him through dark tunnels reeking of urine, where rainwater dripped as though in a cave, and along echoing passages, and up into a vast basilica (the old terminal), and further upward by shining stairs into marble halls, he seeming to grow shabbier and smell stronger as they ascended into clean public places.

"Lemme see that again one time," he said as they stood before a rank of swiftly-revolving doors, glass and steel, through which a continual stream of people passed. Auberon and his guide stood directly in their path, the black man unconscious of them as he studied the little card, and the people flowed around them neatly, their faces fixed in angry looks, though whether because of this obstruction or for reasons of their own Auberon couldn't tell.

"Maybe I could ask someone else," Auberon said.

"No," said the black man without rancor. "You got the one. Y'see I'm a messenger." He looked up at Auberon, his snake eyes full of unreadable meaning. "A messenger. Fred Savage is my name, Wingéd Messenger Service, I only am escaped to tell thee." With quick grace he entered the threshing blades of the door. Auberon, hesitating, nearly lost him, threw himself into an empty segment, and was spun out rapidly into a thin cold rain, outdoors at least, and stepped rapidly to catch up with Fred Savage. "My man Duke, y'know," he was saying, "met the Duke 'bout midnight in a lane behind of the churchyard, with the leg of a man over his shoulder. I says hey, Duke, my man. Said he was a *woof*—only difference was, a woof is hairy on the outside, y'see, and he was hairy on the inside—said I could rip up his skin and try . . ."

Auberon dodged after him through the well-drilled march and press of people, doubly afraid of losing him now since Fred Savage hadn't given back the lawyers' card. But still he was distracted, his eye drawn upward to heights of buildings, some lost in the rainy clouds, so chaste and noble at the tops and, at their bases, so ignoble, stuffed with shops, lettered, scarred, imposed upon, overlaid like mammoth oaks on which generations have carved hearts and nailed horseshoes. He felt a tug at his sleeve.

"Don't be gawking upward," Fred Savage said, amused.

"Good way to get your pocket picked. Besides"—his grin was wide, either his teeth were extraordinarily perfect or these were dentures of the cheapest kind—"they're not for *lookin' up at* anyway by the likes of you, y'know, no, they're for *lookin' out of* by the type of folks inside, yunnastan. You'll learn that, heehee." He drew Auberon with him around a corner and along a street where trucks contested with one another and with taxis and people. "Now if you look close," Fred Savage said, "you see this ad-dress seems to be on the avenue, but thass a fake. It's on thisere street, though they don't want you to guess it."

Cries and warnings from above. Out of a second-story window, an enormous ormolu mirror was being extruded, hung on guy-ropes and tackle. On the street below were desks, chairs, filing cabinets, an office in the street, people had to step out into the loathsome gutter to get around it; only just then trucks clogged the street, the warnings increased—"Watcha back, watcha back!"—and no one could move. The mirror swung free out into the air, its face which had before reflected only quiet interiors now filled with shuddering, madly-swinging City. It looked ravished, aghast. It descended slowly, rotating, flinging buildings and backward-reading signs to and fro within it. The people stood gaping, waiting for their own selves, overcoated and umbrella'd, to be revealed.

"C'mon," Fred said, and took Auberon's hand in a strong grip. He dodged amid the furniture, drawing Auberon after him. Shouts of horror and anger from the mirror's attendants. Something was wrong: the ropes suddenly paid out, the mirror tilted madly only feet above the street, a groan from the watchers, worlds came and went as it righted itself. Fred shuffled beneath it, his hat-crown grazing its gilding. There was the briefest moment when Auberon, though looking into the street behind him, felt himself to be looking into the street ahead, a street from which or into which Fred Savage had disappeared. The he crouched and passed under.

On the other side, still followed by the curses of the mirror men, and by some kind of thunder as well from somewhere, Fred led Auberon up the vast arched entrance to a building. "Be prepared is my motto," he said, pleased with himself, "be sure you're right then go ahead." He pointed out the number of the building, which was indeed an avenue number, and handed back the little card; he patted Auberon's back to encourage him in.

"Hey, thanks," Auberon said, and, bethinking himself, dug in his pocket, and came up with a crumpled dollar.

"The service is free," Fred Savage said, but took the dollar anyway delicately in thumb and index. There was a rich history incised in his palm. "Now go ahead. Be sure you're right, then go ahead." He propelled Auberon toward the brass-bound glass doors. As he entered, Auberon heard the thunder, or felt the bombblast, or whatever it was, again, only much huger; it made him duck, a long tearing roll as though the world, starting at one corner, were being bisected. As it rolled away, there came a gasp, a groan from many throats together, with high-shrieking feminine overtones; and Auberon braced himself against the unmistakable noise of an enormous, a great glass smashing—unmistakable though Auberon had never before heard a piece that size shivered.

Now how many years' bad luck is that for someone, he thought, wondering if he had escaped something.

"I'm putting you in the folding bedroom," George said as he led Auberon by flashlight through the mostly empty warren of buildings that surrounded Old Law Farm. "It's got a fireplace at least. Watch that stuff there. Up we go."

A Folding Bedroom

Auberon followed, shivering, carrying his bag and a bottle of Doña Mariposa rum. A sleety rain had caught him on his way downtown, slicing cleanly through his overcoat and, so it felt, through his skinny flesh as well to chill his heart. He had hidden from it for a while in a little liquor store whose red sign—LIQUOR—went on and off in the puddles outside the door. Feeling intensely the shopkeeper's impatience at his free use of a place of business for profitless shelter, Auberon had begun staring at the various bottles, and at last bought the rum because the girl on its label, in a peasant blouse, arms full of green cane-stalks, reminded him of Sylvie; or rather seemed to him what Sylvie would look like if she were imaginary.

George took out his bunch of keys and began hunting through them abstractedly. His manner since Auberon had returned had been glum, distracted, unaccommodating. He talked ramblingly about the difficulties of life. Auberon had questions to ask him, but felt he would get no answers to them from George in this state of mind, so he only followed silently.

The folding bedroom was double-locked, and George was some time opening it. There was electric light inside though, a lamp that on its cylindrical shade carried a panorama, a country scene through which a train moved, its locomotive almost devouring its caboose, like the Worm. George looked around the room, finger to

213

his lips, as though long ago he had lost something here. "Now the thing is," he said, and then nothing more. He gazed at the spines of a shelf of paperbacks. The locomotive on the lampshade began to travel slowly through the landscape, caused to move by the heat of the bulb. "See, we all pull together here," George said. "Everybody does his part. You can dig that. I mean the work's never done and all. So. This is all right, I guess. That john's the closet, the other way around I mean. The stove and stuff is off, but eat with us, everybody chips in. Well. Listen." He counted his keys again, and Auberon had the feeling he was about to be locked in; but George slipped three from the ring and gave them to him. "Don't for God's sake lose them." He managed a bleak smile. "Hey, welcome to Big-town, man, and don't take any wooden nickels."

Wooden nickels? It seemed to Auberon as he closed the door that his cousin's speech was as full of antique rubbish and battered ornament as his Farm. A card, maybe he'd call himself. Well: a peculiarity felt more than perceived about this folding bedroom became clear to him as he looked around: there was no bed in it. There was a wine-red velvet boudoir chair, and a creaky wicker one with pillows tied on; there was a shabby rug, and an enormous wardrobe or something of glossy wood, with a bevelled looking-glass on its front and drawers with brass pulls at the bottom; this he couldn't figure out how to open. But there was no bed. From a wooden apricot crate (Golden Dreams) he took wood and paper and made a fire with trembling fingers, contemplating a night on the chairs; for sure he wasn't going to try threading his way back through Old Law Farm to complain.

When the fire was hot he began to feel somewhat less sorry for himself; in fact as his clothes dried he felt almost an elation. Kind Mr. Petty of Petty, Smilodon & Ruth had been oddly evasive about the status of his inheritance, but they had willingly advanced him a sum against it. He had it in his pocket. He had come to the City and not died or been beaten; he had money, and the prospect of more; real life was beginning. The long, long ambiguity of Edgewood, the stifling sense of mysteries continually propounded, never solved, the endless waiting for purposes to be made clear and directions pointed out—all over. He had taken charge. A free agent, he would make a million, win love, and never go home at bedtime any more. He went to the tiny kitchen attached to the folding bedroom, where the dead stove and a lumpish refrigerator presumably also dead shared the floor with a tub and a sink; he dug up a white coffee mug all crazed, wiped the husk of a bug from it, and got out his bottle of Doña Mariposa rum.

He was holding a mugful of this in his lap, looking into the fire with a grin on his face, when there came a knocking at the door.

It took him a moment to see that the dark shy girl at his door was the same he had seen breaking eggs in a golden gown. Dressed now in jeans faded and soft as homespun, and clutching herself so tightly against the cold that her multiform earrings shook, she looked far less large; that is, she was just as small, but she had hidden the energy that had made her seem so large before under the bushel of her compact shape.

Sylvie
and Destiny

"Sylvie," he said.

"Yah." She looked away down the dark hall, and then back at him, in some kind of hurry, or in some annoyance, or something; what? "I didn't know anybody was in here. I thought it was empty."

He so obviously filled the doorway that there was no answer he could make to this.

"Okay," she said. She allowed one cold hand out from where it hid in her armpit, so it could press her lip against her teeth to be bitten, and glanced away again, as though he were compelling her to stay here and she were impatient to get away.

"Did you leave something here?" She didn't respond. "How's your son?" At this the hand that had been pressing her lip covered her mouth altogether, and she seemed to weep, or laugh, or both, still looking away though it was obvious she had no place to go; at last he saw that. "Come in," he said, and motioned her in, stepping aside so she could enter and nodding encouragement.

"Sometimes I come here," she said as she came in, "when I want to be, you know, alone." She looked around her with what Auberon supposed was a justified air of grievance. He was the intruder. He wondered if he should yield it to her, and go sleep in the street. Instead he said: "Would you like some rum?"

She appeared not to hear. "So listen," she said, and then nothing more. It would be some time before Auberon realized that these words were often as not a mere vocable in City speech, and not intended to roughly command his attention, as they seemed. He listened. She sat on the little velvet chair and said at last, as though to herself, "It's cozy here."

"Mm."

"Nice fire. What are you drinking?"

"Rum. Would you like some?"

215

"Sure."

There was, it appeared, only the one cup, so she and he passed it back and forth between them. "He's not my son," Sylvie said.

"I'm sorry if I . . ."

"He's my brother's kid. I got a crazy brother. Named Bruno. Like the kid." She pondered, staring into the fire. "What a kid. So sweet. And smart. And *bad?*" She smiled. "Just like his *papo.*" She gripped herself more tightly, drawing her knees up almost to her breasts, and he could see she wept inwardly, and only by this constant pressure against herself kept it from spilling out.

"You and he seemed to get along well," Auberon said, nodding in what he realized was an absurdly solemn fashion. "I thought you were his mother."

"Oh, his mother, man," with a look of pure disdain touched only faintly with pity, "she's sad. She's a sad case. Pitiful." She brooded. "The way they treat him, man. He's going to turn out just like his father."

This was apparently not a good thing. Auberon wished he could think of a question that would draw the whole story from her. "Well, sons do turn out like their fathers," he said, wondering if it would ever seem true of him. "After all, they're around them a lot."

She snorted in disgust. "Shit, Bruno hasn't seen this kid in a year. Now he shows up and says, 'Hey, my son,' and all this. Just because he got religion."

"Hm."

"Not religion. But this guy he works for. Or follows. Russell—what is it, I don't know—I go blank. Anyway, he says, love, family, blahblahblah. So here he is on the doorstep."

"Hm."

"They'll kill that kid." Tears did gather in her eyes, but she blinked them away, none fell. "Damn George Mouse. How could he be so dumb?"

"What did he do?"

"He says he was drunk. Had a knife."

"Oh." There being no reflexive in the language Sylvie had to speak here, Auberon was soon lost among the "he"s and had no idea who had a knife or who said who was drunk. He would have to hear the story twice more in the next days before he sorted out that brother Bruno had come drunk to Old Law Farm and, under the press of his new faith or philosophy, demanded nephew Bruno from George Mouse, who in Sylvie's absence and after a prolonged debate which had threatened to turn violent, had yielded him up. And that nephew Bruno was now in the hands of bedeviling and loving and deeply stupid female relatives (brother Bruno wouldn't stay, she was sure of that) who would raise him just as her brother had been raised after *his* father's desertion, to vanity, and wildness, a touchy ungovernability and a sweet selfishness no woman could resist, and few men for that matter; and that (even if the child avoided being put in a Home) Sylvie's plan to rescue him had failed: George had forbidden the Farm to her relatives, he had enough troubles.

"So I can't live with him any more," she said—George this time, doubtless.

A strange hope rose in Auberon.

"I mean it's not *his* fault," she said. "Not his *fault,* really. I just couldn't any more. I'd always think of it. And anyway." She pressed her temples, pressing in the thing there. "Shit. If I had the nerve to tell them off. All of them." Her grief and bedevilment were reaching a climax. "I never want to see them again myself. *Never. Never never.*" She almost laughed. "And that's really stupid, 'cause if I leave here I got no place else to go. No place else."

She wouldn't weep. She hadn't, and the moment was past now; now blank despair was in her face as she looked into the fire, both cheeks in her hands.

Auberon clasped his hands behind him, studied an offhand, neighborly tone, and said, "Well of course you can stay *here,* you're welcome to," and realized he was offering her a place which was much more hers than his, and flushed. "I mean of *course* you can stay here, if you don't mind my staying too."

She looked at him, warily he thought, which was proper considering a certain bass obbligato in his feelings just then which he was in fact trying to conceal. "Really?" she said. She smiled. "I wouldn't take up much room."

"Well, there's not much room to take up." Become host, he looked the place over thoughtfully. "I don't know how we'd arrange it, but there's the chair, and, well, there's my overcoat almost dry, you could use that for a blanket. . . ." He saw that he himself, curled up in a corner, would probably not sleep at all. Now, though, her face had closed somewhat at these cheerless arrangements. He couldn't think what else to yield up to her.

"I couldn't," she said, "have just a corner of the bed? Like down at the foot? I'll curl up real small."

"Bed?"

"The bed!" she said, growing impatient.

217

"What bed?"

Suddenly getting it, she laughed aloud. "Oh wow," she said, "oh no, you were going to sleep on the *flaw*—I don't *believe* it!" She went to the massy wardrobe or highboy which stood against one wall, and, reaching up along its hidden side, she turned a knob or pulled a lever, and enormously pleased, let down the whole tall front of the thing. Counterweighted (the dummy drawers held lead weights), it swung gently, dreamily down; the mirror reflected floor, and then was gone; brass knobs at each upper corner extruded themselves, slipping out as the front came down, and became legs, locking in place by a gravity-worked mechanism whose ingenuity he would later marvel at. It was a bed. It had a carved headboard; the top of it, as wardrobe, had become the footboard, as bed; it had a mattress, bedclothes, and two plump pillows.

He laughed with her. Displayed, the bed took up most the room. The folding bed room.

"Isn't it great?" she said.

"Great."

"Room enough for two, isn't there?"

"Oh sure. In fact. . . ." He was about to offer the whole of it to her; that was only right, and he would instantly have done so in the first place if he'd known it to be hidden there. But he saw that she assumed he was ungentlemanly enough to assume that she would be grateful for half, and assumed that he assumed that she . . . A sudden cunning shut his mouth.

"You're sure you don't mind?" she asked.

"Oh no. If you're sure *you* don't mind."

"Nah. I've always slept with people. My granny and I slept together for years, usually with my sister too." She sat on the bed—it was so plumply high she had to hoist herself up with her hands, and her feet didn't reach the floor from it—and smiled at him, and he smiled back. "So," she said.

The room transformed was the rest of his life transformed, everything not already metamorphosed by the departure and the bus and the City and the lawyers and the rain. Nothing now would ever be the same again. He realized he had been staring wildly at her, and that she had lowered her eyes. "Well," he said, holding up the cup, "how about a little more of this?"

"Okay." While he was pouring it, she said, "So how come you came to the City, by the way?"

"To seek my fortune."

"Huh?"

"Well, I want to be a writer." Rum and intimacy made it

easy to say. "I'm going to look for a job writing. Something. Maybe television."

"Hey, great. Big bucks."

"Mm."

"You could write, like, 'A World Elsewhere'?"

"What's that?"

"You know. The show."

He didn't. An absurdity in his ambitions became clear to him when they bounced back, as it were, from Sylvie, instead of (as they always had before) paying out endlessly into futurity. "Actually, we never had a television set," he said.

"Really? Well, I'll be." She sipped the rum he gave her. "Couldn't afford one? George told me you guys were real rich. Oops."

"Well, 'rich'. I don't know about 'rich' . . . ." Well! *There* was an inflection like Smoky's, which Auberon heard for the first time in his own voice—that putting of imaginary doubt-quotes around a word. Was he growing old? "We could have bought a TV, certainly. . . . What's this show like?"

" 'A World Elsewhere'? It's a daytime drama."

"Oh."

"The endless kind. You just get over one problem and another starts. Mostly dumb. But you get hooked." She had begun to tremble again, and drew her feet up on the bed; she pulled down the quilt and wrapped it around her legs. Auberon busied himself with the fire. "There's a girl on it who reminds me of me." She said it with a self-deprecating laugh. "Boy has *she* got problems. She's supposed to be Italian, but she's played by a P.R. *And* she's beautiful." She said this as though she said She has one leg, and is like me in that. "And she has a Destiny. She knows it. All these terrible problems, but she has a Destiny, and sometimes they show her just looking out misty-eyed while these voices sing in the background—aa-aa-*aaah*—and you know she's thinking of her Destiny."

"Hm." All the wood in the woodbox was scrap, most of it parts of furniture, though there were pieces that bore lettering too. The varnish on fluted and turned wood sizzled and blistered. Auberon felt an exhilaration: he was part of a community of strangers, burning unbeknown to them their furniture and belongings, just as they not knowing him took his money at change-booths and made room for him on buses. "A Destiny, huh."

"Yah." She looked at the locomotive on the lampshade, turning through its little landscape. "I have a Destiny," she said.

"You do?"

219

"Yah." She said this syllable in a way and with an attitude of face and arms that meant Yes, it's true, and a long story, and while possibly to my credit is something I have nothing to do with, and is even a little embarrassing, like a halo. She studied a silver ring on her finger.

"How does somebody know," he asked, "that they have a Destiny?" The bed was so large that to sit in the little velvet chair at its foot would place him absurdly low; so—gingerly—he got up on the bed beside her. She made room. They took up opposite corners, resting in the wings which protruded from the headboard.

"An *espiritista* read mine," Sylvie said. "A long time ago."

"A who?"

"An *espiritista*. A lady with powers. You know. Reads cards, and does stuff with stuff from the *botanica*; a *bruja* sort of, you know?"

"Oh."

"This one was sort of an aunt of mine, well not really mine, I forget whose aunt she was; we called her Titi, but everybody called her La Negra. She scared the shit out of me. Her apartment, way uptown, always had candles lit on these little altars, and the curtains drawn, and these crazy smells; and out on the fire escape she kept a couple of chickens, man, I don't know what she did with those chickens and I don't *want* to know. She was big—not fat, but with these long strong gorilla arms and a little head, and *black*. Sort of blue-black, you know? She couldn't have really been in my family. So when I was a little kid I got malnutritioned real bad—wouldn't eat—Mami couldn't make me—I got so skinny, like this—" she held up a red-nailed pinkie. "The doctor said I was supposed to eat liver. Liver! Can you imagine? Anyway, Granny decided that somebody was maybe doing a number on me, you know? *Brujeria*. From a distance." She waggled her fingers like a stage hypnotist. "Like revenge or something. Mami was living with somebody else's husband then. So maybe his wife had got an *espiritista* to do revenge on her by making *me* sick. Anyway, anyway . . ." She touched his arm lightly, because he had looked away. In fact she touched his arm every time he looked away, which had begun somewhat to annoy him, his attention couldn't have been more riveted; he thought this must be a bad habit of hers, until much later he saw that the men who played dominoes on the street and the women who watched children and gossiped on stoops did it too: a racial, not a personal habit, maintain the contact. "Anyway. She took me to La Negra to get it wiped out or whatever. Man I was never so scared in *my life*. She started pressing me and feeling me up with these big black hands, and sort of

groaning or singing, and talking this stuff, and her eyeballs rolled
back in her head and her eyelids fluttered—creepy. Then she dashes
over to this little burner and throws some stuff on it, powder or
something, and this real strong perfume comes out, and she rushes
back—sort of dances—and feels me some more. She did some other
stuff too that I forget. Then she drops all that, and gets real regular,
like, you know, a day's work, all done, like at the dentist; and she
told Granny, no, nobody had a spell on me, I was just skinny and
ought to eat more. Granny was so relieved. So—" again the brief
wrist-touch, he had stared into the mug for a moment "—so they're
sitting around drinking coffee and Granny's paying, and La Negra
just kept looking at me. Just *looking*. Man I was *freaking out*. What's
she looking at? She could see right through you, she could see your
heart. Your heart of hearts. Then she goes like this—" Sylvie
motioned with a slow large black *bruja* hand for the child to come
close "—and starts talking to me, real slow, about what dreams I had,
and other stuff I forget; and it's like she was thinking real hard. Then
she gets out this deck of cards, real old and worn out; and she puts my
hand on them and her hand over mine; and her eyes roll up again,
and she's like in a trance." Sylvie took the cup from Auberon, who'd
been gripping it, in a trance himself. "Oh," she said. "No more?"

"Lots more." He went to get some.

"So listen, listen. She lays out these cards—thanks—"
She sipped, her eyes rising, looking for a moment like the child she
was telling of. "And she starts reading them for me. That was when
she saw my Destiny."

"And what was it?" He sat again beside her on the bed.
"A big one."

"The biggest," she said, mimicking a confidential, hot-
news tone. "The very biggest." She laughed. "She couldn't believe
it. This skinny, malnutritioned kid in a homemade dress. This big
Destiny. She stared and stared. She stared at the cards, she stared at
me. My eyes got big, and I thought I was going to cry, and Granny's
praying, and La Negra's making noises, and I just wanted *out*. . . ."

"But what," Auberon said, "was the Destiny? Exactly."

"Well, *exactly* she didn't know." She laughed, the whole
thing had become silly. "That's the only trouble. She said a Destiny,
and a biggie. But not what. A movie stah. A queen. Queen of the
World, man. Anything." As quickly as she had laughed, she grew
thoughtful. "It sure ain't come true yet," she said. "I used to picture
it, though. Like in the future, coming true. I had this picture. There
was this table, in the woods? Like a long banquet table. With a white
cloth. And all these goodies on it. End to end, heaped up. But in the

221

woods. Trees and stuff around. And there was an empty place at the middle of the table."

"And?"

"That's all. I just saw it. I thought about it." She glanced over at him. "I bet you never knew anybody who had any big Destiny before," she said, grinning.

He didn't want to say that he had hardly known anyone who didn't. Destiny had been like a shameful secret shared among all of them at Edgewood, which none of them would exactly admit to except in the most veiled terms and only at great need. He had fled his. He had outrun it, he was sure, like the geese outrunning Brother North-wind on strong wings: it couldn't freeze him here. If he wanted a Destiny now, it would be one of his own choosing. He'd like, for instance, for a single simple instance, to have Sylvie's: to be Sylvie's. "Is it fun?" he asked. "Having a Destiny?"

"Not much," she said. She had begun to clutch herself again, though the fire had heated the little room well. "When I was a kid, they all made fun of me for it. Except Granny. But she couldn't resist going around telling everybody about it. And La Negra told. And I was still just a bad skinny kid who didn't do shit that was wonderful." She wiggled within the bedclothes, embarrassed, and turned the silver ring on her finger. "Sylvie's big Destiny. There was a lot of jokes. Once—" she looked away "—once this real old Gypsy guy came around. Mami didn't want to let him in, but he said he'd come all the way from Brooklyn to see me. So he comes in. All bent and sweaty, and real fat. And talking this funny Spanish. And they dragged me out, and showed me off. I was eating a chicken wing. And he stared at me a while with these big goggle eyes and his mouth open. Then—oh, man, it was weird—he got down on his knees—it took him a long time, you know?—and he says: Remember me when you come into your kingdom. And he gave me this." She held up her hand (the palm lined minutely and clearly) and turned it to show the silver ring, back and front. "Then we all had to help him stand up."

"And then?"

"He went back to Brooklyn." She paused, remembering him. "Man I didn't like him." She laughed. "As he was leaving, I put the chicken wing in his pocket. He didn't see. In his coat pocket. In exchange for the ring."

"A wing for a ring."

"Yeah." She laughed, but soon ceased. She seemed restless and plagued again. Changeful: as though her weather blew faster, fair to foul to fair again, than most people's did. "So big deal," she said. "Forget it." She drank, quickly and deeply, and then exhaled rapidly and waved her hand before her open mouth to cool the rum-flames. She gave him the cup and dug more deeply into the bedclothes. "What has it ever got me. I can't even take care of myself. Much less anybody else." Her voice had grown faint; she turned away, and seemed to be trying to disappear; then she rolled back, and yawned hugely. He could see her mouth's interior: her arched tongue, even her uvula. Not the pale rosebud color of white people's interior parts, but a richer color, tinged with coral. He wondered . . . "That kid was probably lucky," she said when she was done. "To get away from me."

"I can't believe that," he said. "You got along so well."

She answered nothing, only stared at her thoughts. "I wish," she said, but then no more. He wished he could think of something to offer her. Besides everything. "Well," he said, "you can stay here as long as you want. As long as you want."

Suddenly she flung off the covers and scrambled across the bed, getting away, and he had a wild impulse to grab her, restrain her. "*Pípí,*" she said. She climbed over his legs, and down to the floor, and pulled open the door of the closet (it opened only wide enough to admit her before striking the edge of the bed) and turned on a light within.

He heard her unzip. "Wow! That seat is *cold!*" There was a pause, and then the hollow hiss of number one. She said when she was done: "You're a nice guy, you know that?" And any answer he might have made to that (he had none to make) was drowned in the roar of waters as she pulled the chain.

Preparing for their mutual bed was a lot of laughs (he made a joke about sleeping with a naked sword between them that she thought hilarious, never having heard of the thing before) but when the locomotive was stilled and darkness around them, he heard her weep, softly, smothering her tears, far away on her allotted side of the bed.

Gate of Horn

He supposed that really neither of them would sleep; but after long search, on this side and then that, after crying out (Ah! Ah!) softly several times as though frightened by her thoughts, Sylvie did find a pathway to the gate of horn; the tears were dry on her black lashes; she was asleep. In her struggle she had wound the bedclothes tortuously around herself, and he didn't dare extract much (not knowing that once passed to the other side she was as

223

good as dead for hours). For sleeping she wore a T-shirt, intended as a souvenir for tourists' children, which showed garish and inaccurate pictures of four or five big City attractions, nothing but this and a pair of panties, patches of black silk on an elastic and no bigger than a blindfold. He lay awake next to her for a long time while her breathing grew regular. He slept briefly, and dreamed that her child's shirt, and her great grief, and the bedclothes twisted protectively around her brown limbs, and the deliberate high sexiness of her nearly nonexistent underwear, were a rebus. He laughed, dreaming, to see the simple puns contained in these items, and the surprising but obvious answer, and his own laugh awoke him.

With the stealth of one of Daily Alice's cats trying to find the warmth and not disturb the sleeper, his arm worked its way under the blankets and over her. For a long time he lay that way, still and wary. He half-dreamt again, this time that his arm, through contact with her, was turning slowly to gold. He woke, and found it asleep, heavy and dead. He withdrew it; it sprouted pins and needles; he caressed it, forgetting why it and not the other should appear in his mind as valuable; slept again. Woke again. She had grown greatly heavy beside him, seemed to weight her side of the bed like a treasure, the richer for its compactness, and richer still for being all unconscious of itself.

When at last he slept for real, though, it was of nothing in Old Law Farm that he dreamt, but of his earliest childhood, of Edgewood and of Lilac.

III

One thought, one grace, one wonder at the least
Which unto words no virtue can digest
     —Marlowe, Tamburlaine

The house Auberon grew up in wasn't quite the same house his mother had grown up in. As Smoky and Daily Alice had come into possession, the natural directors of a household composed of their children and Alice's parents, the reins of an old orderliness were loosened. Daily Alice liked cats, as her mother hadn't, and as Auberon grew up the number of cats in the house grew by geometrical progression. They lay in heaps before the fireplaces, their airborne down coated the furniture and the rugs as though with a dry and permanent hoarfrost, their self-possessed small demon faces looked out at Auberon from the oddest places. There was a calico tiger whose striped pelt made fierce false eyebrows above her eyes, two blacks or three, a white with discrete and complex black patches, like a melting chessboard. On cold nights Auberon would awake oppressed, toss within his bedclothes, and displace two or three compact dense bodies out of a deep enjoyment.

   Besides cats, there was the dog Spark. He was descended from a long line of dogs who all looked (so Smoky said) like natural sons of Buster Keaton: light patches above Spark's eyes gave him the same faintly reproachful, enormously alert, long-nosed face. Spark when fabulously aged impregnated a visiting cousin and fathered three anonymous dogs and another Spark; his lineage assured, he curled up in Doc's favorite chair before the fire for the rest of his life.

   Lilacs and Fireflies

   It wasn't only the animals (and Doc expressed himself clearly enough without ever speaking about his dislike for pets) that pushed Doc and Mom aside. It was as though, while losing no dignity or place, they were being silently sailed into the past on a quick and heaping tide of toys, cookie crumbs, birds' nests, diapers, Band-aids and bunk beds. Mom, since her daughter was a mom too, became Mom Drinkwater, then Mom D., then Momdy, which she couldn't help feeling was an uncomfortable kind of kicking-upstairs for one who had always served hard and well below. And Somehow over the years the many clocks in the house began to chime unsynchronized, though Doc, usually with one or two children around his knees, used to set them and wind them and peer at their mechanisms often.

The house itself aged, gracefully on the whole and still sound at heart, but sagging here and loosening there; its mainte-nance was a huge job and never done. At its perimeters, rooms had to be closed off: a tower, an extravagance, a glass orangery whose barley-sugar panes lay scattered amid the flower-pots, fallen square by diamond out of the icing of white wrought iron into which John Drinkwater had puttied them. Of the many gardens and flowerbeds around the place, the kitchen-garden's was the slowest downfall and the longest decadence. Though whitewash flaked from the pretty cutout porch and the grape-leaves strangled up the ogee arches, though the steps sagged and the flagstone path disappeared under dock and dandelion muscling up through its crevices, still for as long as she was able Great-aunt Cloud tended the flowerbeds and they brought forth blossoms. Three crabapple trees had grown up at the garden's end, grown old and hale and gnarled; every autumn they scattered their hard fruit on the ground to inebriate the wasps as it rotted. Momdy made jelly of a fraction of it. Later on, when he became a collector of words, the word "crabbed" would bring to Auberon's mind those puckered orange apples withering in their useless sourness amid the weeds.

Auberon grew up in the kitchen-garden. When at last the spring came when Cloud decided that trying to keep up the garden, her back and legs being as they were, and failing would be more painful than letting it go altogether, then Auberon liked it better: now the flower beds weren't forbidden him. And as it was aban-doned, the garden and its buildings took on some of the attractions of a ruin: the tools in the earth-smelling potting shed were dusty and remote, and spiders spun webs across the openings of watering cans, giving them the fabulous antiquity of casques in a buried hoard. The pump house had always had for him this quality of the remote, the barbaric, with its useless tiny windows and peaked roof and miniature eaves and cornices. It was a heathen shrine, and the iron pump was the long-crested, great-tongued idol. He would stand on tiptoe to raise the pump-handle, raise it and lower it with all his strength while the idol choked hoarsely, until there came a catch in its throat as the handle met some mysterious resistance, and he must pull himself almost off his feet to draw it down, and again, and then with a magical sudden ease and release the water would sluice down the pump's broad tongue and splash in a continuous smooth clear sheet onto the worn stones.

The garden was huge then to him. Seen from the vast, slightly undulating deck of the porch it went on great as a seascape to the crabapples and then broke in a high surf of overgrown flowers and indomitable weed against the stone wall and the X-gate forever shut in it which led into the Park. It was a sea and a jungle. He alone knew what had become of the flagstone path, because he could go on all fours beneath the overarching leaves where it ran secretly, its stones as cool and gray and smooth as water.

At evening there were fireflies. He was always surprised by them, how one moment there seemed to be none, and then, when evening turned blue and he looked up from some absorbing thing— the making inch by inch of a molehill maybe—they would be alight in the velvet darkness. There was an evening when he decided to sit on the porch as day turned to night, sit and watch only and nothing else, and catch the first one to light itself, and the next and the next: for the sake of some completeness he hankered after—would always hanker after.

The porch steps were that summer just throne height to him, and so he sat, sneakered feet planted firmly, not so rigidly attentive that he didn't look up at the phoebe's nest modeled neatly in the porch rafters, or at the silver pen-stroke of an unseen jet's smoke; he even sang, without a tune, the words a meaningless onomatopoeia of the fading twilight. All the while he kept watch; yet in the end it was Lilac who saw the first firefly.

"There," she said, in her little gravelly voice; and off amid the jungle of the ferns the light did go on, as though created by her pointing finger. When the next lit, she pointed with a toe.

Lilac wore no shoes, she never did, not even in winter, only a pale blue dress without sleeves or a belt that came midway down her satiny thighs. When he told his mother so, she asked didn't Lilac ever get cold, and he couldn't answer; apparently not, she never shivered, it was as though with the blue dress on she was complete, whole, needed no further protection; her dress, unlike his flannel shirts, was part of her, and not put on to cover or disguise.

The whole nation of the fireflies was coming into being. Whenever Lilac pointed and said "there" another one, or many, lit their pale candles, whitey-green like the phosphorescent tip of the light pull in his mother's closet. When they were all present, the only clarity in a garden grown vague and colorless and massy, Lilac circled her finger in the air and the fireflies began to gather, slowly, by jumps, as though reluctant, in the middle of the air where Lilac pointed; and when they had gathered they began to wheel there, at the direction of Lilac's finger, a twinkling circle, a solemn pavane. He could almost hear the music.

"Lilac made the fireflies dance," he told his mother when at length he came in from the garden. He circled his finger in the air as Lilac had and made a hum.

"Dance?" His mother said. "Don't you think it's time for you to go to bed?"

"Lilac stays up," he said, not comparing himself to her— there were no rules for her—but only associating himself with her: even though he had to go to bed, wrongly, when blue light still suffused the sky and not all the birds were yet asleep, still he knew someone who did not; who would sit up in the garden deep into the night as he lay dreaming, or walk in the Park and see the bats, and never sleep at all if she so chose.

"Ask Sophie to turn on your bath," his mother said. "Tell her I'll be up in a minute."

He stood looking up at her a moment, considering whether to protest. Bathing was another thing Lilac never did, though often she sat on the edge of the tub, studying him, aloof and immaculate. His father rattled his paper and made a noise in his throat, and Auberon went out of the kitchen, a good little soldier.

Smoky put down his paper. Daily Alice had fallen silent at the sink, the dishclout in her hand, her eyes elsewhere.

"A lot of kids have imaginary friends," Smoky said. "Or brothers or sisters."

"Lilac," Alice said. She sighed and picked up a cup; she looked at the tea leaves in it as though to divine from them.

That's a Secret

Sophie allowed him a duck. It was often easier to earn such favors from her, not because she was necessarily more kindly but because she was less alert than his mother, and seemed not always to be paying much attention. When he was neck-deep in the Gothic bathtub (large enough almost for him to swim in) she unwrapped a duck from its tissue. He could see that there were five still left in the compartmented box.

The ducks were made of Castile soap, Cloud said who had

bought them for him, and that's why they float. Castile soap, she said, is very pure, and doesn't sting your eyes. The ducks were neatly carved, of a pale lemon yellow which did seem very pure to him, and of a smoothness that inspired a nameless emotion in him, something between reverence and deep sensual pleasure.

"Time to start washing," Sophie said. He set the duck afloat, brooding on an unrealizable dream: to set all the pale yellow ducks afloat at once, without regard, flotilla of supernal smooth carven purity. "Lilac made the fireflies dance," he said.

"Oh? Wash behind your ears."

Why, he wondered or rather did not quite wonder, was he always told to *do* something or other whenever he mentioned Lilac? Once his mother had suggested to him that it might be better not to say too much about Lilac to Sophie, because it might make her feel bad; but he thought it enough if he was careful to make the distinction: "Not *your* Lilac."

"No."

"*Your* Lilac is gone."

"Yes."

"Before I was born."

"That's right."

Lilac, sitting on the episcopal toilet seat, only looked from one to the other, seemingly unmoved, as though none of this concerned her. There was a host of questions Auberon had about the two Lilacs—or was it three?—and every time Sophie's came to his mind a new question budded on the complex bush. But he knew there were secrets he would not be told: only as he grew older would he come to resent that.

"Betsy Bird's getting married," he said. "*Again.*"

"How do you know that?"

"Tacey said so. Lily said she's going to marry Jerry Thorne. Lucy said she's going to have a baby. *Already.*" He mimicked the intrigued, faintly censorious tone his sisters took.

"Well. First I've heard of it," Sophie said. "Out you come."

With reluctance he abandoned the duck. Already its sharply-incised features had begun to soften; in future baths it would grow eyeless, then featureless; its broad beak would dwindle to a sparrow's, then gone; then headless (he would be careful not to break its increasingly skinny neck, not wanting to interfere in its dissolution); at last shapeless, not a duck any more, a duck's heart only, still pure, still floating.

She toweled him roughly, yawning. Her bedtime was

often as not before his. Unlike his mother, she usually left wet spots, on the backs of his arms, his ankles. "Why don't you ever get married?" he asked. This would solve one of the difficulties about one of the Lilacs.

"Nobody ever asked me."

This wasn't true. "Rudy Flood asked you. When his wife died."

"I wasn't in love with Rudy. Where did you hear that, anyway?"

"Tacey told me. Were you ever in love?"

"Once."

"With who?"

"That's a secret."

Books and a Battle

It wasn't until Auberon was past seven years old that his Lilac went away, though long before that he stopped mentioning her existence to anyone. When he was grown up he would sometimes wonder if most children who have imaginary friends have them for longer than they admit. After a child has stopped insisting that a place be set for his friend at dinner, that people not sit in chairs his friend is sitting in, does he usually go on having some intercourse with him? And does the usual imaginary friend fade only slowly, lingering on more and more spectrally as the real world becomes realer, or is it usually the case that on one specific day he disappears, never to be seen again—as Lilac did? The people he questioned said they remembered nothing about it at all. But Auberon thought they might still be harboring the old small ghosts, perhaps ashamed. Why after all should he alone remember so vividly?

That one specific day was a June day, as clear as water, summer fully clothed, the day of the picnic: the day Auberon grew up.

The morning he spent in the library, stretched out along the chesterfield, the leather cool against the backs of his legs. He was reading: or anyway holding a heavy book on his chest and looking at lines of dense print one by one. There had never been a time when Auberon hadn't loved reading; the passion had begun long before he could actually read, when he would sit with his father or his sister Tacey by the fire, feet up, turning when they turned the incomprehensible pages of a big picture-poor volume and feeling inexpressibly cozy and at peace. Learning to decipher words had only added to the pleasures of holding spines and turning pages, measuring the journey to the end with a thumb-riffle, poring over frontispieces.

Books! Opening with a crackle of old glue, releasing perfume; closing with a solid thump. He liked them big; he liked them old; he liked them best in many volumes, like the thirteen on a low shelf, golden-brown, obscure, of Gregorovius's *Medieval Rome*. Those— the big ones, the old ones—held secrets by their very nature; because of his years, though the paragraphs and chapters passed each under his scrutiny (he was no skimmer), he couldn't quite get at those secrets, prove the book to be (as most books after all are) dull, dated, stupid. They kept their magic, mostly. And there were always more on the burdened shelves, the occult volumes John Drinkwater collected no less compelling to his great-great-grandson than the multi-volume stuff he had bought by the yard to fill up the shelves. The one he held at the moment was the last edition of John Drinkwater's *Architecture of Country Houses*. Lilac, bored, flitted from corner to corner of the library, taking poses, as though playing Statue Tag with herself.

"Hey," Smoky said through the open double doors. "What are you doing frowsting in here?" The word was Cloud's. "Have you been outside? What a day." He got no response but a slowly turned page. From where he stood Smoky saw only the back of his son's cropped head (Smoky's own haircutting) with two pronounced tendons, a vulnerable hollow between them; and the top of the book; and two crossed big-sneakered feet. He didn't have to look to know Auberon wore a flannel shirt buttoned at the wrists—he never wore any other kind, or unbuttoned the wrists, no matter how hot the weather. He felt a kind of impatient pity for the boy. "Hey," he said again.

"Dad," Auberon said, "is this book true?"

"What book is that?"

Auberon held it up, waggling it to show the covers. Smoky felt a dense rush of feeling: it had been a day like this one— perhaps this very day of the year, yes—on which long ago he had opened that book. He hadn't looked at it since. But he knew its contents very much better now. "Well, 'true'," he said, " 'true', I don't know exactly what you mean by 'true'." Each time he said it the invisible doubt-quotes around the word became clearer. "Your great-great-grandfather wrote it, you know," he said, coming to sit on the end of the sofa. "With some help from your great-great-grandmother—and your great-great-*great* grandfather."

"Hm." This didn't intrigue Auberon. He read: " 'There, is a realm by definition precisely as large as this one, which should not be—' " he stumbled " '—reducible by any expansion, or enlargeable by any contraction, of this one, *Here*; and yet it must be that inroads

231

have been made on that kingdome of late, that what are called by us Progress, and the growth of Commerce, and the enlargement of the bounds of Reason, have caused a flight further within their borders of that people; so that (though they have—by the nature of things must have—infinite room in which to retreat) their ancient holdings have been reduced by much. Are they angry at this? We cannot tell. Do they plan revenge? Or are they, like the Red Indian, like the African savage, now so debilitated, made so spiritless, so reduced in number, that they will at last be—' " another hard one " '—extirpated entirely; not because they have nowhere left to flee, but because the losses, both of place and sovereignty, which our rapacity has inflicted on them are griefs too great to be borne? We cannot tell; not yet . . .' "

"What a sentence," Smoky said. Three mystics talking at once made for a thickish prose.

Auberon lowered the book from before his face. "Is it so?" he said.

"Well," Smoky said, feeling the trapped embarrassment of a parent before a child demanding to be told the facts of sex or death, "I don't know, really. I don't know if I really understand it. Anyway, I'm not the one to ask about it . . . ."

"But is it *made up*," Auberon insisted. A simple question.

"No," Smoky said. "No, but there are things in the world that aren't made up but which aren't exactly true either, not true like the sky is up and the ground is down, and two and two make four, things like that . . . ." The boy's eyes regarding him took no comfort from this casuistry, Smoky could see that. "Listen, why don't you ask your mother or Aunt Cloud? They know a lot more about that stuff than I do." He grasped Auberon's ankle. "Hey. You know the big picnic's today."

"What's this?" Auberon said, having discovered the chart or map on onion-skin paper tipped into the back of the book. He began to unfold it—turning it wrongly at first so that an old fold tore—and just for a moment Smoky saw into his son's consciousness: saw the expectation of revelations which any chart or diagram promises, and this one more than any; saw the greed for clarity and knowledge; saw the apprehension (in all senses) of the strange, the heretofore-hidden, the about-to-be-seen.

Auberon at last had to climb off the couch and put the book down on the floor in order to open the chart fully out. It crackled like a fire. Time had punched tiny holes in it where folds crossed one another. To Smoky it looked far older and fainter than it had looked fifteen or sixteen years ago when he had first seen it, and

232

burdened with figures and features he didn't remember, complex as it had then seemed to him. But it was (it must be) the same. As he came to kneel beside his son (who was already intently studying it, eyes alight and fingers tracing lines) he saw that he could understand it no better now, though in the intervening years he had learned (had he learned anything else? Oh, much) how best to go about not understanding it.

"I think I know what this is," Auberon said.

"Oh yes?" Smoky said.

"It's a battle."

"Hm."

In old history books Auberon had studied the maps: the oblong blocks labeled with little flags, disposed across a zebra landscape of topographical lines; gray blocks facing a roughly symmetrical disposition of black blocks (the bad guys). And on another page the same landscape hours later: some of the blocks bent aside, penetrated by the opposing blocks, pierced by the broad-arrow of their advance; others reversed entirely and following the broad-arrow of a retreat; and the diagonally-striped blocks of some belated ally appearing on one side. The great pale chart on the library floor was harder to figure out than those; it was as though the entire course of an immense battle (Positions at Dawn; Positions at 2:30 PM; Positions at Sunset) had been expressed here all at once, retreats superimposed on advances and orderly ranks on broken ones. And the topographical lines not squiggled and bent along the rises and declivities of any battleground but regular, and crossing: so many geometries, subtly altering each other as they interlaced, that the whole shimmered like moiré silk and led the eye into mazes of false appraisal: Is this line straight? Is this one curved? Are these nested circles, or a continuous spiral?

"There's a legend," Smoky said, feeling weary.

There was. There were also, Auberon saw, blocks of minute type placed explanatorily here and there (lost allies' regiments), and the hieroglyphs of the planets, and a compass rose, though not of directions, and a scale, though not of miles. The legend said that the thick lines bounded Here, and the thin lines There. But there was no way to be sure which lines on the chart were truly thick, which thin. Below the legend, in italic type underscored to emphasize its importance, was this note: "Circumference = nowhere; center point = everywhere."

In deep difficulties, and in what suddenly seemed like danger as well, Auberon looked up at his father. He seemed to see in Smoky's face and downcast eyes (and it was this face of Smoky's that

in after years Auberon would most often see when he dreamt of him)
a sad resignation, a kind of disappointment, as though he would say,
"Well, I tried to tell you; tried to keep you from going this far, tried
to warn you; but you're free, and I don't object, only now you know,
now you see, now the milk's spilt and the eggs broken, and it's partly
my fault and mostly yours."

"What," Auberon said, feeling a thickness in his throat,
"what . . . what is . . ." He had to swallow, and found himself then
with nothing to say. The chart seemed to make a noise over which
he couldn't hear his own thoughts. Smoky gripped his shoulder and
rose.

"Well, listen," he said. Perhaps Auberon had mistaken
his expression: as he stood and brushed rug lint from his trouser-
knees he looked only bored, perhaps, probably. "I really *really* don't
think this is the day for this, you know? I mean come on. The
picnic's on." He thrust his hands in his pockets and bent slightly over
his son, taking a different air: "Now maybe you don't feel terrifically
enthusiastic about that, but I *think* your mother would appreciate a
little help, getting things ready. Do you want to go in the car, or
bike?"

"Car," Auberon said, still looking down, not sure whether
he was glad or the reverse that though for a moment, just a moment,
his father and he had seemed to venture into strange lands together,
they now resumed their distant relations. He waited for his father's
eyes (which he could feel on the back of his head) to turn away, and
for his father's footsteps to sound on the parquet outside the library,
before he looked up from the chart (or map) which had grown less
compelling though no less confusing, like an answerless riddle. He
folded it up again, closed the book, and instead of replacing it in the
glass-fronted case with its forebears and cousins, he secreted it beneath the chintz skirts of a plump armchair, where he could retrieve
it later.

"But if it's a battle," he said, "which side is which?"

"*If* it's a battle," Lilac said, crosslegged in the armchair.

The Old Geography

Tacey had gone on ahead to the place that for some time
had been decided on as this year's picnic grounds,
flying down old roads and new paths on her well-kept
bike, pursued by Tony Buck for whom she'd begged a
guest's place. Lily and Lucy were coming from another
direction, from a morning visit of some importance
which Tacey had sent them on. So in the aged station wagon were

Alice, at the wheel; Great-aunt Cloud, beside her, and Smoky at the door; in the back Doc and Momdy and Sophie; and yet further back, legs crossed, Auberon, and the dog Spark, who had the habit of pacing back and forth endlessly when the car was in motion (unable to accept, perhaps, scenery flying by his face while his legs did nothing). There was room also for Lilac, who took up none.

"Scarlet tanager," Auberon said to Doc.

"No, a redstart," Doc said.

"Black, with a red . . ."

"No," Doc said, raising a forefinger, "the tanager is all *red*, with a black wing. Redstart is mostly black, with red patches . . ." he patted his own breast pockets.

The station wagon jounced, squeaking protests from every joint, over the roundabout rutted road that led to their chosen site. Daily Alice claimed it was only Spark's back-and-forth that kept this antiquity in motion at all (as Spark himself also believed), and for certain it had done service in recent years that would have affronted most vehicles its age into silence and immobility. Its wooden sides were as gray as driftwood and its leather seats as wrinkled with fine wrinkles as Aunt Cloud's face, but its heart was still strong, and Alice had learned its little ways from her father, who knew them (despite what George Mouse thought) as well as he knew the habits of redstarts and red squirrels. She'd had to learn, in order to do the Brobignagian grocery-shoppings her growing family required. No more semi-monthly shopping lists. These had been the days of six-legged chickens, of cases of this and dozens of that, of giant economy sizes, of ten-pound boxes of Drudge detergent and magnums of oil and jereboams of milk. The station wagon lugged it all, over and over, and bore it about as patiently as Alice herself did.

"Do you think, dear," Momdy said, "you ought to go much further? Will you be able to get out?"

"Oh, I think we can go a ways yet," Alice said. It was mostly for Momdy's arthritis and Cloud's old legs that they drove at all. In former days . . . They passed over a rut, and everyone but Spark was lifted somewhat off his seat; they entered a sea of leaf shadow; Alice slowed, almost able to feel the gentle strokings of the shadows over the hood and the top of the car; she forgot about former days in a sweet accession of summer happiness. The first cicada any of them had heard sang its semi-tune. Alice let the car drift to a halt. Spark stopped pacing.

"Can you walk from here, ma?" she asked.

"Oh, sure."

235

"Cloud?"

There was no answer. They were all silenced by the silence and the green.

"What? Oh, yes," Cloud said. "Auberon'll help me. I'll bring up the rear." Auberon chortled, and so did Cloud.

"Isn't this," Smoky said when they were on foot in twos and threes down the dirt road, "isn't this a road," he shifted his grip on the handle of the wicker basket he carried with Alice, "didn't we come along this road when . . ."

"Yes," Alice said. She glanced sidewise at him with a smile. "That's right." She squeezed her handle of the wicker basket as though it was his hand.

"I thought so," he said. The trees that stood up on the slopes above the gully of the road had grown perceptibly, had become even more noble and huge with arboreal wisdom, more thickly barked, more cloaked in serious garments of ivy; the road, long closed, had fallen into desuetude and was filling up with their offspring. "Around here somewhere," he said, "was a shortcut to the Woods'."

"Yup. We took it."

The Gladstone bag he shared with Alice drew down his left shoulder and made walking difficult. "That shortcut's gone now, I guess," he said. Gladstone bag? It was a wicker basket, the same that Momdy had once packed their wedding breakfast in.

"Nobody to keep it open," Alice said, glancing back at her father, and seeing him glance toward those same woods, "no need to." Both Amy Woods and her husband Chris were ten years dead in this summer.

"It's amazing to me," Smoky said, "how little of this geography I can keep straight."

"Mmm," said Alice.

"I had no idea this road ran here."

"Well," she said, "maybe it doesn't."

One hand around Auberon's shoulder, the other on a heavy cane, Cloud placed her feet carefully among the stones of the road. She had developed a habit of making a small constant chewing motion with her lips, which if she thought anyone noticed, would have embarrassed her greatly, and so she had convinced herself no one noticed it (since she couldn't help making it), though in fact everyone did. "Good of you to struggle with your old aunt," she said.

"Aunt Cloud," Auberon said, "that book your father and mother wrote—was that your father and mother who wrote it?"

"Which book is that, dear?"

"About architecture, only it's not, mostly."

"I *thought*," Cloud said, "that those books were locked up with a little key."

"Well," Auberon said, ignoring this, "is all that it says, true?"

"All what?"

It was impossible to say all what. "There's a plan in the back. Is it a plan of a battle?"

"Well! I never thought it was. A battle! Do you think so?"

Her surprise made him less sure. "What did you think it was?"

"I can't say."

He waited for at least an opinion, a stab, but she made none, only chewed and toiled along; he was left to interpret her remark to mean not that she was unable to say, but Somehow forbidden. "Is it a secret?"

"A secret! Hm." Again her surprise, as though she had never given these matters the least thought before. "A secret, you think? Well, well, perhaps that's just what it is. . . . My, they are getting on ahead, aren't they?"

Auberon gave it up. The old lady's hand was heavy on his shoulder. Beyond, where the road rose and then fell away, the towering trees framed a silver-green landscape; they seemed to bend toward it, exhibit it with leafy hands extended, offering it to the walkers. Auberon and Cloud watched the others top the rise and pass through the portals into that place, enter into sunlight, look around themselves, and, walking downwards, disappear.

"When I was a girl," Momdy said, "we used to go back and forth quite a bit."

The checkered tablecloth around which they were all disposed had been spread in the sun but was now in the shade of the great solitary maple by which they had camped. Great damage had been inflicted on the ham and the fried chicken and a chocolate cake; two bottles lay fallen, and a third canted over, nearly done for. A flying squadron of black ants had just reached the outskirts of the field, and were relaying the message back: great good luck.

Hills and Dales

"The Hills and the Dales," Momdy said, "always had connections with the City. Hill is my mother's name, you know," she said to Smoky, who did. "Oh, it was fun in the thirties, taking the train in; having lunch; going to see our Hill cousins. Now the Hills hadn't always lived in the City. . . ."

"Are these the Hills," Sophie asked from beneath the straw hat she had tilted over her face against the generous sun, "that are still up in Highland?"

"That's a branch," Momdy said. "My Hills never had much to do with the Highland Hills. The story is . . ."

"The story is long," Doc said. He lifted his wineglass to the sun (he always insisted on real glasses and silverware at picnics, the out-of-doors luxury of them made a picnic a feast) and watched the sun caught in it. "And the Highland Hills get the best of it."

"Not so," Momdy said. "How do you know what story the story is?"

"A little bird told me," Doc said, chuckling, indulging himself. He stretched out, back against the maple, and pulled his panama (as old almost as himself) into snooze position. Momdy's reminiscences had in recent years got longer, more rambling and repetitious, as her ears had got deafer; but she never minded being apprised of it. She went right on.

"The Hills in the *City*," she said to all of them, "were really very splendid. Of course back then it was nothing to have a servant or two, but they had flocks. Nice Irish girls. Marys and Bridgets and Kathleens. They had such stories. Well. The City Hills more or less died out. Some of them went out west, to the Rockies. Except one girl about Nora's age then who married a Mr. Townes, and they stayed. That was a wonderful wedding. The first where I cried. She wasn't beautiful, and she was no spring chicken; and she already had a daughter by a previous husband, what was his name, who hadn't lasted, so this Townes man—what *was* his first name— was quite a catch, oh dear you can't talk that way nowadays can you; and all those maids lined up in their starched outfits, congratulations, missus, congratulytions. Her family was so happy for her . . ."

"All the Hills," Smoky said, "danced for joy."

". . . and it was their daughter or rather *her* daughter, Phyllis, you see, who later on, about the time I got married, met Stanley *Mouse,* which is how *that* family and *my* family get connected in a roundabout way. Phyllis. Who was a Hill on her mother's side. George and Franz's mother."

"*Parturient montes,*" Smoky quipped into the void, "*et nascetur ridiculus mus.*"

Momdy nodded thoughtfully. "Ireland in those days was a dreadfully poor place, of course . . . ."

"Ireland?" Doc said, looking up. "How did we get to Ireland?"

"One of those girls, Bridget I think," Momdy said, turning to her husband, "was it Bridget, or Mary? later married Jack Hill when his wife died. Now his wife . . ."

Smoky quietly rolled away from her discourse. Neither Doc nor Great-aunt Cloud were truly listening either, but as long as they stayed in more or less attentive poses, Momdy wouldn't notice his defection. Auberon sat cross-legged apart from them, preoccupied (Smoky wondered if he had ever seen him otherwise occupied) and tossing an apple up and down in his hand. He was looking sharply at Smoky, and Smoky wondered if he meant to shy the apple at him. Smoky smiled, thought of a joke to make, but since Auberon's expression didn't change he decided against it, and, standing up, changed his place again. (In fact Auberon hadn't been looking at him at all; Lilac sat between him and his father, blocking his view of Smoky, and it was her face he looked at: she wore a peculiar expression, he would have called it sad since he had no better word, and he wondered what it meant.)

He sat down next to Daily Alice. She lay with her head pillowed on a hummock and her fingers interlaced over a full tummy. Smoky drew a sedge from its squeaking new casing and bit down on the pale sweetness. "Can I ask you something?" he said.

"What." She didn't quite open her sleepy eyes.

"When we got married," he said, "that day, you remember?"

"Mm-hm." She smiled.

"When we were going around, and meeting people. They gave us some presents."

"Mm-hm."

"And a lot of them, when they gave us things, said 'Thank you.' " The sedge's green ear bounced in rhythm to his speech; he could see it. "What I wondered was, why they said 'Thank you' to us, instead of us saying 'Thank you' to them."

"We said 'Thank you.' "

"But why did they? That's what I mean."

"Well," she said, and thought. He had asked so few things over the years that when he did ask something she thought hard how to answer him, so that he wouldn't brood. Not that he tended to brood. She often wondered why he didn't. "Because," she said, "the marriage had been promised, sort of."

"Yeah? So?"

"Well, they were glad that you'd come. And that the promise had come out like it had been promised."

"Oh."

239

"So that everything would go on like it was supposed to. You didn't have to, after all." She put a hand on his. "You didn't have to."

"I didn't see it that way," Smoky said. He thought. "Why would they care so much what was promised? If it was promised to you."

"Well, you know. A lot of them are relatives, sort of. Part of the family, really. Though you're not supposed to say it. I mean they're Daddy's half-brothers or sisters, or their kids. Or their kids' kids."

"Oh yes."

"August."

"Oh yes."

"So. They had an interest."

"Mm." It wasn't precisely the answer he'd been looking for; but Daily Alice said it as though it were.

"It gets very thick around here," she said.

"Blood's thicker than water," Smoky said, though that had always seemed to him among the dumber proverbs. Of course blood was thicker; so what? Who was ever connected by this water that blood was supposed to be thicker than?

"Tangled," Alice said, her eyes drifting closed. "Lilac, for instance." A lot of wine and sun, Smoky thought, or she wouldn't have let that name fall so casually. "A double dose; a double cousin, sort of. Cousin to herself."

"How do you mean?"

"Well, you know, cousins of cousins."

"I don't," Smoky said, puzzled. "You mean by marriage?"

"What?" She opened her eyes. "Oh! No. No, of course not. You're right. No." Her eyes closed again. "Forget it."

He looked down at her. He thought: follow one hare, and for sure you'll start another; and while you watch that one scamper out of sight, the first one gets away, too. Forget it. He could do that. He stretched himself beside her, propping his head on one arm; they were posed like lovers then, head to head nearly, he above looking down, she basking in his regard. They had married young; they were still young. Only old in love. There was a tune: he raised his eyes. On a rock not quite out of earshot, Tacey sat playing her recorder; now and then she stopped to remember notes, and to brush from her face a long curl of blond hair. At her feet Tony Buck sat, with the transfigured look of a convert to some just-revealed religion, unaware that Lily and Lucy a ways off whispered about him, unaware of anything but Tacey. Should girls as skinny as Tacey, Smoky wondered, and with legs as long, wear shorts that short and tight? Her bare toes, already sun-browned, kept the rhythm. Green grow the rushes-o. And all the hills around them danced.

Doc meanwhile had also drifted away from his wife's discourse, leaving her only Sophie (who was asleep) and Great-aunt Cloud (who was also asleep, though Momdy didn't know it). Doc went with Auberon following the toiling caravan of ants bearing goodies to their hill: a good big new one, when they found it.

A Getaway Look

"Stocks, supplies, inventory," Doc translated, a look of quiet absorption in his face and his ear cocked to the little city. "Watch your step, watch your back. Routes, work-loads, chain of command, upper echelons, front-office gossip; drop it, forget it, circular file, pass the buck, wander off, let George do it; back in line, the old salt mines, in harness, in and out, lost and found. Directives, guidelines, grapevine, schedules, check in, knock off, out sick. Much the same." He chuckled. "Much the same."

Auberon, hands on his knees, watched the miniature armored vehicles (driver and vehicle in one, and radio antenna too) tumble in and out. He imagined the congress within: endless busyness in the dark. Then he half-saw something, as though there were a darkness or a brightness in the corner of his vision, gathering until it was large enough for him to notice. He looked up and around.

What he had seen or noticed was not something, but something missing. Lilac was gone.

"Now up, or down, at the Queen's, that's very different," Doc said.

"Yeah, I see," Auberon said, looking around. Where? Where was she? Though there were often long periods when he didn't exactly notice her presence, he had always been aware of her, had always sensed she was there by him somewhere. Now she was gone.

"This is very interesting," Doc said.

Auberon caught sight of her, down the hill, just going around a group of trees antechamber to the woods. She looked back for a moment, and (seeing that he saw her) hurried out of sight. "Yes," Auberon said, sidling away.

"Up at the Queen's," Doc said. "What is it?"

"Yes," Auberon said, and ran, racing toward the place where Lilac had disappeared, apprehension in his heart.

He didn't see her when he entered that stand of trees. He had no idea which way to follow further, and a panic seized him: that look she had given him as she turned away into the woods had been a getaway look. He heard his grandfather's voice calling him. He stepped carefully. The beechwood he stood in, smooth-floored and regular as a pillared hall, showed him a dozen vistas down which she could have fled. . . .

He saw her. She stepped out from behind a tree, quite calmly, she even had what appeared to be a bunch of dog-tooth violets in her hand, and seemed to be looking around herself for more. She didn't look back at him, and he stood confused, knowing deeply that she had run away from him, though she didn't look now like she had, and then she was gone again, she'd tricked him with the bouquet into standing still one moment too long. He raced to the place she'd disappeared, knowing even as he ran that she was gone for good now, but calling: "Don't go, Lilac!"

The woods into which she had escaped were various, dense and briary, dark as a church, and showed him no prospects. He plunged in blindly, stumbling, torn at. Very quickly he found himself deeper in The Wood than he had ever been, as though he had shot through a door without noticing that it opened on a flight of cellar stairs to pitch him headlong down. "Don't," he called out, lost. "Don't go." An imperious voice, such as he had never used to her before, such as he had never had to, such as she could not conceivably have refused. But nothing answered him. "Don't go," he said again, not imperiously, afraid in the dark of the wood and more bereft more suddenly than his young soul could have conceived possible. "Don't go. Please, Lilac. Don't go, you're the only secret I ever had!"

Gigantic, aloof, not much disturbed but quite interested, old ones looked down like trees at the small one who had so suddenly and fiercely come in among them. Hands spread on their enormous knees, they considered him, insofar as they could consider someone or something so minute. One put his finger to his lips; silently they watched him stumble amid their toes; they cupped huge hands behind their ears, and with eavesdroppers' slight smiles they heard his cry and his grief, though Lilac could not.

Two Beautiful Sisters

"Dear Parents," Auberon in the Folding Bedroom wrote (typing featly with two fingers on an old, old machine he had discovered there), "Well! A winter here in the City is going to be quite an experience! I'm glad it won't last forever. Though today temp. is 25, and it snowed again yesterday. No doubt it's worse where you are, ha ha!" He paused, having made this gay exclamation carefully out of the single-quote mark and the period. "I've been twice now to see Mr. Petty at Petty, Smilodon & Ruth, Grandpa's lawyers as you know, and they've been kind enough to advance me a little more against the settlement, but not much, and they can't say when the darn thing will be straightened out at last. Well Im sure everything will turn out fine." He was not sure, he raged, he had shouted at Mr. Petty's automaton of a secretary and nearly balled up the paltry check and thrown it at her; but the persona whacking out this letter, tongue between teeth and searching fingers tense, didn't make admissions like that. Everything was fine at Edgewood; everything was fine here too. Everything was fine. He made a new paragraph. "I've already about worn out the shoes I came in. Hard City streets! As you know, things have got very expensive here and the quality is no good. I wonder if you could send the pair of tall lace-up ones in my closet. Theyre not very dressy but anyway Il'l be spending most of my time working here at the Farm. Now that winters here theres a lot to do, cleaning up, stableing the animals and so on. George is pretty funny in his galoshes. But hes been very good to me and I appreciate it even if I do get blisters. And there are other nice people who live here." He stopped, as before a precipice he was about to tumble over, his finger hovering above the S. The machine's ribbon was old and brownish, the pale letters staggered drunkenly above and below the line they should be walking. But Auberon didn't want to display his school hand to Smoky; it had degenerated, he had lately taken up ball-points and other vices; what now about Sylvie? "Among them are:" He ran down in his mind the current occupancy of Old Law Farm. He wished he hadn't taken this route. "Two sisters, who are Puerto Rican and very beautiful." Now what the hell had he done that for? An old secret-agent obfuscation inhabiting his fingers. Tell them nothing. He sat back, unwilling to go on; and at that moment, there was a knock at the door of the Folding Bedroom, and he drew the page out, finish it later (though he never did) and went—two steps across the floor was all it took his long legs—to admit the two beautiful Puerto Rican sisters, wrapped into one and all his, all his.

But it was George Mouse who stood on the threshold. (Auberon would soon learn not to mistake anyone else at the door for Sylvie, because Sylvie instead of knocking always scratched or drummed at the door with her nails; it was the sound of a small animal wanting admission.) George had an old fur coat over his arm, an antique lady's peau-de-soi black hat on his head, and two shopping bags in his hands. "Sylvie not here?" he said.

"No, not just now." With all the practiced skills of a secretive nature Auberon had managed to avoid George Mouse for a week in his own farm, coming and going with a mouse's forethought and haste. But now here he was. Never had Auberon experienced such embarrassment, such a terrible caught-out feeling, such an awful sense that no common remark he could make would not carry a load of hurt and rejection for another, and that no pose, solemn, facetious, offhand, could mitigate that. And his host! His cousin! Old enough to be his father! Usually not at all intensely aware of the reality of others or of others' feelings, Auberon just then felt what his cousin must feel as though he inhabited him. "She went out. I don't know where."

"Yeah? Well, this stuff is hers." He put down the shopping bags and plucked the hat from his head. It left his gray hair standing upright. "There's some more. She can come get it. Well, a load off my mind." He tossed the fur coat over the velvet chair. "Hey. Take it easy. Don't hit me, man. Nothing to do with me."

Auberon realized he had taken a rigid stance in a corner of the room, face set, unable to find an expression to suit the circumstance. What he wanted to do was to tell George he was sorry; but he had just enough wit to see that nothing could be more insulting. And besides, he wasn't sorry, not really.

"Well, she's quite a girl," George said, looking around (Sylvie's panties were draped over the kitchen chair, her unguents and toothbrush were at the sink). "Quite a girl. I hope yiz are very happy." He punched Auberon's shoulder, and pinched his cheek, unpleasantly hard. "You son of a bitch." He was smiling, but there was a mad light in his eye.

"She thinks you're terrific," Auberon said.

"Izzat a fact."

"She said she doesn't know what she would have done without you. Without your letting her stay here."

"Yeah. She said that to me too."

"She thinks of you like a father. Only better."

"Like a father, huh?" George burned him with his coaly eyes, and without looking away began to laugh. "Like a father." He laughed louder, a wild staccato laugh.

"Why are you laughing?" Auberon asked, not certain he was meant to join, or whether it was he who was being laughed at.

"Why?" George laughed all the harder. "Why? What the hell do you want me to do? Cry?" He threw back his head, showing white teeth, and roared. Auberon couldn't help joining in then, though tentatively, and when George saw that, his own laugh diminished. It went on in chuckles, like small waves following a breaker. "Like a father, huh. That's rich." He went to the window and stared out at the iron day. A last chuckle escaped him; he clasped his hands behind his back and sighed. "Well, she's a hell of a girl. Too much for an old fart like me to keep up with." He glanced over his shoulder at Auberon. "You know she's got a Destiny?"

"That's what she said."

"Yeah." His hands opened and closed behind him. "Well, it looks like I ain't in it. Okay by me. Cause there's a brother in it, too, with a knife, and a grandmother and a crazy mother . . . And some babies." He was silent awhile. Auberon almost wept for him. "Old George," George said. "Always left with the babies. Here, George, do something with this. Blow it up, give it away." He laughed again. "And do I get credit? Damn right I do. You son of a bitch, George, you blew up my baby."

What was he talking about? Had he slipped into madness under the pressure of grief? Would losing Sylvie be like that, would it be so awful? A week ago he wouldn't have thought so. With a sudden chill he remembered that the last time Great-aunt Cloud had read the cards for him, she had predicted a dark girl for him; a dark girl, who would love him for no virtue he had, and leave him through no fault of his own. He had dismissed it then, as he was in the process of dismissing all of Edgewood and its prophecies and secrets. He dismissed it now again, with horror.

"Well, you know how it is," George said. He pulled a tiny spiral notebook from his pocket and peered in it. "You're on for the milking this week. Right?"

"Right."

"Right." He put away the book. "Hey listen. You want some advice?"

He didn't, any more than he wanted prophecy. He stood to receive it. George looked at him closely, and then around the room. "Fix the place up," he said. He winked at Auberon. "She likes it nice. You know? Nice." He began to be caught by a fit of laughing again, which burbled at the back of his throat as he took a handful of jewelry from one pocket and gave it to Auberon, and a handful of change from another and gave him that too. "And keep clean," he said. "She thinks us white people are a little on the foul side most of the time." He headed for the door. "A word to the wise," he said, and chuckling, left. Auberon stood with jewels in one hand and money in the other, hearing, down the hall, Sylvie pass George on her way up; he heard them greet each other in a volley of wisecracks and kisses.

IV

It often happens that a man cannot
recall at the moment, but can search
for what he wants and find it. . . .
For this reason some use places for the
purposes of recollecting. The reason
for this is that men pass rapidly from
one step to the next: for instance
from milk to white, from white to air,
from air to damp; after which one
recollects autumn, supposing that one
is trying to recollect that season.

—*Aristotle,* De anima

riel Hawksquill, greatest mage of this age of the world
(and a match, she was not too modest to think, of
many great ones of the so-called past, with whom she
now and then discoursed), possessed no crystal ball; judicial astrology
she knew to be a fraud, though she had uses for the old pictured
heavens; she disdained spells and geomancies of all kinds, except at
great need, and the sleeping dead and their secrets she let sleep. Her
one Great Art, and it was all she needed, was the highest Art of all,
and required no vulgar tools, no Book, no Wand, no Word. It could
be practiced (as, on a certain rainy afternoon of the winter in which
Auberon came to Old Law Farm, she was practicing it) before the
fire, with feet up, and tea and toast at hand. It required nothing but
the interior of her skull: that and a concentration and an acceptance
of impossibility which saints would have found admirable and chess
masters difficult.

The Art of Memory, as it is described by ancient writers, is
a method by which the Natural Memory we are born with can be

improved tremendously, beyond recognition in fact. The ancients agreed that vivid pictures in a strict order were the most easily remembered. Therefore, in order to construct an Artificial Memory of great power, the first step (Quintillian and other authorities agree on this, though they diverge at other points) is to choose a Place: a temple, for instance, or a city street of shops and doorways, or the interior of a house—any place that has parts which occur in a regular order. This Place is committed to memory carefully and well, so well that the rememberer can scurry around it backwards, forwards, any which way at will. The next step is to create vivid symbols or images for the things one wishes to remember—the more shocking and highly-colored the better, according to the experts: a ravished nun, say, for the idea of Sacrilege, or a cloaked figure with a bomb for Revolution. These symbols are then cast onto the various parts of the memory Place, its doors, niches, forecourts, windows, closets, and other spaces; and then the rememberer has simply to go around his memory Place, in any order he wishes, and take from each spot the Thing which symbolizes the Notion which he wishes to remember. The more one wishes to remember, of course, the larger the house of memory must be; it usually ceases to be an actual place, as actual places tend to be too plain and incommodious, and becomes an imaginary place, as large and varied as the rememberer can make it. Wings can be added at will (and with practice); architectural styles can vary with the subject-matter they are meant to contain. There were even refinements of the system whereby not Notions but actual words were to be remembered by complex symbols, and finally individual letters: so that a collection of sickle, millstone, and hacksaw instantly brings the word God to mind when gathered from the appropriate mental nook. The whole process was immensely complicated and tedious and was for the most part rendered obsolete by the invention of the filing-cabinet.

But the greatest practitioners of the old art discovered some odd things about their memory houses the longer they lived in them, and modern practitioners (or practitioner, really, there being only one of any skill, and she keeps it to herself) have improved on and even further complicated the system for reasons of their own.

The Art of Memory

It was discovered, for instance, that the symbolic figures with vivid expressions, once installed in their proper places, are subject to subtle change as they stand waiting to be called forth. That ravished nun who meant Sacrilege might, when one passes her again, have acquired a depraved air about the mouth and eyes one hadn't

247

thought he had bestowed on her, and something wanton about her *deshabille* that looks Somehow purposeful rather than forced: and Sacrilege changes to Hypocrisy, or at least borrows some of its aspects, and thus the memory she symbolizes alters perhaps in instructive ways. Also: as a memory house grows, it makes conjunctions and vistas that its builder can't conceive of beforehand. When out of necessity he throws up a new wing, it must abut the original place in some way; so a door in the original house that previously opened on a weedy garden might suddenly blow open in a draught and show its astonished owner his grand new gallery full of just-installed memories from the backside, so to speak, at a left-hand turning, facing in the wrong direction—also instructive; and that new gallery might also turn out to be a shortcut to the ice-house where he had put a distant winter once and then forgot.

Yes, forgot: because another thing about a memory house is that its builder and occupier can lose things in it just as you can in any house—the ball of string which you were certain you kept either with the stamps and the tape in the desk-drawer or in the hall closet with the tackhammer and the picture-wire, but which isn't in either place when you go to look for it. In the ordinary or Natural Memory such things can simply vanish; you don't even remember you forgot them. The advantage of a memory house is that you know it's in there somewhere.

So it was that Ariel Hawksquill was rooting around in one of the oldest attics of her memory mansions, looking for something she had forgotten but knew was there.

She had been re-reading an *ars memorativa* of Giordano Bruno's called *De umbris idearum*, a huge treatise on symbols and seals and signs to be used in the highest forms of the art. Her first-edition copy had marginal notes in a neat Italic hand, often illuminating but more often puzzling. On a page where Bruno treats of the various orders of symbols one might use for various purposes, the commentator had noted: "As in ye cartes of ye returne of R.C. are iiiij Personnes, Places, Thynges &c., which emblemes or cartes are for remembering or foretelling, and discoverie of smalle worldes." Now this "R.C." could stand for "Roman Church", or—just possibly— "Rosicrucian." But it was the persons and places and things that had rung a distant bell: a bell here, she thought, where she had stored her distant childhood long ago.

She moved carefully but with increasing impatience through the miscellany there, her dog Spark, a trip to Rockaway, her first kiss; she became intrigued with the contents of chests and went off down useless corridors of reminiscence. In one place she had put a battered cowbell, why she at first had no idea. Then she rang it tentatively. It was the bell she had heard, and instantly she remembered her grandfather (whom the cowbell was—of course!—to represent, since he had been a farm laborer in England till he emigrated to this vast and cowless city). She saw him distinctly now, where she had put him, below the mantel with the Toby jugs on it which resembled him, in a battered armchair; he turned the cowbell in his hands as he had used to turn his pipe.

"Did you," she questioned him, "tell me once about cards, with persons and places and things?"

"I might have."

"In what connection?"

Silence. "Well, small worlds then."

It grew clearer in that attic, lit with a past sun, and she sat at Grandpa's feet in the old apartment. "It was the only thing I ever found had any value, like," he said, "and I threw it away on a silly girl. Would've brought twenty bob in any dealer's, I can tell you that, they were that old and fine. I found them in an old cottage that the squire wanted pulled down. And she was a girl who said she saw fairies and pixies and such, and her father was another like her. Violet her name was. And I said, 'Tell my fortune then with these if you can.' And she like riffled through them—there were pictures on them of persons and places and things—and she laughed and said I'd die a lonely old man on a fourth storey. And wouldn't give me back the cards I'd found."

There it was then. She put the cowbell back in its place in the order of her childhood (put it next to a well-thumbed deck of Old Maid cards from the same year, just to keep the connection clear) and shut up that room.

Small worlds, she thought, staring out the rain-crazed window of her parlor. To discover small worlds. In no other connection had she ever heard of these cards. The persons and places and things were reminiscent of the Art of Memory, in which a place is established, and a vivid person imagined, holding his emblematic things. And "the return of R. C.": if that meant the "Brother R. C." of the Rosicrucians, it would place the cards in the first flush of Rosicrucian enthusiasms; which—she pushed away the tray of tea and toast, and wiped her fingers—might make some sense of the small worlds, too. The arcane thought of those years knew of many.

The athenor of the alchemists, for instance, the Philosopher's Egg within which the transformation from base to gold took place—was it not a microcosm, a small world? When the black-books said that the Work was to be begun in the sign of

Aquarius and completed in Scorpio, they meant not those signs as they occurred in the heavens, but as they occurred in the universe of the world-shaped, world-containing Egg itself. The Work was not other than Genesis; the Red Man and the White Lady, when they appeared, microscopic in the Egg, were the soul of the Philosopher himself, as an object of the Philosopher's thought, itself a product of his soul, and so on, *regressus ad infinitum,* and in both directions too. And the Art of Memory: had not the Art introjected into the finite circle of her, Hawksquill's, skull the mighty circles of the heavens? And did not that cosmic engine within then order her memory, thus her perception, of things sublunar, celestial, and infinite? The immense laughter of Bruno when he understood that Copernicus had inverted the universe—what was it but joy in the confirmation of his knowledge that Mind, in the center of all, contains within it all that it is the center of? If the Earth, the old center, now was seen truly to revolve somewhere halfway between the center and the outside; and the Sun, which before had revolved on a path halfway to the outside, were now the center, then a half-turn like that in a Möbius strip was thrown into the belt of the stars: and what then became of the old circumference? It was, strictly, unimaginable: the Universe exploded into infinitude, a circle of which Mind, the center, was everywhere and the circumference nowhere. The trick-mirror of finitude was smashed, Bruno laughed, the starry realms were a jewelled bracelet in the hand.

Well, all that was old. Every schoolboy (in the schools that had schooled Hawksquill) knew small worlds were great. If these cards were in her hands, she had no doubt she could quickly learn just what small worlds they were intended to discover: had little doubt that she herself had traveled in them. But were these cards the cards her grandfather had found and lost? And were they as well the cards Russell Eigenblick claimed to be in? A coincidence of that magnitude didn't seem inherently unlikely to Hawksquill; there was no chance in her universe. But she had no idea how further to search for them, and learn. In fact that alley seemed just at the moment so blind that she decided to walk no further up it. Eigenblick was no Roman Catholic, and the Rosicrucians, as everybody knows, were invisible—and whatever else Russell Eigenblick was, he was very visible. "The hell with it," she was saying under her breath when the doorbell rang.

She consulted her watch. The Maid of Stone still slept, though the day was already as dark as night. She went to the hall, took a heavy stick from the umbrella-stand, and opened the door.

Overcoated and broad-hatted, windblown and rain-swept, the black figure on her doorstep momentarily frightened her.

"Wingéd Messenger Service," he said. "Hello, lady."

"Hello, Fred," Hawksquill said. "You gave me a start." For the first time she had understood the pejorative "spook." "Come in, come in."

He would come no further than the vestibule, because he dripped; he stood dripping while Hawksquill fetched him a wine-glass of whiskey.

"Dark days," he said, taking it.

"St. Lucy's," Hawksquill said. "Darkest of all."

He chuckled, knowing very well she knew he meant more than the weather. He drained his glass at a gulp, and drew from his plastic-sheathed carrier a thick envelope for her. It bore no sender's address. She signed Fred Savage's book.

"Bad day to be working," she said.

"Neither rain nor sleet nor snow," said Fred, "and the owl for all his feathers was a-cold."

"You won't stay a moment?" she said. "The fire's lit."

"If I stayed a *moment*," Fred Savage said, leaning to one side, "I'd stay an *hour*," leaning to the other side, rain running from his hat; "and thad be that." He straightened, and bowed out.

No man more faithful, when he was working, which wasn't often. Hawksquill shut the door on him (thinking of him as a dark shuttle or bobbin stitching up the rainy City) and returned to her parlor.

The fat envelope contained a deck of new bills in large denominations, and a brief note on the stationery of the Noisy Bridge Rod and Gun Club: "Payment per agreement in the matter of R. E. Have you come to any conclusions?" It was unsigned.

She dropped this note on the open folio of Bruno she had been studying, and was going back to the fire, counting her huge and as yet unearned fee, when a lurking connection was made within her consciousness. She went to the table, turned on a strong light, and looked closely at the marginal note which had originally stoked this long train of thought, a train which had just been shunted by the note from the Club.

The Italic hand is notable for its legibility. Yet now and then the swash capitals, if written quickly, can confuse. And yes: looked at closely there was no doubt that what she had read as "the return of R. C." should be read "the return of R. E.".

Where on earth, if on earth at all, were those cards?

LITTLE BIG

As she grew older, Nora Cloud seemed to those around her to take on greater mass and solidity. To herself also—though she gained no physical weight—she seemed to grow great. As her age reached toward three digits and she moved slowly through Edgewood on two canes to support her massy years, she bent—so it seemed—less from weakness than to accommodate herself in the narrow corridors of the house.

A Geography

She came with four-footed deliberateness down from her room toward the drum-table in the many-sided music-room, where beneath a brass and green glass lamp the cards in their bag in their box waited for her—and where Sophie, these several years her student, waited too.

Cloud let herself down into her chair, her sticks rattling and the bones of her knees popping. She lit a brown cigarette and placed it in a saucer beside her, where its smoke rose ribbony and curling like thought. "What's our question?" she asked.

"Like yesterday," Sophie said. "Just to continue."

"No question," Cloud said. "All right."

They were silent awhile together. A moment of silent prayer, Cloud had been delighted and surprised to hear Smoky describe this as; a moment for considering the question, or no question, as today.

Sophie with her long soft hand over her eyes thought of no question. She thought of the cards, dark in their bag in their box. She didn't think of them as units, as individual pieces of paper, could no longer think of them that way even if she chose to. She didn't think of them either as notions, as persons, places, things. She thought of them as one thing, like a story or an interior, something made of space and time, lengthy and vast but compact; jointed, dimensional, ever-unfolding.

"Well," Cloud said with gentle finality. Her brown-spotted hand hovered over the box. "Shall I lay out a Rose?"

"May I?" Sophie asked. Cloud withdrew her hand before it touched the box, which might spoil Sophie's control. Attempting Cloud's wasteless gestures, her calm attention, Sophie laid out a Rose.

Six of cups and four of wands, the Knot, the Sportsman, ace of cups, the Cousin, four of coins and queen of coins. The Rose grew out across the drum-table with an iron yet an organic force. If there was no question, as today, the question always was: what is this Rose the answer to? Sophie laid down the central card.

252

"The Fool again," Cloud said.

"Contention with the Cousin," Sophie said.

"Yes," Cloud said. "But whose cousin? His own, or ours?"

The Fool card in the center of the Rose showed a full-bearded man in armor crossing a brook. Like the White Knight he was in the act of pitching head-first and straight-legged from his brawny horse. His expression was mild, and he looked not into the shallow stream he fell toward, but outward at the viewer, as though what he was doing were intentional, a trick, or possibly an example of something: gravity? In one hand he held a scallop-shell; in the other, some links of sausage.

Before interpretation of any fall could be considered, Cloud had taught Sophie, they must decide how the cards themselves must at this moment be construed. "You can think of them as a story, and then you must find the beginning, middle, and end; or a sentence, and you must parse it; or a piece of music, and you must find the tonic and signature; or anything at all that has parts and makes sense."

"It may be," she said, looking down now at this Rose with a Fool in the middle, "that what we have here isn't a story or an interior, but a Geography."

Sophie asked her what she meant by that, and Cloud said she wasn't at all sure. Her cheek was in her hand. Not a map, or a view, but a Geography. Sophie's cheek was in her hand too, and for a long time she gazed down at the Rose she had made and only wondered; she thought, a Geography, and wondered if it might be that here, that this, that—but then she closed her eyes and paused a moment, no, there was no question today, please, and not that question of any one.

Life—her own life anyway, Sophie had come to think, as it grew longer—was like one of those many-storied houses of dreams she had once been able to build, where the dreamer, with a slow or sudden rush of understanding like a wash of cool water, knows himself to have been merely asleep and dreaming, to have

Wakings-up

merely invented the pointless task, the grim hotel, the flight of stairs; they go away, tattered and unreal; the dreamer awakes relieved in his own bed (though the bed for a reason he can't quite remember is laid in a busy street or afloat in a calm sea), and rises yawning, and has odd adventures, which go on until (with a slow or sudden rush of understanding) he awakes, he had only fallen asleep here in this

253

desert place (Oh I remember) or (Oh I see) in this palace antechamber, and it's time to be up and about life's business; and so on and on: her life had been of that kind.

There had been a dream about Lilac, that she had been real, and Sophie's. Then she had awakened, and Lilac wasn't Lilac at all: she came to see that, came to see that something dreadful had happened, for no reason she could imagine or remember, and Lilac was neither Lilac nor hers, but something else instead. That dream—one of the awful kind, the kind where something terrible and irrevocable has happened, something that oppresses the soul with a special, unrelievable grief—had gone on for nearly two years, and had not truly ended on the night (the night she could still not think about without shudders and involuntary moans, no, not after twenty years) when in desperation, telling no one, she had brought the false thing to George Mouse: and the fireplace: and the blasts, and the phosphorescence, and the rain and the stars and the sirens.

But anyway, awake or not, she had no more Lilac then at all; her dream was another kind then, the Endless Search, that one where some goal recedes forever, or changes when it is approached, leaving you always with further work to do and, though pressing always on your attention, is never nearer to completion. It was then that she had begun to seek for answers from Cloud and her cards: not only *Why*, but also *How; Who*, she supposed she knew, but not *Where*; and, most important of all, would she ever see, have, hold her real daughter again, and *When*? Cloud, try as she might, could give no clear answers to these questions, though she held that still the answers must be in the deck and its conjunctions somewhere; and so Sophie began to study their falls herself, feeling that the intensity of her desire might allow her to discover what Cloud could not. But no answer came for her either, and soon she gave it up, and took to her bed again.

But life is wakings-up, all unexpected, all surprising. On a certain November afternoon, twelve years ago, from a certain nap (why that day? Why that nap?) she had awakened from sleeping: from eyes-closed, blankets-up-to-chin, pillow-sleep Sophie awakened, or had been awakened, for good. As though someone (while she slept) had stolen them, her powers of sleeping and escaping into the small dreams within the large had gone away; and Sophie, startled and lost, had had to dream from then on that she was awake, and that the world was around her, and to think what to do with it. It was only then, because her sleepless mind had to have an Interest, any Interest, that (without any hard question, without any question at all) she had taken up the study of the cards, beginning at the beginning humbly as Cloud's tutee.

And yet, though we wake, though there is no end to waking and saying *Oh I see*, not ever (Sophie knew it and was patient), still within the dream in which we find ourselves every other dream is nested, every one we have awakened from. Sophie's hard first question to the cards had not, precisely, gone without an answer, it had been transmuted into questions about the question. It had branched and rooted like a tree, growing questions like buds, and then at some moment all the questions had become one question: what tree is this? And as her study progressed, as she shifted and shuffled and laid out in geometrical figures the greasy, cornerless, speaking cards, the question intrigued her further, involved her, at last absorbed her utterly. What tree is this? And yet always at its base, between its roots, beneath its branches, still unfound and growing unfindable, a lost child lay asleep.

Six of cups and four of wands, the Knot, the Sportsman. The queen of coins reversed. The Cousin: contention with the Fool in the middle of the deck. A Geography: not a map, or a view, but a Geography. Sophie looked down at the puzzle of it, shifting her consciousness across it, paying attention without quite paying attention, pricking up the ears of her thought and easing them again as hints of speech proceeded from and then retired back into the gabble of the cards' alignments.

No Going Back Out

Then:

"Oh," Sophie said, and again "Oh," as though suddenly in receipt of bad news. Cloud looked up at her questioningly, and saw Sophie pale and shocked, eyes wide with surprise and pity—pity for her, Cloud. Cloud looked down again at the Geography, and yes, in a twinkling it had contracted, like those optical illusions where a complex urn becomes without your choosing it two faces regarding each other. Cloud was used to these vagaries, and to this message; Sophie evidently was not yet.

"Yes," she said softly, and smiled at Sophie, reassuringly she hoped. "You hadn't seen that before?"

"No," Sophie said, both in answer and in denial of what was there in the linked gavotte of cards. "No."

"Oh, I've seen it before." She touched Sophie's hand. "I don't think, though, that we need tell the others, do you? Not just yet." Sophie was weeping, softly, but Cloud chose to ignore it. "It's

255

the difficult thing, the hard thing, about secrets," she said, as though in some small annoyance at the fact, but really passing on to Sophie in the only way she could hope to, the last, the only important lesson about reading these cards. "Sometimes you really don't want to know them. But once you do, there's no going back out; no unlearning them. Well. Now buck up. There's still a lot you can learn."

"Oh. Aunt Cloud."

"Shall we study our Geography?" Cloud said, and picked up her cigarette, and inhaled smoke gratefully, voluptuously, and breathed it out again.

Cloud moved crabwise amid the furniture of the house, down three stairs (the note of her sticks changing as she went from wood to stone) and through the puzzle of the imaginary drawing-room where a tapestry on the wall moved in a draft with spooky life. Then the stairs upward.

Slow Fall of Time

There were three hundred and sixty-five stairs within Edgewood, her father told her. The left-hand stick, the right-hand foot, right-hand stick, left-hand stick, left-hand foot. There were as well seven chimneys, fifty-two doors, four floors, and twelve—twelve what? There must be twelve of something, he wouldn't have left that out. Right-hand stick, left-hand foot, and a landing where a lancet window poured a pearly stain of winter light on the dark wood. Smoky had seen an ad in a magazine for a sort of chair-elevator to move old folks up and down stairs; it even tilted up to deposit the aged body at its chosen floor. Smoky pointed this out to Cloud, but she had said nothing. An object of perhaps some abstract interest, but why was he showing it to her? That's what her silence said.

Upward again, the minute risers—nine inches exactly— growing ever more cliffy no matter how big she was herself, no matter that the banisters shouldered her and the coffered ceiling pressed on her bent neck. It was wrong in her, she thought as she toiled, not to have warned Sophie of what she, Cloud, had for a long time known about, what had become a kind of recurrent obbligato in her recent readings of the cards, a *memento mori* that could show up in any fall cast for any person; but it was so constant lately that Cloud had really ceased to notice it. She didn't anyway need, at her huge age, any reminders in her cards of what was obvious to anyone, and most of all to her. It was no secret. She was packed and ready.

Those of her treasures which had not already been distributed were all labeled for the ones they were meant for, the jewelry, Violet's things, stuff she had never really considered hers anyway.

And the cards would of course be Sophie's; that was a relief. She had made over the house and grounds and rents to Smoky, an unwilling Smoky; he would be caretaker, good conscientious man! Not that the house couldn't in the main take care of itself. It couldn't come apart, not anyway until the Tale was all told, if then—but there was no thinking about that, that was no excuse not to execute legal instruments, make wills and make repairs. Alone of them all, Great-aunt Cloud still remembered Violet's instructions: forget. She had acted so well on those instructions that she supposed that her nieces and nephews and grand- and great-grand-nieces and nephews really *had* forgotten, or never quite learned, what they must forget or needn't learn. Perhaps, like Daily Alice, they thought it had all Somehow slipped out of their reach, each generation slipping further from it as the inexorable slow fall of time was consumed to embers, the embers to ashes, the ashes to cold clinkers, each generation losing something of the last's close connection, or easy access, or quick understanding, the times when Auberon could photograph them or Violet wander in their realms and return with news now the dim fabulous past: and yet (Cloud knew it to be so) each generation in fact grew closer to it, and only ceased to search or bother themselves about it because they felt fewer and fewer distinctions between themselves and it. And, upon a time, there would be no searching at all for a way in. Because there they would be.

The Tale, she thought, would end with them: with Tacey, and Lily, and Lucy; with lost Lilac, wherever she was; with Auberon. Or with their children at the latest. This conviction grew, as she grew older, rather than fading; and that was the clue in these matters that she knew to trust. And it was a shame, a damn shame, she thought, that she had lived nearly to a hundred (at the cost of great effort, and not only on her part) and yet wouldn't live to see the end.

Last stair. She put her stick on it, one foot, the other stick, the other foot. She stood stock still while the clamor of effort subsided in her body.

A Fool, and a Cousin; a geography, and a death. She had been right, that every fall of the cards was related to every other. If she read a fall for George Mouse and saw a vista of corridors, or for Auberon and saw the dark girl he would love and lose, that was not different from searching for lost Lilac, or glimpsing the dim lineaments of the Tale, or reading the fate of the Great World itself. How that could be, how each secret revealed could encode another, or all others, why behind a fall that showed a grand Geography—empires, frontiers, a final battle—there should appear one old woman's death, she couldn't tell; perhaps, probably, it couldn't be told. Her dismay at this was mitigated by her old resolution, her promise to Violet: that even if she could tell, she wouldn't.

She looked down the mountain of stairs she had just barely, had almost not conquered; and, weakened and slowed more by sad understanding than by any arthritis, she turned toward her room, certain now she would not ever go down them again.

The next morning Tacey came, packed for a long visit, bringing needlework to pass the time. Lily and the twins were already there. Lucy came at evening, not surprised to find her sisters there, and settled in with them, with her needlework, to help and watch and wait.

Before anyone else could have perceived morning in the somber air above Old Law Farm, the cock crew, and woke Sylvie. Auberon beside her stirred. She was
Princess pressed against his long, unconscious warmth, and felt a mystery in being awake next to his sleep. She contemplated it, rooting gently in the warmth, thinking that it was odd that she knew she was awake and he asleep, and that he knew neither; and in thinking so, she slept again. But the cock called her name.

She rolled over carefully, so as not to enter the colder frontier of the bed's edge, and put her head out. She should wake him. It was his turn to milk, his last day. But she couldn't bring herself to do that. How would it be if she did it for him, a gift. She imagined his gratitude, and weighed it against the cold dawn and the stairs downward, the wet farmyard and the labor. The gratitude seemed to win, she could feel it the more intensely, could feel it almost as a gratitude of hers toward him. "Aw," she said, grateful for her own kindness, and slipped out of bed.

Swearing terribly and softly she took the stool in the closet, not quite putting her flesh against its iciness, and then in a quick, Chinese-stepping crouch, blowing through her chattering teeth, hunted up her clothes and put them on. Her hands shook with cold and hurry as she did up buttons.

A hard life, she thought with pleasure as she breathed the foggy air out on the fire escape, pulling on brown gardener's gloves; a hard life, this farm-laborer's life. She went down. Outside the door of George's kitchen hallway was a bag of selected garbage for the goats, to be mixed with their meal. She shouldered this, and slopped across the yard to the goats' apartment, hearing them stirring.

"Hi, guys," she said. The goats—Punchita and Núni, Blanca and Negrita, Guapo and La Gráni and the unnamed ones

(George had never named any of them, and Sylvie's inspiration hadn't yet reached two or three, of course they must all have names but the *right* names)—looked up, clattered on the linoleum, shat, and gave voice. The smell of their garden apartment was vivid. Sylvie wondered if she remembered it from childhood, it seemed to suit her nostrils so well.

She fed them, measuring grain and garbage into the bathtub with a nice eye and mixing it carefully as though it were a child's formula; she talked to them, criticizing faults and praising virtues even-handedly but reserving special affection for the black kid and for the oldest, La Gráni, a granny indeed, all backbone and shin, "like a bicycle," Sylvie said. Arms crossed, leaning on the jamb of the bathroom door, she watched them chew with a sidewise motion and raise their heads in rotation to look at her and then down again to their breakfast.

Morning light had begun to enter the apartment. The flowers on the wallpaper awoke, and those on the linoleum, neglected beds and growing indiscernible year by year under dirt, even with all of Brownie's sweeping and mopping in the night. She yawned widely. Why do animals get up so early? "Up and at 'em, huh," she said. "Late for work. Dummies."

She thought, as she prepared for milking: look what love makes me do. And she stopped for a moment, feeling warmth suddenly poured into her heart and loins, for she hadn't before used the word about her feelings for Auberon. Love, she said again to herself; and yes, there was the feeling, the word was like a swallow of rum. For George Mouse, her buddy for life, no matter what, who had taken her in when she had no place else, she felt deep gratitude and a complex of other feelings, mostly good; but not this heat, like a flame with a jewel held at its heart. The jewel was a word: love. She laughed. Love. Nice to be in love. Love disguised her in a peacoat and brown gloves, love sent her to the goats and warmed her hands in her armpits for the goats' udders. "Okay, okay, take it easy," she said, gently, to them and to the love disguised in labor. "Take it easy, we're coming."

She stroked Punchita's udders. "Hey, big tits. Ay *mami*. Where'd you get them big tits. You find them under a bush?" She worked, thinking of Auberon asleep in his bed, and George asleep in his; she alone awake, and all unknown. Found under a bush: a foundling. Saved from the City, taken within these walls, and put to work. In the stories, the foundling always turns out to be some high type person left for dead or something by mistake; a princess no one knows. Princess: that's what George always called her. Hey Princess.

259

A lost princess, enchanted and robbed of her memory of being a princess; a goat-girl, but if you tore off the dirty goat-girl clothes, there would be the sign, the jewel, the birthmark, the silver ring, everybody amazed, everybody laughing. Quick streams of milk rang against the bucket, and then hissed in rising foam, left, right, left, right, calming and bemusing her. And then come into her kingdom, after all the work: grateful for the humble shelter, and humbled herself to have found true love there: so all you guys get to be free, and get gold. And the hand of the princess. She leaned her head against Punchita's hairy warm flank, and her thoughts turned into milk, to wet leaves, baby animals, snails' shells, faun's feet.

"Some princess," Punchita said. "Lots of labor there."

"Whudjoo say?" Sylvie said, looking up, but Punchita only turned her long face to Sylvie, and went on chewing her endless gum.

Brownie's House

Out into the yard, with a jar of fresh milk and a new-laid brown egg she had taken from under a hen who nested in the exploded sofa which stood still in the living room of the goats' apartment. She crossed the humpy vegetable patch to a building on the other side, a building clad in brown vines, with tall sad blind windows and stairs that led up to no door. Behind and below the stairs a tiny damp areaway led to the basement; miscellaneous broken boards and gray slats were nailed up over its entrance and windows; you could peek in, but could see nothing in the darkness. Hearing Sylvie's approach, there swarmed out from within the basement several mewling cats, some of the Farm's cat troops, George said sometimes that at his Farm they grew mostly bricks and raised mostly cats. A big, flat-headed, one-eyed thug was king down there; he didn't deign to appear. But a delicate calico did, hugely pregnant the last time Sylvie had seen her. Not now, though; skinny, depleted, with flaccid stomach and big pink titties. "You got kittens, you?" Sylvie said in reproach. "And didn't tell nobody? You!" She stroked her, and poured milk for them, and, hunkering down, peered through the slats. "Wish I could see," she said. "Kitties."

They roamed around her for a time as she looked in, but she could see only a pair of big yellow eyes: the old guy's? Or Brownie's? "Hi, Brownie," she said, for that was Brownie's house too, she knew, though no one had ever seen him in it. Leave him alone, George always said, he gets along okay. But Sylvie always said hello. She sealed the jar of milk, half-full, and with the egg put it just inside the basement, on a ledge there. "Okay, Brownie," she said. "I'm going. Thanks."

That was a ruse, in a way, for she waited, hoping to catch a glimpse. Another cat appeared. But Brownie stayed within. She rose then, and stretching, started back toward the Folding Bedroom. Morning had come to the Farm, foggy and soft, not so cold after all. She stopped a moment, in the center of the high-walled City garden, feeling sweetly blessed. Princess. Hmp. Under her dirty goat-girl clothes were only yesterday's underwear. Soon she's have to think about getting a job, making some plans, getting her story under way again. But for this moment, in love and safe, chores done, she felt she needn't go anywhere at all, or do anything else, and her story would unfold anyway, clearly and happily.

And endlessly. She knew, for a moment, that her story *was* endless: more endless than any kid's fairy-tale, more endless than "A World Elsewhere" and all its complications. Endless. Somehow. She strode across the Farm, hugging herself, breathing in the farm's rich animal and vegetable exhalations, and smiling.

From deep within his house, Brownie watched her go, smiling too. He took, with his long hands and without a sound, the jar of milk and the egg from the shelf where Sylvie had put them; he drew them within his house, he drank the milk, he sucked the egg, he blessed his queen with all his heart.

She undressed as quickly as she had dressed, leaving only her panties, as Auberon, awaking, watched from within the bedclothes; then she hurried, making small cries, to climb in with him, climb down into warmth, warmth she deserved (she felt) as no other did, warmth where she ought always to be. Auberon re-treated, laughing, from her cold hands and feet that sought him, sought his sleep-soft and helpless flesh, but then surrendered; she pressed her cold nose into the crook of her neck to warm it, moaning like a dove, as his hands took hold of her panties' elastic.

A Banquet

At Edgewood, Sophie laid one card on another, knight of wands on queen of cups.

Later Sylvie said: "Do you have thoughts?"

"Hm?" said Auberon. His nakedness draped in his over-coat, he was building a fire.

"Thoughts," Sylvie said. "Then. I mean during then. I have lots, almost like a story."

He saw what she meant, and laughed. "Oh, *thoughts*," he

said. "Then. Sure. Crazy thoughts." He built the fire hurriedly, heedlessly throwing in most of the wood left in the woodbox. He wanted it hot in the Folding Bedroom, hot enough to draw Sylvie out from the blankets she sheltered beneath. He wanted to see her.

"Like now," she said. "This time. I was wandering."

"Yes," he said, for he had been too.

"Children," she said. "Babies, or baby animals. Dozens, all sizes and colors."

"Yes," he said. He'd seen them too. "Lilac," he said.

"Who?"

He blushed, and stabbed the fire with a golf club that was kept there for that purpose. "A friend," he said. "A little girl. An imaginary friend."

Sylvie said nothing, only wandered in thought, still not quite returned. Then, "Who again?" she said.

Auberon explained.

At Edgewood, Sophie turned down a trump, the Knot. She was looking, not having chosen to look but once again looking, for a lost child of George Mouse's and her fate, but couldn't find them. Instead she found, and the more she looked the more she went on finding, another girl, and not lost; not lost now, but searching. Past her the kings and queens marched, rank on rank, speaking each his message: I am Hope, I am Regret, I am Idleness, I am Unlooked-for Love. Armed and mounted, solemn and minatory, they went on progress through the dark wood of the trumps; but apart from them, unseen by them, glimpsed only by Sophie, moving brightly amid dark dangers, a princess none of them knew. But where was Lilac? She turned down the next card: it was the Banquet.

"So whatever happened to her?" Sylvie asked. The fire was hot, and the room warming.

"Just what I told you," Auberon said, parting the skirts of his coat to warm his buttocks. "I never saw her again after that day, at the picnic . . ."

"Not *her*," Sylvie said. "Not the made-up one. The real one. The baby."

"Oh." He seemed to have been propelled forward several centuries since his arrival in the City; trying to remember Edgewood at all now was an effort, but to search in childhood was to dig up Troy. "You know, I don't really know. I mean I don't think I was ever told the whole story."

"Well, what *happened*, though." She moved luxuriously within the sheets, warming too. "I mean did she die?"

"I don't think so," Auberon said, shocked at this notion.

For a moment he saw the whole story through Sylvie's eyes, and it seemed grotesque. How could his family have lost a baby? Or if it hadn't been lost, if the explanation were simple (adoption, death even) then how could it be that he didn't know it? In Sylvie's family history there were several lost babies, in Homes or fostered; all were minutely remembered, all mourned. If he had been capable just then of any emotion other than that directed toward Sylvie and his plans for her in the next moments, he would have felt anger at his ignorance. Well, it didn't matter. "It doesn't matter," he said, glad to know it didn't. "I give up on it all."

She yawned hugely, and tried to speak at the same time, and laughed. "I said so you're not going back?"

"No."

"Even after you find your fortune?"

He didn't say *I've found it,* though it was true; he'd known it since they'd become lovers. Become lovers: like a wizardry, like frogs become princes.

"You don't want me to go back?" he said, doffing the overcoat and climbing on the bed.

"I'd follow you," she said. "I would."

"Warm?" he said, drawing down the quilt that covered her.

"Hey," she said. "Ay, *que grande.*"

"Warm," he said, and took the neck and shoulders he had revealed by turns between his lips, sucking and munching like a cannibal. Flesh. But all alive, all alive. "I'm melting," she said. He entwined her in him as though his long body could swallow hers, a morsel but endless. He bent to her nakedness, a banquet. "In fact I'm cooking," she said, and she was, her warmth and comfort deep as it was heated further and made more perfect by the incandescent jewel within her; she watched him for a moment, amazed and gratified, watched him swallow her endlessly toward his hollow heart; then she went wandering, and he too, both again in the same realm (later they would speak of it, and compare the places they had been, and find them the same); a realm where they were led, so Auberon thought, by Lilac; coupled, not walking, but still wandering, they were led down concave weed-spined lanes in an endless land, down the twists and turns of a long, long story, a boundless and-then, toward a place something like the place Sophie at Edgewood contemplated in the dark-etched trump called the Banquet: a long table clothed in just-unfolded linen, its claw-feet absurd in the flowers beneath twisted and knotty trees, the tall compote overflowing, the symmetrical candelabra, the many places set, all empty.

Book Four

The Wild Wood

I

They neither work nor weep;
in their shape is their reason.

—*Virginia Woolf*

The years after baby Lilac was rapt from her sleeping mother's arms were the busiest Mrs. Underhill could remember in a long (in fact as-good-as-eternal) life. Not only was there Lilac's education to attend to, and a watch kept just as ever on the rest of them, but there were as well all the councils, meetings, consultations and celebrations, multiplying as the events they had all so long nursed into being came more and more rapidly to pass; and all this in addition to her usual tasks, each composed of countless details no one of which could be skimped or scamped.

But look how she had succeeded! On a day in November a year after the boy Auberon followed imaginary Lilac into the dark of the woods, and lost her, Mrs. Underhill quite otherwhere measured the real Lilac's golden length with a practiced eye. She was, at just past eleven years old, as tall as bent Mrs. Underhill; her chicory-blue eyes, clear as brook water, were level with the old ones which studied her. "Very good," she said. "Very, very good." She circled Lilac's slim wrists with her fingers. She tilted up Lilac's chin and held a buttercup beneath it. She measured with thumb and forefinger the span from aureole to aureole, and Lilac laughed, tickled. Mrs. Underhill laughed too, pleased with herself and with Lilac. There wasn't a tinge of green to her biscuity skin, not a trace of absence in her eyes. So often Mrs. Underhill had seen these things go wrong, seen changelings grow dim and marrowless, become at Lilac's age attenuated pieces of vague longing and good for nothing

A Time and
a Tour

ever after. Mrs. Underhill was glad she had taken on the hand-rearing of Lilac. What if it had worn her to a raveling? It had succeeded, and there would be aeons in which to rest soon enough.

Rest! She drew herself up. There must be strength for the end. "Now, child," she said. "What was it you learned from the bears?"

"Sleep," Lilac said, looking doubtful.

"Sleep indeed," said Mrs. Underhill. "Now . . ."

"I don't want to sleep," Lilac said. "Please."

"Well, how do you know till you've tried it? The bears were comfortable enough."

Lilac, pouting, overturned a darkling beetle which was just then crossing her instep, and righted it again. She thought of the bears in their warm cave, oblivious as snow. Mrs. Underhill (who knew the names of many creatures, as every naturalist should) intro-duced them to her: Joe, Pat, Martha, John, Kathy, Josie, and Nora. But they made no response, only drew breath all together, and let it out, and drew it again. Lilac, who had never closed her eyes except to blink or play hide-and-seek since the night she woke in Mrs. Underhill's dark house, stood bored and repelled by the seven sleep-ers, like seven sofas in their lumpish indifference. But she took her lesson from them; and when Mrs. Underhill came for her in the spring, she had learned it well, and for a reward Mrs. Underhill showed her sea-lions asleep in northern waters bobbing in the waves, and albatrosses in southern skies asleep on the wing; still she hadn't slept, but at least she knew how.

But now the time had come.

"Please," Lilac said, "I will if I must, only . . ."

"No ifs, ands, or buts," Mrs. Underhill said. "There are times that just go by, and times that come. This time's come."

"Well," Lilac said, desperate, "can I kiss everyone good-night?"

"That would take years."

"There are bedtime stories," Lilac said, her voice rising. "I want one."

"All the ones I know are in this one, and in this one it's now the time you fall asleep." The child before her crossed her arms slowly, still thinking; a dark cast came over her face; she would fight this one out. And like all grannies faced with intransigence, Mrs. Underhill bethought her how she might give in—with dignity, so as not to spoil the child. "Very well," she said. "I haven't time to argue. There's a tour I was to take, and if you'll promise to be good, and after take your nap, I'll take you too. It might be educational. . . ."

"Oh yes!"

"And education after all was all the point. . . ."

"It was!"

"Well then." Seeing her excitement, Mrs. Underhill felt for the first time something like pity for the child, how she would be long bound up in the vines and tendrils of sleep, as quiescent as the dead. She rose. "Listen now! Hold tight to me, great thing though you've become, and nor eat nor touch a single thing you see. . . ." Lilac had leapt up, her nakedness pale and alight as a wax candle in Mrs. Underhill's old house. "Wear this," she said, taking a tiny green three-clawed leaf from within her clothes, licking it with a pink tongue, and sticking it to Lilac's forehead, "and you'll see what I say you'll see. And I think . . ." There was a heavy beating of wings outside, and a long broken shadow passed over the windows. "I think we can go. I needn't tell you," she said, raising a warning finger, "that no matter what you're not to speak to anyone you see, not *anyone*," and Lilac nodded solemnly.

The stork they rode flew high and fast over swift-unfolding brown and gray November landscapes, but still perhaps Somehow within other borders, for Lilac naked on her back felt neither warm nor cold. She held tight to folds of Mrs. Underhill's thick clothing, and clutched the stork's heaving shoulders with her knees, the smooth oiled feathers beneath her thighs soft and slippery. With taps of a stick, here, there, Mrs. Underhill guided the stork up, down, right and left.

Rainy-day Wonder

"Where do we go first?" Lilac asked.

"Out," Mrs. Underhill said, and the stork dove and twisted; beneath, far off but coming closer, a large and complex house appeared.

Since babyhood, Lilac had seen this house many times in dreams (how it could be she dreamt but didn't sleep she never thought about; there was much that Lilac, raised the way she had been, had never thought about, knowing no different way the world and selfhood might be organized, just as Auberon never wondered why three times a day he sat at a table and put food into his face). She didn't know, though, that when she dreamt she walked the long halls of that house, touching the papered walls hung with pictures and thinking What? What could this be?, that then her mother and her grandmother and her cousins dreamt—not of her, but of someone like her, somewhere else. She laughed when, now, from the stork's back, she saw the house entire and recognized it instantly: as when the blindfold was lifted from her in a game of blindman's-bluff and the mysterious features she had been touching, the nameless garments, were revealed to be those of someone well-known, someone smiling.

It grew smaller as they grew closer. It shrank, as though running away. If that goes on, Lilac thought, by the time we're close enough to look in its windows, one of my eyes only will be able to see in at a time, and won't they be surprised inside as we go by, darkening the windows like a stormcloud! "Well, yes," Mrs. Underhill said, "if it were one and the same; but it's not, and what they'll see, or rather not see (I should think), is stork, woman and child about a midge's size or smaller, and never pay it the least never-mind."

"I can't," said the stork beneath them, "quite feature that."

"Neither can I," Lilac said laughing.

"Doesn't matter," Mrs. Underhill said. "See now as I see, and it's all one for the purpose."

Even as she spoke, Lilac's eyes seemed to cross, then right themselves; the house rushed greatly toward them, rose up house-sized to their stork's size (though she and Mrs. Underhill were smaller—another thing for Lilac not to think to ask about). From on high they sailed down to Edgewood, and its towers round and square bloomed like sudden mushrooms, bowing neatly before them as they flew over, and the walls, weedy drives, porte-cocheres and shingled wings altered smoothly in perspective too, each according to its own geometries.

At a touch of Mrs. Underhill's stick the stork tipped its wings and fell sharply to starboard like a fighter plane. The house changed faces as they swooped, Queen Anne, French Gothic, American, but Lilac didn't notice; her breath was snatched away; she saw the house's trees and angles uptilt and right themselves as the stork pulled out of her dive, saw the eaves rush up, then closed her eyes, clinging tighter. When her maneuver was completed and the stork was steady again, Lilac opened her eyes to see they were in the shadow of the house, circling to perch on a flinty belvedere outcropping on the house's most Novembery side.

"Look," Mrs. Underhill said when the stork had folded her wings. Her stick like a knuckly finger indicated a narrow ogive window, casements ajar, kitty-corner to where they stood. "Sophie asleep."

Lilac could see her mother's hair, very like her own, displayed on the pillow, and her mother's nose peeking from under the coverlet. Asleep . . . Lilac's bringing-up had trained her to pleasure (and to purpose, though she didn't know it), not to affection and attachments; rainy days could bring tears to her clear eyes, but wonder, not love, shook her young soul most. So for a long time as she looked within the dim bedroom at her motionless mother, a chain of feelings was knitted within her for which she had no name. Rainy-day wonder. Often they had told her, laughing, how her hands had gripped her mother's hair, and how with scissors they had cut the hair to free her, and she'd laughed too; now she wondered what it would be like to be laid against that person; down within those covers, her cheek on that cheek, her fingers in that hair, asleep. "Can we," she said, "go closer to her?"

"Hm," said Mrs. Underhill. "I wonder."

"If we're small as you say," the stork said, "why not?"

"Why not?" Mrs. Underhill said. "We'll try."

They fell from the belvedere, the stork laboring under her load to rise, neck straining, feet climbing. The casements ahead grew big as though they came closer, but for a long time they came no closer; then, "Now," said Mrs. Underhill, and tapped with her stick, and they swooped in a vertiginous arc through the open casement and into Sophie's bedroom. As they flew between floor and ceiling toward the bed, they would have appeared to an observer (if such a one were possible) to be the size of the bird one makes of two linked hands waving.

"How did that work?" Lilac asked.

"Don't ask me how," Mrs. Underhill said. "Anywhere but here it wouldn't." She added thoughtfully, as they circled the bedpost: "And that's the point, about the house, isn't it?"

Sophie's flushed cheek was a hill, and her open mouth a cave; her head was forested in golden curls. Her breathing was as slow and low a sound as a whole day makes together. The stork stalled at the bed's head and turned to coast back toward the arable lands of the patchwork quilt. "What if she woke?" Lilac said.

"You dasn't!" Mrs. Underhill cried out, but it was too late; Lilac had loosed her grip of Mrs. Underhill's cloak and as they passed, inspired by an emotion like mischief but fiercer by far, had taken hold of a coiling rope of golden hair and tugged. The jolt nearly upset them; Mrs. Underhill flailed with her stick, the stork squawked and stalled, they circled Sophie's head again, and still Lilac hadn't released the hank she held. "Wake up!" she shouted.

"Bad child! Oh horrible!" Mrs. Underhill cried.

"Squawk!" said the stork.

"Wake up!" Lilac called, hand cupped by her cheek.

"Away!" cried Mrs. Underhill, and the stork beat strongly

271

toward the casement, and Lilac, if she weren't to be pulled from the stork's back, had to release her mother's hair. One thick strand as long as a towline came away in her fingers, and laughing, shrieking with fear of falling, and trembling head to foot, she had time to see the bedclothes heave vastly before they reached the casement again. Just outside, like a sheet suddenly shaken open, and with a noise like that, they became again stork-sized to the house, and mounted quickly to the chimney-pots. The hair that Lilac held, three inches long now and so fine she couldn't hold it, slipped from her fingers and sailed away glittering.

Sophie said "What?" and sat bolt upright. More slowly she lay back again amid the pillows, but her eyes didn't close. Had she left that casement open? The end of a curtain was waving goodbye madly out of it. It was deathly cold. What had she dreamt? Of her great-grandmother (who died when Sophie was four). A bedroom full of pretty things, silver-backed brushes and tortoise-shell combs, a music-box. A glossy china figurine, a bird with a naked child and an old woman on its back. A big blue glass ball as fine as a soap bubble. Don't touch it, child: a voice dim as the dead's from within the ivory-lace bedclothes. Oh do be careful. And all the room, all of life, distorted, made blue, in the ball; made strange, gorgeous, unified because spherical, within the ball. Oh child, oh careful: a weeping voice. And the ball slipping from her grasp, falling as slow as a soap bubble toward the parquet.

She rubbed her cheeks. She put out a foot, wondering, toward her slippers. (Smashing on the floor, without a sound, only her great-grandmother's voice saying Oh, oh, child, what a loss.) She ran a hand through her hair, impossibly tangled, elf-locks Momdy called them. A blue glass ball smashing; but what had come before that? Already it had fled from her. "Well," she said, and yawned, and stood upright. Sophie was awake.

That's the Lot

The stork was fleeing Edgewood when Mrs. Underhill pulled herself together.

"Hold hard, hold hard," she said soothingly. "The harm's been done."

Lilac behind her had fallen silent.

"I just want," the stork said, leaving off her furious wing-beats, "none of the blame for this to fall on *me*."

"No blame," Mrs. Underhill said.

"If punishments are to be handed out . . ." the stork said.

"No punishments. Don't worry your long red beak about it."

The stork fell silent. Lilac thought she should volunteer to take whatever blame there might be, and soothe the beast, but didn't; she pressed her cheek into Mrs. Underhill's coarse cloak, filled again with rainy-day wonder.

"Another hundred years in this shape," the stork muttered, "is all I need."

"Enough," said Mrs. Underhill. "It may be all for the best. In fact how could it be otherwise? Now"—she tapped with her stick—"there's still much to see, with time a-wasting." The stork banked, turning back toward the multiple housetops. "Once more around the house and grounds," said Mrs. Underhill, "and then off."

As they climbed over the broken, every-which-way mountains and valleys of the roof, a small round window in a particularly peculiar cupola opened, and a small round face looked out, and down, and up. Lilac (though she had never seen his real face before) recognized Auberon, but Auberon didn't see her.

"Auberon," she said, not to call him (she'd be good now), but only to name him.

"Paul Pry," said the stork, for it was from this window that Doc had used to spy on her and her chicks when she had nested here. Thank it all, that part was over! The round window closed.

Mrs. Underhill pointed out long-legged Tacey as they came over the house. Gravel spun from beneath her bike's slim tires as she shot around a corner of the house, making for the once-trim little Norman farmhouse which had been stables once and then garage—the old wooden station wagon slept here in the dark—and was now also where Bumbum and Jane Doe and their many offspring had their hutches. Tacey dropped her bike at the back entrance (seeming, to Lilac over her head, to be a complex scurrying figure suddenly coming apart into two pieces) and the stork with a wingbeat rose out over the Park. Lily and Lucy walked a path there, arm in arm, singing; the sounds they made rose up to Lilac faintly. The path they walked intersected another, which ran past the leafless hedges wild now as madman's hair, stuck full of dead leaves and small birds' nests. Daily Alice loitered there, a rake in her hand, watching the hedge where perhaps she had seen a bird's or an animal's movement; and, when they had gained a bit more altitude, Lilac could see Smoky far down the same path, eyes on the ground, books under his arm.

"Is that . . ." Lilac asked.

"Yes," Mrs. Underhill said.

"My father," Lilac said.

"Well," Mrs. Underhill said, "one of them anyway," and

guided the stork to swoop that way. "Now mind you mind, and no tricks."

How odd people looked from right above, the egg of the head in the center, a left foot seeming to emerge from the back of it, a right foot from the front, then the reverse. Smoky and Alice at last saw each other, and Alice waved, her hand also seeming extruded from the head, like an ear. The stork swooped low beside them as they met, and they took on more human shape.

"How's tricks?" Alice said, putting the rake under her arm like a shotgun and thrusting her hands in the pockets of her denim jacket.

"Tricks is good," Smoky said. "Grant Stone threw up again."

"Outside?"

"At least outside. Amazing how it quiets things down. For a minute. An object-lesson."

"About. . ."

"Stuffing a dozen marshmallows into your face on the way to school? I don't know. The ills that flesh is heir to. Mortality. I look very grave and say, 'I guess we can go on now.' "

Alice laughed, and then looked sharply left, where a movement had caught her eye, either a far-off bird or a last fly nearby; saw nothing. Did not hear Mrs. Underhill, who had been regarding her tenderly, say *Bless you, dear, and watch the time;* only she didn't speak again all the way to the house, nor did she hear much of what Smoky told her about school; she was absorbed in a feeling she had felt before, that the earth, unimaginably massy as it was, turned beneath her only because she walked it, like a treadmill. Peculiar. When they came close to the house, she saw Auberon flee from it as though pursued; he gave a glance at his parents, but no acknowledgement, turning a corner and disappearing. And from an upstairs window she heard her name called: Sophie stood at her casement window. "Yes?" Alice called, but Sophie said nothing, only looked down at them both in wonderment, as though it had been years and not hours since she'd seen them last.

The stork glided over the Walled Garden and then, wings cupped, skimmed the ground between the avenue of sphinxes, all but featureless now and more silent than ever. Ahead, running the same way, was Auberon. In two flannel shirts (one like a jacket) grown somewhat small in a burst of growing he was doing, but still buttoned at the wrist; his long-skulled head balanced on a skinny neck, his sneakered feet pigeon-toed a bit. He ran a few steps, walked, ran again, talking to himself in a low voice.

"Some prince," Mrs. Underhill said in a low voice as they caught up to him. "A lot of labor there." She shook her head. Auberon ducked, hearing wingbeats at his ear as the stork rose up past him, and though he didn't stop walk-running, his head swiveled to see a bird he couldn't see. "That's the lot," said Mrs. Underhill. "Away!"

Lilac looked down as they rose away, and kept on looking down at Auberon growing smaller. In her growing-up Lilac (no matter that Mrs. Underhill strictly forbade it) had spent long days and nights alone. Mrs. Underhill herself had her enormous tasks, and the attendants set to wait on Lilac as often as not had games of their own they wanted to play, amusements the thick, fleshly, stupid human child could never grasp or join. Oh, they had caught it when Lilac was found wandering in halls and groves she had no business to be in yet (startling once with a thrown stone her great-grandfather in his melancholy solitude) but Mrs. Underhill could think of no help for it, and muttered "All part of her Education," and went off to other climes and spaces that needed her attention. But in all this there was one playmate who had always been with her when she liked, who had always done her bidding without a moment's hesitation, who had never grown tired or cross (the others could be, sometimes, not only cross but cruel) and always felt as she did about the world. That he had also been imaginary ("Who's the child always talking to?" asked Mr. Woods, crossing his long arms, "and why amn't I allowed to sit in my own chair?") hadn't really distinguished him from a lot that went on in Lilac's odd childhood; that he had gone away, one day, on some excuse, hadn't really surprised her; only now, as she watched Auberon lope toward the castellated summer house on an urgent mission, she did wonder what this real one—not very like her own Auberon really, but the same, there was no doubt of it—had been doing through all her growing up. He was very small now, pulling open the door of the Summer House; he glanced behind him as though to see if he had been followed; then "Away!" cried Mrs. Underhill, and the Summer House bowed beneath them (showing a patched roof like a tonsured head) and they were off, high and gaining speed.

In the Summer House Auberon unscrewed his fountain pen even before he sat down at the table there (though he firmly shut and hooked the door). He took from the table's drawer a locked imitation-leather five-year diary from some other five years, opened it with a tiny key from his pocket, and, flipping to a

A Secret
Agent

275

page in a long-ago unrecorded March, he wrote: "And yet it does move."

He meant by this the old orrery at the top of the house, from whose round window he had looked out as the stork bearing Lilac and Mrs. Underhill had passed. Everyone told him that the machinery which operated the planets in this antiquity was clabbered thick with rust and had been immovable for years. Indeed Auberon had tried the cogs and levers himself and couldn't move them. And yet it did move: a vague sense he had had that the planets, sun and moon were not, on one visit, in quite the same places they had been on a previous visit he had now confirmed by rigorous tests. It does move: he was sure. Or pretty sure.

Just why they should all have lied to him about the orrery didn't just at the moment concern him. All he wanted was the goods on them: proof that the orrery moved, and (much harder to get, but he would get it, the evidence was mounting) proof that they all knew very well that it moved and didn't want him to know.

Slowly, after glancing at the entry he had made and wishing he had more to state, he shut and locked the diary and put it in the table drawer. Now what question could he think of, what seemingly chance remark could he let fall at dinner, that would cause someone—his great-aunt, no, far too practiced in concealments, expert at looks of surprise and puzzlement; or his mother; or his father, though there were times when Auberon thought his father might be as excluded as he was—to confess inadvertently? As the bowl of mashed potatoes went around, he might say "Slowly but surely, like the planets in the old orrery," and watch their faces. . . . No, too brazen, too obvious. He pondered, wondering what anyway would be for supper.

The Summer House he sat in wasn't much changed from the time his namesake had lived and died there. No one had been able to think what to do with the boxes and portfolios of pictures, or felt up to disturbing what seemed a careful order. So they only patched the roof against leaks, and sealed the windows; and thus it stayed while they thought. The image of it would now and then pass through one or another of their minds, particularly Doc's and Cloud's, and they would think of the past stored up there, but no one got around to unsealing it, and when Auberon came to take possession no one disputed him. It was headquarters now, and contained all things necessary for Auberon's investigations: his magnifying glass (old Auberon's in fact), his clack-clack folding measure and roll-up tape measure, the final edition of *The Architecture of Country Houses*, and the diary which contained his conclusions. It also contained all of Auberon's pictures, which Auberon the younger had not yet begun to look into; the pictures that would end his quest as it had the elder's, through vast superfluity of ambiguous evidence.

Even as it was he wondered if the thing about the orrery weren't dumb after all, and his arrangement of string and pencil-marks open to more than one conclusion anyway. A blind alley, as lined with mum sphinxes as the others he had gone up. He stopped tilting back the old chair he sat in, stopped vigorously chewing the end of his pen. Evening was gathering; no evening more oppressive than one like this, in this month, though at nine years old he didn't attribute his oppression to the day and the hour, or call it by that name. He only felt how hard it was to be a secret agent, to go in disguise as a member of his own family, trying to so insinuate himself among them that, without his ever asking a question (that would expose him instantly) the truth would be spilled in his presence because they would have no reason to doubt he was already privy to it.

Crows cawed away toward the woods. A voice, blown around the Park with odd alteration, called his name, and announced dinner. He felt, hearing the long-drawn melancholy vowels of his own name, at once sad and hungry.

Lilac saw sunset elsewhere.

"Magnificent!" Mrs. Underhill said. "And terrifying. Doesn't it make your heart beat high?"

"But it's all made of cloud," Lilac said.

"Hush, dear," Mrs. Underhill said. "Someone's feelings could be hurt."

The Worm Turned

Made of sunset was more correct: all of it, the thousand striped war-tents obscured in the wreathing smokes of orange watch-fires, and their curling pennants striped the same in sunset colors; the black lines of horse or foot or both, picked out with silver weapon-glint, that receded as far as the eye could see; the bright coats of captains and the dark gray of guns being drawn up under their command against empurpled barricadoes—the whole vast encampment, or was it a great flotilla of galleons, armed and under sail?

"A thousand years," Mrs. Underhill said grimly. "Defeats, retreats, rear-guard actions. But no more. Soon . . ." The knobby stick was under her arm like a commander's baton, her long chin was held high. "See?" she said. "There! Isn't he brave?"

A figure, burdened with armor and with weighty responsibilities, walked the poop, or toured the breastworks; wind stirred his white whiskers as long almost as himself. The Generalissimo of all

277

this. In one hand he held a wand; just then, the sunset altered, the tip of the wand caught fire. He gestured with it toward where the touch-holes on his guns would be, had they been guns, but then thought better of it. He lowered the wand, and it went out. From his broad belt he drew out a folded map, unfolded it, peered near-sightedly at it for some time, then refolded it, replaced it, and took up his heavy tread again.

"The die's cast now," Mrs. Underhill said. "No more re-treating. The worm's turned."

"If you don't mind," the stork said, her voice faint be-tween labored pants, "this altitude's too much for me."

"Sorry," Mrs. Underhill said. "All done now."

"Storks," the stork panted, "are accustomed to sit down, once a league or so."

"Don't sit down there," Lilac said. "You'll sink right through."

"Downward then," Mrs. Underhill said. The stork ceased to pump her short wings, and began to descend, with a sigh of relief. The Generalissimo, hands on his gunwales or his machicolated belvedere, stared eagle-eyed into the distance, but failed to see Mrs. Underhill salute him smartly as they passed.

"Oh, well," she said. "He's as brave as they come, and it's a fine show."

"It's a fake," Lilac said. It had already shape-shifted into something even more harmless as they sank.

Curse the child, Mrs. Underhill thought irritably. It was convincing, convincing enough. . . . Well. Perhaps they oughtn't to have entrusted it all to that Prince: he was just too old. But there it is, she thought: we're all old, all too old. Could it be they had waited too long, been too long patient, retreated one final furlong too many? She could only hope that, when the time at last came, the old fool's guns would not all misfire, would at least give heart to their friends and frighten briefly those on whom they were trained.

Too old, too old. For the first time she felt that the out-come of it all, which could not be in doubt, *could* not, was in doubt. Well, it would all be over soon. Did not this day, this very evening, mark the beginning of the last long vigil, the last watch, before the forces were at last joined? "Now that's the tour I promised you," she said over her shoulder to Lilac. "And now . . ."

"Aw," Lilac said.

"With no complaints . . ."

"Aaaawww . . ."

"We'll take our nap."

Lilac's long-drawn note of complaint altered, surprisingly, in her throat, to something else, a sudden mouth-opening thing that stole over her like a spirit. It went on opening her mouth wider and wider—she hadn't thought it could open so wide—and made her eyes close and water, and sucked a long draft of air into her lungs, which expanded with a will of their own to take it in. Then, just as suddenly, the spirit was gone, releasing her jaws and letting her exhale.

She blinked, smacking her lips, wondering what it was.

"Sleepy," said Mrs. Underhill.

For Lilac had just yawned her first yawn. Her second came soon after. She put her cheek against the rough stuff of Mrs. Underhill's broad cloak, and, Somehow no longer unwilling, closed her eyes.

When he was very young, Auberon had begun a collection of postmarks. On a trip with Doc to the post office in Meadowbrook, he had begun idly examining the wastebaskets, having nothing else to do, and had immediately come up with two treasures: envelopes from places that seemed fantastically distant to him, and looking remarkably crisp for having come so far.

Hidden Ones Revealed

It soon developed into a small passion, like Lily's for bird's nests. He insisted on accompanying whoever was traveling near a post office; he conned his friends' mail; he gloated over distant cities, far states whose names begin with I, and, rarest of all, names from across the sea.

Then one day Joy Flowers, whose granddaughter had lived abroad for a year, gave him a fat brown bag full of envelopes sent her from every part of the world. He could hardly find on the map a place which had not stamped its name on one of these pieces of blue flimsy. Some of them came from places so distant they weren't even in the alphabet he knew. And at a stroke his collection was complete, and his pleasure in it over. No discovery he could make in Meadowbrook's post office could add to it. He never looked at it again.

It was the same with old Auberon's photographs, when at last young Auberon discovered them to be more than a record of a large family's long life. Beginning with the last, of a beardless Smoky in a white suit beside the birdbath made of dwarves which still stood by the Summer House door, he had dipped tentatively, then sorted curiously, and at last hunted greedily through the thousands of pictures big and small, elated with wonder and horror (here! Here was the secret, the hidden ones revealed, each image worth a thousand words) and for a week was almost unable to speak to his family for fear of revealing what he had learned—or rather thought he was about to learn.

For in the end the pictures illuminated nothing, because nothing illuminated them.

"Note thumb," old Auberon would write on the back of a dim view of gray and black shrubbery. And there was, in the undisentanglable convolvulus, something that looked very much like a thumb. Good. Evidence. Another, though, would annul this evidence entirely, because (with only speechless exclamation marks on its back) here was an entire figure, a ghostly little miss in the leaves, with a trailing skirt of dew-glistening cobweb, pretty as a picture; and in the foreground, out of focus, the excited figure of a blond human child looking at the camera and pointing out the wee stranger. Now who could believe that? And if it was true (it couldn't be, how it had been faked Auberon had no idea, but it was just too stupidly real not to be fake) then what good was the maybe-a-thumb-in-the-shrubbery and a thousand others just as obscure? When he had sorted a dozen boxes into the few impossible and the many unintelligible, and saw that there were dozens of boxes and portfolios yet to go, he shut them all up (with a mixed sense of relief and loss) and rarely thought about them again.

He never again opened the old five-year diary in which his own notes had been made either, after that. He returned the last edition of the *Architecture of Country Houses* to its place in the library. His own humble discoveries, or what had seemed like discoveries—the orrery, a few interesting slips of the tongue made by his great-aunt and his grandmother—heart-startling as they had once seemed, had been swamped by the thick flood of torturous pictures and worse notes on them which his namesake had made. He forgot about it all. His secret-agentry was over.

His secret-agentry was over, but he had by this time gone so long in disguise indetectably as a member of his family that by slow stages he had actually become one. (It often happens so with secret agents.) The secret that was not revealed in Auberon's photographs lay, if it lay anywhere, in the hearts of his relatives; and Auberon had for so long pretended to know what they all knew (so that they would reveal it to him by accident) that he came to suppose he did know it as well as any of them; and like his evidences, and about the same time, he forgot about it. And since, if they had ever really known anything that he didn't know, they too had all forgotten it or seemed to have forgotten it, then they were all equal and he was one of them. He even felt, just below consciousness, that he was aligned with all the rest of them in a conspiracy that excluded only his father: Smoky didn't know, and didn't know they knew he didn't know. Somehow, rather than separating them from him, this joined them to Smoky all the more, as though they kept from him the secret of a surprise party planned for Smoky himself. And so for a while Auberon's relations with his father grew a little easier.

But even though he stopped scrutinizing others' motives and movements, a habit of secrecy about his own persisted in Auberon. He often put false faces over his actions, for no good reason. Certainly it wasn't to mystify; even as a secret agent he hadn't wanted to mystify anybody, a secret agent's task is just the reverse of that. If he had a reason at all, it may have been only a desire to present himself in a milder, clearer light than he might otherwise have appeared in: milder and clearer than the dim-flaring lamps by which he perceived himself.

"Where are you off to in such a tear?" Daily Alice asked him as he wolfed his milk and cookies at the kitchen table after school. He was in this autumn the last Barnable still a scholar in Smoky's school. Lucy had stopped going the year before.

"Play ball," he said, his mouth full. "With John Wolf and those guys."

"Oh." She half-refilled the glass he held out to her. Good lord he had gotten big lately. "Well, tell John to tell his mother I'll be over tomorrow with some soup and things, and see what she needs." Auberon kept his eyes on his cookies. "Is she feeling any better, do you know?" He shrugged. "Tacey said . . . oh, well." It seemed unlikely from Auberon's air that he would go tell John Wolf that Tacey had said his mother was dying. Probably her simple message wouldn't even be passed. But she couldn't be sure. "What do you play?"

"Catcher," he said quickly. "Usually."

"I was a catcher," Alice said. "Usually."

Auberon put down the glass, slowly, thinking. "Do you think," he said, "that people are happier when they're alone, or with other people?"

She carried his glass and plate to the sink. "I don't know," she said. "I guess . . . Well, what do *you* think?"

"I don't know," he said. "I just wondered if . . ." What he wondered was whether it was a fact everyone knew, every grown-up anyway: that everyone is of course happiest alone, or the reverse, whichever it was. "I guess I'm happier with other people," he said.

"Oh yes?" She smiled; since she faced the sink, he couldn't see her. "That's nice," she said. "An extrovert."

"I guess."

"Well," Alice said softly, "I just hope you don't creep back in your shell again."

He was already on his way out, stuffing extra cookies in his pockets, and didn't stop, but a strange window had suddenly been flung open within him. Shell? Had he been in a shell? And—odder still—had he been seen to be in one, was it common knowledge? He looked through this window and saw himself for a moment, for the first time, as others saw him. Meanwhile his feet had taken him out the broad swinging doors of the kitchen, which grump-grumped behind him in their way, and through the raisin-odorous pantry, and out through the stillness of the long dining room, going toward his imaginary ball-game.

Alice at the sink looked up, and saw an autumn leaf blown by the casement, and called out to Auberon. She could hear his footsteps receding (his feet had grown even faster than the rest of him) and she picked up his jacket from the chair where he had left it, and went after him.

He was gone out of sight on his bike by the time she got out the front door. She called again, going down the porch stairs; and then noticed that she was outdoors, for the first time that day, and that the air was clear and tangy and large, and that she was aimless. She looked around herself. She could just see, extending beyond the corner of the house, a bit of the walled garden around the other side. On the stone ornament at its corner a crow was perched. It looked at her looking around herself—she couldn't remember ever having seen one so close to the house before, they were fearless but wary—and flopped from its perch, and flapped with heavy wings away over the park. *Cras, cras:* that's what Smoky said crows say in Latin. *Cras, cras:* "tomorrow, tomorrow."

She walked around the walled garden. Its little arched door stood ajar, inviting her in, but she didn't go in. She went around to the funny little walk bordered by hydrangeas that had once been in training to be ornamental shrubs, tall and orderly and cabbage-headed, but which had declined over the years into mere hydrangeas, and smothered the walk they were supposed to border, and obscured the view they were supposed to exhibit: two Doric pillars, leading to the path that went up the Hill. Still aimless, Alice walked along that walk (brushing from the last hydrangea blossoms a shower of papery petals like faded confetti) and started up the Hill.

Auberon circled back along the road that ran around Edgewood's guardian stone wall, and at a certain point, dismounted. He climbed the wall (a fallen tree there and a weedy hummock on the other side made a stile) and hauled his bike over, wheeled it through the rustling gilded beechwood to the path, mounted again, and, glancing behind him, rode to the Summer House. He concealed the bike in the shed old Auberon had built.

Glory

The Summer House, warmed by September sun poured in through its big windows, was still and dusty. On the table where once his diary and spying equipment had lain, and where later he had sorted through Auberon's pictures, there lay now a mass of scribbled-over papers, the sixth volume of Gregorovius's Medieval Rome, a few other large books, and a map of Europe.

Auberon studied the top sheet, which he had written the day before:

> The scene is in the Emperor's tent outside Iconium. The
> Emperor is seated alone in an X-kind of chair. His sword is
> across his knees. He is wearing his armor but some of it has
> been taken off, and a servant is slowly polishing it, and
> sometimes he looks at the Emperor, but the emperor just
> looks straight ahead and doesn't notice him. The emperor
> looks tired.

He considered this, and then mentally crossed out the last sentence. Tired wasn't what he meant at all. Anybody can look tired. The Emperor Frederick Barbarossa on the eve of his last battle looked . . . well, what? Auberon uncapped his pen, thought, and recapped it again.

His play or screenplay (it might end up either, or be transmogrified into a novel) about the Emperor Frederick Barbarossa had in it Saracens and papal armies, Sicilian guerillas and potent paladins and princesses too. A congeries of romantic place-names where battles were fought by mobs of romantic personages. But what Auberon loved in these doings wasn't anything that could be called romantic. In fact all that he wrote was only to bring forth that figure, that single figure on a chair: a figure seen in a moment of repose snatched between two desperate actions, exhausted after victory or defeat, hard clothes stained with war and wear. Above all it was a gaze: a calm, appraising look, without illusions, the look of someone coming to see that the odds against a course of action were insurmountable but the pressures to execute it irresistible. He was indifferent to the weather around him, and as Auberon described it, it was like him: harsh, indifferent, without warmth. His landscape was empty, save for a far tower with an aspect like his own, and perhaps a distant muffled rider bearing news.

Auberon had a name for all this: Glory. If it wasn't what was meant by Glory, he didn't care. His plot—who was to be master, that's all—didn't really much interest him; he was never able to grasp just what the Pope and Barbarossa were arguing about anyway. If someone had asked him (but no one would, his project had been begun in secrecy and years later would be burned in secrecy) what it was that had drawn him to this particular emperor, he wouldn't have been able to say. A harsh ring in the name. The picture of him old, mounted, armed, on his last futile crusade (all crusades were futile to young Auberon). And then swept away by chance in that armor under the waters of a nameless Armenian river when his charger shied in the middle of the ford. Glory.

"The Emperor doesn't look tired exactly, but . . ."

He marked this out too, angrily, and recapped his pen again. His huge ambition to delineate seemed suddenly insupportable, as though he might weep that he had to bear it alone.

I just hope you don't creep back into your shell.

But he had worked so hard to make that shell look just like him. He thought everyone had been fooled, and they hadn't been.

Dust swam in the sunlight still being cast into weighty blocks by the windows of the Summer House, but the place was growing chilly. Auberon put his pen away. Behind him on the shelves, old Auberon's boxes and portfolios stared at the back of his head. Would it always be so? Always a shell, always secrets? For his own secrets seemed likely to separate him from the rest of them as surely as any secret they had kept from him could have. And all he wanted was to be the Barbarossa he imagined: without illusions, without confusions, without shameful secrets: ferocious sometimes, embittered maybe, but all of a piece from breast to back.

He shivered. What had become of his jacket, anyway?

His mother was drawing it over her shoulders as she climbed the hill, thinking: Who plays baseball in weather like this? Young maples along the path, surrendering early, had already flamed beside still-green sisters and brothers. Wasn't this football or soccer weather? An extrovert, she thought, and smiled and shook her head: the glad hand, the easy smile. Oh dear . . . Since

Not Yet

284

her children had stopped growing up quite so fast, the seasons had started going by Daily Alice faster: once, her children were different people in spring and fall, so much learning and sensing and laughing and weeping were packed into their age-long summers. She had hardly noticed that this fall had come. Maybe because she had only one child now to be readied for school. One and Smoky. Practically dutiless on autumn mornings with only one lunch to make, one sleepy body to chivvy from bath to breakfast, one bookstrap and one pair of boots to find.

And yet, as she went up the Hill, she felt huge duties calling to her.

She reached the stone table at the peak of the Hill, a little out of breath, and sat on the stone bench by it. Beneath it—a sorry mess, decayed and autumnal-looking—she glimpsed the pretty straw hat that Lucy had lost in June and mourned all summer. Seeing it, she felt sharply her children's fragility, their danger, their helplessness before loss, before pain, before ignorance. She named them in order in her mind: Tacey, Lily, Lucy, Auberon. They rang like bells of different pitch, some truer than others, but all answering her pull: they were fine, really, all four, just as she always told Mrs. Wolf or Marge Juniper or whoever else inquired after them: "They're fine." No: the duties she felt calling her (and she felt them more intensely now, seated in the sunlight above a wide landscape) didn't have to do with them, or with Smoky either. They had, Somehow, to do with that path upward, and this windy hill-top, and that sky raddled with fast-moving, pigeon-feather gray-and-white cloud, and this young autumn full (as every autumn so strangely is) of hope and expectation.

The feeling was intense, as though she were being drawn in or swept away; she sat motionless in its grip, marveling and a little frightened, expecting it to pass in a moment, like sensations of *déjà vu*. But it didn't pass.

"What?" she said to the day. "What is it?"

Mute, the day couldn't answer: but it seemed to gesture to her, to tug at her familiarly, as though it had mistaken her for someone else. It seemed, and it would not stop seeming, just about to turn all at once to face in her direction, having heard her voice—as though she had all this time been looking at the wrong or back side of it (and of everything, always) and was now about to see it plain, as it really was: and it she, too: and still it couldn't speak.

"Oh, what," Daily Alice said, not knowing she spoke. She felt that she was dissolving helplessly into what she beheld, and at the same time had grown imperious enough to command it in every part; light enough to fly, yet so heavy that not the stone bench but the whole stone hill was her seat; awed, yet for some reason not surprised as she came to know what was being asked of her, what she was summoned to.

"No," she said in reply; "no," she said, softly, as she might have to a child who had by mistake taken hold of her hand or the skirt of her dress, thinking her its mother, turning up to her, inquiringly, its wondering face. "No."

"Turn away," she said, and the day did.

"Not yet," she said, and rang the bells of her children's names again. Tacey Lily Lucy Auberon. Smoky. Too much, too much yet to do; and yet there would come a time when, no matter how much was left to do, no matter how her daily duties had grown or shrunk away, a time when she could no longer refuse. She wasn't unwilling, or afraid, though she thought that when the time came she would be afraid, and yet could not refuse. . . . Astonishing, astonishing that there could be no end to growing bigger, she had thought years ago that she had grown so huge that she could grow no more, and yet she hadn't even begun. But: "Not yet, not yet," she said, as the day turned away; "not yet, there's too much to do still; please, not yet."

The Black Crow (or someone like him), far off invisible through the turning trees, called its call, heading home.

Cras. Cras.

II

Wild above rule or art, enormous bliss.

—Milton

What Smoky liked about his girls' growing up was that, though they moved away from him, they did so (it seemed to him) less from any distaste or boredom than simply to accommodate a growth in their own lives: when they were kids, their lives and concerns—Tacey's rabbits and music, Lily's bird's-nests and boy-friends, Lucy's bewilderments—could all fit within the compass of his life, which was then replete; and then as they grew up and out, they no longer fit, they needed room, their concerns multiplied, lovers and then children had to be fitted in, he could no longer contain them unless he expanded too, and so he did, and so his own life got larger as theirs did, and he felt them to be no further from him than ever, and he liked that. What he didn't like about their growing up was the same thing: that it forced him to grow, to enlarge, sometimes beyond what he felt the character he had come over the years to be encased in could stand.

There had been one great advantage in having grown up anonymous when he had come to have children: for they could make out of him what they wanted, could think him kindly or strict, evasive or frank, jolly or glum, as their own tempers required. That was great, great to be Universal Father, nothing withheld from him, he bet (though he had no way to prove it) that his daughters had told him more of their secrets, grave, shameful, or hilarious, than most men's did. But there were limits even to his flexibility, he couldn't as time went on stretch as much as he had once done, he found himself less and less able to ignore it when his character, growing ever more lobsterlike and unsheddable, disapproved of or could not understand the Young.

Tossing and Turning

287

Perhaps it was chiefly that which had come between him and his youngest child, his son Auberon. Certainly the commonest emotions Smoky remembered feeling about the boy were a sort of baffled irritation, and a sadness over the mysterious gulf that seemed fixed between them. Whenever he got up the nerve to try to learn what was with his son, Auberon had produced a complex and well-practiced secretiveness that Smoky was helpless and even bored before; when Auberon had come to him, on the other hand, Smoky had seemed unable not to retreat into a bluff, know-nothing, standard-issue parent costume, and Auberon would too quickly retire. And it had grown not better but worse as the years went by, until at last Smoky, with outward head-shaking and reluctance, and inward relief, had seen him off on his strange quest to the City.

Maybe if they'd played ball more. Just gone out, son and dad, and tossed the old pill around on a summer afternoon. Auberon had always liked to play ball, Smoky knew, though he himself had never been either good at it or happy doing it.

He laughed at the insufficiency of this reverie. Just the sort of thing his character might suggest, in the face of his children's inexplicability. Maybe, though, it had occurred to him because he sensed that some common touch, some ordinary gesture, might have crossed over what lay between him and his son; if there were something as wide that lay between him and his daughters, he had never noticed it, but of course it might well be there, disguised in the daily strangenesses of growing up today with a father who had grown up yesterday, or even the day before that.

None of his daughters had married, or seemed likely to, though he had now two grandchildren, Lily's twins, and Tacey seemed ready to bear a child by Tony Buck. Smoky held no particular brief for marriage, though he couldn't imagine life without his own, odd as it had proved to be; and as for fidelity, he had no right to speak at all. But he did find it distressing to think that his offspring would be more or less nameless, and that if this kept up might one day be describable only as race-horses are, by so-and-so out of so-and-so. And he couldn't help thinking that there was something embarrassingly obvious in the couplings of his daughters with their lovers, a shamelessness that marriage would have decently hid. Or rather his character thought so. Smoky himself mostly cheered their daring, their bravery, and wasn't ashamed to admire their sexuality as he had always admired their beauty. Big girls now, after all. But still . . . well, he hoped they could ignore it when his character made noises, or caused him, for instance, to decline to visit Tacey and what's-his-name when they were living together in a cave. A cave!

His children seemed bent on recapitulating in their own lives the whole history of the race. Lucy gathered herbs for simples and Lucy read the stars and hung coral around her babies' necks to ward off evil; Auberon with a knapsack set out to seek his fortune. And in her cave Tacey discovered fire. Just when the supply of electricity in the world seemed to be running out for good, too. Thinking of which, he listened to the clock chime the quarter hour, and wondered if he should go down and shut down the generator.

He yawned. The single lamp lit in the library made a pool of light he was reluctant to leave. There was a pile of books by his chair from which he had been choosing for school; the old ones had grown repulsive to the hand and eye from years of use, and boring beyond expression. Another clock chimed, one o'clock, but Smoky didn't trust it. Outside in the corridor, a candle in her hand, a familiar wraith of nighttime passed: Sophie, still awake.

She went away—Smoky watched the changeful light on walls and furniture flash and dim—and then came back again.

"You still up?" she said, and at the same moment he asked the same of her.

"It's awful," she said, coming in. She wore a long white nightgown which gave her even more the air of an unlaid ghost. "Tossing and turning. Do you know that feeling? As though your mind's asleep but your body's awake—and won't give in—and has to keep jumping from one position to another. . . ."

"Just barely waking you up every time. . ."

"Yes, so your head can't—can't dive down, sort of, and really sleep, but it won't give up either and wake up, and just keeps repeating the same dream, or the beginnings of one, and not getting anywhere. . . ."

"Sorting over and over the same handful of nonsense, yup; until you have to give in, and get up. . . ."

"Yes, yes! And you feel like you've been lying there for hours, struggling, and not sleeping at all. Isn't that awful?"

"Awful." He felt, but would never admit to, a sense of fitness that Sophie, long the champion sleeper, had come in recent years to be a fair insomniac, and knew now even better than Smoky, a chancy sleeper at the best of times, the pursuit of fleeing oblivion. "Cocoa," he said. "Warm milk. With a little brandy. And say your prayers." He'd given her all this advice before.

She knelt by his chair, covering her bare feet with the nightgown, and rested her head on his thigh. "I thought," she said, "when I sort of snapped out of it, you know, the tossing and turning? I thought: she must be cold."

"She?" he said. And then: "Oh."

"Isn't that dumb? If she's alive, she's not cold, probably; and if she's—well, not alive . . ."

"Mm." There was, there was Lilac, of course: he had been thinking with such self-satisfaction of how well he knew his daughters, and how well they liked him, his son Auberon the only grain of grit in his oyster: but there was his other daughter, his life was odder than it often appeared to him, Lilac was a dimension of mystery and grief he sometimes forgot. Sophie never forgot.

"You know what's funny?" Sophie said. "Years ago, I used to think of her growing up. I knew she got older. I could feel it. I knew just what she looked like, how she'd look as she got older. But then it stopped. She got to be about . . . nine, or ten, I guess; and then I couldn't imagine her getting any older."

Smoky answered nothing, only stroked Sophie's head softly.

"She'd be twenty-two now. Think of that."

He thought of it. He had (twenty-two years ago) sworn before his wife that her sister's child would be his, all the responsibility his. Her disappearance hadn't altered that, but it had left him with no duties. He couldn't imagine how to search for the real Lilac lost, when he had at length been told that she *was* lost, and Sophie had hid her awful ordeal with the false Lilac from him, and from all of them. He still didn't know how it had ended: Sophie was gone for a day, and when she returned there was no more Lilac, false or true; she took to her bed, a cloud was lifted from the house, and a sadness entered it. That's all. He was not to ask.

So much not to ask. It was a great art, that one. He had learned to deploy it as skillfully as a surgeon his art, or a poet his. To listen; to nod; to act on what he was told as though he understood it; not to offer criticism or advice, except of the mildest kind, just to show his interest and concern; to puzzle out. To stroke Sophie's hair, and not try to deflect her sadness; to wonder how she had gone on with such a life, with such a sorrow at its heart, and never ask.

Well, if it came to that, though, his other three daughters were as great a mystery to him, really, as his fourth, only not a mystery it grieved him to contemplate. Queens of air and darkness, how had he come to engender them? And his wife: only he had so long ceased (since his honeymoon, since his wedding day) to question her that she was now no more a mystery (and no less) than clouds and stones and roses. If it came to that, the only one he could begin to understand (and criticize, and intrude on, and study) was his only son.

"Why do you suppose that is?" Sophie asked.

"Why what is?"

"That I can't imagine her getting any older."

"Well, hm," Smoky said. "I don't really know."

She sighed, and Smoky stroked her head, running his fingers through her curls, sorting them out. They would never exactly go gray; though the gold faded from them, they still seemed like golden curls. Sophie was not one of those maiden aunts whose unused beauty comes to seem dried and pressed, like a flower—for one thing she was no maiden—but it did seem that her youth couldn't be outgrown, that she had never and would never become a person of mature years. Daily Alice looked now, at almost fifty (fifty, good Lord) just as she ought, as though she had shed the successive skins of childhood and youth and come forth thus, whole. Sophie looked sixteen: only burdened with a lot of unnecessary years, almost unfairly, it seemed. Smoky wondered which, over the years, he had oftenest thought the more beautiful. "Maybe you need another Interest," he said.

"I don't need another Interest," she said. "I need to sleep."

It had been Smoky who, when Sophie had discovered with surprise and disgust how many hours there are in the day when it isn't half-filled with sleep, had said that most people fill those hours with Interests of some kind, and had suggested Sophie take some up. Out of desperation she'd done so; the cards, of course, first, and when she wasn't working with them she gardened, and paid visits, canned, read books by the dozen, made repairs around the house, always resenting that these Interests should be forced on her in the absence of her lost (why? why lost?) sweet sleep. She turned her head restlessly on Smoky's thigh as though it were her unquiet pillow. Then she looked up at him. "Will you sleep with me?" she said. "I mean sleep."

"Let's make cocoa," he said.

She got up. "It seems so unfair," she said, casting her eyes upward at the ceiling. "All of them up there fast asleep and I have to haunt the place."

But in fact—besides Smoky leading the way by candlelight to the kitchen—Momdy had just awakened with arthritic pains, and was thinking whether it would hurt more to get up and get aspirin or lie there and ignore them; and Tacey and Lucy had never gone to bed at all, but sat up by candlelight in quiet talk about their lovers and friends and family, about the fate of their brother and the shortcomings and virtues of the sister not present, Lily. Lily's twins had just awakened, one because he'd wet the bed, and the other because she felt the wetness, and their wakefulness was about to wake Lily. The only one asleep then in the house was Daily Alice, who lay on her stomach with her head deep in two feather pillows, dreaming of a hill where there stood an oak tree and a thorn in deep embrace.

On a winter day, Sylvie paid a visit to her old neighborhood, where she had not lived since her mother had gone back to the Island and farmed Sylvie out to

La Negra

aunts. In a furnished room down that street, with her mother, her brother, a child of her mother's, her grandmother and the odd visitor, Sylvie had grown, and grown Somehow the Destiny that she had today brought back with her to these littered streets.

Though only a few subway stops away from Old Law Farm, it seemed a great distance, across a border, another country altogether; so dense was the City that it could contain many such foreign countries cheek by jowl; there were several which Sylvie had never visited at all, their old Dutch or quaintly rural names suggestive and remote to her. But these blocks she knew. Hands in the pockets of her old black fur, double socks on her feet, she went down streets she walked often in her dreams, and they weren't much different than she dreamed them to be, they were preserved as though in memory: the landmarks by which she had mapped them as a child were mostly still there, the candy store, the evangelical church where women with moustaches and powdered faces sang hymns, the squalid credit grocer, the *notária* scary and dark. She found, by following these markers, the building where the woman called La Negra lived; and though it was smaller, dirtier, with darker and more urinous hallways than it had been or than she remembered it, it was the same, and her heart beat fast with apprehension as she tried to remember what door was hers. From out an apartment, as she climbed up, a family argument accompanied by *jíbaro* music suddenly burst, husband, wife, crying children, mother-in-law. He was drunk, and going out to get drunker; the wife railed at him, the mother-in-law railed at the wife, the music sang of love. Sylvie asked where La Negra's house was. They all fell silent, all but the radio, and pointed upward, studying Sylvie. "Thanks," she said, and went up; behind her the sextet (well and long rehearsed) resumed.

From behind her door studded with locks La Negra questioned Sylvie, unable, apparently, despite her powers, to place her. Then Sylvie remembered that La Negra had known her only by a childhood diminutive, and she gave that. There was a shocked silence (Sylvie could sense it) and the locks were opened.

"I thought you were gone," the black woman said, eyes wide, mouth corners drawn down in fearful surprise.

"Well, I am," Sylvie said. "Years ago."

"I mean far," La Negra said. "Far, far."

"No," Sylvie said. "Not so far."

She herself was a shock to Sylvie, for she had grown a lot smaller, and a lot less fearsome as she was smaller. Her hair had grown gray as steel wool. But the apartment, when La Negra at last stood aside and let Sylvie enter, was the same: mostly a smell, or many smells together, that brought back, as though she inhaled them with the odors, the fear and wonder she had felt here.

"*Tití*," she said, touching the old woman's arm (for La Negra still stared at her in something like surprise and didn't speak), "*Tití*, I need some help."

"Yes," La Negra said. "Anything."

But Sylvie, looking around the small, small apartment, was less sure than she had been an hour ago about what help she wanted. "Gee, the same," she said. There was the bureau, done up as a composite altar, with the chipped statues of black Santa Barbara and black Martín de Porres, the red candles lit before them, the plastic lace tablecloth beneath; there was the picture of Our Lady pouring blessings that turned to roses into the gas-flame-colored sea. On another wall was the Guardian Angel picture which also hung, oddly, on George Mouse's kitchen wall: the dangerous bridge, the two children, the potent angel watching to see that they crossed safely. "Who's that?" Sylvie asked. Between the saints, before the talismanic hand, was a picture shrouded in black silk, a candle before it also, burning low.

"Come sit, come sit," La Negra said quickly. "She's not being punished, even if it looks like it. I never meant that."

Sylvie decided not to question this. "Oh, hey, I brought some stuff." She offered the bag, some fruit, some *dulces*, some coffee she had begged from George, who got it when no one else could, for she had remembered her aunt drinking it with relish, hot white and sweet.

La Negra, blessing her profusely, grew easier. When she had, as a precaution, taken the glass of water she kept on the bureau to catch evil spirits in and flushed it down the noisy toilet and replaced it, they made the coffee and talked about old things, Sylvie in her nervousness rattling on a little.

293

"So I heard from your mother," La Negra said. "She called long-distance. Not me. But I heard. And your father."

"He's not my father," Sylvie said, dismissively.

"Well . . ."

"Just somebody my mother married." She smiled at her aunt. "I got no father."

"Ay, *bendita.*"

"A virgin birth," Sylvie said, "just ask my mother," and then, though laughing, clapped her hand over her mouth at the blasphemy.

Coffee made, they drank it and ate the *dulces,* and Sylvie told her aunt why she had come: to get the Destiny that once upon a time La Negra had seen in the cards and in her child's palm removed from her: to have it pulled, like a tooth.

"See, I met this man," she said, looking down, suddenly shy to feel the warmth that bloomed in her heart. "And I love him, and . . ."

"Is he rich?" La Negra asked.

"I don't know, I think his family is, sort of."

"Then," her aunt said, "maybe he's the Destiny."

"Ay, *tití,*" Sylvie said. "He's not *that* rich."

"Well . . ."

"But I love him," Sylvie said. "And I don't want some big Destiny coming along and snatching me away from him."

"Ay, no," La Negra said, "but where would it go? If it left you."

"I don't know," Sylvie said. "Couldn't we just throw it away?"

La Negra slowly shook her head, her eyes growing round. Sylvie felt suddenly both afraid and foolish. Wouldn't it have been easier to simply cease believing that any destiny was hers; or to believe that love was as high a destiny as anyone could want or have, and which she did have? What if messing in it with spells and potions didn't ward it off at all, but only turned it bitter, and sour, and cost her love as well. . . . "I don't know, I don't know," she said. "All I know is that I love him, and that's enough; I want to be with him, and be good to him, and make him rice and beans and have his babies and . . . and just go on and on."

"I'll do what you ask," La Negra said in a low voice that didn't sound like hers. "Whatever you ask."

Sylvie looked at her, a *frisson* of blue magic stealing up her spine. The old black woman sat in her chair as though enervated, her eyes not leaving Sylvie but not quite seeing her either. "Well,"

294

Sylvie said doubtfully. "Like the time you came to our house, and put the evil spirits on a coconut, and rolled them out the door? And down the hall and out to the garbage?" She had told this story to Auberon, laughing uproariously over it with him, but here it didn't seem funny. "*Tití?*" she said. But her aunt (though sitting in her plastic-covered armchair all the time) was no longer there.

No, the Destiny could not be put on a coconut, it was too heavy; it could not be rubbed away with oils or washed off in herb-baths, it went too deep. La Negra, if she were to do what Sylvie commanded, if her old heart could bear it, would have to draw it from Sylvie and swallow it herself. Where was it, first of all? She approached Sylvie's heart with careful steps. Most of these doors she knew: love, money, health, children. That portal there, ajar, she didn't know. "*Bueno, bueno,*" she said, desperately afraid that when the Destiny she let out of Sylvie rushed upon her it would kill her, or so transform her that she might as well be dead. Her spirit guides, when she turned to look for them, had fled in terror. And yet she must do what Sylvie had commanded. She put her hand on the door, and began to open it, glimpsing a golden daylight beyond, a rush of wind, the murmur of many voices.

"No!" Sylvie shouted. "No, no, no, I was wrong, don't!"

The portal slammed shut. La Negra, with heart-sickening vertigo, tumbled back into her armchair in her little apartment. Sylvie was shaking her.

"I take it back, I take it back!" Sylvie cried. But it hadn't ever left her.

La Negra, recovering, patted her heaving breast with her hand. "Don't ever do that again, child," she said, weak with relief that Sylvie had done it this time. "You could kill a person."

"I'm sorry, sorry," Sylvie said, "but this was all just a big mistake. . . ."

"Rest, rest," La Negra said, still immobile in the chair, watching Sylvie scramble into her coat. "Rest." But Sylvie wanted only to get out of this room, where strong currents of *brujería* seemed to play around her like lightning; she was desperately sorry she'd even thought of this move and hoping against hope that her foolishness hadn't wounded her Destiny, or caused it to turn on her, or waked it at all, why hadn't she just let it sleep where it lay, peaceful, not bothering anybody? Her invaded heart thudded reproachfully, she pulled out her purse with trembling fingers, looking for the wadded bills she had brought to pay for this crazy operation.

La Negra drew away from the money Sylvie offered her as though it might sting her. If Sylvie had offered her gold coins, potent herbs, a medallion heavy with power, a book of secrets, she would have taken them, she had passed the test put to her and deserved something: but not dirty bills for buying groceries, not money passed through a thousand hands.

Out on the street, hurrying away, Sylvie thought: I'm all right, I'm all right; and hoped that it was so. Sure she could have her Destiny removed; she could cut off her nose, too. No, it was with her for good, she was still burdened with it, and if not glad to be then glad anyway that it hadn't been taken from her; and though she still knew little enough of it she had learned one thing when La Negra had tried to open her, one thing that made her hurry fast away, searching for a train station that would take her downtown: she had learned that whatever her Destiny was, Auberon was in it. And for sure she would not want it at all if he were not.

La Negra rose heavily from her armchair, still baffled. Had that been she? It could not have been, not in the flesh, not unless all of La Negra's calculations were wrong; yet there on the table lay the fruits she had brought, and the half-eaten *dulces*.

But if that had been her who had been with La Negra just now, then who was it who had these many years helped La Negra in her prayers and spells? If she was still here, untransmogrified still in the same City La Negra inhabited, then how could she, at La Negra's invocation, have cured, and told truths, and brought lovers together?

She went to her bureau and drew off the scrap of black silk that covered the central image of her spirit altar. She half-expected it to be gone, but it was there: an old cracked photograph, an apartment much like the one La Negra stood in; a birthday party, and a dark, skinny, pigtailed girl seated (on a thick phone book no doubt) behind her cake, a paper crown on her head, her large eyes compelling and weirdly wise.

Was she so old now, La Negra wondered, that she could no longer tell spirits from flesh, visitors from visitations? And if that were so, what might it portend for her practice?

She lit a fresh candle, and pressed it down into the red glass before the picture.

The Seventh Saint

Long years before, George Mouse had showed the City to Auberon's father, making him a City man; now Sylvie did the same for Auberon. But this was a changed town. The difficulties that everywhere had been cropping up in even the best laid plans of men, the inexplicable yet Somehow inevitable failure that seemed built into their manifold schemes, were sharpest in the City, and caused the greatest pain and anger there—the fixed anger Smoky hadn't seen but which Auberon saw in nearly every City face he looked into.

For the City, even more than the nation, lived on Change: rapid, ruthless, always for the better. Change was the life-blood of the City, the animator of all dreams there, the power that coursed in the veins of the men of the Noisy Bridge Rod and Gun Club, the fire that boiled up wealth and bustle and satisfaction. The City Auberon came to, though, had slowed. The quick eddies of fashion had grown sluggish; the great waves of enterprise had become a still lagoon. The permanent depression that the Noisy Bridge Rod and Gun Club struggled against but was unable to reverse began in this grinding-to-a-halt, this unwonted cumbersome loginess of the greatest City, and spread outward from it in slow ripples of weary exhaustion to benumb the republic. Except in small ways (and that as constantly and pointlessly as ever) the City had stopped changing: the City Smoky knew had changed utterly, had changed by ceasing to change.

Sylvie assembled from the aged pile a city for Auberon's mind's eye that would anyway have been very different from the one George built for Smoky. A landlord, however odd, and an old, even a charter member (on his grandfather's side) of the great changer families, George Mouse felt the decline in his beloved Apple, and was sometimes bitter, and sometimes indignant at it. But Sylvie had come from a different strain, from what had been in Smoky's time the dark underside of a glamorous dream, and was now (though still raddled with violence and desperation) its least depressed enclave. The last cheerful streets of the City were the streets where the people lived who had always been at the changers' mercy, and who now, in the midst of everyone else's sense of decline into stagnancy and ir-remediable mess, lived much as they always had, only with a longer history and a surer tradition: hand-to-mouth, day to day, with a musical accompaniment.

She took him to the clean, crowded apartments of her relatives, where he sat on the plastic coverings of outlandish furni-ture and was given glasses of iceless soda (not good to chill the blood, they thought) set in saucers, and inedible *dulces,* and listened to himself praised in Spanish: a good husband, they thought, for Sylvie, and though she objected to the honorific they went on using it for decency's sake. He was confused by the many and, to his ear, similar-sounding diminutives used among them. Sylvie, for reasons she remembered but he could never keep straight, was called Tati by some members of the family, a branch that included the dark aunt not-really-an-aunt who had read Sylvie's Destiny, the aunt called La Negra. Tati in some child's mouth had become Tita, which had also stuck, and which in its turn became (a grand diminutive) Titania. Often enough Auberon didn't know that the subject of anecdotes told him in hilarious Spanglish was his own beloved under another name.

"They think you're great," Sylvie said to him after a visit, out on the street, her hand thrust deep into his overcoat pocket where he held it for warmth.

"Well, they're very nice too. . . ."

"But *papo*, I was so embarrassed when you put your feet up on that—*esta* thing—that coffee-table thing."

"Oh?"

"That was very bad. Everybody noticed."

"Well, why the hell didn't you say something?" he said, embarrassed. "I mean at home we lay all over the furniture, and it was . . ." He stopped himself from saying *And it was real furniture*, but she heard it anyway.

"I *tried* to tell you. I was *looking* at you. I mean I couldn't say, Hey take your feet off that. They'd think I treated you like Titi Juana treats Enrico." Enrico was a henpecked husband, and a laughingstock. "You don't know what they go through to get that ugly stuff," she said. "It costs a lot, believe it or not, *muebles* like that." They were silent a while, bent into a cruel wind. *Muebles*, he thought, "movables," strange formal-sounding language for such a people. She said, "They're all crazy. I mean some of them are crazy crazy. But they're all crazy."

He knew that, for all the great affection she had for her complex family, she was trying desperately to extricate herself from the long, almost Jacobean tragicomedy of their common life, charged as it was with madness, farce, corrosive love, even murder, even ghosts. In the night she would often toss and turn, and cry out in anguish, imagining terrible things that might, or might have already, happened to one or another of that accident-prone crowd; and often, though Auberon dismissed them as night terrors (for nothing—not one thing he knew of—had ever happened in his family's life that could be called terrible), her imaginings were not far from wrong. She hated it that they were in danger; she hated to be bound to them; her own Destiny shone like a flaring lamp amid their hopeless confusions, always just about to gutter, or be blown out, but still alight.

"I need a coffee," he said. "Something hot."

"I need a drink," she said. "Something strong."

Like all lovers, they had soon assembled (as on a revolving stage) the places where the scenes of their drama alternately took place: a little Ukrainian diner whose windows were always occluded with steam, where the tea was black and so was the bread; the Folding Bedroom of course; a vast gloomy theater encrusted with Egyptian decoration, where the movies were cheap and changed often and played into the morning; the Nite Owl market; the Seventh Saint Bar & Grill.

The great virtue of the Seventh Saint, besides the price of its drinks and its nearness to Old Law Farm, a train stop away, was its wide front windows, nearly floor to ceiling, in which as in a shadow-box or on a movie screen the life of the street outside passed. The Seventh Saint must once have been somewhat splendid, for this glass wall was tinted a rich, expensive brown, which added a further unreality to the scene, and which darkened the interior like dark glasses. It was like being in Plato's cave, Auberon told Sylvie, who listened to him lecture on the subject; or rather watched him talk, fascinated by his strangeness and not paying inordinately close attention to the words. She loved to learn, but her mind wandered.

"The spoons?" he said, lifting one up.

"Girls," she said.

"And the knives and forks are boys," he said, glimpsing a pattern.

"No, the forks are girls too."

They had café-royale before them. Outside, hatted and scarved in the deathly cold, people hurried home from jobs, bent before the unseen wind as before an idol or a lofty personage. Sylvie was herself between jobs at the moment (a common dilemma for one with a Destiny as high as hers) and Auberon was living on his advances. They were poor but leisured.

"The table?" he asked. He couldn't imagine.

"A girl."

It was no wonder, he thought, that she was so sexy, when all the world was boys and girls to her. In the language she had been born into there were no neuters. In the Latin Auberon had learned, or at least studied, with Smoky, the genders of nouns were an abstraction that he at any rate could never feel; but to Sylvie the world was a constant congress of male and female, boy and girl. The world: that was *el mundo*, a man; but *la terra*, the earth, was a woman. That seemed right to Auberon; the world of affairs and notions, the name of a newspaper, the Great World; but mother earth, the fructifying soil, Dame Kind. Such appropriated divisions didn't extend very far, though: the lank-haired mop was a girl, but so was his bony typewriter.

They played that game for a while, and then commented on the people passing by. Because of the tint of the glass, those passing by outside saw, not the cave's interior, but themselves reflected; and, not knowing they were observed from inside, sometimes stopped to adjust their clothing, or admire themselves. Sylvie's strictures on the common run of people were harsher than his; she had a great taste for all eccentricities and oddities, but stern standards of physical beauty and a finely-honed sense of the ridiculous. "Oh, *papo*, check this one out, check him out. . . . *That's* what I meant by a soft-boiled egg, you see what I mean?" And he did see, and she dissolved in her sweet raucous laughter. Without ever knowing he did so, he adopted for life her standards of beauty, could even feel himself drawn to the lean, brown, soft-eyed, strong-wristed men she favored, like Leon the café-crème-colored waiter who had brought their drinks. It was a relief to him when she decided (after long thought) that their children would be beautiful.

The Seventh Saint was preparing for the dinner hour. The bus-boys glanced at their messy table. "You ready?" Auberon said.

"I'm *ready*," she said. "Let's blow this joint." A phrase of George's, full of aged double-entendres more reminiscent of wit than exactly funny. They bundled themselves up.

"Train or walk?" he asked. "Train."

"Hell yes," she said.

In their rush to the warmth they leapt by mistake onto the express, which (full of sheeplike, sheep-smelling riders bound for the Bronx) didn't stop before it reached the old Terminus, mixing it up there with twenty other trains bound in all directions.

Whispering Gallery

"Oh hey wait a sec," she said as they were changing trains. "There's something here I want to show you. Oh yeah! You gotta see this. Come on!"

They went down along passages and up ramps, the same complex Fred Savage had first threaded him through, though whether in the same direction he had no idea. "What," he said.

"You'll love it," she said. She paused at a turning. "Now if I can only find it . . . There!"

What she pointed to was an empty space: a vaulted intersection where four corridors met in a cross.

"What," he said.

"C'mere." She took him by the shoulders and steered him

300

into a corner of the place, where the ribbed vaulting descended to the floor, making what seemed to be a slot or narrow opening but which was only joined bricks. She faced him into this joint. "Just stand there," she said, and she went away. He waited, obediently facing into the corner.

Then, startling him profoundly, her voice, distinct yet hollow and ghostly, sounded from directly in front of him: "Hi there."

"What," he said, "where . . ."

"Sh," her voice said. "Don't turn around. Talk real soft: whisper."

"What is it?" he whispered.

"I don't know," she said. "But if I stand over here in this corner, and whisper, you can hear me over there. Don't ask me how."

Weird! It sounded as though Sylvie were speaking to him from some realm within the corner, through a crack in an impossibly narrow door. A whispering gallery: hadn't there been some speculation about whispering galleries in the *Architecture*? Probably. There wasn't much that book didn't speculate about.

"Now," she said. "Tell me a secret."

He paused a moment. There was a privacy about the corner, the disembodied whispering, that tempted confidences. He felt bared, or barable, though he could see nothing: the opposite of a voyeur. He said: "I love you."

"Aw," she said, touched. "But that's not a secret."

A new fierce heat flew up his spine and erected his hair as a notion came to him. "Okay," he said, and told her of a secret desire he'd had but hadn't dared express to her before.

"Oh, hey, wow," she said. "You devil."

He said it again, adding a few details. It was just as though he were whispering the words into her ear in the darkest privacy of bed, but more abstract, more perfectly intimate even than that: right into her mind's ear. Someone walked past between them; Auberon could hear the footsteps. But the someone couldn't hear his words: he felt a shiver of glee. He said more.

"Mm," she said, as at the prospect of great comfort or satisfaction, a small sound that he couldn't help answering with a sound of his own. "Hey, what are you doing over there," her whisper said, insinuatingly. "Bad boy."

"Sylvie," he whispered. "Let's go home."

"Yah."

They turned away from their corners (each appearing to

the other very small and bright and far away after the dark intimacy of their whispers) and came to meet in the center, laughing now, pressing into each other as much as their heavy coats allowed them to, and with many smiles and looks (God, he thought, her eyes are so bright, flashing, deep, full of promise, all those things eyes are in books but never are in life, and she was his) they caught the right train and rode home amid self-absorbed strangers who didn't notice the two of them, or if they noticed (Auberon thought) knew nothing, nothing of what he knew.

Sex, he had found out, was really terrific. A terrific thing. Anyway the way Sylvie managed it. In him there had always been a split between the deep desires enchained within him and the cool circumspection which seemed to him required in the adult world he had come to inhabit (he felt, sometimes, by mistake). Strong desire seemed to him childish; childhood (his own, anyway, as far back as he could remember almost, and he could tell stories of others') was darkly aflame, burdened with heavy passions; adults had passed beyond all that, into affections, into the calmer enjoyments of companionability, into a childlike innocence. Weirdly backward he knew this to be, but it's how he had felt it. That adult desire, its exigency, its greatness, had been kept a secret from him like all the rest, he didn't wonder at; he didn't even bother to feel cheated or enraged at the long deception, since with Sylvie he had learned otherwise, broken the code, turned the thing inside-out so that it was right-side-up, and caught fire.

He hadn't come to her exactly a virgin, but he may as well have; with no one else had he shared this huge, this necessitous child's greed, no one had ever lavished hers on him or eaten him up so complacently and with such simple relish. There was no end to it and it was all gratified; if he wanted more (and he discovered in himself astonishing, long-compacted thicknesses of desire to be unfolded) he had more. And what he wanted he was as greedy to give and she as greedy to take. It was all so *simple*! Not that there were no rules, oh yes there were, they were like the rules of children's spontaneous games, strictly adhered to but often made up on the spot out of a sudden desire to change the game and please yourself. He remembered Cherry Lake, a dark-browed imperious little girl he had used to play with: she, unlike all the others he played with who said "Let's pretend," always used another formula—she said "We must." We must be bad guys. I must be captured and tied to this tree, and you must rescue me. I must be queen now, and you must be my servant. Must! yes . . .

Sylvie, it seemed, had always known, had never been in the dark about it all. She told him of certain shames and inhibitions she'd had as a kid where he'd had none, because all that stuff, she knew—kissing, taking off clothes with boys, the rush of feeling—was really for grown-ups, and she would come to it truly only when she was older, and had breasts and high heels and make-up. So there was not in her the division he felt; while he had been told that Mom and Dad had loved each other so much that they had subjected themselves to these childish indignities (so it seemed to him) in order to make babies, and could not connect these reported (and only half-believed-in) acts to the huge lashings of feeling invoked in him by Cherry Lake, by certain photographs, by mad games played naked, Sylvie had all along known the real story. Whatever other terrible problems life put before her, and they were many, that one at least she had solved; or rather she had never felt it to be posed. Romance was real, as real as flesh; love and sex were not even woof and warp in it, they were one indissoluble thing, like the seamless fabric of her scented brown skin.

It was he only, then—though in stark numbers she was not more experienced than he—who was astonished, amazed, that this indulgence like a greedy infant's turned out to be just what grown-ups do, turned out to be adulthood itself: the solemn bliss of strength and capability as well as the mad infant bliss of self-satisfaction unending. It was manliness, womanliness, certified again and again by the most vivid of seals. *Papi* she called him in her bliss. *Ay Papi yo vengo.* Papi! Not daytime papo, but strong nighttime daddy, big as a *platano* and father of pleasures. He almost skipped to think of it, she pressed to his side, her head just reaching his shoulder; but he kept a steady, long-legged, grown-up pace. Was he right that men sensed his potency as he strode along with her, and deferred to him, was it true that women glanced at him covertly, admiringly? Why didn't everyone they passed, why didn't the very bricks and blank white sky bless them?

And so they did: at that moment, as they turned onto the street where Old Law Farm could be entered, between one footfall and another something anyway occurred, something that he thought at first to be within himself, a seizure or a heart attack, but instantly felt all around them: something enormous that was like a sound but wasn't one, was either a demolition (a whole block of dirty brick and wallpapered interiors gone to powder if it was) or a burst of thunder (breaking the sky at least in two, the sky which remained inexplicably blank winter white above, if it was) or both at once.

They stopped, clutching each other.

"What the *hell* was that?" Sylvie said.

"I don't know," he said. They waited a moment, but no roiling smokes arose from the buildings around them, no sirens wailed, ignited by catastrophe; and still the shoppers and loungers and criminals went their ways, unalarmed, unmoved, their faces filled with private wrongs.

They went on warily to Old Law Farm, holding each other, each feeling that the sudden blow had been meant to separate them (why? how?) and had only barely failed, and might come again at any moment.

"Tomorrow," Tacey said, turning her embroidery-frame, "or the next day or the next."

"Oh," Lily said. She and Lucy were bent over a crazy-quilt, enriching its surface with different stitcheries, flowers, crosses, bows, esses. "Saturday or Sunday," Lucy said.

What a Tangle

At that moment match was put to touch-hole (perhaps by accident, there would be some trouble about it afterwards) and the thing that Sylvie and Auberon in the City heard or felt rolled over Edgewood, booming the windows, rattling knickknacks on etagères, cracking a china figurine in Violet's old bedroom and making the sisters duck and raise their shoulders to protect themselves.

"What on earth," Tacey said. They looked at one another.

"Thunder," Lily said; "midwinter thunder, or maybe not."

"A jet plane," Tacey said, "breaking the sound barrier. Or maybe not."

"Dynamite," Lucy said. "Over at the Interstate. Or maybe not."

They bent to their work again, silent for a while.

"I wonder," Tacey said, looking up from her frame half turned back-to-front. "Well," she said, and chose a different thread.

"Don't," said Lucy. "That looks funny," she said critically, of a stitch Lily was making.

"This is a crazy-quilt," Lily said. Lucy watched her, and scratched her head, not convinced. "Crazy isn't funny," she said.

"Crazy *and* funny." She worked. "It's a big zigzag."

"Cherry Lake," Tacey said. She held her needle to the

wan light of the window, which had ceased to tremble. "Thought she had two boys in love with her. The other day . . ."

"Was it some Wolf?" Lily asked.

"The other day," Tacey went on (slipping at the first try a silk thread green as jealousy through the needle's eye), "the Wolf boy had a terrible fight—with . . ."

"The rival."

"A third one; Cherry didn't even know. In the woods. She is . . ."

"Three," Lucy sang, and on the second "three" Lily joined her an octave lower: "Three, three, the rivals; two, two, the lily-white boys, Clothed all in green-o."

"She is," Tacey said, "a cousin of ours, sort of."

"One is one," her sisters sang.

"She'll lose them all," Tacey said.

". . . And all alone, and ever more shall be so."

"You should use scissors," Tacey said, seeing Lucy face down on the quilt to bite a thread.

"You should mind your own . . ."

"Business," Lily said.

"Beeswax," Lucy said.

They sang again: Four for the gospel-makers.

"Run off," Tacey said. "All three."

"Never to return."

"Not soon anyway. As good as never."

"Auberon . . ."

"Great-grandfather August."

"Lilac."

"Lilac."

The needles they drew through cloth glittered when they pulled them out to the full extension of the thread; each time they pulled them through the threads grew shorter until they were all worked into the fabric, and must be cut, and others slipped through the needles' eyes. Their voices were so low that a listener would not have known who said what, or whether they talked at all or only murmured meaninglessly.

"What will be fun," Lily said, "is to see them all again."

"All come home again."

"Clothed all in green-o."

"Will we be there? Will all of us be? Where will it be, how long from now, what part of the wood, what season of the year?"

"We will."

"Nearly all."

"There, soon, not a lifetime, every part, midsummer."

"What a tangle," Tacey said, and held up for them to see a handful of stuff from her workbox, which a child or a cat had got into: silk thread bright as blood, and black cotton darning-stuff, a hank of sheep-colored wool, a silkpin or two, and a bit of sequined fabric dangling from it all, spinning on a thread-end like a descending spider.

She heard a note in Elmond's wood
And wished she had been there.

—*Buchan*, Hynde Etin

Hawksquill could not at first determine whether by the operations of her Art she had cast herself into the bowels
of the earth, the bottom of the sea, the heart of the fire
or the middle of the air. Russell Eigenblick would later tell her that
he had often suffered from the same confusion in his long sleep, and
that perhaps it was in all four places that he had been hidden, in all
four corners of the earth. The old legend always put him in the
mountain, of course, but Godfrey of Viterbo said no, the sea; the
Sicilians had him ensconced in the fires of Etna, and Dante put him
in Paradise or its environs though he might just as well (if he had
been feeling vindictive) have stuck him in the Inferno with his
grandson.

Since taking this assignment, Hawksquill had gone far,
though never quite this far, and little of what she had
begun to suspect about Russell Eigenblick could be put
into a form understandable to the Noisy Bridge Rod
and Gun Club, which almost daily now importuned
her for a decision concerning the Lecturer. His power

The Top of
a Stair

and appeal had grown enormously, and soon it would be impossible
for them to dispose of Eigenblick tidily, if dispose of him they must;
not much longer and it would be impossible to dispose of him at all.
They raised Hawksquill's fees, and spoke in veiled terms of perhaps
seeking other sources of advice. Hawksquill ignored all this. So far
from malingering, she now spent nearly every waking and many
sleeping hours in pursuit of whoever or whatever it was that claimed

to be Russell Eigenblick, haunting her own memory mansions like an unlaid ghost, and following flying scraps of evidence farther than she had ever gone before, pulling up at times before powers she would rather not have started into wakefulness, and finding herself in places that she had not before known she knew existed.

Where she found herself just now was at the top of a stair.

Whether she mounted or descended these stairs she wouldn't afterwards be able to determine; but they were long. At the end of them was a chamber. The broad studded door stood flung open. A great stone, by its track in the dust, had not long ago been rolled away from barring shut the door. Dimly within she could see a long feast-table, spilled cups and scattered chairs iced with ancient dust; from the chamber came an odor as of a messy bedroom just opened. But there was no one within.

She made to pass the broken door to investigate, but noticed then seated on the stone a figure in white, small, pretty, head bound in a golden fillet, paring its nails with a small knife. Not knowing what language to speak to this person, Hawksquill raised her brows and pointed within.

"He is not here," the person said. "He is risen."

Hawksquill considered a question or two, but understood before she asked that this personage would not answer them, that he (or she) was an embodiment only of that one remark: He is not here, he is risen. She turned away (the stair and the door and the message and the messenger fading from her attention like a shape momentarily perceived in changeful clouds) and set off further, bethinking herself where she might go for answers to many new questions, or questions to fit the many new answers she was quickly garnering.

"The difference," Hawksquill had long ago written in one of the tall marbled folios filled with her left-handed script which stood or lay on the long lamplit study table far behind her now, "the difference between the Ancient concept of the nature of the world and the New concept is, in the Ancient concept the world has a framework of Time, and in the New concept, a framework of Space.

Daughter of Time

"To look at the Ancient concept through the spectacles of the New concept is to see absurdity: seas that never were, worlds claimed to have fallen to pieces and been created newly, a congeries of unlocatable Trees, Islands, Mountains and Maelstroms. But the Ancients were not fools with a poor sense of direction; it was only not Orbis Terrae that they were looking at. When they spoke of the four corners of the earth, they meant of course no four physical places; they meant four repeated situations of the world, equidistant in time from one another: they meant the solstices and the equinoxes. When they spoke of seven spheres, they did not mean (until Ptolemy foolishly tried to take their portrait) seven spheres in space; they meant those circles described in Time by the motions of the stars: Time, that roomy seven-storey mountain where Dante's sinners wait for Eternity. When Plato tells of a river girdling the earth, which is somewhere (so the New concept would have it) up in the air and somewhere also in the middle of the earth, he means by that river the same river Heraclitus could never step in twice. Just as a lamp waved in darkness creates a figure of light in the air, which remains for as long as the lamp repeats its motion exactly, so the universe retains its shape by repetition: the universe is Time's body. And how will we perceive this body, and how operate on it? Not by the means we perceive extension, relation, color, form—the qualities of Space. Not by measurement and exploration. No: but by the means we perceive duration and repetition and change: by Memory."

a reason to write, to remember

Knowing this to be so, it could not matter to Hawksquill that on her travels her gray-bunned head and nerveless limbs did not probably change place, remained (she supposed) in the plush chair in the middle of the Cosmo-Opticon at the top of her house which stood in a hexagram of lower City streets. The wingéd horse she had summoned to bear her away was not a wingéd horse but that Great Square of stars pictured above her, and "away" was not where she was borne; but the greatest skill (perhaps the only skill) of the true mage is to apprehend these distinctions without making them, and to translate time into space without an error. It's all, said the old alchemists quite truthfully, so simple.

"Away!" said the voice of her Memory when the hand of her Memory was on the reins again and her seat was sure, and away they went, vast wings beating through Time. They traversed oceans of it while Hawksquill thought; and then her steed plunged, at her command, unhesitatingly, without a blink, which took the breath of her Memory away, into either the southern sky below the world or into the limpid-dark austral waters, in any case making for there where all past ages lie, Ogygia the Fair.

Her Steed's silver-shod feet touched that shore, and his great head sank; his strong wings, billowing like draperies, now emptied of the air of time, sank too with a whisper and trailed along the eternal grass, which he cropped for strength. Hawksquill dismounted, patted her steed's enormous neck, whispered that she would return, and started off, following the footprints, each longer than herself, pressed on these shores at the end of the Golden Age and petrified long since. The air was windless, yet the gigantic forest under whose eaves she entered soughed with a breath of its own, or perhaps with His breath, expelled and drawn with the long regularity of immemorial sleep.

She came no closer than the entrance of the vale he filled. "Father," she said, and her voice startled the silence; aged eagles with heavy wings rose up and settled sleepily again. "Father," she said again, and the vale stirred. The great gray boulders were his knees, the long gray ivy his hair, the precipice-gripping massy roots his fingers; the eye he opened to her was milky-gray, a dim-glowing stone, the Saturn of her Cosmo-Opticon. He yawned: the inhalation turned the leaves of trees like storm-wind and stirred her hair, and when he exhaled his breath was the cold black breath of a bottomless cave.

"Daughter," he said, in a voice like earth's.

"I'm sorry to disturb your sleep, Father," she said, "but I have a question only you can answer."

"Ask it then."

"Does a new world now begin? I see no reason why it should, and yet it seems it does."

Everyone knows that when his sons overthrew their ancient Father, and cast him here, the endless Age of Gold ended, and Time was invented with all its labors. Less well known is how the young, unruly Gods, frightened or ashamed at what they had done, gave the ruling of this new entity into the hands of their Father. He was asleep in Ogygia then and didn't care, so ever since it has been here in this isle, where the five rivers have their common wellspring, that all the used years accumulate like fallen leaves; and when the Ancientest One, troubled by a dream of overthrow or change, shifts his massy limbs and smacks his lips, scratching at the rock-ribbed muscles of his hams, a new age issues, the measures alter which he gives to the dance of the universe, the sun is born in a new sign.

Thus the airy scheming Gods contrived to put the blame for the calamity on their old Father. In time, Kronos, king of the happy Timeless Age, became old busybody Chronos with his sickle and hourglass, father of chronicles and chronometers. Only his true sons and daughters know better—and some adopted ones, Ariel Hawksquill among them.

"Does a new age now begin?" she asked again. "It's beforehand if it does."

"A New Age," said Father Time in a voice that could create one. "No. Not for years and years." He brushed away a few of these that had gathered in withered piles on his shoulders.

"Then," Hawksquill said, "who is Russell Eigenblick, if he isn't King of a new age?"

"Russell Eigenblick?"

"The man with the red beard. The Lecturer. The Geography."

He lay back again, his rocky couch groaning beneath him. "No King of a new age," he said. "An upstart. An invader."

"Invader?"

"He is their champion. That's why they waked him." His milky-gray eye was drifting closed. "Asleep for a thousand years, lucky man. And now awakened for the conflict."

"Conflict? Champion?"

"Daughter," he said. "Don't you know there's a war on?"

War . . . There had been, all along, one word she had sought for, one word under which all the disorderly facts, all the oddities she had gathered up concerning Russell Eigenblick and the random disturbances he seemed to cause in the world might be subsumed. She had that word now: it blew through her consciousness like a wind, uprooting structures and harrying birds, tearing leaves from trees and laundry from lines, but at least, at last, blowing from one direction only. War: universal, millennial, unconditional War. For God's sake, she thought, he'd said as much himself in every recent Lecture; she'd always thought it was merely a metaphor. Merely! "I didn't know, Father," she said, "until this moment."

"Nothing to do with me," said the Ancientest One, his words muffled in a yawn. "They applied to me once for his sleep, and I granted it. A thousand years ago, give or take a century . . . They are after all children of my children, related by marriage. . . . I do them a favor once and again. No harm in that. Little enough to do here anyway."

"Who are they, Father?"

"Mm." His enormous vacant eye was shut.

"Who are they whose champion he is?"

But the vast head was bent backward on its bouldered pillow, the vast throat swallowed a snore. The hoary-headed eagles who had risen shrieking when he woke settled again on their crags. The windless forest soughed. Hawksquill, reluctantly, turned her steps toward the shore again. Her steed (sleepy himself, even he) raised his head at her approach. Well! No help for it. Thought must

311

conquer this, Thought could! "No rest for the weary," she said, and leapt smartly onto his broad back. "On! And quickly! Don't you know there's a war on?"

She thought as they ascended, or descended: who slept for a thousand years? What children of the children of Time would make war on men, to what end, with what hope of success?

And who (by the way) was that golden-haired child she had glimpsed curled up asleep in the lap of Father Time?

The child turned, dreaming; dreaming of what had come of all she had seen on her last day awake, dreaming it all and altering it in her dreaming even as, elsewhere, it came to pass; plucking apart her bright and dark dream-tapestry and knitting it up again with the same threads in a way she liked better. She dreamt of her mother awaking and saying "What?", of one of her fathers on a path at Edgewood; she dreamt of Auberon, in love somewhere with a dream-Lilac of his own invention; she dreamt of armies made of cloud, led by a red-bearded man who startled her nearly awake. She dreamt, turning, lips parted, heart beating slowly, that at the end of her tour she came riding down from the air, came coursing with vertiginous speed along an iron-gray and oily river.

The ghastly red round sun was sinking vaporously amid the elaborate smokes and scorings of jets that had made the false armies in the west. Lilac could only hold her tongue: the brutal esplanades, the stained blocks of buildings, the clamor brought to her ears, silenced her. The stork turned inward; Mrs. Underhill's stick seemed uncertain in the rectangular valleys; they went east, then south. A thousand people seen from above are not as one or two: a heaving queasy sea of hair and hats, the odd bright muffler blown back. Hell-holes in the street shot up steam; crowds were swallowed up in clouds of it, and (so it seemed to Lilac) didn't emerge, but there were countless others to replace them.

"Remember these markers, child," Mrs. Underhill shouted back at Lilac over the keening sirens and the turmoil. "That burned church. Those railings, like arrows. That fine house. You'll pass this way again, alone." A caped figure just then detached itself from the crowd and made to enter the fine house, which didn't seem fine to Lilac. The stork, at Mrs. Underhill's direction, topped the house, cupped her wings to stop, and with a grunt of relief put her red feet down amid the weather-obscured detritus of the rooftop. The three of them looked down into the middle of the block just as the caped figure came out the back door.

The Child Turned

"Now mark him, dear," Mrs. Underhill said. "Who do you suppose he is?"

With arms akimbo beneath the cloak, and a wide hat on his head, he was a dark lump to Lilac. Then he took off the hat, and shook out long black hair. He turned clockwise in a circle, nodding, and looked around at the rooftops, a white grin on his dark face. "Another cousin," Lilac said.

"Well, yes, and who else?"

He put his finger thoughtfully to his lips, and scuffed the dirt of the untidy garden. "I give up," Lilac said.

"Why, your other father!"

"Oh."

"The one who engendered you. Who'll need your help, as much as the other."

"Oh."

"Planning improvements," Mrs. Underhill said with satisfaction, "just now."

George paced out his garden. He went and chinned himself on the board fence which separated his yard from the next building's, and looked over like Kilroy into the even less well-kept garden there. He said aloud, "God *damn!* All *right!*" He let himself down, and rubbed his hands together.

Lilac laughed as the stork stepped to the roof's ledge to take off. Like the stork's white wings opening, George's black cape flew outward and then closed more tightly around him as he laughed too. This, Lilac decided, delighted by something about him which she couldn't name, was the father which, of the two of them, she would have chosen to have: and with the instant certainty of a solitary child about who is and who is not on its side, she chose him now.

"There's no choosing, though," said Mrs. Underhill as they ascended. "Only Duty."

"A present for him!" she cried to Mrs. Underhill. "A present!"

Mrs. Underhill said nothing—the child had been indulged quite enough—but as they coursed down the shabby street, in their wake there sprang up from the sidewalk at even intervals a row of skinny and winter-naked saplings, one by one. This street is ours, anyway, thought Mrs. Underhill, or as good as; and what's a farm without a row of guardian trees along the road that passes it?

"Now for the door!" she said, and the cold city tumbled beneath them as they fled uptown. "It's long past your bedtime—there!" She pointed ahead to an aged building that must once have been tall, overweening even, but no more. It had been built of white stone, white no longer, carved into a myriad of faces, caryatids, birds and beasts, all coal-miners now and weeping filthily. The central part of it was set back from the street; wings on either side framed a dark dank courtyard into which taxis and people disappeared. The wings were linked, high up at the top, by an archlike course of masonry, an arch for a giant to pass under: and they three did pass under it, the stork ceasing to beat its wings, coasting, wing-tipping slightly to arrow accurately into the darkness of the courtyard. Mrs. Underhill cried " 'Ware heads! Duck, duck!" and Lilac, feeling a *whoosh* of stale air rush up at her from the interior, ducked. She closed her eyes. She heard Mrs. Underhill say, "Nearly done now, old girl, nearly done; you know the door," and the darkness behind her lids grew brighter, and the noise of the City vanished, and they were elsewhere again.

So she dreamed; so it came to have been; so the saplings grew, dirty-faced urchins, tough, neglected and sharp. They grew, fattening in the trunk, buckling the sidewalk that ran beneath them. They wore broken kites and candy-wrappers, burst balloons and spar-rows' nests in their hair, unmindful; they shouldered each other for a glimpse of sun, they shook their sooty snow winter after winter on passersby. They grew, penknife-scarred, snaggle-branched, dog-manured, unkillable. On a mild night in a certain March, Sylvie, returning to Old Law Farm at dawn, looked up at their branches outlined against a raw pale sky and saw that every twig-tip bore a heavy bud.

She said goodnight to the one who had seen her home, though he was importunate, and sought the four keys she needed to get herself into Old Law Farm and the Folding Bedroom. He'll never believe this crazy story, she thought laughing, never believe the crazy but essentially innocent, nearly innocent, chain of events that had had her up till dawn. Not that he would grill her; he'd only be glad she was safe, she wished he wouldn't worry. She got whirled away, sometimes, is all; everybody put a claim in on her, and most of them seemed to her good. It was a big city, and its revels ran till late when the moon was full in March, and hey, one thing just led to another. . . . She unlocked the door into the Farm, and made her way up through the sleeping warren of it; at the hall that led to the Folding Bedroom she slipped off the high-heeled shoes from her dancing feet and tiptoed to the door. She unlocked the locks quietly as a burglar, and peeked in. Auberon lay in a heap on the bed, obscure in the dawn light and (for some reason she was sure) only feigning untroubled sleep.

314

The Folding Bedroom and its little kitchen were so small that Auberon, in order to have some quiet and isolation in which to work, had to create out of it an imaginary study.

An Imaginary Study

"A what?" Sylvie asked.

"An imaginary study," he said. "Okay. Look. This chair." He had found somewhere in the ruined habitations of Old Law Farm an old schoolhouse chair with one broad paddle arm for a student to use as a desk. Underneath the seat was a compartment for the student's books and papers. "Now," he said. He positioned the chair carefully. "Let's pretend I have a study in this bedroom. This chair is in it. Now really all we have is this chair, but . . ."

"What are you talking about?"

"Well will you please just listen a minute?" Auberon said, blazing up. "It's very simple. There were lots of imaginary rooms at Edgewood where I grew up."

"I bet." She stood arms akimbo, a wooden spoon in one hand, head bound in a bright hussy kerchief beneath which her earrings trembled amid escaping curls of raven hair.

"The idea is," Auberon said, "that when I say 'I'm going into my study, babe,' and then sit down in this chair, then it's as though I've gone into a separate room. I shut the door. Then I'm alone in there. You can't see me or hear me, because the door is closed. And I can't see or hear you. Get it?"

"Well, okay. But how come?"

"Because the imaginary *door* is *closed*, and . . ."

"No, I mean how come you need this imaginary study? Why don't you just sit there?"

"I'd rather be in private. You see, we have to make a deal, that whatever I do in my imaginary study is invisible to you; you can't comment on it or dwell on it or . . ."

"Gee. What are you going to do?" A smile, and she made a rude gesture with the spoon. "Hey." But what he intended to do, though no less private and self-indulgent, was mostly to daydream, though he wouldn't have put it that way; to court, on long woolgathering rambles, Psyche his soul; put two and two together, and perhaps write down the sum, for he would have sharpened pencils in the pencil-well of the desk and a clean pad before him. But mostly, he knew, he would only sit, twist a lock of hair between his fingers, suck his teeth, scratch himself, try to catch the flying speckles that swam in his vision, mutter the same half-line of someone else's verse

315

over and over and generally behave like the quieter sort of nut. He might also read the papers.

"Thinkin' and readin' and writin', huh," Sylvie said with great affection.

"Yes. You see, I have to be alone sometimes . . . ."

She was stroking his cheek. "For thinkin' and readin' and writin'. Yes, baby. Okay." She backed away, watching him with interest.

"I'm going into my study now," Auberon said, feeling foolish.

"Okay. 'Bye."

"I'm shutting the door."

She waved the spoon. She began to say something further, but he cast his eyes upward, and she returned to the kitchen.

In his study, Auberon rested his cheek in the cup of his hand and stared at the old grainy surface of his desk. Someone had scratched an obscenity there, and someone else had priggishly altered it into BOOK in block letters. Probably all done with the point of a compass. Compass and protractor. When he started in at his father's little school his grandfather gave him his old pencil-case, leather with a snap closure and weird Mexican designs cut in it—a naked woman was one, you could run your finger over her stylized breast and feel the leather button of her nipple. There were pencils with dowdy pink hats for erasers, which pulled off to reveal the naked pencil end; there was another rhomboid dialectical gray eraser, half for pencil and a grittier half for ink, which macerated the paper it was used on. Pens black and cork-tipped like Aunt Cloud's cigarettes, and a steel box of points. And a compass and protractor. Bisect an angle. But never trisect it. With his fingers he moved an imaginary compass above the desk-top. When the little yellow pencil wore down, the compass leaned at a useless angle. He could write a story about those long afternoons in school, in May, say the last day, hollyhocks growing outside and vines clambering in at the open windows; the smell of the outhouse. The pencil box. Mother West-wind and the Little Breezes. Those protracted afternoons . . . He could call the story *Protractor*. "Protractor," he said aloud, and then shot a glance at Sylvie to see if she had overheard him. He caught her just having shot *him* a glance, and now looking back at her task unconcernedly.

Protractor, protractor . . . He drummed his fingers on the oak. What was she up to in there anyway? Making coffee? She had heated a big kettle of water, and now dumped heedlessly into it several big shakes of coffee, right from the bag, and threw in this morning's used grounds as well. A rich, boiling-coffee smell filled the air.

"You know what you ought to do?" she said, stirring the pot. "You ought to try to get a job writing on 'A World Elsewhere.' It's really degenerating."

"I . . ." he began to say, but then studiously turned away.

"Oops, oops," she said, stifling a laugh.

George had said that all that TV was written on the other coast. But how would he know anyway? The real difficulty was that he had come to see, through Sylvie's elaborate retellings of the events of "A World Elsewhere," that he could never have thought up the myriad and (to him) incongruous passions that seemed to fill it. Yet for all he knew the terrible griefs, great sufferings, accidents and windfalls it told of were all true to life—what did he know about life, about people? Maybe most people were as wilful, as overmastered by ambition, blood, lust, money, passion as the TV showed them. People and life weren't his strengths as a writer anyway. His strengths as a writer were . . .

"Knock-knock," Sylvie said, standing before him.

"Yes?"

"Can I come in?"

"Yes."

"Do you know where my white outfit is?"

"In the closet?"

She opened the door of the toilet. They had screwed into the door of this little chamber a collapsing clothes-rack, which held most of their clothes. "Look inside my overcoat," he said.

There it was, a two-piece white cotton outfit, jacket and skirt, an old nurse's uniform in fact with an identifying patch on the shoulder. Sylvie had ingeniously altered it into something at once stylish and improvised: her taste was sure, her skills didn't match it quite, he wished not for the first time that he could give her thousands to lavish on herself, it would be a joy to watch.

She looked over the outfit critically.

"Your coffee's going to boil away," he said.

"Huh?" With a pair of tiny scissors in the shape of a long-beaked bird she was removing the identifying shoulder patch. "Oh, yike!" She hurried to turn it down. Then she returned to her outfit. Auberon returned to his study.

His strengths as a writer were . . .

"I wish I could write," Sylvie said.

"Maybe you can," Auberon said. "I bet you'd be good at it. No, really"—she had snorted in contempt at this notion—"I bet you would." He knew with love's certainty that there was little she couldn't do, and that little wasn't worth doing. "What would you write?"

"I bet I could think up better stuff than they think up on 'A World Elsewhere.' " She carried the steaming kettle of coffee to the tub (as in all old-law tenements this sat squat and unembarrassed in the middle of the kitchen) and began straining the liquid through a cloth into an even bigger cauldron set in the tub. "It's not *touching*, y'know? It doesn't touch your heart." She started to undress.

"Do you mind," Auberon said, abandoning as hopeless the imaginary walls and door that separated him from Sylvie, "if I ask you what the hell you're doing?"

"I'm dying," she said calmly. Shirtless now, the globes of her breasts swinging gently with their pendular momentum as she moved, she picked up the two parts of the white outfit, looked them over a final time, and thrust them into the cauldron of coffee. Auberon got it, and laughed delightedly.

"Sort of a beige," Sylvie said, pronouncing the "g" as though it were in "badge". She plucked from the dish-drainer by the sink the little sock-like cotton strainer—*el colador*, a boy—which she used to make strong Spanish coffee, and showed it to him. It had turned a rich tan color he had himself often admired. She began stirring the cauldron slowly with a long-handled spoon. "Two shades lighter than me," she said, "is what I want. Café-con-leche."

"Pretty," he said. Coffee spattered her brown skin. She wiped it off and licked her fingers. With the spoon in both hands she lifted the garment up, her breasts tautening, and looked at it; it was already deep brown, browner than she, but rinsings (he could see her think it) would lighten it. She dropped it back in, with a quick finger tucked a lock of hair that had got away back under her snood, and stirred again. Auberon wouldn't ever decide whether he loved her more when her attention was on him, or when as now it was fixed on some task or thing in the real world. He couldn't write a story about her: it would consist only of catalogues of her actions, down to the most minute. But he had no real desire to write of anything else. He was standing now in the door of the little kitchen.

"Here's an idea," he said. "Those soap-operas always need writers." He said this as though it were a fact he was sure of. "We could collaborate."

"Huh?"

"You think up some stuff that might happen on the show—coming out of what's happening now—only better than what they'll do—and I can write it."

"Really?" she said, doubtful but intrigued.

"I mean I'll write the *words*, and you write the *story*."
What was odd (he came closer) was that he meant by this offer to
seduce her. He wondered how long lovers are lovers before they stop
having to plot each other's seduction. Never? Perhaps never.
Perhaps the lures get smaller, more perfunctory. Or maybe just the
reverse. What did he know?

"Okay," she said with quick decision. "*But*," she said with
a secret smile, "I might not have a lot of time, because *I'm* going to
get a *job*."

"Hey, terrific."

"Yeah. That's what this outfit's for, if it comes out."

"Gee, that's great. What kind of job?"

"Well, I didn't want to tell you since it's not for *sure*. I
have to get interviewed. It's in the movies." She laughed at the
absurdity of it.

"A star?"

"Not right away. Not the first day. Later for that." She
moved the sodden brown mess to a corner of the tub. She poured out
the cold coffee. "A producer, sort of, I met. Sort of a producer or
director. He needs an assistant. But not like a secretary exactly."

"Oh yeah?" Where was she meeting producers and directors and not telling him about it?

"Like sort of a script girl and assistant."

"Hm." Surely Sylvie, even more alert than he was to such
things, would have sensed whether this sort-of producer's offer was
real or mere predation; it sounded doubtful to him, but he made
encouraging noises.

"*So*," she said—turning cold water full force over the
now-tan outfit, "I got to look *good* or at least as good as I can look, to
go see him. . . ."

"You always look good."

"No, really."

"You look good to me now."

She flashed him the briefest and brightest of her smiles.
"So we'll get famous together."

"Sure," he said, coming closer. "And rich. And you'll
know all about movies, and we'll make a team." He circled her.
"Let's make a team."

"Oh. I got to finish this."

"Okay."

"It'll be a while."

"I can wait. I'll just watch."

"Oh, *papo*. I get embarrassed."

"Mm. That's nice." He kissed her throat, smelling the biscuity odor of her exertion, and she allowed him to, her wet hands held out over the tub. "I'm going to let down the bed," he said in a low voice, something between a threat and the promise of a treat.

"Mm." She watched him do so, her hands in the water but her mind not now on her task. The bed, lowered, intruded suddenly into the room, very bedlike but also like the prow of a laden ship that had just come in: had just sailed through the far wall and hove to there, waiting to be boarded.

Nevertheless Spring

In the end, though—whether because she came to doubt that her producer really was one, or because the false spring of that week vanished and March went out like a lion freezing her tender marrow, or because the dyed outfit didn't ever please her quite (there lingered about it after no matter how many washings a faint smell of stale coffee)—Sylvie never did go to be interviewed for the movies. Auberon encouraged her, bought her a book to read on the subject, but this only seemed to plunge her into further gloom. The klieglit visions faded. She sank into a torpor that alarmed Auberon. She lay till late in a huge tangle of bedclothes, his winter coat atop them all, and when she did rise, mooned around the little apartment with a sweatshirt over her nightgown and thick socks on her feet. She'd open the refrigerator and stare irritatedly within at a container of moldy yogurt, nameless leftovers in tinfoil, a flat soda.

"*Coño,*" she said. "There's never anything in here."

"Yeah? Is that so," he said with heavy irony from within the imaginary study. "I guess it must be broken." He rose, and reached for his coat. "What do you want?" he said. "I'll go get something."

"No, *papo* . . ."

"I have to eat too, you know. And if the refrigerator won't supply it."

"Okay. Something good."

"Well what? I could get some cereal . . . ."

She made a face. "Something *good,*" she said, with a two-handed, chin-uplifted gesture that certainly expressed her desire, but left him no wiser. He went out into a new-fallen still-falling snow.

As soon as she closed the door on him, Sylvie was swept by a tide of gloomy feeling.

It amazed her that he, brought up the baby boy in a household of sisters and aunts, could be so endlessly solicitous, take so much of their daily domestic life on himself, and bitch so little.

White people were strange. Among her relatives and their neighbors a husband's chief domestic duties were eating, beating, and playing dominoes. Auberon was so *good*. So understanding. And smart: official forms and the endless paper of an aged and paralytic welfare state held no terror for him. And not jealous. When early on she'd developed a pressing crush on sweet brown Leon who waited at the Seventh Saint, and indulged it a while, and lain then next to Auberon every night rigid with guilt and fear till he'd wormed the secret out of her, he'd only said he didn't care what she did with others as long as she was happy with him when she was with him: now how many guys could you find, she asked herself in the clouded mirror over the sink, who would act like that?

So good. So kind. And how did she repay him? Look at you, she insisted. Bags under your eyes. Losing pounds every day, pretty soon—she held up a warning pinkie in the mirror—like *this*. *Flacca*. And not bringing home shit, useless to herself as to him, *un' boba*.

She'd work. She'd work *hard* and pay him back everything he'd done for her, the whole oppressive relentless treasure of his goodness. Toss it back in his face. There. "I'll wash fuckin' dishes," she said aloud, turning away from the small pile of them by the squalid sink, "I'll turn tricks . . . ."

And was it to that that her Destiny led her? Bitter-faced and rubbing her horripilated arms, she paced from bed to stove like a caged thing. What should free her bound her, bound her to await it amid a poverty, an impoverished day-to-day existence different from the long, hopeless poverty of her growing up, but poverty nonetheless. Sick of it, sick sick sick! Self-pitying tears sprang to her eyes. Damn her Destiny anyway, why couldn't she trade it for a little decency, a little freedom, a little fun? If she couldn't throw it away, why could she get nothing in exchange for it either?

She climbed back into bed, black resolution in her mind. She drew up the covers, staring accusatorily at the middle distance. Dark, asleep, far-off but built into her very stuff, her Destiny couldn't be resigned, she'd learned that. But she was tired of waiting. It had not one single feature she could determine, except that Auberon was in it (but not this squalor; Somehow, not even this Auberon), but she'd discover it now. Now. "*Bueno,*" she said, "All right," and took a stern attitude under the covers with arms crossed. She'd wait no more. She'd learn her Destiny and begin it or die; she'd drag it out of the future where it lay by main strength.

Auberon meanwhile plodded to the Nite Owl market (surprised to find this was Sunday and nothing else open, what do weekends mean to the leisured poor?) through snow that lay just for this hour virginal and new, his the first feet to begin its long defilement into rotten slush more black than white. He was angry. In fact he was furious, though he had kissed Sylvie gently farewell, and would kiss her again in ten minutes when he got back, just as gently. Why didn't she ever even acknowledge the equability of his temper, the sunniness of his disposition? Did she think it was easy to maintain, easy to press down honest indignation into a soft answer, every time, every single time? And what credit did he get for his efforts? He could sock her sometimes. He'd like to give her one good punch, quiet her down a little, show her just how far his patience had been tried. Oh God how awful even to think it.

Happiness, he had come to see, his happiness anyway, was a season; and in that season, Sylvie was the weather. Everyone within him talked about it, among themselves, but no one could do anything about it, they could only wait till it changed. The season of his happiness was spring, a long, skittish, changeful spring, as often withdrawn as proffered—like any spring: but nevertheless spring. He was sure of it. He kicked the wet snow. Sure.

He mooched indecisively among the few and expensive goods the Nite Owl offered—one of those places that keep up a marginal existence by being open on Sundays and deep into the night—and when he had made his choices (two kinds of exotic juices for Sylvie's tropical palate, to make up for punching her) he drew out his wallet and found it empty. As in the antique joke, a moth should lazily fly out. He scrabbled in his pockets, inside, outside, under the eyes (reserving terrible judgment) of the counterman, and at last, though having to resign one of the juices, made up the amount in found silver and linty pennies.

"Now what?" he said when, snow on his hat and shoulders, he opened the door of the Folding Bedroom and found Sylvie in bed. "Having a little nap?"

"Leamee alone," she said. "I'm thinking."

"Thinking, huh." He took his sodden paper bag into the kitchen and messed around for a time with soup and crackers, but when he offered her these she refused them; in fact for the rest of that day he could hardly get a word out of her, and grew afraid, thinking of her familial streak of madness. Dulcet, kind, he spoke to her, and her retreating soul fled from his words as from a cutting edge.

So he only sat (his imaginary study moved into the kitchen since the bed remained opened and occupied) and thought of how further to indulge her, and of ingratitude; and she struggled on the bed, and sometimes slept. Winter deepened. Black clouds formed over their heads; lightnings answered lightnings; north winds blew; cold rain poured down.

"Hold hard," Mrs. Underhill said, "hold hard. Somewhere here a slip's been made, a turning missed. Don't you feel that?"

Let Him
Follow Love

"We do," said the others gathered there.

"Winter came," Mrs. Underhill said, "and that was right; and then . . ."

"Spring!" they all shouted.

"Too fast, too fast." She beat her temple with her knuckles. A dropped stitch could be fixed, if it could be found; a certain unraveling was in her power; but where along the long, long way had it been? Or—she cast her eye along the vast length of Tale unfolding from the to-come with the steady grace of a jewelled and purposeful serpent—was it yet to be? "Help me, children," she said.

"We will," they said, in all their various voices.

This was the problem: if what had to be discovered lay in what-was-to-be, then they could discover that easily enough. It was what-had-been that was hard to keep in mind. That's the way it is for beings who are immortal or nearly so; they know the future, but the past is dark to them; beyond the present year is the door into aeons-ago, a darkling span lit with solemn lights. As Sophie with her cards probed an unfamiliar future, pressing on the thin membrane that separated her from it, pressing here and there to feel the advancing shapes of things to come, so Mrs. Underhill felt blindly among the things that had been, searching for the shape of what was wrong. "There was an only son," she said.

"An only son," they echoed, thinking hard.

"And he came to the City."

"And he came to the City," they said.

"And there he sits," Mr. Woods put in.

"That's it, isn't it," Mrs. Underhill said. "There he sits."

"Won't be moved, won't do his duty, wants to die of love instead." Mr. Woods clutched his skinny knee in his long hands. "It could be this winter will go on, and never stop."

"Never stop," Mrs. Underhill said. A tear was in her eye. "Yes, yes, that's just how it appears."

"No, no," they all said, seeing it so. The freezing rain beat on the deep small windows, crying in mourning, the trees lashed their branches at the implacable wind, the Meadow Mouse was seized in the Red Fox's desperate jaws. "Think, think," they said.

She knocked again at her temple, but no one answered.

323

She rose, and they retreated. "I'll need advice," she said, "that's all."

The black water of the mountain pool was just unfrozen, though jags of ice like broken stone projected around its margins; on one of these projections Mrs. Underhill stood and sent down her summons.

Sleepy, stupid, too cold even to be angry, Grandfather Trout rose from the dark depths.

"Leamee alone," he said.

"Answer up," Mrs. Underhill said sharply, "or it'll go hard with you."

"What," he said.

"This child in the City," Mrs. Underhill said. "Great-grandson of yours. Won't be moved, won't do his duty, wants to die of love instead."

"Love," Grandfather Trout said. "There is no force on earth left stronger than love."

"He won't follow the others."

"Then let him follow love."

"Hm," said Mrs. Underhill, and then "hmmm." She put her thumb to her chin and her finger along her cheek, resting her elbow in the cup of her other hand. "Well, perhaps he ought to have a Consort," she said.

"Yes," Grandfather Trout said.

"Just to trouble him, and keep his interest up."

"Yes."

"It is not good for man to be alone."

"No," said Grandfather Trout, though whether in agreement or denial was hard to tell when the word issued from a fish's mouth. "Now let me sleep."

"Yes!" she said. "Yes, of course a Consort! What have I been thinking of? Yes!" At every word her voice grew greater. Grandfather Trout sank quickly in fear, and the very ice melted away by inches from beneath Mrs. Underhill's feet as she cried "Yes!" in a voice of thunder.

"Love!" she said to the others. "Not in the Was, not in the Will Be, but Now!"

"Love!" they all cried. Mrs. Underhill threw open a humpbacked trunk bound in black iron and began rummaging in it. She found what she wanted, wrapped it featly in white paper, bound it with red-and-white twine, neatly waxed the ends of the twine to keep them from raveling, took pen and ink, and on Mr. Woods's bent back addressed a label: all in less time than it took to think of it.

"Let him follow love," she said when the package was made. "And so he'll come. Willy." She dotted a final i. "Nilly."

"Aaaah," they all said, and began to drift away, talking in low voices.

"You'll never believe this," Sylvie said to Auberon, bursting through the door into the Folding Bedroom, "but I got a job." She'd been out all day. Her cheeks were red with March wind, her eyes bright.

"Hey." He laughed, astonished, pleased. "Your Destiny?"

"Fuck destiny," she said. She tore from its hanger the coffee-dyed outfit and flung it trashcanwards. "No more excuses," she said. She pulled out work shoes, sweatshirt, muffler. She banged the shoes on the floor. "Have to dress warm," she said. "I start tomorrow. No more excuses."

"That's a good day," he said. "April Fool's."

"Just my day," she said. "My lucky day."

He laughed, raising her. April had come. And she in his embrace felt a thing that was at once relief at a danger avoided and a foreboding of that same danger, and her eyes filled at the safety she felt, within his arms, and at its fragility too. *"Papo,"* she said: "You're the greatest, you know that? You really really are."

"But tell me, tell me," he said. "What's this job?"

She grinned, hugging him. "You'll never believe it," she said.

IV

Methinks there be not impossibilities
enough in Religion for an active faith.

—*Sir Thomas Browne*

In the tiny offices of Wingéd Messenger Service were: a
counter or partition, behind which the dispatcher sat,
chewing always an unlit cigar and plugging and unplug-
ging the cords of the oldest PBX in the world and bellowing
"Wingéd" into his headset; a line of gray metal folding chairs on
which those messengers not at the moment carrying messages sat,
some as still and lifeless as unplugged machines, some (like Fred
Savage and Sylvie) engaged in conversation; a huge and ancient
television on a chain-flown platform out of reach, forever on (Sylvie,
if she wasn't running, caught episodes of "A World Elsewhere");
some urns full of sand and cigarette butts; a crackle-finish brown time
clock; a back office, containing a boss, his secretary, and at odd
hours a hearty but ill-looking salesman; a metal door with a bar; no
windows.

It wasn't a place Sylvie liked to stay in much. In its bare,
fluorescent, hard-finish shabbiness she recognized too
many places where she had spent too much of her
childhood: the waiting rooms of public hospitals and
asylums, welfare offices, police stations, places where
a congress of faces and bodies in poor clothes
gathered, dispersed, were replaced always by others. She didn't, for-
tunately, have to spend much time there: Wingéd Messenger Service
was as busy as it had ever been, and out on the cold spring streets,
bound in work-boots and hooded sweatshirt (looking, she told Auberon, like a teenage dyke, but cute), she made time, glorying in the
crowds, the posh offices, and the oddly-assorted secretaries (snooty,
harsh, and mannered; slovenly; kind) whom she gave to and took

**More Would
Happen**

326

away from. "Wingéd Messenger!" she shouted at them, no time to waste. "Sign here please." And away, in elevators crowded with soft-voiced, fine-suited men on their way to lunch, or loud-voiced back-slappers returning. Though she never learned midtown as Fred Savage knew it—every underground access, every passageway, every building which, facing on one avenue, evacuated onto another, saving half a block for a walker—she did grasp the general, and find shortcuts; and she made her lefts and rights, ups and downs, with an accuracy she was proud of.

On a day early in May that had begun rainy (Fred Savage beside her wore a vast fedora swaddled in plastic) she sat restless on the edge of her chair, crossing her legs right over left and then left over right, watching "A World Elsewhere" and waiting for her name to be called.

"*That* guy," she explained to Fred, "was the one who pretended to be the father of the kid whose real father was the *other* guy, who divorced the wife who fell for the girl who crashed the car that crippled the kid that lived in the house that *this* guy built."

"Mm," Fred said. Sylvie's eyes hadn't left the screen nor her ear the story, but Fred looked only at Sylvie.

"That's him," she said as the scene changed to a smooth-haired man sipping coffee and studying, silently, for a very long time, a letter addressed to someone else, trying apparently to decide whether he dared open it. He had been, Sylvie told Fred, wrestling with this temptation since April ended.

"If I was writing it," she said, "more would happen."

"I just bet it would," Fred said, and the dispatcher said "Sylvie!"

She leapt up, though her eyes didn't leave the screen; she took the dispatcher's slip and started out.

"See ya," she said to Fred and to an unresponsive overcoat and hat at the end of the row of chairs.

"More would happen, mm-mm," said Fred, who still looked only at Sylvie. "I bet now it would at that."

The pickup was from a suite in a tall hotel of glass and steel, chill, sinister even, despite the factitious gaiety of its tropical lounges and English chophouse and hustle and bustle. She rode upward alone in a silent, thickly carpeted elevator in which nameless music played. At the thirteenth floor, the doors slid open, and Sylvie said "A! A!", startled, because facing her was a vast blowup in color of Russell Eigenblick's face, bushy eyebrows over limpid eyes, red red beard sprouting from his cheeks almost up to his

Something
Going

eyes, mouth knowing, stern and kindly. The nameless elevator music became a radio, loud: a *merengue*.

She looked down the long plush corridor of the suite. Instead of a secretary of any sort, four or five young guys, black and P.R., made dance steps and drank Cokes around a vast rosewood desk. Those not in a sort of military undress wore bright loose shirts or jackets of many colors, Eigenblick's troops' insignia. "Hi," she said, at ease now. "Wingéd Messenger Service."

"Hey. Check the messenger."

"Saayy . . ."

One of the dancers strutted toward her as the others laughed, and Sylvie did a step or two with him; another, with an expert air, manipulated the intercom. "A messenger's here. We got something going?"

"So listen," Sylvie said. "What about this guy—" thumb toward the vast portrait. "What's with him?"

Some laughed; one looked solemn; the dancer fell back in astonishment at Sylvie's ignorance. "Oh wow man," he said, "oh *man* . . ."

He had just begun to put right forefinger into left palm to begin an explanation (cute, Sylvie thought him, well-muscled, real neighborhood) when double doors behind them were flung open. Sylvie caught a glimpse of huge rooms glossily furnished. A tall white guy with blond hair cut severely came out. With a quick gesture he ordered the radio silent. The young men drew together protectively, taking stances tough but wary. The blond man raised his chin and eyebrows at Sylvie inquiringly, too busy to say actual words.

"Wingéd Messenger."

He considered her for a long moment, almost insolently. He had a good five inches on everybody else present, more than that on Sylvie. She crossed her arms, placed her booted feet in a "So?" attitude, and returned his look. He turned back into the rooms he had come from.

"What's *his* problem?" she asked the others, but they seemed subdued. He was back anyway in a moment, with a parcel, oddly shaped, tied with an old-fashioned red-and-white twine Sylvie hadn't seen in years, and addressed in a hand so fine and antique as to be almost illegible. Altogether it was one of the odder things she had been asked to carry.

"Don't delay," the man said, with what Sylvie thought might be the trace of an accent.

"I'm not gonna de*lay*." Turkey. "Sign here please." The blond man drew back from her book as though it were repellent; he gestured to one of the boys, and backed through the doors, closing them after him.

"Wow," she said as the good-looking one signed her book with a flourish and a final dot. "You work for *him?*"

Big gestures all around indicating resentment, defiance, resignation. The black one essayed a quick imitation, and the others fell out in exaggerated but silent laughter. "Okay," Sylvie said, seeing that the address was far uptown, a good long time away from the office, "see ya."

The dancer accompanied her to the elevator, bringing out a quick line, listen I could use a message if you got one, no message for me, hey, listen, I wanna ask you sumpm, no this is serious; and after further chaff (she would have liked to stay, but the package under her arm seemed Somehow needful and exigent) he struck a comic pose as the elevator doors extinguished him to her. She did a few steps alone in the elevator, hearing other music than was playing there. Long time since she'd been dancing.

Riding uptown, hands thrust in her sweatshirt's front pockets and the weird package beside her.

She should have asked those guys if they knew Bruno. She had heard nothing of her brother in some time; he wasn't living with his wife and her mother, she knew that. Hustling somebody somewhere . . . But those guys weren't together. Just something to do. Instead of hanging around the block. She thought of little Bruno: *pobricito.* She had vowed that, once a week at least, she would make the long journey out to Jamaica and visit him, take him away from them for a day. She hadn't, not as often as she'd intended to: not at all in the last busy month. She renewed her vow, sensing at her back, pressing on her, a history of such neglects and their cumulative damage—the ones she had been subjected to, and her mother before her; and Bruno; her other nieces and nephews. Smothered with love, and left to sink or swim: what a system. Kids. And why did she think she could do it any differently? And yet she thought she could. With Auberon she might have kids. Sometimes her ghost children implored her to be born; she could almost see and hear them; she couldn't resist forever. Auberon's. She couldn't do better, such a sweetie, good good man at heart, and for sure a hot number too: and yet. Often enough he treated her like a child herself. Not that she sometimes wasn't one. But a child a mother . . . Uncle Daddy they both called him when he was in that mode or mood. He'd wiped her tears, though. He'd wipe her ass if she asked him to. . . . What a mean thing to think.

Uncle Daddy

What if they grew old together? How would that be? Two little old people, apple-cheeked and crinkly-eyed and white haired, full of years and affection. Nice . . . She'd like to see that big house and all that it contained. But his family. His mother was almost six feet tall, *coño*. She imagined the vast race of them towering over her, looking down. Sport model. George said they were a sweet bunch. He'd got lost more than once in that house. George: Lilac's father, though Auberon didn't know it, and George had sworn her to secrecy. Lost. What was that about? George knew more, but what he wouldn't say. What if Auberon lost one of *her* kids? White people. She'd have to keep a sharp eye out, running around at knee level to them, holding on to her babies.

But if all that weren't her Destiny: or if she really had escaped Destiny, refused it, turned it down . . . If she had, then, oddly, she seemed to have more future, rather than less. Anything could happen if she were free of the cramp of Destiny. Not Auberon, not Edgewood, not this town. Visionary men and pursuits, visionary places, visionary selves crowded up on the borders of her train-lulled consciousness. Anything . . . And a long table in the woods, dressed in a white cloth, set for a banquet; and everybody waiting; and an empty place in the middle . . .

Her head, falling suddenly breastwards, dipped her in vertigo, and she snapped awake.

Destiny, destiny. She yawned, covering her mouth, and then looked at her hand, and the silver ring on it. She'd worn it for years and years. Would it come off? She turned it. She tugged. She put her finger in her mouth to wet it. She pulled harder. Nope: stuck on good. But gently: yes, if she pushed gently from below . . . the silver circle slid upwards, over the big knuckle, and off. A strange lightness glowed around the naked finger, spreading outward from it to the rest of her; the world, the train, seemed to grow pale and insubstantial. She looked slowly around herself.

The package that had been beside her on the seat was gone.

She leapt up, filled with horror, jamming the ring back on her finger. "Hey! Hey!" she said out loud, to alarm the thief if he was still nearby; she charged out into the middle of the car, sweeping the other riders with her glance, they looked up at her curious and guiltless. She looked again at where she had been sitting.

The package was right there where it had been.

She sat again slowly, wondering. She put her ringed hand on the smooth white paper of the package, just to make sure it was really there. It was: though it seemed, unaccountably, to have grown larger as it traveled uptown.

Definitely larger. Out on the street, where breezes had blown away the rain and clouds and brought in a real spring day, first one of the few the City was ever allowed, she chased down the address written on the package, which no longer quite fit beneath her arm. "What is *with* this thing," she said aloud as she walked briskly through a neighborhood she hadn't ever visited much, a neighborhood of great, dark-stained apartment-hotels and aged brownstones. She tried holding the package this way, then that; never had she been given anything so clumsy to carry. But the spring was vivifying; she couldn't have wished for a better day on which to carry messages through the streets; wingéd was just what she felt. And summer would come soon, hot as hell, she couldn't wait; she unzipped, tentatively, then boldly, the front of her sweatshirt, felt the breeze lick at her throat and breast, and found the feeling good. And there, ahead, must be the building she had been sent to.

It was a tall, white building, or a building that had once been white; it was covered with gloomy cast figures of every description. Two wings of it stuck out, forming a dank dark courtyard between them. Far above, at the top of the building, a course of masonry joined these two wings, making an arch absurdly high, an arch for a giant to pass under.

Lost for Sure

Sylvie glanced up at this monstrous fancy, and then quickly away. Tall buildings gave her the willies, she didn't like looking up at them. She stepped into the courtyard, where puddles from the recent rain showed lurid rainbows of oil, but then had no idea how to find Room 001 as she must. An ancient porter's lodge there by the entrance seemed to have been shuttered up tight for years and years, but she went to it anyway and pressed a rusted bell, if this thing works I'll . . .

She didn't get to complete her condition, for even as she pressed down the bell's black nipple a small shutter flew open in the little lodge, and showed her the top half of a head, long nose, small eyes, bald dome. "Hi, can you tell me . . ." she began, but before she could ask further, the eyes crinkled up in a smile or a grimace, and a hand arose; with a long index finger, the hand indicated Left, then Down, and the shutter banged shut.

She laughed. What the hell do they pay him for? That? She followed his instructions, and found herself going in, not the central entrance with its steps and glass doors, but a wrought-iron grille or gate that led to stairs, which went down into an open areaway. Sun didn't reach that narrow place, a sort of slot made by the rising towers. She went down, down, down to the echo-y, cavern-smelling bottom, where there was a small door, let into the wall. A *very* small door; but there was no other exit. "This can't be right," she said, shifting the impossible package (it seemed to be changing shape, and had grown very heavy too). "I'm lost for sure." But she pushed open the door.

It opened on a narrow, low-ceilinged corridor. Down at the far small end, someone was standing before a door, doing something: painting the door? He had a brush, and a paint-pot. Super, or super's helper. Sylvie thought she'd ask further instructions from him, but when she called "Hi," he looked back at her in alarm, and vanished through the door he'd been working on. She marched up to it anyway, reaching it with surprising suddenness, the corridor was shorter than it seemed, or seemed longer than it was, whichever; and the door at its end was even smaller than the one she'd come in by. If this keeps up, she thought, I'll be crawling next. . . . On the door, in fresh white paint in an antique style, the number 001 was painted.

Laughing a little, a little nervously, uncertain now and not at all sure that an elaborate joke wasn't being played on her, Sylvie knocked at the little door. "Wingéd Messenger," she called.

The door opened a crack. A strange, outdoor, summer-gold light seemed to come through it from beyond. A very long, very knuckly hand was put around the door to open it further, and then a very widely grinning face looked out.

"Wingéd Messenger?" Sylvie said.

"Yes? What is it? What can we do for you?" He was the man she'd seen painting the number on the door, or someone just like him; or he was the man who'd directed her here. Or someone just like him.

"Package for you," she said.

"Aha," the little man said. His grin unabated, he opened the door wider so she could stoop to enter. "Do come in, then."

"Are you sure," she said, looking within, "that this is where I'm spose to be?"

"Oh, it certainly is."

"Boy. It's real little in here."

"Oh, yes it is. Won't you please step right on in."

Out on the same May streets at evening, Auberon dawdling Farmwards through the brand-new spring thought of fame, and fortune, and love. He was returning from the offices of the production company that created and sustained "A World Elsewhere" and several other less successful ventures. He had there given into the manicured hands of a remarkably friendly but some-

The Wild Wood

332

what absent man of not much more than his own age two scripts for imaginary episodes of their famous soap. Coffee had been pressed on him, and the young man (who didn't seem to have a lot of business on hand) had talked ramblingly about television, and writing, and production; huge figures of money were mentioned, and arcana of the business touched on—Auberon tried hard not to be astonished at the first and nodded sagely at the latter though he understood little enough of it; and then he'd been shown out, with invitations to drop around any time, by a secretary and a receptionist of near-legendary beauty.

Amazing and wonderful. Large vistas opened before Auberon on the crowded street. The scripts, his and Sylvie's collaboration through long, hilarious and excited evenings, were shapely and thrilling, he thought, though not exquisite to look at, typed as they were on George's old machine; no matter, no matter, his future was filled with expensive office equipment, and with long lunches, prize secretaries, hard work for great rewards. He would seize, from between the claws of the dragon who was denned in the heart of the Wild Wood, the golden treasure it guarded.

The Wild Wood: yes. There had been a time, he knew, say when Frederick Barbarossa was emperor of the West, a time when it had been beyond the log walls of tiny towns, beyond the edges of the harrowed land, that the forest began: the forest, where there lived wolves, and bears, witches in vanishing cottages, dragons, giants. Inside the town, all was reasonable and ordinary; there were safety, fellows, fire and food and all comforts. Dull, maybe, more sensible than thrilling, but safe. It was beyond, in the Wild Wood, that anything could happen, any adventure could be had; out there you took your life in your hands.

No more though. It was all upside down now. At Edgewood, upstate, night held no terrors; the woods there were tame, smiling, comfortable. He didn't know if there were any locks that still worked on the many doors of Edgewood; certainly he'd never seen any of them locked. On hot nights, he'd often slept out on open porches, or in the woods themselves, listening to the sounds and the silence. No, it was on these streets that you saw wolves, real and imagined; here you barricaded your door against whatever fearful thing might be Out There, as once the doors of woodsmen's huts were barred; horrid stories were told of what could happen here after the sun has set; here you had the adventures, won the prizes, lost your way and were swallowed up without a trace, learned to live with the fear in your throat and snatch the treasure: this, this was the Wild Wood now, and Auberon was a woodsman.

Yes! Greed for treasure bred daring in him, and daring

made him strong; errant, armed, he strode through the crowd. Let the weak be gobbled up, he would not be. He thought of Sylvie, clever as a fox, woods-bred though born in the complacent safety of a jungle island. She knew this place; her greed was as great as his, greater, and her cunning matched it. What a team! And to think that not many weeks ago they two had seemed stuck in a deadfall, to have lost each other in trackless undergrowth, to be on the point of surrendering to it all, and parting. Parting. God, what chances she took! How narrow the odds were!

But he could believe, just now, this evening, that they would grow old together. The joy they took in each other, in abeyance all that cold bitter March, had flowered again bright and tough as clustered dandelions—that very morning, in fact, she had been late for work for a reason, a new reason; late, because a certain elaborate process had had to be successfully brought to conclusion—oh, God, the fabulous exertions they required of one another, and the rests those exertions required, a life could be spent in the one and then the other, he felt that his nearly had been so spent all in that morning. And yet unending: he felt it could be, saw no reason why it should not be. He drifted to a halt in the middle of an intersection, grinning, blind; his heartbeats seemed to be minted in gold as moment upon moment of that morning was relived within his breast. A truck blared at him, a truck desperate not to miss the light, its light, which Auberon was flouting. Auberon leapt from its path and the driver yelled something pointed but unintelligible at him. Struck down blinded by love, Auberon thought (laughing and safe on the far sidewalk), that's how I'll die, struck by a truck when I'm whelmed with lust and love and forget where I am.

He took up a quick City stride, still grinning but trying to be alert. Keep your wits about you. After all, he thought, but got no further in the thought, for there came at that moment, crashing down the avenue or swarming up the side-streets or descending from the balmy sky like a ton of shrieking laughter, a thing that was like a sound but wasn't one: the bomb that had fallen once on him and Sylvie, but double that or greater. It rolled over him, it might have been the truck that had missed him, yet it seemed to burst from his own person. Coursing away from him up the avenue, leaving him sundered, the thing seemed to make a vacuum behind it or within it that tugged at his clothes and ruffled his hair. Still his feet fell in good order—the thing had no power to hurt him physically at least—but the smile was quite wiped from his face.

Oh boy, they really mean business now; that was his thought. But he didn't know why he thought it, or what business he thought they meant, or for that matter who he thought they were.

At that moment, far to the west in a state whose name begins with I, Russell Eigenblick, the Lecturer, was on the point of rising from his folding chair to address another immense gathering. He had a small deck of index cards in his hands, a pimento-flavored belch in his throat (chicken a la king again) and a throbbing pain in his left leg, just below the buttock. He wasn't feeling particularly justified. That morning, in the stables of his wealthy hosts, he had mounted a horse and trotted sedately around a small enclosure. Posing for photographers thus, he had looked confident (as always) and somewhat too small (as always, nowadays; upon a time, he had been well above average height). Then he had been induced to take a gallop over fields and meadows as barbered and neat as any chase he had ever ridden. A mistake, that. He hadn't explained that it had been centuries since he'd last been on a horse; he seemed lately to have lost the strength for such provocative remarks. Now he wondered if an ungainly limp would mar his approach to the dais.

How long, how long, he thought. It wasn't that he shunned the work, or resented the trials that were part of it. His paladins strove to ease the process for him, and he was grateful, but the squalid intimacies of this age, the backslapping and arm-taking, didn't really bother him. He had never stood on ceremony. He was a practical man (or thought himself to be so), and if this was what his people—as he already thought of them—wanted of him, he could give it. A man who without complaint had slept amid the wolves of Thuringia and the scorpions of Palestine could suffer motels, could service aging hostesses, could catnap on planes. Only there were times (as now) when the strangeness of his long journey, too impossible to seize, bored him; and the great sleep with which he had grown so familiar tugged at him, and he longed to lay his heavy head once again on his comrades' shoulders, and close his eyes.

His eyes were drifting closed even at the thought.

Then there came, bowling outward in all directions from its starting place, the thing Auberon in the City had felt or heard: a thing that turned the world for a moment to shot silk, or changed in a wink the changeable taffeta of its stuff. A bomb, Auberon had thought it to be; Russell Eigenblick knew it wasn't a bomb but a bombardment.

Like a sharp restorative it shot throught his veins. His weariness vanished. He heard the end of the encomium which introduced him, and he sprang from his chair, eyes alight, mouth grim. He let flutter away, dramatically, the handful of notes for this Lecture as he mounted the dais; the vast audience, seeing this, gasped and cheered. Eigenblick gripped the edges of the lectern with both hands, leaned forward, and bellowed into the microphones that gaped before him to receive his words: "You must change your lives!"

A wave of astonishment, the wave of his own amplified voice washing the crowd, lifted them up, struck the back wall, and returned to break over him. "You must. Change. Your lives!" The wave curled back on them, a tsunami. Eigenblick gloried, sweeping the crowd and seeming to look deeply into every eye, into every heart: they knew it, too. Words crowded into his brain, formed sentences, platoons, regiments against whom resistance was hopeless. He unleashed them.

"The preparations are finished, the votes are in, the die is cast, the chips are down! Everything you most dreaded has already occurred. Your ancientest enemies have the whip hand now. To whom will you turn? Your fortress is all chinks, your armor is paper, your old laughter is a reproach in your throat. Nothing—nothing is as you supposed it to be. You have been deeply fooled. You have been staring into a mirror and supposing it to be the old road's long continuation, but the road has run out, dead end, no through traffic. You must change your lives!"

He drew upright. Such winds were blowing in Time that he had difficulty hearing himself speak. In those winds rode the armed heroes, mounted at last, sylphs in battle-dress, hosts in the middle of the air. Eigenblick, as he harangued the open-mouthed mass before him, lashed them, threshed them, felt himself bursting restraints and coming forth whole at last. As though in a moment he had grown too large for an old worn carapace, with delicious itchy relief he felt it split and crack. He paused, until he knew it had all been shed. The crowd held its breath. Eigenblick's new voice coming forth, loud, low, insinuating, made them shiver as one: "Well. *You* didn't know. Oh, no. How were *yoouu* to know? You never *thought.* You for*got.* You hadn't *heard.*" He leaned forward, looking out over them like a terrible parent, speaking rapidly, as though he spoke a curse: "Well, there will be no forgiveness this time. This time is once too often. Surely you see that, surely you knew it all along. You might, in your secretest heart, if you ever allowed yourself to suspect that this would happen, and you did suspect it, you did, you might have hoped that once again, once again there would be mercy, however undeserved; another chance, however badly bungled every other chance had been; that at the very last you would be ignored, you, only you would be missed out, overlooked, not counted, lost blameless in the cracks of the catastrophe that must engulf all else. No! Not this time!"

"No! No!" They cried out to him, afraid; he was moved,

deep love for their helplessness, deep pity for their state filled him and made him powerful and strong.

"No," he said softly, cooing to them, rocking them in the arms of his bottomless wrath and pity, "no, no; Arthur sleeps in Avalon; you have no champion, no white hope; nothing is left to you but surrender, don't you see that, you do, don't you? Surrender; that's your only chance; show your rusted sword, useless as a toy; show yourselves, helpless, innocent of any of the causes or conclusions of this, aged, confused, weak as babes. And still. And still. Helpless and pitiable as you are"—he held out commiserating arms to them with great slowness, he could hold them all and comfort them— "eager to please as you are, full of love, asking only with softest tears in your big babe's eyes for mercy, pity peace; still, still." The arms descended, the big hands again gripped the lectern as though it were a weapon, a huge fire burst within Russell Eigenblick's bosom, horrid gratitude engulfed him that he could lean down upon these microphones at last and say this: "Still it will not draw their pity, none of it, for they have none; or stay their awful weapons, for they have already been loosed; or change anything at all: for this is war." Lower he bent his head, closer his satyr's lips came to the aghast microphones, and his whisper boomed: "Ladies and *gentle*-MEN, *THIS IS WAR.*"

Ariel Hawksquill, in the City, had felt it too: a change, like a flash of menopause, but not happening to herself but to the world at large. A Change, then; not a change but a Change, a Change glimpsed bowling along the course of space and time, or the world stumbling over a thick and unexpected seam in the seamless fabric.

Unexpected Seam

"Did you feel that?" she said.

"Feel what, my dear?" said Fred Savage, still chuckling over the ferocious headlines of yesterday's paper.

"Forget it," Hawksquill said softly, thoughtful. "Well. About cards, now. Anything at all about cards? Think hard."

"The ace of spades reversed," Fred Savage said. "Queen of spades in your bedroom window, fierce as any bitch. Jack of diamonds, on the road again. King of hearts, that's me, baby," and he began to sing-hum through his ivory teeth, his buttocks moving slightly but snappily on the long, buttock-polished bench of the waiting room.

Hawksquill had come to the great Terminus to question this old oracle of hers, knowing that most evenings after work he could be found here, confiding strange truths to strangers; pointing out with an index finger brown, gnarled, and dirt-clogged as a root, certain items in yesterday's paper which the train-takers around him might have missed, or discoursing on how a woman who wears a fur takes on the propensities of the animal—Hawksquill thought of timid suburban girls wearing rabbit-furs dyed to look like lynx, and laughed. Sometimes she brought a sandwich to share with him, if he were eating. Usually she went away wiser than she had come.

"Cards," she said. "Cards and Russell Eigenblick."

"That fella," he said. He was lost awhile in thought. He shook out his paper as though shaking a troublesome notion from it. But it wouldn't go.

"What is it?" she said.

"Now damn if there *wasn't* a change just now," he said, looking upward. "Sumpm . . . What was it, did you say?"

"I didn't say."

"You said a name."

"Russell Eigenblick. In the cards."

"In the cards," he said. He folded his paper carefully. "That's enough," he said. "That'll do."

"Tell me," she said, "what you think."

But she had pressed him too hard, always a danger, ask the great virtuosi for one more encore and they will turn petulant and surly. Fred rose—as far as he ever rose, remaining bent like a quizzical letter—and felt for something nonexistent in his pockets. "Gotta go see m'uncle," he said. "You wouldn't have a buck for the bus? Some kinda buck or change?"

From East
to West

She walked back through the vast arching hall of the Terminus no wiser this time than when she had come, and more troubled. The hundreds who hurried there, eddying around the shrinelike clock in the center and washing up in waves against the ticket booths, seemed distracted, hard-pressed, uncertain of their fates: but whether more so than on any other day she wasn't sure. She looked up: grown faint with age and long watching, the Zodiac painted in gold marched biaswise across the night-blue dome, pricked out with tiny lights, many of them extinguished. Her steps slowed, her mouth fell open; she turned, staring, unable to believe what she saw.

The Zodiac ran the proper way across the dome from east to west.

Impossible. It had always been one of her favorite jokes about this mad City that its grand center was watched over by a

Zodiac that was backwards, the mistake of a star-ignorant muralist, or some sly pun on his star-crossed City. She had wondered what reversals might happen if—with proper preparation—one were to walk backwards through the Terminus beneath this backwards cosmos, but propriety had always kept her from trying it.

But look now. Here was the ram in his right place, and the hindquarterless bull, the twins and the crab, King Lion and the virgin and the double-panned scales. The poised scorpion next, with red Antares in his sting; the centaur with his bow, the fish-tailed goat, the man with the water-jug. And the two fishes bow-tied at the tails. The crowds flowed around her where she stood gawking, flowed without pause as they did around any fixed object in their path. Her looking upward was infectious, as in the hoary trick; others looked upward too, searching briefly, but, unable to see the impossible thing she saw, hurried on.

The ram, the bull, the twins . . . She struggled to retain her memory that they had been otherwise, had not always had this order, for they looked as old and immutable as the stars they pictured. She grew afraid. A Change: and what other changes would she find, out on the streets; what others lay in the to-come, yet to be manifested? What anyway was Russell Eigenblick doing to the world; and why on earth was she sure that it was Russell Eigenblick who was Somehow at fault? A sweet baritone bell struck, and echoed around her as she stared, not loud but clear, calm as though possessed of the secret: the Terminus clock, ringing the small time of the hour.

The same hour was being rung in the pyramidal steeple of a building which Alexander Mouse had built downtown, the only steeple in the City that rang the hours for the public enlightenment. One of the four notes of its four-note tune was silenced, and the others fell irregularly into the channel of streets below, blown away by wind or muffled by traffic, so it was no help usually, but Auberon (unbarring and unbolting a door into Old Law Farm) didn't care what time it was anyway. He gave a glance around himself to see that he wasn't followed by thieves. (He'd already been robbed once, by two kids who, since he'd had no money, had taken the bottle of gin he was carrying, and then took and flung his hat to the ground and stepped on it with long sneakered feet as they went away.) He slipped in, and bolted and barred the door behind him.

Down the hall, through a brick-toothed rent George had made in the wall to give access to the next building, up that hall, up the stairs, gripping the banister iced thickly with generations of

Sylvie?

339

paint. Out a hall window onto a fire escape, a wave to the happy farmers at work with shoots and trowels down below, and back into another building, another hall, absurdly narrow and close, familiar in its gloom and joyful, for it led home. He glimpsed himself in the pretty mirror Sylvie had hung on the wall at the end of the hall, with a tiny table below it and a bowl of dried flowers, *bien* nice. The door-knob didn't open the door. "Sylvie?" Not home. Not back from work, or out farming; or just out, the reborn sun caused the blue island lagoon in her blood to rise. He hunted out his three keys and peered at them in the dark, growing impatient. Ovoid-ended for the top lock, keystone-ended for the middle, oh hell! He dropped one, and had to get down on hands and knees, furious, and feel for it amid the irremediable antique filth of all City nooks and crannies. Here it was: huge, round-ended one for the police lock, which kept the police out, ha ha.

"Sylvie?"

The Folding Bedroom seemed oddly large, and, though sunlight poured in through all its little windows, Somehow not cheerful. What was it? The place seemed swept, but not tidy; cleaned, but not clean. There was a lot of stuff missing, he gradually realized; a lot of stuff. Had they been robbed? He went gingerly into the kitchen. Sylvie's collection of unguents and such that clustered above the sink was gone. Her shampoos and hairbrushes, gone. It was all gone. All but his own old Gillette.

In the bedroom likewise. Her totems and pretty things, gone. Her china señorita, with a dead-white face and black spit-curls, whose top half separated from her flaring skirt which was really a jewel box, gone. Her hats hung on the back of the door, gone. Her crazy envelope of important papers and assorted snapshots, gone.

He tore open the closet door. Empty coat-hangers clanged, and his own overcoat hung on the door flung out startled sleeves, but there was nothing at all of hers there.

Nothing at all.

He looked around him, and then looked around him again. And then stood still in the middle of the empty floor.

"Gone," he said.

Book Five

THE ART OF MEMORY

*The fields, the caves, the dens of
Memory cannot be counted; their
fullness cannot be counted nor the
kinds of things counted that fill
them . . . I force my way in amongst
them, even as far as my power
reaches, and nowhere find an end.*

—Augustine, Confessio

Upon a deep midnight, the Maid of Stone knocked with a heavy fist on the tiny door of the Cosmo-Opticon on the top floor of Ariel Hawksquill's townhouse.
"The Noisy Bridge Rod and Gun Club to see you."
"Yes. Have them wait in the parlor."
The moon behind the mirrored moon of the Cosmo-Opticon, and the dull glow of the City lights, were all that illuminated the heavens of glass; the blackish Zodiac and the constellations could not be read. Odd, she thought, how (reversing the natural order) the Cosmo-Opticon was intelligible, ablaze, in the day, and obscure at night, when the real heaven's panoply is full. . . . She rose and came out, the iron Earth with its enameled rivers and mountains clanging beneath her feet.

A year had passed since she had looked up to see that the Zodiac painted on the night-blue ceiling of the Terminus had changed its old wrong order of march and went the way the world went. In that year, her investigations into the nature and origins of Russell Eigenblick had grown only more intense, though the Club had fallen oddly silent; no longer lately did they send her cryptic telegrams urging her on, and though Fred Savage showed up

The Hero
Awakened

343

as usual at her door with the installments of her fee, these weren't accompanied by the usual encouragements or reproaches. Had they lost interest?

If they had, she thought she could awaken it this night.

She had broken the case, in fact, some months before; the answer came, not from her occult researches, but from such mundane or sublunary places as her old encyclopaedia (tenth Britannica), the sixth volume of Gregorovius on Medieval Rome, and (a great folio in double columns, with a hasp to lock it up) the Prophecies of Abbot Joachim da Fiore. It was certainty that had taken all her arts, and that had to be bought at the cost of much labor, and much time. There was no doubt, now, though. She knew, that is, Who. She did not know How, or Why; she knew no more than she had known who the children of the children of Time were, whose champion Russell Eigenblick might be; she didn't know where those cards were which he was in, or in what sense he was in them. But she knew Who: and she had summoned the Noisy Bridge Rod and Gun Club to hear that news.

They had disposed themselves around the chairs and sofa of her dimly-lit and crowded drawing-room or study on the ground floor.

"Gentlemen," she said, gripping the back of an upright leather chair like a lectern, "more than two years ago you gave me the assignment of discovering the nature and intentions of Russell Eigenblick. You have had an unconscionable wait, but I think to-night I can at least provide you with an identification; a recommendation as to the disposition of the case will be far harder. If I can make one at all. And if I can make one, then you—yes, even you—may be incapable of acting on it."

There was an exchange of glances at this, subtler than one sees on stage, but with the same effect of registering mutual surprise and concern. It had once before occurred to Hawksquill that the men she dealt with were not the Noisy Bridge Rod and Gun Club at all, but actors hired to represent them. She suppressed the notion.

"We all know," she went on, "the tales, found in many mythologies, of a hero who, though slain on the field of battle or otherwise meeting a tragic end, is said not to have died at all, but to have been borne away to somewhere, elsewhere, an isle or a cave or a cloud, where he sleeps; and from where, at his people's greatest need, he will issue, with his paladins, to aid them, and to rule then over a new Golden Age. *Rex Quondam et Futurus.* Arthur in Avalon; Sikander somewhere in Persia; Cuchulain in every other fen or glen of Ireland; Jesus Christ himself.

"All these tales, moving as they are, are not true. No trials

344

of his people awakened Arthur; Cuchulain is able to sleep through the mutual slaughter of his, protracted over centuries; the Second Coming, continually announced, has been delayed past the virtual end of the Church that so much counted on it. No: whatever the next World-Age brings (and that age lies anyway well in the to-come) it will not bring back a hero whose name we know. But . . ." She paused, assailed by a sudden doubt. Said aloud, the absurdity of it seemed greater. She even flushed, ashamed, as she went on: "But it happens that one of these stories *is* true. It's not one we would ever have thought to be true, even if it were one we remember and tell, and for the most part it isn't; it and its hero are much forgotten. But we know it to be true because the necessary conclusion of it has occurred: the hero has awakened. Russell Eigenblick is he."

This shot fell less heavily among her hearers than she had expected it to. She felt them withdraw from her; she saw, or perceived, their necks stiffen, their chins draw down doubtfully into expensive haberdashery. There was nothing for it but to go on.

"You may wonder," she said, "as I did, what people Russell Eigenblick has returned to aid. We as a people are too young to have cultivated stories like those told of Arthur, and perhaps too self-satisfied to have felt the need of any. Certainly none are told of the so-called fathers of our country; the idea that one of those gentlemen is not dead but asleep, say, in the Ozarks or the Rockies is funny but not anywhere held. Only the despised ghost-dancing Red Man has a history and a memory long enough to supply such a hero; and the Indians have shown as little interest in Russell Eigenblick as in our Presidents, and he as little in them. What people then?

"The answer is: no people. No people: but an Empire. An Empire which could, and once did, comprise any people or peoples regardless, and had a life, a crown, borders and capitals of the greatest mutability. You will remember Voltaire's dig: that it was neither holy, nor Roman, nor an empire. Yet in some sense it existed until (as we have thought) its last Emperor, Francis II, resigned the title in 1806. Well: my contention is, gentlemen, that the Holy Roman Empire did not pass away then either. It continued to exist. It continued, like an amoeba, to shift, crawl, expand, contract; and that while Russell Eigenblick slept his long sleep (exactly eight hundred years by my reckoning)—while, in effect, we all slept—it has crept and slid, shifting and drifting like the continents, until it is now located here, where we sit. How exactly its borders should be drawn I have no idea, though I suspect they may be identical with this country's. In any case we are well within it. This city may even be its Capital: though probably only its Chief City."

345

She had ceased looking at them.

"And Russell Eigenblick?" she asked of no one. "He was once its Emperor. Not its first, who was of course Charlemagne (about whom the same sleep-wake story was for a while told) nor its last, nor even its greatest. Vigorous, yes; talented; uneven in temperament; no administrator; steady, but generally unsuccessful, in war. It was he who, by the way, added the 'holy' to his Empire's name. About 1190 he chose, with the Empire generally at peace and the Pope for the moment off his back, to go on crusade. The Infidel only briefly felt his scourge; he won a battle or two, and then, crossing a stream in Armenia, he fell from his horse, and was too weighted down by his armor to get out. He drowned. So says Gregorovius, among other authorities.

"The Germans, though, after many later reverses, came to disbelieve this. He hadn't died. He was only asleep, perhaps beneath the Kyffhauser in the Hartz Mountains (the place is still pointed out to tourists) or perhaps in Domdaniel in the sea, or wherever, but he would return, one day; return to the aid of his beloved Germans, and lead German arms to victory and a German empire to glory. The hideous history of Germany in the last century may be the working-out of this vain dream. But in fact that Emperor, despite his birth and his name, was no German. He was Emperor of all the world, or at least all Christendom. He was heir to French Charlemagne and Roman Caesar. And now he has shifted like his ancient borders, and has changed no allegiances in doing so, only his name. Gentlemen, Russell Eigenblick is the Holy Roman Emperor Frederick Barbarossa, yes, *die alte Barbarossa,* reawakened to rule over this strange latter age of his Empire."

This last sentence she had spoken, her voice rising, against a growing swell of murmurs, protests, and standings-up among her hearers.

"Absurd!" said one.

"Preposterous!" said another, like a spit.

"Do you mean to say, Hawksquill," said a third, more reasonably, "that Russell Eigenblick supposes himself to be this resurrected Emperor, and that . . ."

"I have no idea who he supposes himself to be," Hawksquill said. "I'm only telling you who he in fact is."

"Then answer me this," said the member, raising his hand to silence the hubbub Hawksquill's insistence raised. "Why is it just now that he returns? I mean didn't you say that these heroes return at the time of their people's greatest need, and so on?"

"Traditionally they are said to, yes."

"Then why now? If this futile Empire has lain doggo for so long . . ."

Hawksquill looked down. "I said it would be hard for me to make a recommendation. I'm afraid that there are essential pieces of this puzzle still withheld from me."

"Such as."

"For one," she said, "the cards he speaks of. I can't now go into my reasons, but I must see them, and manipulate them. . . ." There was an impatient uncrossing and recrossing of legs. Someone asked why. "I supposed," she said, "you would need to know his strength. His chances. What times he considers propitious. The point is, gentlemen, that if you intend to suppress him, you had better know whether Time is on your side, or on his; and whether you are not futilely ranging yourselves against the inevitable."

"And you can't tell us."

"I'm afraid I can't. Yet."

"It doesn't matter," said the senior member present, rising. "I'm afraid, Hawksquill, that, your investigations in this case being so prolonged, we've had to come to a decision ourselves. We came tonight chiefly to discharge you of any further obligation."

"Hm," said Hawksquill.

The senior member chuckled indulgently. "And it doesn't really seem to me," he said, "that your present revelations do much to alter the case. As I remember my history, the Holy Roman Empire had not a lot to do with the life of the peoples who supposedly comprised it. Am I right? The real rulers liked having the Imperial power in their hands or under their control, but in any case did what they liked."

"That was often so."

"Well then. The course we decided on was the right one. If Russell Eigenblick turns out to be in some sense this Emperor, or convinces enough people of it (I notice, by the way, he continually puts off announcing just who he is, big mystery), then he might be more useful than the reverse."

"May I ask," Hawksquill said, motioning forward the Maid of Stone who stood mumchance in the doorway with a tray of glasses and a tall decanter, "what course of action you decided on?"

The Noisy Bridge Rod and Gun Club settled back in their seats, smiling. "Co-optation," said a member—one of those who had most vigorously protested Hawksquill's conclusions. "The power of certain charlatans," he went on, "isn't to be despised. We learned that in last summer's marches and riots. The Church of All Streets fracas. Et cetera. Of course such power is usually short-lived. It's not real power. All wind, really. A storm soon passed. They know it, too. . . ."

"But," said another member, "when such a one is introduced to *real* power—promised a share in it—his opinions indulged —his vanity flattered . . ."

"Then he can be enlisted. He can be used, frankly."

"You see," said the senior member, waving away the drink-tray offered him, "in the large scheme, Russell Eigenblick has no real powers, no strong adherents. A few clowns in colored shirts, a few devoted men. His oratory moves; but who remembers next day? If he stirred up great hatreds, or mobilized old bitternesses—but he doesn't. It's all vagueness. So: we'll offer him real allies. He has none. He'll accept. There are lures we have. He'll be ours. And damn useful he might prove, too."

"Hm," Hawksquill said again. Schooled as she had been in the purest of studies, on the highest of planes, she had never found deception and evasion easy. That Russell Eigenblick had no allies was, anyway, true. That he was a cat's-paw for forces more powerful, less namable, more insidious than the Noisy Bridge Rod and Gun Club could imagine, she ought by rights to inform them: though she herself could not yet name those forces. But she had been released from the case. They wouldn't anyway—she could see it in their smug faces—probably listen to her. Still she blushed, fiercely, at what she withheld from them, and said, "I think I'll have a drop of this. Will no one join me?"

"The fee," said a member, watching her closely as she poured for him, "need not be returned, of course."

She nodded at him. "When exactly do you put your plan into execution?"

"This day next week," said the senior member, "we have a meeting with him in his hotel." He rose, looking around him, ready to go. Those members who had accepted drinks swallowed them hastily. "I'm sorry," the senior member said, "that after all your labors we've gone our own way."

"It's no doubt just as well," Hawksquill said, not rising.

They looked at each other—all standing now—in that unconvincing manner, this time expressing thoughtful doubt or doubtful thought, and took a muted leave of her. One hoped aloud as they went out that she had not been offended; and the others, as they inserted themselves into their cars, pondered that possibility, and what it might mean for them.

Hawksquill, alone, pondered it too.

Released from her obligation to the Club, she was a free

agent. If a new old Empire were rearising in the world, she couldn't but think it would give her new and wider scope for her powers. Hawksquill was not immune to the lure of power; great wizards rarely are.

And yet no New Age was at hand. Whatever powers stood behind Russell Eigenblick might not, in the end, be as strong as the powers the Club could bring against them.

Whose side then, supposing she could determine which side was which, would she be on?

She watched the legs her brandy made on the sides of the glass. A week from today . . . She rang for the Maid of Stone, ordered coffee, and readied herself for a long night's work: they were too few now to spend one asleep.

Exhausted by fruitless labor, she came down some time after dawn and went out into the bird-loud street.

Opposite her tall and narrow house was a small park which had once been public but which was now sternly locked; only the residents of those houses and private clubs which faced on it, viewing it with calm possessiveness, had keys to the wrought-iron gates. Hawksquill had one. The park, too chock-full of statues, fountains, birdbaths and such fancies, rarely refreshed her, since she had more than once used it as a sort of notepad, sketching quickly on its sunwise perimeter a Chinese dynasty or a Hermetic mathesis, none of which (of course) she was now able to forget.

A Secret Sorrow

But now in the misty dawn on the first day of May it was obscure, vague, not rigorous. It was air mostly, almost not a City air, sweet and rich with the exhalation of newborn leaves; and obscurity and vagueness were just what she required now.

As she came up to the gate she used, she saw that someone was standing before it, gripping the bars and staring within hopelessly, obverse of a jailed man. She hesitated. Walkers-abroad at this hour were of two kinds: humdrum hard workers up early, and the unpredictable and the lost who had been up all night. Those seemed to be pajama bottoms protruding from beneath this one's long overcoat, but Hawksquill didn't take this to mean that he was an early riser. She chose a grand-lady manner as best suited to the encounter and, taking out her key, asked the man to excuse her, she'd like to open the gate.

"About time too," he said.

"Oh, I'm so sorry," she said; he had stood aside only slightly, expectantly, and she saw that he intended to follow her in.

"It's a private park. I'm afraid you can't come in. It's only for those who live around it, you see. Who have the key."

She could see his face now clearly, with its desperate growth of whisker and its wrinkles etched deeply with filth; yet he was young. Above his fierce yet vacant eyes a single eyebrow ran.

"It's damned unfair," he said. "They've all got houses, what the hell do they need a park for too?" He stared at her, rageful and frustrated. She wondered if she should explain to him that there was no more injustice in his being locked out of this park than out of the buildings that surrounded it. The way he looked at her seemed to require some plea; or then on the other hand perhaps the injustice he complained of was the universal and unanswerable kind, the kind Fred Savage liked to point up, needing no spurious or ad-hoc explanations. "Well," she said, as she often did to Fred.

"When your own great-grandfather built the damn thing." His eyes looked upward, calculating. "Great-*great*-grandfather." He pulled, with sudden purpose, a glove from his pocket, put it on (his medicus extending naked from an unseamed finger) and began brushing away the new-leaving ivy and obscuring dirt from a plaque screwed to the rusticated red-stone gate-post. "See? Damn it." The plaque said—it took her a moment to work it out, surprised she had never noticed it, the whole history of Beaux-Arts public works could have been laid on its close-packed Roman face and the floweret nailheads that held it in place—the plaque said "Mouse Drinkwater Stone 1900."

He wasn't a nut. City-dwellers in general and Hawksquill in particular have a sure sense, in these encounters, of the distinction—fine but real—between the impossible imaginings of the mad and the equally impossible but quite true stories of the merely lost and damned. "Which," she said, "are you, the Mouse, the Drinkwater, or the Stone?"

"I guess you wouldn't know," he said, "how impossible it is to get a little peace and quiet in this town. Do I look like a bum to you?"

"Well," she said.

"The fact is you can't sit down on a God damn park bench or a doorway without ten drunks and loudmouths collecting as though they were blown together. Telling you their life stories. Passing around a bottle. Chums. Did you know how many bums are queer? A lot. It's surprising." He said it was surprising but in fact he seemed to feel it was just what was to be expected and no less infuriating for that. "Peace and quiet," he said again, in a tone so genuinely full of longing, so full of the dewy tulip-beds and shadowed walks within the little park, that she said: "Well, I suppose an exception can be made. For a descendant of the builder." She turned her key in the lock and swung open the gate. For a moment he stood as before those final gates of pearl, wondering; then he went in.

Once inside his rage seemed to abate, and though she hadn't intended it, she walked with him along the curiously curving paths that seemed always about to lead them deeper within the park but in fact always contrived to direct them back to its perimeters. She knew the secret of these—which was, of course, to take those paths which seemed to be heading outward, and you would go in; and with subtle motions she directed their steps that way. The paths, though they didn't seem to, led them in to where a sort of pavilion or temple—a tool shed in fact, she supposed—stood at the park's center. Overarching trees and aged bushes disguised its miniature size; from certain angles it appeared to be the visible porch or corner of a great house; and though the park was small, here at the center the surrounding city, by some trick of planting and perspective, could hardly be perceived at all. She began to remark on this.

"Yes," he said. "The further in you go, the bigger it gets. Would you like a drink?" He pulled from his pocket a flat clear bottle.

"Early for me," she said. She watched, fascinated, as he undid the bottle and slid a good bit of it down a throat no doubt now so flayed and tanned it couldn't feel. She was surprised then to see him shaken by big involuntary shudders, and his face twisted in disgust just as hers would have been if she'd tried that gulp. Just a beginner, she thought. Just a child, really. She supposed he had a secret sorrow, and was pleased to contemplate it; it was just the change she needed from the hugeness she had been struggling with.

They sat together on a bench. The young man wiped the neck of his bottle on his sleeve and recapped it carefully. He slid it into the pocket of his brown overcoat without haste. Strange, she thought, that glass and clear cruel liquid could be so comforting, so tenderly regarded. "What the hell is that supposed to be?" he said.

They faced the square stone place that Hawksquill supposed to be a tool shed or other facility, disguised as a pavilion or miniature pleasure-dome. "I don't know exactly," she said, "but the reliefs on it represent the Four Seasons, I think. One to a side."

The one before them was Spring, a Greek maiden doing some potting, with an ancient tool very like a trowel and a tender shoot in her other hand. A baby lamb nestled near her and like her looked hopeful, expectant, new. It was all quite well done; by varying the depth of his cutting, the artist had given an impression of distant fields newly turned and returning birds. Daily life in the

351

ancient world. It resembled no spring that had ever come to the City, but it was nonetheless Spring. Hawksquill had more than once employed it as such. She had for a time wondered why the little house had been placed off-center on its plot of ground, not square with the streets around the park; and after a little thought saw that it faced the compass points, Winter facing north and Summer to the south, Spring east, and Autumn west. It was easy to forget, in the City, that north was only very approximately uptown—though not easy for Hawksquill, and apparently this designer had thought a true orientation important too. She liked him for it. She even smiled at the young man next to her, a supposed descendant, though he looked like a City creature who didn't know solstice from equinox.

"What good is it?" he said, quietly but truculently.

"It's handy," said Hawksquill. "For remembering things."

"What?"

"Well," she said. "Suppose you wanted to remember a certain year, and the order in which events happened then. You could memorize these four panels, and use the things pictured in them as symbols for the events you want to remember. If you wanted to remember that a certain person was buried in the spring, well, there's the trowel."

"Trowel?"

"Well, that digging tool."

He looked at her askance. "Isn't that a little morbid?"

"It was an example."

He regarded the maiden suspiciously, as if she were in fact about to remind him of something, something unpleasant. "The little plant," he said at length, "could be something you began in the spring. A job. Some hope."

"That's the idea," she said.

"Then it withers."

"Or bears fruit."

He was thoughtful a long time; he drew out his bottle and repeated his ritual exactly, though with less grimace. "Why is it," he said then, his voice faint from the gin that had washed it, "that people want to remember everything? Life is here and now. The past is dead."

She said nothing to this.

"Memories. Systems. Everybody poring over old albums and decks of cards. If they're not remembering, they're predicting. What good is it?"

An old cowbell rang within Hawksquill's halls. "Cards?" she said.

"Brooding on the past," he said, regarding Spring. "Will that bring it back?"

"Only order it." She knew that, reasonable as they might seem, people like this who live on the street are differently composed from people who live in houses. They have a reason for being where they are, expressed in a peculiar apprehension of things, a loss of engagement with the ordinary world and how it goes on, often unwilled. She knew she must not press questions on him, pursue a subject, for like the paths in this place that would only lead her away. Yet she wanted very much now not to lose contact. "Memory can be an art," she said schoolmarmishly. "Like architecture. I think your ancestor would have understood that."

He lifted eyebrows and shoulders as though to say Who knows, or cares.

"Architecture, in fact," she said, "is frozen memory. A great man said that."

"Hm."

"Many great thinkers of the past"—how she had caught this teachery tone she didn't know, but she couldn't seem to relinquish it, and it seemed to hold her hearer—"believed that the mind is a house, where memories are stored; and that the easiest way to remember things is to imagine an architecture, and then cast symbols of what you wish to remember on the various places defined by the architect." Well, that surely must have lost him, she thought, but after some thought he said:

"Like the guy buried with the trowel."

"Exactly."

"Dumb," he said.

"I can give you a better example."

"Hm."

She gave him Quintillian's highly-colored example of a law-case, freely substituting modern for ancient symbols, and spreading them around the parts of the little park. His head swiveled from side to side as she placed this and that here and there, though she had no need to look. "In the third place," she said, "we put a broken toy car, to remind us of the driver's license that expired. In the fourth place—that arch sort of thing behind you to the left—we hang a man, say a Negro all dressed in white, with pointed shoes hanging down, and a sign on him: INRI."

"What on earth."

"Vivid. Concrete. The judge has said: unless you have documentary proof, you will lose the case. The Negro in white means having it on paper."

"In black and white."

"Yes. The fact that he's hanged means we have captured this black-and-white proof, and the sign, that it is this that will save us."

"Good God."

"It sounds terribly complicated, I know. And I suppose it's really not any better than a notebook."

"Then why all that guff? I don't get it."

"Because," she said carefully, sensing that despite his outward truculence he understood her, "it can happen—if you practice this art—that the symbols you put next to one another will modify themselves without your choosing it, and that when next you call them forth, they may say something new and revelatory to you, something you didn't know you knew. Out of the proper arrangement of what you *do* know, what you *don't* know may arise spontaneously. That's the advantage of a system. Memory is fluid and vague. Systems are precise and articulated. Reason apprehends them better. No doubt that's the case with those cards you spoke of."

"Cards?"

Too soon? "You spoke of brooding over a deck of cards."

"My aunt. Not *my* aunt really," as though disclaiming her. "My grandfather's aunt. She had these cards. Lay them out, think about them. Brood on the past. Predict things."

"Tarot?"

"Hm?"

"Were they the Tarot deck? You know, the hanged man, the female pope, the tower . . ."

"*I* don't know.. How would *I* know? Nobody ever explained anything to *me*." He brooded. "I don't remember *those* pictures, though."

"Where did they come from?"

"I dunno. England, I guess. Since they were Violet's."

She started, but he was lost in thought and didn't see. "And there were some cards with pictures? Besides the court cards?"

"Oh yeah. A whole slew of 'em. People, places, things, notions."

She leaned back, interlacing her fingers slowly. It had happened before that a place which she had put to multiple memory uses, like this park, came to be haunted by figments, hortatory or merely weird, called into being simply by the overlap of old juxtapositions, speaking, sometimes, of a meaning she would not otherwise have seen. If it were not for the sour smell of this one's overcoat, the undeniable this-worldness of the striped pajamas beneath it, she might have thought him to be one of them. It didn't matter. There is no chance. "Tell me," she said. "These cards."

"What if you wanted to forget a certain year?" he said. "Not remember it, but forget it. No help there, is there? No system for that, oh no."

"Oh, I suppose there are methods," she said, thinking of his bottle.

He seemed sunk in bitter reflection, eyes vacant, long neck bent like a sad bird's, hands folded in his lap. She was casting about for words to form a new question about the cards when he said: "The last time she read those cards for me, she said I'd meet a dark and beautiful girl, of all cornball things."

"Did you?"

"She said I'd win this girl's love through no virtue I had, and lose her through no fault of my own."

He said nothing else for a time, and (though not sure now that he heard or registered much of anything she said to him) she ventured softly: "That's often the way, with love." Then, when he didn't respond: "I have a certain question that a certain deck of cards might answer. Does your aunt still . . ."

"She's dead."

"Oh."

"My aunt, though. I mean *she* wasn't my aunt, but *my* aunt. Sophie." He made a gesture which seemed to mean This is complex and boring, but surely you catch my drift.

"The cards are still in your family," she guessed.

"Oh, yeah. Never throw out anything."

"Where exactly . . ."

He raised a hand to stop her question, suddenly wary. "I don't want to go into family matters."

She waited a moment and then said: "It *was* you who mentioned your great-great-grandfather, who built this park." Why suddenly was she visted with a vision of Sleeping Beauty's castle? A chateau. With a hedge of thorn, impassable.

"John Drinkwater," he said, nodding.

Drinkwater. The architect . . . A mental snap of fingers. That hedge wasn't thorn. "Was he married to a woman named Violet Bramble?"

He nodded.

"A mystic, a seer of sorts?"

"Who the hell knows what she was."

Urgency suddenly compelled her to a gesture, rash perhaps, but there was no time to waste. She took from her pocket the key to the park and held it up before him by its chain, as old mesmerists used to do before their subjects. "It seems to me," she said, seeing him take notice, "that you deserve free access here. This is my key." He held out a hand, and she drew the key somewhat away. "What I require in exchange is an introduction to the woman who is or is not your aunt, and explicit directions as to how to find her. All right?"

As though in fact mesmerized, staring fixedly at the glinting bit of brass, he told her what she wanted to know. She placed the key in his filthy glove. "A deal," she said.

Auberon clutched the key, his only possession now, though Hawksquill couldn't know that, and, the spell broken, looked away, not sure he hadn't betrayed something, but unwilling to feel guilt.

Hawksquill rose. "It's been most illuminating," she said. "Enjoy the park. As I said, it can be handy."

A Year to Place Upon It

Auberon, after another scalding yet kindly draught, began, closing one eye, to measure out his new demesne. The regularity of it surprised him, since its tone was not regular but bosky and artless. Yet the benches, gates, obelisks, marten-houses on poles, and the intersections of paths had a symmetry easily adduced from where he sat. It all depended from or radiated outward from the little house of the seasons.

That was all hopeless guff she had instructed him in, of course. He did feel bad about inflicting such a lunatic on his family, not that they would notice probably, hopeless themselves; and the price had not been resistable. Odd how a man of wide sympathies like himself started such hares and harebrains wherever he went.

Outside the park, framed in sycamores from where he sat, was a small classical courthouse (Drinkwater's too for all he knew), surmounted with statues of lawgivers at even intervals. Moses. Solon. Etc. A place to put a law-case, certainly. His own infuriating struggle with Petty, Smilodon & Ruth. Those coffered brass doors not yet open for business the locked entrance to his inheritance, the egg-and-dart molding the endless repetition of delay and hope, hope and delay.

Stupid. He looked away. What was the point? No matter how gracefully the building accepted his case in all its complexity (and as he glanced again sidelong at it he saw that it could and did) it was needless. How could he forget all that? The doles they eked out to him, enough to keep him from starvation, enough to keep him signing (with an increasingly furious scrawl) the instruments, waivers, pleas and powers they presented him with as those stony-eyed immortals there proffered tablets, books, codices: the last of the last had bought this gin he now drank of, and more than was left in the bottle would be necessary for him to forget the indignity of his pleading for it, the injustice of it all. Diocletian counted out wrinkled bills from petty cash.

Hell with that. He left the courthouse outside. In here there was no law.

A year to place upon it. She had said that the value of her system was how it would cast up, spontaneously, what you didn't know out of the proper arrangement of what you did.

Well: there was a thing he didn't know.

If he could believe what the old woman had said, if he could, wouldn't he then set to work here, commit every tulip-bed and arrowheaded fence-post, every whitewashed stone, every budding leaf to memory, so that he could distribute among them every tiny detail of lost Sylvie? Wouldn't he then march furiously sniffing up and down the curving paths, like this mutt that had just entered with his master, searching, searching, going sunwise then antisunwise, searching until the one single simple answer arose, the astonishing lost truth, that would make him clutch his brow and cry *I see*?

No, he would not.

He had lost her; she was gone, and for good. That fact was all that excused and made reasonable, even proper, his present degradation. If her whereabouts were revealed to him now, though he had spent a year trying to learn them, he would avoid them of all places.

And yet. He didn't want to find her, not any more; but he would like to know why. Would like to know (timidly, subjunctively) why she had left him never to return, without a word, without, apparently, a backward glance. Would like to know, well, what was up with her nowadays, if she was all right, whether she thought of him ever, and in what mode, kindly or otherwise. He recrossed his legs, tapping one broken shoe in the air. No: it was just as well, really; just as well that he knew the old woman's batty and monstrous system to be useless. That Spring could never be the spring she had blossomed for him, nor that shoot their love, nor that trowel the tool by which his rageful and unhappy heart had been scored with joy.

357

He hadn't at first found her disappearance all that alarm-
ing. She'd run off before, for a few nights or a
weekend, where and for what reasons he never pressed
her about, he was cool, he was a hands-off guy. She
hadn't ever before taken every stitch of clothes and
every souvenir, but he didn't put it beyond her, she
could bring them all back in an hour, at any hour, having missed a
fleeing bus or train or plane or been unable to bear whatever relative
or friend or lover she had camped with. A mistake. The greatness of
her desires, of her longing for life to come out right even in the
impossible conditions under which hers was lived, led her into such
mistakes. He rehearsed fatherly or avuncular speeches with which,
unhurt and unalarmed and not angry, he would counsel her after he
welcomed her back.

In the First Place

    He looked for notes. The Folding Bedroom though small
was such a chaos that he might easily have overlooked one; it had
slipped down behind the stove, she had propped it on the windowsill
and it had blown out into the farmyard, he had closed it up in the
bed. It would be a note in her huge, wild round hand; it would start
"Hi!" and be signed with x's for kisses. It had been on the back of
something inconsequential, which he had thrown out even as he
searched through inconsequential papers for it. He emptied the
wastebasket, but when its contents lay around his ankles he stopped
the search and stood stock still, having suddenly imagined another
sort of note entirely, a note with no "Hi!" and no kisses. It would
resemble a love letter in its earnest, overwrought tone, but it
wouldn't be a love letter.

    There were people he could call. When (after endless
trouble) they had had a phone put in, amazing George Mouse, she
had used to spend a good amount of time talking to relatives and
quasi-relatives in a rapid and (to him) hilarious mixture of Spanish
and English, shouting with laughter sometimes and sometimes just
shouting. He had taken down none of the numbers she called; she
herself often lost the scraps of paper and old envelopes she had
written them on, and had to recite them out loud, eyes cast upward,
trying out different combinations of the same numbers till she hit on
one that sounded right.

    And the phone book, when (just hypothetically, there
was no immediate need) he consulted it, listed surprising columns,
whole armies in fact, of Rodriguezes and Garcias and Fuenteses, with
great pompous Christian names, Monserrate, Alejandro, such as he
had never heard her use. And talk about pompous names, look at
this last guy, Archimedes Zzzyandottie, what on earth.

He went to bed absurdly early, trying to hurry through the hours till her inevitable return; he lay listening to the thump and hum and squeak and wail of night, trying to sort from it the first intimations of her footfalls on the stair, in the hall; his heart quickened, banishing sleep, as he heard in his mind's ear the scratch of her red nails on the door. In the morning he woke with a start, unable to remember why she wasn't next to him; and then remembered that he didn't know.

Surely around the Farm someone would have heard something, but he would have to be circumspect; he restricted himself to inquiries that, if they ever got back to her, would reveal no possessive distress or fussy prying on his part. But the answers which he got from the farmers raking muck and setting out tomatoes were even less revealing than his questions.

"Seen Sylvie?"

"Sylvie?"

Like an echo. A kind of propriety kept him from approaching George Mouse, for it could be that it was to him she had fled, and he didn't want to hear that from George, not that he had ever felt competition from his cousin, or jealousy, but, well, he didn't like any of the possible conversations he could imagine himself and George having on the subject. A weird fear was growing in him. He saw George once or twice, trundling a wheelbarrow in and out of goat sheds, and studied him secretly. His state seemed unchanged.

At evening he fell into a rage, and imagined that, not content with leaving him flat, she had engineered a conspiracy of silence to cover her tracks. "Conspiracy of silence" and "cover her tracks," he said aloud, more than once that long night, to the furnishings of the Folding Bedroom which were none of them hers. (Hers were at that moment being exclaimed over, one by one, elsewhere, as they were taken from the drawstring bags of the three brown-capped flat-faced thieves who had abstracted them; exclaimed over in cooing small voices one by one before being put away in a humpbacked trunk bound in black iron, to wait for their owner to come and claim them.)

The bartender at the Seventh Saint, "their" bartender, didn't appear for work that night or the next or the next, though Auberon came every night to question him. The new guy wasn't sure just what had happened to him. Gone to the Coast, maybe. Gone, anyway. Auberon, having no better post from which to keep

And in the Second Place

vigil when he could no longer bear the Folding Bedroom or Old Law

Farm, ordered another. One of those periodic upheavals in bar life had taken place among the clientele lately. As evening drew on, he recognized few regulars; they seemed to have been swept away by a new crowd, a crowd that did superficially resemble the crowd Sylvie and he had known, were in fact the same people in every respect except that they were not. The only familiar face was Leon's. After an inward struggle and several gins, he managed a casual question.

"Seen Sylvie?"

"Sylvie?"

It might well be, of course, that Leon was hiding her in some apartment uptown. It might be that she had gone to the Coast with Victor the bartender. Sitting his stool before the broad brown window night after night, watching the crowds outside pass, he concocted these and several other explanations of what had happened to Sylvie, some pleasing to him, some distressing. He fitted each out with motives planted in the past, and a resolution; what she would do and say, and what he. These would grow stale, and like a failing baker he would remove them, still pretty but unsold, from his case, and replace them with others. He was at this on the Friday after her disappearance, the place packed with laughing folks more bent on pleasure, more exquisite than the diurnal crowd (though he couldn't be sure they weren't the same). He sat his stool as on a solitary rock amid their foamy rushing back and forth. The sweet scent of liquor mingled with their mingled perfumes, and all together they made the soughing sea-noise which, when he became a television writer, he would learn to call "walla". Walla walla walla. Far away, waiters tended to the banquettes, drawing corks and laying cutlery. An older man, white-templed less it seemed from age than by choice but with an air of subtle ruin about his nattiness, poured wine for a dark, laughing woman in a broad-brimmed hat.

The woman was Sylvie.

One explanation that had occurred to him for her disappearance was her disgust with her poverty; often she had said, as she pawed furiously through her thrift-shop clothes and dime-store valuables, makeshifting an outfit, that what she needed was a rich old man, that she'd turn tricks if she only had the nerve—I mean *look* at this *clothes,* man! He looked now at her clothes, nothing he had ever seen before, the hat shading her face was velvet, the dress nicely constructed—lamplight fell, as though guided there, into its decolletage and lit the amber roundness of her breast; he could see it from where he sat. A small roundness.

Should he leave? How could he? Turmoil nearly blinded him. They had ceased laughing together, and raised their glasses now, topped up with lurid wine, and their eyes met like voluptuaries greeting. Good God, what nerve to bring him here. The man took an oblong case from within his jacket, and opened it to her. It would contain icy jewels blue and white. No, it was a cigarette case. She took one and he lit it for her. Before he could be harrowed by the characteristic way she had of smoking her occasional cigarette, as individual as her laugh or her footstep, thronging crowds intervened. When they parted, he saw her take up her purse (also new) and rise. The john. He hid his head. She would have to pass by him where he sat. Flee? No: there was a way, he thought, to greet her, there must be, but only seconds in which to find it. Hi. Hello. Hello? Heh-lo, fancy meeting . . . His heart was mad. Having calculated the moment at which she must pass by, he turned, supposing his face to be composed and his heart-thuds invisible.

Where was she? He thought a woman just then passing near him in a black hat was she, but it wasn't. She had disappeared. Passed by him quickly? Hidden from him? She would have to pass him again on her return. He'd keep watch now. Maybe she'd leave, covered with shame, sneak away sticking Mr. Rich with the bill but no favors. The woman he had for a moment thought to be her—in fact years and inches different, with a practised lurch and a gravel-voiced excuse-me—worked her way past him, and through the massed exquisites, and took her seat with Mr. Rich.

How could he even for a moment have thought . . . His heart turned to an ember, to a cold clinker. The cheerful walla of the bar faded away into a sound of silence, and Auberon had a sudden horrible percipience, like a dropped ball of mental string madly unwinding, of what this vision meant, and what would now, must now, become of him; and he raised a trembling hand for the bartender, pushing bills urgently across the bar with the other.

He arose from his bench in the park. Traffic had grown loud as day grew bright, the City flinging itself against this enclave of morning. Without reservations now, but with a strange hope in his heart, he moved sunwise around the small pavilion and sat again, before Summer.

And in the Third

Bacchus and his pards; the flaccid wineskin and the checkered shade. The faun that follows, the nymph that flies. Yes: so it was, so it had been, so it would be. And below all this pictured lassitude was a sort of fountain, the sort where water gushes from a lion's or a dolphin's mouth: only this wasn't a lion or a dolphin but a man's face, a medallion of grief, a tragic mask with snaky hair; and the water was not issuing from his sad-clown mouth but from his eyes, falling in two slow and constant trickles down his cheeks and chin into a scummy pool below. It made a pleasant sound.

Hawksquill meanwhile had gone to her car in its underground den, and slipped into its waiting seat which was clad in leather as smooth as the backless gloves she then drew on. The wooden wheel carved for her grip and polished by her hands backed the long wolflike shape neatly around and faced it outward; with a clanking the garage door opened and the car's growl opened fanwise into the May air.

Violet Bramble. John Drinkwater. The names made a room: a room where pampas grass stood in heavy floor vases purple and brown, and there were Ricketts drawings on the lily-patterned walls, and the drapes were drawn for a seance. In the fruitwood bookcases were Gurdjieff and other frauds. How could anything like a world-age be born there, or one die? Moving uptown in knight's-moves as the clotted traffic forced her, her impatient tires casting up filth, she thought: yet it may well be; may well be that they have kept a secret for all these years, and a very great secret too; and it may be that she, Hawksquill, had come close to a very great mistake. It would not be the first time . . . . The traffic around her loosened as she set out on the wide north road; her car threaded through it like a needle through old cloth, picking up speed. The boy's directions had been eccentric and wandering, but she wouldn't forget them, having impressed each one in place on an old folding Monopoly board she kept in her memory for just such a use.

II

The Thirst that from the Soul doth rise
Doth ask a drink divine;
But might I of Jove's nectar sip
I would not change for thine.

—Ben Jonson

E arth rolled its rotundity around, tilting the little park where Auberon sat one, two, three days more face-upwards to the changeless sun. The warm days were growing more frequent, and though never matching quite the earth's regular progress, the warmth was already more constant, less skittish, soon not ever to be withdrawn. Auberon, hard at work there, hardly noticed; he kept on his overcoat; he had ceased to believe in spring, and a little warmth couldn't convince him.

Press on, press on.

The struggle was, as it had always been, to think rightly about what had happened, to come to conclusions that took in all aspects, that were mature; to be *objective*. There were multitudes of reasons why she might have left him, he knew that well, his faults were as numerous as the paving-stones of those walks, as rooted and thorny as that blooming hawthorn. There was after all no mystery in the end of love, no mystery but the mystery of love itself, which was large certainly but as real as grass, as natural and unaccountable as bloom and branch and their growth.

> Not Her
> But This Park

No, her leaving him was sad, and a puzzle; it was her disappearance that was insane and maddening. How could she leave not a wrack behind? He had thought of her abducted, murdered; he had thought of her planning her own vanishing, just to drive him mad with bafflement, but why would she want such a madness?

Certainly he had raged, frantic, at George Mouse, unable to bear it, tell me you son of a *bitch* where she is, what you've done with her, and saw his madness reflected in George Mouse's honest fear as he said "Now now, now now," and groped amid his souvenirs for a baseball bat. No, he had not gone about his searching in the most lucid frame of mind, but what the hell was to be expected?

What the hell was to be expected, when after four gins at the Seventh Saint he would see her passing by in the crowds outside the window, and after five find her sitting on the adjacent stool?

One trip only to Spanish Harlem, where he had seen her replicated on a dozen street corners, in halter tops, with baby carriages, chewing gum on crowded stoops, dusky roses all of them and none of them her, and he had abandoned that search. He had forgotten utterly, if he ever really knew, just which of these buildings on highly individual but at the same time identical streets had been the ones she had taken him to; she might be in any of those aqua living rooms, watching through the plastic lace of curtains as he passed, any of those rooms lit by aeqeous television and the red points of votive candles. Even worse was the checking of jails, hospitals, madhouses, in all of which the inmates had obviously taken over, his calls were shunted from thug to loony to paralytic and finally cut off, by accident or on purpose, he had not made himself clear. If she had fallen into one of those public oubliettes . . . No. If it was madness to choose to believe she had not, he would rather be mad.

And in the street his name would be called. Softly, shamefacedly; happily, with relief; peremptorily. And he would stand looking up and down the avenue, searching, stock still amid the traffic, unable to see her but unwilling to move lest she lose sight of him. Sometimes it was called again, even more insistently, and still he would see nothing; and after a long time move on, with many halts and backward glances, having at last to say out loud to himself that it wasn't her, wasn't even his name that had been called, just *forget* it; and curious passersby would covertly watch him reason with himself.

Mad he must have seemed, but whose God damn fault was that? He had only tried to be *sensible,* not to become fixated and obsessed with the imaginary, he had struggled against it, he had, though he had succumbed in the end; Christ it must be hereditary, some taint passed down to him through the generations like color-blindness. . . .

Well, it was over now. Whether or not it was possible for the park and the Art of Memory to yield up to him the secret of her whereabouts didn't interest him; that was not what he was at work on there. What he hoped and believed, what seemed to him promised by the ease with which the statuary and greenery and footpaths accepted his story, was that once he had committed the whole of his year-long agony to them—no hope or degradation, no loss, no illusion unaccounted for—then he would someday remember, not his search, but these intersecting pathways that, leading always inward, led always away.

Not Spanish Harlem but that wire basket just outside the fence, with a *cerveza Schaefer* and a mango pit and a copy of *El Diario* crushed in it, MATAN as always in the headline.

Not Old Law Farm but that old marten-house on a pole, and its battling noisy occupants coming and going and building nests.

Not the Seventh Saint Bar & Grill but Bacchus in bas-relief, or Silenus or whoever that was supported by goat-footed satyrs nearly as drunk as their god.

Not the weird pursuing pressure of his madness, inherited and inescapable, only that plaque fixed to the gate where he had entered: Mouse Drinkwater Stone.

Not the false Sylvies that had afflicted him when he was drunk and defenseless but the little girls, skipping rope and playing jacks and whispering together as they eyed him suspiciously, who were always the same yet always different, perhaps only in different outfits.

Not his season on the street but the seasons of this pavilion.

Not her but this park.

Press on, press on.

The cold compassion of bartenders, he came to see, was like that of priests: universal rather than personal, with charity for all and malice toward almost none. Firmly situated (smiling and making ritual and comforting gestures with glass and cloth) between sacrament and communicant, they commanded rather than earned love, trust, dependence. Best always to placate them. A big hello, and the tips subtle but sufficient.

Never Never
Never

"A gin, please, Victor, I mean Siegfried."

Oh God that solvent! A season's worth of summer afternoons dissolved in it as his father once, in a rare burst of enthusiasm for the sciences, had in school dissolved something blue-green (cop-

per?) in a beaker of clear acid till it did not exist at all, didn't stain its
solvent with even the faintest veridical residue; what had become of
it? What had become of that July?

The Seventh Saint was a cool cavern, cool and dark as
any burrow. Through the windows the white heat showed the more
blank and violent to his eyes when they were accustomed to the dark;
he looked out at a parade of blinking, harrowed faces, bodies as
nearly unclothed as decency and contrivance allowed them to be.
Negroes turned gray and oily and white people red; only the Spanish
bloomed, and even they sometimes looked a little blown and wilted.
The heat was an affront, like winter's cold; all seasons were errors
here, two days only excepted in spring and a week in autumn full of
huge possibilities, great glamor and sweetness.

"Hot enough for you?" said Siegfried. This was he who
had replaced Auberon's first friend Victor behind the Seventh Saint
bar. Auberon had never enjoyed any rapport with this thick, stupid
one, named Siegfried. He sensed an unpastoral cruelty in him, an
enjoyment almost in others' weaknesses, a *Schadenfreude* shadowing
his ministry.

"Yes," Auberon said. "Yes, it is." Somewhere, far off,
guns were fired. The way to avoid being disturbed by these, Auberon
had decided, was to regard them as fireworks. You never anyway saw
the slain in the streets, or as rarely as you saw the dead bodies of
rabbits or birds in the woods. Somehow they were disposed of. "Cool
in here, though," he said with a smile.

Sirens wailed, going elsewhere. "Trouble someplace,"
Siegfried said. "This parade."

"Parade?"

"Russell Eigenblick. Big show on. You didn't know?"

Auberon made gestures.

"Jeez, where you been? Did you know about the arrests?"

"No."

"Some guys with guns and bombs and literature. Found
them in the basement of some church. They were a church group.
Planning some assassination or something."

"They were going to assassinate Eigenblick?"

"Who the hell knows? Maybe they were his guys. I forget
exactly. But he's in hiding, only there's this big march on today."

"For him or against him?"

"Who the hell knows?" Siegfried moved off. If Auberon
wanted details, let him get a paper. The bartender had just been
making conversation; he had better things to do than be grilled.
Auberon drank, abashed. Outside, people were hurrying by, in

groups of two and three, looking behind them. Some were shouting, others laughing.

Auberon turned from the window. Surreptitiously, he counted his money, contemplating the evening and the night ahead. Soon he would have to move downward in the drinker's scale, from this pleasant—more than pleasant, necessary, imperative—retreat to less pleasant places, brightly-lit, naked, with sticky plastic bars surmounted by the waxy faces of aged patrons, their eyes fixed on the absurdly cheap prices posted on the mirror before them. Dram shops, as old books had it. And then? He could drink alone, of course, and wholesale so to speak: but not in Old Law Farm, not in the Folding Bedroom. "Another of these," he said mildly, "when you get a chance."

He had that morning decided, not for the first time, that his search was over. He wouldn't sally forth today to follow illusory clues. She couldn't be found who wanted not to be found. His heart had cried out, But what if she does? What if she is only lost, and searching for you even as you search for her, what if only yesterday you came within a block of one another, what if at this moment she sits somewhere nearby, on a park bench, a stoop, Somehow unable to find her way back to you, what if she is even now thinking *He'll never believe this crazy story* (whatever it would be) *if only I find him, if only;* and the tears of loneliness on her brown cheeks . . . But that was all old. It was the Crazy Story Idea, and he knew it well; it had once been a bright hope, but it had over time condensed to this burning point, not a hope but a reproach, not even (no! No more!) a spur; and that was why it could be snuffed.

He'd snuffed it, brutally, and come to the Seventh Saint. A day off.

There was only one further decision then to make, and he would (with the help of this gin, and more of the same) make that today. She hadn't ever existed at all! She was a figment. It would be hard, at first, to convince himself of how sensible a solution this was to his difficulty; but it would grow easier.

"Never existed," he muttered. "Never never never."

"Wazzat?" said Siegfried, who usually couldn't hear the plainest request for replenishment.

"Storm," Auberon said, for just then there was a sound which if it wasn't cannon was thunder.

"Cool things off," said Siegfried. What the hell could he care, Auberon thought, aestivating in this cave.

Out of the roll of thunder came the more rhythmic beats of a big bass drum far downtown. More people were in the streets, driven forward by or perhaps heralding the oncoming of something big which they looked now and again over their shoulders at. Police cruisers shot into the intersections of street and avenue, blue lights revolving. Among those coming up the street—they were walking heedlessly in the middle of the roadway, that looked exhilarating to Auberon—were several wearing the blousy shirts of many colors worn by Eigenblick's adherents; these, and others in dark glasses and narrow suits, with what could have been hearing aids stuck into their ears but probably were not, discussed things with the sweating policemen, making gestures. A portable conga band, contrapuntal to the far-off beating bass drum, proceeded northward, surrounded by laughing brown and black people and by photographers. Their rhythms hurried the negotiators. The suited men seemed to command the police, who were helmeted and armed but apparently will-less. The thunder, more distinct, rolled again.

It seemed to Auberon that he had discovered, since coming to the City, or at least since he had spent a lot of time staring at crowds, that humanity, City humanity anyway, fell into only a few distinct types—not physical or social or racial, exactly, though the qualities that could be called physical or social or racial helped qualify people. He couldn't say just how many of these types there were, or describe any of them at all precisely, or even keep any of them in his mind when he didn't have an actual example before him; but he found himself continually saying to himself, "Ah, there's one of *that* sort of person." It certainly hadn't helped in his search for Sylvie that, however distinct she was, however utterly individual, the vague type she belonged to could throw up cognates of her everywhere to torment him. A lot of them didn't even look like her. They were her sisters, though; and they harrowed him, far more than the *jovens* and *lindas* that superficially resembled her, like those that, on the lean muscled arms of their boyfriends or honorary husbands, now followed the conga band up the street, dancing. A larger group, of some status, was coming into view behind them.

These were decently dressed matrons and men, walking abreast, black women with broad bosoms and pearls and glasses, men in humble pork-pie hats, many skinny and stooped. He had often wondered how it is that great fat black women can grow faces, as they get older, that are hard, chiseled, granitic, tough and leathery, all that is associated with the lean. These people supported a street-wide banner on poles, with half-moon holes cut in it to keep it from being filled like a sail and carrying them off, whose letters, picked out in sequins, spelled out CHURCH OF ALL STREETS.

"That's the church," Siegfried said—he had moved his

glass-wiping activities nearer the window in order to watch. "The church where they found those guys."

"With the bombs?"

"They got a lot of nerve."

Since Auberon still didn't know whether the bombers found in the Church of All Streets were for or against whoever this parade was for or against, he supposed this could be true.

The Church of All Streets contingent, the decent poor mostly as far as Auberon could see but with one or two Eigenblick blousons marching beside them, and one of the hearing-aides watching them too, was escorted by the many-eyed press on foot and in vans, and by armed horsemen, and by the curious. As though the Seventh Saint were a tidepool, and the tide were rising, two or three of these spilled through its doors, bringing in the hot breath of day and the odor of their marching. They complained loudly of the heat, more in high-pitched whistles and low groans than in words, and ordered beers. "Here you are, take this," said one, and held out something to Auberon on his yellow palm.

It was a narrow strip of paper, like a Chinese cookie fortune. Part of a sentence was crudely printed on it, but the sweat of the man's hand had obscured part of that, and all Auberon could make out was the word "message". Two of the others were comparing similar strips of paper, laughing and wiping beer-foam from their lips.

"What's it mean?"

"That's for *you* to figure out," the man said gaily. Siegfried put a drink in front of Auberon. "Maybe if you make a match, you win a prize. A lottery. Huh? They're handing 'em out all over town."

And indeed now outside Auberon saw a line of white-faced mimes or clowns cakewalking along in the wake of the Church of All Streets, doing simple acrobatics, firing cap pistols, tipping battered hats, and distributing among the jostling crowd that thronged around them these small strips of paper. People took them, children begged for more, they were studied and compared. If no one took them, the clowns let them flutter away into a breeze that was beginning to rise. One of the clowns turned the handle of a siren he had hung around his neck, and an eerie wail could be faintly heard.

"What on earth," Auberon said.

"Who the hell knows," Siegfried said.

With a crash of brass instruments, a marching band began, and the street was suddenly filled with bright silken flags, barred, starred, snapping and furling in the thunder-wind. Great cheers rose. Double eagles screamed from some banners, double eagles with double hearts aflame in their bosoms, some clutching roses in their beaks, myrtle, swords, arrows, bolts of lightning in their talons; surmounted with crosses, crescents, or both, bleeding, effulgent or aflame. They seemed to stream and flutter on the terrific wave of military sound rising from the band, which was not uniformed but dressed in top hats, tails, and paper bat-wing collars. A royal-blue gold-fringed gonfalon was born before them, but was gone before Auberon could read it.

The bar patrons went to the window. "What's going on? What's going on?" The mimes or clowns worked the borders of the march, handing out slips, avoiding grabbing hands dexterously as they somersaulted or rode each other's shoulders. Auberon, well oiled by now, was exhilarated, as they all were, but he as much because he had no idea for what all this crazy energy was being expended as for the quick-stepping, flag-waving thing itself. More refugees barged through the doors of the Seventh Saint. For a moment the music grew loud. They weren't a good band, cacaphonous in fact; but the big drum kept the time.

"Good God," said a haggard man in a wrinkled suit and a nearly brimless straw fedora. "Good God, those people."

"Check it out," said a black man. More entered, black, white, other. Siegfried looked startled, at bay. He'd expected a quiet afternoon. A sudden chattering roar drowned out their orders, and outside, descending right into the valley of the street, a sharp-stuttering helicopter hove, hovered, reascended, scanning, raising winds in the streets; people clutched their hats, running in circles like farmyard fowl beneath a hawk. Commands issued from the copter in meaningless shouts of gravelly static, repeated over and over just as meaninglessly but more insistently. In the street, people shouted back defiance, and the helicopter rose away, turning carefully. Cheers and raspberries for the dragon's going.

"Whaddy say whaddy say?" the partrons asked each other.

"Maybe," Auberon said to no one, "warning them it's about to rain."

It was. They didn't care. More conga artists were passing, nearly swamped by throngs, all chanting to their beat: "Let it fall, let it rain; let it fall, let it rain." Fights were breaking out, shoving contests mostly, girl-friends shrieked, bystanders pulled apart contestants. The parade seemed to be turning into a swarming culture, and growing a riot. But car horns honked, insistently, and the millers were parted by several black limousines with fast-fluttering pennants on their fenders. Hurrying beside the cars were many of the suited, dark-spectacled men, looking everywhere and nowhere, faces grim, not having fun. The scene had darkened, quickly, ominously, the harsh dusty orange light of late afternoon snuffed like a klieg-light. Black clouds must have extinguished the sun. And even the neat haircuts of the suited aides were ruffled by the rising wind. The band had ceased, only the drum went on, sounding threnodic and solemn. Crowds pressed closely around the cars, curious, perhaps angry. They were warned away. Wreaths of dark flowers dressed some of the cars. A funeral? Nothing could be seen within their tinted windows.

The patrons of the Seventh Saint had grown quiet, respectful or resentful.

"The last best hope," the sad man in the straw fedora said. "The goddam last best goddam hope."

"All over," said another, and drank deeply. "All over but the shouting." The cars passed away, the crowds falling in behind them, filling up their wake; the drum was like a dying heartbeat. Then, as uptown the band rang out again, there was a terrific crash of thunder, and everyone in the bar ducked at once, and then looked at one another and laughed, embarrassed to have been startled. Auberon finished his fifth gin in a gulp, and, pleased with himself for no reason but that, said "Let it fall, let it rain." He thrust his empty glass toward Siegfried, more commandingly than he usually did. "Another."

The rain began all at once, big drops spattering audibly on the tall window and then falling in great volumes, hissing furiously as though the city it fell on were red-hot. Rain coursing down the tinted glass obscured the parade's events. It looked now like ranks of people wearing hoods, holes cut out for eyes, or paper masks like welder's masks, carrying clubs or batons, were coming behind the limos and meeting some resistance; whether they were part of the parade or another show in opposition to it was hard to tell. The Seventh Saint filled rapidly with clamoring folk fleeing the rain. One of the mimes or clowns, his white face running, came in bowing, but certain shouts of greeting seemed to him hostile; he bowed out again.

Thunder, rain, sunset swallowed up in stormy darkness; crowds pouring through the pouring streets in the glare of streetlights. Breaking of glass, shouts, tumult, sirens, a war on. Those in the bar rushed out, to see or join in, and were replaced by others fleeing, who had seen enough. Auberon held his stool, calm, happy, lifting his drink with a suggestion of extended pinkie. He smiled beatifically at the troubled man in the straw fedora, who stood next to him. "Drunk as a lord," he said. "Quite literally. I mean lunk as a drord is when a lord is drunk. If you follow me." The man sighed and turned away.

"No, no," Siegfried shouted, waving his hands before him

371

like shutters: for barging in were a bunch of Eigenblick adherents, their colored shirts plastered to their bodies with rain, supporting one among them who had been hurt: a spiderweb of blood over his face. They ignored Siegfried; the crowd, murmuring, let them in. The man next to Auberon stared openly and truculently at them, speaking in his mind to them in unguessable words. Someone vacated a table, upsetting a drink, and the wounded one was lowered into a chair.

They left him there to recuperate, and pushed to the bar. The man in the fedora was displaced elsewhere. A brief mood seemed to pass over Siegfried's face that he wouldn't serve them, but he thought better of it. One mounted the stool next to Auberon, a small person over whose shivering back was draped someone else's colored shirt. Another rose on tiptoe, glass raised high, and gave a toast: "To the Revelation!" Many cheered, for or against. Auberon leaned toward the person next to him and said, "What revelation?"

Excited, shivering, brushing rain from her face, she turned to Auberon. She'd got her hair cut, very short, like a boy's. "The Revelation," she said, and handed him a slip of paper. Not wanting to look away from her now that she was next to him, afraid if he looked away she would not be there when he looked back, he held the paper up to his near-blinded eyes. It said: *No fault of your own.*

In fact there were two Sylvies beside him, one for each eye. He clapped a hand over one eye and said, "Long time no see."

"Yah." She looked around at her companions, smiling, still shivering, but caught up in their excitement and glory.

Doesn't Matter

"So where did you get to anyway?" Auberon said. "Where've you been? By the way." He knew he was drunk, and must speak carefully and mildly so that Sylvie wouldn't see and be ashamed of him.

"Around," she said.

"I don't suppose," he said, and would have gone on to say *I don't suppose if you weren't really Sylvie here now that you'd tell me so,* but this was drowned out by further toasts and comings and goings, and all he said was, "I mean if you were a figment."

"What?" Sylvie said.

"I mean how've you been!" He felt his head wobbling on his neck, and stopped it. "Can I buy you a drink?" She laughed at that: drinks for Eigenblick's people were not to be bought tonight. One of her companions caught her up and kissed her. "Fall of the City!"

he cried hoarsely, been shouting all day no doubt. "Fall of the City!"

"Heeeey!" she answered, a kind of agreement with his enthusiasm rather than exactly with his sentiment. She turned back to Auberon then; she lowered her eyes, she moved her hand toward him, she was about to explain everything; but no, she only picked up his drink, sipped from it (raising her eyes to him over its rim) and put it down again with a grimace of disgust.

"Gin," he said.

"Tastes like *alcolado*," she said.

"Well, it's not supposed to be good," he said, "only good for you," and heard in his own voice a joking Auberon-and-Sylvie tone that had been so long absent from it that it was like hearing old music, or tasting a long-untasted food. Good for you, yes, for a further thought about her figmentary nature was trying to crack his consciousness like an oyster-knife, so he drank again, beaming at her as she beamed at the merry madness that boiled around them. "How's Mr. Rich?" he said.

"He's okay." Mum, not looking at him. He wasn't to pursue such subjects. But he was desperate to know her heart.

"You've been happy, though?"

She shrugged. "Busy." A small smile. "A busy little girl."

"Well, I mean . . ." He stopped. The last dim bulb of reason in his brain showed him Silence and Circumspection, and then went out. "It doesn't matter," he said. "I've been thinking about this a lot, lately, you know, well, you could've guessed, about us and all, I mean you and me; and what I figured out is that really it's basically okay, and all right, really." She had cupped her cheek in her hand, and was looking up at him rapt yet inattentive, as she had always been at his disquisitions. "You moved on, is all, right? I mean things change, life changes; how could I complain about that? I couldn't have any argument with that." It was suddenly sweetly clear: "It's as though I were with you like in one stage of your development—like a pupa stage, or a nymph stage. But you outgrew that. Became a different person. Like a butterfly does." Yes: she had broken from the transparent shell which was the girl he had known and touched; and (as he had the empty isinglass sculptures of locusts when he was a kid) he had preserved the shell, all he had of her, all the more precious for its terrible fragility and the perfect abandonment it embodied. She meanwhile (though out of his sight and ken, imaginable only by induction) had grown wings and flown: was not only elsewhere but something else as well.

She wrinkled her nose and opened her mouth in a *huh?* "What stage?" she said.

"Some early stage," he said.

"What was the word, though?"

"Nymph," he said. Thunder crashed; the eye of the storm had passed; rain wept again. And was this before him then nothing but the old transparency? Or her in the flesh? It was important to get these things straight right off the bat. And how anyway could it be that her flesh was what he was most intensely left with, and was it the flesh of her soul or the soul of her flesh? "It doesn't matter, doesn't matter," he said, his voice thick with happiness and his heart awash in the gin of human kindness; he forgave her everything, in exchange for this presence, whatever it was. "Dozen madder."

"Listen, it really doesn't," she said, and raised his own glass to him before sipping it gingerly again. "Go with the flow, y'know."

"Trooty is booth, booth trooty," he said "that is all ye know on earth, and all . . ."

"I need to go," she said. "To the john."

That was the last thing he clearly remembered, that she returned from the john, though he hadn't expected her to; when he saw her returning, his heart rose as it had when she had turned to face him on the stool next to him; he forgot that he had denied her thrice, had decided to decide she had never existed; that was absurd anyway, when here she was, when in the pelting rain outside (this glimpse only he had) he could kiss her: her rain-wet flesh was as cold as any ghost's, her nipples as hard as unripe fruit, but he imagined that she warmed.

There are charms that last, keeping the world long suspended in their power, and charms that do not last, that drain quickly away and leave the world as it was. Liquor is well known for not lasting.

Sylvie & Bruno Concluded

Auberon was wrenched awake just after dawn, after a few hours of deathlike unconsciousness. He knew instantly that he should be dead, that death was his only appropriate condition, and that he was not dead. He cried out softly and hoarsely, "No, oh God no," but oblivion was far away and even sleep had fled utterly. No: he was alive and the wretched world was around him; his staring eyeballs showed him the Folding Bedroom's crazed map of a ceiling, so many Devil's Islands in plaster. He didn't need to investigate to find that Sylvie wasn't next to him.

There was, however, someone next to him, bound up in the damp sheet (it was hot as hell already, chill sweat circled Auberon's neck and brow). And someone else was speaking to him; speaking from a corner of the Folding Bedroom, soothingly, confidentially: "Oh for a draught of vintage, that hath been Cooled a long age in the deep delved earth, Tasting of Flora and the country green . . ."

The voice came from a small red plastic radio, an antique with the word Silvertone across it in bas-relief script. Auberon had never known it to work before. The voice was black, a silky DJ's voice, black but cultured. God, they're everywhere, Auberon thought, overwhelmed with horrid strangeness, as a traveler sometimes is to find so many foreigners in other lands. "Away! Away! For I will fly to thee, Not charioted by Bacchus and his pards, But on the viewless wings of Poesy . . ."

Auberon climed slowly like a cripple from the bed. Who the hell was this beside him anyway. A brown shoulder big with muscle could be seen; the sheet breathed softly. Snored. Christ what have I done. He was about to draw down the sheet when it moved of its own accord, snuffling, and a shapely leg, flat-shinned, with curly dark hair, came out like a further clue; yes it was a man, that was certain. He carefully opened the door of the toilet, and took out his overcoat. He put it on over his nakedness, feeling with loathing the clammy touch of its lining against his skin. In the kitchen he opened cupboards with trembling skeleton's hands. The dusty vacuity within the cupboards was for some reason ghastly. In the last he opened there was a bottle of Doña Mariposa rum with an inch or two of amber fluid in it. His stomach turned, but he took it out. He went to the door, with a glance at the bed—his new friend still slept— and then out.

He sat on the stairs in the hallway, staring into the stair-well, the bottle in both hands. He missed Sylvie and comfort so dreadfully, with such a parched thirst, that his mouth hung open and he leaned forward as though to scream or vomit. But his eyes wouldn't yield tears. The vivifying fluids had all been drawn from him; he was a husk; the world was a husk too. And this man in the bed. He unscrewed (it took some application) the cap of the rum bottle, and, turning its accusatory label away from him, he poured fire on his sands. Darkling I listen. Keats, in smoothie blackface, slid out under the door and insinuatingly into his ear. Now more than ever seems it rich to die. Rich: he drank the last of the rum and rose, gasping and swallowing bitter spittle. To thy high requiem become a sot.

He recapped the empty bottle and left it on the stair. In the mirror hung over the pretty table at the hall's end he caught a glimpse of someone forlorn. The very word is like a bell. He looked away. He went into the Folding Bedroom, a golem, his dry clay animated briefly by rum. He could speak now. He went to the bed. The person there had thrown off his sheet. It *was* Sylvie, only modeled in male flesh, and no charm: this goatish boy was real. Auberon shook his shoulder. Sylvie's head rolled on the pillow. Dark eyes opened momentarily, saw Auberon, and closed again.

Auberon bent over the bed and spoke into his ear. "Who are you?" He spoke carefully and slowly. Might not understand our lingo. "What is you *name*?" The boy rolled over, woke, brushed his hand over his face from forehead to chin as though to magic away the resemblance to Sylvie (but it stayed) and said in a morning-roughened voice, "Hey. What's happening?"

"What is your name?"

"Hey, hi. Jesus Christ." He lay back on the pillow, smacking his lips. He rubbed his knuckles in his eyes like a child. He scratched and stroked himself shamelessly, as though pleased to find himself to hand. He smiled at Auberon and said, "Bruno."

"Oh."

"You membah."

"Oh."

"We got frone outta dap bah."

"Oh. Oh."

"Boy you was drunk."

"Oh."

"Membah? You coont even . . ."

"Oh. No. No." Bruno was looking at him with easy affection, still stroking himself.

"You said Jus wait," Bruno said, and laughed. "That was you lass words, man."

"Oh yes?" He didn't remember; but he felt a weird regret, and almost laughed, and almost wept, that he had failed Sylvie when she was Sylvie. "Sorry," he said.

"Hey listen," Bruno said generously.

He wanted to move away, he knew he ought; he wanted to close his coat, which hung open. But he couldn't. If he did so, if he let this cup pass away from him, then the last dry dregs of last night's charm within it would not be licked up, and they might be all he had forever. He stared at Bruno's open face, simpler and sweeter than Sylvie's, unmarked by his passions, strong though Sylvie had always said they were. Friendly: tears, double-distilled because there was so little water within to draw on, burned the orbits of his eyes: friendly was the word to describe Bruno. "Do you," he said, "have a sister?"

"Shichess."

"You wouldn't happen to know," Auberon said, "where she is?"

"Nah." He dismissed her with an easy gesture, her own gesture translated. "Ain't seen her in munce. She gets around."

"Yes." If he could just put his hands in Bruno's hair. Just for a moment; that would be enough. And close his burning eyes. The thought made him faint, and he leaned against the headboard.

"A real mof," Bruno said. With an unself-conscious languor he disposed himself on the bed so that there would be room there for Auberon.

"A what?"

"A mof. Sylvie." Laughing, he linked his thumbs together, and with his hands made a winged creature. He made it fly a little, smiling at Auberon; and then made it, wings fluttering, summon Auberon to follow it.

Fled is that music.

Sure that Burno slept as his sister did, dead to the world, Auberon took no precautions to be quiet; he hauled out his belongings from chest and closet and flung them around. He unfolded his crushed green knapsack and into it put his poems and the rest of the contents of his study, his razor and his soap, and as many of his clothes as would go wadded in; he stuffed what money he could find into the pockets of it.

How Far You've Gone

Gone, gone, he thought; dead, dead; empty, empty. But by no incantation could he exorcise even the palest, most illusory ghost of her from this place; and so there was only one thing to do, and that was flee. Flee. He strode from side to side of the room, looking hastily into drawers and shelves. His abused sex swung as he walked; at last he drew shorts and pants over it, but it glowed reproachfully even hidden. The deed had proved more operose than he'd expected. Oh well, oh well. Forcing a pair of socks into the knapsack's pocket he found something he had left there: something wrapped in paper. He dug it out.

It was the present he had had from Lily the day that he had left Edgewood to come to the City and seek his fortune; a small present, wrapped in white paper. Open it when you think of it, she'd said.

He looked around the Folding Bedroom. Empty. Or as empty as it would ever be. Bruno weighted the dishonored bed, and his coat of many colors hung on the velvet chair. A mouse, or a brief hallucination of one (had it already come to that? He felt that it had) sped across the floor of the kitchen and hid itself. He tore open Lily's little package.

It turned out to be a small machine of some sort. He stared at it uncomprehendingly for some time, turning it in his sticky and still-trembling fingers, before he realized what it was: it was a pedometer. The handy kind that attaches to your belt and tells you, whenever you look at it, how far you've gone.

The little park was filling up.

Bottom of a Bottle

Why had he not known that love could be like that? Why hadn't anyone told him? If he had known, he would never have embarked on it; or at least not so gladly.

Why did he, a young man of some intelligence after all, and of good family, know nothing about anything at all?

He had even been able to suppose, when he left Old Law Farm for the streets of the City foul with summer and decline, that he fled Sylvie rather than merely pursuing her farther and in even less warm directions. Drunkards, Great-aunt Cloud had used to say, drink to escape their troubles. If that was his case—and surely he had tried his best to become a drunkard—then how could it be that, not every time but often enough, he found Sylvie there, just there where Cloud said drinkers find surcease, at the bottom of a bottle?

Well: press on. Autumn was harvest, of course, the bound wheat-sheaf, the hale fruit. And faintly in the distance, cheeks puffed out and eyebrows fierce, Brother North-wind came on apace.

Was the girl who with a sickle cut the heavy-eared grain the same one who set out shoots in spring with a little trowel? And who was the oldster, huddled up on the earth piled with riches, brooding in profile? Thinking of winter . . .

In November the three of them—he, and she, and Fred Savage, his mentor in bumhood, who had begun appearing to him as often in that season as Sylvie did, though more solidly than she—rode a park bench, somewhat afloat in the darkening city, huddled up but not uncomfortable; the newspapers inside Fred Savage's overcoat crackled when he moved, though he moved only to lift brandy to his lips. They had done singing, and reciting drinker's poetry—

You know, my friends, with what a gay Carouse
I took a Second Mortgage on my house

—and sat quiet now contemplating that fearful hour before the City's lights are lit.

"Old Man Hawk's in town," Fred Savage said.

"Wazzat?"

"Winter," Sylvie said, thrusting her hands into her armpits.

"Gonna move these bones," Fred Savage said, crackling, sipping. "Gonna move these old cold bones to Florida."

"All *right*," Sylvie said, as though at last somebody had said something sensible.

"Old Man Hawk is *not* my friend," Fred Savage said. "Price of a Greyhound to outrun that boy. Philly, Baltimore, Charleston, Atlanta, J'ville, St. Pete. Miami. Ever see a pelican?"

He hadn't. Sylvie, from ancientest childhood, summoned them up, frigates of the Caribbean evening, absurd and beautiful. "Yas yas," Fred Savage said. "Beak holds more than his belican. Tears out the feathers of his bosom, and feeds they young ones on the blood of his heart. His heart's blood. Oh Forida."

Fred had taken the autumn off, and perhaps the rest of his life as well. He had come to Auberon's aid, in his most need to be by his side, just as he had said he would on the day when he had first guided him through the City to the offices of Petty, Smilodon & Ruth. Auberon didn't question this providence, or any other the City gave. He had thrown himself on the City's mercy, and found that, like a strict mistress, she was kind to those who submitted utterly, held nothing back. By degrees he learned to do that; he who had always been fastidious, and more fastidious than that for Sylvie's sake, grew filthy, City dirt worked itself into his fabric ineradicably, and though when drunk he would walk for blocks to find public facilities, damn few of them and dangerous too, between these spurts of scrupulosity he mocked himself for them. By autumn his knapsack was a useless rag, a cerement, and anyway had ceased to be large enough to hold a life lived on the streets; so like the rest of the secret City's epopts he carried paper shopping bags, one inside the other for strength, advertising in his degraded person many great establishments in turn.

And so he went on, hooded in gin, sleeping in streets sometimes full of riot, sometimes quiet as a necropolis, always as far as he was concerned empty. He learned from Fred and from ancients who had instructed Fred that the great days of the secret commonwealth of bums were over, the days when there were kings and wise men on Lower Broadway, the days when the City was marked with their glyphs whose code only the initiate could read, when the drunk, the gypsy, the madman and the philosopher had their ranks, as firm as deacon, sexton, priest and bishop. Of course, over. Join any enterprise, Auberon thought, and you'll find its great days are over.

He didn't need to beg. The money he extracted from Petty, Smilodon & Ruth was given him as much to rid their offices of his noisome figure as for any right he had to it—he knew that, and took to appearing there only at his most hideous, often with Fred Savage in tow—but it was enough for a drunk's few dietary needs, and the odd flop when he feared freezing to death pillowed in booze as some of his buddies' buddies had reportedly done, and for gin. He never sank to fulsome wine, he gave himself credit for that, he resisted that final degradation even though it was apparently only in the transparent fire of gin that Sylvie (like a Salamander) could sometimes appear.

His topside knee was growing cold. Why his knee should grow cold first he didn't know; neither his toes nor his nose had felt it yet. "Greyhound, huh," he said. He recrossed his legs and said, "I can raise the price." He asked Sylvie: "You want to go?"

"Sure I do," Sylvie said.

"Sure I do," said Fred.

"I was speaking to, I wasn't speaking to you just then," Auberon said.

Fred put his arm gently around Auberon's shoulder. What ghosts plagued his friends he was always careful to be kind to. "Well, sure she do," he said, his yellow eyes opening enough to gaze on Auberon in a way Auberon had never decided was predatory or kindly. "And bes' of all," he said, smiling, "she don't need a ticket."

Door into Nowhere

Of all the lapses and losses of his sodden memory, the one that troubled Auberon most later on was that he couldn't remember whether or not he had gone to Florida. The Art of Memory showed him a few ragged palms, some stucco or concrete-block buildings painted pink or turquoise, the smell of eucalyptus; but if that was all, solid and unremovable though it seemed, it might well be imagination only, or only remembered pictures. Just as vivid were his memories of Old Man Hawk on avenues as wide as wind, perched on the gloved wrists of doormen along the Park, his beard of feathers rimy and his talons sharp to grip the entrails. But he had, somehow, not frozen to death; and surely even more than palms and jalousies, a City winter survived on the street would, he thought, stick in the memory. Well: he hadn't been paying close attention: the only thing that really engaged him were those islands where red neon signs beckoned to the wanderer (they were always red, he learned) and the endless replication of those flat bottles clear as water, in some of which, as in a box of children's cereal, there would be a prize. And the only thing he vividly recalled was how, at the end of winter, there were no more prizes. His drunkenness was empty. There were only the lees left to drink; and he drank them.

Why had he been in the bowels of the old Terminus? Had he just returned by train from the Sunshine State? Or was it chance? Seeing three of most things, a damp leg where he had pissed himself some time before, in the small hours he strode purposefully (though going nowhere; if he didn't stride purposefully he would take a header; this walking business was more complicated than most people supposed) down ramps and through catacombs. A fake nun, wimple filthy and eyes alert (Auberon had long ago realized this figure was a man) shook a begging cup at him, more in irony than expectation. He passed on. The Terminus, never silent, was as silent now as it ever was; the few travelers and the lost gave him a wide berth, though he glowered at them only to make them singular, three of each was too many. One of the virtues of drink was how it reduced life to these simple matters, which engaged all the attention; seeing, walking, raising a bottle accurately to the hole in your face. As though you were two years old again. No thoughts but simple ones. And an imaginary friend to talk to. He stopped walking; he had come up against a more-or-less solid wall; he rested and thought *Lost*.

A simple thought. One simple singular thought, and the rest of life and time a great flat featureless gray plain extending in all directions; consciousness a vast ball of dirty fuzz filling it to its limits, with only the hooded fire of that one thought alive within it.

"What?" he said, starting away from the wall, but no one had spoken to him. He looked around at the place where he stood: a vaulted intersection where four corridors met in a cross. He stood in a corner. The ribbed vaulting, where it joined in descending to the floor, made what seemed to be a slot or narrow opening, but which was only joined bricks; a sort of slot, which, it seemed, if you faced into it you might peer through . . .

"Hello?" he whispered to the darkness. "Hello?"

Nothing.

"Hello." Louder this time.

"Softer," she said.

"What?"

"Speak real soft," Sylvie said. "Don't turn around now."

"Hello. Hello."

"Hi there. Isn't this great?"

"Sylvie," he whispered.

"Just like you were right next to me."

"Yes," he said; "yes," he whispered. He pressed his consciousness forward into the darkness. It folded up closed for a moment, then opened again. "What?" he said.

"Well," she said, in a small voice, and after a darkling pause, "I think I'm going."

"No," he said. "No, I bet not, I bet not; why?"

"Well, I lost my job, see," she whispered.

"Job?"

"With a ferry. A real old guy. He was nice. But bo-ring. Back and forth all day . . ." He felt her withdraw somewhat. "So I guess I'll go. Destiny calls," she said; she said it self-mockingly, making light of it to cheer him.

"Why?" he said.

"Whisper," she whispered.

"Why do you want to do this to me?"

"Do what, baby?"

"Well why don't you just God damn go then? Why don't you just go and leave me alone? Go go go." He stopped, and listened. Silence and vacuity. A deep horror flew over him. "Sylvie?" he said. "Can you hear me?"

"Yes."

"Where? Where are you going?"

"Well, further in," she said.

"Further in where?"

"Here."

He gripped the cold bricks to steady himself. His knees were falling back and forth from locked to loose. "Here?"

"The further in you go," she said, "the bigger it gets."

"God damn it," he said. "God damn it, Sylvie."

"It's weird here," she said. "Not what I expected. I've learned a lot, though. I guess I'll get used to it." She paused, and the silence filled the darkness. "I miss you, though."

"Oh god," he said.

"So I'll go," she said, her whisper already fainter.

"No," he said, "no no no."

"But you just said . . ."

"Oh god Sylvie," he said, and his knees gave way; he knelt heavily, still facing into the darkness. "Oh god," and he thrust his face into the nonexistent place he spoke into, and said other things, apologizing, begging abjectly, though for what he no longer knew.

"No, listen," she whispered, embarrassed. "I think you're

great, really, I always did. Don't say that stuff." He was weeping now, uncomprehending, incomprehensible. "Anyway I have to," she said. Her voice was already faint and distant, and her attention turning elsewhere. "Okay. Hey, you should see all the stuff they gave me. . . . Listen, *papo. Bendicion.* Be good. G'bye."

Early train-takers and men come to open tawdry shops passed him later, still there, long unconscious, on his knees in the corner like a bad boy, face wedged into the door into nowhere. With the ancient courtesy or indifference of the City, no one disturbed him, though some shook their heads sadly or in disgust at him as they passed: an object-lesson.

Tears were on his cheeks too in the little park where he sat, having salvaged this, the last of Sylvie, the living end. When he had at last awakened in the Terminus still in that position, he didn't know how or why he had come to be there; but he remembered now. The Art of Memory had given it all back to him, all, to do with what he could.

Ahead and Behind

What you didn't know; what you didn't know arising, spontaneously, surprisingly, out of the proper arrangement of what you did: or rather what you knew all along but didn't know you knew. Every day here he had come closer to it; every night, lying awake at the Lost Sheep Mission, amid the hawkings and nightmares of his fellows, as he walked these paths in memory, he approached what he didn't know: the simple single lost fact. Well, he had it now. Now he saw the puzzle complete.

He was cursed: that's all.

Long ago, and he knew when though not why, a curse had been laid on him, a charm, a disfigurement that made him for good a searcher, and his searches at the same time futile. For reasons of their own (who could say what, malevolence only, possibly, probably, or for a recalcitrance in him they wanted to punish, a recalcitrance they had however not punished out of him, he would never give in) they had cursed him: they had attached his feet on backwards, without his noticing it, and then sent him out that way to search.

That had been (he knew it now) in the dark of the woods, when Lilac had gone away, and he had called after her as though his heart would break. From that moment he had been a searcher, and his searching feet pointed Somehow in the wrong direction.

He'd sought Lilac in the dark of the woods, but of course he'd lost her; he was eight years old and only growing older, though against his will; what could he expect?

383

He'd become a secret agent to plumb the secrets withheld from him, and for as long as he sought them, for just so long were they withheld from him.

He'd sought Sylvie, but the pathways he found, seeming always to lead to her heart, led always away. Reach toward the girl in the mirror, who looks out at you smiling, and your hand meets itself at the cold frontier of the glass.

Well: all done now. The search begun so long ago ended here. The little park his great-great-grandfather made he had remade into an emblem as complete, as fully-charged, as any trump in Great-aunt Cloud's deck or any cluttered hall in Ariel Hawksquill's memory mansions. Like those old paintings where a face is made up of a cornucopia of fruit, every wrinkle, eyelash, and throat-fold made of fruits and grains and victuals realistic enough to pluck up and eat, this park was Sylvie's face, her heart, her body. He had dismissed from his soul all the fancies, laid here all the ghosts, deposited the demons of his drunkenness and the madness he'd been born with. Somewhere, Sylvie lived, chasing her Destiny, gone for reasons of her own; he hoped she was happy. He had lifted the curse from himself, by main strength and the Art of Memory, and was free to go.

He sat.

Some sort of tree (his grandfather would have known what kind, but he didn't) was just in that week casting off its leaflike blooms or seeds, small silver-green circles that descended all over the park like a million dollars in dimes. Fortunes of them were rolled toward him by wastrel breezes, piled against his unmoving feet, filled his hat-brim and his lap, as though he were only another fixture of the park to be littered, like the bench he sat on and the pavilion he looked at.

When he did rise, heavily and feeling Somehow still inhabited, it was only to move around from Winter, which he was done with, back to Spring, where he had begun; where he now was. A year's circuit. Winter was old Father Time with sickle and hourglass, his ragged domino and beard blown by chappy winds, and a disgusted expression on his face. A lean, slavering dog or wolf was at his phthisical feet. Green coins fell across them, catching in the relief; green coins fell whispering from Auberon as he rose. He knew what Spring, just around the corner, would be; he'd been there before. There seemed suddenly little point in doing anything any more but making this circuit. Everything he needed was here.

Brother North-wind's Secret. Ten steps was all it took. If Winter comes, can Spring be far behind? He'd always thought that was put wrong. Shouldn't it be, If Winter comes can Spring be far *ahead?* Ahead: as you advance through the seasons, first winter comes, and then spring is not far ahead. "Right?" he said aloud to no one. Ahead, behind. It was probably he who had it wrong, who saw it from some peculiar useless personal point of view no one else shared, no one. If winter comes . . . He turned the corner of the pavilion. Can spring be far ahead, behind . . . Someone was just then turning the other corner, from Spring into Summer.

"Lilac," he said.

She glanced back at him, half gone around the corner; glanced back at him with a look he knew so well yet had for so long not seen that it made him feel faint. It was a look which said, *Oh I was just going away somewhere, but you caught me,* and yet it didn't mean that, was just pretty coquetry mixed with some shyness, he'd always known that. The park around him grew unreal, as though in the act of silently blowing away. Lilac turned toward him, her clasped hands swinging before her, her bare feet taking small steps. She had (of course) grown no older; she wore (of course) her blue dress. "Hi," she said, and brushed her hair away from her face with a quick motion.

"Lilac," he said.

She cleared her throat (long time since she'd spoken) and said, "Auberon. Don't you think it's time for you to go home?"

"Home," he said.

She took a step toward him, or he one toward her; he held out his hands to her, or she hers toward him. "Lilac," he said. "How do you come to be here?"

"Here?"

"Where did you go," he said, "that time you went?"

"Go?"

"Please," he said. "Please."

"I've been here all the time," she said, smiling. "Silly. It's you who've been in motion."

A curse; only a curse. No fault of your own.

"All right," he said, "all right," and took Lilac's hands, and lifted her up, or tried to, but that wouldn't work; so he linked his hands like a stirrup, and bent down, and she put her small bare foot into his hands, and her hands on his shoulders, and so he hoisted her up.

"Kind of crowded in here," she said as she made her way within. "Who are all these people?"

"Doesn't matter, doesn't matter," he said.

"Now," she said, settled in, her voice already faint, more his than hers, as it had always been, after all, after all; "now where do we go?"

He drew out the key the old woman had given him. It was necessary to unlock the wrought-iron gate in order to leave, just as it was in order to enter. "Home, I guess," Auberon said. Little girls playing jacks and plucking dandelions along the path looked up to watch him talk to himself. "I guess, home."

III

Despising, for your sake, the City, thus
I turn my back: there is a world elsewhere.

—*Coriolanus*

Hawksquill's powerful Vulpes translated her back to the City in a near-record time, and yet (so her watch told her) perhaps still not under the wire. Though she was now in possession of all the missing parts of the problem of Russell Eigenblick, the learning of those parts had taken longer than she had expected.

All along the road north she had planned how she might present herself to the heirs of Violet Drinkwater in such a way—as antiquarian, collector, cultist—that the cards would be shown her. But if she had not herself been predicted in them (Sophie knew her at once, or recognized her very quickly) they would certainly not have been yielded up to her at all. That she proved to be as well a tenuous cousin of Violet Bramble's descendants had helped too, a coincidence that surprised and delighted that strange family as much as it interested Hawksquill. And even so days went by as she and Sophie pored over the cards. More days she spent with the last edition of *The Architecture of Country Houses*, whose peculiar contents none of them seemed to be very familiar with; and though, as she studied and pored, the whole story—or as much of it as had so far happened—gradually came clear under her cockatoo scrutiny, still all the while the Noisy Bridge Rod and Gun Club advanced toward the fateful meeting with Russell Eigenblick, and still Hawksquill's loyalties remained unplaced, and her path obscure.

It was obscure no more. The children of the children of Time: who would have thought? A Fool, and a Cousin; a Journey,

Not a Moment Too Soon

and a Host. The Least Trumps! She smiled grimly, circling around the mammoth Empire Hotel in which Eigenblick had installed himself, and decided on a charm, a thing she rarely resorted to.

She inserted the Vulpes into the cavernous parking garage beneath the hotel. Armed guards and attendants patrolled the doors and elevators. She found herself in a line of vehicles being checked and examined. She stilled the car's growl, and took a Morocco-leather envelope from the glove-box. From this she extracted a small white fragment of bone. It was a bone taken from a pure black cat which had been boiled alive in the tenement kitchen of La Negra, an *espiritista* for whom Hawksquill had once had occasion to do a great favor. It might have been a toebone, or part of the maxillary process; certainly La Negra didn't know; she'd hit on it only after a whole day's experimenting before a mirror, separating the bones carefully from the stinking carcass and putting each in turn into her mouth, searching for the one that would make her image in the mirror disappear. It was this one. Hawksquill found the processes of witchcraft vulgar and the cruelty of this one especially repellent; she wasn't herself convinced that there was one bone among the thousand-odd bones in a pure black cat that could make one invisible, but La Negra had assured her that the bone would work whether she believed it or didn't; and she was glad to have the gift just now. She looked around her; the attendants had not yet noticed her car; she left the keys in the lock, thoughtfully; put the little bone into her mouth with a grimace of disgust, and disappeared.

Extracting herself unnoticed from the car took some doing, but the attendants and guards paid no attention to the elevator doors opening and closing on no one (who could predict the vagaries of empty elevators?) and Hawksquill walked out into the lobby, going carefully in the company of the visible so as not to brush against them. The usual unsmiling raincoated men stood at intervals along the walls or sat in lobby armchairs behind dummy newspapers, fooling no one, being fooled by no one but she. At an unseen signal, they began to change their stations just then, like pieces on a board. A large party was coming through the swift-bladed revolving doors, preceded by underlings. Not a moment too soon, Hawksquill thought, for this was the Noisy Bridge Rod and Gun Club proceeding into the lobby. They didn't gaze around themselves inquiringly as ordinary men might on entering such a place, but, spreading out slightly as though more fully to take possession here, they kept their eyes ahead, seeing the future and not the transitory forms of the present. Under each arm was the glove-soft case, on each head the potent homburg long ridiculous on any but men like these.

THE ART OF MEMORY

They sorted themselves into two elevators, those with the highest standing holding the doors for the others, as ancient male ritual dictates; Hawksquill slipped into the less crowded one.

"The thirteenth?"

"The thirteenth."

Someone punched the button for the thirteenth floor with a forceful forefinger. Another consulted a plain wristwatch. They ascended smoothly. They had nothing to say to one another; their plans were made, and the walls, they well knew, had ears. Hawksquill remained pressed against the door, facing their blank faces. The doors opened, and neatly she sidled out; just in time too, for there were hands thrust forward to take the hands of the club members.

"The Lecturer will be right with you."

"If you could wait in this room."

"Can we order anything up for you. The Lecturer has ordered coffee."

They were shepherded leftward by alert suited men. One or two young men, in colored blouses, hands clasped behind them in an uneaseful at-ease, stood by every door. At least, Hawksquill thought, he's wary. From another elevator a red-coated waiter came out carrying a large tray which bore a single tiny cup of coffee. He went rightwards, and Hawksquill followed him. He was admitted through double doors and past guards, and so was Hawksquill at his heels; he came up to an unmarked door, knocked, opened it, and went in. Hawksquill put an invisible foot in the door as he closed it behind him, and then slipped in.

It was an impersonally-furnished sitting-room with wide windows looking out over the spiky city. The waiter, muttering to himself, passed Hawksquill and exited. Hawksquill took the fragment of bone from her mouth and was carefully putting it away when a farther door opened and Russell Eigenblick came out, yawning, in a blackish, bedragoned silk dressing-gown. He wore on his nose a pair of tiny half-glasses which Hawksquill hadn't seen before.

Needle in The Haystack of Time

He started when he saw her, having expected an empty room.

"You," he said.

Without much grace (she couldn't remember ever having done quite this before), Hawksquill lowered herself onto one knee, bowed profoundly, and said, "I am your Majesty's humble servant."

"Get up," Eigenblick said. "Who let you in here?"

389

"A black cat," Hawksquill said, rising. "It doesn't matter. We haven't much time."

"I don't talk to journalists."

"I'm sorry," Hawksquill said. "That was an imposition. I'm not a journalist."

"I thought not!" he said, triumphantly. He snatched the spectacles from his face as though he had just remembered they were there. He moved toward an intercom on the phony Louis Quatorze desk.

"Wait," Hawksquill said. "Tell me this. Do you want, after eight hundred years of sleep, to fail in your enterprise?"

He turned slowly to regard her.

"You must remember," Hawksquill went on, "how once you were abased before a certain Pope, and were forced to hold his stirrup, and run beside his horse."

Eigenblick's face was suffused. It grew a bright red different from the red of his beard. He rifled fury at Hawksquill from his eagle eyes. "Who are you?" he said.

"At this moment," Hawksquill said, gesturing toward the farther end of the suite, "men await you who intend to abase you in just such a degree. Only more cleverly. So that you will never notice being clipped. I mean the Noisy Bridge Rod and Gun Club. Or have they presented themselves to you under some other name?"

"Nonsense," Eigenblick said. "I've never heard of this so-called club." But his eyes clouded; perhaps, somewhere, somewhen, he had been warned. . . . "And what *could* you mean about the Pope? A charming gentleman who I've never met." His eyes not meeting hers, he picked up his little coffee and drank it off.

But she had him: she saw that. If he didn't ring to have guards eject her, he would listen. "Have they promised you high position?" she asked.

"The highest," he said after a long pause, gazing out the window.

"It might interest you to know that for some years those gentlemen have employed me on various errands. I think I know them. Was it the Presidency?"

He said nothing. It was.

"The Presidency," Hawksquill said, "is no longer an office. It's a room. A nice one, but only a room. You must refuse it. Politely. And any other blandishments they may offer. I'll explain your next moves later. . . ."

He turned on her. "How is it you know these things?" he said. "How do you know me?"

Hawksquill returned his gunlike look with one of her own,

and said, in her best wizard's manner, "There is much that I know."

The intercom buzzed. Eigenblick went to it, looked thoughtfully at the array of bottons on it, finger to his lips, and then punched one. Nothing happened. He pushed another, and a voice made of static spoke: "Everything is ready, sir."

"Ja," Eigenblick said. "Moment." He released the button, realized he hadn't been heard, pressed another, and repeated himself. He turned to Hawksquill. "However it is you've found out these things," he said, "you have obviously not found out all. You see," he went on, a broad smile on his face and his eyes cast upward with the look of one confident of his election, "I'm in the cards. Nothing that can happen to me can deflect a destiny set elsewhere long ago. Protected. All this was meant to be."

"Your Majesty," Hawksquill said, "perhaps I haven't made myself clear. . . ."

"Will you stop calling me that!" he said, furious.

"Sorry. Perhaps I haven't made myself clear. I know very well that you are in the cards—a deck of very pretty ones, with trumps at least obstensibly designed to foretell and encourage the return of your old Empire; designed and drawn, I would guess, some time in the reign of Rudolf II, and printed in Prague. They have been put to other uses since. Without your being, so to speak, any the less in them."

"Where are they?" he said, suddenly coming toward her, avaricious hands like claws held out. "Give them to me. I must have them."

"If I may go on," Hawksquill said.

"They're my property," Eigenblick said.

"Your Empire's," she said. "Once." She stared him into silence, and said: "If I may go on: I know you're in the cards. I know what powers put you there, and—a little—to what end. I know your destiny. What you must believe, if you are to accomplish it, is that I am in it."

"You."

"Come to warn you, and to aid you. I have powers. Great enough to have discovered all this, to have found you out, needle in the haystack of Time. You have need of me. Now. And in time to come."

He considered her. She saw doubt, hope, relief, fear, resolution come and go in his big face. "Why," he said, "was I never told about you?"

"Perhaps," she said, "because they didn't know about me."

"Nothing is hidden from them."

"Much is. You would do well to learn that."

He chewed his cheek for a moment, but the battle was over. "What's in it for you?" he said. The intercom buzzed again.

"We'll discuss my reward later," she said. "Just now, before you answer that, you'd better decide what you will tell your visitors."

"Will you be with me?" he said, suddenly needful.

"They mustn't see me," Hawksquill said. "But I'll be with you." A cheap trick, a cat's bone; and yet (she thought, as Eigenblick punched at the intercom) just the thing to convince the Emperor Frederick Barbarossa, if he remembered his youth at all, that indeed she did have the powers she claimed. With his back to her, she disappeared; when he turned to face her, or the place where she had been, she said, "Shall we go meet the Club?"

The day was gray, a certain pale and moist gray, when Auberon descended from the bus at the crossroads. He had had words with the driver about being let off at this particular place; had had difficulty at first in describing it, then in convincing the driver that he actually passed such a spot. The driver shook his head slowly in negative as Auberon described, his eyes not meeting Auberon's, and said "Nope, nope," softly, as though lost in thought; a transparent lie, Auberon knew, the man simply didn't want to make the slightest variation in his routine. Coldly polite, Auberon described the place again, then sat in the first place behind the driver, his eyes peeled; and tapped the driver when the place approached. Got out, triumphant, a sentence forming on his tongue about the hundreds of times the man must have passed this place, if that was the level of observation to be found in the men the public was urged to leave the driving to, etc.; but the door hissed shut and the long gray bus ground its gears like teeth and lurched away.

The fingerboard he stood by pointed as always down the road toward Edgewood; more haggard, leaning at a more senescent angle, the name more time-erased than he remembered or than it had been when he had last seen it, but the same. He started down the looping road, brown as milk-chocolate after the rain, stepping along cautiously and surprised by the loudness of his footfalls. He hadn't understood how much he had been deprived of during his months in the City. The Art of Memory could make a plan of his past where all this had perhaps a place, but it couldn't have restored to him this fullness: these odors, sweet and moist and vivifying, as though the air had a clear liquid texture; the constant low nameless

Crossroads

sound filling up the air, whispering loud to his dull ear, pricked out with birdsong; the very sense of volume, of far distances and middle distances made up out of lines and groups of new-leaving trees and the roll and heap of the earth. He was able to survive outside all this well enough—air was air, after all, here or in the City—but, once plunged down within it again, he might have felt returned to a native element, might have uncurled within it, soul expanding like a butterfly sprung from its confining coccoon. In fact he did stretch his arms out, breathe deeply, and quote a few lines of verse. But his soul was a cold stone.

As he went along, he felt himself to be accompanied by someone: someone young, someone not in a lank brown overcoat, someone not hung over, someone who tugged at his sleeve, reminding him that here he'd used to pull his bike over the wall to return by secret ways to the Summer House and the Emperor Frederick Barbarossa, there he'd fallen out of a tree, there bent down with Doc to hear the mutter of closeted woodchucks. It had all happened once, to someone, to this insistent someone. Not to him . . . The gray stone pillars topped with gray oranges rose up where and when they always would. He reached up to one to touch the pitted surface, clammy and slick with spring. Down at the end of the drive his sisters awaited him on the porch.

Now for God's sake. His homecoming was to be no more secret than his leaving—and as he thought this, he realized for the first time that he had intended it to be secret, had supposed himself able to slip back into the house without anyone's noticing he had been gone for some eighteen months. Foolish! And yet the last thing he wanted was a fuss made over him. Too late, anyway, for as he stood by the gate-posts uncertainly, Lucy had spied him and leapt up waving. She pulled Lily after her to run and greet him; Tacey more regally kept to the peacock chair, dressed in a long skirt and one of his old tweed jackets.

"Hi, hi," he said, casual but suddenly aware of the figure he must cut, unshaven and bloodshot, with his shopping bag and the City dirt beneath his nails and in his hair. So clean and vernal Lucy and Lily seemed, so glad, that he was torn between drawing back from them and kneeling before them to beg their forgiveness; and though they embraced him and took his bag from him, talking both at once, he knew they read him.

"You'll never guess who came here," Lucy said.

"An old woman," Auberon said, glad that once in his life he could be sure he guessed right, "with a gray bun. How's Mom? How's Dad?"

"But *who* she is you'll never guess," Lily said.

"Did she tell you I was coming? I never said it to her."

"No. But we knew. But *guess*."

"She is," Lucy said, "a cousin. In a way. Sophie found out. It was years ago . . ."

"In England," Lily said. "Do you know the Auberon you're named after? Well, he was Violet Bramble Drinkwater's son . . ."

"But not John Drinkwater's! A love child . . ."

"How do you keep all these people straight?" Auberon asked.

"Anyway. Back in England Violet Bramble had an affair. Before she married John. With someone named Oliver Hawksquill."

"A swain," Lily said.

"And got pregnant, and that was Auberon. And *this* lady . . ."

"Hello, Auberon," Tacey said. "How was the City?"

"Gee, just great," Auberon said, feeling a hard lump rise in his throat and water spring to his eyes. "Great."

"Did you walk?" Tacey asked.

"No, the bus, actually." They were silent a moment at that. No help for it. "So listen. How's Mom? How's Dad?"

"Fine. She got your card."

A horror swept him as he thought of the few cards and letters he had sent from the City, evasive and bragging, or uncommunicative, or horribly facetious. The last one, Mom's birthday, he had found, oh God, unsigned in a trash can he was examining, a bouquet of smarmy sentiments; but his silence had been long and he was drunk and he sent it. He saw now that it must have been to her like being stabbed cruelly with a butter knife. He sat down on the steps of the porch, unable just for the moment to go further.

"Well, what do you think, Ma?" Daily Alice asked as she stood looking into the dank darkness of the old icebox.

An Awful Mess

Momdy was examining the stock inside the cupboards. "Tuna wiggle?" she said doubtfully.

"Oh dear," Alice said. "Smoky will give me a look. You know that look?"

"Oh, I do."

"Well." Beneath her gaze the few damp items on the slatted metal shelves seemed to shrink away. There was a constant drip, as in a cave. Daily Alice thought of the old days, the great white refrigerator chock-full of crisp vegetables and colorful containers, perhaps a varnished turkey or a diamondback ham, and neatly wrapped meats and meals asleep in the icy-breathing freezer. And a cheerful light that winked on to show it all, as on a stage. Nostalgia. She put her hand on a luke-cold milk bottle and said, "Did Rudy come today?"

"No."

"He's really getting too old for that," Alice said. "Lifting big blocks of ice. And he forgets." She sighed, still looking within; Rudy's decline, and the general falling-off in the amenities of life, and the not-so-hot dinner probably awaiting them all, all seemed contained within the zinc-lined icebox.

"Well, don't hold the door open, dear," Momdy said softly. Alice was closing it when the swinging doors of the pantry opened.

"Oh my God," Alice said. "Oh, Auberon."

She came quickly to embrace him, hurrying to him as though he were in deep trouble and she must instantly rescue him. His harrowed look, though, came less from the trouble he was in than from the trip he had just taken through the house, which had assaulted him unmercifully with memories, odors he'd forgotten he knew, scarred furniture and worn rugs and garden-exhibiting windows that filled his eyesight to the brim, as if it had been half a lifetime and not a year and a half he'd been away.

"Hi," he said.

She released him. "Look at you," she said. "What is it?"

"What's what?" he said, attempting a smile, wondering what degradation she read in his features. Daily Alice raised a wondering finger and traced the line of his single eyebrow across his nose. "When did you grow that?"

"Huh?"

Daily Alice touched the place above her own nose where (though faintly, because of her lighter hair) she bore the mark of Violet's descendants.

"Oh." He shrugged. He hadn't actually noticed; he hadn't been studying mirrors much lately. "I dunno." He laughed. "How do you like that?" He stroked it himself. Soft and fine as baby hair, with one or two coarser hairs springing from it. "I must be getting old," he said.

She saw that that was so; that he had crossed in his absence some threshold beyond which life is consumed faster than it increases; she could see the marks of it in his face and the backs of his hands. A hard lump formed in her throat, and she embraced him again so that she wouldn't have to speak. Over her shoulder, to his grandmother, Auberon said, "Hi Momdy, listen, listen, don't get up, don't."

"Well, you're a bad boy, not to have written your mother," Momdy said. "To tell us you were coming. Not a thing for supper."

"Oh, that's okay, that's okay," he said, releasing himself from his mother and coming to kiss Momdy's feathery soft cheek. "How have you been?"

"The same, the same." She looked up at him from where she sat, studying him shrewdly. He'd always had the sense his grandmother knew some discreditable secret about him, and if she could just squeeze it between the thick layers of her usual discourse, it would be revealed. "I go on," she said. "You've grown."

"Gee, I don't *think* so."

"Either that or I'd forgotten how big you'd got."

"Yeah, that's it. . . . Well." The two women looked him over from the heights of two generations, seeing different views. He felt examined. He knew he ought to take off his overcoat, but he had forgotten exactly what was underneath it; he sat instead at the far end of the table and said again, "Well."

"Tea," Alice said. "How about some tea? And you can tell us all your adventures."

"Tea would be great," he said.

"And how's George?" Momdy asked. "And his people?"

"Oh, fine." He hadn't been to Old Law Farm in months. "Fine, same as ever." He shook his head in amusement at funny George. "That crazy farm."

"I remember," she said, "when that was really such a nice place. Years ago. The corner house, that was the one the Mouse family first lived in . . ."

"Still do, still do," Auberon said. He glanced at his mother, who was busy with teapot and water at the big stove; surreptitiously she brushed her eyes with the sleeve of her sweatshirt, and then saw that he caught her at it, and turned to face him, teapot in her hands.

". . . and after Phyllis Townes died," Momdy was going on, "well that was a protracted illness, her doctor thought he'd chased it down to her kidneys, but *she* thought . . ."

"So how was it, really?" Alice said to her son. "Really."

"Really it wasn't so hot," Auberon said. He looked down. "I'm sorry."

"Oh, oh well," she said.

"For not writing and all. There wasn't much to say."

"That's okay. We were afraid for you, that's all."

He lifted his eyes. He really hadn't thought of that. Here he'd been swallowed down by the teeming terrible City, swallowed as by a dragon's mouth and hardly been heard of again; of course they'd been afraid for him. As it had once before in this kitchen, a window rose within him and he saw, through it, his own reality. People loved him, and worried about him; his personal worth didn't even enter into it. He lowered his eyes again, ashamed. Alice turned back to the stove. His grandmother filled the silence with reminiscence, the details of dead relatives' sickness, remission, relapse, decline and death. "Mm, mm-hm," he said, nodding, studying the scarred surface of the table. He had sat, without choosing to, at his old place, at his father's right hand, Tacey's left.

"Tea," Alice said. She put the teapot on a trivet, and patted its fat belly. She put a cup before him. And waited, then, hands folded, for him to pour it, or for something; he glanced up at her and was about to try to speak, to answer the question he saw posed in her, if he could, if he could think of words, when the double doors of the pantry flew open and Lily and the twins came in, and Tony Buck.

"Hi Uncle Auberon," the twins (Bud the boy and Blossom the girl) shouted in unison, as though Auberon hadn't quite arrived yet and they had to call far to be heard. Auberon stared at them: they seemed to be twice the size they had been, and they could talk: they hadn't been able to when he left, had they? Hadn't he last seen them still carried fore and aft by their mother in a canvas carrier? Lily, at their insistence, began to go through cupboards, looking for good things to eat, the twins were unimpressed by the solitary teapot but certainly it was time for *some*thing. Tony Buck shook Auberon's hand and said, "Hey, how was the City?"

"Oh, hey, swell," Auberon said in a tone like Tony's, hearty and no-nonsense; Tony turned to Alice and said, "So Tacey said maybe we should have a couple rabbits tonight."

"Oh, Tony, that would be terrific," Alice said.

Tacey herself came through the door then, calling Tony's name. "Is that okay, Ma?" she said.

"It's great," Alice said. "Better than tuna wiggle."

"Kill the fatted calf," Momdy said, the only one there to whom the phrase would have occurred. "And fricassee it."

"Smoky'll be so happy," said Alice to Auberon. "He loves rabbit, but he can't ever feel it's his place to suggest it."

"Listen," Auberon said, "don't make any fuss just for . . ."

He couldn't, in his self-effacement, bring himself to say personal pronouns. "I mean just because . . ."

"Uncle Auberon," said Bud, "did you see any muggerds?"

"Hm?"

"Muggerds." He curved his fingers predatorily at Auberon. "Who get you. In the City."

"Well, as a matter of fact . . ." But Bud had noticed (he hadn't ever quite taken his eyes from her) that his sister Blossom had acquired a cookie of a sort that hadn't been offered to him, and he had to hurry to put in a claim.

"Now out, out!" said Lily.

"You wanna go see the rabbits die?" her daughter asked her, taking her hand.

"No, I don't," said Lily, but Blossom, wanting her mother with her for the dread and fascinating event, pulled her by the hand.

"It only takes a *second*," she said reassuringly, drawing her mother after her. "Don't be afraid." They went out through the summer kitchen and the door that led to the kitchen-garden, Lily, Bud and Blossom, and Tony. Tacey had filled a cup for herself and one for Momdy, and with them backed out the pantry doors; Momdy followed her.

Grump grump grump said the doors behind them.

Alice and Auberon sat alone in the kitchen, the storm of them having passed as quickly as it came on.

"So," Auberon said. "It seems like everybody's fine here."

"Yes. Fine."

"Do you mind," he said, rising slowly like an old man, much tried, "if I get myself a drink?"

"No, sure," Alice said. "There's some sherry there, and other things, I think."

He got down a dusty whiskey bottle.

"No ice," said Alice. "Rudy didn't come."

"He still cuts ice?"

"Oh yes. But he's been sick lately. And Robin, you know, his grandson—well, you know Robin; he isn't much help. Poor old man."

Absurdly, this was the last straw. Poor old Rudy . . . "Too bad, too bad," he said, his voice shaky. "Too bad." He sat, his glassful of whiskey the saddest thing he had ever seen. His vision was clouded and sparkling. Alice rose slowly, alarmed. "I made a real mess of it, Ma," he said. "A real awful mess." He put his face in his hands, the awful mess a harsh, gathering thing in his throat and breast. Alice, unsure, came and put her arm tentatively around his shoulder, and Auberon, though he hadn't done so in years, never even for Sylvie, not once, knew he was about to sob like a child. The awful mess gathered weight and force and, pressing its way out, opened his mouth and shook his frame violently, causing sounds he had not known he could make. There there, he said to himself, there there: but it wouldn't stop, release made it grow, there were vast volumes of it to be expelled, he put his head down on the kitchen table and bawled.

"Sorry, sorry," he said when he could speak again. "Sorry, sorry."

"No," Alice said, her arm around his resistant overcoat; "no, sorry for what?" He raised his head suddenly, throwing off her arm, and, after another gasping sob, ceased, his chest heaving. "Was it," Alice said softly, warily, "the dark girl?"

"Oh," Auberon said, "partly, partly."

"And that stupid bequest."

"Partly."

She saw peeking from his pocket a hanky, and pulled it out for him. "Here," she said, shocked to see in his streaming face not her baby boy in tears, but a grownup she hardly knew transformed by grief. She looked at the hanky she offered him. "What a pretty thing," she said. "It looks like . . ."

"Yes," Auberon said, taking it from her and mopping his face. "Lucy made it." He blew his nose. "It was a present. When I left. Open it when you come home, she said." He laughed, or cried again, or both, and swallowed. "Pretty, huh." He stuffed it back in his pocket and sat, back bent, staring. "Oh God," he said. "Well, that's embarrassing."

"No," she said, "no." She put her hand over his. She was in a quandary; he needed advice, and she couldn't give it to him; she knew where advice could be got, but not whether it could be given to him there, or whether it was right for her to send him. "It's all right, you know," she said, "it really is, because," and then bethought herself. "Because it's all right; it'll be all right."

"Oh sure," he said, sighing a great, shuddering sigh. "All over now."

"No," Alice said, and took his hand more firmly. "No, it's not all over, but . . . Well, whatever happens, it'll all be part of, well part of what's to be, won't it? I mean there's nothing that couldn't be, isn't that right?"

"I don't know," Auberon said. "What do I know."

She held his hand, but oh, he was too big now for her to gather him to her, hug him, cover him up with herself and tell him all, tell him the long, long tale of it, so long and strange that he would fall asleep long before it was over, soothed by her voice and her warmth and the beat of her heart and the calm certainty of her telling: and then, and then, and then: and more wonderful than that: and strange to say: and the way it all turns out: the story she hadn't known how to tell when he was young enough to tell it to, the story she knew now only when he was too big to gather up and whisper it to, too big to believe it, though it would all happen, and to him. But she couldn't bear to see him in this darkness, and say nothing. "Well," she said, not releasing his hand; she cleared her throat of the huskiness that had gathered there (was she glad, or the reverse, that all her own storms of tears had been wept, years ago?) and said, "Well, will you do something for me, anyway?"

"Yes, sure."

"Tonight, no, tomorrow morning—do you know where the old gazebo is? That little island? Well, if you follow that stream up, you come to a pool—with a waterfall?"

"Sure, yes."

"Okay," she said. She took a deep breath, said "Well" again, and gave him instructions, and pledged him to follow them exactly, and told him something of the reasons why he must, but not all; and he agreed, in a cloud, but having wept out before her any reservations he might have had to such a scheme, and such reasons.

The door to the kitchen-garden opened, and Smoky came in through it; before he came around the corner of the summer kitchen, though, Alice had patted Auberon's hand, smiled, and pressed her forefinger to her lips, and then to his.

"Rabbit tonight?" Smoky was saying as he came into the kitchen. "What's all the excitement?" He did an extravagant double-take when he saw Auberon, and books slipped from beneath his arm to the floor.

"Hi, hi," said Auberon, glad at least to have taken one of them by surprise.

Slowly I Turn

Sophie had also known that Auberon was on his way home, though the bus had thrown off her calculations by a day. She was full of advice, and had many questions to ask; but Auberon wanted no advice, and she saw that her questions would get no answers either, so she didn't ask them: what information he chose to offer was all she would get for the moment, scantily though it clothed his City months.

At dinner she said: "Well. It's nice to have everybody back. For one night."

Auberon, devouring victuals like a man who's lived for months on hot dogs and day-old Danish, looked up at her, but she had looked away, not conscious apparently of having said anything odd; and Tacey began a story about Cherry Lake's divorce after only a year of marriage.

"This is delicious, Ma," Auberon said, and helped himself again, wondering.

Later, in the library, he and Smoky compared cities: Smoky's, from years ago, and Auberon's.

"The best thing," Smoky said, "or the exciting thing, was the feeling you always had of being at the head of the parade. I mean even if all you did was sit in your room, you felt it, you knew that outside in the streets and in the buildings it was going forward, boom boom boom, and you were part of it, and everybody everywhere else was just stumbling along behind. Do you know what I mean?"

"I guess," Auberon said. "I guess things have changed." Hamletish in a black sweater and pants he'd found among his old clothes, he sat somewhat folded up in a tall buttoned leather chair. One light lit shone on the brandy bottle Smoky had opened. Alice had suggested he and Auberon have a long talk; but they were having difficulty finding subjects. "It always felt to me like everybody everywhere else had forgotten all about us." He held out his glass, and Smoky put an inch of brandy in it.

"Well, but the crowds," Smoky said. "The bustle, and all the well-dressed people; everybody hurrying to appointments . . ."

"Hm," Auberon said.

"I think it's . . ."

"Well I mean I think I know what you say you thought, I mean that you think it was . . ."

"I think I thought . . ."

"I guess it's changed," Auberon said.

A silence fell. Each stared into his glass. "So," Smoky said. "Anyway. How did you meet her?"

"Who?" Auberon stiffened. There were subjects he had no intention of discussing with Smoky. That with their cards and their second sight they could probe his heart and learn his business was bad enough.

"The lady who came," Smoky said. "That Miss Hawksquill. Cousin Ariel, as Sophie says."

"Oh. In a park. We fell into conversation. . . . A little

401

park that said it was built by, you know, old John and his company, back when."

"A little park," Smoky said, surprised, "with funny curving paths, that . . ."

"Yeah," Auberon said.

"That lead in, only they don't, and . . ."

"Yeah."

"Fountains, statues, a little bridge . . ."

"Yeah, yeah."

"I used to go there," Smoky said. "How do you like that."

Auberon didn't, really. He said nothing.

"It always reminded me," Smoky said, "for some reason, of Alice." Suddenly flung back into the past, Smoky with great vividness remembered the small summery park, and felt—tasted, almost, with the mind's tongue—the season of his first love for his wife. When he was Auberon's age. "How do you like that," he said again, dreamily, tasting a cordial in which a whole summer's fruits were long ago distilled. He looked at Auberon. He was staring into his glass gloomily. Smoky sensed that he was approaching a sore spot or subject. How odd, though, the same park . . . "Well," he said, and cleared his throat. "She seems like quite a woman."

Auberon ran his hand over his brow.

"I mean this Hawksquill person."

"Oh. Oh, yes." Auberon cleared *his* throat, and drank. "Crazy, I thought, maybe."

"Oh? Oh, I don't think so. No more than . . . She certainly had a lot of energy. Wanted to see the house from top to bottom. She had some interesting things to say. We even crawled up into the old orrery. She said she had one, in her house in the City, different, but built on the same principles, maybe by the same person." He had grown animated, hopeful. "You know what? She thought we could get it working again. I showed her it was all rusted, because, you know, the main wheel for some reason sticks out into the air, but she said, well, she thought the basic works are still okay. I don't see how she could tell that, but wouldn't that be fun? After all these years. I thought I'd have a shot at it. Clean it up, and see . . ."

Auberon looked at his father. He began to laugh. That broad, sweet, simple face. How could he have ever thought . . . "You know something?" he said. "I used to think, when I was a kid, that it *did* move."

"What?"

"Sure. I thought it did move. I thought I could prove that it moved."

"You mean by itself? How?"

"I didn't know *how*," Auberon said. "But I thought it did, and that you all knew it did, and didn't want me to know."

Smoky laughed too. "Well, why?" he said. "I mean why would we keep it a secret? And anyhow, how could it? What would be the power?"

"*I* don't know, Dad," Auberon said, laughing more, though the laughter seemed likely to deliquesce into tears. "By itself. I don't know." He rose, unfolding himself from the buttoned chair. "I *thought*," he said, "oh, hell, I can't recreate it, why I thought it was important, I mean why *that* was important, but I thought I was going to get the goods on you. . . ."

"What? What?" Smoky said. "Well why didn't you ask? I mean a simple question . . ."

"Dad," Auberon said, "do you think there's ever been a simple question around here you could ask?"

"Well," Smoky said.

"Okay," Auberon said. "Okay, I'll ask you a simple question, okay?"

Smoky sat upright in his chair. Auberon wasn't laughing any more. "Okay," he said.

"Do you believe in fairies?" Auberon asked.

Smoky looked up at his tall son. Through the whole of their lives together, it had been as though he and Auberon had been back to back, fixed that way and unable to turn. They had had to communicate by indirection, through others, or by craning their necks and talking out the sides of their mouths; they had had to guess at each other's faces and actions. Now and then one or the other would try a quick spin around to catch the other unawares, but it never worked, quite, the other was still behind and facing away, as in the old vaudeville act. And the effort of communication in that posture, the effort of making oneself clear, had often grown too much for them, and they'd given it up, mostly. But now—maybe because of what had happened to him in the City, whatever that was, or maybe only increase of time wearing away the bond that had both held them and held them apart, Auberon had turned around. Slowly I turn. And all that was left then was for Smoky himself to turn and face him. "Well," he said, " 'believe', I don't know; 'believe', that's a word . . ."

"*Uh* uh," said Auberon. "No quotes."

Auberon stood over him now, looking down, waiting. "Okay," Smoky said. "The answer is no."

"Okay!" Auberon said, grimly triumphant.

LITTLE, BIG

"I never did."

"Okay."

"Of course," Smoky said, "it wouldn't have been right to *say* so, you know, or really ask right out what was what here; I never wanted to spoil anything by not—not joining in. So I never said anything. Never asked questions, never. Especially not simple ones. I just hope you noticed that, because it wasn't always easy."

"I know," Auberon said.

Smoky looked down. "I'm sorry about that," he said; "about deceiving you—if I did, I suppose I didn't; and sort of spying on you all the time, trying to figure it out—when all the time I was supposed to know about it all, the same as you." He sighed. "It's not so easy," he said. "Living a lie."

"Wait a sec," Auberon said. "Dad."

"None of you seemed to *mind*, really. Except you, I think. Well. And it didn't seem that *they* minded, that I didn't believe in them, the Tale went on and all, just the same—didn't it? Only I did, I admit, feel a little jealous; anyway I used to. Jealous of you. Who knew."

"Listen, Dad, listen."

"No, it's all right," Smoky said. If he were going to face front then he would by God face front. "Only . . . Well, it always seemed to me that *you*—just you, not the others—could have explained it. That you wanted to explain it, but couldn't. No, it's all right." He held up his hand to forestall whatever evasion or equivocation his son was about to make. "They, I mean Alice, and Sophie, and Aunt Cloud—even the girls—they said everything they could, I think, only nothing they could say was ever an explanation, not an *explanation*, even though maybe they thought it was, maybe they thought they'd explained it over and over and I was just too dumb to grasp it; maybe I was. But I used to think that *you*—I don't know why—that I could maybe understand you, and that you were always just about to spill the beans. . . ."

"Dad . . ."

"And that we got off on the wrong foot, way back, because you had to hide it, and so you sort of had to hide from me. . . ."

"No! No no no . . ."

"And I'm sorry, really, if you felt I was always spying on you and intruding and all, but . . ."

"Dad, Dad, will you please just listen a second?"

"But well, as long as we're asking simple questions, I'd like to know what it was that you . . ."

404

"I didn't know anything!" His shout seemed to awaken Smoky, who looked up to see his son twisted up in an attitude of recrimination or confession, and a mad light in his eye.

"What?"

"I didn't know anything!" Auberon knelt suddenly before his father, his whole childhood giddily inverted; it made him want to laugh insanely. "Nothing!"

"Cut it out," Smoky said, puzzled. "I thought we were getting down to brass tacks here."

"Nothing!"

"Then how come you were always hiding it?"

"Hiding *what?*"

"What you knew. A secret diary. And all those weird hints . . ."

"Dad. Dad. If I knew anything you didn't know—if I did—would I have thought that old orrery was going around and nobody was admitting to it? And what about the *Architecture of Country Houses,* that you wouldn't explain to me . . ."

"*I* wouldn't explain! It was *you* who thought you knew what it was. . . ."

"Well, and what about Lilac?"

"What about her?"

"Well, what happened to her? Sophie's, I mean. Why didn't anybody tell me?" He gripped his father's hands. "What happened to her? Where did she go?"

"*Well?*" Smoky said, frustrated beyond endurance. *"Where did she?"*

They stared at each other wildly, all questions, no answers; and at the same moment saw that. Smoky clapped his hand to his brow. "But how could you have thought I . . . that *I* . . . I mean wasn't it obvious I didn't *know.* . . ."

"Well, I wondered," Auberon said. "I *thought* maybe you were pretending. But I couldn't be sure. How could I be sure? I couldn't take a chance."

"Then why didn't you . . ."

"Don't say it," Auberon said. "Don't say, Why didn't you ask. Just don't."

"Oh, God," Smoky said, laughing. "Oh, dear."

Auberon sat back on the floor, shaking his head. "All that work," he said. "All that effort."

"I think," Smoky said, "I think I'll have another taste of that brandy, if you can reach the bottle." He hunted up his empty snifter, which had rolled away into the darkness. Auberon poured for him, and for himself, and for a long time they sat in silence, glancing now and again at each other, laughing a little, shaking their heads. "Well, isn't that something," Smoky said.

"And wouldn't it *really* be something," he added after a while, "if *none* of us knew what was what. If we, if you and I, marched up now to your mother's room . . ." He laughed at the idea. "And said, Hey . . ."

"I don't know," Auberon said. "I bet . . ."

"Yes," Smoky said. "Yes, I'm sure. Well." He remembered Doc, years ago, on a hunting expedition Smoky and he had made one October afternoon: Doc, who was himself Violet's grandson, but who had advised Smoky that day that it was best not to inquire into some things too deeply. Into what's given; what can't be changed. And who could tell now just what Doc himself had known, after all, what he had carried with him to the grave. On the very first day he had come to Edgewood, Great-aunt Cloud had said: The women feel it more deeply, but the men perhaps suffer from it more. . . . He had come to spend his life with a race of expert secret-keepers, and he had learned much; it was no wonder really that he'd fooled Auberon, he'd learned from masters how to keep secrets, even if he had none to keep. Yet he did have secrets, he suddenly thought, he did: though he couldn't tell Auberon what had happened to Lilac, there was more than one fact about her and about the Barnable family that he still kept to himself, and had no intention of ever telling his son; and he felt guilty about that. Face to face: well. And was it suspicion of some such thing which made Auberon rub his brow, staring again into his glass?

No; Auberon was thinking of Sylvie, and of what his mother had instructed him to do tomorrow in the woods above the lake island, the outlandish thing; and how she had pressed her finger to her lips, and then to his, enjoining silence on him when his father came into the room. He raised his forefinger and stroked the new hair that had recently and unaccountably joined his two eyebrows into one.

"In a way, you know," Smoky said, "I'm sorry you made it back."

"Hm?"

"No, of course I don't mean I'm sorry, only . . . Well, I had a plan; if you didn't write or show up soon, I was going to set out to find you."

"You were?"

"Yup." He laughed. "Oh it would have been quite an expedition. I was already thinking of what to pack, and all."

"You should have," Auberon said, grinning with relief that he had in fact not.

"It might have been fun. Seeing the City again." He was lost a moment in old visions. "Well. I probably would have got lost myself."

"Yes." He smiled at his father. "Probably. But thanks, Dad."

"Well," Smoky said. "Well. Gosh, look at the time."

He followed his father up the wide front staircase.

The stairs creaked where and when they always had. The nighttime house was as familiar to him as the day-house, as full of details he had forgotten he knew.

Embracing Himself

They parted at a turning of the corridor.

"Well, sleep well," Smoky said, and they stood together in the pool of light from the candle Smoky held. Perhaps if Auberon hadn't been encumbered with his squalid bags and Smoky with the candle, they would have embraced; perhaps not. "You can find your room?"

"Sure."

"Goodnight."

"Goodnight."

He took the fifteen and a half steps—bumping his flank against the absurd commode he always forgot was there—and put out his hand, and it touched his faceted glass knob. He lit no light once inside, though he knew that a candle and matches were there on the night-table, knew how to find them, knew the scarred underside of the table where he could strike the match. The odor (his own, cold, faint, but familiar, with an admixture of child's smell, Lily's twins who had camped there) spoke in a constant old murmur to him of past things. He stood unmoving for a moment, seeing by smell the armchair where much of his childhood's happiness had been had, the armchair just large enough and unsprung enough for him to curl in with a book or a pad of paper, and the calm lamp beside it, and the table where cookies and milk or tea and toast could glow warmly in the lamplight; and the wardrobe from out whose door, when left ajar, ghosts and hostile figures used to steal to frighten him (what had become of those figures, once so familiar? Dead, dead of loneliness, with no one to spook); and the narrow bed and its fat quilt and its two pillows. From an early age he'd insisted on having two pillows, though he'd only rested his head on one. He liked the rich luxury of them: inviting. All there. The weight of the odors was heavy on his soul, like chains, like old burdens reassumed.

He undressed in the dark and crawled into the cold bed. It was like embracing himself. Since the adolescent spurt of growing that had brought him to Daily Alice's height, his feet, when he was in this bed, curled down over the end, and had made two depressions there in the mattress. His feet found them now. The lumps were where they had always been. There was in fact only one pillow, and it smelled vaguely pissy. Cat? Child? He wouldn't sleep, he thought; he couldn't decide whether he wished he had been bold enough to gulp more of Smoky's brandy or glad that this agony was his now, a lot to make up for, starting tonight. He had, anyway, plenty to occupy his wide-awake thoughts. He rolled over carefully into Position Two of his unvarying bedtime choreography, and lay that way long awake in the suffocating familiar darkness.

You talk like a Rosicrucian, who
will love nothing but a sylph, who does
not believe in the existence of a
sylph, and who yet quarrels with the whole
universe for not containing a sylph.

—Peacock, Nightmare Abbey

No, I understand now," Auberon said, calm in the woods—it was so simple, really. "I didn't, for a long time, but I do now. You just can't *hold* people, you can't *own* them. I mean it's only natural, a natural process really. Meet. Love. Part. Life goes on. There was never any reason to expect her to stay always the same—I mean 'in love,' you know." There were those doubt-quotes of Smoky's, heavily indicated. "I don't hold a grudge. I can't."

"You do," Grandfather Trout said. "And you don't understand."

He had gone out at dawn, awakened by that abrasive thing like thirst or need that always awoke him at dawn since he'd become a drunkard. Unable to recapture sleep, unwilling to stare at the room, his room, which in the untender dawn looked alien and unfamiliar, he'd dressed. Put on his overcoat and hat against the misty chill. And climbed up through the woods, past the lake island where the white gazebo stood up to its knees in mist, up to where a falls fell melodiously into a deep dark pool. There, he'd done as his mother had instructed him, though believing none of it or trying to believe none of it. But, believe it or not, he was after all a Barnable, Drinkwater on his mother's side; his great-grandfather didn't refuse his summons. He couldn't have if he'd wanted to.

Nothing for Something

409

"Well, though, but I'd like to explain to her," Auberon said. "Tell her . . . Tell her, anyhow. That I don't mind. That she has my *respect* for making the decision she did. So I thought if you knew where she was, even approximately where . . ."

"I don't," said Grandfather Trout.

Auberon sat back from the pool's edge. What was he doing here? If the one piece of information he had wanted—the one piece which of all pieces he should not any longer care to seek—was to be still withheld from him? How could he anyway have asked for it? "What I *don't* understand," he said at last, "is why I have to go on making such a big deal out of it. I mean there are lots of fish in the sea. She's gone, I can't find her; so why do I cling to it? Why do I keep making her up? These ghosts, these phantoms . . ."

"Oh, well," said the fish. "Not your fault. Those phantoms. Those are their work."

"Their work?"

"Don't want you to know it," said Grandfather Trout, "but yes, their work; just to keep you sharp set; lures; no worry there."

"No worry?"

"Just let 'em pass by. There'll be more. Just let 'em pass by. Don't tell them I told you so."

"Their work," Auberon said. "Why?"

"Oh, well," Grandfather Trout said guardedly. "Why; well, *why* . . ."

"Okay," Auberon said. "Okay, see? See what I mean?" An innocent victim, tears sprang to his eyes. "Well, hell with them anyway," he said. "Figments. I don't care. It'll pass. Phantoms or no phantoms. Let 'em do their worst. It won't last forever." That was saddest of all; sad but true. A trembling sigh covered him and passed. "It's only natural," he said. "It won't last forever. It can't."

"It can," Grandfather Trout said. "It will."

"No," Auberon said. "No, you *think* it will sometimes. But it passes. You think—Love. It's such a whole, such a permanent thing. So big, so—separate from you. With a weight of its own. Do you know what I mean?"

"I do."

"But that's not so. It's just a figment too. I don't have to do its bidding. It just withers away on its own. When its over after all you don't even remember what it was like." That's what he had learned in his little park: that it was possible, reasonable even, to discard his broken heart like a broken cup; who needed it? "Love: It's all *personal.* I mean my love doesn't have anything to do with her—

not the *real* her. It's just something *I* feel. I think it connects me to her. But it doesn't. That's a myth, a myth I make up; a myth about her and me. Love is a myth."

"Love is a myth," Grandfather Trout said. "Like summer."

"What?"

"In winter," Grandfather Trout said, "summer is a myth. A report, a rumor. Not to be believed in. Get it? Love is a myth. So is summer."

Auberon raised his eyes to the crook-fingered trees that rose above the sounding pool. Leaves were uncurling from ten thousand tips. What he was being told, he saw, was that he had accomplished nothing in the little park by Art of Memory, nothing at all; that he was as burdened as ever, unrelievably. That couldn't be so. Could he really love her forever, live in the house of her forever, inescapably?

"In summer," he said, "winter is a myth. . . ."

"Yes," said the trout.

"A report, a rumor, not to be believed."

"Yes."

He had loved her and she had left him, without reason, without farewell. If he loved her always, if there was no death of love, then she would always leave him, always without reason, always without farewell. Between those eternal stones bright and dark he would be ground small forever. It couldn't be so.

"Forever," he said. "No."

"Forever," said his great-grandfather. "Yes."

It was so. He knew, eyes blind with tears and heart black with terror, that he had exorcised nothing, not one moment, not one glance, no, he had by his Art only refined and burnished every moment of Sylvie that he had been given, not one of them was returnable now forever. Summer had come, and all serene autumns and all winters peaceful as any grave were myth and no help.

"No fault of your own," Grandfather Trout said.

"I must say," Auberon said, wiping tears and snot from his face with the sleeve of his coat, "you're not a lot of comfort."

The trout answered nothing. He hadn't expected thanks.

"You don't know where she is. Or why I should be done by this way. Or what I should do. And then you tell me it won't pass." He sniffed. "No fault of my own. Big help that is."

There was a long silence. The fish's wavering white form regarded him and his grief unblinking. "Well," he said at last. "There *is* a gift in it for you."

411

"Gift. What gift."

"Well, I don't know. Exactly. But I'm sure there's a gift. You don't get nothing for something."

"Oh." Auberon could sense the fish's effort to be kind. "Well. Thanks. Whatever it is."

"Nothing to do with me," Grandfather Trout said. Auberon stared into the water's silky folded surface. If he had a net. Grandfather Trout sank slightly and said, "Well, listen." But after that he said nothing more; and by slow degrees sank out of sight.

Auberon rose. The morning mist had burned away, the sun was hot, and the birds were ecstatic—it was all that they had hoped it would be. He made his way down the stream through all this gladness, and out along the path to the pasture. The house, beyond whispering trees, was pastel in the morning, and seemed to be just opening its eyes. A dark smudge in the spring, he stumbled through the pasture, wet to his knees with dew. It can last forever: it will. There would be a bus he could catch at evening, a bus that by a roundabout path met another bus that went south along the gray highways, through thickening suburbs, to the broad bridge or to the tiled tunnel, and then out onto the horrid streets that led by old geometries smoked and full of wretchedness to Old Law Farm and the Folding Bedroom in the City where Sylvie was or was not. He stopped walking. He felt himself to be a dry stick, that dry stick that the Pope in the story gave to the sinful knight who had loved Venus, and who would not be redeemed until it blossomed. And there was no blossoming in him.

Grandfather Trout, within whose pool spring was also unfolding, fringing his private holes with tender weed and bringing bugs to term, wondered if there really would be a gift for the boy. Probably not. They didn't give out such things when they didn't have to. But the boy had been so sad. What harm in telling him? Give him heart. Grandfather Trout's was not an affectionate soul, not now, not after all these years; but this was after all spring, and the boy was after all flesh of his flesh, or so they said. He hoped anyway that if there *was* a gift in it, it wouldn't be one that would cause the boy any great suffering.

Quite
Long-Sighted

"Of course I'd always known about them," Ariel Hawksquill said to the Emperor Frederick Barbarossa. "In the practical, or experimental, stage of my studies, they were always a nuisance. Elementals. The experiments seemed to draw them, like a bowl of peaches drawing a cloud of fruit flies from nowhere, or a walk in the woods drawing chickadees. There were times I couldn't go up and down the stairs to my sanctum—where I worked with the glasses and mirrors and so on, you know—without a crowd of them at my heels and head. Annoying. You couldn't ever be sure they weren't affecting your results."

She sipped at the sherry the Emperor had ordered for her. He was pacing the parlor of his suite, not paying close attention. The Noisy Bridge Rod and Gun Club had departed in some confusion, not sure whether any conclusion had been come to, and feeling vaguely fleeced. "What," Barbarossa said, "do we do now? That's the question. I think the time is ripe to strike. The sword's unsheathed. The Revelation should come soon."

"Hm." The difficulty was that she had never thought of them as having *wills*. Like angels, they were forces only, emanations, condensations of occult energy, natural objects really and no more wilful than stones or sunlight. That they had shapes which seemed to be able to contain wills, had voices and faces with changeful expressions and flitted about with apparent purpose, she had ascribed to that quiddity of human perception that sees faces in the blotches of plaster walls, hostility or friendliness in landscapes, creatures in clouds. Once see a Force, and you will see it with a face, and a character; no help for it. But the *Architecture of Country Houses* saw the matter very differently: it seemed to state that if there were creatures who were merely expressions of natural forces, the will-less emanations of shaping wills, the medium of spirits who knew what they were doing, then those creatures were men and not fairies. Hawksquill was unwilling to go so far, but she was forced to think that yes, they did have wills as well as powers, and desires as well as duties, and weren't blind, no, quite long-sighted in fact; and where did that leave her?

She really didn't feature being a mere link in a chain woven by other powers, and having nothing to say in the matter, as her upstate cousins apparently thought of themselves. For sure she had no intention of being a subaltern in their army, which is how she supposed they thought of the Emperor Frederick Barbarossa, whatever *he* thought of the matter. No: with no side was she ready to throw in her lot that completely. The mage is by definition he who manipulates and rules those forces at whose direction the common run blindly live.

She was on thin ice, in fact. The Noisy Bridge Rod and Gun Club could never have been an opponent worthy of her powers. And by as much as she outclassed those gentlemen, by just as much, perhaps, was she outclassed by those who operated Russell Eigenblick. Well: it was anyway to be a contest worthy of her, at last; at last she and what she knew, now when her powers were at their height and her senses sharpest, would be tested as far as they could be tested; and if found wanting, there would at least be no dishonor in the losing.

"Well? Well?" said the Emperor, sitting down heavily.

"No Revelation," she said, and rose. "Not now, if ever."

He started, and his eyebrows shot up.

"My mind is changed," Hawksquill said. "It might be just the thing to be a President for a while."

"But you said . . ."

"As far as I know," Hawksquill said, "that office's powers are legally intact; only disused. Once installed, you could turn them on the Club. They'd be surprised. Throw them . . ."

"Into prison. Have them done secretly to death."

"No; but perhaps into the toils of the Legal System at least; from which, if recent history is any guide, they will not emerge for a long time, and then considerably weakened, and much poorer—nickeled and dimed to death, as we used to say."

He grinned at her from his chair, a long, wolfish, conspirator's grin which almost made her laugh. He crossed his large blunt fingers over his stomach and nodded, pleased. Hawksquill turned to the window, thinking Why him? Why him of all people? And thought: if the mice in a household were suddenly given some vote or say in its management, whom would they elect housekeeper?

"And I suppose," she said, "in many ways, being President of this country, just now, wouldn't be altogether different from being Emperor of your old Empire." She smiled at him over her shoulder, and he looked up at her from under his red brows to see if he were being mocked. "The same splendors, I mean," Hawksquill said mildly, raising her glass to the window light. "The same joys. The same sorrows . . . How long, in any case, did you expect to reign now?"

"Oh, I don't know," he said. He yawned hugely, complacently. "From now on, I suppose. Ever after."

"That's what I thought," Hawksquill said. "In that case, there's no need to be hasty, is there?"

From the east, across the ocean, evening was gathering; a complex, lurid sunset was spilled in the west as from a broken vessel. From this window's height, out of its orgulous expanse of glass, the struggle between them could be observed, a show laid on for the rich and mighty who lived in high places. Ever after . . . It seemed to Hawksquill, watching the battle, that the whole world was just at that moment lapsing into a long dream, or perhaps awaking from one; it was impossible to tell which. But when she turned from the window to remark on this, she saw that the Emperor Frederick Barbarossa was asleep in his chair, snoring softly, his faint breath blowing out the hairs of his red moustache and his face as peaceful as any sleeping child's: as if, Hawksquill thought, he had never really awakened at all.

"Oho," George Mouse said when at last he opened the door of Old Law Farm to find Auberon on the stoop. Auberon had been long pounding and calling (somewhere in his wanderings he had lost all his keys) and now faced George ashamed, the prodigal cousin.

Ever After

"Hi," he said.

"Hey," George said. "Long time no hear from."

"Yeh."

"You had me worried, man. What the hell was that about, running off? Hell of a thing."

"Looking for Sylvie."

"Oh, yeah, hey, you left her brother in the Folding Bedroom. A sweet guy, really. So you find her?"

"No."

"Oh."

They stood facing each other. Auberon, still bemused by his own sudden reappearance in these streets, could not think of a way to ask George to take him back, though it seemed that it was for that that he stood before him. George only smiled and nodded, his black eyes alert to something not present: stoned again, Auberon supposed. Though May was just unfolding in Edgewood, the City's single week of spring had come and passed, and summer was full there already, putting forth its richest odors, like a lover in heat. Auberon had forgotten.

"So," George said.

"So," Auberon said.

"Back in Bigtown, huh?" George said. "Were you thinking . . ."

"Can I come back?" Auberon said. "I'm sorry."

"Hey, no. Swell. Lot's to do just now. The Folding Bedroom's empty . . . How long were you thinking? . . ."

"Oh, I don't know," Auberon said. "From now on, I guess. Ever after."

He was a flung ball, that's all, he saw that clearly now; flung outward from Edgewood at first, leaping high, bounding to the

City, then ricocheting madly within that maze, the walls and objects he struck the determiners of his way, until (not by his choice) he had been flung back Edgewoodwards again to carom there, angles of incidence equaling angles of reflection; and then back again to these streets, to this Farm. And even the most tensile of balls must have a stop, must bounce more lowly, then more lowly, and at last roll only, parting the grass; then, resisted even by the grass, must slow, and with a little rocking motion come to rest.

George seemed then to realize that they stood there in an open door, and, darting his head out for a quick look down the fearful street to see who might be approaching, drew Auberon within and locked the door behind them, as he had once before on a winter night in another world.

Three Lilacs

"You got some mail and stuff," he said as he led Auberon down the hall and down the stairs to the kitchen; and then said something more, about goats and tomatoes, but Auberon heard nothing more because of a sudden roaring of blood in his ears and a fearful thought about a gift, which filled up his head; a roaring and a thought which continued to fill up his head while George aimlessly searched amid the treasures of the kitchen for the letters, stopping to put questions and make remarks. Only when he saw that Auberon neither heard nor answered did he apply himself and come up with two long envelopes, which had been put in a toast-rack along with some ancient dunning letters and souvenir menus.

A glance told Auberon that neither was from Sylvie. His fingers trembled, though pointlessly now, as he opened them. Petty, Smilodon & Ruth were pleased to inform him that Doctor Drinkwater's will had at last been settled. They included an accounting which showed that, less advances and costs, his share of the settlement was $34.17. If he would come in and sign some papers he would receive this amount in full. The other envelope, a heavy wove paper with an expensive-looking logo, yielded up a letter from the producers of "A World Elsewhere." They had gone very carefully over his scripts. The story ideas were terrific and vivid but the dialogue was somewhat unconvincing. Still, if he cared to work over these scripts or try another, they thought a place could be found for him soon among the show's junior writers; they hoped to hear from him, or were anyway hoping last year. Auberon laughed. At least he'd have, perhaps, a job; perhaps he *would* continue Doc's endless chronicle of the Green Meadow and the Wild Wood, though not in the way Doc would have.

"Good news?" George said, making coffee.

"You know," Auberon said, "There's some very strange things going on in the world lately. Very strange."

"Tell me about it," George said, meaning the opposite.

Auberon realized that coming out of his long drunk he was just now noticing things that everyone else had already learned to live with. As though he were suddenly to turn to his fellow man and announce that, hey, the sky is blue, or point out that the aged trees along the street were in leaf. "Were there always big trees along this street?" he asked George.

"That ain't the worst of it," George said. "The roots are breaking up my basements. And just try to get through to the Parks Department. Hopeless." He put coffee before Auberon. "Milk? Sugar?"

"Black."

"Curiouser and curiouser," George said, stirring his coffee with a tiny souvenir coffee-spoon though he had put nothing in it. "Sometimes I think I'll blow this burg. Go back into fireworks. There's going to be big bucks in fireworks now, I bet, with all the celebrations."

"Hm?"

"Eigenblick and all that. Parades, shows. He's very into that stuff. And fireworks."

"Oh." Since his night and morning with Bruno, it had been a policy of Auberon's not to think or ask questions about Russell Eigenblick. Love was strange: it could color whole passages of the world, and ever after they retained the color of love, whether that color was bright or dark. He thought of Latin music, souvenir T-shirts, certain City streets and places, the nightingale. "You were in fireworks?"

"Sure. You didn't know that? Hey. The biggest. Name in the papers, man. It was a lot of laughs."

"It wasn't ever mentioned at home," Auberon said, feeling the familiar exclusion. "Not to me."

"No?" George looked at him strangely. "Well, it all came to a kind of sudden end. Just about the time you were born."

"Oh yeah? How come?"

"Circumstances, man, circumstances." He stared into his coffee, a pensiveness odd for George having fallen on him. Then, seeming to come to a decision, he said, "You know you had a sister, named Lilac."

"Sister?" This was a new idea. "Sister?"

"Well, yeah, sister."

417

"No. Sophie had a baby, named Lilac, that went away. I had an imaginary friend, named Lilac. But no sister." He pondered. "I always kind of thought there were three, though. I don't know why."

"Sophie's baby's the one I'm talking about. I always thought the story up there was . . . Well, never mind."

But Auberon had had enough. "No, uh-uh, wait a minute. No 'never mind.'" George looked up startled and guilty at Auberon's tone. "If there's a story, I want to hear it."

"It's a long one."

"All the better."

George pondered. He got up, put on his old cardigan and sat down again. "Okay. You asked for it." He thought for a time how to begin. Decades of odd drugs made him a vivid but not always a coherent story-teller. "Fireworks. Three Lilacs, did you say?"

"One was imaginary."

"Shit. I wonder what makes the other two. Anyway, there was one in there that was false: like a false nose. I mean exactly like. That's the fireworks story: that one.

"See, a long time ago, one day, Sophie and I . . . Well, it was one winter day when I went up to Edgewood, and she and I . . . But I didn't think anything *came* of it, you know? Sort of a crazy fling. I wrote it off. I mean she had *me* fooled. Meanwhile, I knew there was a thing between her and Smoky." He looked at Auberon. "Common knowledge, right?"

"Wrong."

"You didn't . . . They didn't . . ."

"They never told me anything. I knew there'd been a baby, Lilac, of Sophie's. Then she was gone. That's all I knew."

"Well, listen. As far as I know, Smoky still thinks he's Lilac's father. So, you know, mum is definitely the word on this story. Wazza matter?"

Auberon was laughing. "No, nothing," he said. "Yeah, sure, mum's the word."

"Anyway. This is—what?—twenty-five years ago maybe. I'd gotten heavily into fireworks, because of Act Theory. Remember Act Theory? No? Jesus, things don't last long in that line these days, do they. Act Theory, dig—God, I don't know if I remember now how it worked myself, but it was this idea about how life works—how life is acts, and not thoughts or things: an act is a thought and a thing both at once, only it has this shape, see, so it can be analyzed. Every act, no matter what kind, pick up a cup, or a whole life, or like all of evolution, every act has the same shape; two acts together are another act with the same shape; all life is only one big act, made up of a million smaller ones, follow?"

"Not really."

"Don't matter. It was the reason I got into fireworks though, because a rocket has the same form as an act: initiation, burning, explosion, burning out. Only sometimes that rocket, that act, sets off another initiation, burning, explosion, and so on, get the picture? And so you can set up a display that has the same form as life. Acts, acts, all acts. Shells: inside one shell you can pack a bunch of others, which go off after the big one, packed in like a chicken is packed inside an egg, and inside that chicken more eggs with more chickens, and so on odd infinooty. Gerbs: a gerb has the same form as the feeling of being alive: a bunch of little explosions and burnings going on all the time, burning out, initiating, burning out, that all together make a picture, like thought makes pictures in the middle of the air."

"What's a gerb?"

"A gerb, man. Chinese fire. You know, that makes a picture of two battleships shooting at each other, and that turns into Old Glory."

"Oh, yeah."

"Yeah. Lancework we call those. Just like thinking. A few people got that, too. Some critics." He said nothing for a time, remembering vividly the river barge where he'd set off *The Act Entrained* and other shows. Darkness, and the slap of oily water; the smell of punk. And then the sky filled up with fire, which is like life, which is light that ignites and consumes and goes out and for a moment traces a figure in the air that can't be forgotten but which, in a sense, was never there. And he racing around like a madman, shouting at his assistants, firing shells from the mortar, his hair singed, throat burning, coat motheaten from cinders, while his thought took shape above.

"About Lilac," Auberon said.

"Yeah? Oh, yeah. Well, I'd been working for weeks for a new show. I had some new ideas about garnitures, and it was—well, it was my life, man, night and day. So one night . . ."

"Garnitures?"

"Garnitures are the part of the rocket that goes blooey at the end, like a flower. Y'see, you got your rocket, and here's your case with your composition that burns and gets it aloft; and up here you got your, what you call your cap, and that's where your garniture goes—stars, pinched stars, pumped stars—"

"Okay. Go on."

"So I'm up on the third floor in this workshop I had fitted out up there—top floor, in case anything went, you know, the whole building wouldn't go—it's late, and I hear the bell ring. Bells still worked in those days. So I put down the case and stuff—you can't just walk away from a roomful of fireworks, you know—and all the time the bell's going, and I go down, who is this wise guy leaning on the bell. It was Sophie.

"It was a cold night, raining, I remember, and she had this shawl on, and that face in the shawl. She looked about dead, like she hadn't slept for days. Big eyes like saucers, and tears, or maybe it was the rain on her face. She had this big bundle in her arms in another shawl, and I said what's up and so on, and she said, 'I've brought Lilac,' and she pulled the shawl away from this thing she had."

George shuddered, deeply, the shudder seeming to start at his loins and work upward till it flew off the top of his head, making his hair rise—the shudder of one whose future grave, they say, is somewhere stepped on. "Remember, man, I never *knew* about any of this. I didn't know I was a daddy. I hadn't heard from up that way in a year. And suddenly there's Sophie, standing on the stoop like a bad dream saying Here's your daughter, man, and showing me this baby, if that's what it was.

"Man, this baby was in *trouble.*

"It looked *old.* I guess it was supposed to be about two now, but it looked about forty-five, a little withered bald guy, with this *sly* little face like some middle-aged furrier with troubles." George laughed, a strange laugh. "It was supposed to be a girl, remember. God, it gave me a start. So we're standing there, and the kid *puts out its hand* like this"—palm up, flat—"and checks the rain, and pulls the scarf over its head. Hey. What could I say? The kid made itself clear. I brought them in.

"We came in here. She set the kid up in that high chair. I couldn't look at it, but I like couldn't look away. And Sophie told me the story: her and me, that afternoon, strange as it may seem, she's figured the dates blahblahblah, Lilac is my kid. But—dig this—*not this one.* She's figured it out: the true Lilac got changed, one night, for this one. This one isn't real at all. Not the real Lilac, not even a real baby. I'm stunned. I'm reeling around saying What! What! And all the time"—he started laughing again, helplessly—"this kid is sitting there with this attitude—I can't describe it—this *sneer* on its face like okay, okay, I've heard this tripe a million times—like it was *bored*—and all I could think was that it needed a cigar in its mouth, just to complete the picture.

"Sophie was like in shock. Shivering. Trying to tell me all

this stuff at once. Then she stopped, couldn't go on. It seems the kid
was all right at first, she never knew the difference; she couldn't even
tell what night it was when it happened, 'cause she seemed so normal. And beautiful. Only quiet. Real quiet. Like passive. Then—a
few months before—it started to change. Very slowly. Then faster. It
started to sort of *wither*. But it wasn't sick. Doc checked it at first, all
okay, big appetite, smiling—but getting old, like. Oh God. I put an
afghan around her and started making tea and I'm saying Calm
down! Calm down! And she's telling me how it dawned on her what
must have happened—I just wasn't convinced yet, man, I thought
this kid should see a specialist—and then how she started hiding it
from everybody, and they started asking hey, how's Lilac, how come
we never see her around anymore." Another fit of unwilled laughter.
George was on his feet now, acting out the parts of the story, especially his own bewilderment, and suddenly he turned wide-eyed to
the empty high chair. "Then we look. The kid is gone.

"Not in the chair. Not underfoot.

"The door's open. Sophie's dazed, she lets out a little
cry—Ah!—and looks at me. See, I was its *daddy*. I was supposed to
do something. That's why she'd come and all. God. Just the thought
of this thing running around loose in my house gave me the willies. I
went out in the hall. Nobody. Then I saw it climbing up the stairs.
Stair by stair. It looked—what's the word—purposeful: like it knew
where it was going. So I said, 'Hey, wait a second, buster—' I
couldn't think of it as a girl—and I reached for its arm. It felt weird,
cold and dry, like leather. It looked back at me with this look of
hate—who the fuck are *you*—and it gave a pull away, and I pulled
back, and—" George sat again, overcome. "It tore. I tore a hole in
the god damn thing. Rrrrip. A hole opened up near its shoulder, and
you could look in, like into a doll—empty. I let go *fast*. It didn't seem
to be hurt, it just flapped the arm, like damn now it's busted, and
crawled on; and its blanket was coming off, and I could see there
were some other cracks and splits here and there—at the knees, you
know, and the ankles. This kid was falling apart.

"Okay. Okay. What could I think then? I came back in
here. Sophie's bundled up, with these big eyes. 'You're right,' I said.
'It ain't Lilac. And it ain't mine, either.'

"She broke down. Like dissolved. That was the last straw.
She just melted, man it was the saddest thing I've ever seen—'You've
got to help me, you've got to'—you know. Okay, Okay, I'll help; but
what in hell am I supposed to do? She didn't know. Up to me.
'Where is she?' Sophie asked me.

" 'Went upstairs,' I said. 'Maybe it's cold. There's a fire up there.' And she suddenly gave me this look—horrified, but just too tired to do anything or even really feel anything—I can't describe it. She grabbed my hand and said, 'Don't let her go near the fire, please, please!'

"Now what's *that* about? I said, 'Look, you just sit here and get warm and I'll see.' What the hell I was going to *see* I didn't know. I picked up the baseball bat—be prepared, you know—and I went out, and she was still pleading: 'Don't let her get near the fire.' "

George mimed creeping up the stairs, and entering the second-floor drawing-room. "I go in, and there it was. By the fire. Sitting on the whatchacallit, the hearth there. And I can *not believe* my *eyes:* because as it sits there it's reaching into the fire—yes!—*reaching into the fire* and picking out, you know, *glowing embers:* picking them out, and popping them into its mouth."

He came close to Auberon, this could not be believed unless he gripped Auberon's wrist in pledge of his truthfulness. "And *crunching* them." George made the gesture: like eating a walnut. "Ca-runch. Ca-runch. And smiling at me—smiling. You could see the coals glowing inside its head. Like a jack o'lantern. Then they'd go out, and it'd pick out another. And boy, it was getting a *lot* livelier behind this. Chipper, you know, a little refreshment; it jumps up, does a little dance. Naked now, too. Like a little broken evil plaster cherub. I swear-to-god *nothing:* nothing has ever scared me like that. I was so scared I couldn't think, I just *moved.* You know? Too scared to be scared.

"I went over to the fire. I picked up the shovel. I dug up a whole lotta hot stuff from deep inside the fire. I showed it: mmm mmm good. Follow me, follow me. Okay, it wants to play this game, hot chestnuts, *very* hot chestnuts, come on, *come* on, we went out and up the stairs, it keeps reaching for the shovel; uh-uh, no no, I keep leading it on.

"Now listen, man. I don't know if I was crazy or what. All I knew was that this thing was *evil:* I mean not evil evil, because I don't think it *was* anything, I mean it was like a doll or a puppet or a machine, but moving on its own, like awful things in dreams that you know aren't alive, piles of old clothes or mounds of grease that suddenly get up and start threatening you, okay? Dead, but moving. *Animated.* But evil, I mean an awful evil thing to have in the world. All I could think of was: get rid of it. Lilac or no Lilac. Just. Get. Rid of it.

"So anyway it's following me. And up on the third floor across from the library is my, you know, my studio. Okay? Get the picture? The door is closed, of course; I closed it when I came down, always did, can't be too careful. So I'm fumbling with it, and the thing is looking at me with these eyes that weren't eyes, and oh shit any minute now it's going to figure out the scam. I shove the shovel under it's nose. The damn door won't open, won't open, then it does—*and*—"

With a mighty imaginary gesture, George heaved the shovelful of live coals into the studio filled with charged fireworks. Auberon held his breath.

"And then for the *kid*—"

With a swift, careful kick, side of the foot, George propelled the false Lilac into the studio also.

"And then the *door!*" He flung shut the door, staring at Auberon with the same wild horror and hurry that must have been in his eyes that night. "So done! Done! I flew down the stairs. 'Sophie! Sophie! Run!' She's still sitting in that chair—right there—paralyzed. So I picked her up—not exactly carried her, but like a bum's rush, because I can already hear the noises upstairs—and get her out into the hall. Bang! Blooey! Out the front door.

"And we stood out there in the rain, man, just looking up. Or anyway I looked up, she just sort of hid her head. And out the studio windows comes my whole show. Stars. Rockets. Magnesium, phosphorus, sulfur. Light for days. Noise. Stuff is falling all around us, hissing in the puddles. Then blowey! Some big cache goes up, and puts a hole right through the roof. Smoke and stars, boy we lit up the neighborhood. But the rain had got a lot worse; and pretty soon it was out, about the time the cops and the fire-trucks got there.

"Well, I had the studio pretty well reinforced, you know, steel door and asbestos and stuff, so the building didn't go. But by God if there was anything left of that kid, or whatever it was . . ."

"And Sophie?" Auberon said.

"Sophie," George said. "I told her: 'Listen, it's all right. I got it.'

" 'What?' she says. 'What?'

" 'I got it,' I said. 'I blew it up,' I said. 'Nothing left of it.'

"And hey: do you know what she said to me?"

Auberon could not say.

"She looked up at me—and man I don't think anything I saw that night was as bad as her face just then—and she said: 'You killed her.'

"That's what she said. 'You killed her.' That's all."

George sat down, weary, depleted, at the kitchen table. "Killed her," he said. "That's what Sophie thought, that I'd killed her only child. Maybe that's what she still thinks, I don't know. That old George killed her only child, and his too. Blew her up, in stars and stripes forever." He looked down. "Man, I don't want to see somebody look at me the way she did that night, not ever again."

"What a story," Auberon said, when he could find his voice again.

"See, *if*," George said. "If it *was* Lilac, but just transformed in some weird way . . ."

"But she knew," Auberon said. "She knew it wasn't really Lilac."

"Did she?" George said. "Who knows what the hell she knew." A dark silence rose. "Women. How do you figure 'em."

"But," Auberon said, "what I don't understand is, why they would have brought her that thing in the first place. I mean if it was such a fake."

George eyed him suspiciously. "What 'they' is this?" he asked.

Auberon looked away from his cousin's inquiry. "Well, they," he said, surprised and oddly embarrassed that this explanation was coming out of his mouth. "The ones who stole the real one."

"Hm," George said.

Auberon said nothing further, having nothing further to say on that head, and seeing quite plainly and for the first time in his life just why silence had been kept so well among those whom he had used to spy on. Having them for explanation felt in fact like having none at all, and he found himself now, willy-nilly, sworn to the same silence; and yet he thought he would not ever again be able to explain a single thing in the world without recourse to that collective pronoun: they. Them.

"Well, anyway," he said at last. "That accounts for two."

George raised his eyebrow in question.

"Two Lilacs," Auberon said. He counted them off: "Of the three I thought there were, one was imaginary, mine, and I know where she is." In fact he felt her, deep within, take notice of his mention of her. "One was false. That's the one you blew up."

"But if," George said, "if that *was* the real one, only Somehow changed . . . Naaah."

"No," said Auberon. "That's the one that's left, the one that's unaccounted for: the true one." He looked out the casement at the gloaming which was stealing now over Old Law Farm as well as over the high towers of the City. "I wonder," he said.

"I wonder . . ." George said. "I'd give a lot to know."

"Where," Auberon said. "Where, where."

Far, far, and dreaming: turning in her sleep, restless, and thinking of waking, though she would not wake yet for many a year; an itch in her nose, and a yawn in her throat. She even blinked, but saw nothing through sleeping eyes but dream: a dream, amid the spring she slept in, of autumn: of the gray vale where, on the day of her tour, the stork that bore her and Mrs. Underhill had at last put its feet on *terra firma* or something like it, and how Mrs. Underhill had sighed and dismounted, and how she, Lilac, had reached out to put her arms around Mrs. Underhill's neck and be helped down. . . . She yawned; having learned how to do it, she was now apparently unable to stop, and couldn't decide whether she liked the sensation or not.

Thinking of Waking

"Sleepy," Mrs. Underhill said.

"Where is this?" Lilac said when she had been set on her feet.

"Oh, a place," Mrs. Underhill said softly. "Come along."

A broken arch, roughly carved, or finely carved and roughly weathered, stood before them; no walls extended from it, it stood alone astride the leaf-littered path showing the only way into the sere November wood beyond. Lilac, apprehensive yet resigned now, put her young small hand in Mrs. Underhill's old huge one, and like any granny and child in a chill park from which summer and fun have fled, they went on to the gate; the stork stood alone on one red leg, preening her rumpled and disordered feathers.

They passed under the arch. Old birds' nests and moss filled its coffers and reliefs. The carving was obscure, creatures inchoate or returning to chaos. Lilac passed her hand over it as they passed: the stuff it was made of was not stone. Glass? Lilac wondered. Bone?

"Horn," said Mrs. Underhill. She took off one of her many cloaks, and dressed Lilac's nakedness in it. Lilac kicked the brown leaves of the vale, thinking it might be nice to lie down in them, for a long time.

"Well, a long day," said Mrs. Underhill, as though sensing this thought.

"It went too fast," Lilac said.

Mrs. Underhill put her arm around Lilac's shoulder. Lilac stumbled against her, her feet seeming to have lost contact with her will. She yawned again. "Aw," said Mrs. Underhill tenderly, and she picked up Lilac with a single swift motion of her strong arms. She drew the cloak more tightly around her as Lilac nestled against her.

425

"And was it fun?" she asked.

"It was fun," Lilac said.

They had stopped before a great oak at whose foot a whole summer's worth of leaves was piled. From a hollow in it an owl, just awakened, boomed softly to itself. Mrs. Underhill bent to lay her burden in the rustling leaves.

"Dream of it," she said.

Lilac said something that made no sense, about clouds and houses, and then no more, for she was asleep. Asleep, never having noticed the moment when she began, dreaming of it already as she would go on dreaming of it from now on; dreaming of all that she had seen, and all that would come of it; dreaming of the spring when she would dream of the autumn when she fell asleep, and dreaming of the winter when she would wake; in the involution of her dream, turning and altering those things she dreamed even as she dreamed them and as elsewhere they came to pass. She drew up, though unaware she did so, her knees; she drew her hands close to her chin, which drew down, till she took the same S-shape she had taken when she had lived within Sophie. Lilac was asleep.

Mrs. Underhill tucked the cloak once more carefully around her, and then straightened up. With both hands she pressed the small of her back and bent backwards, as weary as she had ever been. She pointed to the owl, whose soft-blooming eyes were looking out from its house, and said, "You. Take care, watch well," which those eyes could do as well as any pair she knew. She looked upward. Twilight, even the endless twilight of this November day, had nearly ended, and she with all her tasks left undone: the last of the year still unburied, and the rains that were to bury it (and a million insect larvae, a million bulbs and seeds) yet unpoured; the floor of heaven unswept of dirty cloud and its winter lamps still to be lit. Brother North-wind, she was sure, champed at his bit to be unleashed. It was a wonder, she thought, that day followed night, that the very earth turned at all, she had given it so little thought of late. She sighed, turned away, and (growing huger and older and more puissant than Lilac had ever supposed, or could imagine or even dream her to be) she expanded upward and outward toward these tasks without a backward look at her adopted grand-daughter asleep among the leaves.

Book Six

THE FAIRIES' PARLIAMENT

High on the hilltop
  The old King sits;
He is now so old and gray
  He's nigh lost his wits.

—Allingham, The Fairies

The first years after what Russell Eigenblick thought of as his accession were the hardest anyone then alive would live to see—so it would seem to them, looking back. Sudden snowstorms raged on the November day when against token opposition he was elected President, and seemed scarcely to abate thereafter. It could not have been always winter in those years, summer must have come around duly as ever, yet universally people remembered winters: the longest, coldest, deepest winters ever known; one continuous winter. Every hardship the Tyrant regretfully imposed or his opponents wilfully inflicted in their uprisings against him was made worse by winter, by months of frozen mud and sleety rain that continually mired every enterprise. Winter made ghastly and hopeless the movements of trucks, traffic, brown-clad troops; everywhere, deeply marking the memory, were the huddled clots and queues of refugees, rag-bound against the cold; the stalled trains, grounded planes; the new frontiers at which lines of slush-bound cars, tailpipes breathing cold clouds, waited to be examined by muffled guards; the shortages of everything, the awful struggle, the difficulties and uncertainties made more awful by the isolating endless cold. And the blood of martyrs and reactionaries frozen on the dirty snow of city squares.

At Edgewood, the old house submitted to indignities: antique plumbing froze; a whole floor was closed up, cold dust collecting in its disused rooms; glum black stoves were set to squat in front of marble fireplaces; and, worst, sheets of plastic for the first time were stapled up over dozens of windows, making every day a foggy day. One night, Smoky, hearing noises in the wilderness of the kitchen-garden, went out and surprised with his flashlight a starveling, an animal long, gray, red-eyed and slavering, mad with cold and hunger. A stray dog, the others said, or something; but only Smoky had seen it, and Smoky wondered.

Winters

There was a pan of water on the stove which sat in the old music room, to help keep the plaster of the ceiling from cracking further from the dryness. A big wooden box roughly carpentered by Smoky held logs to feed the stove, and the two together, stove and woodbox, gave a Klondike air to the pretty room. Rudy Flood had cut the logs, and been felled himself doing so; had pitched face forward, chain saw still gripped in his hands, dead before he struck the ground, which (so Robin said, who was much changed by witnessing it) shook when he met it. Sophie, whenever she rose from her place at the drum-table to feed the insatiable Moloch, had an unpleasant or at least odd sensation that it was pieces of Rudy and not of his woodlot that she thrust into its maw.

Fifty-Two

Work consumed men. It hadn't been so in Sophie's youth. Not only Robin, but Sonny Noon and many others who in the old expansive days might have given up the farms their parents had worked, now drew in, thinking that if they had not these acres, and this labor, they'd have nothing. Rudy had after all been an exception; the older generation's experience had mostly been with endless possibility, sudden change for the better, vistas of freedom and ease. The younger saw things differently. Their motto was, perforce had to be, the old one about Use it up, wear it out and so on. That applied all around: doing his part, Smoky had decided that rents would be reduced or in abeyance indefinitely. And the house showed it: it was, or seemed to be, wearing out. Sophie, pulling her thick shawl more closely around her, looked up at the skeleton's hand and arm drawn in cracks across the ceiling, and then returned to her cards.

Being used up, worn out, and not replaced. Could that be it? She looked at the fall she had made.

Nora Cloud had left Sophie not only her cards, but her sense that every fall made with them was Somehow contiguous with every other, that they made only one geography, or told only one story, though it could be read or viewed differently to different purposes, which made it seem discontinuous. Sophie, taking up Cloud's view at the point where she had left it, had taken it further: if it were all one thing, then one question continually proposed to it should come eventually to have a whole answer, however lengthy and encyclopaedic; should come to have the whole thing for an answer. If only she could concentrate hard enough, continue to formulate the question properly and with the right variations and qualifications, and not be distracted by the shadow answers to unasked small questions which lurked within the falls—yes, Smoky's angina will worsen, Lily's baby will be a boy—then perhaps she could reach it.

The question she had was not exactly the one that Ariel Hawksquill had come to have answered, though that lady's sudden appearance and importunity had jolted Sophie into beginning to try and ask it. Hawksquill had had no trouble locating in the cards the huge events that had lately been taking place in the world, and the reasons for them, and her own part in them too, cutting them from the trivia and puzzlements like a surgeon finding and excising a tumor. Sophie's difficulty in doing such a thing had been that, ever since her search for Lilac, question and answer with these cards had seemed to her to be one; all answers seemed to her to be only questions about the question, every question only a form of the answer it sought. Hawksquill's long training had allowed her to overcome this difficulty, and any Gypsy fortune-teller could have explained to Sophie how to ignore it or evade it: but perhaps if one had, Sophie wouldn't have struggled so with the question, through years, through long winters, and would not now be as close as she felt herself to be to a sort of great dictionary or guidebook or almanac of answers to her (strictly speaking unaskable) single question.

Being used up, one by one, and not being replaced; dying, in fact, though they couldn't die, or anyway Sophie had always supposed they couldn't, she didn't know why. . . . Could it be so? Or was it just a winter thought in a time of hardship and shortage?

Cloud had said: it only seems as though the world is getting old and worn out, just as you are yourself. Its life is far too long for you to feel it age during your own. What you learn as you get older is that the world *is* old, and has been old for a long time.

Well: all right. But what Sophie felt to be aging wasn't a world, but only its inhabitants: if there were such a thing as a world which they inhabited, distinct from them, which Sophie couldn't imagine really—but anyway, suppose there was such a world, old or young didn't matter, what Sophie knew for sure was that however densely populated those lands may have been in Dr. Bramble's time or in Paracelsus's, they weren't populated at all any longer in any large sense, Sophie thought it would be possible eventually—soon!—if not to name at least to number all of them, and that the total number wouldn't be a large one; two digits only, possibly, probably. Which (since everyone without exception quoted in the *Architecture*, and everyone else for that matter who had considered the question at all, supposed there to be uncounted milliards of them, one for every harebell and thorn-bush at least) might mean that Somehow lately they were being one by one consumed, like the split muscled logs Sophie fed into the fire, or worn down to ravelings by grief and care and age, and blown away.

Or reduced by war. War was what Ariel Hawksquill had determined to be the relation at work, the thing that had made the world or this Tale (if there was a difference) turn so sad and puzzling and uncertain. Like all wars, an unchosen thing, however inevitable, with awful losses on their side at least, Sophie couldn't imagine what losses they might themselves have inflicted, or how . . . War: could it be then that all that remained of them was one last forlorn hope, a brave band caught in a desperate rearguard action and going down to the last man?

No! It was too awful to think of: dying. Dying out. Sophie knew (none better) that they had not ever thought of her with love, didn't in any human sense care about her at all, or any being like her. They had stolen Lilac from her, and though that had not been for any intention of hurting Sophie, it hadn't been for any love they bore Lilac either, presumably, but only for reasons of their own. No, Sophie had no reason to love them; but the thought of their passing away utterly was unbearable: like thinking of a winter with no end.

And yet she thought she could soon count out the few remaining.

She assembled her deck, and spread it all in a fan before her; then she drew out court cards one by one to represent the ones she already knew of, laying them in groups with low cards for their courts or children or agents, insofar as she could guess at them.

One for sleep, and four for seasons; three to tell fates, two to be Prince and Princess; one to go messages, no, two to go messages, one to go and one to come back again . . . It was a matter of discriminating between functions, and learning which were whose, and how many were needed for it. One to bring gifts; three to bear gifts away. Queen of Swords and King of Swords and Knight of Swords; Queen of Coins and King of Coins and ten low cards for their children . . .

Fifty-two?

Or was it only that at that number (with only the Least Trumps, the plot which they acted out, left uncounted) her deck ran out?

There was a sudden clanging noise above her head, and Sophie ducked; it sounded as though a full and heavy set of fire-irons had tumbled over in the attic. Smoky, at work in the orrery. She glanced up. The crack in the ceiling seemed to have lengthened, but she doubted that it really had.

Three for labor, two to make music, one to dream dreams . . .

She thrust her hands into her sleeves. Few, anyway; not hosts. The taut plastic over the window was a drumskin, tapped on by wind. It seemed—it was hard to tell—that it had begun to snow again. Sophie, abandoning the count (she still didn't know enough; it was wrong, and more than wrong on an afternoon like this, to speculate when you knew so little) gathered up the cards and put them away in their bag in their box.

She sat for a while, listening to the taps of Smoky's hammer, hesitant at first, then more insistent, then ringing as though he struck a gong. Then they fell silent, and the afternoon returned.

"Summer," Mrs. MacReynolds said, lifting her head slightly from the pillow, "is a myth."

The nieces and nephews and children around her looked at each other in thoughtful doubt or doubtful thought.

Carrying a Torch

"In winter," the dying old woman went on, "summer is a myth; a report, a rumor, not to be believed. . . ."

The others drew closer to her, watching her fine face, her fluttering blue lids. Her head lay so lightly on its pillow that her blue-rinsed coiffure was unmussed, but this was for sure her last gasp; her contract had run out, and would not be renewed.

"Never," she said, and then paused a long time in limbo while Auberon thought further: never forget me? Never break faith, never say die, never never never? "Never *long,*" she said. "Only wait; only have patience. Longing is fatal. It will come." They had begun to weep around her, though they hid it, for the old lady would have been impatient with tears. "Be happy," she said, even more faintly. "For the things . . ." Yes. There she goes. Bye, Mrs. MacR. "The things, children—the things that make us happy—make us wise."

One last look around. Lock glances with Frankie MacR., the black sheep: he won't forget this, a new leaf turns for him. Music up. And dead. Auberon skipped two spaces and made three memorial asterisks across the page, and drew it out.

"Okay," he said.

"Okay?" said Fred Savage. "Done?"

"Done," Auberon said. He shuffled the twenty or so pages together, his hands clumsy in gloves from which the ends of the fingers had been cut off, and jammed them in an envelope. "G'ahead."

Fred took the envelope, thrust it smartly beneath his arm, and with a mocking suggestion of salute, made to leave the Folding Bedroom. " 'M I spose to wait?" he asked, hand on the door. "While they reads over this?"

"Ah, don't bother," Auberon said. "It's too late now. They'll have to just do it."

"Oookay," Fred said. "Later, m'man."

Auberon built up the fire, pleased with himself. Mrs. MacReynolds was among the last of the characters whom he had inherited from the creators of "A World Elsewhere." A young divorcée thirty years ago, she had tenaciously and cleverly held on to her part, through alcoholism, remarriage, religious conversion, grief, age and illness. Done now though. Contract terminated. Frankie was about to go off on a long trip, too; he would return—his contract had years to run, and he was the producer's boyfriend as well—but he would return a changed man.

A missionary? well, yes, in a sense; perhaps a missionary . . .

More ought to happen, Sylvie had said once on a certain day to Fred Savage; and in the long interpenetration of Auberon's vision of "A World Elsewhere" and the show as he had found it, a lot had. He couldn't believe it at first to be so, but it seemed that the turgid, long-drawn-out pointlessness of its plot had been due simply to a lack of inventiveness on the writers' parts. Auberon, in the beginning anyway, suffered from no such lack, and besides, there were all those tedious and unlikable people who had to be disposed of, whose passions and jealousies Auberon had a hard time understanding. The death rate had therefore been high for a while; the shriek of tires on rainy roads, the horrid crunch of steel on steel, the shout of sirens had been nearly continuous. One young woman, a drug-addicted Lesbian with an idiot child, he could not contractually eliminate; so he magicked her away in favor of her identical twin sister, long-lost and a very different character. That had taken a few weeks to accomplish.

The producers blanched at the speed with which crises came and passed in those days; the audience, they said, couldn't bear such storms, they were used to tedium. But the audience seemed to disagree, and while eventually it came to be a somewhat different audience, it was no smaller, or not measurably so, and more fiercely devoted than ever. Besides, there were few enough writers who could produce the amounts of work Auberon could, at the new and sharply reduced salaries being offered, and so the producers, struggling for the first time in their profession with tight budgets, flirting with bankruptcy, counting assets and debits late into the night, gave Auberon his head.

So the actors spoke the lines which Fred Savage carried to them from Old Law Farm every day, meekly trying to infuse some reality and humanity into the strange hopes, intimations of high events, and secret expectancy (calm, sad, impatient, or resolved) which had come to infect characters they had played for years. There were not the many secure berths for actors that there had been in the days of the old affluence, and for every character released from the box of Auberon's foreknowledge there were scores of applicants, even at fees that would have been scoffed at in the now-lost Golden Age. They were grateful to be embodying these peculiar lives, working toward or away from whatever huge thing it was which seemed always in preparation, yet never revealed, and which had kept their audience on gentle tenterhooks now for years.

Auberon laughed, staring into the fire and already formulating new gins and defeats, embroglios and breakthroughs. What a form! Why hadn't anyone before caught the secret of it? A simple plot was required, a single enterprise which concerned all the characters deeply, and which had a grand sweet simple single resolution: a resolution, however, that would never be reached. Always approached, keeping hopes high, making disappointments bitter, shaping lives and loves by its inexorable slow progress toward the present: but never, never reached.

In the good old days, when polls were as common as house-to-house searches were now, pollsters asked viewers why they liked the bizarre torments of the soap operas, what kept them watching. The commonest answer was that they liked soap operas because soap operas were like life.

Like life. Auberon thought "A World Elsewhere," under his hands, was coming to be like a lot of things: like truth, like dreams; like childhood, his own anyway; like a deck of cards or an old album of pictures. He didn't think it was like life—not anyway like his own. On "A World Elsewhere," when a character's greatest hopes were dashed, or his task all accomplished, or his children or friends saved by his sacrifice, he was free to die or at least to pass away; or he changed utterly, and reappeared with a new task, new

435

troubles, new children. Except for those whose embodying actors were on vacation or ill, none simply came to a stop, all their important actions over, haunting the edges of the plot with their final scripts (so to speak) still in their hands.

That was like life, though: like Auberon's.

Not like a plot, but like a fable, a story with a point, which had already been made. The fable was Sylvie; Sylvie was the sharply-pointed, unenigmatic yet brimful and undepletable allegory or tale that underlay his life. Sometimes he was conscious that this view robbed Sylvie of the intense and irreducible reality which she had had, and no doubt somewhere went on having, and when he saw that he felt a sudden shame and horror, as though he had been told or had told a shocking and defaming lie about her; but those times grew less frequent as the story, the fable, grew more perfect, took on other and more intricately refracting facets even as it grew shorter and more tellable; underlying, explaining, criticizing and defining his life even as it grew less something that had actually happened to him.

"Carrying a torch," George Mouse called it, and Auberon, who had never heard the old phrase, thought it just, because he thought of the torch he carried not as a penitential or devotional one, but as Sylvie. He carried a torch: her. She flared brightly sometimes, sank low other times; he saw by her, though he had no path in particular he wanted to see. He lived in the Folding Bedroom, he helped out on the Farm; one year was not different from the next. Like a long-time cripple, he put aside the better part of the world, not always aware he did so, as not being for the use of such as he: he was not any longer someone to whom things happened.

He suffered from some odd disorders, living as he did in his most vigorous years. He couldn't sleep much beyond dawn on any but the deepest of winter mornings. He grew able to see faces in the chance arrangements of his room's fixtures and furnishings, or rather unable not to see them: faces wicked, wise or foolish, figures gesturing to him, weirdly distorted or wounded, able to express emotions that affected him without themselves having them, animated without being alive, which he found faintly disgusting. He pitied, against his will, the ceiling light fixture, two blank Phillips-head screws the eyes, and a light bulb stuck in its stupid, gaping ceramic mouth. The flowered curtains were a crowd, a congress, or rather two: the flower people, and the people made of background, outlined by flowers, peering through flowers. When the whole room had become unrelievably populated, he actually visited a psychiatrist, though he told no one about it. The man said he suffered from man-in-the-moon syndrome, not uncommon, and suggested that he get out more; a cure, though, he said, would take years.

Years.

Get out more: George, a constant and a choosy philanderer, not much less successful now than he had been in youth, introduced him to many women, and the Seventh Saint provided others. But talk about ghosts. Now and then two of these real women rolled into one (when on occasion he could persuade them to be so rolled) gave him a rude bliss, if he concentrated, that was intense. But his imaginings, working on the sturdy though desperately fine stuff of memory, were of a different order of intensity altogether.

He would not have had it so; he honestly believed that. He even knew, in moments of great clarity, that it would not have been so had he not been who he was, that his disability didn't lie in what had happened to him at all, but in his flawed nature, that not everyone, perhaps no one but he, would have ended up thus becalmed after being touched only by Sylvie as though in passing— what a stupid and antique disease that was, and one that had been all but eliminated from the modern world, he resented deeply at times that he should be, apparently, the last victim of it and thus excluded, as though by some rule of common hygiene, from the broad banquet that the City, even in decline, could still show. He wished, he wished he could do as Sylvie had done: say Fuck destiny, and escape. And so he could, too, he just wasn't trying very hard; he knew that, too, but there it was: flawed. And it was no comfort to think that perhaps to have such a flaw, to be thus inadequate to the world, was just what it was to be in the Tale he could no longer deny that he was in: that perhaps the Tale *was* the flaw, that the flaw and the Tale were the same thing; that being in the Tale meant nothing more than being suited to your role in it and good for nothing else, like having a cast in your eye, by which you saw always something elsewhere, but which to everyone else (even most of the time to yourself) seemed only a disfigurement.

He rose, annoyed with his thoughts for having fallen into that old bag. There was work to do; that should be enough; most of the time it was, and he was grateful. The amount he accomplished, and the pittance he was paid, would have astonished the mild and affable man (dead now of an accidental overdose) to whom Auberon had first shown scripts. Life had been easy then. . . . He poured himself a small whiskey (gin was *verboten*, but his adventure had left him with a persistent small habit, more like a sweet tooth than an addiction) and addressed himself to the mail which Fred had brought from uptown. Fred, his old guide, was his associate now, and so described

437

to Auberon's employers. He was farmhand as well, and *memento mori* or at least an object-lesson of some kind for Auberon; he could not now any longer get along without him, or so it seemed to him. He tore open an envelope.

"Tell Frankie he's going to break his mother's HEART carrying on like that. Doesn't he see that, how can he be so BLIND. Why doesn't he get a good woman and settle down." Auberon never got used to the suspension of disbelief his viewers were capable of, it always gave him a guilty thrill. Sometimes he felt the MacReynolds's *were* real, and it was the viewers, like this lady, who were imaginary; pale fictions hungering after the flesh-and-blood life Auberon created. He tossed the letter into the woodbox. Settle down, huh; a good woman. Not a chance. Lot of blood under the bridge before Frankie settles down.

He saved for the last a letter from Edgewood, some weeks in transit, a good long one from his mother, and settled to it like a squirrel to a large nut, hoping to find something within he could use for next month's episodes.

Something He Could Steal

"You asked what happened to the Mr. Cloud that Great-aunt Cloud was married to," she wrote. "Well, that's really sort of a sad story. It happened a long time before I was born. Momdy sort of remembers. His name was Harvey Cloud. His father was Henry Cloud, the inventor and astronomer. Henry used to spend his summers up here, he had that pretty little cottage where the Junipers later lived. I think he had a lot of patents he lived on. Old John had put some money into his inventions—engines, I think, or astronomical things, I guess; I don't know what. One of his things though was the old orrery at the top of the house—you know. That was an invention of Henry's—I mean not orreries in general, they were invented by a Lord Orrery believe it or not (Smoky told me that). But Henry died before it was finished (it cost a lot of money I think) and about that time Nora, Great-aunt Cloud, married Harvey. Harvey was working on it too. His father's son. I saw a picture of him once that Auberon took, in his shirtsleeves and a stiff collar and tie (I guess he wore them even when he was working), looking very fierce and thoughtful, standing next to the engine of the orrery before they installed it. It was HUGE and complicated and took up most of the picture. And then when they were done installing it (John was long dead by then) there was an accident, and poor Harvey fell off the very tip-top of the house and was killed. I guess then everybody forgot about the orrery, or didn't want to think about it. I know Cloud never talked about it. You used to hide out up there, I remember. Now, you know, Smoky's up there all the time, trying to see if it will ever run, and studying books on machinery and clockwork—I don't know how he's doing.

"So he used to just live here, Harvey I mean, with Nora, in her room; and go up and work on the orrery; and then he fell off. So there you are.

"Sophie says to tell you to be careful of your throat because of bronchitis, in March.

"Lucy's baby's going to be a boy.

"Isn't the winter dragging on!

"Your loving mother."

Well. Still further dark or at least odd corners in his family's life he hadn't known about. He remembered saying once to Sylvie that nothing terrible had ever happened in his family. That was before he had learned much about the true and false Lilacs, of course; and here now was poor Harvey Cloud, a young husband, tumbling off the roof at the moment of his greatest triumph.

He could work that in. There was nothing, he had begun to think, that he couldn't work in. He had a gift for such work: a real gift. Everybody said so.

But meanwhile, his scene switched back to the City. This was the easy part, a rest from the other, more complex scenes; it was all simple in the City—predation, chase, escape, triumph and defeat; the weak to the wall, and only the strong survive. He chose, from a long row of them which had replaced George's anonymous paperbacks on the shelf, one of Doc's old books. He had sent to Edgewood for them when he had become a writer, and they had proved very useful, as he had thought they might. The one he had was one of the Gray Wolf's adventures; and, sipping his whiskey, he began to thumb through it, looking for some material he could steal.

The moon was silver. The sun was gold, or at least gold-plated. Mercury was a mirrored globe—mirrored with mercury, of course. Saturn was heavy enough to be lead. Smoky remembered something from the *Architecture* that associated various metals with various planets; but those weren't these planets, they were the dream-planets of magic and astrology. The orrery, brass-bound and oak-cased, was one of those turn-of-the-century scientific instruments that couldn't have been more solidly rational, material, engineered: a patented universe, made of rods and balls, meshing gears and electroplated springs.

Escapements

439

Then why couldn't Smoky understand it?

He stared hard again at the mechanism, a sort of detached escapement, which he was about to disassemble. If he disassembled it before he understood its function, though, he doubted whether he could put it back together. On the floor, on tables in the hall below, there were several such, all cleaned and wrapped in oily rags, and wrapped too in mystery; this escapement was the last. He supposed (not for the first time) that he should never have begun this. He looked again at the diagram in the Cyclopedia of Mechanics which most resembled the dusty, rusted thing before him.

"Let E be a four-leaved scape-wheel, the teeth of which as they come around rest against the bent pall GFL at G. The pall is prevented from flying too far back by a pin H and kept up to position by a very delicate spring K." God it was cold in here. Very delicate spring: this thing? Why did it seem to be in here backwards? "The pall B engages the arm FL, liberating the scape-wheel, a tooth of which, M . . . ." Oh dear. As soon as the letters got past the middle of the alphabet, Smoky began to feel helpless and bound, as though tangled in a net. He picked up a pliers, and put it down again.

The ingenuity of engineers was appalling. Smoky had come to understand the basic principle of clockwork, upon which all those ingenuities were based: that a motive force—a falling weight, a wound spring—was prevented by an escapement from expending all its energy at once, and made to pay it out in ticks and tocks, which moved hands or planets around evenly until the force was all expended. Then you wound it up. All the foliots, verges, pallets, stackfreeds and going-barrels were only ingenuities, to keep the motion regular. The difficulty, the maddening difficulty, about Edgewood's orrery was that Smoky couldn't discover a motive force that made it go around—or rather he had discovered where it was, in that huge circular case, as black and thick as an old-time safe, and he had examined it, but still couldn't conceive how it was supposed to drive anything; it looked like something meant itself to be driven.

There was just no end to it. He sat back on his heels and clutched his knees. He was eye-level now to the plane of the solar system, looking at the sun from the position of a man on Saturn. No end to it: the thought stirred in him a mixture of itchy resentment and pure deep pleasure he had never felt before, except faintly, when as a boy he had been presented with the Latin language. The task of that language, when he had begun to grasp its immensity, had seemed likely to fill up his life and all the blank interstices of his anonymity; he had felt at once invaded and comforted. Well, he had

440

abandoned it somewhere along in the middle of it, after having mostly licked off its magic, like icing; but now his old age would have this task: and it was a language too.

The screws, the balls, the rods, the springs were a syntax, not a picture. The orrery didn't model the Solar System in any visual or spatial way, if it had the pretty green-and-blue enameled Earth would have been a crumb and the whole machine would have needed to be ten times the size it was at least. No, what was expressed here, as by the inflections and predicates of a tongue, was *a set of relations:* and while the dimensions were fictional, the relations obtained all through, very neatly: for the language was number, and it meshed here as it did in the heavens: exactly as.

It had taken him a long time to figure that out, being unmathematical as well as unmechanical, but he had its vocabulary now, and its grammar was coming clear to him. And he thought that, not soon perhaps but eventually, he would be able to read its huge brass and glass sentences with some comprehension, and that they would not be as Caesar's and Cicero's had turned out to be, mostly dull, hollow and without mystery, but that something would be revealed equal to the terrific encoding it had received, something he very much needed to know.

There were quick footsteps on the stairs outside the orrery door, and his grandson Bud put his red head in. "Grampa," he said, looking over the mystery there, "Gramma sent you a sandwich."

"Oh, great," Smoky said. "Come on in."

He entered slowly, with the sandwich and a mug of tea, his eyes on the machine, better and more splendid than any Christmas-window train set. "Is it done?" he asked.

"No," Smoky said, eating.

"When will it be?" He touched one sphere, and then quickly drew his hand away when, with the smooth ease of heavy counterweighting, it moved.

"Oh," Smoky said, "about the time the world ends."

Bud looked at him in awe, and then laughed. "Aw come on."

"Well, I don't know," Smoky said. "Because I don't know yet what makes it go around."

"That thing," Bud said, pointing to the black case like a safe.

"Okay," Smoky said, and went to it, cup in hand, "but then the question is what makes *this* go around?"

He pushed up the lever that opened the gasketed door

(dust-proof, but why?) and swung the case open. Inside, cleaned and oiled and ready to go if it could, which it couldn't, was the impossible heart of Harvey Cloud's machine: the impossible heart, so Smoky sometimes thought, of Edgewood itself.

"A wheel," Bud said. "A bent wheel. Wow."

"I think," Smoky said, "it's supposed to go by electricity. Down under the floor, if you lift up that door, there's a big old electric motor. Only—"

"What?"

"Well, it's backwards. It's in there backwards, and not by mistake."

Bud looked over the arrangement, thinking hard. "Well," he said, "maybe this makes this go around, and this makes this go around, and this makes that go around."

"A good theory," Smoky said, "only you've just come full circle. Everything's making everything else go around. Taking in each other's washing."

"Well," Bud said. "If it went fast enough. If it was smooth enough."

Fast, and smooth, and heavy it certainly was. Smoky studied it, his mind crossing in paradox. If this made that go around, as it was obviously meant to do; and that made this go around, which wasn't unreasonable; and this and that powered that and this. . . . Almost he saw it, jointed and levered, its sentences reading backwards and forwards at once, and couldn't just for a moment think why it was impossible, except that the world is as it is and not different. . . .

"And if it ever slowed down," Bud said, "you could come up once in a while and give it a push."

Smoky laughed. "Should we make that your job?" he asked.

"Yours," Bud said.

A push, Smoky thought, one constant small push from somewhere; but whosoever that push was, it couldn't be Smoky's, he had nothing like the strength, he would Somehow have to inveigle the whole universe to look away for a moment from the endless task of itself and reach out an enormous finger to touch these wheels and gears. And Smoky had no reason to think that such a special mercy would be his, or Harvey Cloud's, or even Edgewood's.

He said, "Well, anyway. Back to work." He pushed gently on the leaden sphere of Saturn, and it moved, ticking a few degrees, and as it moved all the other parts, wheels, gears, rods, spheres, moved too.

"But perhaps," Ariel Hawksquill said, "perhaps there's no war on at all."

"What do you mean?" asked the Emperor Frederick Barbarossa, after a moment's startled thought.

Caravans

"I mean," Hawksquill said, "that perhaps what we think of as a war is in fact not one. I mean that perhaps there is no war on at all, after all; and perhaps there never was one."

"Don't be absurd," the President said. "Of course there's a war on. We're winning."

The Emperor sat sunk in a broad armchair, chin resting on his breast. Hawksquill was at the grand piano which took up much of the far end of the room. She had had this piano altered to make quarter-tones, and on it she liked to play plangent old hymn-tunes harmonized according to a system of her own devising, rendered oddly, sweetly discordant by the altered piano. They made the Tyrant sad. Outside, snow was falling.

"I don't mean," Hawksquill said, "that you have no enemies. Of course you have. I was speaking of the other, the long war: the Great War. Perhaps that's not a war at all."

The Noisy Bridge Rod and Gun Club, though exposed (their drawn cold faces and dark overcoats appearing in every newspaper) had not fallen easily, as Hawksquill had known they would not. Their resources were great; for whatever they were charged with they had countercharges, and they had the best legal counsel; but (they hadn't listened when Hawksquill had warned them it might be so) their part in the story was over. Struggle only prolonged the end, it was never in doubt. Money gathered at junctures of the case and went off like bombs sometimes, causing temporary outlandish reversals of members' fortunes, but these firebreaks never seemed to give the Club time to recoup. Petty, Smilodon & Ruth, after accruing enormous fees all around, withdrew from their defense amid mysterious circumstances and bitter recriminations; shortly thereafter, masses of paper came to light whose provenance couldn't successfully be denied. Men once made of power and cold blood were seen on every television screen to weep tears of frustration and despair as they were led away to trial by the gloved hands of marshals and indifferent plainclothesmen. The end of the story was not widely known, for it was in the winter of its most shocking revelations that the universal grid of communications which had for a glorious seventy-five years or so lit up the nation like the strung lights of a Christmas tree was for the most part roughly cut: by Eigenblick himself, to forestall its

443

takeover by his enemies; elsewhere, by his enemies, to forestall its takeover by the Tyrant.

That war—the war of the People against the Beast who had seized power and trodden on the institutions of democracy, and of the Emperor-President against the Interests on the people's behalf—was real enough. The blood shed in it was real. The fractures that had run through the society when it had been struck thus hard were deep. But: "If," Hawksquill said, "if those whom we have thought to be at war with men came here to this new world in the first place at about the same time the Europeans did—at about the time, that is, that your latter Empire began to be predicted; and if they came for the same reasons, freedom and space and scope; then they must have eventually been disappointed, just as the men were. . . ."

"Yes," said Barbarossa.

"The virgin forests where they hid themselves gradually logged, cities built on the river-banks and lake shores, the mountains mined, and with no old European regard for wood-sprites and kobolds either. . . ."

"Yes."

"And, if they are in fact as long-sighted as they seem to be, then they must have themselves seen this result, known about it, long ago."

"Yes."

"Before the migration even began. As long ago, in fact, as your Majesty's first reign. And, since they could see it, they prepared for it: they begged your long sleep of him who keeps the years; they sharpened their own weapons; they waited. . . ."

"Yes, yes," Barbarossa said. "And now at last, though much reduced, having been patient for centuries, they strike! Issue from their old strongholds! The robbed dragon stirs in his sleep, and wakes!" He was on his feet; flimsy sheets of computer printout, strategies, plans, figures, slid from his lap to the floor.

"And the bargain made with you," Hawksquill said. "Help them in this enterprise, distract the nation's attention, reduce it to warring fragments (much like your old Empire, they counted on you to do that part well), and, when the old woods and bogs had crept back, when the traffic stopped, when they had recouped as much of their losses as would satisfy them, you could have the rest as your Empire."

"Forever," Eigenblick said, stirred. "That was the promise."

"Fine," Hawksquill said thoughtfully. "That's fine." She stroked the keys; something like *Jerusalem* came from beneath her ringed fingers. "Only none of it's true," she said.

"What?"

"None of it's true; it's false, a lie, not in fact the case."

"What . . ."

"It's not *odd* enough, for one thing." She struck a twanging chord, grimaced, tried it again a different way. "No, I think something quite different is occurring, some motion, some general shift that is no one's choice, no one's . . ." She thought of the dome of the Terminus, its Zodiac reversed, and how she had at the time blamed that on the Emperor who stood before her. Foolish! And yet . . . "Something," she said, "something like the shuffling together of two decks of cards."

"Speaking of cards," he said.

"Or one cut deck," she said, ignoring him. "You know the way small children will sometimes, in trying to shuffle, get one-half the deck upside down? And then there they all are, shuffled together, inextricably mixed backs and faces."

"I want my cards," he said.

"I don't have them."

"You know where they are."

"Yes. And if you were meant to have them, so would you."

"I need their counsel! I need it!"

"Those who have the cards," Hawksquill said, "prepared the way for all this, for your victory such as it is or will be, as well or better than you could have yourself. Long before you appeared, they were a fifth column for that army." She struck a chord, sweet-sour, tart as lemonade. "I wonder," she said, "if they regret that; if they feel bad, or traitorous to their own kind. Or if they ever knew they were taking sides against men."

"I don't know why you say there's no war," the President said, "and then talk like that."

"Not a war," Hawksquill said; "but something *like* a war." Something like a storm, perhaps; yes, like the advancing front of a weather system, which alters the world from warm to cold, gray to blue, spring to winter. Or a collision: *mysterium coniunctionis*, but of what with what? "Or," she said—the thought suddenly struck her—"something like two caravans, two caravans that meet at a single gate, coming from different far places, going toward different far places; mixing it up, jostling through that gate, for a time one caravan only, and then, on the far side, unwinding again toward their destinations, though perhaps with some few having changed places; a saddle bag or two stolen; a kiss exchanged. . . ."

"What," Barbarossa said, "are you talking about?"

She turned her stool to face him. "The question is," she said, "just what kingdom it is you've come into."

"My own."

"Yes. The Chinese, you know, believe that deep within each of us, no larger than the ball of your thumb, is the garden of the immortals, the great valley where we are all king forever."

He turned on her, suddenly angry. "Now listen," he said.

"I know," she said, smiling. "It would be a damned shame if you ended up ruling, not the Republic that fell in love with you, but some other place entirely."

"No."

"Someplace very small."

"I want those cards," he said.

"Can't have 'em. Not mine to give."

"You'll get them for me."

"Won't."

"How would you like it," Barbarossa said, "if I *got* the secret out of you? I do have power, you know. Power."

"Are you threatening me?"

"I could have you—I could have you killed. Secretly. No one would be the wiser."

"No," Hawksquill said calmly. "Killed you could not have me. Not that."

The Tyrant laughed, his eyes catching lurid fire. "You think not?" he said. "Oh ho, you think not?"

"I *know* not," Hawksquill said. "For a strange reason which you couldn't guess. I've hidden my soul."

"What?"

"Hidden my soul. An old trick, one which every village witch knows how to do. And is wise to do: you never know when those you serve may turn resentful, and fall on you."

"Hidden? Where? How?"

"Hidden. Elsewhere. Exactly where, or in what, I won't of course tell you; but you see that unless you knew, it would be useless trying to kill me."

"Torture." His eyes narrowed. "Torture."

"Yes," Hawksquill rose from her stool. Enough of this. "Yes, torture might work. I'll say goodnight now. There's much to do."

446

She turned back, at the door, and saw him standing as though stuck in his threatening pose, glaring at her but not seeing her. Had he heard, or understood, anything she had tried to tell him? A thought took hold of her, a strange and fearful thought, and for a moment she only looked at him as he looked at her, as though they were both trying to remember where, or whether, they had ever met before; and then, alarmed, Hawksquill said, "Goodnight, your Majesty," and left him.

Later that night, in the Capital, the episode of Mrs. Mac-Reynolds' death appeared on "A World Elsewhere." In other places the time of its showing varied; it was no longer in many places a daytime drama, often it was a post-midnight one. But shown it was, broadcast or cabled or—where that wasn't possible, where lines had been cut or transmission interdicted—smuggled into small local stations, or copied and carried overland by hand to hidden transmitters, the precious tapes beamed feebly to far small snowy towns. A walker on this night through such a town could pass along its single street and glimpse, in every living room, the bluish glow of it; might see, in one house, Mrs. MacReynolds carried to her bed, in the next, her children gathered, in the next, her parting words spoken; in the last house before the town ran out and the silent prairie began, her dead.

New-Found-Land

In the Capital, the Emperor-President watched too, his eagle-browed but soft brown eyes dimmed. Never long; longing is fatal. A cloud of pity, of self-pity, rose in him, and took (as clouds can do) a form: the form of Ariel Hawksquill's aloof, amused and unyielding face.

Why me? he thought, raising his hands as though to exhibit shackles. What had he ever done that this awful bargain should have been struck with him? He had been earnest and hard-working, had written a few cutting letters to the Pope, had married his children well. Little else. Why not his grandson, Frederick II, now there was a leader; why not him? Had not the same story after all been told of him, that he was not dead but slept, and would awake to lead his people?

But that was legend only. No, he was here, it was his to suffer this, insufferable though it seemed.

A king in Fairyland: Arthur's fate. Could it be true? A realm no larger than the ball of his thumb, his earthly kingdom nothing but wind, the wind of his passage from here to there, from sleep to sleep.

No! He drew himself up. If there had been no war so far, or only a phony war, well, that time was over. He would fight; he would extract from them every jot of the promises so long ago made to him. For eight hundred years he had slept, doing battle with dreams, laying siege to dreams, conquering dream Holy Lands, wearing dream crowns. He had hungered eight hundred years for the real world, the world he could just sense but not see beyond all the dissolving kingdoms of dream. Hawksquill might be right, that they had never intended him to have it. She might (might well, oh yes, it was all coming quite, quite clear to him) have been in league with them from the beginning to deprive him of it. He almost laughed, a dreadful laugh, to think that there had been a time when he had trusted her, leaned on her even. No more. He would fight. He would get those cards from her by whatever means, yes, though she unleashed her terrible powers on him, he would. Alone, helpless it might be, he would fight, fight for his great, dark, snow-burdened new-found-land.

"Only hope," Mrs. MacReynolds said, dying; "only have patience." The lone walker (refugee? salesman? police spy?) passed the last house on the outskirts, and stepped out along the empty highway. In the houses behind, one by one the bluish eyes of sets were closed; a news broadcast had begun, but there was no news any longer. They went to bed; the night was long; they dreamed of a life that wasn't theirs, a life that could fill theirs, a family elsewhere and a house that could make the dark earth once again a world.

It was still snowing in the Capital. The snow whitened the night, obscuring the far monuments that could be seen through the President's mullioned windows, piling up at the feet of heroes, choking the entrances to underground garages. Somewhere a stuck car was crying rhythmically and helplessly to escape a drift.

Barbarossa wept.

"What do you mean," Smoky asked, "just about over?"

"I mean I think it's just about over," Alice said. "Not over, not yet; but just about."

Just About Over

They had gone to bed early—they did that often nowadays, since their big bed with its high-piled quilts and comforters was the only place in the house they could be truly warm. Smoky wore a nightcap: draughts were draughts, and no one could see how foolish he looked. And they talked. A lot of old knots were untangled in those long nights: or at least shown to be for sure unentanglable, which Smoky supposed was more or less the same thing.

"But how can you say that?" Smoky said, rolling over toward her, lifting as on a big wave the cats who sailed the foot of the bed.

"Well, good heavens," Alice said, "it's been long enough, hasn't it?"

He looked at her, her pale face and nearly white hair just distinguishable in the dark against the white pillowcase. How did she always come up with these un-answers, these remarks struck off with such an air of logical consequence, that meant nothing, or as good as nothing? It never ceased to amaze him. "That's not what I meant, exactly. I guess I meant how do you know it's just about over? Whatever it is."

"I'm not sure," she said, after a long pause. "Except that after all it's happening to me, partly anyway; and I feel about over, some ways; and . . . ."

"Don't say that," he said. "Don't even joke about it."

"No," she said. "I don't mean dying. Is that what you thought I meant?"

He had; he saw now that he didn't understand at all, and rolled over again. "Well, hell," he said. "It never really had anything to do with me anyway."

"Aw," she said, and moved closer to him, putting an arm around him. "Aw, Smoky, don't be that way." She placed her knees up behind his, so that they lay together like a double S.

"What way."

She said nothing for a long time. Then: "It's a Tale, is all," she said; "and tales have beginnings and middles and ends. I don't know when the beginning was, but I know the middle. . . ."

"What was the middle?"

"You were in it! What was it? It was you!"

He drew her familiar hand around him closer. "What about the end?" he said.

"Well that's what I mean," she said. "The end."

Quick, before a looming something he saw darkly huge in her words could steal over him, he said, "No no no no. Things don't have ends like that, Alice. Any more than they have beginnings. Things are all middles in life. Like Auberon's show. Like history. One damn thing after another, that's all."

"Tales have ends."

"Well, so you say, so you say, but . . . ."

"And the house," she said.

"What about the house?"

"Couldn't it have an end? It seems like it will, not long from now; if it did . . ."

"No. It'll just get older."

"Fall apart . . ."

He thought of its cracked walls, its vacant rooms, the seep of water in its basements; its paintless clapboards growing warped, masonry rotting; termites. "Well, it's not its *fault*," he said.

"No, sure."

"It's *supposed* to have electricity. Lots of it. That's how it was made. Pumps. Hot water in the pipes, hot water in the heaters. Lights. Ventilators. Things freeze and crack, because there's no heat, because there's no electricity."

"I know."

"But that's not *its* fault. Not our fault either. Things have gotten so bad. Russell Eigenblick. How can you get things fixed when there's a war on? His domestic policy. Crazy. And so things run out, and there's no electricity, and so . . ."

"And whose fault," she said, "do you think Russell Eigenblick is?"

For a moment, just for a moment, Smoky allowed himself to feel the Tale closing around him, and around all of them; around everything that was. "Oh, come on," he said, a charm to banish the idea, but it persisted. A Tale: a monstrous joke was more like it: the Tyrant installed, after God knows how many years' preparation, amid bloodshed and division and vast suffering, just so that one old house could be deprived of what it needed to live on, so that the end of some convoluted history, which coincided with the house's end, could be brought about, or maybe only hastened; and he inheriting that house, maybe lured there in the first place by love only so that eventually he could inherit it, and inheriting it only so that (though he struggled against it, tools were never far from his hapless hands, all to no good) he could preside over—maybe even, through some clumsiness or inadequacy he could easily imagine himself capable of, insure—its dissolution; and that dissolution in turn bringing about . . . "Well, what then?" he asked. "If we couldn't live here any more."

She didn't answer, but her hand sought his and held it.

Diaspora. He could read it in her hand's touch.

No! Maybe the rest of them could imagine such a thing (though how, when it had always been more their house than his?), maybe Alice could, or Sophie, or the girls; imagine some impossible imaginary destination, some place so far . . . But he could not. He remembered a cold night long ago, and a promise: the night they had

450

first been in the same bed, he and Alice, bedclothes drawn up, lying together like a double S, when he saw that in order to go where she would go, and not be left behind, he would have to find within himself a child's will to believe that had never been much exercised in him and was even then long in disuse; and he found himself no more ready to follow now than he had ever been. "Would you leave?" he asked.

"I think," she said.

"When."

"When I know where it is I'm supposed to go." She drew even closer to him, as though in apology. "Whenever that is." Silence. He felt her breath tickle his neck. "Not soon, maybe." She rubbed her cheek against his shoulder. "And maybe not leave; I mean *leave*-leave; maybe not ever."

But that was just to placate him, he knew. He had after all never been more than a minor character in that destiny, he had always expected to be left in some sense behind: but that fate had been for so long in abeyance, causing him no grief, that (without ever quite forgetting it) he had chosen to ignore it; had even sometimes allowed himself to believe that he had made it, by his goodness and acquiescence and fidelity, go away. But he had not. Here it was: and, as gently as she could consonant with there being no mistake about it, Alice was telling him so.

"Okay, okay," he said. "Okay." That was a code-word between them, meaning I don't understand but I have come to the limit of my strength to try to understand, and I trust you to this point anyway, and let's talk of something else. But—

"Okay," he said again, and this time meant a different thing by it: because he saw just then that there was one way, an impossible unfollowable way but the only way there was, for him to fight this—yes! Fight!—and that Somehow he would have to find it.

It was his damn house now, damn it, and he would have to keep it alive, that's all. For if it lived, if it could, then the Tale couldn't end, could it? No one would have to leave, maybe no one could leave (what did he know about it?) if the house held together, if there was some way to halt its decline, or reverse it. So he would have to do that. Strength alone wouldn't be enough, not anyway his strength; cunning would be needed. Some huge thought would have to be thought (did he feel it, down deep, trying to be born, or was that just blind hope?) and nerve would be necessary, and application, and tenacity like grim death's. But it was the way; the only way.

Access of energy and resolve spun him in the bed, the tassel of his nightcap flying. "Okay, Alice, okay," he said again. He kissed her fiercely—his too!—and then again firmly; and she laughed, embracing him, not knowing (he thought) that he had just resolved to spend his substance subverting her; and she kissed him back.

How could it be, Daily Alice wondered as they kissed, that to say such things as she had said to the husband she loved, on this darkest night of the year, made her not sad but glad, filled in fact with happy expectation? The end: to have the Tale end meant to her to have it all forever, no part left out, complete and seamless at last—certainly Smoky couldn't be left out, not as deeply woven into its stuff as he had become. It would be good, so good to have it all at last, start to finish, like some long, long piece of work that has been executed in dribs and dabs, in the hope and faith that the last nail, the last stitch, the last tug at the strings, will make it all suddenly make sense: what a relief! It didn't, quite, not yet; but now in this winter Alice could at last believe, with no reservations, that it would: they were that close. "Or maybe," she said to Smoky, who paused in his attentions to her, "maybe just beginning." Smoky groaned, shaking his head, and she laughed and clasped him to her.

When there was no more talk from the bed, the girl who had for some time been watching the bedclothes heave and listening to their words turned to go. She had come in through the door (left open for the cats to go in and out) silently, on bare feet, and then stood in the shadows watching and listening, a small smile on her lips. Because a mountain-range of quilts and coverlets rose between their heads and the room, Smoky and Alice hadn't seen her there, and the incurious cats, who had opened big eyes when she had entered, had returned to fitful sleep, only now and then regarding her through narrowed lids. She paused a moment now at the door, for the bed had begun to make noises again, but she couldn't make anything of these, mere low sounds, not words, and she slipped through the door and into the hall.

There was no light there but a faint snowlight coming in through the casement at the hall's end, and slowly, like someone blind, she went with small silent steps, arms extended, past closed doors. She considered each dark blank door as she passed it, but shook her blond head at each in turn, thinking; until, rounding a corner, she came to an arched one, and smiled, and with her small hand turned its glass knob and pushed it open.

II

To remark the folly of the fiction,
the absurdity of the conduct, the
confusion of the names and manners of
different times, and the impossibility
of the events in any system of life,
were to waste criticism upon unresisting
imbecility, upon faults too evident for
detection, and too gross for aggravation.

—*Johnson on* Cymbeline

Sophie too had gone to bed early and not to sleep.

In her old figured bed-jacket, and a cardigan over that, she lay huddled close to the candle which stood on the bedside table, two of her fingers only allowed out from the bedclothes to hold open the pages of the second volume of an ancient three-volume novel. When the candle began to gutter, she reached into the table's drawer, took out another, lit it from the first, pressed it down into the candlestick, sighed, and turned the page. She was far, far from the final weddings; only now had the will been secreted in the old cabinet; the bishop's daughter thought of the ball. The door of Sophie's room opened, and a child came in.

She wore only a blue dress, without sleeves or a belt. She came a step through the door, her hand still on its knob, smiling the smile of a child who has a terrific secret, a secret which she's not sure will amuse or annoy the grown-up she stands before; and for a time she only stood in the doorway, glowing faintly in the candlelight, her chin lowered and her eyes raised to Sophie turned to stone on the bed.

What a Surprise

Then she said: "Hello, Sophie."

She looked just as Sophie had imagined she would, at the

453

age she would have been when Sophie had been unable to imagine her further. The candle-flame shivered in the draft from the open door, which cast strange shadows over the child, and Sophie grew for a moment as afraid and struck with strangeness as she had ever in her life been, but this was no ghost. Sophie could tell that by the way the child, having come in, turned to push the heavy door closed behind her. No ghost would have done that.

She came slowly toward the bed, hands clasped behind her, with her secret in her smile. She said to Sophie: "Can you guess my name?"

That she spoke was for some reason harder for Sophie to take in than that she stood there, and Sophie for the first time knew what it was not to believe her ears: they told her that the child had spoken, but Sophie didn't believe it, and couldn't imagine answering. It would have been like speaking to some part of herself, some part that had suddenly and inexplicably become detached from her and then turned to face her, and question her.

The child laughed a small laugh; she was enjoying this. "You don't," she said. "Do you want me to give you a hint?"

A hint! Not a ghost, and not a dream, for Sophie was awake; not her daughter, certainly, for her daughter had been taken from her over twenty-five years ago, and this was a child: yet for sure Sophie knew her name. She had raised her hands to her face, and between them now she said or whispered: "Lilac."

Lilac looked a little disappointed. "Yes," she said. "How did you know?"

Sophie laughed, or sobbed, or both at once. "Lilac," she said.

Lilac laughed, and made to climb up on the bed with her mother, and Sophie perforce had to help her up: she took Lilac's arm, wondering, afraid that perhaps she would herself feel her own touch, and if she did, then—then what? But Lilac was flesh, cool flesh, it was a child's wrist her fingers circled; she drew up Lilac's real solid weight with her strength, and Lilac's knee pressed the bed and made it jounce, and every sense Sophie had was certain now that Lilac was here before her.

"Well," Lilac said, brushing the golden hair from before her eyes with a quick gesture. "Aren't you surprised?" She watched Sophie's stricken face. "Don't you say hello or kiss me or anything?"

"Lilac," Sophie only said again; for there had been for many, many years one thought forbidden to Sophie, one unimaginable scene, this one, and she was unrehearsed; the moment and the child were just as she would have imagined them to be if she had allowed herself to imagine them at all, but she had not, and now she was unready and undone.

"*You* say," Lilac said, indicating Sophie—it hadn't been easy memorizing all this, and it should come out right—"*you* say, 'Hello, Lilac, what a surprise,' because you haven't seen me since I was a baby; and then I say, 'I came a long way, to tell you this and this,' and you listen, *but* first before that part you say how much you missed me since I was stolen, and we hug." She flung open her arms, her face pretending to radiant, poignant joy to cue Sophie; and there was nothing then for Sophie to do but to open her arms too, no matter how slowly and tentatively (not fearful now but only deeply shy before the impossibility of it) and take Lilac in them.

"You say, 'What a surprise,' " Lilac reminded her, whispering close to her ear.

Lilac's odor was of snow and self and earth. "What a surprise," Sophie began to say, but couldn't finish it, because tears of grief and wonderment flew up her throat behind the words, bringing with them all that Sophie had been denied and had denied herself all these years. She wept, and Lilac, surprised herself now, thought to draw away, but Sophie held her; and so Lilac patted her back gently to comfort her.

"Yes," she said to her mother, "yes, I came back; I came a long way, a long long way."

She may have come a long, long way; for sure she remembered that this was what she was to say. She remembered no long journey, though; either she had awakened only after most of it had been sleepwalked away, or in fact it had really been quite short. . . .

Walking
from There

"Sleepwalked?" Sophie asked.

"I've been asleep," Lilac said. "For so long. I didn't know I'd sleep so long. Longer than the bears even. Oh, I've been asleep ever since a day, since the day I woke you up. Do you remember?"

"No," Sophie said.

"On a day," Lilac said, "I stole your sleep. I shouted 'Wake up!' and pulled your hair."

"Stole my sleep?"

"Because I needed it. I'm sorry," she said gleefully.

"That day," Sophie said, thinking How odd to be so old and full of things, and have your life inverted as a child's can be. . . . That day. And had she slept since then?

"Since then," Lilac said. "Then I came here."

"Here. From where?"

"From there. From sleep. Anyway . . ."

She awoke, anyway, out of the longest dream in the world, forgetting all of it or nearly all of it as she did so, to find herself stepping along a dark road at evening, silent fields of snow on either side and a still cold pink-and-blue sky all around, and a task she'd been prepared for before she slept, and which her long sleep had not forgotten, ahead of her to do. All that was clear enough, and Lilac didn't wonder at it; often enough in her growing up she'd found herself suddenly in strange circumstances, emerging from one enchantment into another like a child carried sleeping from a bed to a celebration and waking, blinking, staring, but accepting it all because familiar hands hold him. So her feet fell one after the other, and she watched a crow, and climbed a hill, and saw the last spark of a red sun go out, and the pink of the sky deepen and the snow turn blue; and only then, as she descended, did she wonder where she was, and how much further she had to go.

There was a cottage at the bottom of the hill, amid dense small evergreens, from whose windows yellow lamplight shone out into the blue evening. When Lilac reached it she pushed open the little white gate in its picket fence—a bell tinkled within the house as she did so—and started up the path. The head of a gnome, his high hat doubled by a hat of snow, looked out over the drifted lawn, as he had been doing for years and years.

"The Junipers'," Sophie said.

"What?"

"It was the Junipers'," Sophie said. "Their cottage."

There was an old, old woman there, the oldest (except for Mrs. Underhill and her daughters) Lilac had ever seen. She opened her door, held up a lamp, and said in a small old voice, "Friend or Foe? Oh, my," for she saw then that a nearly naked child, barefoot and hatless, stood before her on the path.

Margaret Juniper did nothing foolish; she only opened the door so that Lilac could enter if she liked, and after a moment Lilac decided that she would, and went in and down the tiny hall across the scatter rug and past the knickknack shelf (long undusted, for Marge was afraid of breaking things with her old hands, and couldn't any longer see the dust anyway) and through the arched doorway into the parlor, where a fire was lit in the stove. Marge followed with the lamp, but then at the doorway wasn't sure she wanted to enter; she watched the child sit down in the maple chair with broad paddle arms that had been Jeff's, and put her hands flat on the arms, as though they pleased or amused her. Then she looked up at Marge.

456

"Can you tell me," she said, "am I on the right road for Edgewood?"

"Yes," Marge said, Somehow not surprised to be asked this.

"Oh," Lilac said. "I have to bring a message there." She held up her hands and feet to the stove, but didn't seem to be chilled through; and Marge didn't wonder at that either. "How far is it?"

"Hours," Marge said.

"Oh. How many."

"I never walked there," Marge said.

"Oh. Well, I'm a fast walker." She jumped up then, and pointed inquiringly in a direction, and Marge shook her head No, and Lilac laughed and pointed in the opposite direction. Marge nodded Yes. She stood aside for the child to pass her again, and followed her to the door.

"Thank you," Lilac said, her hand on the door. Marge chose, from a bowl by the door of mixed dollar bills and candy with which she paid the boys who shoveled her walk and split her wood, a large chocolate, and offered it to Lilac, who took it with a smile, and then rose on tiptoe and kissed Marge's old cheek. Then she went out and down the path, and turned toward Edgewood without looking back.

Marge stood in the door watching her, filled with the odd sensation that it had been only for this tiny visit that she had lived her whole long life, that this cottage by the roadside and this lamp in her hand and the whole chain of events which had caused them to be had always and only had this visit for their point. And Lilac too, walking fast, remembered just then that of *course* she was to have visited that house, and said what she did say to the old woman there—it was the taste of the chocolate that reminded her—and that by next evening, an evening as still and blue as this one or stiller, everyone in the pentacle of five towns around Edgewood would know that Marge Juniper had had a visitor.

"But," Sophie said, "You can't have walked here since evening. . . ."

"I walk fast," Lilac said; "or maybe I took a shortcut."

Whatever way she had taken had led her past a frozen lake and a lake island all glittering in starlight, where a little pillared gazebo stood up, or perhaps it was only snow-shapes that suggested such a place; and through woods, waking a chickadee; and past a place, a sort of castle iced with snow . . .

"The Summer House," Sophie said.

457

. . . a place she'd seen before, from above, in another season long ago. She came toward it through what had been the flower beds that bordered its lawn, gone wild now and with only the tall dead stalks of hollyhock and mullein standing above the snow. There were the gray bones of a canvas sling-chair in the yard. She thought, seeing them: wasn't there some message, or some comfort, she was to deliver here? She stood for a moment, looking at the derelict chair and the squat house where not a single footprint went through the snow up to the half-engulfed door, a summery screen door, and for the first time she shivered in the cold, but couldn't remember what the message was or whom it had been for, if there really had been one at all; and so passed on.

"Auberon," Sophie said.

"No," Lilac said. "Not *Auberon*."

She walked through the graveyard, not knowing it to be such; the plot of ground where John Drinkwater had first been buried and then others beside him or near him, some known to him and some not. Lilac wondered at the big carved stones placed at random here and there, like giant forgotten toys. She studied them a while, walking from one to another and brushing off their caps of snow to look at sad angels, and deep-incised letters, and granite finials, while beneath her feet, beneath the snow and black leaves and earth, stiff bones relaxed, and hollow chests would have sighed if they could have, and old attitudes of attention and expectancy undissolved by death were softened; and (as sleepers do when a troublesome dream passes or a bothering noise, the crying of a cat or a lost child, ceases) those asleep there rested more deeply and slept at last truly as Lilac walked above them.

"Violet," Sophie said, her tears flowing freely and pain-lessly now, "and John; and Harvey Cloud, and Great-aunt Cloud. Daddy. And Violet's father too, and Auberon. And Auberon."

Yes: and Auberon: that Auberon. Standing above him, on the bosom of earth that lay on his bosom, Lilac felt clearer about her message, and her purpose. It was all getting clearer, as though she continued to wake further all the time after waking. "Oh, yes," she said to herself; "oh, yes . . ." She turned to see, past black firs, the dark pile of the house with not a light showing, as snow-burdened as the firs, but unmistakable; and soon she found a path to there, and a door to go in by, and steps to go up, and glass-knobbed doors to choose from.

"And then, and now," she said, kneeling on the bed before Sophie, "I have to tell you what.

"If I can remember it all."

"I was right, then," Sophie said. A third candle was burn-ing down. Deep cold midnight was in the room. "Only a few."

"Fifty-two," Lilac said. "Counting them all."   A Parliament
"So few."

"It's the War," Lilac said. "They've all gone. And the ones left are old—so old. You can't imagine."

"But why?" Sophie said. "Why if they knew they must lose so many?"

Lilac shrugged, looking away. It didn't seem part of her mission to explain, only to give news, and a summons; she couldn't explain to Sophie either exactly what had become of her when she had been stolen, or how she had lived: when Sophie questioned her, she answered as all children do, with hasty references to strangers and events unknown to her hearer, expecting it all to be understood, to be as familiar to the grown-up as to the child: but Lilac was not as other children. "*You* know," she only said, impatiently, when Sophie questioned her, and returned to the news she had come to bring: that the War was to end; that there was to be a peace confer-ence, a Parliament, to which all who could come must come, to resolve this, and end the long sad time.

A Parliament, where all who came would meet face to face. Face to face: when Lilac said it to her, Sophie felt a hum in her head and a pause in her heartbeat, as though Lilac had announced to her her death, or something as final and unimagined.

"So you must come," Lilac said. "You have to. Because they're so few now, the War has to end. We have to make a Treaty, for everybody."

"A Treaty."

"Or they'll *all* be lost," Lilac said. "The winter might go on, and never end. They could do that, they could: the last thing they could do."

"Oh," Sophie said. "No. Oh, no."

"It's in your hands," Lilac said, stately, minatory; and then, solemn message done, she threw her arms wide. "So all right?" she said happily. "You'll come? All of you?"

Sophie put her cold knuckles to her lips. Lilac, smiling, alive and alight in the winter-dusty room: and this news. Sophie felt vacant, disappeared. If there were a ghost here, it was Sophie and not her daughter.

Her daughter!

"But how?" she said. "How are we to go there?"

Lilac looked at her in dismay. "You don't know that?" she said.

459

"Once I did," Sophie said, tears gathering again in her throat. "Once I thought I could find it, once . . . Oh, oh, why did you wait so *long!*" With a pang she saw, dead, buried within her, the possibilities that Lilac spoke of: dead because Sophie had crushed all possibility that Lilac could ever sit here and speak them. She had lived long with terrible possibilities—Lilac dead, or utterly transformed—and had faced them; but Tacey and Lily's ancient prediction (though she had counted years, and even studied the cards for a date) she had never allowed herself to believe. The effort had been huge, and had cost her terribly; she had lost, in her effort not to imagine this moment, all her childhood's certainties, all those commonplace impossibilities; had lost, even, without quite noticing it, every vivid memory she had ever had of those daily impossibilities, of the sweet unreasonable air of wonder she had once lived in. Thus she had protected herself; this moment hadn't been able to injure her— kill her, for it would have!—in her imagining it; and so she had at least been able to go on from day to day. But too many thin and shadowed years had gone by now, too many. "I can't," she said. "I don't know. I don't know the way."

"You must," Lilac said simply.

"I don't," Sophie said, shaking her head. "I don't, and even if I did I'd be afraid." Afraid! That was the worst: afraid to take steps away from this dark old house, as afraid as any ghost. "Too long," she said, wiping her wet nose on the sleeve of her cardigan, "too long."

"But the house is the door!" Lilac said. "Everybody knows that. It's marked on all their maps."

"It is?"

"Yes. So."

"And from here?"

Lilac looked at her blankly. "Well," she said.

"I'm sorry, Lilac," Sophie said. "I've had a sad life, you see. . . ."

"Oh? Oh, *I* know," Lilac said, brightening. "Those cards! Where are they?"

"There," Sophie said, pointing to where the box of different woods from the Crystal Palace lay on the night table. Lilac reached for them, and pulled open the box. "Why did you have a sad life?" she asked, extracting the cards.

"Why?" Sophie said. "Because you were stolen, partly, mostly . . ."

"Oh, *that.* Well, that doesn't matter."

"Doesn't matter?" Sophie laughed, weeping.

"No, that was just the beginning." She was shuffling the big cards awkwardly in her small hands. "Didn't you know that?"

"No. No, I thought . . . I think I thought it was the end."

"Oh, that's silly. If I hadn't been stolen, I couldn't have had my Education, and if I hadn't had my Education I couldn't have brought this news now, that it's *really* beginning; so that was all right, don't you see?"

Sophie watched her shuffle the cards, dropping some and sticking them back in the deck, in a sort of parody of careful arrangement. She tried to imagine the life Lilac had led, and couldn't. "Did you," she asked, "ever miss me, Lilac?" Lilac shrugged one shoulder, busy.

"There," she said, and gave the deck to Sophie. "Follow that." Sophie slowly took the cards from her, and just for a moment Lilac seemed to see her—to see her truly, for the first time since she had entered. "Sophie," she said. "Don't be sad. It's all so much larger than you think." She put her hand over Sophie's. "Oh, there's a fountain there—or a waterfall, I forget—and you can wash there— oh it's so clear and icy cold and—oh, it's all, it's all so much bigger than you think!"

She climbed down from the bed. "You sleep now," she said. "I have to go."

"Go where? I won't sleep, Lilac."

"You will," Lilac said. "You can, now; because I'm awake."

"Oh?" She lay back slowly on the pillows Lilac plumped up behind her.

"Because," Lilac said, with the secret in her smile again, "because I stole your sleep; but now I'm awake, and you can sleep."

Sophie, exhausted, clasped the cards. "Where," she said, "will you go? It's dark and cold."

Lilac shuddered, but she only said, "You sleep." She raised herself on tiptoe beside the tall bed and, brushing the pale curls from Sophie's cheek, kissed her lightly. "Sleep."

She stepped noiselessly across the floor, opened the door, and with a glance back at her mother, went out into the still, cold hall. She closed the door behind her.

Sophie lay staring at the blankness of the door. The third candle guttered out with a hiss and a pop. Still holding the cards, Sophie wiggled slowly down within the quilts and coverlets, thinking—or perhaps not thinking, not thinking at all but feeling certain—that Lilac had, in some regard, been lying to her; in some regard misleading her at least; but in what regard?

461

Sleep.

In what regard? She was thinking, like a mental breathing: in what regard? She was breathing this when she knew, with a gasp of delight in her soul that almost woke her, that she was asleep.

Auberon, yawning, glanced first through the mail that Fred Savage had brought the night before from uptown.

Not All Over

"Dear World Elsewhere," a lady with peacock-green ink wrote, "I am writing now to ask you a question I have long pondered. I would like to know, if at all possible, *where is that house where the MacReynolds and the others live?* I must say that it is very important to me personally to know this. Its exact location. I wouldn't bother you by writing except that I find it impossible to imagine. When they used to live at Shady Acres (way back when!) well, I could imagine that easily enough, but I cannot imagine this other place they've ended up. Please give me some kind of hint. I can hardly think of anything else." She signed herself his hopefully, and added a postscript: "I sincerely promise not to *bother* anybody." Auberon glanced at the postmark—way out West—and tossed it in the woodbox.

Now what the hell, he wondered, was he doing awake so early? Not to read mail. He glanced at Doc's old square-faced wristwatch on the mantelpiece. Oh, yes: milking. All this week. He roughly pulled the covers of the bed in place, put a hand under the footboard, said *"Up* we go," and magicked it into a mirror-fronted old wardrobe. The click of its locking into upright place he always found satisfying.

He pulled on tall boots and a heavy sweater, looking out the window at a light snow falling. Yawning again (would George have coffee? Yours hopefully) he pushed his hat on his head and went out clumping, locking the Folding Bedroom's doors behind him and making his way down the stairs, out the window, down the fire escape, into the hall, through the wall and out onto the stairs that led down to the Mouse kitchen.

At the bottom he came on George.

"You're not going to believe this," George said.

Auberon stopped. George said nothing more. He looked like he'd seen a ghost: Auberon at once recognized the look, though he'd never before seen anyone who'd seen a ghost. Or like a ghost himself, if ghosts can look stricken, overcome by conflicting emotions, and amazed out of their wits. "What?" he said.

"You are *not*. Gonna believe this." He was in socks of

great antiquity and a quilted boxer's dressing gown. He took
Auberon's hand and began to lead him down the hall toward the
door of the kitchen. "What," Auberon said again. The back of
George's dressing gown said it belonged to the Yonkers A.C.

At the door—which stood ajar—George turned again to
Auberon. "Now just for God's sake," he whispered urgently, "don't
say a word about, you know, that story. That story I told you,
about—you know—" he glanced at the open door—"about Lilac,"
he said, or rather did not say, he only moved his lips around the
name silently, exaggeratedly, and winked a frightened warning wink.
Then he pushed open the door.

"Look," he said. "Look, look," as though Auberon were
capable of not looking. "My kid."

The child sat on the edge of the table, swinging her
crossed bare legs back and forth.

"Hello, Auberon," she said. "You got big."

Auberon, feeling a feeling like crossed eyes in his soul but
looking steadily at the child, touched the place in his heart where his
imaginary Lilac was kept. She was there.

Then this was—

"Lilac," he said.

"My kid. Lilac," George said.

"But how?"

"Don't ask me how," George said.

"It's a long story," Lilac said. "The longest story I know."

"There's this meeting on," George said.

"A Parliament," Lilac said. "I came to tell you."

"She came to tell us."

"A Parliament," Auberon said. "What on earth."

"Listen, man," George said. "Don't ask me. I came down
to brew a little coffee, and there's a knocking at the door. . . ."

"But why," Auberon asked, "is she so young?"

"You're asking me? So I peeked out, and here's this kid in
the snow. . . ."

"She should be a lot older."

"She was asleep. Or some damn thing. What do I know.
So I open the door . . ."

"This is all kind of hard to believe," Auberon said.

Lilac had been looking from one to the other of them,
hands clasped in her lap, smiling a smile of cheerful love for her
father, and of sly complicity at Auberon. The two stopped talking
then, and only looked at her. George came closer. The look he wore
was an anxious, joyful wonderment, as though he'd just hatched

Lilac himself. "Milk," he said, snapping his fingers. "How about a glass of milk? Kids like milk, right?"

"I can't," Lilac said, laughing at his solicitude. "I can't, here."

But George was already bustling with a jelly jar and a canister of goat's milk from the refrigerator. "Sure," he said. "Milk."

"Lilac," Auberon said. "Where is it you want us to go?"

"To where the meeting is," Lilac said. "The Parliament."

"But where? Why? What . . ."

"Oh, Auberon," Lilac said, impatient, "they'll explain all that when you get there. You just have to come."

"They?"

Lilac turned up her eyes in mock-stupefaction. "Oh, come on," she said. "You just have to hurry, that's all, so as not to be late. . . ."

"Nobody's going anywhere now," George said, putting the milk in Lilac's hands. She looked at it curiously, and put it down. "Now you're back, and that's great, I don't know from where or how, but you're here and safe, and we're staying here."

"Oh, but you *must* come," Lilac said, taking the sleeve of his dressing gown. "You have to. Otherwise . . ."

"Otherwise?" George asked.

"It won't come out right," Lilac said softly. "The Tale," she said, even more softly.

"Oho," George said. "Oho, the Tale. Well." He stood before her arms akimbo, nodding a skeptical nod but lost for an answer.

Auberon watched them, father and daughter, thinking: *It's not all over, then.* That had been the thought he had begun to think as soon as he entered the old kitchen, or rather not to think but to know, to know by the rising of the hair on his nape and the weird swarm of feeling, the feeling that his eyes were crossing and yet seeing more clearly than before. Not all over: he had lived long in a small room, a folding bedroom, and had explored its every corner, had come to know it as he knew his own bowels, and had decided: this is all right, this will do, a sort of life can be lived here, here's a chair by the fire and a bed to sleep in and a window to look out of; if it was constricted, that was made up for by how much simple sense it made. And now it was as though he had lowered the front of the mirrored wardrobe and found not a bed clothed in patched sheets and an old quilt but a portal, a ship in full sail raising anchor, a windy dawn and an avenue beneath tall trees disappearing far out of sight.

He shut it up, fearful. He'd had his adventure. He'd followed outlandish paths, and hadn't for no good reason given them up. He got up, and clumped to the window in his rubber boots. Unmilked, the goats bewailed in their apartments.

"No," he said. "I'm not going, Lilac."

"But you haven't even heard the *reasons,*" Lilac said.

"I don't care."

"The War! The Peace!" Lilac said.

"Don't care." He'd stick. He wouldn't miss the whole world if it passed him by on the way there, and it probably would; or perhaps he would miss it, but he'd rather that than take his life in his teeth and pass into that sea again, that sea Desire, now that he'd escaped it, and found a shore. Never.

"Auberon," Lilac said softly. "Sylvie will be there."

Never. Never never never.

"Sylvie?" George said.

"Sylvie," Lilac said.

When there had been no further word from either of them for some time, Lilac said, "She told me to tell you . . ."

"She didn't!" Auberon said, turning on her. "She didn't, it's a lie! No! I don't know why you want to fool us, I don't know why or for what you came, but you'll say anything, won't you, won't you? Anything but the truth! Just like all of them, because it doesn't *matter* to you. No, no, you're just as bad as they are, I know it, just as bad as that Lilac that George blew up, that fake one. No different."

"Oh, *great,*" George said, casting his eyes upward. "That's just great."

"Blew up?" Lilac said, looking at George.

"It was *not* my *fault,*" George said, rifling a furious look at Auberon.

"So *that's* what happened to it," Lilac said thoughtfully. Then she laughed. "Oh, they were mad! When the ashes drifted down. It was hundreds of years old, and the last one they had." She climbed down from the table, her blue skirt riding up. "I have to go now," she said, and started toward the door.

"No," Auberon said. "Wait."

"Go! No," George said, and took her arm.

"There's so much to do," Lilac said. "And this is all set-tled here, so . . . Oh," she said. "I forgot. *Your* way is mostly in the forest, so it would be best if you had a guide. Somebody who knows the woods, and can help you along. Bring a coin, for the ferryman; dress warm. There are lots of doors, but some are quicker than others. Don't be too long, or you'll miss the banquet!" She was at the door, but rushed back to leap into George's arms. She circled his neck in her thin golden arms, kissed his lean cheeks, and scrambled down again. "It's going to be so much fun," she said; she glanced once at them, smiling a smile of simple sweet wickedness and pleasure, and was gone. They heard the pat of her bare feet on the old linoleum outside, but didn't hear the street door open, or shut.

George took from a leaning hatrack his overalls and coat, pulled them on, and then his boots; he went to the door, but when he reached it he seemed to forget what he was about, or why he hurried. He looked around himself, found no clue, and went to sit at the table.

Auberon slowly took the chair opposite him, and for a long time they sat silent, sometimes starting, but seeing nothing, while a certain light or meaning was subtracted from the room, returning it to ordinariness, turning it to a kitchen where porridge was made and goat's milk drunk and two bachelors sat rubber-boot to rubber-boot at the table, with chores still to be done.

And a journey to go: that was left.

"Okay," George said. "What?" He looked up, but Auberon hadn't spoken.

"No," Auberon said.

"She said," George said, but then couldn't exactly say what; couldn't forget what she had said but (what with the goats bawling, what with the snow outside, what with his own heart emptying and filling) couldn't remember it either.

"Sylvie," Auberon said.

"A guide," George said, snapping his fingers.

There were footsteps in the hall.

"A guide," George said. "She said we'd need a guide."

They both turned to look at the door, which just then opened.

Fred Savage came in, wearing *his* rubber boots, and ready for his breakfast.

"Guide?" he said. "Somebody goan someplace?"

"Is it her?" Sophie asked. She pushed aside the window's drape further to look.

"It must be," Alice said.

Not often enough now did headlights turn in at the stone gateposts for it to be very likely anyone else.

The long, low car, black in the twilight, swept the house with its brilliant eyes as it bounced up the rutty drive; it pulled around in front of the porch, its lights went out but its impatient burble went on for a while. Then it fell silent.

Lady with the Alligator Purse

466

"George?" Sophie asked. "Auberon?"

"I don't see them. No one but her."

"Oh dear."

"All right," Alice said. "Her at least." They turned away from the window to the expectant faces of those gathered in the double drawing room. "She's here," Alice said. "We'll start soon."

Ariel Hawksquill, after stilling the car's motor, sat for a moment listening to the new silence. Then she worked her way out of the seat's grasp. She took from the seat next to her an alligator shoulder bag, and stood in the slight drizzle that was falling; she breathed deeply of the evening air, and thought: Spring.

For the second time she had driven north to Edgewood, this time over the ruts and potholes of a degenerated road system, and passing this time checkpoints where passes and visas had to be shown, a thing that would have been unthinkable five years before when she had come here. She supposed that she had been followed, at least part way, but no tail could have kept up with her through the tangle of rainy roads that led from the highway to here. She came alone. The letter from Sophie had been odd but urgent: urgent enough, she hoped, to justify sending it (Hawksquill had insisted her cousins never write to her at the Capital, she knew her mail was scanned) and to justify a journey and a long absence from the Government at a critical time.

"Hello, Sophie," she said, when the two tall sisters came out on the porch. There was no welcoming light lit there. "Hello, Alice."

"Hello," Alice said. "Where's Auberon? Where's George? We asked . . ."

Hawksquill mounted the steps. "I went to the address," she said, "and knocked a long time. The place looked abandoned . . ."

"It always does," Sophie said.

". . . and no one answered. I thought I heard someone behind the door; I called their names. Someone, someone with an accent, called back that they had gone."

"Gone?" Sophie said.

"Gone away. I asked where, for how long; but no one answered. I didn't dare stay too long."

"Didn't dare?" Alice said.

"May we go in?" Hawksquill said. "It's a lovely night, but damp." Her cousins didn't know, and, Hawksquill supposed, couldn't really imagine the danger they might put themselves in by association with her. Deep desires reached out toward this house, not knowing of its existence, yet sniffing closer all the time. But there was no need (she hoped) to alarm them.

There was no light in the hall but a dull candle, making the place shadowy and vast; Hawksquill followed her cousins down, around, up through the impossible insides of the house into a set of two big rooms where a fire burned, lights were lit, and many faces looked up interested and expectant at her arrival.

"This is our cousin," Daily Alice said to them. "Long-lost, sort of, her name is Ariel. This is the family," she said to Ariel, "you know them; and some others.

"So, I guess everybody's here," she said. "Everybody who can come. I'll go get Smoky."

Sophie went to a drum-table where a brass, green-glass-shaded lamp shone, and where the cards lay. Ariel Hawksquill felt her heart rise or sink to see them. Whatever other fates they held or did not hold, Hawksquill knew at that moment that hers was surely in them: was them.

"Hello," she said, nodding briefly to the assembly. She took a straight-backed chair between a very, a remarkably old and bright-eyed lady and two twin children, boy and girl, who shared an armchair.

"And how," said Marge Juniper to her, "do you come to be a cousin?"

"As nearly as I can tell," Hawksquill said, "I'm not, really. The father of the Auberon who was Violet Drinkwater's son was my grandfather by a later marriage."

"Oh," Marge said. "That side of the family."

Hawksquill felt eyes on her, and gave a quick glance and a smile at the two children in the armchair, who were staring at her with uncertain curiosity. Rarely see strangers, Hawksquill supposed; but what Bud and Blossom were seeing, in the flesh, with wonder and a little trepidation, was that enigmatic and somewhat fearsome figure who in a song they often sang comes at the crux of the story: the Lady with the Alligator Purse.

Alice climbed quickly up through the house, negotiating dark stairways with the skill of a blind man.

Still Unstolen

"Smoky?" she called when she stood at the bottom of a narrow curl of steep stairs that led up into the orrery. No one answered, but a light burned up there.

"Smoky?"

She didn't like to go up; the small stairs, the small arched door, the cramped cold cupola stuffed with machinery, gave her the willies, it wasn't designed to amuse someone as big as she was.

"Everyone's here," she said. "We can start."

She waited, hugging herself. The damp was palpable on this neglected floor; and brown stains spread over the wallpaper. Smoky said, "All right," but she heard no movement.

"George and Auberon didn't come," she said. "They're gone." She waited more, and then—hearing neither noise of work nor preparations to come down—climbed up the stairs and put her head through the little door.

Smoky sat on a small stool, like a petitioner or penitent before his idol, staring at the mechanism inside the black steel case. Alice felt somewhat shy, or intrusive into a privacy, seeing him there and it exposed.

"Okay," Smoky said again, but when he rose, it was only to take a steel ball the size of a croquet ball from a rack of them in the back of the case. This he placed in the cup or hand of one of the extended jointed arms of the wheel which the case contained and sheltered. He let go, and the weight of the ball spun the arm downward. As it moved, the other jointed arms moved too; another, clack-clack-clack, extended itself to receive the next ball.

"See how it works?" Smoky said, sadly.

"No," Alice said.

"An overbalancing wheel," Smoky said. "These jointed arms, see, are held out stiff on this side, because of the joints; but when they come around to this side, the joints fold up, and the arm lies along the wheel. So. This side of the wheel, where the arms stick out, will always be heavier, and will always fall down, that is, around; so when you put the ball in the cup, the wheel falls around, and that brings the next arm into place. And a ball falls into the cup of *that* arm, and bears it down and around, and so on."

"Oh." He was telling all this flatly, like an old, old story or a grammar lesson too often repeated. It occurred to Alice that he'd eaten no dinner.

"Then," he went on, "the weight of the balls falling into the cups of the arms on *this* side carries the arms far enough up on *this* side so that they fold up, and the cup tips, and the ball rolls out"—he turned the wheel by hand to demonstrate—"and goes back into the rack, and rolls down and falls into the cup of the arm that just extended itself over on *this* side, and that carries that arm around, and so it goes on endlessly." The slack arm did deposit its ball; the ball did roll into the arm that extended itself, clack-clack-clack, out

from the wheel. The arm was borne down to the bottom of the
wheel's cycle. Then it stopped.

"Amazing," Alice said mildly.

Smoky, hands behind his back, looked glumly at the unmoving wheel. "It's the stupidest thing I've ever seen in my life," he
said.

"Oh."

"This guy Cloud must have been just about the stupidest
inventor or genius who ever . . ." He could think of no conclusion,
and bowed his head. "It never worked, Alice; this thing couldn't
turn anything. It's not going to work."

She moved carefully among the tools and oily disassembled works and took his arm. "Smoky," she said. "Everybody's
downstairs. Ariel Hawksquill came."

He looked at her, and laughed, a frustrated laugh at a
defeat absurdly complete; then he grimaced, and put his hand
quickly to his chest.

"Oh," Alice said. "You should have eaten."

"It's better when I don't," Smoky said. "I think."

"Come on," Alice said. "You'll figure this out, I bet.
Maybe you can ask Ariel." She kissed his brow, and went before him
out the arched door and then down the steps, feeling released.

"Alice," Smoky said to her. "Is this it? Tonight, I mean.
Is this it?"

"Is this what?"

"It is, isn't it?" he said.

She said nothing while they went along the hall and down
the stairs toward the second floor. She held Smoky's arm, and
thought of more than one thing to say; but at last (there wasn't any
point any longer in riddling, she knew too much, and so did he) she
only said. "I guess. Close."

Smoky's hand, pressed to his chest beneath his breast-
bone, began to tingle, and he said "Oh-oh," and stopped.

They were at the top of the stairs. Faintly, below, he could
see the drawing-room lights, and hear voices. Then the voices went
out in a hum of silence.

Close. If it were close, then he had lost; for he was far
behind, he had work to do he could not even conceive of, much less
begin. He had lost.

An enormous hollow seemed to open up in his chest, a
hollow larger than himself. Pain gathered on its perimeter, and
Smoky knew that after a moment, an endless moment, the pain
would rush in and fill the hollow: but for that moment there was

nothing, nothing but a terrible premonition, and an incipient revelation, both vacant, contesting in his empty heart. The premonition was black, and the incipient revelation would be white. He stopped stock still, trying not to panic because he couldn't breathe; there was no air within the hollow for him to breathe; he could only experience the battle between Premonition and Revelation and listen to the long loud hum in his ears that seemed to be a voice saying Now you see, you didn't ask to see and this is not the moment in which you would anyway have expected sight to come, here on this stair in this dark, but Now: and even then it was gone. His heart, with two slow awful thuds like blows, began to pound fiercely and steadily as though in rage, and pain, familiar and releasing, filled him up. The contest was over. He could breathe the pain. In a moment, he would breathe air.

"Oh," he heard Alice saying, "oh, oh, a bad one"; he saw her pressing her own bosom in sympathy, and felt her grip on his left arm.

"Yeah, wow," he said, finding voice. "Oh, boy."

"Gone?"

"Almost." Pain ran down the left arm she held, diminishing to a thread which continued down into his ring finger, on which there was no ring, but from which, it felt, a ring was being torn, pulled off, a ring worn so long that it couldn't be removed without severing nerve and tendon. "Quit it, quit it," he said, and it did quit, or diminish further anyway.

"Okay," he said. "Okay."

"Oh, Smoky," Alice said. "Okay?"

"Gone," he said. He took steps downward toward the lights of the drawing-room. Alice held him, supported him, but he wasn't weak; he wasn't even ill, Dr. Fish and Doc Drinkwater's old medical books agreed that what he suffered from wasn't a disease but a condition, compatible with long life, even with otherwise good health.

A condition, something to live with. Then why should it appear to be revelation, revelation that never quite came, and couldn't be remembered afterwards? "Yes," old Fish had said, "premonition of death, that's a common feeling with angina, nothing to worry about." But was it of death? Would that be what the revelation was, when it came, if it came?

"It hurt," Alice said.

"Well," Smoky said, laughing or panting, "I think I would have preferred it not to happen, yes."

"Maybe that's the last," Alice said. She seemed to think

471

of his attacks on the model of sneezes, one big last one might clear the system.

"Oh, I bet not," Smoky said mildly. "I don't think we want the last one. No."

They went down the stairs, holding each other, and then into the drawing room where the others waited.

"Here we are," said Alice. "Here's Smoky."

"Hi, hi," he said. Sophie looked up from her table, and his daughters from their knitting, and he saw his pain reflected in their faces. His finger still tingled, but he was whole; his long-worn ring was for a time yet unstolen.

A condition: but like revelation. And did theirs, he wondered for the first time, hurt like his did?

"All right," Sophie said. "We'll start." She looked around at the circle of faces which looked at her, Drinkwaters and Barnables, Birds, Flowers, Stones, and Weeds, her cousins, neighbors and relatives. The brightness of the brass lamp on the table made the rest of the room obscure to her, as though she sat by a campfire looking at the faces of animals in the surrounding dark, whom by her words she must charm into consciousness, and into purpose.

"Well," she said. "I had a visitor."

III

But how could you have expected
to travel that path in thought alone;
how expect to measure the moon by
the fish? No, my neighbors, never think
that path is a short one; you must
have lions' hearts to go by that way, it
is not short and its seas are deep;
you will walk it long in wonder, some-
times smiling, sometimes weeping.

—Attar, Parliament of the Birds

It had been easier than Sophie would have thought to assemble her relatives and neighbors here on this night, though it hadn't been easy to decide to assemble them, or to decide what to tell them: for an old, old silence was being broken, a silence so old that they at Edgewood did not even remember that it had been sworn to, a silence at the heart of many stories, broken into like a locked chest to which the key is lost. That had taken up the last months of winter: that, and getting the word out then to mudbound farms and isolated cottages, to the Capital and the City, and setting a date convenient to all.

They had almost all agreed, though, to come, oddly untaken-aback, when the word reached them; it had been almost as if they had long expected a summons like this. And so they had, though most of them didn't realize it until it had come.

Is It Far?

When Marge Juniper's young visitor passed through the pentacle of five towns which, once upon a time, Jeff Juniper had connected with a five-pointed star to show Smoky Barnable the way to Edgewood, more than one of the sleeping househol-

473

ders had awakened, feeling someone or something go by, and a kind of expectant peace descend, a happy sense that all their lives would not end, as they had supposed, before an ancient promise was Somehow fulfilled, or some great thing anyway come to pass. Only spring, they told themselves in the morning; only spring coming: the world is as it is and not different, and contains no such surprises. But then Marge's story went from house to house, gathering details as it went, and there were guesses and supposings about that; and then they were unsurprised—surprised to be unsurprised—when they were summoned here.

For it was with them, with all those families touched by August, taught by Auberon and then by Smoky, and visited by Sophie on her endless spinster's rounds, just as Great-aunt Nora Cloud supposed it would come to be with Drinkwaters and Barnables. There had been, after all, a time, nearly a hundred years ago, when their ancestors had settled here because they knew a Tale, or its tellers; some had been students, disciples even. They had been, people like the Flowers had been or had felt themselves to be, in on a secret; and many had been wealthy enough to do little but ponder it, amid the buttercups and milkweed of the farms they bought and neglected. And though hard times had reduced their descendants, turning many of them into artisans, into odd-jobbers, pickup-truckers, hard-scrabble farmers, inextricably intermarried now with the dairymen and handymen whom their great-grandparents had hardly spoken to, still they had stories, stories told nowhere else in the world. They were in reduced circumstances, yes; and the world (they thought) had grown hard and old and desperately ordinary; but they were descended from a race of bards and heroes, and there had been once an age of gold, and the earth around them was all alive and densely populated, though the present times were too coarse to see it. They had all gone to sleep, as children, to those old stories; and later they courted with them; and told them to their own children. The big house had always been their gossip, they could have surprised its inhabitants by how much they knew of it and its history. At table and by their fires they mused on these things, having not much other entertainment in these dark days, and (though altering them in their musing into very different things) they did not forget them. And when Sophie's summons came, surprised to be unsurprised, they put down their tools, and put off their aprons, they bundled up their children and kicked up their old engines; they came to Edgewood, and heard about a lost child returned, and an urgent plea, and a journey to go on.

"And so there's a door," Sophie said, touching one of the

cards (the trump Multiplicity) which lay before her, "and that's the house here. And," touching the next, "there's a dog who stands by the door." The silence was utter in the double drawing-room. "Further on," she said, "there's a river, or something like one. . . ."

"Speak up, dear," Momdy said, who sat almost next to her. "No one will hear."

"There's a river," Sophie said again, almost shouted. She blushed. In the darkness of her bedroom, with Lilac's certainty before her, it had all seemed—not easy, no, but clear at least; the end was still clear to her, but it was the means that had to be considered now, and they weren't clear. "And a bridge to cross it by, or a ford or a ferry or anyway some way to cross it; and on the other side an old man to guide us, who knows the way."

"The way where?" someone behind her ventured timidly; Sophie thought it was a Bird.

"There," someone else said, "Aren't you listening?"

"There where they are," Sophie said. "There where the Parliament's to be."

"Oh," said the first voice. "Oh. I thought *this* was the Parliament."

"No," Sophie said. "That's there."

"Oh."

Silence returned, and Sophie tried to think what else she knew.

"Is it far, Sophie?" Marge Juniper asked. "Some of us can't go far."

"I don't know," Sophie said. "I don't think it can be far; I remember sometimes it seemed far, and then sometimes near; but I don't think it could be too far, I mean too far to get to; but I don't know."

They waited; Sophie looked down at her cards, and shifted them. What if it was too far?

Blossom said softly: "Is it beautiful? It must be beautiful."

Bud beside her said, "No! Dangerous. And awful. With things to fight! It's a war, isn't that so, Aunt Sophie?"

Ariel Hawksquill glanced at the children, and at Sophie. "Is it, Sophie?" she asked. "Is it a war?"

Sophie looked up, and held out empty hands. "I don't know," she said. "I think it's a war; that's what Lilac said. It's what *you* said," she said to Ariel, a little reproachfully. "I don't know, I don't know!" She got up, turning around to see them all. "All I know is that we have to go, we have to, to help them. Because if we don't, there won't be any more of them. They're dying, I know it! Or going away, going away so far, hiding so far that it's like dying, and because of us! And think what that would be, if there weren't any more."

They thought of that, or tried to, each coming to a different conclusion, or a different vision, or to none at all.

"I don't know where it is," Sophie said, "or how it is we're to go there, or what we can do to help, or why it is that it's us that have to go; but I know we must, we have to try! I mean it doesn't even matter if we want to or don't want to, really, don't you see, because we wouldn't even *be* here if it wasn't for them; I know that's so. Not to go, now—that's like, it's like being born, and growing up, and marrying and having children, and then saying well, I've changed my mind, I'd rather not have—when there wouldn't be a person there even to *say* he'd rather not have, unless he *had* already. Do you see? And it's the same with them. We couldn't refuse unless we were the ones who were meant to go, unless we were all *going* to go, in the first place."

She looked around at them all, Drinkwaters and Barnables, Birds, Stones, Flowers, Weeds, and Wolfs; Charles Wayne and Cherry Lake, Bud and Blossom, Ariel Hawksquill and Marge Juniper; Sonny Moon, ancient Phil Flowers and Phil's girls and boys, August's grandchildren and great- and great-great-grandchildren. She missed her aunt Cloud very much, who could have said these things so simply and incontrovertibly. Daily Alice, chin in her hand, was only looking at her smiling; Alice's daughters were sewing calmly, as though all that Sophie had said were just as clear as water, though it had seemed nonsense to Sophie even as she had said it. Her mother nodded sagely, but perhaps she hadn't heard aright; and the faces of her cousins around her were wise and foolish, light and dark, changed or unchanged.

"I've told you all I can," Sophie said helplessly. "All that Lilac said: that there are fifty-two, and that it's to be Midsummer Day, and that this is the door, as it always was; and the cards are a map, and what they say, as far as I can tell, about the dog and the river and so on. So. Now we just have to think what next."

They all did think, many of them not much used to the exercise; many, though their hands were to their brows or their fingertips together, drifted away into surmise, wild or common, or sank into memory; gathered wool, or knitted it; felt their pains, old or new, and thought what those might portend, this journey or a different one; or they simply ruminated, chewing and tasting their own familiar natures, or counting over old fears or old advice, or remembering love or comfort; or they did none of these things.

"It might be easy," Sophie said wildly. "It could be. Just a step! Or it might be hard. Maybe," she said, "yes, maybe it's not one way, not the same way for all—but there *is* a way, there must be. You have to think of it, each of you, you have to *imagine* it."

They tried that, shifting in their seats and crossing their legs differently; they thought of north, of south, east, west; they thought of how they had come to be here anyway, guessing that if a path *there* could be seen, then perhaps its continuation would be clear; and in the silence of their thinking they heard a sound none had heard yet this year: peepers, suddenly speaking their one word.

"Well," Sophie said, and sat. She pushed the cards together as though their story were all told. "Anyway. We'll go step by step. We've got all spring. Then we'll just meet, and see. I can't think what else."

"But Sophie," Tacey said, putting down her sewing, "if the house is the door . . ."

"And," Lily said, putting down hers, "if we're in it . . ."

"Then," Lucy said, "aren't we traveling anyway?"

Sophie looked at them. What they had said made perfect sense, common sense, the way they said it. "I don't know," she said.

"Sophie," Smoky said from where he stood by the door. He hadn't spoken since he'd come in and the meeting had started. "Can I ask something?"

"Sure," Sophie said.

"How," Smoky said, "do we get back?"

In her silence was his answer, the one he'd expected, the one thing everyone present had suspected about the place she spoke of. She bowed her head in the silence she had made, and no one broke it; they all heard her answer, and in it, hidden, the true question that was being put to them, which Sophie could not quite ask.

They were all family, anyway, Sophie thought; or if they came, they counted, and if they didn't, they didn't, that's all. She opened her mouth to ask: Will you come? but their faces abashed her, so various, so familiar, and she couldn't frame it. "Well," she said; they had grown indistinct in the sparkling tears that came to her eyes. "That's all, I guess."

Blossom jumped from her chair. "I know," she said. "We all have to take hands, in a circle, for strength, and all say 'We will!' " She looked around her. "Okay?"

There was some laughter and some demurrers, and her mother drew her to her and said that maybe everyone didn't want to do that, but Blossom, taking her brother's hand, began to urge her cousins and aunts and uncles to come closer to take hands, avoiding only the Lady with the Alligator Purse; then she decided that perhaps the circle would be stronger if they all crossed arms and took hands with opposite hands, which necessitated an even smaller circle, and when she got this linked in one place it would break in another. "Nobody's *listening*," she complained to Sophie, who only gazed at her unhearing, thinking of what might become of her, of the brave ones, and unable to imagine; and just then Momdy stood up tottering, who hadn't heard the plan Blossom had urged, and said, "Well. There's coffee and tea, and other things, in the kitchen, and some sandwiches," and that broke the circle further; there was a scraping of chairs, and a general movement; they went off kitchenwards, talking in low voices.

"Coffee sounds good," Hawksquill said to the ancient lady beside her.

Only
Pretending

"It does," Marge Juniper said. "Only I'm not sure whether it's worth the trouble of going for it. You know."

"Will you allow me," Hawksquill said, "to bring you a cup?"

"That's very kind," Marge said with relief. It had been quite a trouble to everyone getting her here, and she was glad to keep to the seat she'd been put in.

"Good," Hawksquill said. She went after the others, but stopped at the table where Sophie, cheek in hand, stared down as in grief, or wonder, at the cards. "Sophie," she said.

"What if it's too far?" Sophie said. She looked up at Hawksquill, a sudden fear in her eyes. "What if I'm wrong about it all?"

"I don't think you could be," Hawksquill said, "in a way. As far as I understood what you meant, anyway. It's very *odd*, I know; but that's no reason to think it's wrong." She touched Sophie's shoulder. "In fact," she said, "I'd only say that perhaps it's not yet odd enough."

"Lilac," Sophie said.

"That," Hawksquill said, "was odd. Yes."

"Ariel," Sophie said, "won't you look at them? Maybe you could see something, some first step. . . ."

"No," Hawksquill said, drawing back. "No, they're not for me to touch. No." In the figure Sophie had laid out, broken now, the Fool did not show. "They're too great a thing now."

"Oh, I don't know," Sophie said, spreading them idly around. "I think—it seems to me I've about got to the end of them.

478

Of what they have to tell. Maybe it's only me. But there doesn't seem to be any more in them." She rose, and walked away from them. "Lilac said they were the guidebook," she said. "But I don't know. I think she was only pretending."

"Pretending?" Hawksquill said, following her.

"Just to keep our interest up," Sophie said. "Hope."

Hawksquill glanced back at them. Like the circle Blossom had tried to make, they were linked strongly, even in disorder, by their opposite hands. The end of them . . . She looked quickly away, and signalled reassuringly to the old woman she had sat by, who didn't seem to see.

In fact Marge Juniper didn't see her, but it wasn't fading eye-sight or failing attention that blinded her. She was only absorbed in thinking, as Sophie had abjured them, how she might walk to that place, and what she might take with her (a pressed flower, a shawl embroidered with the same kind of flowers, a locket containing a curl of black hair, an acrostic valentine on which the letters of her name headed sentiments faded now to sepia and insincerity) and how she might husband her strength until the day she should set out.

For she knew what place it was that Sophie spoke of. Lately Marge's memory had grown weak, which is to say that it no longer contained the past time on deposit there, it was not strong enough to keep shut up the moments, the mornings and evenings, of her long life; its seals broke, and her memories ran together mingling, indistinguishable from the present. Her memory had grown incontinent with age; and she knew very well what place it was she was to go to. It was the place where, eighty-some years ago or yesterday, August Drinkwater had run off to; and the place also where she had remained when he had gone. It was the place all young hopes go when they have become old and we no longer feel them; the place where beginnings go when endings have come, and then themselves passed.

Midsummer Day, she thought, and made to count out the days and weeks remaining until them; but she forgot what season this was she counted from, and so gave it up.

In the dining room Hawksquill came upon Smoky, loitering in the corner, seeming lost in his own house and at loose ends.

"How," she said to him, "do you understand all this, Mr. Barnable?"

Where Was She Headed?

"Hm?" He took a time to focus on her. "Oh. I don't. I don't understand it." He shrugged, not as though in apology but as though it were a position he found himself taking, one side of a question, the other side had lots to be said for it too. He looked away.

"And how," she said then, seeing she ought not to pursue that further, "is your orrery coming? Have you got it working?"

This too seemed to be the wrong question. He sighed. "Not *working*," he said. "All ready to go. Only not working."

"What's the difficulty?"

He thrust his hands in his pockets. "The difficulty is," he said, "that it's circular. . . ."

"Well, so are the Spheres," Hawksquill said. "Or nearly."

"I didn't mean that," Smoky said. "I mean that it depends on itself to go around. Depends on its going around to go around. You know. Perpetual Motion. It's a perpetual motion machine, believe it or not."

"So are the Spheres," Hawksquill said. "Or nearly."

"What I can't understand," Smoky said, growing more agitated as he contemplated this, and jingling the small objects he had in his pockets, screws, washers, coins, "is how someone like Henry Cloud, or Harvey either, could have come up with such a dumb idea. Perpetual motion. Everybody knows . . ." He looked at Hawksquill. "How does yours work," he said, "by the way? What makes is go around?"

"Well." Hawksquill said, setting down the two coffee cups she carried on a sideboard, "not, I think the way yours does. Mine shows a different heavens, after all. Simpler, in many ways . . ."

"Well, but how?" Smoky said. "Give me a hint." He smiled, and Hawksquill thought, seeing him, that he had not often done so lately. She wondered how he had come among this family in the first place.

"I can tell you this," she said. "Whatever makes mine go around now, I have the definite impression that it was designed to go around by itself."

"By itself," Smoky said doubtfully.

"It couldn't, though," Hawksquill said. "Perhaps because it's the wrong heavens, because it models a heavens that never did go by themselves, but were always moved by will: by angels, by gods. Mine are the old heavens. But yours are the new, the Newtonian, self-propelling, once-wound-up-forever-ticking type of heavens. Perhaps it does move by itself."

Smoky stared at her. "There's a machine that looks like it's supposed to drive it," he said. "But it needs to be driven itself. It needs a push."

"Well, " Hawksquill said, "once properly set . . . I mean if
it had the star's motions, they'd be irresistible, wouldn't they?
Forever." A strange light was dawning in Smoky's eyes, a light that
looked like pain to Hawksquill. She should shut up. A little learning.
If she hadn't felt Smoky to be effectively outside the scheme the rest
of her cousins were proposing, which Hawksquill had no intention of
furthering, she would not have added: "You may well have it backwards, Mr. Barnable. Drive and driven. The stars have power to
spare."

She picked up her coffee cups, and when he reached out a
hand to keep her, she showed them to him, nodded and escaped; his
next question would be one she couldn't answer without breaking old
vows. But she wanted to have helped him. She felt, for some reason,
the need of an ally here. Standing confused at a juncture of hallways
(she had taken a wrong turning away from the dining room) she saw
him hurrying away upstairs, and hoped she hadn't set him on fruit-
lessly.

Now where was it she was headed? She looked around
herself, turning this way and that, the coffee cooling in her hands.
Somewhere there was a murmur of voices.

A turning, a juncture where many ways could be seen at
once; a Vista. No memory mansion of her own was built more over-
lappingly, with more corridors, more places that were two places at
once, more precise in its confusions, than this house. She felt it rise
around her, John's dream, Violet's castle, tall and many-roomed. It
took hold of her mind, as though it were in fact made of memory; she
saw, and it swept her into a fearful clarity to see, that if this *were* her
own mind's house, all her conclusions would now be coming out
quite differently; quite, quite differently.

She had sat this night smiling among them, listening politely, as though she were attending someone else's religious service,
mistaken for a member of the congregation, feeling at once embarrassed at their sincerity and aloof from emotions she was glad not to
share, and perhaps just a little sad to be excluded, it looked like fun
to understand things so simply. But the house had meanwhile been
all around them as it was all around her now, great, grave, certain
and impatient: the house said it was not so, not so at all. The house
said (and Hawksquill knew how to hear houses speak, it was her chief
skill and great art, she only wondered how she had been deaf to this
huge voice so long), the house said that it was not they, not
Drinkwaters and Barnables and the rest, who had understood things
too simply. She had thought that the great cards they played with
had come to them by chance, a Grail stashed amusingly with the

481

daily drinking cups, an historical accident. But the house didn't believe in accidents; the house said she had been mistaken, again, and this time for the last time. As though while sitting aloof in some humble church, among ordinary parishioners who sang corny hymns, she had witnessed some concrete and terrible miracle or grace, she trembled in denial and fear: she could not have been so horribly mistaken, reason couldn't bear it, it would turn dream and shatter, and in its shattering she would awake into some world, some house so strange, so new. . . .

She heard Daily Alice call to her, from an unexpected direction. She heard the coffee cups she still held rattling faintly in their saucers. She composed herself, took courage, and pulled herself out of the tangle of the imaginary drawing-room where she had got stuck.

"You'll stay the night, won't you, Ariel?" Alice said. "The imaginary bedroom's made up, and . . ."

"No," Hawksquill said. She delivered Marge's coffee to her where she still sat. The old woman took it abstractedly, and it seemed to Hawksquill that she wept, or had been weeping, though perhaps it was only the watering of aged eyes. "No, it's very kind of you, but I must leave. I have to meet a train north of here. I should be on it now, but I managed to get away to here first."

"Well, couldn't you . . ."

"No," Hawksquill said. "It's a Presidential train. Waiting on princes, you know. He's taking one of his tours. I don't know why he bothers. He's either shot at, or ignored. Still."

The guests were leaving, pulling on heavy coats and ear-flap hats. Many stopped to talk with Sophie; Hawksquill saw that one of these, an old man, wept too as he talked, and that Sophie embraced him.

"They'll all go, then?" she asked Alice.

"I think," Alice said. "Mostly. We'll see, won't we?"

Her eyes on Hawksquill, so clear and brown, so full of serene complicity, made Hawksquill look away, afraid that she too would stutter and weep. "My bag," she said. "I'll get it, then I must go. Must."

The drawing-rooms where they had all met were empty now, except for the dim figure of the old woman, drinking her coffee in tiny sips like a clockwork figure. Hawksquill took up her purse. Then she saw that the cards still lay spread out beneath the lamp.

The end of their story. But not of hers; not if she could help it.

She glanced up quickly. She could hear Alice and Sophie,

saying goodbye to guests at the front door. Marge's eyes were closed. Almost without thinking she turned her back to Marge, snapped open the purse, and swept the cards into it. They burned the fingertips that touched them like ice. She snapped the purse shut and turned to leave. She saw Alice standing in the drawing-room door, looking at her.

"Goodbye, then," Hawksquill said briskly, her icy heart thudding, feeling as helpless as a naughty child in a grown-up's grip who's yet unable to quit his tantrum.

"Goodbye," Alice said, standing aside to let her pass. "Good luck with the President. We'll see you soon."

Hawksquill didn't look at her, knowing that she would read her crime in Alice's eyes, and more too that she wanted even less to see. There was an escape from this, there had to be; if wit couldn't find it, power must make it. And it was too late now for her to think of anything but escape.

Daily Alice and Sophie watched from the front door as Hawksquill climbed quickly, as though pursued, into her car, and gunned the motor. The car leapt forward like a steed, and arrowed out between the stone gateposts and into the night and fog.

Too Simple to Say

"Late for her train," Alice said.

"Do you think she'll come, though?" Sophie said.

"Oh," Alice said, "she will. She will."

They turned away from the night, and shut the door. "But Auberon," Sophie said. "Auberon, and George . . ."

"It's okay, Sophie," Alice said.

"But . . . ."

"Sophie," Alice said. "Will you come sit up with me a while? I'm not going to sleep."

Alice's face was calm, and she smiled, but Sophie heard an appeal, even something like a fear. She said, "Sure, Alice."

"How about the library?" Alice said. "Nobody will go in there."

"Okay." She followed Alice into the great dark room; Alice lit a single lamp with a kitchen match and turned it low. Out the windows the fog seemed to contain dull lights, but nothing else could be seen. "Alice?" she said.

Alice seemed to wake from thought, and faced her sister.

"Alice, did you know all what I was going to say, tonight?"

"Oh; most of it, I guess."

483

"Did you? How long ago?"

"I don't know. In a way," she said, sitting slowly on one end of the long leather chesterfield, "in a way I think I always knew it; and it just kept getting clearer. Except when . . ."

"When?"

"When it got darker. When—well, when things didn't seem to be going as you thought they would, or even the opposite. Times when—when it all seemed taken away."

Sophie turned away, though her sister had spoken only with a deep thoughtfulness, and in no way in reproach; she knew what times it was that Alice spoke of, and grieved that she had, even for a day, for an hour, deflected her certainties. And all so long ago!

"Afterwards, though," Alice said, "when things seemed, you know, to make sense again, they made an even bigger sense. And it seemed funny that you could ever have thought it wasn't all right, that you could have been fooled. Isn't that right? Wasn't it like that?"

"I don't know," Sophie said.

"Come sit," Alice said. "Wasn't it like that with you?"

"No." She sat by Alice, and Alice pulled a multi-colored afghan, Tacey's work, over the two of them; it was cold in the fireless room. "I think it just kept making less sense ever since I was little." So hard to speak of it, after so many years of silence; once, years ago, they had chatted about it endlessly, not making sense and not caring to, mixing it with their dreams and with the games they played, knowing so surely how to understand it because they made no distinction between it and their desires, for comfort, for adventure, for wonder. Very suddenly she was visited with a memory, as vivid and as whole as though present, of her and Alice naked, and their uncle Auberon, at the place on the edge of the woods. For so long had her memories of those things come to be in effect replaced by Auberon's photographs that recorded them, beautiful pale and still, that to have one return in all its fullness took her breath away: heat, and certainty, and wonder, in the deep real summer of childhood. "Oh, why," she said, "why couldn't we have just gone then, when we knew? When it would have been so *easy*?"

Alice took her hand under the comforter. "We could have," she said. "We could have gone any time. When we did go is the Tale."

She added after a time: "But it *won't* be easy." Her words alerted Sophie, and she took her sister's hand more tightly. "Sophie," Alice said, "you said Mid-summer Day."

"Yes."

"But—all right," Alice said. "Only. I have to go sooner."

Sophie raised her head from the sofa, not relinquishing her sister's hand, and afraid. "What?" she said.

"I," Alice said, "have to go sooner." She glanced at Sophie, and then away; a glance Sophie knew meant that Alice was telling her now a thing she had long known about and had kept a secret.

"When?" Sophie said, or whispered.

"Now," Alice said.

"No," Sophie said.

"Tonight," Alice said, "or this morning. That's why—that's why I wanted you to sit with me, because . . ."

"But why?" Sophie said.

"I can't say, Sophie."

"No, Alice, no, but . . ."

"It's okay, Soph," Alice said, smiling at her sister's bafflement. "We're all to go, all of us; only I have to go sooner. That's all."

Sophie stared at her, a very strange thought invading her, invading her wide eyes and open mouth and hollowed heart: strange, because she had heard Lilac say it, and had read it in the cards, and then spoken of it to all her cousins, but had only now come to truly think it. "We *are* going, then," she said.

Alice nodded, a tiny nod.

"It's all true," Sophie said. Her sister, calm or at least not shaken, ready or seeming to be, grew huge before Sophie's eyes. "All true."

"Yes."

"Oh, Alice." Alice, grown so great before her, frightened her. "Oh, but Alice, don't. Wait. Don't go now, not so soon. . . ."

"I have to," Alice said.

"But then I'll be left, and . . . everybody . . ." She threw off the comforter and stood to plead. "No, don't go without me, wait!"

"I have to, Sophie, because . . . Oh, I can't say it, it's too strange to say, or too simple. I have to go, because if I don't, there won't be any place to go *to*. For you, and everybody."

"I don't understand," Sophie said.

Alice laughed, a small laugh like a sob. "I don't either, yet. But. Soon."

"But all alone," Sophie said. "How can you?"

Alice said nothing to that, and Sophie bit her lip that she'd said it. Brave! A huge love, a love like deepest pity, filled her

up, and she took Alice's hand again; she sat again beside her. Somewhere in the house, a clock rang a small morning hour, and the bells
stabbed one by one through Sophie. "Are you afraid?" she said,
unable not to.

"Just sit with me awhile," Alice said. "It's not long till
dawn."

Far above them then there were footsteps, quick ones,
heavy. They both looked up. The steps went overhead, down a hall,
and then came rapidly and noisily down the stairs. Alice squeezed
Sophie's hand, in a way that Sophie understood, though what she
understood Alice to be telling her by it shocked her more deeply than
anything her sister had so far said.

Smoky opened the door of the library, and gave a start
seeing the two women on the sofa.

"Hey, still up?" he said. His breath was labored. Sophie
was sure he would read her stricken face, but he didn't seem to; he
went to the lamp, picked it up, and began going around the library,
peering at the dark-burdened shelves.

"You wouldn't happen to know," he said, "whereabouts
the ephemeris might be?"

"The what?" Alice said.

"Ephemeris," he said, pulling out a book, pushing it back.
"The big red book that gives the positions of the planets. For every
date. You know."

"You used to look at it when we were stargazing?"

"Right." He turned to them. He was still faintly panting,
and seemed in the grip of a fierce excitement. "No guesses?" He held
aloft the lamp. "You're not going to believe this," he said. "I don't,
yet. But it's the only thing that makes sense. The only thing crazy
enough to make sense."

He waited for them to question him, and at last Alice
said, "What."

"The orrery," he said. "It'll work."

"Oh," Alice said.

"Not only that, not only that," he said in astonished
triumph. "I think it'll *do* work. I think it was *meant* to. It was so
simple! I never thought of it. Can you imagine if that's so? Alice, the
house will be all right! If that thing will turn, it'll turn belts! It'll turn
generators! Lights! Heat!"

The lamp he held showed them his face, transformed, and
seeming so close to some dangerous limit that it made Sophie shrink.
She supposed that he couldn't see the two of them well; she glanced
at Alice, who still tightly held her hand, and thought that Alice's

eyes might fill with tears, if they could, but that they could not; that
Somehow they never would again.

"That's nice," Alice said.

"Nice," Smoky said, resuming his search. "You think I'm
crazy. *I* think I'm crazy. But I think just maybe Harvey Cloud wasn't
crazy. Maybe." He pulled a thick book from under others, which fell
noisily to the floor. "This is it, this is it, this is it," he said, and
without looking back at them, he made to leave.

"The lamp, Smoky," Alice said.

"Oh. Sorry." He had been carrying it off absently. He put
it down on the table, and smiled at them, so infinitely pleased that
they couldn't not smile back. He left almost at a run, the thick book
under his arm.

The two women sat without speaking for some time after
he had gone. Then Sophie said: "You won't tell him?"

"No," Alice said. She began to say something further, a reason perhaps, but then didn't, and
Sophie dared say nothing more. "Anyway," Alice said,
"I won't be *gone,* not really. I mean I'll be gone, but
still I'll be here. Always." She thought that was true; she thought,
looking up at the dark ceiling and the tall windows, at the house
around her, that what called to her, calling from the very heart of
things, called to her as much from here as from any other place; and
that the feeling she felt was not loss, it was only that sometimes she
mistook it for loss. "But Sophie," she said, and her voice had grown
rough, "Sophie, you have to take care of him. Watch out for him."

"How, Alice."

"I don't know, but—well, you must. I mean it, Soph. Do
that for me."

"I will," Sophie said. "But I'm not much good at that, you
know, watching out, and taking care."

"It won't be long," Alice said. That too she was sure of, or
believed or hoped she was sure of; she tried, searching in herself, to
find that certainty: to find the calm delight, the gratitude, the exhilaration she had felt when she had begun to understand what conclusion it was all to have, the half-scared, half-puissant sense that she
had lived her whole life as a chick inside an egg, and then got too big
for it, and then found a way to begin to break it, and then had
broken it, and was now about to come forth into some huge, airy
world she could have had no inkling of, yet bearing wings to live in it
with that were still untried. She was sure that what she knew now,
they would all come to know, and other things still more wonderful,

487

and more wonderful yet; but in the cold old room at the dark end of night, she couldn't quite feel it alive within her. She thought of Smoky. She was afraid; as afraid as if . . .

"Sophie," she said softly. "Do you think it's death?"

Sophie had fallen asleep, her head resting against Alice's shoulder. "Hm?" she said.

"Do you think that dying is what it really is?"

"I don't know," Sophie said. She felt Alice trembling beside her. "I don't think so. But I don't know."

"I don't think so either," Alice said.

Sophie said nothing.

"If it is, though," Alice said, "it isn't . . . what I thought."

"You mean dying isn't? Or that place?"

"Either." She pulled the afghan more closely around them. "Smoky told me, once, about this place, in India or China, where ages ago when somebody got the death sentence, they used to give him this drug, like a sleeping drug, only it's a poison, but very slow-acting; and the person falls asleep first, deep asleep, and has these very vivid dreams. He dreams a long time, he forgets he's dreaming even; he dreams for days. He dreams that he's on a journey, or that some such thing has happened to him. And then, somewhere along, the drug is so gentle and he's so fast asleep that he never notices when, he dies. But he doesn't know it. The dream changes, maybe; but he doesn't even know it's a dream, so. He just goes on. He only thinks it's another country."

"That's spooky," Sophie said.

"Smoky said he didn't think it was so, though."

"No," Sophie said. "I bet not."

"He said, if the drug was always supposed to be fatal in the end, how would anybody know that's what its effect was?"

"Oh."

"I was thinking," Alice said, "that maybe this is like that."

"Oh, Alice, how awful, no."

But Alice had meant nothing awful; it seemed to her no dreadful issue, if you were condemned to death, to make out of death a country. That was the similarity she saw: for she had perceived, what none of the others had and Sophie only dimly and backwardly, that the place they had been invited to was no place. She had perceived in her own growing larger that there was no place there distinct from those who lived in it: the fewer of them, the smaller their country. And if there were now to be a migration to that land, each emigrant would have to make the place he traveled to, make it out of himself. It was what she, pioneer, would have to do: make out of her own death, or what just now seemed like her death, a land for the rest of them to travel to. She would have to grow large enough to contain the whole world, or the whole great world turn out to be small enough after all to fit within the compass of her bosom.

Smoky for sure wouldn't believe in that either. He'd find it hard, anyway. She thought then that he had found the whole thing hard; that however patient he had grown, however well he had learned to live with it, he had never and would never find it easy. Would he come? More than anything else she wanted to be sure of that. Could he? She was sure of so many things, but not sure of that; long ago she had seen that the very thing that had earned Smoky for her might be the cause of her losing him, that is, her place in this Tale. And there it still was, the bargain held; she felt him even now to be at the end of a long and fragile cord, that might part if she tugged it, or slip from her fingers, or from his. And she would leave now without farewell lest it be for good.

Oh Smoky, she thought; oh death. And for a long time thought nothing else, only wishing, without making the wish, that this issue were not the issue it must have, the only issue it could have or ever had.

"You will watch out for him," she whispered; "Sophie, you have to see that he comes. You have to."

But Sophie was asleep again, the afghan drawn up to her chin. Alice looked around herself, as though waking; the windows were blue. Night was passing. Like someone coming to consciousness with the cessation of pain, she gathered around herself the world, the dawn, and her future. She stood then, easing herself away from her sleeping sister. Sophie dreamed that she did so, and partly woke to say, "I'm ready, I'll come," and then other words that made no sense. She sighed, and Alice tucked the afghan around her.

Above her, there were footsteps again, coming downward. Alice kissed her sister's brow, and blew out the dim lamp; blue dawn filled the room when the yellow flame was gone. It was later than she had thought. She went out into the hall; Smoky came running down to the landing on the stairs above her.

"Alice!" he said.

"Yes, hush," she said. "You'll wake everybody."

"Alice, it works." He gripped the newel at the stair's turning, as though he might fall. "It works, you have to come see."

"Oh?" Alice said.

"Alice, Alice, come see! It's all right now. It's all right, it works, it goes around. Listen!" And he pointed upward. Far, far off, barely discernible amid the dawn noises of peepers and first birds, there was a steady metallic clacking, like the ticking of a vast clock, a clock inside which the house itself was contained.

"All right?" Alice said.

"It's all right, we don't have to leave!" He paused again to listen, rapt. "The house won't fall apart. There'll be light and heat. We don't have to go anywhere!"

She only looked up, from the bottom of the stair.

"Isn't that great?" he said.

"Great," she said.

"Come see," he said, already turning back up the stairs.

"Okay," she said. "I'll come. In a minute."

"Hurry," he said, and started upwards.

"Smoky, don't run," she said.

She heard his climbing footsteps recede. She went to the hall-mirror, and from a peg beside it took her heavy cloak, and threw it around her. She glanced once at the figure in the mirror, who looked aged in the dawn light, and went to the great front door with its oval glass, and opened it.

The morning was huge, and went on in all directions before her, and blew coldly past her into the house. She stood a long time in the open doorway, thinking: one step. One step, which will seem to be a step away, but which will not be; one step into the rainbow, a step she had long ago taken, and which could not be untaken, every other step was only further. She took one step. Out on the lawn, amid the rags of mist, a little dog ran toward her, leaping and barking excitedly.

IV

Itur in antiquam silvam, stabula alta ferrarum.
—Aeneid, *Book VI*

While Daily Alice thought and Sophie watched and slept, while Ariel Hawksquill flew along foggy country roads to meet a train at a northern station, Auberon and George Mouse sat close to a small fire, wondering what place it was that Fred Savage had led them to, and unable to remember in any clear way just how they had got there.

They'd started off some time ago, it seemed to them; they'd begun by making preparations, going through George's old trunks and bureaus outfitting themselves, though since they had had not much idea at all of what dangers or difficulties they would meet, this had been haphazard; George found and tossed out sweaters, flaccid knapsacks, knitted caps, galoshes.

Storm of Difference

"Say," Fred said, tugging a cap over his wild hair. "Long time since I wore one of these here."

"What good is all this, though?" Auberon said, standing aside, hands in his pockets.

"Well, listen," George said. Better safe than sorry. Forewarned is forearmed."

"You'd about need to be four-armed," said Fred, holding up an immense poncho, "for thisere to do you much good."

"This is stupid," Auberon said. "I mean . . ."

"Okay, okay," George said angrily, flourishing a large pistol he had just then found in the trunk, "okay, *you* decide, Mr. Know-it-all. Just don't say I didn't warn you." He thrust the gun in his belt, then changed his mind and tossed it back. "Hey, how about this?" It was a twenty-bladed jackknife with a thousand uses. "God, I haven't seen this in *years.*"

491

"Nice," Fred said, levering out the corkscrew with a yellow thumbnail. "Ver' nice. *And* handy."

Auberon went on watching, hands in pockets, but made no further objection; after a moment he no longer watched. Ever since Lilac's appearance at Old Law Farm he had had immense difficulty in remaining for any length of time in the world; he seemed only to enter and leave particular scenes, which had no connection with each other, like the rooms of a house whose plan he couldn't fathom, or didn't care to try to fathom. He supposed, sometimes, that he was going mad, but though the thought seemed reasonable enough and an explanation of sorts, it left him oddly unmoved. For sure an enormous difference had suddenly come over the nature of things, but just what that difference was he couldn't put his finger on: or rather, any individual thing he did put his finger on (a street, an apple, any thought, any memory) seemed no different, seemed to be now just what it had always been, and yet the difference remained. "Same difference," George often said, about two things that were more or less alike; but for Auberon the phrase had come to designate his sense of one thing, one thing that had Somehow become—and was probably now for good—more or less different.

Same difference.

Probably, though (he didn't know, but it seemed likely) this difference hadn't come about suddenly at all, it was only that he had suddenly come to notice it, to inhabit it. It had dawned on him, is all; it had grown clear to him, like breaking weather. And he foresaw a time (with only a faint shudder of apprehension) when he would no longer notice the difference, or remember that things had ever been, or rather not been, different; and after that a time when storms of difference would succeed one another as they liked, and he would never notice.

Already he found himself forgetting that something like an occluded front seemed to have swept over his memories of Sylvie, which he had thought as hard and changeless as anything he owned, but which when he touched them now seemed to have turned to autumn leaves like fairy gold, turned to wet earth, staghorn, snails' shells, fauns' feet.

"What?" he said.

"Put this on," George said, and gave him a sheath knife on whose sheath, dimly printed in gold, were the words "Ausable Chasm," which meant nothing to Auberon; but he looped it through his belt, not able to think just then why he might rather not.

Certainly this drifting in and out of what seemed to be chapters of fiction with blank pages in between had helped out with a hard task he had had to do: wrapping up (as he had thought he would never need to) the tale told on "A World Elsewhere." To wrap up a tale whose wrapping-up was in the very nature of it not conceivable—hard! And yet he had only had to sit before the nearly-shot typewriter (so much had it suffered) for concluding chapters to begin to unfold as clearly, as cleverly, as impossibly as an endless chain of colored scarves from the empty fist of a magician. How does a tale end that was only a promise of no ending? In the same way as a difference comes to inhabit a world that is otherwise the same in all respects; in the same way that a picture which shows a complex urn alters, as you stare at it, to two faces contemplating each other.

He fulfilled the promise, that it wouldn't end: and that was the end. That's all.

Just how he had done it, just what scenes he stabbed out on the twenty-six alphabetical buttons and their associates, what words were said, what deaths came to pass, what births, he couldn't remember afterwards; they were the dreams of a man who dreams he dreams, imaginary imagination, insubstantialities set up in a world itself gone insubstantial. Whether they would be produced at all, and what effect they would have Out There if they were, what spell they might cast or break, he couldn't imagine. He only sent Fred off with the once-unimaginable last pages, and thought, laughing, of that schoolboy device he had once used, that last line that every schoolboy had once used to complete some wild self-indulgent fantasy otherwise uncompletable: *then he woke up.*

Then he woke up.

The phrases of his fugue with the world touched each other. The three of them, he, George, and Fred, stood booted and armed before the maw of a subway entrance: a cold spring day like a messy bed where the world still slept.

"Uptown? Downtown?" George asked.

Auberon had suggested other doors, or what had seemed to him might be doors: a pavilion in a locked park to which he had the key; an uptown building that had been Sylvie's last destination as a Wingéd messenger; a barrel vault deep beneath the Terminus, nexus of four corridors. But Fred was leading this expedition.

Watch Your Step

"A ferry," he said. "Now if we's to take a ferry, we surely will cross a river. So now not countin' the Bronx and the Harlem, not countin' no Kills and no Spuyten Duyvil which is really th'ocean, not goan so far north as the Saw Mill, and settin' aside the East and the Hudson which got bridges, you still got a mess more of rivers to consider, yunnastan, only, here's the thang, they runnin' *under-ground* now all unseen; covered up with streets and folks' houses and plays-a-business; shootin' through ser-pipes and pressed down to trickles and rivulets and like that; stopped up, drove down deep into the rock where they turn into seep and what you call your groundwater; still there though, y'see, y'see, so we gots to first *find* the river to cross, and then we gots to *cross* it next; and if the mose of 'em is underground, underground is where we gots to go."

"Okay," George said.

"Okay," Auberon said.

"Watch your step," Fred said.

They went down, stepping carefully as though in an unfamiliar place, though all of them were familiar with it, it was only The Train with its caves and dens, its mad signs pointing in contradictory directions, no help for the lost, and its seep of inky water and far-off borborygmic rumbles.

Auberon stopped, half-way down the stairs.

"Wait a sec," he said. "Wait."

"Wazza matter?" George said, looking quickly around.

"This is crazy," Auberon said. "This can't be right." Fred had gone ahead, had rounded the corner, waving them on. George stood between, looking after Fred and up at Auberon.

"Let's go, let's go," George said.

This would be hard, very hard, Auberon thought, following reluctantly; far harder to yield to than to the blank passages and discomfitures of his old drunkenness. And yet the skills he had learned in that long binge—how to yield up control, how to ignore shame and make a spectacle of himself, how not to question circumstances or at least not be surprised when no answers to questions could be found—those skills were all he had now, all the gear he could bring to this expedition. Even with them he doubted he would get to the end; without them, he thought, he would not have been able to start off.

"Okay, wait," he said, turning after the others into deeper places. "Hold on."

And what if he had been put through that awful time, basic training, only so that now (snow-blind, sun-struck) he could live through this storm of difference, make his way through this dark wood?

No. It was Sylvie who had set him on that path; or rather Sylvie's absence.

Sylvie's absence. And what if Sylvie's absence, what if her

presence in his life in the first place, God what if her very love and beauty had been plotted from the beginning, to make him a drunk, to teach him those skills, to train him in pathfinding, to immure him at Old Law Farm for years to wait for news without knowing he waited, to wait for Lilac to come with promises or lies to stir his heart's ashes into flame again, and all for some purpose of their own, which had nothing to do with him, or with Sylvie either?

All right: supposing there was to be this Parliament, supposing that that wasn't just lies as well and that he would come Somehow face to face with them, he had some questions to ask, and some good answers to get. Come to that, let him only find Sylvie, and he had some tough questions he could put to her about her part in all this, some damn tough questions; only let him find her. Only, only let him find her.

Even as he thought this he saw, leaping from the last stair of a rachitic escalator, down there, a blond girl in a blue dress, bright in the brown darkness.

She looked back once and (seeing that they saw her) turned around a stanchion where a notice was posted: HOLD ONTO YOUR HATS.

"I think this is the way," George called. A train roared through just at that moment, as they were gathering to run downward; the wind of its passage snatched at their hats, but their hands were quicker. "Right?" George said, hand on his hat, shouting over the trains enfilade.

"Yup," Fred said, holding his. "I was about to say."

They went down. Auberon followed. Promises or lies, he had no choice, and for sure they had known that all along too, for had it not been they who had at first thus cursed him? He sensed with a terrible clarity all the circumstances of his life, not excepting this foul underground now and these stairs down, take hands in a chain one after another, not one left out; they linked up, they unmasked, they seized him by the throat, they shook him, shook him, shook him till he woke up.

Fred Savage was returning from the woods with a bundle of sticks to feed the fire.

"Mess o' folks out there," he said with satisfaction as he stuck sticks into the embers. "Mess o' folks."

"Oh yeah?" George said with some alarm. "Wild animals?"

"Could be," Fred said. His white teeth shone. In watch cap and poncho he looked ancient, a shapeless hump, like a wise old

495

stumpwater toad. George and Auberon hunched a little closer to the feeble flames, and pricked up their ears, and looked around them into the complex darkness.

They had not come very far into this wood from the river's edge, where the ferry had let them off, before darkness overtook them and Fred Savage called a halt. Even as the ancient, gray, knocking, creaking boat had slid downstream along its line they watched the red sun sinking behind the still-leafless great trees, bitten into rimson bits by undergrowth, and then swallowed. It had all looked fearsome and strange, yet George said:

A Family Thing

"I think I've been here. Before."

"Oh yeah?" Auberon said. They stood together in the bow. Fred, sitting astern, legs crossed, made remarks to the aged aged ferryman, who said nothing in response.

"Well, not *been* here," George said. "But sort of." Whose adventures here, in this boat, in those woods, had he known about, and how had he come to know about them? God, his memory had turned to a dry sponge lately. "I dunno," he said, and looked curiously at Auberon. "I dunno. Only—" He looked back at the shore they had come from, and at the one they slid toward, holding his hat against the river breezes. "Only it seems—aren't we going the wrong way?"

"I can't imagine that," Auberon said.

"No," George said, "can't be . . ." Yet the feeling persisted, that they travelled back-toward and not away-from. It must be, he thought, that same disorientation he sometimes experienced emerging from the subway into an unfamiliar neighborhood, where he got uptown and downtown reversed, and could not make the island turn around in his mind and lie right, not the street-signs nor even the sun's position could dissuade him, as though he were caught in a mirror. "Well," he said, and shrugged.

But he had jogged Auberon's memory. He knew this ferry too: or at any rate he had heard of it. They were approaching the bank, and the ferryman laid up his long pole and came forward to tie up. Auberon looked down on his bald head and gray beard, but the ferryman didn't look up. "Did you," Auberon said, "did you once," now how was he to put this, "was there a girl, a dark girl once, who, a time some time ago, well worked for you?"

The ferryman with long, strong arms hauled on the ferry's line. He looked up at Auberon with eyes as blue and opaque as sky.

"Named Sylvie?" Auberon asked.

"Sylvie?" said the ferryman.

The boat, groaning against its stub of dock, came to rest. The ferryman held out his hand, and George put into it the shiny coin he had brought to pay him with.

"Sylvie," George said by the fire. His arms were around his drawn-up knees. "Did you think," he went on, "I mean I sort of thought, didn't you, that this was sort of a family thing?"

"Family thing?"

"All this, I mean," George said vaguely. "I thought it might only be the family that got into this, you know, from Violet."

"I did think that," Auberon said. "But then, Sylvie."

"Yeah," George said. "That's what I mean."

"But," Auberon said, "it still might, I mean all that about Sylvie might be a lie. They'll *say* anything. Anything."

George stared into the fire a time, and then said: "Mm. Well, I think I have a confession to make. Sort of."

"What do you mean?"

"Sylvie," George said. "Maybe it *is* family."

"I mean," he went on, "that maybe she's family. I'm not sure, but . . . Well, way back when, twenty-five years ago, oh more, there was this woman I knew. Puerto Rican. A real charmer. Bats, completely. But beautiful." He laughed. "A spitfire, in fact. The only word. She was renting at the place, this was before the Farm, she was renting this little apartment. Well, to tell the truth she was renting the Folding Bedroom."

"Oh. Oh," Auberon said.

"Man, she was something. I came up once and she was doing the dishes, in a pair of high heels. Doing the dishes in red high heels. I dunno, something clicked."

"Hm," Auberon said.

"And, well." George sighed. "She had a couple of kids somewhere. I got the idea that whenever she got pregnant she'd go nuts. In a quiet way, you know. So, hey, I was careful. But."

"Jeez, George."

"And she did sort of go off the deep end. I *don't* know why, I mean she never told me. She just went—and went back to P.R. Never saw her again."

"So," Auberon said.

"So." He cleared his throat. "So Sylvie did look a lot like her. And she did find the Farm. I mean she just showed up. And never told me how."

"Good grief," Auberon said, as the implications of this sank in. "Good grief, is this true?"

George held up an honest palm.

"But did she . . ."

"No. Said nothing. Name wasn't the same, but then it wouldn't have been. And her mother was off, she said, gone, I never met her."

"But surely you, didn't you . . ."

"To tell you the truth, man," George said, "I never really inquired into it too closely."

Auberon was silent a time, marveling. She *had* been plotted, then; if all their lives were, and she was one of them. He said: "I wonder what she . . . I mean I wonder what she thought."

"Yeah." George nodded. "Yeah, well, that's a good question all around, isn't it. A damn good question."

"She used to say," Auberon said, "that you were like a . . ."

"I know what she used to say."

"God, George, then how could you have . . ."

"I wasn't *sure*. How could I be sure? They all look sort of alike, that type."

"Boy, you're really given to that, aren't you?" Auberon said in awe. "You really . . ."

"Gimme a break," George said. "I wasn't sure. I thought, hell, probably not."

"Well." The two cousins stared into the fire. "That does explain it, though," Auberon said. "This. If it is family."

"That's what I thought," George said.

"Yeah," Auberon said.

"Yeah?" Fred Savage said. They looked up at him, startled. "Then what in hell 'm I doin' here?"

He looked from one to the other, grinning, his dull, living eyes amused. "Y'see?" he said.

"Well," George said.

"Well," Auberon said.

"Y'see?" Fred said again. "What in hell 'm *I* doin here?" His yellow eyes closed and opened, and so did the many yellow eyes in the woods behind him. He shook his head as though at a puzzle, but he wasn't really puzzled. He never seriously asked such a question, what was he doing where he was, except when it amused him to watch others consider it in consternation. Consternation, and considering, thought itself in fact, were mostly a spectacle to him; a man who had long since given up making any distinction between the place behind his closed black lids and the place before him when they were open, he was hard to confuse, and as for this place, Fred

Savage didn't really wonder; he didn't bother himself supposing he had ever lived anyplace else.

"Teasin'," he said softly and kindly to his two friends. "Teasin'."

He kept vigil for a while, or slept, or both, or neither. Night passed. He saw a path. In the blue dawn, birds awaking, fire cold, he saw the same path, or another, there between trees. He woke George and Auberon, a huddled pile, and with his index brown and gnarled and dirt-clogged as a root, he pointed it out to them.

George Mouse looked around himself, swept with uneasy wonder. He had been feeling, since the first steps they had taken on the path which Fred had found, that none of it was as strange as it ought to be, or as unknown to him. And here in this spot (no different otherwise, as thick with undergrowth, as overwhelmed with towering trees) the feeling had grown much stronger. His feet had stood in this place before. In fact they had rarely been far from it.

A Watch and a Pipe

"Wait," he said to Fred and Auberon, who were stumbling ahead, looking for the path's continuation. "Wait a sec."

They stopped, looking back.

George looked up, down, left, right. Right: there, he could sense more than see it, was a clearing. Air more gold and blue than the forest's gray was beyond that row of guardian trees.

That row of guardian trees . . .

"You know," he said, "I get the feeling we haven't come all that far, after all."

But the others were too far on to hear him. "Come on, George," Auberon called.

George pulled himself from the spot, and followed. But he had taken only a few steps when he felt himself drawn back.

Damn. He stopped.

The forest was, it was hard to believe it of a mess of vegetation but it was so, the forest was like a huge suite of rooms, you stepped through doors continually out of one place into a very different place. Five steps were all it had taken him to leave the place where he had felt so familiar. He wanted to go back; he wanted very much to go back.

"Well, just *wait* a second," he called out to his companions, but they didn't turn back, they were already elsewhere. The calls of birds seemed louder than George's own call. In a quandary, he took two steps in the direction they had gone, and then, drawn by

499

a curiosity stronger than fear, returned to the place where the clearing could be glimpsed.

It didn't seem far. There seemed even to be a path in that direction.

The path led him down, and almost at once the guardian trees and the patch of sunlight he had seen were gone. Very soon after that the path was gone too. And very soon after that George forgot completely what had caused him to take this way.

He walked on a bit, his boots sinking into soft earth, and his coat clawed at by harsh, marsh-living bushes. Where? For what? He stood stock still, but began to sink, and pulled himself forward. The forest sang all around him, blocking his ears to his own thoughts. George forgot who he was.

He stopped again. It was dark yet bright, the trees all in a moment seemed to have bloomed a chartreuse cloudiness, spring had come. And why was he here, afraid, in this place, when and where was this, what had become of him? Who was he? He began searching in his pockets, not knowing what he would find but hoping for a clue as to who this was here and what he was doing.

From one pocket he pulled out a blackened pipe, which meant nothing to him though he turned it and turned it in his hand; from the other he pulled out an old pocket watch.

The watch: yes. He couldn't read its moustached face, which was grinning at him disconcertingly, but this was definitely a clue. A watch in his hand. Yes.

He had, no doubt (he could almost remember it) taken a pill. A new drug he was experimenting with, a drug of astonishing, of just unheard-of potency. That had been some time ago, yes, by the watch, and the pill had done this to him: had snatched away his memory, even his memory of having taken the pill, and set him to struggle in a wholly imaginary landscape, my God a pill so potent that it could build a forest complete with bilberries and birdsong inside his head for the homunculus of himself to wander in! But this imaginary woods was still interpenetrated, faintly, by the real: he had in his hand the watch, the watch by which he had intended to time the new drug's working. He had had it in his hand the whole time, and had only now, because the pill's effect was wearing off, imagined that he had taken it out of his pocket to consult it—had imagined that he had taken it out because with the pill's wearing off he was coming to himself again, by slow stages, and the real watch was intruding into the unreal forest. In a moment, any moment, the terrible leaf-jewelled forest would fade and he would begin to see through it the room where he in fact sat with the watch in his hand:

the library of his townhouse, on the third floor, on the couch. Yes! Where he had sat motionless for who knew how long, the pill made it seem a lifetime; and around him, waiting for his response, his description, would be his friends, who had watched with him. Any second now their faces would swim into reality, as the watch had: Franz and Smoky and Alice, coalescing in the dusty old library where they had so often sat, their faces anxious, gleeful, and expectant: what was it like, George? What was it like? And he would for a long time only shake his head and make inarticulate round noises, unable till firm reality reasserted itself to speak of it.

"Yes; yes," George said, near to tears of relief that he remembered, "I remember, I remember;" and even as he was saying that, he slipped the watch back into his pocket, turning his head in the greening landscape. "I remember . . ." He pulled a boot from the mud, and the other boot, and no longer remembered.

A row of guardian trees, and a clearing where sunlight fell, and a suggestion of cultivation. On ahead. Ahead: only now he was stumbling downward over mossy rocks black with wetness, stumbling toward a ravine through which a cold stream ran rushing. He breathed its moist breath. There was a rude bridge there, much fallen, where floating branches caught and white water swirled; looks dangerous; and a hard climb beyond that; and as he put a cautious foot on the bridge, afraid and breathing hard, he forgot what it was he toiled toward, and at the next step (a loose crosspiece, he steadied himself) forgot who he was that toiled or why, and at the next step, the middle of the bridge, realized that he had forgotten.

Why did he find himself staring down into water? What was going on here anyway? He put his hands into his pockets hoping to find something that would give him a clue. He took out an old pocket watch, which meant nothing to him, and a blackened, small-bowled pipe.

He turned the pipe in his hands. A pipe: yes. "I remember," he said vaguely. The pipe, the pipe. Yes. His basement. Down in the basement of a building on his block he had discovered an ancient cache, an amazing, a hilarious find. Amazing stuff! He had smoked some, in this pipe, that must be it: there in that blackened bowl. He could see bits of cindery consumed resin, it was all in him now, and this—this!—was the effect. Never, never had he known a rush so total, so involving! He had been swept away; he was no longer standing where he had been standing when he had put match to the pipe's contents—on a bridge, yes, a stone bridge up in the Park, where he had gone to share a pipe with Sylvie—but in some weird woods, so real he could smell them, so swept away that he seemed to have been clambering forgetful of who he was in this woods for hours, forever, when in fact (he remembered, he remembered clearly) he had only at this moment lowered the pipe from his lips —here it still was in his hands, before his eyes. Yes: it had reappeared first, first sign of his alighting from a no doubt quite short but utterly ravishing rush; Sylvie's face, in an old peau-de-soie black hat, would come next. He was even now about to turn to her (the hash-created woods discreating themselves and the littered brownish winter Park assembling itself around him) and say: "Hm, ha, strong stuff, watch it, STRONG stuff;" and she, laughing at his swept-away expression, would make some Sylvie remark as she took the pipe from him:

"I see, I remember," he said, like a charm, but he had already a terrible percipience that this was not the first time he had remembered, no indeed, once before he had remembered it all but remembered it all differently. Once before? No, oh no, perhaps many times, oh no oh no: he stood frozen as the possibility of an endless series of remembrances, each one different but all made out of a small moment in the woods, occurred to him: an infinite series endlessly repeated, oh *I* remember, *I* remember, each one extending a lifetimewards out from one small, one *very* small moment (a turn of the head only, a step of the foot) in an absolutely inexplicable woods. George, seeing it so, felt he had been suddenly—but not suddenly, for a long, an immemorial time—condemned to hell.

"Help," he said, or breathed. "Help, oh help."

He took steps across the rickety bridge beneath which the forest stream foamed. There was a glassless picture framed in an old gilt frame on his kitchen wall (though George had forgotten just now that it was there) which showed just such a dangerous bridge as this, and two children, innocent, unafraid or perhaps unaware of their danger, crossing it hand in hand, a blond girl, a dark, brave boy, while above them, watching, ready to stretch out a hand to them if a loose crosspiece broke or a foot was placed wrong, was an angel: a white angel, crowned with a gold fillet, vapid-faced in gauzy draperies but strong, strong to save the children. Just such a power George felt behind him then (though he didn't dare turn to see it) and, taking Lilac's hand, or was it Sylvie's, he stepped bravely across the creaking slats to reach the other side.

Then came a long, an endless because unremembered time; but at last George gained the top of the ravine, knees torn and hands weary. He came out between two rocks like upraised knees, and found himself—yes!—in a small glade spangled with flowers; and in the near distance, the row of guardian trees. Beyond them, it was clear now, was a fence of wattles, and a building or two, and a curl of smoke from a chimney. "Oh, yes," George said, panting, "oh, yes." Near him in the glade, a lamb stood; the noise George heard was not his own lost heart but its crying voice. It had got caught in some wicked trailing briar, and was hurting itself to free its leg.

"There, there," George said. "There, there."

"Baa, baa," said the lamb.

George freed its fragile black leg; the lamb stumbled forward, still crying—it was just newborn, how had it strayed from its mother? George went to it, and picked it up by its legs, he had seen this done but he forgot where, and slung it over his neck, holding it by its feebly kicking feet. And with it turning its silly sad face to try and look into his, he went on up to the gate in the fence of wattles beyond the row of guardian trees. The gate stood open.

"Oh, yes," George said, standing before it. "Oh, yes; I see. I see."

For this was clear enough; there was the small ramshackle house with horn windows, there the byre, there the goat shed; there was the plot of new-planted vegetables, in which someone was digging, a small brown man who when he saw George approach threw down his tool and hurried away muttering. There was the wellhouse and the root cellar, there the woodpile, with its axe upright in the block. And there, the hungry sheep shouldered at their fences, looking up to be fed. And all around the little clearing, there was the Wild Wood looking down, indifferent and dark.

How he had come here he didn't know, any more than he knew now where he had started from; but it was plain now where he was. He was home.

He set down the lamb within the fold, and it skipped to where its mother scolded it. George wished that he could remember, just a little; but what the hell, he'd spent a lifetime in one enchantment or another, or one enchantment in another, in another; he was too old now to worry when it changed. This was real enough.

"What the hell," he said. "What the hell, it's a living." He turned to close his gate of palings, barring it and tying it closely in good husbandry against the dark Wild Wood and what lived there, and, brushing his hands together, went to his door.

A heaven, Ariel Hawksquill thought, deep within, a heaven no larger than the ball of one's thumb. The island-garden of the Immortals, the valley where we are all kings forever. The rocking, clacking rhythm of the train drove the thought again and again around the track of her mind.

Middle of Nowhere

Hawksquill was not one of those who find the motion of trains soothing. Rather it prodded and grated on her hideously, and though a dull rainy dawn looked to be near breaking in the flat landscape beyond the window, she had not slept, though she had given out, on boarding, that she would—that was only to keep the President, for a time, away from her door. When the aged, kindly porter had come to make up her bed, she had sent him away, and then called him back, and asked that a bottle of brandy be brought her, and that no one disturb her.

"Sure you don't want that bed made up, miz?"

"No. That's all." Where had the President's staff found these gentle, bowed black men, who had been old and slow and few even in her own youth? Come to that, where did he find these grand old cars, and where tracks that could still be traveled on?

She poured brandy, grinding her teeth in nervous exhaustion, feeling that even her sturdiest memory mansions were being shaken to earth by this motion. Yet she needed, more than she had ever needed, to think clearly, fully, and not in circles. On the luggage rack above and opposite her was the alligator purse containing the cards.

A heaven deep within, the island-garden of the Immortals. Yes: if it were so, and if it were in fact heaven or someplace like it, then the one thing that could be said with certainty about it was that, whatever other delightful qualities it might have, it must be more spacious than the common world we leave to reach it.

More spacious: skies less limited, mountain peaks less reachable, seas deeper and less plumbable.

But there, the Immortals themselves must dream and ponder too, and take their spiritual exercises, and search for an even smaller heaven within that heaven. And that heaven, if it exist, must be yet more wide, less limited, higher, broader, deeper than the first. And so on . . . "And the vastest point, the center, the infinity—Faëry, where the gigantic heroes ride across endless landscapes and sail sea upon sea and there is no end to possibility—that circle is so tiny it has no doors at all."

Yes, old Bramble might be right, only too simple—or rather too complex, with his fundibular other-worlds with doors attached. No, not two worlds; with Occam's old razor she could slit the throat of that idea. One world only, but with different modes; what anyway was a "world?" The one she saw on television, "A World Elsewhere," could fit without multiplication of entities into this one, it was molecule-thin but whole: it was only another mode, it was fiction.

And in a mode like fiction, like make-believe, existed the

land to which her cousins said she was invited to—no, told she must!—journey. Yes, journey; for if it was a land, the only way to get there was to travel.

All that was clear enough, but no help.

For Chinese heavens and make-believe lands had this in common, that however you reached them, it was your choice so to travel; in fact endless preparations were almost always required for such journeys, and a will or at least a dream of iron. And what had that to do with a mode which, against this world's will, or without anyway asking its leave at all, invaded it piecemeal, siezing an architect's fancy, a pentacle of five towns, a block of slum buildings, a Terminus ceiling—the Capital itself? Which fell on the citizens of this common mode and bore them away, or at least absorbed them willy-nilly in the advancing tide of its own being? The Holy Roman Empire, she had called it; she had been mistaken. The Emperor Frederick Barbarossa was only flotsam borne on this wave that moved the waters of Time, his sleep had been broken into as graves are broken into by the waters of a flood and the dead borne out, he was headed elsewhere.

Unless she, who had no intention of ending up in some place ruled by who knew what masters, masters who might well take her revolt against them very badly, could turn him. Turn him, as a secret agent is turned by the side he is spying on. For this she had stolen the cards. With them she might rule him, or at least make him see reason.

There was one great flaw in that scheme, however.

What a pickle, what a pickle. She glanced up at the purse over on the luggage rack. She felt that her shift against this storm was as hopeless as any, as any sad hopeless shift of those caught in the path of something, something uncaring and oncoming, and far huger than they had imagined. Eigenblick had said it in every speech, and he had been right, and she blind. To welcome it was as futile as to defy it, it would have you anyway if it wanted you, Hawksquill was very sorry she had been smug but still she must escape. Must.

Footsteps: she sorted their progress down the corridor toward her bedroom from the regular clatter of the train wheels' turning.

No time to hide the cards, nowhere better anyway than in plain sight. This was all coming too rapidly to a head, she was after all only an old lady and no good at this, no good at all.

Do not, she counseled herself, do *not* look toward the alligator purse.

The door was flung open. Holding the jamb in his two

hands to steady himself against the train's motion, Russell Eigenblick stood before her. His somber tie was pulled awry, and sweat glistened on his forehead. He glared at Hawksquill.

"I can smell them," he said.

There, there was the flaw in her scheme. She had glimpsed it first in the Oval Office on a certain snowy night. Now she was certain. The Emperor was mad: as mad as any hatter.

"Smell what, sir?" she asked mildly.

"I can smell them," he said again.

"You're up very early," she said. "Too early for a glass of this?" She showed him the brandy bottle.

"Where are they?" he said, stumbling into the tiny chamber. "You have them, now, here somewhere."

Do *not* look toward the alligator purse. "Them?"

"The cards," he said. "You bitch."

"There's a matter I must speak to you about," she said, getting up. "I'm sorry I was delayed boarding last night until late, but . . ."

He was lunging around the room, eyes shifting rapidly, nostrils flaring. "Where," he said. "Where."

"Sir," she said, drawing up but feeling hopelessness swim up in her, "sir you must listen."

"The cards."

"You're acting on the wrong side." She blurted it out, unable to frame it cleverly, feeling horribly drawn to stare at the purse which he had not seen on the luggage rack. He was tapping the walls for hiding places. "You must listen. Those who made promises to you. They have no intention of keeping them. Even if they could. But I . . ."

"You!" he said, turning to her. "You!" He laughed hugely. "That's rich!"

"I want to help you."

He paused in his search. He looked at her, depths of sad reproach in his brown eyes. "Help," he said. "You. Help. *Me.*"

It had been an unfortunate choice of words. He knew— she could see it in his face—that helping him had never been what Hawksquill had intended, nor was it her intention now. Mad he might be, but he wasn't stupid. The betrayal in his face made her look away. It was apparent that nothing she could say would move him. All he wanted from her now was what was useless to him without her, though even that she couldn't think how to explain.

She found herself staring at them, in their purse on the luggage rack. She could almost see them looking back at her.

506

She snatched her look away, but the Tyrant had seen her. He made to shove her aside, reaching up.

"Stop!" she said, flinging into the word powers she had once vowed never to use except at deepest need, and for good ends only. The Emperor stopped. He was still in mid-grasp; his bull's strength struggled against Hawksquill's command, but he couldn't move. Hawksquill grabbed the alligator purse and fled from the room.

In the corridor, she nearly collided with the stooped and slow-moving porter. "Ready to sleep, now, miz?" he inquired gently.

"You sleep," she said, and pushed past him. He slid down the wall, mouth open, eyes closed, asleep. Hawksquill, already crossing into the next car, heard Eigenblick roar out in rage and dismay. She shoved aside a heavy curtain that barred her way, and found herself in a sleeper, where at Eigenblick's cry men had awakened and were now pulling aside the curtains on upper and lower berths and looking out, sleepy, alert, pale. They saw Hawksquill. She backed out through the curtain and into the car she had come from.

There, in a niche in the wall, she saw that cord which she had often studied in her train-going, the cord that when pulled in fun or malice set the puller up for a stiff fine. She had never really believed that these slim ropes could actually stop a train, but, hearing steps and clamor in the far car, she pulled it now, and stepped quickly to the door, and grasped its handle.

Within seconds the train came to a thrashing, crashing, jolting stop. Hawksquill, astonished at herself, wrenched open the door.

Rain struck her. They were in the middle of nowhere, amid rainy, dark woods where last hillocks of snow melted. It was fiercely cold. Hawksquill leapt to the ground with a fainting heart and a cry. She struggled up the embankment, hampered by her skirt, hurrying herself lest the impossibility of her doing this at all catch up with her.

Dawn was gray, almost in its paleness more opaque than night. At the top of the embankment, within the woods, panting, she looked back at the dark length of the stopped train. Lights were coming on inside. From the door she had left, a man jumped down, signalling behind him to another. Hawksquill, stumbling in snow-obscured undergrowth, ran deeper in. She heard calls behind her. The hunt was up.

She turned behind a great tree and rested her back against it, sobbing painful cold breaths, listening. Twigs crackled, the woods were being beaten for her. A glance around showed her a dim figure, far off to the left, with something blunt, pointed and black in a gloved hand.

Done secretly to death. No one the wiser.

With trembling hands she opened the alligator purse. She clawed out from amid the loose cards a small morocco-leather envelope. Her breath condensing before her made it difficult to see, and her fingers shook uncontrollably. She pulled open the envelope and fumbled within it for the sliver of bone that it contained, one bone chosen from among the thousand-odd bones of a pure black cat. Where was the wretched thing. She felt it. She pinched it between two fingers. A crackle of brush that seemed close by startled her, she threw up her head, the tiny charm slipped from her fingers. She almost caught it as it fell catching along the stuff of her skirt, but her eager hand grasping for it brushed it away. It fell amid snow and black leaves. Hawksquill, crying a hopeless no, stepped unwittingly on the place where it had fallen.

The calling of those who followed her was soft, confident, coming closer. Hawksquill fled from her shelter, glimpsing as she did so the shade of another of Eigenblick's soldiers, or the same one, anyway armed; and he saw her too.

She had never given much thought to what in fact might happen to her mortal body, its soul securely hidden, if fatal things were done to it; if projectiles were passed violently through it, if its blood were spilled. She couldn't die, she was certain of that. But what, exactly? What? She turned, and saw him aim. A shot was fired, she turned to run again, unable to tell if she had been struck or only shocked by the noise.

Struck. She could distinguish the warm wetness of her blood from the cold wetness of the rain. Where was the pain? She ran on, plunging hopelessly out-of-kilter, one leg seemed not to be working. She fell against tall trees, hearing her pursuers guiding each other with brief words. They were quite near.

There were escapes from this, there were other exits she could find, she was sure of it. But just at the moment she could remember none of them.

Could not remember! All her arts were being taken from her. Well, that was just; for she had dishonored them, had lied, had stolen, had sought power with them in her height of pride; she had used powers she had forsworn, for ends of her own. It was quite just. She turned, at bay; she saw on all sides the dark shapes of her pursuers. They wanted to get quite close, no doubt, so as not to make a great fuss. One or two shots. But what would become of her? The pain she had thought not to feel was just now surging up her body, and was ghastly. Pointless to run any more; black mists were passing before her eyes. Yet she turned again to run.

There was a path.

There was a path, quite clear in the twilight. And there—well, she could go there, couldn't she? To that little house in the clearing. A shot jolted her horribly, but as though a shaft of sunlight struck it, the house became clearer: a funny sort of house, indeed the oddest little house that she had ever seen. What house did it remind her of? Gingerbreaded and many-colored, with chimney-pots like comic hats, and cheerful firelight showing in the deep small windows, and a round green door. A welcoming, a friendly green door; a door that just then opened; a door from which a broadly grinning face looked out to welcome her.

Fifty-two Pickup

They shot her, in fact, several times, being superstitious themselves; and certainly she looked as dead as any dead person they had ever seen, the same doll-like, heedless appearance to the limbs, the same vacated face. She didn't move. No cloud of breath condensed above her lips. Satisfied at last, one snatched up the alligator purse, and they returned to the train.

Weeping, shouting hoarse gouts of laughter, with the old cards (mixed backs and faces) pressed in a messy clutch against his bosom, at last, at last, Russell Eigenblick, the President, pulled at the cord which would start the train again. Blinded with fear and joy, he plunged through the cars of the train, almost knocked over when the train with a jolt started up again; the train plunged through his country, swept with rain, breathing clouds of steam. Between Sandusky and South Bend the rain turned unwillingly to snow and sleet and deepened to blizzard; the baffled engineer could see nothing. He cried out when there loomed up before him with great suddenness the mouth of a lightless tunnel, for he knew there could be no tunnel in this landscape, nor had ever been, but before he could take action (what action?) the train had roared into limitless darkness louder and darker even than Barbarossa's triumph.

When it arrived, quite empty of passengers, at the following station (an Indian-named town where no train had stopped for years) the porter whom Ariel Hawksquill had shouldered aside in her haste awoke.

Now what on earth?

He arose, and, slow with forty years' service, walked the train, as astonished at himself for having slept, and at the train for having stopped unscheduled, as at the absence of his passengers.

509

Midway through the silent cars, he met the white-faced engineer, and they consulted, but said little. There was no one else aboard; there had been no conductor; it was a special train, everyone aboard had known where they were going. So the porter said to the engineer. "They knew," he said, "where they were going."

The engineer returned to his cab, to use the radio, though he hadn't yet decided what to say. The porter continued through the cars, feeling ghostly. In the bar car he found, amid empty glasses and crushed cigarettes, a deck of cards, old-fashioned cards, flung about as though in rage.

"Somebody playin' fifty-two pickup," he said.

He gathered them up—the figures on them, knights and kings and queens such as he had not seen before, seemed to plead with him from their scattered places to do so. The last one—a joker maybe, a character with a beard, falling from a horse into a stream—he found caught in the window's edge, face outward, as though in the act of escaping. When he had assembled them all, and squared them up, he stood unmoving in the car with them in his hands, filled with a deep sense of the world, the whole world, and his place in it, somewhere near the center; and of the value which later ages would put on his standing here alone, at this moment, on this empty train, at this deserted station.

For the Tyrant, Russell Eigenblick, would not be forgotten. A long bad time lay ahead for his people, a bitter time when those who had contended against him would turn, in his absence, to contend with each other; and the fragile Republic would be broken and reshaped in several different ways. In that long contention, a new generation would forget the trials and hardships their parents had suffered under the Beast; they would look back with growing nostalgia, with deep pain of loss, to those years just beyond the horizon of living memory, to those years when, it would seem to them, the sun always shone. His work, they would say, had gone unfinished, his Revelation unmade; he had gone away, and left his people unransomed.

But not died. No; gone off, disappeared, one night between dawn and day slipped away: but not died. Whether in the Smokies or the Rockies, deep in a crater lake or far beneath the ruined Capital itself, he lay only asleep, with his executive assistants around him, his red beard growing longer; waiting for the day (foretold by a hundred signs) when his people's great need should at last awake him again.

V

*Are you, or are you not? Have
you the taste of your existence,
or do you not? Are you within
the country or on the border? Are
you mortal or immortal?*

—Parliament of the Birds

'I want a clean cup,' the Hatter
interrupted. *'Everyone move one place.'*

—Alice in Wonderland

That the Dog predicted by Sophie which greeted Daily Alice at the door should turn out to be Spark didn't surprise Alice much, but that the old man whom she found to guide her on the far side of the river should be her cousin George Mouse was unexpected.

"I don't think of you as old, George," she said. "Not *old.*"

"Hey," George said, "older than you, and you're no spring chicken, you know, kid."

"How did you get here?" she asked.

"How did I get where?" he replied.

They walked together through dark woods, talking of many things. They walked a long way; spring came on more fully; the woods deepened. Alice was glad of his company, although she had not been sure she needed a guide; the woods were unknown to her, and scary; George carried a thick stick, and knew the path. "Dense," she said; and as she said it she remembered her wedding journey: she remembered Smoky asking, about a stand of trees over by Rudy Flood's, whether those were the woods Edgewood was on the

Her Blessing

511

edge of. She remembered the night they had spent in the cave of moss. She remembered walking through the woods on the way to Amy and Chris's house. "Dense," he had said; "Protected," she'd answered. As each of these memories and many others awoke in her, unfolding as vivid as life, Alice seemed to remember them for the last time, as though they faded and dropped as soon as they blossomed; or rather that each memory she called up ceased, as soon as she called it up, to be a memory, and became instead, Somehow, a prediction: something that had not been but which Alice, with a deep sense of happy possibility, could imagine one day being.

"Well," George said. "This is about as far as I go."

They had approached the edge of the wood. Beyond, sunny glades went on like pools, sunlight falling in square shafts upon them through tall trees; and beyond that, a white, sunlit world, obscure to their eyes accustomed to the dimness.

"Goodbye, then," Alice said. "You'll come to the banquet?"

"Oh, sure," George said. "How could I help it?"

They stood a moment in silence, and then George, a little embarrassed for he'd never done this before, asked her blessing; and she gave it gladly, on his flocks and on his produce, and on his old head; she bent and kissed him where he knelt, and went on.

So Big

The glades like pools, one after another, continued a long way. This part, Alice thought, was the best so far: these violets and these new moist ferns, those gray-lichened stones, these bars of benevolent sun. "So big," she said. "So big." A thousand creatures paused in their spring occupations to watch her pass; the hum of newborn insects was like a constant breath. "Dad would have liked this place," she thought, and even as she thought it she knew how it was that he had come (or would come) to understand the voices of creatures, for she understood them herself, she needed only to listen.

Mute rabbits and noisy jays, gross belching frogs and chipmunks who made smart remarks—but what was that in the further glade, standing on one leg, lifting alternately one wing and then the other? A stork, wasn't it?

"Don't I know you?" Alice asked when she had entered there. The stork leapt away, startled and looking guilty and confused.

"Well, I'm not sure," the stork said. It looked at Alice first with one eye, and then with both eyes down its long red beak, which gave it a look at once worried and censorious, as though it peered

512

over the tops of pince-nez spectacles. "I'm not sure at all. I'm not sure of much at all, to tell you the truth."

"I think I do," Alice said. "Didn't you once raise a family at Edgewood, on the roof?"

"I may have," the stork said. It made to preen its feathers with its beak, and did it very clumsily, as though surprised to find it had feathers at all. "This," Alice heard it say to itself, "is going to be just an enormous trial, I can see that."

Alice helped her loose a primary that had got folded the wrong way, and the stork, after some uncomfortable fluffing, said, "I wonder—I wonder if you would mind my walking a ways with you?"

"Of course you may," Alice said. "If you're sure you wouldn't rather fly."

"Fly?" said the stork, alarmed. "Fly?"

"Well," Alice said, "I'm not really sure where I'm going at all. I sort of just got here."

"No matter," the stork said. "I just got here myself, in a manner of speaking."

They walked on together, the stork as storks do taking long, careful steps as though afraid to find something unpleasant underfoot.

"How," Alice asked, since the stork said nothing more, "*did* you just get here?"

"Well," the stork said.

"I'll tell you my story," Alice said, "if you'll tell me yours." For the stork seemed to want to speak, but to be unable to bring itself to do it.

"It depends," the stork said at last, "on whose story it is you want to hear. Oh, very well. No more equivocation.

"Once," it said, after a further pause, "I was a real stork. Or rather, a real stork was all I was, or she was. I'm telling this very badly, but at all events I was also, or we were also, a young woman: a very proud and very ambitious young woman, who had just learned, in another country, some very difficult tricks from masters far older and wiser than herself. There was no need, no need at all, for her to practice one of these tricks on an unwitting bird, but she was young and somewhat thoughtless, and the opportunity presented itself.

"She performed her trick or manipulation very well, and was thrilled at her new powers, though how the stork bore it—well, I'm afraid she, I, never gave much thought to that, or rather I, the stork, I thought about nothing else.

"I had been given consciousness, you see. I didn't know that it was not my own but another's, and only loaned to me, or rather given or hidden in me for safe-keeping. I, I the stork, thought—well, it's very distressing to think of, but I thought that I was not a stork at all; I believed myself to be a human woman, who by the malice of someone, I didn't know whom, had been transformed into a stork, or imprisoned in one. I had no memory of the human woman I had been, because of course *she* retained that life and its memories, and went gaily on living it. I was left to puzzle it out.

"Well, I flew far, and learned much; I passed through doors no stork before had ever passed through. I made a living; I raised young—yes, at Edgewood once—and I had other employments, well, no need to speak of them; storks, you know . . . Anyway, among the things I learned, or was told, was that a great King was returning, or re-awaking; and that after his liberation would come my own, and that then I would truly be a human woman."

She paused in her tale, and stood staring; Alice, not knowing whether storks can weep or not, looked closely at her, and though no drop fell from her pinkish eye Alice thought that in some storkish sense she did weep.

"And so I am," she said at length. "And so I am, now, that human woman. At last. And still only, and for always, the real stork I always and only was." She lowered her head before Alice in sorrowful confession. "Alice, you do know me," she said. "I am, or was, or we were, or will be, your cousin Ariel Hawksquill."

Alice blinked. She had promised herself to be surprised by nothing here; and indeed, after she had contemplated the stork, or Hawksquill, for an astonished moment, it did seem that she had heard this tale before, or to have known that it would happen, or had happened. "But," she said, "where, I mean how, where is . . .."

"Dead," said the stork. "Dead, spoilt, ruined. Murdered. I really, she really, had no place else to go." She opened her red beak, and clacked it shut again, a sort of sigh. "Well. No matter. Only it will take time to get used to. Her disappointment, the stork's I mean. My new—body." She raised a wing and looked at it. "Fly," she said. "Well. Perhaps."

"I'm sure," Alice said, putting her hand on the stork's soft shoulder. "And I should think you could share, I mean share it with Ariel, I mean share it with the stork. You can accommodate." She smiled; it was like arbitrating a dispute between two of her children.

The stork stepped on in silence a time. Alice's hand on her shoulder seemed to soothe her, she had stopped her irritable fluffing. "Perhaps," she said at length. "Only—well. Forever and ever." There was a catch in her throat; Alice could see the long apple move. "It does seem hard."

"I know," Alice said. "It never comes out like you think it will; or even like you thought they *said* it would, though maybe it does. You learn to live with it," she said. "That's all."

"I'm sorry now," Ariel Hawksquill said, "of course too late, that I didn't accept your invitation of that night, to go with you. I should have."

"Well," Alice said.

"I thought I was separate from this fate. But I've been in this Tale all along, haven't I? With all the rest."

"I suppose," Alice said. "I suppose you have, if here you are now. Tell me though," she added, "whatever became of the cards?"

"Oh dear," said Hawksquill, turning her red beak away in shame. "I do have a lot to make up for, don't I?"

"It doesn't matter," Alice said. They were coming to the end of the forest glades; beyond lay a land of a different sort. Alice stopped. "I'm sure you can. Make up for it, I mean. For not coming and all." She looked out over the land she must now travel. So big, so big. "You can be a help to me, I think. I hope."

"I'm sure of it," Hawksquill said with conviction. "Sure."

"Because I'll need help," Alice said. There somewhere, beyond those hedges, over those green waves of earth where the new-risen grass-sea turned silver in the sunlight, Alice remembered or foresaw the knoll to be, on which there stood an oak tree and a thorn in deep embrace; and, if you knew the way, there was a small house there built underside, and a round door with a brass knocker; but there would be no need to knock, for the door would stand open, and the house would anyway be empty. And there would be knitting to take up, and duties, duties so large, so new. . . . "I'll need help," she said again. "I will."

"I'll help," said her cousin. "I can help."

Somewhere there, beyond those blue hills, how far? An open door, and a small house big enough to hold all this spinning earth; a chair to rock away the years, and an old broom in the corner to sweep away winter.

"Come along," the stork said. "We'll get used to it. It'll be all right."

"Yes," said Alice. There would be help, there must be; she couldn't do it all alone. It would be all right. Still she didn't take the first step beyond the woods' edge; she stood a long time, feeling the asking breezes on her face, remembering or forgetting many things.

Smoky Barnable, in the warm glow of many electric lights, sat down in his library to turn over once again the pages of the last edition of the *Architecture of Country Houses*. All the windows had been opened, and a cool fresh May night came and went unhindered as he read. The last of winter had been swept away as by a new broom.

More, Much More

Far upstairs, as silently as the stars it modeled, the orrery turned, passing its tiny but unresistable motion through many oiled brass gears to give impetus to the twenty-four-handed fly-wheel, shut up once again in its black case but delivering its own force to generators, which in turn fed the house with light and power, and would go on doing so until all the jewelled bearings, all the best-quality nylon and leather belts, all the hardened-steel points themselves wore away: years and years, Smoky supposed. The house, his house, as though from the effects of a tonic, had perked up, refreshed and strengthened; its basements had dried, its attics were ventilated; the dust that had filled it had been sucked up by a potent and ancient whole-house vacuum-cleaner whose existence in the walls of the house Smoky had vaguely known about but which no one had thought would ever work again; even the crack in the music-room ceiling seemed on the way to healing, though why was a mystery to Smoky. The old stocks of hoarded light-bulbs were brought out, and Smoky's house alone, the only one for miles, was lit up continuously, like a beacon or the entrance to a ballroom. Not out of pride, not really, though he had been very proud of his arrangements, but because he found it easier to expend the limitless energy than to store it (why store it, anyway?) or to disengage the machine.

And besides, lit up, the house might be easier to find: easier for someone lost, or gone off, who might be returning on a moonless night, to find in the darkness.

He turned a heavy page.

Here was a horrid idea of some vindictive spiritualist's. There is, of course, no hell after death, only a progress through higher and higher Levels. No eternal suffering, though there might be a difficult, or at least lengthy, Re-education for recalcitrant or stupid souls. Generous: but this had apparently not been enough coals to heap on the heads of sceptics, so the idea was conceived that those who refuse to see the light in this life will refuse to see it, or be blind to it, in the next as well; they will stagger alone eternally in cold darkness, believing that this is all there is, while all around them unbeknown the happy bustle of the communion of saints goes

516

on, fountains and flowers and whirling spheres and the striving souls of the great departed.

Alone.

It was clear that he could not go where all of them were summoned unless his desire were as strong as faith. But how could he desire another world than this one? He studied again and again the descriptions in the *Architecture,* but he found nowhere anything to convince him that There he would find a world anything like as rich, as deeply strange yet just as deeply familiar, as this one he lived in.

Always Spring there: but he wanted winter too, gray days and rain. He wanted it all, nothing left out; he wanted his fire, his long memories and what started them in his soul, his small comforts, his troubles even. He wanted the death he had often lately contemplated, and a place beside the others he had dug places for.

He looked up. Amid the constellation of the library's lamps reflected in the windows the moon had risen. It was just crescent, fragile and white. When it was full, Midsummer Day, they would depart.

Paradise. A world elsewhere.

He didn't really mind that there was a long Tale being told, didn't even object any longer that he had been put to its uses; he only wanted it to continue, not to stop, to go on being muttered out endlessly by whatever powers they were who spun it, putting him to sleep with its half-heard anecdotes and going on still while he slept in his grave. He didn't want it to snatch him up in this way, startle him with high, sad, harrowing conclusions he wasn't equal to. He didn't want it to have taken his wife from him.

He didn't want to be marched off to another world he couldn't imagine; a little world that couldn't be as big as this one.

Yet it is, said the breezes that passed his ears.

It couldn't contain all seasons in their fullness, all happinesses, all griefs. It couldn't contain the history of his five senses and all that they had known.

But it does, said the breezes.

Not all of that, which was his world; and then more too.

Oh more, said the Breezes; *more, much more.*

Smoky looked up. The drapes at the window moved. "Alice?" he said.

He got up, pushing the heavy book to the floor. He went to the tall window and looked out. The walled garden was a dark vestibule; the door open in the wall led to moonlit turf and misty evening.

She's far, she's there, a Little Breeze said.

"Alice?"

She's near, she's here, said another; but whatever it was that seemed to proceed toward him through the windy darkness and the garden, he didn't recognize it. He stood a long time looking into the night as into a face, as though it might converse with him, and explain many things: he thought it could, but all he heard it say, or himself say, was a name.

The moon rose out of sight above the house. Smoky climbed slowly up to his bed. About the time the moon set, pale horns indicating the place where the sleepy sun would soon rise, Smoky awoke, feeling he hadn't been asleep for a moment, as insomniacs do; he dressed himself in an old frayed dressing gown with braided edges around the cuffs and pockets, and climbed up to the top of the house, turning on as he went the hall-sconces that some thoughtless person had left off.

Lit by planetshine and daybreak, the sleepless system didn't seem to move, any more than the morning star outside the round window seemed to: and yet it did move. Smoky watched it, thinking of the night when by lamplight he had read out from the Ephemeris the degrees, minutes and seconds of the stars' ascensions, and felt, when he had set the last moon of Jupiter, the infinitesimal shudder of its quickening. And heard the first steel croquet-ball fall otherwise unaided into the waiting hand of the absurd overbalancing wheel. Saved. He remembered the feeling.

He put his hand on the wheel's black case, feeling it tick over far more steadily than his own heart; and more patient too, and a hardier thing altogether. He pushed open the round window, letting in a glad rush of birdsong, and looked out over the tiled roofs. Another nice day. What is so rare. You could see a long way south from this height, he noticed; you could see the steeple at Meadowbrook, the roofs of Plainfield. Amid them the greening clumps of woods were misty; beyond the towns the woods thickened into the great Wild Wood on whose edge Edgewood stood, which went on growing always deeper and thicker toward the South far farther than the eye could see.

Only the Brave

They came to the heart of the forest, but it was a deserted kingdom. They had come no closer to any Parliament, or any closer either to her whom Auberon sought, whose name he had forgotten.

"How far can you go into the woods?" Fred asked.

Auberon knew the answer to that. "Halfway," he said. "Then you start coming back out again."

"Not this woods though," Fred said. His steps had slowed; he plucked up moss and wormy earth with every footstep. He put his feet down.

"Which way?" Auberon said. But from here all ways were one.

He had seen her: he had seen her more than once: had seen her far off, moving brightly amid the forest's dark dangers, seeming at home there; once standing alone pensive in the tigery shade (he was sure, almost sure, it had been she), once hurrying away, a crowd of small beings at her feet, she hadn't turned to see him though one of those with her had, sharp ears, yellow eyes, a beast's unmeaning smile. Always she seemed to be headed elsewhere, purposefully; and when he followed she wasn't where he went.

He would have called to her, if he hadn't been unable to remember her name. He had sorted through the alphabet to jog his memory, but it had turned to wet leaves, to staghorn, snails' shells, fauns' feet; it all seemed to spell her, but gave him no name. And then she had escaped, not having noticed him, and he was only deeper in than before.

Now he was at the center, and she wasn't there either, whatever her name was.

Brown breasts? Brown something. Laurel, or cobweb, something like that; bramble, or something that began with a bee, or a sea.

"Annaway," Fred said. "This looks like as far as I go." His poncho was stiff and tattered, his pant-legs all fray; his toes protruded from the mouths of his ruined galoshes. He tried to raise one foot from the ground, but it wouldn't rise. His toes gripped earth.

"Wait," said Auberon.

"No help for it," Fred said. "Nest of robins in my hair. Nice. Okay."

"But come on," Auberon said. "I can't go on without you."

"Oh, I'm comin'," said Fred, budding. "Still comin', still guidin'. Oney not walkin'." Between his great rooting toes a crowd of brown mushrooms had sprung up. Auberon looked up, up, up at him. His knuckles doubled, tripled, turned to hundreds. "Hey m'man," he said. "Lookin' at God all day, yunnastan. Gots to catch some rays, scuse me," and his face tilted back disappearing into bole as he reached up toward the treetops with a thousand greening fingers. Auberon gripped his trunk.

"No," he said. "Damn it now, don't."

He sat down, helpless, at Fred's foot. Now he was lost for

sure. What stupid, stupid madness of desire had propelled him here, here where she was not, this princedom of nobody's where she had never been, where he was unable to remember anything of her but his desire for her. He put his head in his hands, despairing.

"Hey," said the tree, with a woody voice. "Hey, what's that about. I got counsel. Listen up."

Auberon raised his head.

"Oney the brave," said Fred, "jes' oney the brave deserve the fair."

Auberon stood. Tears made rivulets in his dirty cheeks. "All right," he said. He ran his hands through his hair, combing out dead leaves. He too had grown rank, as though he had lived years in the woods, mould in his cuffs, berry-juice in his beard, caterpillars in his pockets. A derelict.

He would have to start all over again, that's all. Brave he was not, but he had arts. Had he learned nothing at all? He must get a grip on this, he must get power over this. If this were a deserted princedom, then he could install himself in its seat, if he could think how, and then he would be lost no more. How?

Only by reason. He must *think*. He must make order here where there was none. He must get bearings, make a list, number everything and arrange it all in ranks and orders. He must, first of all, erect in the heart of the forest a place where he knew *where* he was, and what was what; then he might remember *who* he was, he who was here at the seat and center; and then what he should do here thereupon. He would, Somehow, have to turn back and start again.

He looked around the place he was, trying to think which of the ways away from it would lead him back.

All would, or none would. Warily he peered down leafy flowered avenues. Whatever way looked most like leading him away would only turn in some subtle way and lead him back, he knew that much. There was an expectant, an ironic silence in the woods, a few brief questions from the birds.

He took a seat on a fallen log. Before him, in the center of the glade, amid the grasses and violets, he set up a little stone shed or pavilion, facing in four directions, north, south, east and west. On each of its faces he put a season: winter, summer, spring and fall. Radiating away from it were the curving, tricksome ways; he metalled them in gravel, and bordered them with white-painted stones, and led them toward or away from statues, an obelisk, a marten-house on a pole, a little arched bridge, beds of tulips and day-lilies. Around it all he drew a great square of wrought-iron fence studded with arrow-headed posts, and four locked gates to go in and out of.

There. Traffic could be heard, though far off. Carefully he shifted his look: there beyond the fence was a classical courthouse, surmounted with statues of lawgivers. A hint of acrid smoke mixed in his nostrils with spring air. Now he needed only to go around the place he had made, to each of its parts in strict order, and demand from each the part of Sylvie he had put there.

The part of whom?

The park trembled in unreality, but he put it back. Don't grasp, don't hurry. The first place first, then the second place. If he didn't do this properly, he would never find out how the story came out: whether he found her, and brought her back (back where?) or lost her for good, or whatever the end was, or would be, or had been. He began again: the first place, then the second place.

No, it was hopeless. How could he ever have thought to have contained her in this place, like a princess in a tower? She had fled, she had arts of her own. And what anyway did his ragbag of memories amount to? Her? No way. They had grown over time even more crushed, faded and tattered than he remembered them being when he had put them here. It was no use. He rose from his park bench, feeling in his pocket for the key that would let him out. The little girls who played jacks along the path looked up at him warily as he chose a gate to go out of.

Locks. That's all this damn City is, he thought, inserting his key; locks upon locks. Rows, clusters, bouquets of locks knotted against the edges of doors, and the pocket weighed down as with sin by keys, to open them and lock them up again. He pushed open the heavy gate, swinging it aside like a jail door. On the rusticated red stone gatepost was a plaque: it said Mouse Drinkwater Stone 1900. And from the gate the street stretched out, townhouse-lined for a block, then marching into the brown uptown distance between vague castles, old in power, that scraped the sky, wreathed in smoke and noise.

He walked. People hurried past him, they had destinations, he was aimless and slower. And from a side street ahead of him, a package under her arm, booted feet quick, Sylvie turned on to the avenue and away uptown.

Small, alone but assured on the hectic street, her kingdom. And his. Her retreating back: she was still on her way away, and he was behind. But he was pointed now, at last, in the right direction. He opened his mouth, and her name came out. It had been on the tip of his tongue.

"Sylvie," he called.

521

Quite Close

She heard that, and it seemed to be a name she knew; her feet slowed, and she partly turned but did not; it had been a name, a name she remembered from somewhere, somewhen. Had a bird called it, calling to its mate? She looked up into the sunshot leaves. Or a chipmunk, calling its friends and relations? She watched one scamper and freeze on the knobby knees of an oak, then turn to look at her. She walked on, small, alone but assured beneath the tall trees, her naked feet falling quick one after the other among the flowers.

She walked far, and fast; the wings she had grown were not wings, yet they bore her; she didn't stop to amuse herself, though pleasures were shown her and many creatures implored her to stay. "Later, later," she said to all, and hurried on, the path unfolding before her night by day as she went.

He's coming, she thought, I know it, he'll be there, he will; maybe he won't remember me, but I'll remind him, he'll see. The present she had for him, chosen after long thought, she held tight under her arm and had let no one else carry, though many had offered.

And if he wasn't there?

No, he would be; there could be no banquet for her if he wasn't present, and a banquet had been promised; everybody would be there, and surely he was one. Yes! The best seat, the choicest morsels, she would feed him by hand just to watch his face, he'd be so surprised! Had he changed? He had, but she'd know him. She was sure.

Night sped her. The moon rose, waxing fat, and winked at her: party! Where was she now? She stopped, and listened to the forest speak. Near, near. She had never been here before, and that was a sign. She didn't like to go further without sure bearings, and some word. Her invitation was clear, and she need defer to none, but. She climbed a tall tree to its tip-top, and looked out over the moon's country.

She was on the forest's edge. Night breezes browsed in the treetops, parting the leaves with their passage. Far off, or near, or both, anyway beyond the roofs of that town and that moonlit steeple, she saw a house: a house decked out in lights, every window bright. She was quite close.

Mrs. Underhill on that night looked one last time around her dark and tidy house, and saw that all was as it should be. She went out, and pulled the door shut; she looked up into the moon's face; she drew from her deep pocket the iron key, and locked the door, and put the key under the mat.

Give way, give way, she thought; give way. It was all theirs, now. The banquet was set with all its places, and very pretty it was too, she almost wished she could be there. But now that the old king had come at last, and would sit on his high throne (whenever it was, she had never been exactly sure) there was nothing more for her to do.

Give Way
Give Way

The man known as Russell Eigenblick had had, when he alighted, only one question for her: "Why?"

"*Why*, for goodness' sake," Mrs. Underhill had said. "why, why. Why does the world need three sexes, when one of them doesn't help out? Why are there twenty-four kinds of dreams and not twenty-five? Why is there always an even number of ladybugs in the world and not an odd, an odd number of stars visible and not an even? Doors had to be opened; cracks had to be forced; a wedge was needed, and you were it. A winter had to be made before spring could come; you were the winter. Why? Why is the world as it is and not different? If you had the answer to that, you wouldn't be here now asking it. Now do calm yourself. Do you have your robe and crown? Is everything as you like it, or near enough? Rule wisely and well; I know you'll rule long. Give my best to them all, when they come to make their obeisance, in the fall; and don't, please don't, ask them hard questions; they've had enough of those to answer these many years."

And was that all? She looked around herself. She was all packed; her unimaginable trunks and baskets had been sent on ahead with those strong young ones who had gone first. Had she left the key? Yes, under the mat; she had just done that. Forgetful. And was that all?

Ah, she thought: one thing left to do.

"We're going," she said, when near dawn she stood on the point of rock that jutted out over a pool in the woods into which a waterfall fell with a constant song.

Come or
Stay

Spears of moonlight were broken by the pool's surface; new leaves and blossoms floated there, gathering in the eddies. A great white trout, pink-eyed, without speckle or belt, rose slowly at her words. "Going?" he said.

"You can come or stay," said Mrs. Underhill. "You've been so long on this side of the story that it's up to you by now."

The trout said nothing, alarmed beyond words. At last Mrs. Underhill, growing impatient with his sad goggling, said sharply, "Well?"

"I'll stay," he said quickly.

"Very well," Mrs. Underhill said, who would have been very surprised indeed if he had answered differently. "Soon," she said, "soon there will come to this place a young girl (well, an old, old lady now, but no matter, a girl you knew) and she will look down into this pool; she will be the one you've so long waited for, and she won't be fooled by your shape, she'll look down and speak the words that will free you."

"She will?" said Grandfather Trout.

"Yes."

"Why?"

"For love's sake, you old fool," Mrs. Underhill said; she struck the rock beneath her stick so hard it cracked; a dust of granite drifted onto the stirred surface of the pool. "Because the story's over."

"Oh," said Grandfather Trout. "Over?"

"Yes. Over."

"Couldn't I," said Grandfather Trout, "just stay as I am?"

She bent down, studying his dim silver shape in the pool. "As you are?" she said.

"Well," said the fish. "I've got used to it. I don't remember this girl, at all."

"No," said Mrs. Underhill, after some thought. "No, I don't think you can. I can't imagine that." She straightened up. "A bargain's a bargain," she said, turning away. "Nothing to do with me."

Grandfather Trout retreated into the weed-bearded hidey-holes of his pool, fear in his heart. Remembrance, against his will, was coming fast on him. She; but which she would it be? And how could he hide from her when she came, not with commands, not with questions, but with the words, the only words (he would have shut his eyes tight against the knowledge, if only he had had lids to shut) that would stir his cold heart? And yet he could not leave; summer had come, and with it a million bugs; the torrents of spring were done and his pool the old familiar mansion once again. He would not leave. He laved his fins in agitation, feeling things come and go along his thin skin he had not felt in decades; he worked himself deeper into his hole, hoping and doubting that it would be deep enough to hide him.

"Now," Mrs. Underhill said, as dawn rose around her. "Now."

"Now," she heard her children say, those near and those far off too, in all their various voices. Those near gathered around

524

her skirts; she put her hand to her brow and spied those already journeying, caravans down the valley toward dawn, dwindling to invisibility. Mr. Woods took her elbow.

"A long way," he said. "A long, long way."

Yes, it would be long; longer, she thought, though not so hard, as the way for those who followed her here, for at least she knew the way. And there would be fountains there to refresh her, and all of them; and there would be the broad lands she had dreamed of so often.

There was some trouble getting the old Prince helped onto his broken-winded charger, but when he was aloft he raised a feeble hand, and they all cheered; the war was over, more than over, forgotten, and they had won. Mrs. Underhill, leaning on her staff, took his reins, and they set out.

It was the year's longest day, Sophie knew, but why should it be called Midsummer when summer had just begun? Maybe only because it was the day, the first day, on which summer seemed endless; seemed to stretch out before and behind limitlessly, and every other season was out of mind and unimaginable. Even the stretch of the screen-door's spring and the clack of its closing behind her as she went in, and the summer odor of the vestibule, seemed no longer new, and were as though they had always been.

Not Going

And yet it might have been that this summer could not come at all. It was Daily Alice who had brought it, Sophie felt sure; by her bravery had saved it from never occurring, by going first had seen to it that this day was made. It should therefore seem fragile and conditional, and yet it didn't; it was as real a summer day as Sophie had ever known, it might be the only real summer day she had known since childhood, and it vivified her and made her brave too. She hadn't felt brave at all for some time: but now she thought she could feel brave, Alice all around, and she must. For today they set out.

Today they set out. Her heart rose and she clutched more tightly to her the knitted bag that was all the luggage she could think to bring. Planning and thinking and hoping and fearing had taken up most of her days since the meeting held at Edgewood, but only rarely did she feel what she was about; she forgot, so to speak, to feel it. But she felt it now.

"Smoky?" she called. The name echoed in the tall vestibule of the empty house. Everyone had gathered outdoors, in the walled garden and on the porches and out in the Park; they had been gathering since morning, bringing each whatever they could think of for the journey, and as ready for whatever journey they imagined as they could be. Now afternoon had begun to go, and they had looked to Sophie for some word or some direction, and she had gone to find Smoky, who at times like this was always behind-hand, for picnics and expeditions of every kind.

Of every kind. If she could go on thinking that it was a picnic or an expedition, a wedding or a funeral or a holiday, or any ordinary outing at all which of course she knew quite well how to manage, and just go on doing what needed to be done just as though she knew what that was, then—well, then she would have done all that she could, and she had to leave the rest to others. "Smoky?" she called again.

She found him in the library, though when at first she glanced in there she didn't perceive him; the drapes were drawn, and he sat unmoving in a big armchair, hands clasped before him and a big book open, face down, on the floor by his feet.

"Smoky?" She came in, apprehensive. "Everybody's ready, Smoky," she said. "Are you all right?"

He looked up at her. "I'm not going," he said.

She stood for a moment, unable to understand this. Then she put down her knitted bag—it contained an old album of pictures, and a cracked china figurine of a stork with an old woman and a naked child on its back, and one or two other things; it should have contained the cards, of course, but did not—and came to where he sat. "What, no," she said. "No."

"I'm not going, Sophie," he said, mildly enough, as though he simply didn't care to. And looked down at his clasped hands.

Sophie reached for him, and opened her mouth to expostulate, but then didn't; she knelt by him and said gently, "What is it?"

"Oh, well," Smoky said. He didn't look at her. "Somebody ought to stay, shouldn't they? Somebody ought to be here, to sort of take care of things. I mean in case—in case you wanted to come back, if you did, or in case of anything.

"It *is* my house," he said, "after all."

"Smoky," Sophie said. She put her hand over his clasped ones. "Smoky, you have to come, you have to!"

"Don't, Sophie."

"Yes! You can't not come, you can't, what will we do without you?"

He looked at her, puzzled by her vehemence. It didn't seem to Smoky to be a remark anyone could fitly make to him, what would they do without him, and he didn't know how to answer. "Well," he said. "I can't."

"Why?"

He sighed a long deep sigh. "It's just, well." He passed his hand over his brow; he said, "I don't know—it's just . . ."

Sophie waited through these preambles, which put her in mind of others, long ago, other small words eked out before a hard thing was said; she bit her lip, and said nothing.

"Well, it's bad enough," he said, "bad enough to have Alice go. . . . See," he said, stirring in his chair, "see, Sophie, I was never really part of this, you know; I can't . . . I mean I have been *so lucky*, really. I never would have thought, I never really would have thought, back when I was a kid, back when I came to the City, that I could have had so much happiness. I just wasn't made for it. But you—Alice—you—you took me in. It was like—it was like finding out you'd inherited a million dollars. I didn't always understand that—or yes, yes I did, I did, sometimes I took it for granted maybe, but underneath I knew. I was grateful. I can't even tell you."

He pressed her hand. "Okay, okay. But now—with Alice gone. Well, I guess I always knew she had a thing like that to do, I knew it all along, but I never *expected* it. You know? And Sophie, I'm not suited for that, I'm not made for it. I wanted to try, I did. But all I could think was, it's bad enough to have lost Alice. Now I have to lose all the rest, too. And I can't, Sophie, I just can't."

Sophie saw that tears had started in his eyes, and over-flowed the old pink cups of his lids, a thing she didn't think she'd ever seen before, no, never, and she wanted with all her heart to tell him No, he wouldn't lose anything, that he went away from nothing and toward everything, Alice most of all; but she didn't dare, for however much she knew it was true for her, she couldn't say it to Smoky, for if it wasn't true for him, and she had no certainty that it was, then no terrible lie could be crueler; and yet she had promised Alice to bring him, no matter what; and couldn't imagine leaving without him herself. And still she could say nothing.

"Anyway," he said. He wiped his face with his hand. "Anyway."

Sophie, at a loss, oppressed by the gloom, rose, unable to think. "But," she said helplessly, "it's too nice a day, it's just such a nice day. . . ." She went to the heavy drapes that made a twilight in the room, and tore them open. Sunlight blinded her, she saw many in the walled garden, around the stone table beneath the beech; some looked up; and a child outside tapped on the window to be let in.

Sophie undid the window. Smoky looked up from his chair. Lilac stepped over the sill, looked at Smoky arms akimbo, and said, "Now what's the matter?"

"Oh, thank goodness," Sophie said, weak with relief. "Oh, thank goodness."

"Who's that?" Smoky said, rising.

Sophie hesitated a moment, but only a moment. There were lies, and then there were lies. "It's your daughter," she said. "Your daughter Lilac."

"All right," Smoky said, throwing up his hands like a man under arrest, "all right, all right."

"Oh good," Sophie said. "Oh Smoky."

Land Called the Tale

"It'll be fun," Lilac said. "You'll see. You'll be so surprised."

Defeated in his last refusal, as he might have known he would be. He really had no arguments that could stand against them, not when they could bring long-lost daughters before him to plead, to remind him of old promises. He didn't believe that Lilac needed his fathership, he thought she probably needed nothing and no one at all, but he couldn't deny he'd promised to give it. "All right," he said again, avoiding Sophie's radiantly pleased face. He went around the library, turning on lights.

"But hurry," Sophie said. "While it's still day."

"Hurry," Lilac said, tugging at his arm.

"Now wait a minute," Smoky said. "I've got to get a few things."

"Oh, Smoky!" Sophie said, stamping her foot.

"Just hold on," Smoky said. "Hold your horses."

He went out into the hall, turning on lamps and wall-sconces, and up the stairs, with Sophie at his heels. Upstairs, he went one by one through the bedrooms, turning on lights, looking around, moving just ahead of Sophie's impatience. Once he looked out a window, and down on many gathered below; afternoon was waning. Lilac looked up, and waved.

"Okay, okay," he muttered. "All right."

In his and Alice's room, when he had lit all the lights, he stood a time, angry and breathing hard. What the hell do you take? On such a trip?

"Smoky . . ." Sophie at the door said.

528

"Now, damn it, Sophie," he said, and pulled open drawers. A clean shirt, anyway; a change of underwear. A poncho, for rain. Matches and a knife. A little onion-skin Ovid, from the bedside table. *Metamorphoses*. All right.

Now what to put them in? It occurred to him that it had been so many years since he had gone anywhere from this house that he owned no luggage whatever. Somewhere, in some attic or basement, lay the pack he had first carried to Edgewood, but just where he had no idea. He threw open closet doors, there were half a dozen deep cedar-lined closets around this room that all his and Alice's clothes had never come close to filling. He tugged at the light-pulls, their phosphorescent tips like fireflies. He glimpsed his yellowed white wedding suit, Truman's. Below it in a corner—well, maybe this would do, odd how old things pile up in the corners of closets, he hadn't known this was in here: he pulled it out.

It was a carpetbag. An old, mouse-chewed Gladstone carpetbag with a cross-bones catch.

Smoky opened it, and looked with a strange foreboding or hindsight into its dark insides. It was empty. An odor arose from it, musty, the odor of leaf-mould or Queen-Anne's-lace or the earth under an upturned stone. "This'll do," he said softly. "This'll do, I guess."

He put the few things in it. They seemed to disappear in its capacious insides.

What else should go in?

He thought, holding open the bag: a twine of creeper or a necklace, a hat heavy as a crown; chalk, and a pen; a shotgun, a flask of rum-tea, a snowflake. A book about houses; a book about stars; a ring. With the greatest vividness, a vividness that stabbed him deeply, he saw the road between Meadowbrook and Highland, and Daily Alice as she had looked on that day, the day of the wedding trip, the day he was lost in the woods; he heard her say *Protected*.

He closed the bag.

"All right," he said. He took it up by its leather handles, and it was heavy, but an ease entered him with its weight, it seemed a thing he had always carried, a weight without which he would be unbalanced, and unable to walk.

"Ready?" Sophie said from the door.

"Ready," he said. "I guess."

They went down together. Smoky paused in the hall to push in the ivory buttons of the lights that lit the vestibule, the porches, the basement. Then they went out.

Aaaah, said everyone gathered there.

Lilac had drawn them all after her, from the Park, from the walled garden, from the porches and parterres where they had gathered, to this front of the house, the wooden porch that faced a weedy drive leading to stone gateposts topped with pitted balls like stone oranges.

"Hi, hi," said Smoky.

His daughters came up to him smiling, Tacey, Lily and Lucy, and their children after them. Everyone rose, everyone looked at one another. Only Marge Juniper kept her seat on the porch stairs, unwilling to rise till she knew steps must be taken, for she didn't have many. Sophie asked Lilac:

"Will you lead us?"

"Part way," Lilac said. She stood in the center of the company, pleased, yet a little awed too, and not sure herself which of these would keep on till the end, and having not enough fingers to count. "Part way."

"Is it that way?" Sophie asked, pointing to the stone gateposts. They all turned and looked that way. The first crickets' voices began. Edgewood's swifts cut the air, air blue and turning green. Exhalations of the cooling earth made the way beyond those gateposts obscure.

Had that been the moment, Smoky wondered; had it been that moment, when he had turned in at those stone gateposts for the first time, that the charm had fallen on him, not ever after that to release him? The arm and hand with which he held the carpetbag tingled like a warning bell, but Smoky didn't hear it.

"How far, how far?" asked Bud and Blossom hand in hand.

On that day: the day he had first gone in at Edgewood's door and then in some sense never again back out.

Perhaps: or it may have been before that, or after it, but it wasn't a matter of figuring out when exactly the first charm had invaded his life, or when he had stumbled unwittingly into it, because another had come soon after, and another, they had succeeded one another by a logic of their own, each one occasioned by the last and none removable; even to try to disentangle them would only be the occasion for further charms, and anyway they had never been a causal chain but a series of removes, Chinese boxes one inside the other, the further in you went the bigger it got. And it didn't end now: he was about to step into a new series, endless, infundibular, utter. Apalled by a prospect of endless variation, he was only glad that some things had remained constant: Alice's love chief among them. It was toward that that he journeyed, the only thing that could draw him; and yet he felt that he left it behind; and still he carried it with him.

"A dog to meet us," Sophie said, taking his hand. "A river to cross."

Something began to open in Smoky's heart as he stepped from the porch: a premonition, or the intimation of a revelation.

They had all begun to move, taking up their bags and belongings, talking in low voices, down the drive. But Smoky stopped, seeing he could not go out by that gate: could not go out by the gate through which he had come in. Too many charms had intervened. The gate wasn't the same gate; he wasn't the same either.

"A long way," Lilac said, drawing her mother after her. "A long, long way."

They passed him on either side, burdened and holding hands, but he had stopped: still willing, still journeying, only not walking.

On his wedding day, he and Daily Alice had gone among the guests seated on the grass, and many of them had given gifts, and all of them had said "Thank you." Thank you: because Smoky was willing, willing to take on this task, to take exception to none of it, to live his life for the convenience of others in whom he had never even quite believed, and spend his substance bringing about the end of a Tale in which he did not figure. And so he had; and he was still willing: but there had never been a reason to thank him. Because whether *they* knew it or not, he knew that Alice would have stood beside him on that day and wed him whether they had chosen him for her or not, would have defied them to have him. He was sure of it.

He had fooled them. No matter what happened now, whether he reached the place they set out for or didn't, whether he journeyed or stayed behind, he had his tale. He had it in his hand. Let it end: let it end: it couldn't be taken from him. He couldn't go where all of them were going, but it didn't matter, for he'd been there all along.

And where was it, then, that all of them were going?

"Oh, I see," he said, though no sound came from his lips. The something that had begun to open in his heart opened further; it let in great draughts of evening air, and swifts, and bees in the hollyhocks; it hurt beyond pain, and wouldn't close. It admitted Sophie and his daughters, and his son Auberon too, and many dead. He knew how the Tale ended, and who would be there.

"Face to face," Marge Juniper said, passing by him. "Face

to face." But Smoky heard nothing now but the wind of Revelation blowing in him; he would not, this time, escape it. He saw, in the blue midst of what entered him, Lilac, turning back and looking at him curiously; and by her face he knew that he was right.

The Tale was behind them. And it was to there they journeyed. One step would take them there; they were there already.

"Back there," he tried to say, unable himself to turn in that direction, back there, he tried to tell them, back to where the house stood lit and waiting, the Park and the porches and the walled garden and the lane into the endless lands, the door into summer. If he could turn now (but he could not, it didn't matter that he could not but he could not) he would find himself facing summer's house; and on a balcony there, Daily Alice greeting him, dropping from her shoulders the old brown robe to show him her nakedness amid the shadows of leaves: Daily Alice, his bride, Dame Kind, goddess of that land behind them, on whose borders they stood, the land called the Tale. If he could reach those stone gateposts (but he never would) he would find himself only turning in at them, Midsummer Day, bees in the hollyhocks, and an old woman on the porch there turning over cards.

A Wake

Under an enormous moon full to bursting Sylvie traveled toward the house she had seen, which seemed to be further and further off the closer she came to it. There was a stone fence to climb, and a beech-wood to go through; there was finally a stream to cross, or an enormous river, rushing and gold-foamed in the moonlight. After long thought on its banks, Sylvie made a boat of bark, with a broad leaf for a sail, spider-web lines and an acorn-cup to bail with, and (though nearly swept into the mouth of a dark lake where the river poured underground) she reached the far bank; the flinty house, huge as a cathedral, looked down on her, its dark yews pointing in her direction, its stone-pillared porches warning her away. And Auberon always said it was a cheerful house!

Just as she was thinking that she never would quite reach it, or if she did would reach it as such an atomy that she would fall between the cracks of its paving-stones, she stopped and listened. Amid the sounds of beetles and nightjars, somewhere there was music, somber yet Somehow full of gladness; it drew Sylvie on, and she followed it. It grew, not louder but more full; she saw the lights of a procession gather around her in the furry darkness of the under-wood, or saw anyway the fireflies and night-flowers as though in procession, a procession she was one of. Wondering, her heart filled with the music, she approached the place to which the lights tended; she passed through portals where many looked up to see her enter. She put her feet in the sleeping flowers of a lane, a lane that led to a glade where more were gathered, and more coming: where beneath a flowering tree the white-clothed table stood, many places set, and one in the center for her. Only it was not a banquet, as she had thought, or not only a banquet; it was a wake.

Shy, sad for those saddened by whosoever death it was they mourned, she stood a long time watching, her present for Auberon held tight under her arm, listening to the low sounds of their voices. Then one turned at the end of the table, and his black hat tilted up, and his white teeth grinned to see her. He raised a cup to her, and waved her forward. Gladder than she could have imagined to see him, she made her way through the throng to him, many eyes turning toward her, and hugged him, tears in her throat. "Hey," she said. "Heeeey."

"Hey," George said. "Now everybody's here."

Holding him, she looked around at the crowded table, dozens present, smiling or weeping or draining cups, some crowned, some furred or feathered (a stork or somebody like one dipped her beak in a tall cup, eying with misgivings a grinning fox beside her) but Somehow room for all. "Who are all these people?" she said.

"Family," George said.

"Who died?" Sylvie whispered.

"His father," George said, and pointed out a man who sat, bent-backed, a handkerchief over his face, and a leaf stuck in his hair. The man turned, sighing deeply; the three women with him, looking up and smiling at Sylvie as though they knew her, turned him further to face her.

"Auberon," Sylvie said.

Everyone watched as they met. Sylvie could say nothing, the tears of Auberon's grief were still on his face, and he had nothing that he could say to her, so they only took hands. *Aaaah,* said all the guests. The music altered; Sylvie smiled, and they cheered her smile. Someone crowned her with odorous white blooms, and Auberon likewise, taking chaplets of locust-flower from the locust-tree which overhung the feast-table. Cups were raised, and toasts shouted; there was laughter. The music pealed. With her brown ringed hand, Sylvie brushed the tears from her prince's face.

The moon sailed toward morning; the banquet turned from wake to wedding, and grew riotous; the people stood up to dance, and sat down to eat and drink.

"I knew you'd be here," Sylvie said. "I knew it."

In his certainty that she was here now, the fact that
Auberon had himself not known at all that she
would be here dissolved. "I was sure too," he said.
"Sure.

A Real Gift

"But," he said, "why, a while ago—" he had no
sense of how long ago it had been, hours, ages "—
when I called your name, why didn't you stop, and turn around?"

"Did you?" she said. "Did you call my name?"

"Yes. I saw you. You were going away. I called 'Sylvie!' "

"Sylvie?" She looked at him in cheerful puzzlement.
"Oh!" she said at length. "Oh! Sylvie! Well, see, I forgot. Because
it's been so long. Because they never call me that here. They never
did."

"What do they call you?"

"Another name," she said. "A nickname I had when I was
a kid."

"What name?" he said.

She told him.

"Oh," he said. "Oh."

She laughed to see his face. She poured foaming drink
into his cup and offered it to him. He drank. "So listen," she said. "I
want to hear all your adventures. All of them. Don't you want to
hear mine?"

All of them, all of them, he thought, the honeyed liquor
he drank washing away any sense he might have had of what they
could be, it was as though they were all yet to happen, and he would
be in them. A prince and a princess: the Wild Wood. Had she then
been there, in that kingdom, their kingdom, all along? Had he?
What anyway had his adventures been? They vanished, crumpling
into broken nothings even as he thought of them, they became as
dim and unreal as a gloomy future, even as the future opened before
him like a storied past.

"I should have known," he said laughing. "I should have
known."

"Yes," she said. "Just beginning. You'll see."

Not one story, no, not one story with one ending but a
thousand stories, and so far from over as hardly to have begun. She
was swept away from him then by laughing dancers, and he watched
her go, there were many hands importuning her, many creatures at
her quick feet, and her smile was frank for all of them. He drank,
inflamed, his feet itching to learn the antic-hay. And could she, he
thought watching her, still cause him pain, too? He touched the gift
which in their revels she had placed on his brow, two handsome,

534

broad, ridged and exquisitely recurving horns, heavy and brave as a crown, and thought about them. Love wasn't kind, not always; a corrosive thing, it burned away kindness as it burned away grief. They were infants now in power, he and she, but they would grow; their quarrels would darken the moon and scatter the frightened wild things like autumn gales, would do so, had long done so, it didn't matter.

Doesn't matter, doesn't matter. Her aunt was a witch, but his sisters were queens of air and darkness; their gifts had once aided him, and would again. He was heir to his father's bafflements, but he could touch his mother for strength. . . . As though turning the pages of an endless compendium of romances, all read long ago, he saw the thousands of her children, generations of them, most of them his, he would lose track of them, meet them as strangers, love them, lie with them, fight them, forget them. Yes! They would blunt the pens of a dozen chroniclers with their story and the stories their story generated, tedious, hilarious, or sad; their feasts, their balls, their masques and quarrels, the old curse laid on him and her kiss that mitigated it, their long partings, her vanishings and disguises (crone, castle, bird, he foresaw or remembered many but not all), their reunions and couplings tender or lewd: it would be a spectacle for all, an endless and-then. He laughed a huge laugh, seeing that it would be so: for he had a gift for that, after all; a real gift.

"Y'see?" said the black locust-tree that overhung the feast-table, the locust from which the flowers that decked Auberon's horned head had been taken. "Y'see? Jes' oney the brave deserve the fair."

The dance whirled around the prince and princess, marking a wide circle in the dewy grass; the fireflies, toward dawn, turned in a great circle in obedience to the turning of Lilac's finger, wheeling in the opulent darkness. *Aaaah,* said all the guests.

She's Here, She's Near

"Just the beginning," Lilac said to her mother. "You see? Just like I told you."

"Yes, but Lilac," Sophie said. "You lied to me, you know. About the peace treaty. About meeting them face to face."

Lilac, elbow on the littered table, rested her cheek in the cup of her hand, and smiled at her mother. "Did I?" she said, as though she couldn't remember that.

"Face to face," Sophie said, looking along the broad table. How many were the guests? She'd count them, but they moved around so, and diminished uncountably into the sparkling darkness;

some were crashers, she thought, that fox, maybe that gloomy stork, certainly this clumsy stag-beetle that staggered amid the spilled cups flourishing its black antlers; anyway she didn't need to count in order to know how many were here. Only—"Where's Alice, though?" she said. "Alice should be here."

She's here, she's near, said her Little Breezes, moving among the guests. Sophie trembled for Alice's grief; the music altered once again, and a sadness and a stillness came over the company.

"Call for the robin-redbreast an' the wren," said the locust-tree, dropping white petals like tears on the feast-table. "Keep m'man Duke far hence that's foe to man."

The breezes rose to dawn winds, blowing away the music. "Our revels now are ended," sighed the locust-tree. Alice's white hand blotted out the grieving moon like clouds, and the sky grew blue. The stag-beetle fell off the edge of the table, the ladybug flew away home, the fireflies turned down their torches; the cups and dishes scattered like leaves before the coming day.

Come from his burial, none knew where but she, Daily Alice came among them like daybreak, her tears like day-odorous dew. They swallowed tears and wonder before her presence, and made to leave; but no one would say later that she hadn't smiled for them, and made them glad with her blessing, as they parted. They sighed, some yawned, they took hands; they took themselves by twos and threes away to where she sent them, to rocks, fields, streams and woods, to the four corners of the earth, their kingdom new-made.

Then Alice walked alone there, by where the moist ground was marked with the dark circle of their dance, her skirts trailing damp in the sparkling grasses. She thought that if she could she might take away this summer day, this one day, for him; but he wouldn't have liked her to do that and she could not do it anyway. So instead she would make it, which she could do, this her anniversary day, a day of such perfect brilliance, a morning so new, an afternoon so endless, that the whole world would remember it ever after.

Once Upon a Time

The lights of Edgewood which Smoky had left burning paled to nothing on that day; in the night that followed they shone again, and on every night thereafter. Rain and wind came in through the open windows, though, which they had forgotten to close; summer storms stained the drapes and the rugs, scattering papers, blowing shut the closet doors. Moths and bugs found holes in the screens, and died happily in union with the burning bulbs, or did not die but generated young in the rugs and tapestries. Autumn came, though it seemed impossible, a myth, a rumor not to be believed; fallen leaves piled up on the porches, blew in through the screen-door left unlatched, which beat helplessly against the wind and at last died on its hinges, no barrier any more. Mice discovered the kitchen; the cats had all left for more seemly cir-cumstances, and the pantry was theirs, and the squirrels' who came after and nested in the musty beds. Still the orrery turned, mindlessly, cheerfully whirling, and still the house was lit up like a beacon or the entrance to a ballroom. In winter it shone its lights on snow, an ice palace; snow drifted in its rooms, snow capped its cold chimneys. The light over the porch went out.

That there was such a house in the world, lit and open and empty, became a story in those days; there were other stories, people were in motion, stories were all they cared to hear, stories were all they believed in, life had got that hard. The story of the house all lit, the house of four floors, seven chimneys, three hundred and sixty-five stairs, fifty-two doors, traveled far; they were all travelers then. It met another story, a story about a world elsewhere, and a family whose names many knew, whose house had been large and populous with griefs and happinesses that had once seemed endless, but had ended, or had stopped; and to those many who still dreamed of that family as often as of their own, the two stories seemed one. The house could be found. In spring the basement lights went out, and one in the music-room.

People in motion; stories starting in a dream, and spoken by unwise actors into wanting ears, then ceasing; the story turning back to dream, and then haunting the day, told and retold. People knew there was a house made of time, and many set out to find it.

It could be found. There it was: at the end of a neglected drive, in a soft rain, not what had been expected at all and however long-sought always come upon unexpectedly, for all its lights; sagging porch steps to go up, and a door to go in by. Small animals who thought the place theirs, long in possession, sharing only with the wind and the weather. On the floor of the library, by a certain chair, face down at a certain page, a heavy book spine-broken and warped by dampness. And many other rooms, their windows filled with the rainy gardens, the Park, the aged trees indifferent and only growing older. And then many doors to choose from, a juncture of corridors, each one leading away, each ending in a door that could be gone out by; evening falling early, and a forgetfulness with it, which way was the way in, which now the way out?

Choose a door, take a step. Mushrooms have come out in

the wetness, the walled garden is full of them. There are further lights, there in the twilit bottom of the garden; the door in the wall is open, and the silvery rain sifts over the Park that can just be seen through it. Whose dog is that?

One by one the bulbs burned out, like long lives come to their expected ends. Then there was a dark house made once of time, made now of weather, and harder to find; impossible to find and not even as easy to dream of as when it was alight. Stories last longer: but only by becoming only stories. It was anyway all a long time ago; the world, we know now, is as it is and not different; if there was ever a time when there were passages, doors, the borders open and many crossing, that time is not now. The world is older than it was. Even the weather isn't as we remember it clearly once being; never lately does there come a summer day such as we remember, never clouds as white as that, never grass as odorous or shade as deep and full of promise as we remember they can be, as once upon a time they were.

ABOUT THE AUTHOR

JOHN CROWLEY lives in the hills above the Connecticut River in northern Massachusetts with his wife and twin daughters. He is the author of *Love & Sleep; Aegypt; Beasts; The Deep;* and *Engine Summer.*